Stranger in the Shadows

"There ain't no reason to hurry none." The man stepped forward as he spoke, emerging into moonlight. At his approach, Leanna felt the first whisper of fear brush her soul. For a moment, her fingers paused on her half-buttoned blouse and she glanced in the direction of the distant camp. He was alone.

"I'd have saved me some work, it appears, to have come a mite sooner."

In the moonlight, Leanna had no trouble seeing the way the man's eyes flickered over her half-buttoned blouse, then dipped lower to the dark cloth of her skirt. She felt a moment's utter shock, and took a single, faltering step away from him. "No." At the first realization of the expression glittering in his eyes, her voice was startled, more pleading than angry.

"C'mon, now. Sooner we begin, sooner it's over."

Also by Jessica St. Claire:

A REBEL'S HONOR

WINTER ROSES

JESSICA ST. CLAIRE

PINNACLE BOOKS **NEW YORK**

WINTER ROSES

An original Pinnacle Books edition, published for the first time anywhere.

First printing, January 1984

ISBN: 0-523-42098-6

Can. ISBN: 0-523-43087-6

Cover illustration by Dan Gonzalez

Printed in the United States of America

PINNACLE BOOKS, INC.
1430 Broadway
New York, New York 10018

9 8 7 6 5 4 3 2 1

WINTER ROSES

Chapter One

The moonlight failed behind a high, scudding cloud, leaving
the Atlanta night darker than ever as Major Chase Courtland
rode slowly down the broad, shadowed street. It was always
an uneasy feeling—being a Union officer in a Confederate
city, a Northerner, alien and unwelcome, intruding into the
last, proud bastions of the cotton South. But tonight, there
was additional uneasiness to it. It pricked at him as he rode,
and he concentrated on it, trying to isolate the cause. It was
more than the usual sensation of being a stranger in a strange
land, and more than the darkness—Lord knows soldiers grew
used to night's shadows after long years of war. It was more,
too, than the emptiness of the city—the lack of lamps burning
in shuttered houses, the lack of sounds—those faint, ordinary,
normally hardly heard sounds of any sleeping city—dogs
barking, an infant squalling. Civilians usually fled before the
line of the advancing armies, so after nearly four years of civil
war, he was used to that eerie silence. He glanced over one
dark blue uniformed shoulder at a wrought-iron street sign—
Peachtree, he thought it said. And a faint whiff of fragrance
drifted out from behind it. Roses? He stopped in surprise,
reining the tired horse over a step. Roses climbing on a white
painted trellis.

On impulse, he leaned to pick one, laying the flower across
the saddle in front of him. Maybe that was what had seemed
wrong, he thought suddenly—roses blooming in mid-November.
North of Atlanta, in the edge of the mountains, where
Union and Rebel cavalry had been sparring still until yesterday,
the land was higher, nights were cooler. The mountain hardwoods had begun to turn scarlet and gold, then earlier this
week, to shed their leaves. They'd crackled under the horses'
hooves as the last federal columns had retreated south toward
the city. But here in Atlanta itself, autumn had not yet

1

begun. The live oaks were evergreen, lawns high and summer-colored, and in abandoned gardens, flowers were blooming still among the overgrown weeds. It was a strange land, the South, a land of paradoxes, compelling, beautiful, but to any outsider such as himself, infinitely unknowable. And it had bred an equally enigmatic, equally beautiful woman—one he loved with a deep passion and a reckless disregard for the danger he knew she offered to his sanity, his soul, and his country: Leanna Penley Leighton, Virginia born and bred. Black-haired and violet-eyed, as staunch a Confederate as any Rebel soldier who shouldered a rifle and twice as deadly because he could not regard her as the enemy she was.

A sudden glow lit the city behind him, golden light silhouetting black rooftops. It startled him, and he drew rein on his horse with a frown. Fire? A moment later, the wind shifted and the smell of burning deepened his frown. His horse lifted his head and snorted once, uneasy and concerned, paralleling Chase's own reaction as he kicked the stallion forward into a canter. If they were firing parts of the city, Sherman must be planning on marching out—today probably, maybe at the dawn's light. It didn't give him much time to spend with Leanna. Little time to try to undo the damage done the night he'd left the city back in September before going north to spar with the Rebel cavalry Hood had left behind on his retreat into Tennessee. What he *should* do was forget Leanna Leighton, he told himself for the hundredth time. Forget the insanity that drove him to see her again, to torture himself and her, too, with a last meeting, more bitter words probably to worsen an already festering wound. Hadn't he had enough already? Enough guilt? Enough pain? He ought to turn the horse around and rejoin the rest of the regiment, get some sleep, the first in forty-eight hours and more than welcome. But he kept going straight, only frowning that much more grimly in the dull gray shadows of the Georgia night. The wind seemed to be picking up. The smell of burning was thick on the night air. Now, twin fires lit the horizon behind him. Ahead, he could catch the occasional, distant clamor of activity far to the south, sometimes from the east, too, where the city was still black as pitch; but from the burning part, there came only the silence of a grave. It was reckless to set fires in this sort of wind. This wind was changeable and gusty—dusty-dry, as well. October and November were dry months in Georgia,

2

and the whole city could go up in flames. Leanna, maybe, with it.

The quickening beat of the horse's hooves rang a sharp, metallic beat on the uneven cobblestones of the main street, a loud song in the eerie stillness of the city. If it weren't for the fire that was already spreading ominously, he wouldn't go back to her. Chase told himself that and knew it for a lie even as he thought it. After that near rape that mostly wasn't—at least not by the end—what could he have to say to her? Or she to him? Six weeks had already passed since that bitter and violent night, weeks while he'd waited for the anguish and the guilt to fade, but it never had. Sometimes after a sharp skirmish, a particularly hard ride, it would lessen. But it always came back. He'd roll over in the morning on his blankets, his breath vapor in the cold mountain air, and there it would be . . . haunting him as strong as ever. Haunting him now. Forcing him to seek her out one last time. To try to find some peace in it. To try to say good-bye forever to the woman he had no right to love and couldn't quite seem to stop. A married woman—a Confederate one. Damn you, Leanna Leighton. Damn fate for ever having our paths cross in that beautiful Virginia Valley. I could die and hurt less than this.

"Who goes there?"

Starlight glinted on the muzzle of a raised carbine, and Chase drew rein. "Major Courtland. Eighth Pennsylvania."

The carbine lowered. "Yes, sir. Cavalry's massing at the east end."

"I know. I have some business here first, though."

"Better make it quick, sir." The soldier chuckled softly as he nodded toward the fires on the north side, almost a solid bar by now. Three—no, four to the west, separate blazes. "Uncle Billy ordered all Reb civilians out of town yesterday. Once the fires get caught good, ain't gonna be nobody around to put 'em out again."

Chase glanced almost involuntarily in that direction, and saw faint bright gold sparks of ash rising in the night wind. As shock faded a coldness spread in his gut. It was not merely *parts* of the city that Sherman had planned to burn, after all. Federal command had been all too aware of how recklessly those fires would spread. This war grew uglier by the day. "Thanks soldier. I'll make it quick."

As the Union officer urged his tired mount on to race against the flames, the single rose he'd picked for a beloved enemy—half in apology, half as a farewell gift—had slipped off the saddle to mark the dusty Atlanta street with a drop of wilting scarlet. Before dawn broke, the all-consuming fires would reach it. Too fresh to burn at first, the petals turned slowly to shriveled black and then smoldered at last into crackling ash as the city burned.

It was dark in Philadelphia, too, that night, but colder, and the fires that glowed here were those of crystal chandeliers and Carrara-marble fireplaces. Chase Courtland's father, Joshua, sat at a supper table, deep in thought. It was a meeting of "the coalition," a group of wealthy, unscrupulous businessmen, who had banded together for the purpose of manipulating the war, the intention being to rake the maximum profits from its bloody raging. Joshua was not spiritually one with such men. He had joined the group last spring only in the hope of thwarting plots too horrible to countenance. And just now, he was not even thinking about the traitorous group, not about the profiteering they encouraged, nor the congressmen they'd bought, nor their eventual ambitions to divide the conquered South and rule like feudal kings in unlimited power there. He was thinking instead about his son, Chase, and the last letter he'd received from him only today. A letter sent from Resaca, but dominated still by Atlanta and the woman Chase had so improbably been reunited with there: Leanna Penley Leighton.

Damn it; Joshua frowned wearily. He'd thought that was over. It *should* have been over. His son's involvement with the beautiful Virginia rebel should never have resurfaced again. Chase had fallen in love with Leanna Leighton last year when he and the troops under his command had taken up winter quarters in her Shenandoah Valley home. In the spring, though, Lt. Col. Stewart Leighton had returned and ambushed Chase's federal troops a few days later. Leanna Leighton had made her choice there and then, Joshua thought. She had fled with her Confederate husband to heaven knew where, leaving Chase lying bleeding in a lonely Virginia meadow. Following that, and in a way Joshua thought thanks to that, he had finally pressured Chase into making a long-overdue commitment to his fiancée Susan Stratford. Chase would marry Susan on his very next leave. He would forget the

4

woman he had no right to love and marry the woman he ought to love instead.

Ugly but finished, Joshua had thought at the time. At least it was over. And he had worked hard to make his peace with the whole dismal affair. Complications enough had already been left in the wake of the brief but anguished entanglement. Leanna Leighton was now suspected by the federal government of being a Confederate spy. Blytheswood, her home, had been marked for reprisals by the Valley's Yankee troops. Chase had been wounded and could as easily have been killed. And he, Joshua, was playing host and guardian to Leanna Leighton's brother, who had been captured and then paroled for the duration of the war. Even though Joshua had lost his oldest son to Rebel bullets at Shiloh, his remaining son, Chase, had begged him to offer sanctuary to the Penley brother—for the sister's sake, Joshua knew well, for there was no love lost between Chase and any Rebel officer.

Consequently, last spring in April, ex-Confederate Cavalry Major Jonathon Penley had been offered reluctant sanctuary in Joshua Courtland's own home and work at the Courtland Bank. Both offers had worked out much better than Joshua had anticipated. Jonathon Penley had proven an excellent financier at the bank, and he and his family—Whitney, his wife, and their two young daughters Miranda and Bonnie—had become surprisingly dear to Joshua in the past few months. Joshua had actually congratulated himself just last month that what should have been an utter disaster had become instead a blessing in disguise. And then had come the Chase's first letter from Atlanta, and all Joshua's hard-won complacencies had vanished. Chase had found Leanna Leighton once again. Worse, she was in danger—under suspicion still of treasonous activities, and being hounded by a War Department adjutant named Drake. Damn it, Joshua thought in sudden helpless anger. They had half the bloody country to choose from, a thousand miles from the Gulf of Mexico to the Mason-Dixon line! Couldn't Chase and Leanna Leighton manage to remain just a few hundred miles away from each other? Must the woman insist on being wherever his son Chase was just then campaigning with his federal cavalry? God only knew what agonies such a devil-spawned reunion would produce this time around. Far better if their paths had never crossed again.

"Are you all right, Joshua?"

5

Joshua turned with a start toward Henry Walters, the man who had first extended Joshua the invitation to join the coalition, but in spite of that, the only man here he would still have called friend. "Oh, Henry. Oh, yes, I'm fine. Brooding over a letter I got from my son today, that's all."

"Oh. Well, you looked like one of the Furies, there."

"I had reason to, believe me."

Henry shrugged uneasily, giving Joshua a single curious glance. But when he spoke again, it was to change the subject, and along with his words there was something in his eyes that looked like a kind of fear. "Joshua, have you noticed how strangely some of the men have been acting here tonight? I think something's afoot. Something really important, I mean. I overheard some of Roland Hodges' conversation with that lawyer chap, and I could swear they said something about a kidnapping. And they said Lafayette Baker's name in the next breath, as if he was either *in* on something with them, or as if he must be *convinced* to be."

"Baker's the head of War Department secret intelligence, Henry. He's involved with all sorts of nasty little plots. You know that."

"Yes, of course I know that. But who would they be thinking of kidnapping, for heaven's sake? Jefferson Davis, perhaps? Or Lee? But what good would it do them to capture either of them?"

Joshua paused a moment, frowning. It was not the first time he'd suspected that within the larger evil of the coalition, there was an inner circle, the most callous, the most bloodless men, who rivaled Satan himself for the evils that they would foster. Lord, what men would do in the name of the god called wealth. "Kidnapping either of the Confederacy's two top men might give them leverage to force an end to the war, Henry, though I was unaware they were at all interested in doing that. Maybe they're only speaking about future possibilities." They could not kidnap Davis or Lee anyway, Joshua decided quickly, dismissing the notion. The whole Confederate Army lay between the coalition members and either man. They couldn't get to them until the war had ended and by then there would be no reason for the coalition to bother. By then, their real enemy would be Abraham Lincoln. Lincoln was the main obstacle to any ambitions to bleed the already nearly prostrate South, to cut it up into private princedoms and rule there under guise of martial law. And President Lincoln, thank God, *would* stop them. A sudden, abysmal coldness touched Joshua's soul and he quickly denied its feasibility. No. Impossible. Even men such as these would not dare raise their hand against their own president . . . Would they?

Henry Walters had turned partially away with the look of fear rising more sharply in his eyes. He was not a strong man. He had joined the group, admittedly, to further his own monetary interests in the war but with limits as to how far he would go to do that. Now though he was suddenly aware of being deeply afraid of his own compatriots. They could cut him to ribbons, both personally and financially. For him to turn against a Hodges would be like a ramuda attacking its own shark. Little fish had certain limits. Little fish either followed the predators or served instead as the predator's dinner. Whatever else he owed his conscience, he thought, it did *not* include sure suicide. "No, never mind, Joshua. In fact, I'm sorry I mentioned it. Now that I reconsider, I'm not at all sure anyone said 'kidnap.' Let's just forget about it, please."

Joshua nodded agreeably, to all appearances accepting Henry Walters' sudden equivocating. But tucked carefully away in an inscrutable part of his being was the dim possibility that Henry had not misheard a thing. There might be deeds yet to come that would make anything the coalition had plotted up to now seem benign. God, how much longer could this endless war drag on, Joshua wondered in sudden ominous foreboding. He needed his son Chase home before his health failed to the point where Joshua could no longer keep up with the coalition's dangerous intrigues. Maybe he should simply override Chase's wishes. Insist his son transfer out of the field to take a desk position in Washington instead. That could easily be arranged.

As a matter of fact, that might solve any number of lingering problems, Joshua thought suddenly. And the coalition was only one of them.

In the dark of the same November night, Atlanta was disappearing in fiery chaos, a familiar nightmare on a grander scale. Winship's iron foundry had been among the first touched by a Yankee torch. An oil refinery nearby had caught fire from wind-borne sparks. Then a freight warehouse, the depot, freight sheds and surrounding stores helped spread the flames. Soon the entire square by the main railroad terminal was burning—the Atlanta Hotel, Washington Hall, drugstores, dry-goods, the abandoned slave mart, theaters and taverns. Even churches were not exempt. A stone warehouse, refusing to catch, was detonated by a mine. Other explosions followed. Shells or powder concealed throughout the Rebel city added their horror. The air resounded with the crash of multistory buildings falling in upon themselves in ruin. Many of the soldiers were drunk, others on their way there. The black curtain of night had been all but entirely rolled away by now; the sky was a huge bright heaven of fire and floating ash. Atlanta's two hundred acres lay either in orange flame or burnt-out ruin, and less than four hundred buildings in the entire city would finally survive the Yankee holocaust.

Chase Courtland had reached the rooming house only a few blocks before the ravaging flames, checked the rooms and took the stairs back down at a run. Leanna Leighton wasn't there. In fact, no one was there. The wind was already hot, carrying fiery ash, and he stopped at the bottom of the stairs to frown in growing desperation. Where else could Leanna be? He glanced up and down the dark, deserted street as if it might somehow answer that question, but it didn't. Most houses on the street had long since been abandoned; several had already been burned. Might Leanna be at the town house where he had first found her? It was mostly ruined from the soldiers that had broken in to loot it that first night the federal army had occupied the city, but perhaps, in the face of the spreading fires, she had gone back to collect what few things had been left there. Or maybe Lt. Col. Drake had taken advantage of both Chase's absence and General Sherman's orders to take the beautiful Rebel into federal custody and out of the city. Chase almost preferred to think so; just now it would be, for her, the safest place to be, and for him, the simplest answer to a worrisome question. But what if Leanna weren't with Drake? Then she might be anywhere. Would she have the good sense to flee before the line of flames? Or would she stay, try to fight the inevitable, risking her life to try to save the Confederate city from the Yankee fires? Knowing Leanna, he would guess the latter.

Bright, glowing ash was already beginning to drift down

from the rooming-house roof signaling that it wouldn't be long before the clapboard structure was entirely ablaze. Chase swore softly and reached to grab the reins of his frightened horse, remounting with sudden haste. He couldn't take the chance that Leanna was safely outside the city, somewhere in the adjutant officer's custody. Because if he were wrong . . . He turned the stallion's head toward the east, away from the swiftly approaching flames, and set him into a reckless gallop. Where are you, Lea? God damn you, anyway. Where in the world have you disappeared to?

On the eastern side of Atlanta, about eighteen miles from the city along the McDonough Road, a farmhouse stood cheerless and gray amid poor fields and bramblelike cottonrows. A small wooden sign on the road nearby was obscured by road dust and now by the night's shadows, but in the daylight it announced ROOMS TO LET in crude hand-painted lettering, red paint flaking off a dirty white background. Locally it was known as the MacRaes' place, a farmhouse whose pretensions to hostlery were ludicrous, but it was almost exactly a single day's walk east of the city and as such, before the war, had done a fair to decent business. Weeks before, when Sherman's Yankee cavalry had been ordered back into the northern mountains and Leanna Leighton had fled the nearby city in anguished desperation—fled the Yankees in general and Chase Courtland more particularly—she had found herself here as dusk had forced an end to her first day's journey. Then, almost incomprehensibly, she had dallied here day after day, now week after week, neither going back to Atlanta nor north toward her home in the Virginia Valley. Torn between the two, she had simply ended up staying here at the MacRaes'.

Now she stood on the porch of the sagging, white frame farmhouse and watched a distant glow rising to the west, brightening the dark predawn Georgia sky. Atlanta was burning. It had to be. So the Yankees had finally set fire to the Rebel city. God damn you, Chase Courtland, she thought in a rush of sudden bitter tears, damn you and all your torch-happy bluebelly soldiers. How could she ever have lost her heart to one of the enemy? Loved a man who was part of such wanton Northern devastation? Such careless cruelty to innocent Southern civilians? It made her own husband's guerrilla tactics seem entirely justified in their viciousness. Maybe

9

Stewart hadn't been so wrong after all. Maybe the Yankees deserved every ugly trick he'd pulled on them.

"Mrs. Leighton?"

Leanna half-turned, startled. Jennie MacRae pulled a ragged shawl closer around her shoulders as she stepped out onto the creaking boards of the farmhouse's dark porch. Only for a moment and with no visible sign of reaction, the older woman's eyes went to the western horizon toward the glow of the burning city. Without a word or even any change in expression then, she merely shrugged a kind of indifferent dismissal. "My son John's just got back." She paused only to gesture backward into the house behind them. "You was talkin' 'bout going on to yer house in the Virginia Valley. You might outa talk to John now afore you bother makin' that trip."

Atlanta was momentarily forgotten. The Virginia Valley took instant precedence in Leanna's mind and in her fears. There had been a kind of warning in Jennie MacRae's cold words, and that coldness began to slowly spread through Leanna, replacing the white heat of anger she'd felt while watching Atlanta burn. But the Georgia woman only stood in continued silence, watching the girl, impassive but waiting—for what, Leanna didn't know. In the night shadows, Mrs. MacRae's aged, weathered face looked more carved stone than human flesh, but one edge of her mouth quirked suddenly upward as if in amusement at a private joke. "The Shenandoah Valley?" Leanna heard herself repeat the words and knew it for a stupid question even as she asked it. If the Yankees would burn Atlanta with such cavalier disregard, she realized suddenly, what made her think they would have spared the lush, innocent, rolling hillsides of her beloved Virginia Valley?

Jennie MacRae only shrugged once more for silent reply, turning aside to pull open the shadowed door and standing like a guard while Leanna passed slowly through it. From inside the kitchen now, Leanna could see a dim, flickering glow—the uneven light of a tallow candle. She made her way toward it but awkwardly, reluctantly, her heart hammering with the shock of her sudden fears. Not the Valley, oh God, please . . . not beautiful, beloved Blytheswood. Not that old Valley house that had been home to four generations of Penleys, that guardian of long, lazy summers and the silver river nearby. Jennie MacRae must be mistaken.

10

"Mrs. Leighton?"

At Leanna's entrance, a tall young man had turned to respectfully tip a battered, broad-brimmed hat. Just for a moment, the action startled her badly. It was a Yankee hat, marked by the twin crossed sabers of the federal cavalry insignia. The miniature swords flashed momentarily in the light of the single candle and brought back memories, too many memories. It was the same kind of hat Chase Courtland always wore. Young MacRae had stolen it, perhaps, she realized instantly. Or taken it from a dead soldier perhaps. That was more than possible. So many were dead by now . . . on either side. "Mr. MacRae?"

The young man grinned briefly as he shook his head. "Not 'mister' no more. *Private*. I'm joinin' the Confederate raiders."

From behind Leanna in the primitive, brick-floored kitchen, Jennie MacRae snorted rude disagreement. "Private nothing. Joinin' nothing. I lost two boys already. You're staying here where you belong, to plow and harvest and help yer ma."

The boy's face hardened and his glance at his mother was defiant. "No, Ma! With them Yankees coming, I figure every able-bodied man should fight 'em!"

"Please!" Leanna's voice was sharp with fear. An awful image of Blytheswood burning, its graceful, tall columns falling to ruin against a flaming roof, grew ever more vivid with the passing moments. "Your mother said . . . Do you have news about the Shenandoah Valley of Virginia? I've been in Atlanta, you see. And the Yankees there . . . I heard rumors, but . . ." She couldn't quite make herself speak the question. Her voice faltered, her words echoed and then faded into ominous silence.

The young man half-turned, avoiding her eyes so carefully that Leanna knew the dreaded answer before he even spoke it out loud. "Virginia Valley's been torched, ma'am. All above Harrisonburg."

Leanna felt her breath catch just once, and she closed her eyes against the shock of the searing pain. Blytheswood. Old and gracious. Her beloved home. Cold Spring, too, then would be gone—Jonathon and Whitney's place. All of it gone. "Oh, damn this war." She was aware finally of the overlong silence and numbly shook her head, forcing herself to reopen eyes wet with tears. Only a step away, Jennie MacRae stood

11

staring at her, and astonishingly, malice shone in the Georgia woman's eyes.

"Pretty plantation house all gone?"

Leanna blinked, startled. So close upon the pain of the son's news, Jennie MacRae's enmity added only incomprehensible shock.

"Mother, don't. For God's sake—"

"You hush, boy. What do you know of a ma's grief? Three sons I reared to men. Two are dead in places I never he'erd of afore. And you calling yourself "Private MacRae" and strutting like some rutting banty cock! All for her and the likes of her!" She turned suddenly to Leanna, her face hard as stone in the grotesque shadows of the kitchen's single candle. "You rich folk, with yer fine houses and yer darkies! It's a rich man's war and a poor man's fight, s'all it is, all it ever was. I'm glad you lost something, fancy ma'am. God's justice, is what it is."

Leanna felt something finally. She felt ice cold, then fever hot, and nearly ill. And her hands began to tremble in sudden reaction.

"Now yer husband's comin' round taking boys, damn him, what few is left us poor folks. You go on to him, you fine lady. You go tell him you ain't having my lastborn! Do you understand me? I'll shoot John myself afore I let him go fight for the likes of you!"

Hatred and near madness gleamed suddenly in the woman's eyes, and seeing it, Leanna instinctively moved with a swift backward step. But Jennie MacRae only brushed past her to disappear into the darkness of the hall like an ugly apparition vanishing into nights' concealment.

"Ma don't mean no harm."

Leanna had almost forgotten the boy where he stood nearby her. Now she made the effort to glance at him again, but the movement was slow and oddly difficult. She had the sensation, suddenly, of struggling up out of some kind of paralytic numbness, a kind of dull and disbelieving horror. Atlanta burning. Blytheswood gone. The Southern people turning on one another like mad dogs. God, what else could this war do to them?

"Anyway, it don't matter what she says. I'm a man grown near enough. I can do what I want, fight them damn Yankees if I want."

No, you're too young, Leanna thought suddenly. And then abruptly, she was surprised at her own surprise. God, why should I feel so old, she wondered dazedly. I'll be only twenty-two next July, myself. Far from old. Far from dead. Far from defeated, either, unless she chose to let herself be. Those Yankees would pay and pay dearly for what they'd done to her beloved South. "Your mother talked about my husband, John. Is that Colonel Leighton she really meant? If he's that closeby to us here, is there a way I might get a message to him if I wanted to?"

"I can do better if you please, ma'am. I can go tell him you're here. I figure he might come on down here with me then, and you can talk to him yourself."

Only for one instant more did Leanna allow herself to even hesitate. Chase Courtland touched her mind and unconsciously she raised a hand to her belly. She was nearly a month late now for her monthly flow. It had been one thing keeping her from moving faster on her return to Blytheswood. She'd been so sure that today, maybe tomorrow, she would get it and need to be in somewhere, not out on a dusty roadway begging rides to a distant railroad station. But it had never come. What if, because of that one, terrible, bittersweet night, what if she were with child by Chase and her husband Stewart should somehow guess? And if she were with child . . . Good Lord, could she make war on her own unborn child's father by joining Stewart? But after all the Yankees had done, how could she not? "Yes, John." She spoke her decision aloud before she'd quite made it, but once said, she forced a nod to finalize her words. The lines of the war were drawn in blood and now in fire. The Yankees deserved whatever they got from Stewart; whatever they got from anyone in fact. That even included Chase Courtland now. It had to. "Yes, John, I've a score of my own to settle with the Yankees now, don't I? If you can find my husband Colonel Leighton and ask him to come here with you, I'd be most appreciative."

It was nearly dawn and Chase ash-streaked and infinitely weary by the time he turned the stallion's head toward the distant edge of the city. Even so, the exhausted animal went willingly into a canter, anxious to escape the ever-thickening smoke of the fires. Chase passed people finally, small clusters of civilians struggling to save something from ruin, more rarely a detail of federal soldiers making halfhearted efforts to dampen the blaze. It was a bizarre feeling riding through, reminding him of that first night federal troops had taken the city. There was only the orange glow of fire and the otherwise blackness of night. Strangely, no one even seemed aware of his presence as he passed; they were too intent on their desperation to save their homes. It gave Chase a curious feeling. It seemed oddly as if he were moving in a dream, nothing being quite real, the people merely phantoms, the burning city imagined. Then reality recrystallized abruptly in the form of federal battle flags and shouting soldiers. By the Decatur Road, the army was massing, whole columns already marching out to disappear into the black Georgia night. A staff officer cantered toward Chase out of the noisy chaos, offering him a hurried salute.

"Major! Looking for your regiment?"

Chase started to shake his head. "No. Looking for—" He stopped himself, glancing only once over his shoulder toward the burning, abandoned city. Let her go, he told himself, let her go. But he couldn't. "Where would I find a Lieutenant Colonel Drake, Major? Adjutant staff?"

Major Nichols shrugged, pointing to the east. "Marched out yesterday. With the Seventeenth Corps."

Chase considered the information wearily. Colonel Drake had seemed determined to arrest Leanna for treason back in September when he'd first found her again, and when Chase had been ordered to Resaca early in October, Drake's guards had still been stationed at the door of the rooming house. He could only assume then that Leanna was somewhere in the adjutant's custody, but at least that meant she was outside the danger of the burning city. He'd looked everywhere else for her before he'd finally given up. Tomorrow he would try to catch up to the adjutant lieutenant colonel. Try once more to offer Leanna what little protection he could—welcome, or not. Probably not, he admitted to himself with a sense of futile and anguished repetition. After what had passed between them that bitter night, most probably not.

"Something else, Major?"

Major Nichols was waiting with poorly concealed impatience. He had sixty-two thousand men to get out of Atlanta by

14

dawn—only about an hour left, and a third of them were still waiting.

Chase recollected himself with an effort and shook his head. "Sorry, Major. I'm half asleep, I guess. Thanks." The brassy call of a bugle sounded suddenly to his left, signaling the order to ride out. His brigade was assigned to ride the advance for General Slocum's Twentieth Army Infantry Corps. Soldiers were forming into ragged ranks; cavalry horses were neighing and stamping restlessly. No sleep again tonight. No sleep now until heaven knew when. The coming march would be a bad one, the native Georgians stubborn Rebels who would contest the enemy army's advance in a thousand ways. And the curse of the war—partisan groups like Leanna's husband's—would no doubt continue their vicious, dirty attacks, as would Joe Wheeler's better-respected regulation Rebel cavalry. No one even knew yet where Sherman was taking them. East, obviously, by his choice of roads. But where exactly? Directly on to Richmond to join Grant in the war there? Or the ordnance plants of Macon or Augusta? Maybe Savannah? Charleston, where the Rebels had first fired shots at the federal flag?

Music sounded suddenly behind him as he rode into place at the head of his battalion, and he glanced back toward the sound in surprise. The silver band of the Thirty-Third Massachusetts was playing "John Brown's Body"; brassy and jubilant, it rang out above the distant roar of flames, the crash of falling brick, the popping of bullets exploding in burning arsenals, the occasional wail of despair from a native Atlantan losing his battle to the flames. Behind the Twentieth column, the Fourteenth Corps sang along as they began to group to march, and federal troops moved eastward into the untouched Georgia countryside singing "Glory, Glory, Hallelujah!" with exultant enthusiasm. Behind them, the Confederacy's second most important war city was left in smoldering ashes.

"I seem to have the unhappy faculty of always being in the Yankees' way." Leanna's smile held the hint of bitter memories as she looked toward the western horizon. Dawn had broken, and above where Atlanta would have been, a gray cloud of smoke and ash obscured the morning sky. Other than that, it was a beautiful day—blue and clear and warm.

15

Almost mockingly beautiful, she thought. It favored the Yankees' march.

Jennie MacRae made no reply to Leanna's comment, only continued carding cotton left over from the late summer crop. Leanna herself was hardly aware of the woman's silence; in the weeks she'd been here, Jennie MacRae had hardly said three words. And after the bitter scene of the night before, Leanna expected even less courtesy from her than usual. She had merely spoken aloud, not expecting any answer. "I wonder how long it will be before they'll get here? Atlanta must be fifteen miles, at least. But perhaps I'd better pack my things to go."

"Don't forget you owe me two more weeks board afore you leave here."

That Mrs. MacRae spoke at all was startling enough. What she said only made Leanna turn to stare at her in cold contempt. Money and slaves were still the universally worshiped gods of Georgia, it seemed, despite the war. And evidently, Jennie MacRae was no exception. So unlike Virginia, Leanna thought bitterly. There, at home, the Confederate cause had superceded all else. The war there had unified the people of all classes in fervent comradeship. "No, Mrs. MacRae, I haven't forgotten our financial arrangement. Your son said he might, with luck, make it back by noon or so. But if you're already anxious about receiving your due, perhaps you think I should pay you now."

"Fine thought." The woman looked up from her cotton to extend one work-reddened hand.

That gesture startled Leanna again, for her words had been offered as mockery. Now, her face flaming with contempt, she reached beneath her skirt for the purse she kept concealed there, tied to her petticoat. Angrily, she withdrew several bills. It was an unkind thought, but she hoped the Yankee columns *would* march directly across the MacRaes' place here. Jennie MacRae ought to learn what the Virginians had lived through for the past three years—serving as a buffer for the deeper South for all this time. And apparently for little gratitude. "Here then. I'll pay for today as well, though I don't actually owe—"

"Not with that you ain't paying."

Leanna froze.

16

"You ken keep yer Jeff Davis money. Ain't worth nothin' no more."

"But Confederate money is all I have."

"Yankee greenbacks or gold. You got gold. You got a necklace. I seen it."

Leanna paled with anger. "Two sons given to the cause and that's all it means to you, Mrs. MacRae?"

"Yankee money or gold." The woman repeated herself almost indifferently, still carding the cotton balls with a rhythmic stroke. "Maybe you're a rich lady, still. You can afford your 'hurrah for the bonnie blue flag.' I'm only poor white trash to such as you, but even poor trash get hungry come winter, and them troopers of Wheeler's took most of the grain. You et good, used our bed."

"Magnificent accommodations." Leanna had been helping with the cotton. Now she laid it aside with an abrupt gesture. So this was what Virginia had sacrificed so dearly to defend all these long years, what she had lost Blytheswood for—the likes of Jennie MacRae. "Take this then." Her hands trembled despite her command to them to be steady, and she raised them slowly to the locket around her neck. Chase had given it to her at Blytheswood, centuries ago it now seemed. Engraved on the locket's back were gentle, bittersweet words— "For a Rebel's honor." The inscription was worn in the soft gold, just barely readable. And events after he'd made the gift—Stewart's ambush, the war itself, the bitterness between her and Chase here in Atlanta, Blytheswood itself burned— those events had made a mockery of such idealistic thoughts. The words on a locket could not mean anything to anyone anymore. Such fine, sweet sentiments belonged to an age the war had ended.

Still, it hurt as she pulled the locket from her neck to drop it into Jennie MacRae's faded calico lap, hurt with a searing jolt that faded almost instantly, as if something inside her had gone numb. Like exorcising a demon or defiling a saint, Chase Courtland was abruptly gone—the place in her heart where he had been was only a cold and empty ache. Leanna blinked at the tears that had started to her eyes, and she turned into the house to conceal them. She would await her husband Stewart's return alone; she had given all she cared to give today to a world consumed by selfishness and war.

Chapter Two

Washington, D.C., was celebrating the news of President
Lincoln's reelection. The popular vote had been close, but in
the electoral college, which actually decided the thing, it had
hardly been a contest. In consequence, the always crowded
federal capital was this week literally overflowing with people.
Elinor Courtland Bennington had used all her father's influence to secure her room at the Willard Hotel, at Fourteenth
and E. She could have gotten a room more easily at Brown's,
across from the National at Sixth and Pennsylvania, but
Willard's was *the* hotel in Washington, and Elinor had no
intention of staying anywhere else. She came through the
ornate Victorian lobby now, her flounced crinoline petticoats
and hooped satin skirts rustling, and she smiled faintly to the
maroon-and-black-uniformed doorman who hurried to precede her. Liveried servants, crystal chandeliers, rich carpeting,
wonder of wonders—indoor plumbing. This hick-town capital was finally acquiring a little class, she thought. Not much,
but a little. Her hired coach stood outside, and she allowed
the doorman to hand her up the marble mounting block, then
tossed him a small gold coin as a tip. He didn't quite catch it,
and it amused her to see him on his knees as the carriage
pulled away, hunting for the coin in the Washington dirt.

She had told her father Joshua she'd come down for new
hats—William, on Pennsylvania Avenue, was adequate for
them. Gowns she wouldn't buy except in New York or
imported directly from Europe. Philadelphia was the largest
city in the world second to London, but its sophistication was
second-class. Fortunately, Joshua had consented willingly,
not having the vaguest suspicion of the real reason for his
daughter's trip. That real reason was the promising news that
things might finally be going Elinor's way. She'd had a wire
from a friend at the War Department announcing the fact that

18

they had Jonathon Penley's sister under their thumb . . . they thought. Arrest orders were being drawn up with Leanna Penley Leighton's name on them. At last. Elinor had nothing against the woman personally, but she needed leverage on the Penley brother, needed it badly and needed it now. The war couldn't go on much longer and every month lost was thousands of dollars gone, for gunrunning was only a wartime business. And like any other business, gunrunning required capital. Since her father's heart attack and Jonathon Penley's simultaneous takeover at the bank, the capital had, to be blunt, dried up. But once she had Leanna Leighton walking a federal tightrope, brother Jonathon would reopen the bank vaults and turn a blind eye to Elinor's petty pilfering. He'd have to—or his sister would be rotting in a prison camp, the horrors of which Jonathon knew well from an earlier stay there of his own. As protective as he was of his precious blue-blooded sister, he would never allow that to happen to her. At least Elinor was *gambling* that he wouldn't.

The restaurant at the National was less crowded by now. Elinor recognized Bristol at once and noted he had chosen a table set apart from the others. That was probably second nature she thought, for a man in his profession. Bristol was one of Chief Baker's operatives in the Bureau of Internal Intelligence, that portion of the War Department that was war-created, power-oriented and infinitely accessible to bribery. Patriotism in Washington, D.C., only went so far, war or no war. What a pleasure it was to deal with men of such uncomplicated vision.

"Lady Bennington." Bristol stood as he spoke, impeccably dressed in black with a white starched collar and a black string tie. An expensive watch hung from his waistcoat pocket and swung slowly outward as he reached to offer her chair.

"Mr. Bristol." She smiled, but coolly, for the man was not attractive to her and she could see from his expression that she *was* to him. Complications she didn't want. "I assume you brought what I asked for—something tangible to prove the endangered status of our mutual friend Mrs. Leighton."

There was a second's hesitation. Noting it, Elinor's smile cooled. She glanced over her shoulder for caution, then swiftly took her seat.

"A minor problem, Lady Bennington."

"How minor?" Her smile had faded entirely.

"Well . . ." He merely shrugged. "Nothing we can't circumvent in time."

"Time? If I had time to spare, I wouldn't need you and your damn War Department!" Elinor rarely lost her composure, but she did momentarily now—she had already been imagining the look of fear on Jonathon's face and the feel of more gold pouring into the Richmond vaults.

"There's been a slight complication. A federal cavalry major with an interest in the woman's case." He glanced at a piece of paper as he spoke, unfolding another section. "Yes. Courtland. With the Eighth Pennsylvania, it seems."

"Courtland?"

"Yes. Odd coincidence, isn't it? Same name and—"

"Coincidence?" Elinor interrupted Bristol by laughing in sudden mockery. "You damn *fool*, it's no coincidence. That's my *brother*. Leanna Leighton is in Atlanta then, I gather." She reached for the paper he held, snatching it without apology. "Of all the God-cursed luck." She read it quickly, twice, then began to feel better. There might be a way out yet. "But this says my brother is camped at Resaca, not in the city."

"Still . . ."

"Still nothing. Arrest the damn woman before my brother gets back to Atlanta."

"Impossible. Don't *you* read the newspapers, Lady Bennington?" Bristol was no fool, had never been one. He didn't appreciate being labeled one, and as he returned her barb, he deliberately smiled. "This wire is almost a week old. Sherman's *left* Atlanta. He left on the fifteenth, with all his troops."

"Then wire down and tell your man to—"

"Communications with Sherman's troops were cut on the twelfth. We don't even know for sure where his army is going."

Elinor paused in exasperation. As she considered her alternatives, she stared at the agent coldly, noting and not appreciating the quirk of amusement that was curling his mouth. "*So*, Mister Bristol? What now?"

"So, dear lady, we sit tight and wait until we get further word from Lieutenant Colonel Drake, who is assigned to Sherman's army and is trying his level best to fulfill our wishes in regard to your Leanna Leighton. She fled Atlanta some weeks ago apparently, and she's now at a farmhouse about a day's journey west of the city. Drake has several dozen troopers watching her there, waiting for her Rebel husband to come to claim her. When he does that, Drake will have his reason to arrest the woman as well."

"You mean you've let all this time go by simply so you could use her to bait a trap for her husband?" Elinor threw her gloves down on the white-lined cloth in hissing fury. "You damn fools, you've wasted weeks already! What if she *never* contacts her husband? What if my damn *brother* catches up to her first? Now you listen to me and listen to me good! I don't give a damn about Leanna Leighton's husband. It's *her* I want! Now you make contact somehow with that Drake of yours and tell him that. *Now!*"

"But with your brother involved—"

"I don't give a damn about him either! He *is* only *one* man, isn't he? Outranked by heaven knows how many other officers down there? Send him on trash collection duty if you like, but get me that woman!"

Bristol raised one brow. "But your father, too, complicated the matter by inquiring—"

"My father is a sick man. He may not even live out the year. It's *me* you are dealing with, Bristol. Me you'll *be* dealing with for years to come when my father's in his grave and my brother, if he's even still alive, is doodling away in bank offices." Elinor spoke sweetly again, even softly, having regained her composure momentarily. She even smiled, though Bristol wasn't fooled. The expression in her green eyes was still coldly murderous. "I want Leanna Leighton arrested. And I want no more excuses. *Now* do you understand me?"

"Perfectly." He nodded and rose, reaching for his hat. Bitch, he thought. A rare one at that. Still, he'd been in the War Department long enough to know one thing: personal feelings didn't count. Orders from Secretary Stanton, Major Eckert or Lafayette Baker *did*, and somehow she'd gotten to them. "Your wish is the bureau's command, Lady Bennington. Consider it done. By the end of this month, Leanna Leighton will have been tried and convicted of treason against the federal government."

Stone Mountain was a huge, granite dome east of Atlanta. It thrust up out of brick-red clay into November-blue sky, dominating the Georgia countryside, and Stewart Leighton used it often as a lookout post for his guerrilla rangers, and sometimes as a campground. There, John MacRae had found him this morning just before dawn.

"We've got a problem, gentlemen." The CSA lieutenant colonel spoke softly in his leisurely South Carolinian drawl. As he spoke he halted his horse in the shade of a huge pine and gestured to the woods below. There, when the men looked carefully enough in among the trees, they could see a horse's head, or a leg, or a rump half-covered in dark federal blue. Of the soldiers themselves, there wasn't a sign, but that didn't mean that they weren't there. They were . . . somewhere.

Stewart stood in his stirrups, searching the fields below. "That's MacRaes' place there, isn't it?"

The young officer riding beside him nodded, glancing over one shoulder. The rest of the men were waiting in restless silence. Only horses moved. A canteen jingled as someone raised it to drink and let it fall again.

"So where are the damn Yankees hiding?" Stewart's question was rhetorical, and he searched the countryside for his answer. MacRaes', obviously—it was a Yankee trap. The real question was how to ambush the ambushers. Stewart's lieutenant touched his arm and gestured wordlessly to a dust cloud rising suddenly to the west—distant yet, but heading swiftly closer. The main Yankee army was moving already on the McDonough Road. If he wanted Leanna back, it was now or never to attack the soldiers concealed around the MacRae place below.

"Right, let's go." That quickly, Stewart Leighton had made his decision about the trap. Inconvenience or not, Leanna was his wife still, he owed her something. And he would teach the damn Yanks a lesson, too, about how a Leighton held on to something that belonged to him. He raised one arm to gesture forward and in unison, the Rebel raiders spurred after him down the wooded slope, galloping headlong toward the MacRae farm and the Yankees they knew were concealed somewhere there—thinking *they* were the ones about to spring an ambush. As they rode a single whisper passed among the guerrillas, low and ugly, a whisper not uncommon by this point of the war. "No quarter," it said. There would be no prisoners taken while Stewart Leighton rode in command.

Inside the MacRae farmhouse, the sound of shots rang out with the suddenness of summer thunder. Leanna heard an

22

answering crash from the kitchen below as Jennie MacRae dropped a bowl in startlement, but by then Leanna was on the stairs already, racing for the front door. Yankees, she thought, and the single word echoed and reechoed furiously in her mind. John MacRae hadn't brought Stewart here in time. Like Blytheswood in the Shenandoah Valley, like Atlanta that terrible September night, she was once more to find herself alone and unaided while Yankees came pouring in all around her.

A minié ball splintered the wooden frame of the door as she reached to pull it open and she froze, more surprised than frightened in that first instant of danger, standing motionless for a long minute beside the ruined door. Through the windowpane that lined the doorway, she saw enough to tell her instantly that there were more than Yankees involved out there. Dark blue uniforms showed against the lighter blue sky, but mounted men wearing CSA gray were chasing the federals pell-mell from the wood lines out onto the open crop fields. Confederate Cavalry, she thought with a sudden rush of startled pride. They weren't going to let Sherman march through Georgia unmolested, after all!

A sudden shot snapped her back to her senses as it shattered the window to the left of the door. Then another hit the glass she'd just been standing by, and she shook her head sharply against a rain of flying glass shards as she ran for the comparative safety of the nearby kitchen. "Mrs. MacRae, get down! There's fighting out there and I can't tell yet for sure who's winning."

But even as she cried the warning the back door of the farmhouse flew open with a sudden crash. No Yankees stood there etched against the bright blue sunlight, and even as Leanna gasped in instinctive shock she was beginning to smile in glad relief. Young MacRae and an officer in a battered CSA uniform stood outside on the mossy stone step, and young MacRae was openly grinning.

"Come on, ma'am. Yer husband's waitin' on ya. Yer comin' with us."

"Stewart?" For only a moment, Leanna stood startled. She had thought it was Wheeler's men, seeing gray outside the front door. And before she could gather her senses to think, Jennie MacRae had reacted, screeching a denial to the youngster's words and clawing forward toward the two men like some demented animal.

"No!" She shoved Leanna aside in reckless fury, knocking the startled girl into the doorframe. "No, John, you ain't goin'! Damn you, you ain't, I say!"

Young MacRae returned only a stubborn silence, trying to ease his arm free of his mother's grip. He threw an apologetic glance toward the other man who stood nearby, but the young officer by the boy's side seemed hardly to notice. He had looked up suddenly instead, looking over Leanna's shoulder toward the front of the house, and an expression of something like pain suddenly flickered over his dust-covered features. Distracted, Leanna turned instinctively to follow his gaze and only then began to realize that the sound of shooting had abruptly slackened. There were hoarse cries instead, and the wails of the wounded. Dimly, it seemed to her that she could make out a shouted plea for mercy . . . and then came the sound of a half-dozen more shots. Bewildered, she started to turn toward the distant sounds, but the officer's hand fastened quickly on her arm.

"No, ma'am. You best come this way, I think." The uniformed officer thrust past Jennie MacRae to take Leanna's arm. "Nothing out there for a lady to be seeing."

He spoke in a deep drawl, a cultured tone, and Leanna turned back to find a strange expression darkening his eyes. He seemed deliberately unwilling to answer the question in her gaze and turned his head, gesturing instead to the open back door. "This way, if you please. Colonel Leighton will ride around when he's through."

"Through?" Leanna shook her head, glancing distractedly to where Jennie MacRae still held her son's sleeve in a desperate grip. "Through with what?" The MacRae boy was pulling away from his mother at last . . . embarrassment, now anger, hardening his face as he shook himself harshly free.

"Damn it, Ma, let go! You got nothing more to say in it!" The young man shoved the woman aside with a last angry motion, and as Jennie MacRae scrambled for her balance she turned suddenly to lunge at Leanna instead.

"Yer fault, damn you! I should'ha never taken you in! You rich folk with yer fancy ways!"

With a startled cry, Leanna shrank away from the woman's hands, and the young officer beside her moved instantly to offer protection. He shielded her with one arm and used the other to knock Jennie MacRae backward into her own rough-hewn kitchen table. Another bowl rocked, found the edge and smashed down on to the brick. And that was the last Leanna saw of Jennie MacRae.

An instant later, she felt sunlight on her face and the bracing coolness of the brilliant blue day as the young officer pulled her with him out the farmhouse door. Horsemen were already riding around the edge of the dirty white house. And one of them was her husband Stewart, blond and blue-eyed, handsome as he had been that day in Richmond when she'd first married him—years ago now, in 1861. But Stewart seemed changed somehow. Different. A difference that went deeper than the stains and wear showing on his Confederate-gray officer's coat, she suspected suddenly, and for a single instant, Leanna found herself almost afraid of him. Nonsense, she told herself. He's my own husband. But before either she or Stewart could speak, another rider had abruptly appeared, and Stewart's attention went instantly to him.

"All done, Colonel." The man was just now reholstering a smoking Colt revolver and chuckling as he spoke to his commander. "Them Yanks got real cut by the end. You missed a good 'un. One fella was cryin' for his mammy—now ain't that nice?"

Leanna glanced at the stranger, startled, puzzled, then understanding in a single swift instant of chilling clarity. Oh God. Those cries for mercy. The shots. Now, a total silence. They had shot them all. *Murdered*, really. What had happened to the Southern world?

"I love dead Yankees." The man leaned over his saddle to spit brown tobacco juice, wiping the residue left on his beard with the back of one hand. Suddenly he laughed uproariously, set spurs to his sweating horse and started toward the distant tree line that bordered the far cotton fields.

Appalled, Leanna stood motionless as she watched him go. From across the fields, his laughter was echoing, still, and then from the distance came the shrill cry of a Rebel yell. She shivered convulsively at the madness it conveyed and fought a sudden impulse to turn and run.

"Treejack." Stewart startled her by speaking without preamble and he gestured lazily to the now-distant rider. Then, as if sensing her fear, he smiled a kind of faint amusement.

25

"Why, don't mind him any, Leanna. *You* needn't worry. Treejack only bites Yankees and rabid dogs." He watched her yet a moment longer, then seemed to make a final decision of his own, swinging down off his horse to step toward her. "Let's go, then, my dear. Before the Yankees' main columns get up here. We've already shot our quota for today."

As he lifted her quickly back up to his saddle Leanna glanced involuntarily over Stewart's dust-grayed shoulder—toward the west, where the federal columns were already marching. Oh God, Chase, she found herself thinking in a kind of sudden, frightened anguish. Have I made the wrong decision? Husband or not, should I have stayed with you instead? But I couldn't. You're an enemy now. God help us both, an enemy. I had no other choice.

By the time a Union Cavalry patrol reached the MacRae farmhouse, the sun was low in the deep blue Georgia sky, and shadows were lengthening around the tall pines and oaks that edged the road. Stone Mountain sat a few miles north like a silent giant, brooding and grim against the horizon. It was easy to see there was something amiss. Flies had found the bodies of the ambushed federal ambushers and without riding a step further on, the young lieutenant in command of the federal patrol sent a hasty courier galloping back to fetch the major.

It had already been a long day for Major Courtland. A long ride, without sleep the night before, the hours today moving slowly and heavily with nagging uneasiness—both about the Georgia Confederate troops still prowling the area, and about a courier sent to Drake who had not yet returned. Chase Courtland's face was grim when the young trooper relayed his message. His face was grimmer still when he and his own patrol had finally reached the MacRae place and the butchery that awaited him there. For the first time all day, he totally forgot about Leanna Leighton.

He gave orders, curtly, leaving a detail of men out front to bury the federal soldiers—or what was left of them—as he continued warily on toward the nearby house. This was a trademark of the worst of the partisan raiders, this mutilation of the bodies. Some linked the atrocities to Leighton's crew, though with little real proof. True, it had begun last year in Virginia when Leighton was there, but it had spread since then. It had been both novel and appalling at first. Now, Chase thought grimly, it was merely appalling. Appalling enough that it still made his stomach heave. And several of the younger troopers lost their lunch as they rode through the overgrown little gulley where most of the bodies lay sprawled. Damn war, he thought. Putting men in the midst of this butchery. Twenty-eight men lay dead here by an insignificant farmhouse.

A woman stood in the distant doorway, watching the soldiers come. A ragged shawl lay around her shoulders, and her hair was badly askew.

"Mrs. MacRae?" Chase dismounted as he reached the white frame farmhouse and curtly touched the brim of his hat. He moved slowly and watched the woman carefully. She had a strange vacant look in her eyes.

Jennie MacRae stared at him but never moved. "They took my boy."

It wasn't her words, it was the tone of her voice. From the corner of his eye, Chase noticed Grier suddenly crossing himself. Chase was Episcopalian, not Catholic, but he understood well Grier's action. Jennie MacRae spoke like a dead woman.

"Excuse me." As Chase spoke he gestured to his captain to be alert for trouble. "We're with General Sherman's troops. I'd like your permission to search—"

"They took my boy. My last one. They took my boy."

She was staring past him, over his left shoulder. Almost involuntarily, Chase glanced to follow her gaze. Nothing was there. The burial detail wasn't visible from the house and the men out there were working in silence. He glanced at Grier and nodded once, gesturing him on inside.

"Sorry to intrude, ma'am." Chase reached to an inside pocket and withdrew a paper, a copy of General Sherman's "Special Field Order" Number 120. He didn't think the woman was capable of understanding, but he read it aloud to dispel the odd silence. " 'The army will forage liberally on the country . . . at least ten days' provisions . . . and three days' forage . . . In districts . . . where guerrillas or bushwhackers molest our march . . . or inhabitants otherwise manifest local hostility, then army commanders should order and enforce a devastation more or less relentless. Horses, mules, wagons, etc. belonging to the inhabitants may be appropriated freely

. . . in all foraging of whatever kind, the parties engaged . . . will endeavor to leave each family a reasonable portion for their maintenance.' "

He paused at the end. The woman made no reply. Didn't even blink. He sighed faintly and turned, gesturing men to the barn and sheds. Grier had come out of the house already, shaking his head. So they'd missed the raiders. They were long gone already, as they usually were. It was for the best maybe, he thought, the troopers were tired and edgy and in a mood to lynch Rebels. They'd catch up to them another day—on a better day for Chase's troops. He tried to tell himself that anyway, ignoring a sudden inexplicable sense of denial. He shrugged once, and he turned. "We'll leave enough to see you through the winter."

"You looking for Colonel Leighton, Yankee?"

She startled Chase by speaking at all. Startled him so much that his hand moved instinctively to grip his saber, and he felt its cold metal under his fingers as he turned on one heel. The woman hadn't moved, and he forced his hand from his sword, glancing once again at Grier.

"He left. She left. And they took my boy."

Uncomprehending, Chase watched her for another moment, but no explanation followed her words. Finally, he simply nodded, raising his hand to hastily tip his hat. The woman was more than half crazy, dusk was coming and the main column miles back yet. In the strange silence, it felt as if hostility to the hated Yankees radiated from the red earth itself. Around them, the lengthening shadows felt cold and ominous. The smell of death lay heavy in the air. It was time to get away from both this farm and the madwoman who owned it. He'd swung into the saddle before one of the returning troopers suddenly shouted and stepped forward, grabbing at something in the woman's hand.

"Gold! Lookit here! Rebel—"

"Hazan! Let be!" Grier interceded, snatching the trinket away from the trooper with an effort. "Damn you, Hazan, what the hell . . . ?"

"Forage liberally! S'our orders, Captain, ain't it? She don't need no gold watch to eat this winter!"

Grier shoved the trooper back toward his horse. "Jesus, Hazan. You reek of rotgut whiskey. Hand me that canteen you're carrying."

Hazan did . . . not without an ugly look. Grier took one sniff and dumped it upside down to stain the red dirt dark scarlet. "Forage means *food*, Hazan. Keep that in mind."

Chase nodded once in agreement and began to turn his horse. He stopped suddenly, frowning. "That's no watch." He leaned over the saddle, conscious of a slow growing shock of disbelief that was spreading in his gut. No watch indeed. It was a locket. One he knew well. "Where did you get that?"

Jennie MacRae smiled slowly, strangely. She held the necklace aloft, letting it swing slowly in the falling sunlight. "Purty thing, ain't it?" Her smile widened, she chuckled softly, staring at it. Suddenly, her smile died. Her eyes glazed with venom and she spit at the swinging gold. "Devil woman!" she hissed fiercely. "Gave it to me . . . then took my last boy! Spawn of Satan!"

Maybe it was only the sudden chill of the dusk breeze, but Chase shivered sharply watching her. Leanna's locket . . . Leanna's no more. Jennie MacRae was too crazy to lie. He took a deep breath, his brown eyes growing infinitely cold. All the pieces were coming together, and the whole arrangement was suddenly all too plain. Drake. Leanna. A federal ambush and Stewart Leighton's raiders . . . And what clearer message could Leanna have left for him than this? Twenty-eight soldiers in one grisly grave.

He'd been a fool then all along. A blind, damn fool. Leanna had spoken the truth in Atlanta. It had been the sweetness of Virginia that had been the lie. "Devil woman" was an apt epithet. "C'mon, Grier, let's get moving. It's getting dark." Chase turned his horse without a backward glance, setting his spurs sharply against the animal. The burial detail was done. He saw them up ahead, mounted and waiting, and Grier was following, equally eager to leave the grisly scene well behind. Unnoticed by either, Hazan was the last to depart. He rode hard into Jennie MacRae, knocking her down in the dirt. As she fell he reached for the locket and slipped it into one pocket, never glancing back. Food, hell, he thought. He wasn't leaving the damn Reb's gold, no matter what the high-brow officers said. And if they protested *too* much, well, wouldn't be the first "strap" to catch a bullet in the back from one of his own troopers. When gold glinted like that in Georgia sunlight, Willy Hazan was helping hisself.

Jennie MacRae's mad eyes glazed slowly, staring upward as

29

sunset streaked the blue Southern sky with deepening rose and gold. It was a clear night and cold. Before the dawn broke, she was dead.

Elinor felt better now. The meeting with Bristol had upset her, but a full day had passed since. She'd been extravagant at William's yesterday afternoon, and that had helped. Last night, she'd attended a glittering evening soirée—Secretary of War Stanton himself had sent on the engraved invitation— and she'd enjoyed the evening. Enjoyed the handsome young army captain detailed to escort her as well. She smiled faintly, remembering. He'd been charming at first—carefully courteous. She'd worn a peach gown with a beaded, low bodice. Far outdone the Washington ladies—including Mrs. Lincoln, the President's dowdy wife. Mary Todd Lincoln had a figure like a plug of tobacco. It didn't matter how much she spent on her gowns, she still looked like the Illinois bumpkin she was. Elinor had seen Mrs. Lincoln's expression, overheard the beginning of a nasty, shrill exchange between her and her henpecked husband. Then the Lincolns had left early. Elinor's smile widened, wondering how any of the Washington wives were, this very morning, on their way to their dressmakers, sketches in hand. No matter, she thought. By the time they got their copies made, she'd be wearing something else. Leanna Leighton not withstanding, life did have certain simple pleasures.

Capt. Benjamin Knowles, for instance. Only in Washington on a two-week leave from Grant's Army of the Potomac, he had been hard-pressed to conceal his astonishment at the brazen invitation Elinor had whispered in his ear as they'd danced. He'd had an erection almost instantly. She'd felt it as he'd held her close to turn in the waltz. Long war for young men. She'd played a teasing game after that, staying on at the soirée for another hour at least. He'd been trembling already as they'd seated themselves in the closed carriage. Elinor had ordered the driver to take the long route back to her hotel, and as they'd made the last turn by Lafayette Square, Captain Knowles had forgotten most of what had showed as careful breeding and taken her right there and then—no easy feat with a half-dozen petticoats between them. The night had been long after that—and sweet. Elinor guessed the young man would spend most of today sleeping.

30

Besides that, she had another reason for her greatly improved humor. It had occurred to her that there was more than one way to cook her particular Penley goose. She would write to Hadley, her husband, who was still in Richmond. The CSA government was as anxious to *get* the black-market guns as she was anxious to *sell* them. Hadley surely could convince the desperate Confederates to put Leanna Leighton's name on a certain list, offer a bribe or two if need be. That way, Penley's own people would also be after the girl. And Elinor didn't care a whit which side of the war the woman landed on. It didn't matter to her what color uniforms were worn by the men who took Leanna Leighton into custody. The result would be the same. Leverage, she thought, happily. Either way, Jonathon Penley would dance to a tune of Elinor's piping, the bank vault would reopen, the black-market guns once more start rolling across the Maryland border. It had turned out to be a good trip after all.

Leanna deliberately rode some distance apart from the rest of Stewart's guerrilla raiders, allowing herself the illusion that this was beloved Virginia instead of alien Georgia, trying to escape from the bitter realities of omnipresent war by taking a moment's rest within a world of reconstructed memory. It was all that kept her sane sometimes, she thought, the memory of the world that once had been and the hope that it would someday be again. It was easier here than it might be elsewhere; this part of Georgia reminded her a little of the lush green hills of Virginia. There were rolling, forested hills; narrow, swift-flowing creeks; rich, emerald pastureland; pines with hardwoods mixed in—turning autumn colors, finally, the sumac red, the yellow of goldenrod—a deep blue sky and the soft crackle of dead leaves beneath the horses' hooves. The pecan trees offered ripe, sweet nuts, and in happier days, Jewel would have made sugar pie out of them.

Her horse shied, and Leanna took a tighter rein as she glanced sharply over one shoulder. There was nothing to worry about yet, she was sure. The Yankees were many miles behind them, not even to Covington, yet. She could still keep her position, apart from the main body of men, and that pleased her. Other than her husband, his young Lt. Walker and the MacRae boy, the fifty-odd men of the partisan group were a strange and frightening crew—more dangerous probably than the Yankees who came behind. Leanna made a point of keeping her distance in the daylight, and of keeping close to Stewart's tent at night. If this was the best Georgia had left to offer, they hadn't a prayer of containing Sherman's huge army, she thought with a bitter smile. General Joe Wheeler's Rebel cavalry was only a few thousand men—like a flea attacking an elephant, they would hardly even be a nuisance.

Anyway, more than the Yankees just now, Leanna worried about the child she thought she was carrying inside her still-flat belly. She'd been sick again this morning. Luckily, she was fairly sure that Stewart hadn't even noticed. That was for the best, she thought. In truth, it was the only way she dared to keep things. She must conceal her pregnancy from Stewart until he put her safely on the train to his family's plantation near Charleston and then hope he would eventually accept the child as his own. It could work, she told herself uneasily. It *should* work. Stewart paid little enough attention to her that such a reluctant deception on her part could succeed. He had been courteous enough in the days since MacRaes', but distant, as if Leanna were merely an adjunct to his life, a kind of inconvenience he must bear with grace. There was the odd sensation of being strangers, two strangers trying to remember why they should not feel so strange with one another. And Stewart had grown so cold somehow. So eternally grim. She could remember him smiling in earlier years. Though he had never been a man to indulge in playful humor, there had been at least the occasional smile. Now there was not even that. It was the war, of course. But other men in the war had managed to retain enough of their humanity to smile still. Chase Courtland had, she remembered well. He had smiled in the darkness that last night in Atlanta, lying quiet and weary there in her arms. She had felt the gentle curve of his mouth as he'd laid his face down against her bare shoulder. That was the night she'd conceived the child which lay secreted in her belly. A Yankee's child, but in spite of that, a child almost desperately precious to her—for all that it was a betrayal of her Confederate husband and a betrayal of her Confederate conscience. Stewart was too strange to her now, too distant, for her to try to explain the truth. But she would make it up to him, she promised herself. She would bear him his own children, manage his house, share his bed. From this point forward, she must think of the child as his, not as

Chase's, and her loyalties must be entirely undivided. She was the wife of a Confederate officer, only that. And from now on she would be a model of the loyalty and soul-deep resistance that characterized most other Southern women. In a few days, they would be in Madison, at the railroad depot running from there. Stewart planned to put her on a train heading east and out of the war. To Augusta first, probably, and then on to Charleston to the Leighton family plantation. Like all the rest of the Leighton women, then, Leanna would devote her days to supporting the men who had ridden to war. That much at least, she thought, she owed to her Confederate husband. The ever-worsening atrocities of the Yankees' war had made that decision final for her.

A sudden burst of laughter startled her. Her horse shied violently and instantly began to rear. Caught by surprise, Leanna made a desperate grab for the animal's mane and missed. She felt herself starting to slip sideways on the saddle, had a momentary glimpse of a grinning, gargoyle face hanging upside down on the tree bough above her, and then the horse reared again as the face laughed and then began to sing. She lost the stirrups and the reins both, and as the animal came back to earth stiff-legged, she fell.

Stewart had reached Leanna by the time she'd recovered her senses, but the ground had been hard, and she'd landed almost flat on her back with stunning force. Treejack swung off the bough above her with a final cackle of mirth and disappeared back into the woods, seemingly undismayed by his commander's angry rebuke.

"You all right, Leanna?"

Stewart's anger sounded genuine and she managed to nod, struggling to sit up. A shudder rippled instantly inside her belly, her breath caught in her throat. The baby. Oh my God, the baby.

"Damn that lunatic! If he couldn't smell Yankees five miles away, I'd shoot him where he stands."

"It's all right, I think."

Leanna's voice held a tentative note but Stewart didn't notice in the heat of his own anger. He reached his hand out to help her stand. "I'm sorry, dear. We can still treat a lady better than that, can't we?" His smile was brief and forced. She looked at him and quickly away, fighting secret tears of fright and guilt. "Nothing but trash, of course. In the old days, we'd hang him for that. But I can't now, I'm sorry. I need all of them too badly. Especially Treejack." He helped her up, keeping his hold on her arm. "You're sure you're all right? I'll ride with you for a while, I think."

Leanna managed a nod, but as another cramp rippled deep inside her, she closed her eyes for a moment's prayer. Please, God, she thought, please. Leave me something from this war. Leave me my baby. Please.

"Here, Leanna. I'll help you up."

She felt Stewart's hands strong around her waist, hoisting her back up toward her empty saddle. Almost numbly, she reached out and managed to collect the reins. Then she waited wordlessly while Lt. Walker brought Stewart's horse. They set off again through the pine-needled floor of the woods, but no matter how hard she tried, she couldn't make it feel like Virginia. And once or twice she shuddered, hearing the distant echoes still of Treejack's crazy laughter.

Chapter Three

Dusk was deepening to twilight, and the crackling flames of Madison's burning railroad depot grew ever brighter against a darkening sky. The air was colder today, and the heat of the fire offered welcome warmth to Chase's bare face and hands. He watched the roof of the depot glow in one spot, bursting into reluctant flame. Then the first of the inside timbers burned through with an audible crack, the roof edge nearest it began to sag and the whole building collapsed inward. The cavalry horses clustered nearby snorted and stamped uneasily, and he took a tighter hold on the reins of his own horse as he turned to nod at the man standing heavily silent beside him.

"That's all we're going to do tonight, sir." He tipped his hat courteously as he spoke, for the man beside him was ex-Senator Joshua Hill, a friend of General Sherman's from Washington days and one of the few Georgians who'd voted against Southern secession four years ago. Hill's courageous, personal intercession with the advancing Union Army had saved Madison from the fate of other Georgia towns in the Yankee line of march. The destruction here was limited and carefully controlled. Lucky for Madison, Chase thought, remembering the black smoke rising above Covington, the last town they'd been through. "Foraging" was no longer defined very strictly.

"And the cotton bales in the warehouse, Major? They represent next year's food and dress for many of our people."

Chase shrugged, carefully noncommittal. "General Slocum will decide tomorrow what else needs to be done. I'll post a guard detail tonight on the cotton and the courthouse both, but I imagine the warehouse will be considered contraband, Senator. I'm sorry." He felt Senator Hill's eyes on him still as he remounted and turned his horse away, felt the frustration and the anguish both in the Southerner's eyes and shrugged

35

against an instinctive sympathy for the man. Hell, *they* started it, Chase reminded himself. Fired on the country's flag at Fort Sumter, and nearly two hundred thousand Union soldiers already lay buried—dying to repair the damage done that April day. This was war, and it was as General Sherman said, "Hell." Burning in such a place as hell was only to be expected.

"Major?"

A soft feminine voice caught his ear in the midst of the shouting men and the roar of nearby flames, and he stopped his horse in surprise to glance down. A young woman stood there—pretty, he thought. But in the darkness it was hard to tell. "Ma'am." Wariness hardened his face and the glance he gave her was cold. Another Southern belle, probably. Thinking fluttering eyelashes and a smile would save Daddy's cotton and Mother's silver.

"Have you a supper invitation yet?" The lace shawl covering her high-piled hair and most of her face slipped back a little as she looked up. And she *was* pretty. "I've come to extend one if you'd pause just a moment."

Chase's answering smile was wryly sarcastic, and he shrugged. "I think I must be misunderstanding you, ma'am. Or perhaps in the darkness, you're mistaking the color of my uniform for gray."

"If you're determined to be unpleasant, I'll retract my invitation. Are you?"

"Am I?" He considered a moment, then shrugged again. "My unpleasantness has become habit, I'm afraid. Too long a war."

"Habits can be broken." She kept her smile but it had faded somewhat. "I need a yes or a no, Major. We Southern ladies aren't supposed to remain so long in such rough environs, you know. If you don't make a decision soon, I'll be forced to faint simply to save my reputation."

His gut reaction was to say no, and then almost in the same instant, he checked that impulse. Why not, he demanded harshly to himself? Still saving yourself for Leanna Leighton, you fool? It wasn't Susan Stratford, he knew—he wasn't married to her yet. And as for Leanna, she was only a memory now and a bad one. And the best way to get rid of one memory was to bury it beneath a horde of others. More pleasant ones, hopefully. "I'd be most honored, ma'am. To share dinner—and whatever else you care to offer."

She reached up with one gloved hand in answer, resting it briefly on the hard muscles of Chase's thigh before turning around to gesture the way.

It was a common situation in the war, women fleeing the dangers of isolated country homes to seek refuge with kin or friends in town. Five women shared the single house, and the atmosphere during the meal was most obviously strained. After dinner, though, there was a lovely, moonlit formal garden, fragrant with tea olive, warm where the hedgerow blocked the wind. The distant fires of the railroad depot had finally burned down to glowing red ash, and quiet shadows had claimed the pretty little town. Louisa had offered the first kiss. Chase had taken responsibility for the succeeding ones, finding her mouth sweet, her breasts soft and full, her body pliant in welcome. When the lights from the parlor inside had finally been extinguished, he'd taken her upstairs and enjoyed the remainder of the evening's effort. Louisa did, too, and she smiled contentedly in the bedroom's darkness and listened to Chase slowly regaining his breath.

"Well, now what do you think of our Southern hospitality, Major?" Louisa's voice was laughing and light, her breath tickled the hair by his ear, and Chase smiled back, turning his head to face her. Her face was dark against the white linen sheets, her hair gleamed burnished gold on the pillow and he raised one hand lazily to gather its long strands.

"I hope you don't have cotton in the railroad shed and think you've just saved it." He was only half teasing, and he glanced at her in the darkness to read her face. She was still smiling, and as she moved closer to his bare side he raised his arm carelessly to cover her nakedness.

"We have a few bales." She smiled as if at a joke and glanced up. For one split second, she wore the patented insipidity of the Southern belle and then she laughed again softly and shrugged. "Most of *our* cotton is elsewhere. I hope you'll be gentleman enough not to ask *where* exactly."

Chase smiled and shrugged. "No, I just hope it's well hidden, Louisa. Regardless of your . . . hospitality, I'd burn what I found. I'd have to." There was a short silence, a pleasant enough one, and he raised himself on one elbow to reach for a cheroot. As he leaned over her for the matches a soft scent of rose sachet drifted up from her hair, and he frowned, startled, then angry. Leanna had always used the same scent. It dispelled the easy pleasure of the moment and his smile faded. "Pardon my asking so bluntly, but why aren't you waving Confederate flags and slamming doors in our faces like most of the other women in Madison are doing, Louisa? Don't you believe in the Confederate cause?" Chase new he'd startled her. He felt it in the swift question of her glance, the thoughtfulness of the gaze that followed it.

"That seems an odd question to ask at such a time, Major," she answered finally. "But being unaccustomed to Yankee officers and their ways, I'll try not to wonder at the question but simply to answer it." She moved the pillow to sit higher, watching the hard, handsome lines of his face thoughtfully in the light of the flaring match. "I'm not as staunch a Rebel as most, no. I was raised in France and there's no slavery there, for one thing. But I went to college here in Madison. CSA Vice-President Stephens taught one of my classes as a matter of fact, and I consider this my home, as I consider myself a Southerner. You may be surprised because I'm sharing your bed—all you outsiders see of us is proper gentlewomen and gallant gentlemen, but human nature remains the same beneath it. My college degree is in needlework and the social graces. My evening out may be a cultured reading of the classics or Melissa Jones playing songs of her own composition on the pianoforte—no more interesting to me than it would be to you. It's like a game we play, mostly. A game we *choose* to play, and one we understand, even though you Yankees don't. But the other side of the South's coin is *this*, my handsome major. Plus, white masters taking slave mistresses, raising 'yellow' bastards to do housework. Women desperate to be women, to be warm, to be human, to be really loved. It can't be so different up North, is it? Don't your backstairs servants find plenty to whisper about wherever they go to whisper?"

"To McGillin's Pub on Drury Lane." Chase shrugged, unconvinced. Leanna was on his mind still, and because of that, the expression in his brown eyes stayed hard and dark. "There is a difference, though. We aren't as hypocritical about what we do. We don't pretend to be saints."

"We don't think of it as hypocrisy; we think of it as setting up high ideals for ourselves and for our world. And then trying to live up to them as best we can."

"But it produces a culture riddled with sham. And people who learn too well how to dissemble. And ideals no one gives anything but lip service to."

"But the South is founded on fine ideals whether or not you—"

"Ideals?" Chase startled the girl by the bitterness in his voice. He saw it in the sudden widening of her eyes, her uneasy glance toward the bedroom door as he turned back to face her. "What ideals, for God's sake? What of your slaves? The few free blacks you do have? The poor whites you call trash? What of the people who have no place in your 'ideals'? What does your world offer for them?"

Louisa looked at him silently and finally reached one hand out to gently brush his hair. He flinched at her touch, startled, then looked away. "And you, Major. What has your world offered us but our ruination?" She offered a faint, pensive smile and shook her head. Chase said nothing and finally she shrugged, turning to reach for her dressing gown. "Are all Yankees like you, Major? Kind one minute and cruel the next?"

Chase watched her slip the lace of her gown over her shoulders, still frowning. Finally, he reached out one hand to help her, regretting the bitterness of his outburst. "I'm sorry, Louisa. I didn't mean to be cruel. I only meant—"

"Oh, I know." She glanced over one shoulder as she tied the neck ribbons, then half-turned to face him. "Or I think I know, anyway. You're a very fine lover, Major. A considerate one. That makes its own statement of what kind of man you are. But you're angry about something. And I wonder if it's merely because of the war." She paused as if waiting for Chase to reply. When he only shrugged, she returned the gesture in silence.

Chase still said nothing, only kept frowning, as he reached for his cheroot. Louisa watched him, studying his face in the brief flare of the ash. "All right, then, keep your secrets, whatever they are. Just remember what the gamblers say in New Orleans; don't count your money until you've left the table. Maybe by the time the war ends, you'll find something of the South worth caring for. Odder things have happened."

"Maybe." He only said it to be agreeable and he knew by

her momentary smile that she didn't believe he meant the pleasantry. He hadn't, so he wasted no words trying to sound more convincing. She started for the door and he rose to walk with her. That much courtesy, at least, he did think he owed her. "Louisa—"

"Or maybe it's a woman?" She interrupted what would have been an apology from him, and she turned sharply as she spoke, watching his eyes. They were dark—unreadable—and finally she shrugged at her inability to guess. "If it *is* a woman, Major—one of *us*—you'd better forget her. A Southern woman may cheat a little on her world, but she'll never betray it entirely. You'll save yourself a great deal of anguish to remember that." She smiled faintly, almost sympathetically, and watched him a moment in silence, then turned to go. "I'll wave good-bye in the morning, Major, when you leave. Remember me kindly. And remember my advice." With a faint rustling of her dressing gown and a fainter whiff of roses, Louisa disappeared behind the door, and Chase turned slowly back to bed.

General Slocum's Twentieth Infantry Corps arrived in town before daybreak, broke into the stores looting and shouting, and set fire to the cotton bales Senator Hill had tried to save. As the main column entered, the cavalry was ordered to resume its advance and Louisa kept her promise and waved good-bye from her bedroom window. Two minutes out of Madison, Chase dismissed both Louisa and her advice to memory, counting the town only as another forward step in a march that must, eventually, end at Richmond, Virginia, and mean the end of the CSA and the end of the war. She'd told him nothing he didn't already know about Southern women anyway, and in a strange way, leaving Madison, he left much of the memory of Leanna Leighton there as well. Only the cold bitterness of her betrayal stayed with him after that.

Like Georgia, Philadelphia was enjoying a week of Indian summer. The trees had turned weeks ago, most were bare by now. Lawns were beginning to brown, and roses had given way to fall chrysanthemums blooming white and yellow in the manicured beds. But as November drew toward December a last spell of summer had resurfaced and the day had been hot today in the sun, the night clear but still warm, and Joshua enjoyed the air of the open carriage. He enjoyed the

40

darkness, too, the opportunity to be alone with his thoughts, the time to weigh thoughts carefully, and he directed the driver to take the long way home.

Broad Street tonight held little traffic. They passed the Academy of Music between Locust and Spruce. Carriages were grouped there by the curb three-deep. Jonathon and Whitney were attending a concert tonight, he knew, and he was almost tempted to stop and go in after them—after Jonathon actually. Amazing how he depended on the boy. Perhaps too much so. But with Chase gone still, in Georgia with the federal army, Jonathon was the closest thing Joshua had to a son. And he needed someone. Especially on a night like this, he needed the assurance that he wasn't alone.

The driver had begun to halt, but Joshua waved him on now, shaking his head. The gaslights inside the academy had brightened abruptly, which meant the concert was over. The building would be a madhouse now with people massing to leave. So the carriage continued up Broad to Walnut, passing the ghostly shadows of the nearly completed Union League Club. Joshua had contributed to its building, but whether he would live to see its dedication, he didn't know. Others would and the idea was a good one. He didn't begrudge the money spent. They turned at Sixteenth, and he could see the coach light at the driveway of the house. The inside two of the tall Doric columns gleamed a soft smooth ivory from the inside hallway's chandelier, but the rest of the house was dark still. That meant Elinor had not yet returned from her shopping trip. Joshua felt relief at the thought, guilt at the realization of his relief, and then pushed it all away with a touch of impatience.

Far more important matters waited to be dealt with. There had been another meeting tonight of the coalition, starting with a toast to the success of their management of the president's reelection campaign. That toast had been, for Joshua, the first and last pleasant point in the entire evening. The business meeting that had followed had left him shaken, and—to be absolutely candid—deeply frightened. Not content any longer with merely profiteering off the war in progress, the coalition members were busily formulating future ambitions now. Money, as ever, was the primary goal of the machinations—money and its equally seductive twin, power. No longer were such men content to simply manipulate the war to their best interests, dispersing when that war was ended. Now the coalition was laying far-reaching plans that threatened the future of the government itself, the country as a whole, plans that would outlast the war by decades if not by centuries. Not for them the concept of democracy. Men rich as kings must have the *power* of kings as well. They would keep the republic but only in name. The coalition members would be the actual rulers, a secret oligarchy that pulled the puppet strings of any government elected to Washington. The first steps toward that end had already been taken. *Tonight*, in fact. The coalition had found an unexpected ally for such future plans.

The meeting had begun with a letter read aloud from an "undisclosed Washington source"—probably L. C. Baker, Joshua had guessed, the chief of the War Department's secret intelligence staff. Outlined in that frightening letter were a half-dozen "suggestions" on how Washington and the coalition members might cooperate in firming up support for radical changes come the war's end. And countering Joshua's initial sense of incredulity at such a notion was an uneasy memory of the kidnapping threats Henry Walters had overheard at the last coalition meeting. Ambitions that should have begun and ended both in the same degree of nightmarish impossibility were now becoming all too feasible.

Because, at last, a deep, dangerous realization was beginning to penetrate even the War Department's incredible arrogance. It had finally occurred to someone there that all their awesome power, painstakingly accumulated over the chaotic crises of the past four war years, was going to be taken away pretty quickly now as the war's end drew near. Up to now, that end had been a too-far-distant future to worry much over—but no longer. Richmond and Petersburg both were besieged. The blockade, ocean and river, both, was tight. Sheridan had cleared the Virginia Valley. Sherman had captured Atlanta, and now had arrogantly cut loose from any base of supply and marched off who knew where into the very heart of the Confederacy, leaving behind only his promise to "make Georgia howl."

The CSA had struggled merely to survive to this past presidential election. Had the Democrats been elected, there would have been the hope of a negotiated peace, of independence for the seceded Southern states. That hope was gone now. The hope of military victory over the North—always only a dream of fanatics—was no longer even that, now. The South *must* soon surrender. But a country at peace was far less dependent on and far less tolerant of the abuse of power by any single Cabinet member or his department. So the War Department's kingdom was soon to come tumbling down.

Not without a fight though, Joshua had realized tonight with a sudden fear. And not without some sort of deadly struggle. Like the proverbial people of Crete, the North had created a monster terrible enough to defeat the danger of another—the CSA. But with that danger slain, the monster of the North would still remain. Should they, like the Minoans, build it a labyrinth? Sacrifice young men and maidens every seven years to slake its thirst for blood? He smiled at the whimsy, but not with humor. Tonight, he really wondered. That the War Department, strong and bloated with its power, would turn like a cornered animal and fight viciously for its own survival, he didn't doubt. The only question was how? And when? And with what? After tonight, he knew the answer to the last question at least. With such weapons as the coalition. With the Philadelphia one, and others like it. New York, Boston, Washington, D.C., itself. Men rich and powerful in their own right, whose conscience had long since been sacrificed to ego and to greed. Individually they were a nuisance—but united, a fearful menace. They had dealt with Stanton's department for years, grown ever richer from it, enjoyed its largesse. If President Lincoln in the White House turned now to slay that bloated monster, and if those secret coalitions should back their old friend, the War Department, in the power struggle . . . what then? Good God, what then? Another war? With the South already bleeding and prostrate? With the North already reeling from this war, so many of their finest young men worn out, some wounded, others dead? Could they even gather the spirit to take *on* another war? And if so, would this one even *be* a battlefield war? Or would this be fought quietly instead—in exclusive mens' clubs, in the halls of Congress, on Wall Street and in the bank board rooms? Could they have saved the Union only to see it fall to a grim future so petty dictatorships backed by the War Department's invisible hand?

It seemed improbable, but Joshua found little comfort in

that thought. Before tonight, he would have said *impossible*. God help us, he thought suddenly. God help all of us, North and South, if the War Department turns on *us* now, to save itself. What could we ever do to stop them?

"Something's going wrong, Whit, and I just can't figure out exactly what."

She wasn't surprised to hear him say that; she knew Jonathon awfully well. And all evening there'd been a certain distance, a preoccupation, and she'd wondered how much of the piano concert he'd even heard earlier at the academy tonight. He'd seemed startled when the clapping started, as if he'd not been listening at all. "Why, Jon? Something wrong with what?"

He rolled toward her in the moon-shadowed darkness of the cottage bedroom, raising himself on one elbow. Even in the dimness, Whitney could see concern etched on his handsome face. "With the bank."

She paled. "More money missing?"

"Money miss—oh, no, not that again, thank God." He shook his dark head and Whitney released a silent sigh. "No, it's nothing that definite. More a feeling I have. Sidelong glances. Furtive whispers. Godwyn on the board seems especially . . . odd."

Whitney reached in silence to touch his bare shoulder reassuringly. He responded with a smile, faint and, she had the impression, forced. She began to frown. "And Joshua?"

A more genuine smile touched her husband's mouth. "I haven't said anything to him. No reason yet I should. He has enough troubling him with his heart condition and his son heaven knows where down in the deep South, and no word where Sherman is, where he's headed, or even if the command is still in one piece."

"Not to mention Elinor."

"Of course. That goes without saying." At mention of the Courtland daughter's name, the smile had faded from Jonathon's mouth; grim distaste took its place.

"Well, what are you going to do?"

"Nothing yet. Wait and watch." He seemed discontent with the solution and shrugged uneasily. "After all, as long as Joshua lives, there isn't much anyone can do to make serious trouble. Not even Elinor."

Whitney nodded in the darkness, but not without a qualm. The Courtland daughter, she thought to herself warily, was never more dangerous than when people believed her not to be.

Leanna shivered in the cold rain of the late November day, glanced once without much hope at the leaden gray skies that poured down liquid ice, drenching her, then looked back to the muddy road and the slow file of horses' hooves as they squished haphazard patterns into it, pulling up with soft plops and leaving miniature ponds that almost instantly filled with water. All but the pines had lost their leaves by now and bare-boughed oaks offered no protection as they rode in slow, miserable silence toward the east. They had beaten the Yankees to Madison by only a few hours. No trains had been left there to face Yankee destruction, and Yankee cavalry had ruined the track to the north near Greensboro. Short of riding to Augusta itself, there were no trains running anymore on the Central Georgia Railroad Line. She would find no escape from the war by that route.

Stewart then had turned southeast, toward the state capital of Milledgeville. There they arrived two days ahead of the Yankees, and a detail of General Wheeler's cavalry rode in on their heels to urge evacuation of the city. The single train leaving had been instantly commandeered by Governor Brown and his political cronies. The good governor had fled with his furniture, rugs, portraits and silver, and left behind arms, ammunition, the state archives, government documents and almost a million dollars in new-printed Confederate dollars—those bills not even signed yet. Even if space had been available on that train, Leanna would have disdained taking it. The "car of cowards," disgusted townsfolk had called it. And she agreed. State militia had made a stand in defense of the capital, or tried to, old men and green youngsters, easily slaughtered by Sherman's veteran troops. Leaving a scorched path from forty to sixty miles wide, a hundred miles long behind them, the Yankees took Milledgeville on the twenty-third. She'd heard they'd convened a mock legislature in the abandoned capital, repealed the Secession Act and voted to kick Governor Brown's "respectful ass" whenever they caught up with him. Kilpatrick had chaired the "congress"—the cav-

45

alry had, as usual, been among the first troops in. She wondered if Chase had taken part in it, or later, in the bonfires they had made of the money, or in the destruction of the state penitentiary and the arsenal buildings on the square. Luckily for Milledgeville, it had rained for two solid days, so the isolated fires hadn't spread throughout the town.

Now they were in Sandersville, again only about a day ahead of Sherman's Twentieth Corps. And again, in anticipation of the approaching enemy, all the rolling stock of the Georgia Central Railroad had been withdrawn farther east to Bostwick. To cut due south to Dublin was the best hope of escaping the Yankee columns, but Leanna had learned enough of her husband by now to relinquish that as a forlorn hope. Stewart had changed; the war had changed him, or maybe he'd always been this way and she'd never realized it. The war came first—above her, above his men, above anything else. They could easily have put greater distance between themselves and the marching federals, but Stewart would not. He must first fell trees to block their roads, burn bridges, set snipers in isolated farmhouses and treetops, poison a well or make lightninglike midnight raids at a lonely picket position. The result of all those exertions was minimal. Even Wheeler, with several thousand men, could not do more than waste a few hours along the Yankees' way. But Stewart was relentless. *Vicious*, she could have said. Obsessive. Even when such resistance was useless—or worse, a disadvantage, as the infuriated Yankees took their anger out on helpless farms and townsfolk in the area—still he would not stay his hand. It *was* obsessive. And it was frightening. Leanna had begun to have the feeling she'd wandered into some sort of private nightmare. Even worse, most of the men seemed to thrive on it. Ex-criminals, habitual losers, the dregs of Southern society, they had joined Stewart only for the bounty money and the prospect of looting along the way—the Yankees were not the only ones "foraging liberally" in the Georgia countryside anymore. Even among the ranks of Wheeler's regulation cavalry, discipline was breaking down. It was anarchy; it was chaos. It was dog eat dog and survival of the fittest, and in this once gracious world now gone berserk, a gently reared wife was an encumbrance and an inconvenience. At least, that was the opinion Stewart seemed at pains to offer her. And even though she knew she no longer loved him as she'd once thought she did, still his attitude gave rise to bitter resentment.

"Leanna? We'll be stopping ahead for a little rest."

Stewart startled her as he spoke and she stole a moment to conceal her thoughts before she glanced at him to answer. "Somewhere dry, I hope."

"Pine woods. You should be able to find some cover there." He gestured ahead and she followed his arm with her eyes. "There's a bridge there over the fishing creek. We'll cross and then burn it. I'd like to set some stakes in the bank as well."

Leanna nodded, grateful for the prospect of a rest for whatever reason. Burnt bridges, a half-dozen stakes, what problem would they pose to the Union Army of sixty thousand? But she'd learned not to argue; Stewart would tolerate no treaties in his private war. "Fine." She paused a moment, frowning as she took notice of the country again with more awareness. The earth was less red here. The road stretching ahead was level for longer stretches. Few hardwoods stood in the dense woods, and the huge, white loblolly pines had given way to smaller trees, pines that could almost be called scrub. "The country's changing. Are we going south after all?" She spoke with sudden hope, thinking of the child in her belly, the consequent necessity for her to rest, to stop this riding before it killed a child who'd never had a chance to live.

"No, east." Stewart's eyes changed in that indefinable way they did, closing to show no expression. "We're on the Bostwick Road. They'll have trains there to take you on to Savannah."

Leanna raised her head too sharply and icy rain ran down the brim of her hat to drip down her back. "Savannah? I thought you wanted me in Charleston?"

"Savannah will be safer." He began to turn his horse's head to rejoin the main group of men, and Leanna stared after him. Safer, she thought? Or more convenient?

"The Yankees will turn north soon, to Augusta. There's an ordnance plant there they'll want to take. And then they'll probably go on to Charleston and Fort Sumter on their way to Richmond. Savannah won't interest them. And anyway, General Hardee's got a concentration of regulation troops stationed there."

You'd lie to me, Stewart, and never blink an eye if it suited you, Leanna realized in sudden surprise. Even so, she managed a nod as he rode away. Then, as she urged the horse toward the cover of the woods she shivered a last time, trying to repress a rising sense of panic that the rain and monotonous clip-clop of the horses' hooves behind her did nothing to allay. God help me if there's no train at Bostwick either. Even Stewart will guess eventually. And *his* wife carrying a *Yankee's* bastard . . . there had to be a train. There just simply had to be. She *must* find a way out of this ever-worsening war.

Chapter Four

As that November of 1864 passed into December and Thanksgiving gave way to thoughts of Christmas, the people of the Northern states began to forget the exuberant confidence they'd enjoyed when Sherman's troops had taken Atlanta, and to feel more keenly each passing day of silence from that southernmost army. No one in the North had news. Not Grant, still besieging Lee's army at Richmond. Not the president, worrying aloud by now over the sixty thousand federals who seemed to have vanished into the red Georgia earth without a trace. Confederate newspapers, smuggled north, taunted the anxious Union with hints of disaster, and worse, a flippant disregard for Sherman's "menace." President Lincoln aged by the day—growing gaunter, grayer, preoccupied and desperately worried. General Grant tried to reassure him, knowing no more than anyone else but confident of the abilities of that eccentric, high-strung western general called William Tecumseh Sherman. Even if Sherman was "possibly prevented from reaching the point he had started out to reach, still he would get through somewhere . . . and even if worse came to worst . . . if they cannot get out where they want to, they can crawl back by the hole they went in at."

But such talk was cold comfort with the terrible silence lengthening day by day. Joshua, on a trip to Washington, found President Lincoln badly troubled, his health suffering from the overlong anxiety, and Joshua, too—with a son, now his last and his only son, among those missing soldiers—was no less troubled. The heart pains that had eased earlier with Jonathon Penley's adept management of the Courtland Bank began to worsen again in the growing silence of the raw December days.

Down in Georgia, "worse" had hardly come to the worst. In fact, the federal troops were discovering how pleasant war could be when there was little fighting and much high-living provided at the enemy's expense. Confederate soldiers had made a show of a stand in the streets of Sandersville, just enough to provide a little exercise, and by the time the federals had taken possession of the town, they were about halfway to Savannah. Not that they knew that they were heading for that particular point. Only General Sherman and his personal staff knew that. They issued orders for the march only one day at a time, and the crisscrossing maneuvers, which confused the Confederates as to a final destination, confused the federal officers almost equally. Few of the rank-and-file soldiers cared. About two days east of Atlanta, they had marched into cotton country, the area of great plantations, among the wealthiest counties of the South. Cotton they had little use for and burned it by the hundreds of bales. But land that could grow the greedy cotton plant could and did grow other things equally well: sweet potatoes, wheat, corn, apples, tobacco, sugar cane, tomatoes, vegetables of all kinds, honey, sorghum, rich pasturing for dairy cows and beef cattle, pigs and turkeys and chickens and geese. When the army moved, it looked like a quartermaster's dream come true. Men drove herds of animals for fresh meat. Chickens hung in bunches from saddles. Wagons were overflowing. Runaway slaves from the great plantations accompanied the army as refugees in droves. Strong, young bucks were put to use in the "pioneer" corps—clearing felled trees, rebuilding burnt bridges. Young females—especially the good-looking ones who attached themselves to the columns as mistresses or prostitutes—wore "foraged" ball gowns of priceless French silks and gems that would have made even Tiffany look twice. Those who could not provide such service to the Yankees were treated less kindly, however. When the crowd grew too burdensome, or the troops tired of the company, hundreds were left behind on riverbanks or swamp edges, to survive, starve or be recaptured as their own fates dictated.

All in all, it was practically routine by now. It as much resembled a high-spirited, disorganized picnic as a war. Of course, civilians unfortunate enough to live too near the Yankees' line of march knew it differently. The federal troops had swept through Georgia like a whirlwind, stripping food, clothes, livestock, plate, silver, jewelry and anything else, including even flowers and fenceposts, from the homes as they passed.

Well-meaning officers might leave the milk cow at a poor widow's house. The "bummers," as they came to be called—men almost deserters, who followed like vultures on the fringes of the columns—took that, and occasionally more. When all else was done, burning was good sport and readily practiced. Rape, though, was infrequent—among white women at least, for the penalty was dear. Slave girls, unfortunately, did not enjoy the same protection.

Resistance offered by local militia, partisans, or "Fighting Joe" Wheeler's regulation cavalry hardly intruded on the consciousness of most soldiers. Riding in the cavalry advance, Chase saw it better. There would be a bend in the rutted, winding road, blocked by new-cut trees, and sudden shots would ring out from impenetrable thickets or treetops. Battle lines charged the Confederate positions at a gallop, firing as they went. If the Rebels persisted beyond that point, the cavalry kept up a sharp skirmish fire until the lead regiment of infantry hurried up, bringing whatever artillery pieces were nearest at hand. Rarely did it take more than a half hour. Ambulances were galloped up; shallow graves hastily dug at the tree line; the main column took it as a chance to snack, or rest or play another game of euchre or seven-up; and soon the march resumed.

It was far less predictable for the other side, Southern soldier or civilian alike. Leanna was living proof of that statement. There had been no train at Bostwick. None at Cushingville or Millen, either. Leanna lived now in a kind of numb desperation compounded of cold, hunger, exhaustion and fear. Today, Stewart's band had raided Yankee wagons stuck at a muddy stream crossing, lost three men, and had, for all their pains, captured only a few haversacks stuffed with food and the field desks of some federal adjutants. Around the small fire built against the December night's cold, the men were ransacking the loot in angry disappointment, smashing locks and burning papers. She watched in silent exhaustion, despising them all but too weary to register disapproval. They didn't care for her disapproval anyway—she had voiced it on other occasions with a notable lack of success.

Treejack stepped forward into the uneven firelight, reaching into his belt for the long-bladed, wicked knife he carried there waking or sleeping. Leanna shivered at the sight of him and drew her legs up closer against her chest instinctively.

Few of Stewart's "partisan rangers" were better than mere animals—ruled by greed, by lust, by fear. Lt. Walker was one exception. So, she thought, was young John MacRae, who was fairly new to the group. But Treejack—he was worse than the others, something either inhuman or insane, and he did, quite frankly, terrify Leanna. He was from Louisiana, they said, somewhere near New Orleans, from inside that strange, fey world of moss-draped, impenetrable swamps. He'd come east when New Orleans had fallen to Yankees, east to people unfamiliar with the bayou ways and the bayou speech. Très Jacques, he'd told them. Treejack, he'd become. As cunning as a wolverine and equally cruel. She'd watched him for two weeks now and knew Stewart hadn't been humorous when he'd said the man could smell Yankees five miles distant. And Treejack seemed to watch Leanna constantly. It made her skin crawl, and she wondered in nervous, irrational fear whether the politics of war followed maternal or paternal lines. If paternal, was Treejack watching her because he could smell Yankee growing in her belly?

He suddenly gave a bloodcurdling cry, raising the Bowie knife high in both hands. Firelight flashed silver on the oiled blade, and as he plunged it down into the mahogany desk an obstinate drawer burst asunder with a crack, splinters of wood flying as the brass lock fell at his feet. He disdained to touch it, merely pulled free the knife blade and laughed, disappearing again into the darkness as silently as he'd earlier appeared.

There were some low murmurings among the men, an uneasiness that hadn't been there before; Leanna was not the only one Treejack frightened. Lt. Walker eyed the muttering men for a moment over his battered tin coffee cup, then laid it aside to rise to his feet. He bent down by the desk, taking the wood and tossing it casually into the fire, then reaching inside the desk for a sheaf of papers someone had thought important enough to protect with a very fine lock. Only Leanna noted the swift, wary glance he gave to the others before daring to turn his back on them, walking back to the fire and reseating himself. He noted her gaze and offered Leanna a faint, empathetic smile before the usual grimness fell over his face again.

"What is it, Walker?" Stewart spoke lazily over his own coffee cup, gesturing to the papers by a single glance.

The young officer shrugged, looking down. "Files. Case files, it looks like. More adjutant stuff, I imagine."

Leanna was hardly listening. She'd taken as large a dinner portion as she'd dared and yet her stomach still cried hunger. She wondered if this was normal: the constant, gnawing hunger, the weariness, the sickness every morning. She told herself it was, it must be. But with Blytheswood lost, and Chase; Stewart—what he had become; the CSA teetering on the brink of final ruin; the child had become her existence and her future—her determination to keep it the strength that kept her going day after day in this unholy nightmare. She would escape this war. She would survive it. She had to—and she would. She and the child both.

"Now this should make good reading." The lieutenant pulled one file forward with a wry smile, handing it across Leanna's lap to her husband. "It's about us."

" 'Lieutenant Colonel Drake. Forward to the War Department,' it says." Stewart smiled humorlessly, raising the cover. "Think they'll understand if we don't oblige their request?"

Leanna turned her head sharply in sudden attention at the mention of the federal adjutant's name. Drake—he plagued her still. Would he make reference to Chase Courtland's protection of her in Atlanta? And if so, would Stewart guess her guilty secret?

"It's hard to read it in this light." Stewart frowned, tilting it toward the flames.

Burn it, Leanna prayed in sudden fervency. Burn it, Stewart. Don't read any more.

"What's it say?"

"I'm not sure. Here." *Mrs. Leighton, not surprisingly, denied any involvement in her husband's notorious activities. Following is a transcript of a preliminary hearing held in Atlanta, September of 1864.* Stewart didn't look up. He finished the page with what seemed impossible slowness, then turned to the next in absolute silence. In her ears, Leanna heard nothing but her heart pounding. Her mouth was as dry as cotton. It was worse than she'd feared. It must be. What could Drake have written there?

". . . 'Specifically, we were having an affair.' "

It was barely breathed but it echoed in Leanna's mind like trumpets. Oh God, no, she thought in sudden horror. Chase.

" 'Mrs. Leighton and I were lovers.' Once? Twice? Regularly?" There was an instant of endless, terrible silence. The fire cracked and hissed on green wood. Only fifteen feet away, men still pried at the desks hoping for money. But from where Leanna sat, there was not a sound. Stewart turned one more page, read it, then slowly, with great precision, closed the file and set it beside him. Only then did he look up. "*Regularly*, my dear? No wonder I found Blytheswood in such fine condition."

"Stewart, no. I don't know why he would say such a thing. It wasn't true."

"And in Atlanta as well?" He raised one blond brow, not taking his eyes from hers. "And did you cooperate, then, with the Yankees in arranging that trap at the MacRae place?"

"Stewart, no!" Leanna was trembling too much to speak well; her head felt light, but her lips like wood, clumsy and cold. Part of her was angry at the accusation. Part of her was stunned. And she swallowed against a sickness that had to be from fear.

That one day in Atlanta, she had realized suddenly, when Chase had looked at her so strangely, answered her bitter accusations with such puzzling words . . . Drake must have made an outright attempt to arrest her for treason. And Chase had lied under oath, lied to his own army, saying whatever he thought would serve in the future as Leanna Leighton's best protection. It had protected her from Drake, all right. But it was liable to mean her death now in Stewart's hands. Stewart would never understand her explanations of what Chase Courtland had been trying to offer Leanna by swearing to such damning accusations. Still, she had no choice left but to try. "You know better than that, Stewart. I know you do. I never willingly betrayed you or any other portion of the Confederacy. I never even knew there *were* Yankees there at the MacRaes'."

"But surely if you liked the Yankees well enough to be sharing their beds, my dear, you must have liked them well enough to—"

"I *wasn't* sharing their *beds*! I did accept Major Courtland's protection in Atlanta, yes, but I never willingly—" Her words ended in a startled gasp as Stewart's hand whipped out to slash across her face. She fell sideways with the force of it, half stunned, feeling cold rocky ground beneath her cheek and tasting the salty blood rising swiftly on her tongue.

"Yankee whore."

Leanna was expecting the blow this time before it came. Even so, her head snapped back helplessly, cutting her face on the hard ground and dazing her further.

"You bore my name and *still* you groveled like a bitch in heat beneath some damn Yankee!"

She shook her head desperately, tasting tears and blood, salt and sourness, trying to raise herself off the ground to face him. "That report is a lie! Chase must have been trying to protect me. Or else Colonel Drake himself could have made it up to—oh!" She cried out against Stewart's sudden grip on her hair, his hand pulling her up by it. She twisted in his grasp with a startled cry, trying to reach his hands with her own. "Oh God, Stewart! Are you mad?"

"I'll kill you for this, you whore! Half the damn bluebelly army is probably laughing behind my back! Only first I think I'll give you to *my* men! You ought to at least give the Confederate fellows an equal turn."

"That's enough!"

Leanna tried to turn, hearing the lieutenant's voice interrupt in a kind of vague, distant surprise. She felt Stewart's grip on her tighten and then begin to loosen as Lt. Walker grabbed Stewart's wrist and tried to force his hand free.

"For the love of God, Colonel, I say that's enough! You don't even know how much of it's true!"

"Don't I? I caught them out walking alone that night in Virginia when I came home."

"*Walking* is no crime!"

"I think it is. So get your hands off me, Lieutenant! It's my wife. My affair. You get your damn hands off me before I remember I'm your superior officer and blow your brains out for your insubordination. Nobody tells me what I can or can't do with something that belongs to me."

Walker's face paled in the orange firelight, but he didn't back down. "You can't behave like this on the basis of some damned Yankee papers! You have to listen, at least, to her explanation."

"I know all I need to."

"And I say you don't! Damn it, she's a lady! She's your

own wife, for God's sake! You don't beat her around the ground for a damn guess! No true gentleman would!"

"No one questions my right to be called a gentleman."

Leanna heard the warning in Stewart's voice. It had always been a touchy point with him, his pride. Now with Yankees ravaging the South, winning the war, it had been cut to the quick—dangerously sore. She felt Stewart's sudden release on her and cried in warning to the young officer. But Stewart had begun to move even before she could cry out. A LeMat revolver glinted momentarily in the shadowed light and Lt. Walker's eyes opened wide for an instant of incredulous shock. Then the gun cracked, and the young officer's face instantly changed. She reached out for him as he jerked backward from the blow of the bullet hitting high in his forehead. His eyes met hers for a heartbeat before they glazed and she gasped her horror in a breathless sob. There had been helplessness there— and more astoundingly an apology—as though *he* and not she had been the one at fault. An apology for the way the war had shattered the old ways perhaps. A last attempt to rein-state them. Gradually, the little round hole began to fill with blood and suddenly there was bright, warm scarlet running down into the young officer's hair and into his still-open eyes. But for a moment, all she could feel was astonishment that he should feel so warm when he was so very obviously dead.

She heard a sound suddenly from behind her, a sound that jerked her back to fearful reality—Stewart. She let go of the dead young lieutenant and scrambled forward a few paces with a choking cry, tripping on her skirt, tasting bile in her mouth and retching as she moved, running for the darkness beyond the firelight with desperate haste.

"Leanna."

Stewart stood suddenly in her path—only a step away, a black menace silhouetted in the night. She tried to turn, to twist away, but he moved too quickly. He found and held her wrist with a terrible strength. Leanna gave a single, soft cry and fell slowly to her knees, sinking beneath the pressure of her husband's hand.

"No, my dear. I won't let you run back to your Yankee friends. That would be too easy."

That he smiled as he said it only made it seem worse. "No, Stewart, you're wrong. Why won't you listen to me at least? For God's sake, you've already killed one man! Let me explain it! Listen to me!" Stewart only jerked her back to her feet with a vicious heave. Helplessly, she tried to back away, stumbling in the twigs and rocks of the forest floor, unable to break the hold he maintained on her wrist. An owl hooted suddenly, and she cried out at the sound, biting her lip to blood to maintain any sanity at all. It was as if Stewart didn't notice. His blue eyes glittered pale ice as he watched her, letting her move backward step by step, slowly following her without another word. She stumbled harder on an exposed tree root, almost fell, and suddenly felt the cold, rough bark of a tree trunk against her back. Stewart came closer, and she shivered violently, staring back at his face and reading murder in his eyes. He began to raise one hand, and she cried a futile denial, closing her eyes and twisting away. The blow caught her across her jaw and she fell easily, sobbing as she staggered to her knees and tried to crawl away. His hand gripped her shoulder, wrenching her over to face him, and she screamed out loud, no longer able to stop herself. As his hand moved, black against gray moonlight, she gave a last, desolate moan and helplessly covered her belly with her arms to try to shield her unborn child.

And then there was a sudden, awesome stillness. Not a sound, not a breath, just the slow passage of seconds that had lost all meaning. No blow landed and she forced her eyes open at last. She felt no relief, no hope, nothing. Only a vague wonder at what had stayed his hand. Stewart stood silent, looming in the darkness over her, and staring to where her arms clasped so tightly around her body.

"You're with child. That Yankee's child."

"No . . ." But she didn't move her arms. Couldn't actually. It felt as if they were locked in place.

"Oh, yes, you are—of course. That explains a great deal." His eyes had narrowed. The murderous fury written there had changed to a different sort. If possible, this was worse, and Leanna shuddered seeing it. "Not only did you whore with that damn bluebelly, you're carrying his bastard, as well."

She shivered again and shook her head. His blows had long since loosened all the pins from her long hair. It hung about her face now, half blinding her, and it was coldly wet with tears.

"Get up."

There was a long silence. Leanna lay on the cold, rough wood floor, sobbing for breath.

"I said get up!" He reached down to grab her by the hair once more to haul her upright. She struggled instinctively, futilely trying to escape, and he ignored her resistance to take her wrists in a painful grip, forcing her hands high above her head. Almost at once, she realized, screamed and kicked and tried to break his hold. No, she thought. Oh God! Not that. Not the baby. No!

His knee drove into her stomach with incredible force, driving her upward and slamming her hard against the tree. Her head jerked back against the trunk, and she cried a last sound or thought she did. She felt her mouth open. She half-saw his fists clenched and swinging straight toward her. Then another blow exploded in her belly, and as she doubled over in desperate pain a strange brilliant blackness took her away.

She awoke to faint light. Not dawn, but a warmer glow like a burning candle. Her body was stiff, aching and deeply bruised, her belly rippled with cramping waves. There was a warm wetness between her legs, soaking the heavy folds of her linsey-woolsey skirt. As new pain came the wetness increased. Blood, she realized. It must be blood. She opened her eyes slowly, blinking once, staring up at a tree bough covered by pale canvas tenting. The light came from her right side, and with a great effort, she turned her head to see. It *was* a tent, she realized slowly. And it *was* a candle. And Stewart sat watching her barely an arm's length away.

"One less Yankee brat to spoil the South."

Leanna watched him silently, with no expression on her face. He was smiling and she thought, quite clearly, that she hated him far more than she would ever have dreamed it possible to hate anyone.

"I hope you understand my position, my dear. I would be crushed to find you'd hold this cruel necessity against me in the years to come." He inclined his head once as he spoke, in a voice as charming and cultured as any that had ever graced the halls of fine Southern mansions. But that peculiar, abysmal coldness still glittered in his eyes, and Leanna wasn't fooled. "You are my wife, after all. And I could hardly acknowledge a Yankee's bastard as my heir."

"That Yankee was worth two of you, Stewart. Maybe a

hundred." She spoke in a voice to match her face, softly and with no expression. She studied his face—a face she'd once found handsome, even fancied that she'd loved—and wondered now what it would look like dead. "You were wrong, Stewart. Chase Courtland loved me, yes. And I loved him. But I never willingly betrayed you, Stewart. You murdered an innocent child and your own officer over a report that was nine-tenths a lie."

"A lie?" He raised one brow and gestured crudely to the pooling blood that was staining her skirts. "And that, I suppose, is only a figment of my imagination?"

"No." She refused to follow his gaze, refused to give in to the grief that would unlock. "No, I *was* carrying his child. But it was the product of a single night . . . because I had refused to compromise the South or my vows to you. I could have explained all that to you. I never allowed myself to love him because of you. Or I tried not to, anyway. So we almost hated each other by the end, and he took me once simply out of anger." She paused to watch him, seeing only a mild kind of indifference register on his face. "What you did was a mistake, Stewart, regardless of all of that. I didn't want the child because it was his—but because it was mine. It would have been *ours*. I was determined to be a good wife to you. It doesn't matter now, anyway, but you'd better kill me, too, Stewart. Because if you don't, someday, somehow, I'm going to kill *you*. I swear it."

He looked amused and leaned back lazily. "I doubt that."

"Don't."

Stewart shrugged, the faint smile lingering on his weather-roughened face. "If you're so anxious for babies, my dear, I'll do my best in the future. I'll keep your belly full every year if you like. Only first, I'm going to kill your Yankee lover. War or not, some things a gentleman simply must make time for."

Even in her agony, Leanna almost smiled. "You'll never be able to kill Chase."

"Won't I?"

"No."

Stewart shrugged agreeably. "Well, we'll see, I suppose, won't we?" He rose suddenly to his feet, stepping toward her, and all the feigned pleasantness fell from his face like a mask. "First things first, my dear. I've learned one thing about you. I won't be sending you off to Savannah or anywhere else before you've safely settled with my child. Whether or not your Yankee major is dead by then, whores can always find other customers. Next time, I'll be totally sure you're at least *breeding* Leightons." He dropped to one knee beside her and reached to begin unbuttoning the mud-streaked rags of her blouse. Leanna watched him numbly, uncomprehending. Then saw his smile, the cruelty, the excitement of it, as he reached to pull free her bloody skirt. Her breath caught in her throat and she forced her eyes closed as his hand moved to the buttons of his own trousers. As bruised as she was, as weak from the beating and the blood still flowing, there could be no escape. Animal, she thought numbly. Disgusting, vicious animal.

Quite suddenly he was on her, entering her. He did not trouble himself to gentle his actions any in consideration of her hurts. Consequently, before he'd even quite finished, Leanna had lost consciousness once again.

It was the end of the first week of December and still the weather was holding fine. The Yankee march was sheer luxury compared to the one into Atlanta six months before. Indian summer had started the march; heavy rains had marked its middle; now, nearing the seacoast, warm wet winds from the ocean kept winter again at bay and few of the men even wore overcoats except at night. Even then, being in woods now more scrublike and almost exclusively pine, fragrant fires of still-green pine knots warmed the air, and the scent was remarkably reminiscent of Christmas fires Chase had known at home. He opened his eyes in the darkness, switched the reins to his other hand and stretched the muscles of his back and shoulders. He'd been sleeping in the saddle, something one learned to do early on in service in the cavalry. He thought the horses learned to do it, too, to doze at least, even while they walked along. He glanced around to orient himself, found shadowed, level road stretching ahead of them, the other troopers in what could only be termed a loose formation behind them. The three lone pickets were barely visible up ahead, the omnipresent pine-scrub woods still lining either side of the road. He hadn't missed much, apparently. He almost wondered what had woken him.

"Good morning, Major."

He heard Grier's chuckle to one side and turned to flash a grin, acknowledging the jibe. "Where the hell are we?"

"Who knows? Who cares?" Grier shrugged agreeably as he spoke. "Not to Savannah, yet. Nearing something called the Ogeechee River."

"Wonderful."

"Yes. We might send a stronger detail up front in a while. Liable to be the usual problems when we get into the swampier parts."

Problems with Wheeler's cavalry or partisans again. Chase covered a yawn, and with it the last of the drowsiness left him. His head felt clearer again. For a moment, he almost envied the infantry. They were behind them somewhere, cozily camped for the night. On reflection, he changed his mind. It had been one hell of a long walk from Atlanta to here. Better to be what he was. "Any trouble so far?"

"Nothing special. A couple of trees down. No bridge left over the last creek but it was fordable. Other than that, we did pass a farm. Poor one. All burnt out already. Bummers must have got there first. One old lady and a couple Negroes were still there. I left them a cow and some corn."

"Somebody else will only take it again."

Grier shrugged and fell silent. Chase returned the gesture. It wasn't that he disapproved of his captain's effort. Or that he didn't care. Well, he didn't care a great deal at this point, he admitted frankly to himself, but still, the bummers were a fact of life. Nobody could do much to control them. Wheeler had registered a formal protest, still playing by all the old rules, but Sherman's reply had been common sense: his responsibility was to get his army safely to the sea and he could spare neither the manpower nor the energy to protect the people of Georgia. Actually, Sherman's officers understood another hard reality. The bummers were doing what Sherman really wanted done, namely, the wholesale destruction of the civilian underpinning of the CSA war effort. All the South had to do was surrender. "I want some cows driven ahead when we get near the road to the river. In case they've mined the damn thing with torpedoes." Chase spoke casually, almost distractedly. For him, it was a routine precaution. Almost more than anything else, he hated to lose men to that tactic. It felt like murder, not war, and he resented it the more bitterly because of it.

61

"Good idea. Oh, I heard from a courier that they'd found another prisoner camp up at Millen as they went through."

Chase glanced sharply at his officer, frowning. He remembered Milledgeville, his first sight of the men who'd escaped nearby Andersonville Prison. More than half dead, diseased, open sores, emaciated, rags for clothes. It had infuriated him, infuriated all the Northern troops. Lucky for Milledgeville, it had been raining like a son of a bitch. Whatever sympathy had lingered inside him for the CSA had dissipated entirely there, and his brown eyes were hard as he spoke softly in the night. "Bad as the other?"

"Nobody there. Holes dug in the ground for shelter. About eight hundred graves."

"And they complain about our brutality." Chase's mouth twisted into a colorless line, and he swallowed against a rising anger. Anger was a bad thing to carry around in war. It clouded his judgment and led to mistakes. He forced it away and waited until his emotions had cooled again to speak. "How'd Jenkins say our food supply is holding out?"

"All right. We'll make it to Savannah. If we have to wait there outside the city very long though—well, we'll learn to like rice better, I guess."

Grier delivered the assessment without enthusiasm and Chase grunted agreement. The closer they got to the actual coast, the more sandy and barren the land became—fewer farms to raid, less food at the ones they did pass. They'd come upon a couple of rice fields yesterday, along the swampy banks of a broad river. But after sweet potatoes and fresh meat, rice for breakfast, lunch and dinner seemed utterly unappealing. "While you're managing so splendidly, Grier, maybe I should go back to sleep."

"Hell, no. My turn. We've got about five miles yet from what I understand. And with my luck, it will be light before then. And you know how happy the men are when they catch *all* their officers riding along sound asleep."

Chase chuckled. "Yes. Can't say I blame them much. As a matter of fact—" He stopped speaking suddenly, beginning to frown. Beside him, Grier started to talk and he gestured him abruptly to silence, reining in his horse and cocking his head to try to hear. Now what the devil? Something was wrong. Instinct had rung that subliminal warning bell. But why, he wondered? Not a sound came from either side of the road . . .

not a single . . . "Fall back!" He shouted the order as he grabbed down for the carbine strapped to the saddle beneath his leg. He raised it high, pointing it into the moonlit sky to fire once in warning, shattering the night's guilty quiet. Up ahead, the three lone pickets turned at a gallop, dashing back toward the rest of the troop. Soldiers sleeping behind him awoke instantly, grabbing rifles in reflex before they were even awake, turning their horses in rearing pivots. For just an instant, the night was filled with only the sudden sounding of horses' hooves on the hard-packed roadway. Then shots exploded from the woods ahead, deafening, like too-close thunder. Chase held the dangerous position for what seemed forever, waiting for the pickets to safely rejoin, firing blindly into woods that showed nothing but shadows, vague ones, slate and jet, where nothing moved. But firing guns showed orange bursts of brief flame and he shot at one as he whirled his horse, heard a cry and kept moving, spurring his stallion to greater speed and leaning lower over the animal's lathered neck.

That was it for the night's advance. They'd lost three men and two horses and been lucky to escape that lightly. They'd regroup up the road to camp. Tomorrow when the infantry column caught up, they'd try again. Send some artillery fire into the woods first. It was almost routine for the march through Georgia, and as Chase assigned sentries and rolled out his blankets to sleep he thought nothing more about the incident. Nor did it occur to him to consider the attack in any way personal.

Chapter Five

On the ninth and tenth of December, the first Union soldiers reached the Confederate-held fortifications of the city of Savannah. Rebel infantry contested the last several dozen miles, but outnumbered as the Rebels were by any single one of Sherman's four federal corps, they could do little. Breastworks were easily taken and a few prisoners on either side. But that was as far as the Yankees could go. CSA General Hardee was inside Savannah with about ten thousand Confederate troops, and as long as Fort McAllister—guarding the mouth of the Ogeechee—remained in Rebel hands, Sherman could do little to threaten the city itself.

Consequently, the federal campaign quite literally bogged down. And as Chase waited with his command, encamped in the low, swampy Georgia coast country, there was little to do but watch the days pass with monotonous slowness. It was miserable country to him, alien and charmless to any Northerner's eyes: scrub pines stunted by sandy, poor soil; waxy underbrush, often prickly; great live oaks with ghostly moss, thin and ethereal as spiderwebs or thick and trailing to the ground like rotting burial shrouds. Snakes were everywhere, cottonmouths on the marshy banks; and water moccasins in the green-scummed, brackish pools. Equally omnipresent were mosquitoes, a new breed of the thing and bigger than any he'd ever encountered; they deviled the horses especially nearly to madness. Alligators lay waiting for the unwary, and fever had broken out as well. Dysentery and malaria both were going through the ranks like a whirlwind. Typhus, too, in more isolated cases. To add to those uniquely Georgia-coast delights, it had drizzled cold and miserable rain for three solid days. Savannah rice fields, marshy at best, now were totally flooded and Chase's boots hadn't been dry for days. Still, there was a kind of grim satisfaction in being here, he thought.

In only a month's time, they'd cut hundreds of miles through the heartland of the enemy, gone from Atlanta to Savannah practically unopposed. Forty of the wealthiest counties of the South lay burned and ruined behind them. They'd occupied over two hundred railroad depots, county seats and towns, liberated over fifteen thousand slaves and ten thousand head of livestock, destroyed two hundred miles of irreplaceable Southern railroad. Burned all the gins, cotton mills, sawmills, armories, and CSA government property, about fifty million dollars' worth of baled cotton and Confederate bonds and currency and a great deal else. These were the official figures and didn't count the additional contributions the bummers had made. Sherman had dealt the state a blow Georgia would be reeling from for years. Toppled, with one hard punch, the cotton aristocracy, which had reigned impregnable for a hundred years and which so ardently supported the Southern war. If he wasn't exactly proud of it, Chase didn't regret any of it much either. He was tired. Bone tired. More inside than out. He wanted the war finished. He wanted to go home. He wanted to turn his back on the bleeding South and all she'd cost him in personal anguish these past few years, and try to forget he'd ever been here.

"Major Courtland?"

Chase turned at the voice to find his brigade commander, Colonel Adamson, ducking beneath thick moss to ride toward him. "Here, sir." He gestured toward a greenish pool in weary warning. "Watch the footing, sir. The mud right here is worse than most."

"God-awful place," Adamson swore softly with a grimace. As he drew rein on his horse he lifted one boot up out of the stirrup to show rainwater dripping, mud splashed all the way to the boot's top edge. "What do the Rebels see in this damn place anyway? If it were *mine* and someone wanted it, I'd *give* it away. Cheerfully. Never will understand the Rebel mind, I guess." He paused only for a moment, leaning down to swat a mosquito off his horse's shoulder, getting blood on his hand and wiping it off in disgust on the dark blue of his uniform trousers. Another insect quickly took the first one's place and Adamson merely scowled at it in forced surrender. "I've got an assignment for you, Chase. At least you'll be out of these God-forsaken swamps. You're to move your battalion north about a dozen miles, opposite the Savannah fieldworks."

"Why north?" It wasn't a question Chase usually asked a superior officer but he did so now. Fort McAllister lay to the southeast. And to be ordered so suddenly in the opposite direction hinted of something unusual brewing beneath the surface. "What's going on?"

"Can't say exactly this time, Chase. I'm sorry. Orders for secrecy came from the general's own staff."

Chase glanced at the older man in sharp surprise, holding Adamson's eyes for a long minute before he finally nodded. He didn't like following orders blindly, but Adamson rarely asked him to do that either. "All right. What are we to do along the way? Make trouble or try to stay out of it?"

Adamson allowed a brief wry smile to touch his mouth at the perspicacity of his young cavalry major. "Trouble is irrelevant. Making a lot of fuss along your way is what's required."

"I see." Chase nodded and turned to glance southeast, looking out toward the distant ocean. What Adamson was asking for was a diversion, obviously, a lot of fuss far away from Fort McAllister. Well, he'd known Sherman would take the fort. It had only been a question of when. "When?"

"Start now."

"But it's late afternoon already."

"Now, Major. Please."

Chase hesitated a moment in surprise, then quickly shrugged. Sherman must have made signal contact with the federal blockade ships, then. He would be impatient to capture the Rebel fort that blocked his access to those ships—and so, late as it was, the attack on McAllister would be made at once. "Wish the infantry boys good luck tonight, will you, sir? We've grown sort of fond of them over the past month." Chase spoke only in the quietest undertone, watching as the colonel nodded an acknowledgment. Then he forced a farewell smile and stepped back to let Adamson's horse maneuver more easily in the treacherous footing. "See you in Savannah, Colonel."

"Right." Adamson had returned Chase's faint smile and already begun to turn his horse away. He stopped suddenly, struck by a strange foreboding, turning in his saddle to catch and hold his young major's eyes once more. "And you, son, you take care of yourself now on the way up to Savannah. You understand?"

Adamson had spoken with an unusual urgency. Chase noted it, glancing in surprise to catch the older man's gaze. For a minute, neither man either moved or spoke. Then Chase shrugged a deliberate dismissal to his officer's warning and saluted once in farewell. "I always do, Colonel. You take care, too."

Unaware of the frown he wore, Chase watched the officer go, trying to ignore the uneasiness the colonel's words had left behind. Oh hell, he thought. Forget it. It had been a long campaign and men's emotions were reaching the breaking point, that was all. He gestured sharply to his bugler to sound orders, and he himself turned once again to look toward the distant north. "Ask Grier to come up here, will you, Sergeant? Apparently, we're riding up to the city yet tonight."

Stewart had watched the Yankee battalion for a long time—since his first attack at Millen had failed. He saw them mounting up now, saw the Yankee captain's arm gestures through the lens of the ocular glass—north. That made sense. South was the Ogeechee River. East more flat salt marshes and finally the sea; west was how they'd come. There was one particular swamp about seven miles north that Stewart knew well. The Rebel partisans had camped there before the Yankee columns had begun to arrive around Savannah in strength. A swamp of scattered cypress and tall water oaks; lots of mud and rotting tree trunks beneath the swamp's flooded waters. The Yankees wouldn't outrun them this time because their horses would be lucky to keep their footing even at a walk. He snapped the eyeglass closed and turned, nodding once to the waiting Treejack. At last, the long days of watching Yankees had paid off.

Chase drew rein at the edge of what looked like another swamp—and the worst one yet—and glanced uneasily at the sun already low on the western horizon. Half set already, he thought. Only a soft golden semicircle lingered to light their way. He glanced back to the swamp again, seeing deep shadows already forming, thick, trailing moss, dead trees, ghostly gray and leaning at a dangerous angle, soon to fall. The waters ahead were black and eerily still. Far away, he thought he heard the hoot of an owl, and then another. "What do you think, Grier?"

Grier's expression was answer in itself, and he spoke only a grim denial. "I don't like it."

Chase nodded agreement but still began to calculate quickly. He had his whole battalion with him, four troops, roughly two hundred and fifty men. Each troop on the march covered one hundred yards, so from beginning to end, they were strung out nearly a quarter of a mile long. Figuring forward progress at a walk, usually about four miles an hour, less in such footing: "It's going to be close, Grier. Maybe too close. We ought to have an hour of light left counting dusk, and the swamp shouldn't be more than a few miles wide. Still—" He frowned, glancing toward the setting sun once again. "That leaves Cowles' troop still in the swamp after dark, maybe."

"So we stop here?"

Chase frowned, and sighed his uneasiness. "Orders are to make the Savannah works."

Grier raised one brow in question but said nothing. He saw Chase's glance southeast and his deepening frown, and he spoke softly. "If there were some way to know whether the assault's already begun?"

Chase shook his head sharply and Grier fell silent. There was no way to know. Their job was to make the fort's Rebel defenders think the whole Union column was moving north. That would give the infantry boys the advantage of surprise at least, something they'd need storming the well-fortified Rebel position. So they had to go—there was no real choice. "We go." Chase frowned still but he signaled the advance to the bugler, and the high brassy notes echoed loud in the eerily quiet air. "Like it or not, let's move."

Inside, it was even worse than Chase had feared. The swamp waters were high; horses stumbled over submerged logs and tangled their legs in long, tough marsh grass and invisible vines. Muck turned unexpectedly to deep water, and horses floundered or swam. Men made a desperate grab for their rifles, trying, often failing, to keep the cartridge chambers dry. Snakes hung hissing from low branches, and as the shadows lengthened alligators splashed in the darkest pools. Men got lost; precious minutes were spent in finding them. Formation became nonexistent. Before the first mile ended, forward had come to mean movement in any direction. Now while the sun was sinking fast, men began to lose *all* orientation, going in circles, sometimes back the way they'd come. Whole sections of the swamp were black as night already; horses were sweating and blowing in the darkness, rolling their eyes white in borderline panic. And the men weren't much better. Lose the rest of the light and they'd never get out, any of them, lost in this hell forever. As shadows lengthened, the swamp closed in oppresively like a living thing; moss unseen reached down like ghostly hands, cold and damp, fearsome in that instant before a man identified exactly what it was. Something like claustrophobia began to spread through the ranks like whispered fear. Chase felt it and fought it, riding among small clusters of frightened men to offer a reassurance he did not entirely feel, pointing the direction, offering his own steadiness to guide them. This was where his officers counted—where good ones were gold and the bad ones broke fast. Grier had the head troop. He was irreplaceable. Cowles was good, too, but he had the toughest job, the rear guard, and men already uneasy panicked quickly in that exposed position. Let them get the notion something dangerous lay at their unprotected backs and all hell would break loose. They'd kill themselves and the men in front, too, in a blind scramble to escape. Captain Watson was the weak link—he'd abandoned his troop already to ride alone farther forward. Luckily his lieutenants were good, but they couldn't do the job alone. Enlisted men worshiped rank. Orders they'd refuse from a lieutenant, they'd obey with a cheer from a general. So that left Chase riding among Watson's troop, and keeping an eye on Cowles' men behind.

He tried not to think about how fast even the faint light of dusk was disappearing, but he thought he'd finally heard the distant boom of artillery fire from the south. If so, the assault on Fort McAllister had begun. And once free of the swamp, he could halt the battalion for the night. Once free. Those two words began to assume a great importance—soon to be even greater.

The first shots roared suddenly from the left. Chase's startled troops halted in confusion, calling out as if to friends, but only another burst of fire answered from the right. Men and horses began to go down, screaming and floundering in the scum-covered water, and the swamp was instantly filled with panic. Few of the men even thought to draw weapons. Most of the ones that did were kicked aside by the rush of others. Shots were sent wild in the darkness, hitting friend instead of enemy and worsening the madness. Chase deliberately pushed his own horse back to check the others, grabbing bridles, men's arms, anything he could reach. Shouted orders were scarcely heard more than a dozen yards away. But there were some good men there and those that could hear him tried to obey. Small clusters formed amid the shouting, screaming mass, three or four men to a group regaining their wits, returning the rifle fire instead of trying, blindly and futilely, to outrun it.

As he raised his own rifle, Chase dimly heard Cowles' profane shouting from behind, the captain trying to regroup his own panicky troop. More distantly, from up ahead, he heard Grier. Then Chase's horse sank suddenly into deep water, floundering, then swimming, reaching another higher ridge only to tangle his hooves in vines and becoming nearly unmanageable with fear. Chase kept one fist on the slippery wet reins and fired one-handed in the direction of the shots still pouring in. A man screamed behind him, riding into Chase and nearly unseating him, leaving dark scarlet smeared on Chase's arm as the soldier fell. Chase's Spencer carbine held seven shots—three or four at least were gone, and reloading now was an impossibility. Already, all around him, he began to hear the dull click of hammers hitting empty chambers. It was a dreaded sound and one he had no recourse for. Damn it, he thought. Where in the bloody hell is Cowles? Sudden white-hot pain seared his left arm and he grunted a curse of reaction to it from between clenched teeth. In answer, he fired his own carbine twice more but almost wildly, more intent now on trying to recognize faces whose familiarity was masked by shadows. Most of Watson's troops were through by now, he thought. One of those good young lieutenants lay dead against a nearby hillock. Other dark blue bodies lay sprawled over trees or floating in black water, near enough on either side to touch. But Cowles had made it up at last. They were *his* men passing now, new faces. He sensed more than saw his captain near him, heard the louder roar of troops with still-loaded rifles arriving, finally, and he raised one arm to gesture them forward. "That way! Keep them moving, for God's sakes!"

Something wet and hot trickled down into Chase's eyes as he shouted. It blurred his vision and he tried to wipe it out, surprised to find blood, colored black not red in the darkness.

Then rifle fire roared suddenly in concerted thunder, ahead and to the left. Grier, he realized. Thank God. Grier was using his troop to flank the ambushers. Shots from that section of the swamp grew few; those remaining were aimed in a new direction. He turned his horse as the last third of Cowles' men came up—vague shadows, only a little bit blacker than the surrounding swamps darkness, but firing, thank God, and moving as fast as they could in such hellish conditions.

Chase moved with them, firing the last cartridge from his carbine and reaching for his Remington instead. Powder smell thickened around him, almost obliterating the stink of the swamp, the smell of sulfur and the foulness of dead things unseen and rotting. They aimed for the sound of Grier's shooting, crawling, it felt like, but moving toward it, stumbling and splashing, blind in the blackness.

Chase fought a treacherous and worsening light-headedness, adrenaline failing as it always did after that first rush in danger. That and the blood lost, blood still flowing he thought. It was too dark to see but he thought he felt the warmth of it, the wetness soaking his whole left sleeve, stiffening the navy-blue broadcloth as it dried. There was firm ground suddenly beneath the horse's hooves, then there was muck again and water oaks barring the way. Then at last, there was ground once more, and up ahead the twilight was astonishingly bright after the dead blackness of the swamp's interior. Chase blinked in the sudden light, staring dazedly around him for a moment. He heard Grier's voice and tried to turn toward it.

"Everybody's clear, Major. Everybody, at least, that's coming. Watson's troop was hit pretty hard, almost half dead or missing. Cowles maybe lost a third."

Chase nodded, conscious of an exhaustion that seemed to be sweeping over him in dizzying waves. He felt himself starting to fall and felt hands grabbing for him just before he hit the ground. Vaguely, just before he lost consciousness, he heard Grier calling out for the company medic. And that was all.

Inside the eerie silence that had reclaimed the swamp, Stewart Leighton lit tarred, pine-knot torches and searched the frozen faces of the Yankee dead, shooting the few wounded that remained alive. Only seven of his men had been killed to

71

almost fifty bluebellies. A good exchange—except the one he *most* wanted dead was not. He'd counted on panic, initially had thought he'd had it. But the Yanks had managed to regroup, to return the fire and slow the slaughter down to practically nothing. Why hadn't Courtland died? He'd seen him square in the middle as they'd opened fire. Then he'd lost him in the confusion, found him once more and thought he'd hit him. Damn Yankee, he thought. A man surprisingly hard to kill. Stewart paused a moment more, watching his men rob the Yankee dead of rings, money, everything including the occasional gold tooth. They'd leave the bodies for the alligators to ravage and the water to rot. He glanced to the north with narrowed eyes, then turned to head on back to camp. All in all, it was still a good night's work. There would always be another chance for him to get the Yankee major. Next time, for *sure*.

Chase awoke a day later to a headache, a bandaged left arm, and the report that General Howard's infantry division had captured Ford McAllister just after sunset on the thirteenth. Among the one hundred thirty-five federals lost in the assault there had been Colonel Adamson, struck by cannon shot while observing the battle from a nearby hill. He had found for his own fate what he had feared for his young cavalry major.

Killed at just about the same time as his own battalion had been ambushed in that hellhole of a swamp, Chase reflected now. Like rattlesnakes, rotten luck must come in pairs. The thought brought a frown and Grier, sitting beside him in the hospital tent, returned it.

"Arm hurt?"

"No. Well, no more than to be expected anyway." Chase grimaced as he sat up, raising his good hand to reach for the battered tin cup Grier held. "Give me some of that, though, will you?"

Grier nodded. Even rotgut whiskey was a painkiller held in high esteem by most of the army, and this was good bourbon, long aged in a Southern cellar. He handed it over wordlessly.

"Any news?"

"About Savannah? Or about who ambushed us in the swamp?"

"Swamp," Chase specified.

"No, nothing. Couldn't find many clues the next day when we went back in." Grier grimaced and Chase didn't ask. He could imagine. The water, plus the alligators . . . "It must have been Wheeler's crew."

"No, I don't think so. Wheeler's been sticking close to Kilpatrick's main column lately. And he's up by Louisville." Chase closed his eyes, but kept the frown. It had been days since the incident, but the question continued to nag at him relentlessly, prodding him as if he ought to know the answer. Was there a connection to that first night, for example, on the road after Millen? Hadn't the firing then, too, started from the left? Maybe not. Or maybe it was coincidence. Anyway, who would single out *his* battalion? Not that they hadn't left some bitter enemies foraging their way from Atlanta to here, but on the whole, his troops had been *better* behaved than most. "I don't know."

"What?"

Chase hadn't realized he'd spoken aloud. He forced his eyes open again, making an effort to focus on Captain Grier's face.

"I'd better be going, Major. You look tired." Grier set the cup and the rest of its contents aside on the crude camp table as he stood up. "I'll 'forget' my cup, but you'd better enjoy it before the orderly gets back, Major, or *he'll* drink it."

"Thanks." Chase reached across for the cup in silence. The burning liquor didn't clear his head any but it did fog the pain. Who? he asked himself. *Who?* And why? Grier was at the open flap of the field tent before Chase spoke again, not even sure what had prompted the words. "Grier!" His captain turned, startled. "Don't take the men out. Not for routine patrol or anything else." Chase frowned, uneasy but heeding an instinct he'd learned to trust. "Run up the disabled tally or something, Grier. Just for a few days, until I'm on my feet again. Understand?"

Chase had spoken softly, but the surprise registering on Grier's face showed he'd heard. It was the kind of order most men would have questioned, even *should* have questioned, but Grier didn't. They'd been together too long. There was a moment's silence, and then the captain merely nodded. "All right, Major. I'll do it. Heal quick, though."

Chase nodded, only once, surprised at himself as he watched Grier go. Damn. What in the hell was going on? And why did he feel as though he ought to be able to answer that question himself? He shook it aside and drained the rest of the bourbon, almost impatiently. Whatever it was, Grier was right about not having much time to figure it out. Chase only knew that until they actually got into the city itself, they would continue to be hunted—by whom, and for what reason, he didn't know. But he would know, he promised himself. Before he let his men ride out into yet another trap, he would.

The war seemed to be on Chase's side. Not four days later, in the dead of night, the once proud and mighty Confederate city of Savannah watched General Hardee evacuating his ten thousand beaten troops across the broad, moonlit gray river into South Carolina. Yankee armies blocked any other escape. To the south, Sherman had captured Fort McAllister and federal gunboats sailed the waters of the Ogeechee River. To the east lay the sea and federal blockade ships. To the west lay Sherman's countless thousands, the main body of his troops and his artillery, both being readied for morning bombardment of the besieged city. Strong works had been constructed for the heavy guns. Lighter field pieces were less than a hundred and fifty yards from the Rebel trenches. The flooded rice field that lay between the two armies was rapidly being spanned by bridges and bundles of straw and sticks. Sherman had hinted that the first man to enter Savannah would be its military governor, and even this late at night, isolated, ambitious soldiers were building little platforms and advancing on Rebel gun positions. Officers watched and smiled, but no one interfered.

Whatever Grier had privately thought of his major's strange order, he had obeyed it—the Eighth Pennsylvania was not assigned any part in the general assault Sherman was planning on the city. But Hardee in Savannah was a competent soldier. He understood the futility of asking ten thousand men to stand against sixty thousand. From the docks at the foot of West Broad's cobblestones to the low, marshy Hutchison's Island one thousand feet across, CSA engineers had made a bridge, which, of itself, was proof of what pitiful resources were left to Southern armies. Only cotton flats and rice-field flats—towed by steamboats, positioned by a sympathetic tide—spanned the deep river, anchored by railroad-car

74

wheels and covered by planking ripped from city docks. To try to deaden the sound of the crossing, rice straw was spread on the wood. Beyond that pitiful bridge lay the Middle River and Pennyworth Island, then finally the back portion of the Savannah and the Carolina shores. Troops in night-shrouded trenches were withdrawn slowly, maintaining an unusually brisk fire to conceal one another's absences. The fire also concealed the sad sounds of an army destroying its own arsenals and spiking its own guns, firing the navy yard that had once been the pride and hope of the CSA and sinking or burning what few vessels still remained of the Savannah navy. Only the city's iron-clad namesake—busy removing stores and ammunition to the Carolina shore—was temporarily spared. Later that day, the *Savannah* fired a last defiant shell at the hated federal flag flying high over Fort Jackson, then her commander deliberately fired the ship's magazine. With a single flash of light and an immense tower of flame, the ship then blew to smithereens, literally rocking the city with the awesome detonation of her destruction.

On the twenty-second, Sherman formally entered the captured city with bands playing, and regimental and national colors flying. He rode slowly, taking salutes from his cheering troops who lined the streets. From his headquarters there, he sent the telegram that would reach Washington on December 23 and sweep the North with jubilant relief. "I beg to present to you as a Christmas gift the city of Savannah, with one hundred and fifty heavy guns and plenty of ammunition, also about twenty-five thousand bales of cotton."

The "lost" army had finally been found again.

Chapter Six

To the people of the North, the news of Sherman's capture of Savannah meant many things. To simple farm folk with husbands or sons in Sherman's army, it meant relief, the hope of seeing loved ones on some future day. To Abraham Lincoln, it meant one more crucial step taken toward defeating the Confederacy and securing the preservation of the Union. To the CSA government of Richmond, it meant disaster. To such groups as the Philadelphia coalition and others like it, the news meant rich harvests, the opportunity for profiteering in a new locale. Hardly had the telegraph wires ceased vibrating before such men were scrambling for ship berths, sending their emissaries down to deal in the captured city. Elinor Courtland Bennington, whose avaricious pursuit of wealth knew no limits and whose loyalties knew no cause beyond herself, was one of the people who would be involved in such schemes.

But regardless of what it meant to other people, no one in the North heard war news before the people of Washington did, and in the capital just now were two people who found anguish as well as benefit in the news of Sherman's triumph. One of them was a brilliant young surgeon, assigned to practice medicine in one of Washington's many federal military hospitals. The other was a young woman who had volunteered to work as a war nurse and been assigned to work at that surgeon's side. Thrown together by the chances of war, they had gradually, reluctantly, found themselves falling in love. It was not a love affair that gave either one of them anything other than bittersweet anguish, because the young surgeon's name was Doc Lacey and the woman's name was Susan Stratford. Surgeon Major Roger Lacey was one of Chase Courtland's closest friends; Susan Stratford was Chase Courtland's fiancée.

76

"Sherman's resurfaced?" Doc Lacey was working alone in the Confederate prisoner ward when he heard the shouts of the jubilant newsboy echoing up the hospital's three-story marble facade: 'Sherman in Savannah! Christmas present to the Union!" There was a sudden noticeable silence among the Rebel wounded who filled the ward and an all too palpable sense of remembered enmity. Doc Lacey might exult in the Union triumph. Confederates would not. Not even Confederates such as these men, who were out of the actual war itself, who both liked and respected the federal doctor who treated them. It was, consequently, an uneasy moment in the ward, a moment awkward with the consciousness of men's divisions from one another. Lacey finished bandaging a wound in careful silence and withdrew from the ward a minute later. He would leave the Confederates to express the anguish they must feel in privacy and seek his own side to express his own relief.

Instinctively, as he left the ward he went looking for Susan. She was on break, a short break. That in itself was unusual for she rarely took even that much rest in the course of their grueling day. He found her easily enough as he always did. Lacey had often a kind of sixth sense about where Susan was, and just now she was standing in the dark inside an otherwise deserted staff room—a slender, silent silhouette showing black against the pearl gray of undraped institutional windows. He allowed a smile of pleasure, finally, to break the weary, straight line of his mouth as he began to relay the news. "Susan, I heard a newsboy shouting that Sherman and his troops are—"

"I know, in Savannah. I heard it, too, about a half hour ago." In contrast to Doc Lacey's open pleasure, Susan seemed oddly subdued. She half-turned as she spoke, gesturing toward a newspaper she held folded in one hand. "I checked the casualty lists already, Roger. Chase's name isn't listed, so I'm assuming he is all right."

In the wake of her words there was a sudden silence. For a moment the atmosphere in the staff room seemed a disorienting replay of the awkwardness Lacey had just left behind him in the Confederate ward. Preoccupied there with the Rebels' anguish and preoccupied, too, with his own initial jubilation, Lacey had not associated General Sherman's victory with Chase Courtland's reemergence into his and Susan's lives.

77

Nevertheless Chase was suddenly present again. The Union Cavalry major stood now between Doc Lacey and the woman he loved as ominously as ever and Lacey felt his initial jubilation quickly fading. Chase Courtland was among those Union soldiers now safely arrived in distant Savannah. And with the campaign over, Chase might well be coming home soon to marry the woman Doc Lacey loved. The triangle that had entrapped the three of them—himself, Susan and Chase—nearly a year ago entrapped them still. As a matter of fact, it was farther from resolution now than it had probably ever been. "You can't marry him, Susan. Even if Chase does come home, you simply can't."

"Roger, please don't start that same argument again. Please don't."

Doc Lacey could hear a catch now in Susan's voice as she spoke, and he realized instantly why she'd left the oil lamps of the staff room carefully unlit. She had sought out the darkness to conceal her tears. He was conscious of a single, momentary flash of anger, of jealousy, and then of familiar, rising fear. "Susan, for God's sake, you can't still mean to marry Chase."

"Roger, I am engaged to him!"

"Which is bad enough without compounding the folly by *marrying* him!"

"How can you ask me to betray a man who's probably your own closest friend, Roger! Isn't it bad enough what I've already done to Chase? Haven't I already betrayed too much of my commitment to him?"

"Betrayed Chase?" For only a moment, Doc Lacey paused, poised on the brink of a revelation he'd kept carefully silent for too many months. But if there was ever to be a time to tell her, it was now. *Now*, he thought, before they all sank hopelessly deeper into this solutionless morass. "For the love of God, Susan, you haven't betrayed Chase—you haven't even done anything that Chase himself hasn't already done as well! Chase Courtland is in love with Leanna Leighton, Jonathon Penley's sister! I was there at Blytheswood with the two of them. I saw it happen. You needn't marry Chase because you think you'd break his heart if you didn't. Chase is already in love with another woman!"

Her only reply was silence, as sharp, as bitter as if he'd struck her physically. But in the faint light of the Washington

78

dusk, Doc Lacey could see enough of Susan's face to identify the emotions that instantly played across it, and the one emotion he'd most expected to see—surprise—was not there. For a moment longer, incredulous, he continued to stare at her in silence. "Sweet God, Susan, you *knew* that already, didn't you? You knew about Chase and Leanna Leighton."

Susan met Doc Lacey's eyes for only the briefest of instants as she turned away from the light that issued from the room's single window. And as she moved she made one small gesture with her hand, a gesture that was part bewilderment and part dismissal. "Last spring when Chase was wounded in Virginia and brought up here for you to tend, Roger, he had one particularly feverish night. He called Leanna Leighton's name, not mine. I suppose, in a way, that I knew it then."

"And all these months, I've been walking on eggshells, Susan. Thinking I couldn't hurt you by admitting the truth." In the lingering shock of his disbelief, Doc Lacey was slow to speak, slow to even regather his thoughts. There must be a kind of reason to this, he found himself thinking, some explanation that I can't seem to piece together. There must be an answer here that will make all of this madness make sense. "Susan, what the hell kind of game are you playing here? Chase is in love with Leanna Leighton. You're in love with me. Yet you both go blithely on together as if none of that even *matters* to you. Your engagement to each other is nothing more than a sham. Or is it?"

"It isn't a sham, Roger. It's not . . . nearly as simple a problem as you seem to think." Susan's voice broke once as she began to speak and she paused momentarily to struggle for composure. Doc Lacey instinctively started toward her, one hand outstretched, but she waved him back, waved him away almost too quickly, as if she could not, just now, allow his touch. She started speaking quickly again, as if by doing so she could forestall his approach. "No, listen to me, Roger. You see it all in far-too-simple terms. You say Chase is in love with Leanna Leighton, and I think that may be true, but there are different kinds of love. He may love her, but in another sense, I know Chase cares for me. And even while I love you, in another way, I love him, too. I don't expect you to understand entirely, but none of that is what really matters anyway. Love or the lack of it has never been the deciding factor. My marriage to a Courtland has been assumed for years, Roger. Practically since I was born, I imagine. Our feelings toward one another—Chase's and mine, I mean—have been cultivated and watched and endlessly coaxed. It's part of our world, Roger. Part of how things work. Then this war interrupted it all, changed it even a little. But not enough." Susan's whispered words faded momentarily into absolute silence, and somewhere down the street, Doc Lacey could hear church bells pealing out. It seemed a mocking sound, just now. Their jubilation struck him as bitterly ironic. "Regardless of how I feel about you, or how Chase feels about Leanna Leighton, I am still committed to marry him, Roger. It's a fact of life to me, something like the sun rising or setting every day. And not something I can change."

"Of course you can change it!" Doc Lacey found his voice again in a burst of disbelieving protest. This was utter madness. This was nineteenth-century America not medieval Europe. Women were not blindly bound to follow their families' wishes anymore. He must force Susan, somehow, to find the courage to rebel. "For Gods' sake, Susan, you just open your mouth and tell them all no!"

"I can't, Roger! I can't tell them all no!" Susan's self-control broke with a single desperate, choking sob. "I promised my brother, too. Before Ben died at Chancellorsville, I promised him I would marry Chase."

"Susan, you can't be serious! Chancellorsville was years ago. Before Chase Courtland ever met Leanna. Before you ever met me, or we fell in love!"

"I still promised him!"

"But you can't build your life on that! You can't sacrifice everything else to keep that promise! Susan, can't you see what you are doing? You're running hell-for-leather straight into disaster! And taking Chase Courtland there along with you!" Doc Lacey heard the rush of Susan's sudden sobbing, saw the sudden anguished, helpless shudder that shook her slender body. In two swift steps he had crossed the room to reach toward her, seizing her shoulders and shaking her hard. "I won't let you do this, damn it! You don't owe anyone your future—not yours and not mine either! It *can* be changed and it *will* be changed! Before even more misery comes out of it!" Susan turned suddenly toward him with an anguished cry, pressing against him, trembling, shuddering, her wrenching sobs caught against his shoulder.

Roger wasn't sure how she'd gotten there, whether he'd pulled her or whether she'd come by herself, but too many months of wanting her had drained his resistance. He lowered his head over hers and found her mouth hot with the wet salt of her tears, her lips yielding beneath his in stunning softness. It was like drowning almost. Losing himself. Drawn deeper and deeper, incapable of struggle. But there was no reason to struggle, he thought in sudden realization. This was something that should have happened long before it actually had, something that would put a final end to the course of disaster that Susan seemed hell-bent on continuing to run. This was something that would make the rest of the decisions come easy, because after this, there would not be any other choices left to take.

Only vaguely was he even aware of the moment he lifted her in his arms to take her into his quarters. The room was windowless, and black as coal, and cold, but none of it mattered. Susan was in his arms and Doc Lacey was unaware of anything else. Her breasts were soft and round, peaked from the chill of the air and from his mouth on them, her skin suddenly bare and warm and touching his with unimaginable fire. He murmured her name, over and over again, a prayer almost, and a demand, covering her mouth with his own, tasting her tongue and the salt of her tears. She flinched only once as he entered her, finding her maidenhead and tearing it with desperate, all-consuming need to possess her himself and to deny Chase Courtland's rights to her. He heard Susan's soft cry against his shoulder and turned his head to take her lips again, kissing her until the fear and pain both left her once again.

Susan clung to Roger than in urgent hunger, as desperate as he—unable to stop herself, unable even to feel the shame and the guilt of such a loving. Chase's ring sparkled in the darkness, deathly pale compared to the fire within her as she was swept to the heights of passion, lost in dark, urgent hungers that throbbed in her belly and possessed her soul. There was a single, endless instant of bursting fulfillment, ecstasies that coursed terrible and brilliant as the sun, and suddenly Roger was quiet, still above her, heavy, and only the ragged sound of his breathing and the pounding of his heart intruded on an absolute silence that seemed more terrible to her by the minute. Slow tears gathered finally in her eyes. Her heart, released from passion, thudded sickly in her breast. Oh God, she thought, what have I done? Now what horrors have I set in motion?

Doc Lacey moved finally, touching Susan's lips a last time with his own. He was content and smiling faintly in the darkness. It was over now, he was thinking—so close, maybe, to disaster, but after this, there was no returning, no more choices. In his mind Susan now belonged unequivocally to him.

"May God forgive us. . . ."

Doc Lacey heard Susan's murmured prayer in a kind of startled confusion, lifting his head to watch her face. There he saw the gleam of new tears as she pulled away from beneath him, reaching for her dress, and barely buttoning it halfway before she reached for the door to pull it open. "Susan, wait. No. What are you—"

"Good-bye, Roger."

Too late, he tried to grab for her arm, staring in astonishment as she began to go. "Susan, no! Not after this. Susan, you can't still mean to pursue—"

"I'm leaving now. Washington, I mean. I'm going home to wait. To hear from Chase when he's coming home."

"For God's sake, no! Susan! You can't!" But Lacey found himself speaking only to air as Susan pulled from his grasp and slammed the door closed for answer. He dressed as fast as he could, sick, and stunned, and trying to think. Good God, she couldn't still think to marry another man, especially not Chase. *Especially* not a friend who would think, if he ever knew, that this had been a betrayal of friendship. "Susan!" He called her name to the empty night air as he pulled open the heavy main door and took the marble steps outside at a run. "Susan!"

But she was gone. The streets were beginning to crowd with people walking and in carriages, singing, shouting at darkened houses, celebrating the Christmas news of Sherman's incredible victory in the heart of the Confederacy. And though Roger searched the city until dawn, he never found any further trace of her. He watched the sun rising over the Capitol's white dome in helpless frustration and then slowly turned to head back to the waiting hospital. What had passed between Susan and him tonight was final. Irrevocable. Susan would realize that finally on her own, she had to. For now, perhaps, the kindest thing he could offer her was the time to do just that, to make her own peace with the fact that the future no longer held any choices. For either of them.

As Doc Lacey headed back for the hospital, it never occurred to him to doubt that eventually Susan would accept that as fact.

Whitney was among the first in Philadelphia to hear the news of Savannah's fall. The baby, Bonnie, had had a touch of fever lately and been up fussing in the night, keeping Whitney up as well. Over the baby's wails, she'd heard the cries being shouted outside by a newsboy running down night-shadowed Locust Street. And then she'd gone instantly to wake Jonathon—to tell him and to share that first instant of pain that had flashed so plainly in his drowsy eyes. "God. Maybe they'll surrender now." But the ex-Confederate officer spoke with soft anguish at the prospect, and Whitney reached out in sympathy to catch his hand as he continued. "They ought to, I guess, Whit. Atlanta . . . now Savannah, gone. They haven't enough troops left to fight one army let alone two—Grant and Sherman both."

"Maybe they'll negotiate a peace, Jon. The paper reported rumors that Vice-President Stephens has asked for a meeting."

"Lincoln won't negotiate his Union away. Why should he? And Davis won't accept anything else."

There was a moment of silence, anguished, and Whitney swallowed against a lump in her throat. To have sacrificed so much and for nothing—for only the bitter humiliation of defeat. It was hard for her, harder, she knew, for Jonathon, who carried the curse of the Penley pride. "You should get dressed and go tell Joshua," she urged awkwardly at last. "He's been so desperately concerned for Major Courtland. Go tell him that it appears his son is safe, at least."

Jonathon nodded reluctantly and rose. It was cold in the December nights—especially for someone used to Southern winters—and he shivered as he dressed. Outside, the night air was bitingly cold and clear as a diamond. In the lamplight, snowflakes dusted lawns with crystal glitter. Jonathon shivered harder as he walked, then ran, trying to fight off the shock of the cold and of the pain, both together. A light was already showing in the servants' quarters in back of the mansion. A moment later, the front door opened for his knock. He saw

Elinor already descending the stairs, beautiful as ever and wicked as Satan in a green embroidered silk dressing gown that had to have come from the tea trade of China, her hair undone for sleep and gleaming like gold silk in the mellow chandelier light. She smiled most graciously and never missed a step at his entrance. Joshua's bedroom door opened and clicked sharply closed, unseen, upstairs and down the hall, and Jonathon saw the fear in Joshua's eyes as the older man appeared at the top of the stairs.

"What is it? What's wrong?"

"Nothing's wrong." Jonathon stepped hastily inside, closing the door behind him. He made an effort to conceal both his own anguish and the instinctive rising of his neck hairs as Elinor drew ever nearer to him. "Sherman's army is safely in Savannah. Whitney thought you'd want to know."

There was a heartbeat of startled stillness in the Courtland house, a moment in which Jonathon, Elinor and Joshua reacted to the war news with their own individual biases. To Jonathon Penley, whose own personal anguish at the Confederate defeat was finally subsiding, it seemed as if he sensed a flash of anger or perhaps of disappointment from the Courtland daughter, who stood silently on the steps above him. That startled him, for it was not a reaction he would have expected. Jonathon had not expected any hallelujahs from Elinor either, of course. Regardless of what her father chose to believe, Jonathon Penley knew well that Elinor was no Unionist—Elinor had no loyalties to anything except herself. What Jonathon *had* expected of her was the kind of bored indifference she displayed to anything not directly relevant to either her personal comforts or her personal wealth. What he saw now momentarily on Elinor's all-too-lovely face was anything but that expected indifference.

If Savannah had fallen, then the Confederacy was one step closer to its inevitable grave, Elinor was thinking. And the enormous profits she gained by running black-market guns to the South was therefore also one step closer to *its* end. Damn pity, that. Few businesses were as profitable as gunrunning had proven to be. But on the other hand, there would be money to be made profiteering in Savannah; there was in any newly captured city. Money was money. And after all, money was the point of the whole thing, anyway. Plus, Sherman's army would now be in communication once again with Elinor's contacts at the Washington War Department, and if Drake's post-Atlanta trap had snared as it should have a certain Leanna Leighton, then Elinor would have Leanna Leighton under federal arrest, Jonathon Penley under her thumb, and consequent unchallenged access to the millions that lay in the Courtland bank. Perhaps, she decided—having weighed all the pluses and minuses of Savannah's fall in a single minute of furious thought—perhaps she could sincerely applaud General Sherman's conquest of the Southern city. Glory, glory, Hallelujah. Hip, hip, hooray for the rest of the family's precious Union. As long as it didn't conflict with either her plans or her profits, she wouldn't begrudge them a moment of pride. Elinor regained her composure swiftly to offer a smile, a smile given in obvious and genuine sincerity.

Jonathon Penley, standing watching Elinor still from the bottom of the Courtland stairs, felt more uneasy at seeing that sudden smile than he had at the lack of it. He knew she would not be smiling that way simply because of the Union victory. She would smile to fool her father, of course, but the lack of sincerity in such a smile should be easily spotted. From past experience with her, Jonathon thought this particular smile usually meant gain for her—and trouble, consequently, for someone else. The only real question was trouble for whom?

With an effort, Jonathon turned his gaze and his attention away from the Courtland daughter toward the father. In contrast to his daughter, Joshua's reaction was patently simple. A joy that was deeply real, almost religious, suffused the older man's whole being. Joshua was regaining the color that had initially drained from his face at Jonathon's midnight entrance, and as he began to take the stairs down toward the ex-Confederate officer a smile of relief had quickly formed. But mixed with the relief some sympathy showed as well. As he gained the foyer and reached to clasp Jonathon Penley's cold-chilled hand Joshua nodded once in acknowledgement of another's anguish.

"I'm sorry a bit—for your sake, Jonathon. I don't want you to misconstrue my personal relief, to think I don't understand it means different things to you and Whitney." He held the young Rebel's eyes a moment more, tightening his hand once before he withdrew it. "For myself, I thank God. You understand the difference, I hope."

Jonathon nodded and managed a smile. Joshua's hand had not been much warmer than his own—Major Courtland's overlong absence with Sherman had not improved his father's failing heart. "I understand. That's why I came over to tell you Joshua. Whitney heard a newsboy crying the story and woke me, too."

"Chase must be all right, then. We would have gotten a wire from the War Department by now if he hadn't been." Joshua was showing both his age and his ill health suddenly as he spoke, and Jonathon, standing watching him, was conscious of a sudden rush of answering pain. There was a certain febrile quality in the Courtland father's relief, the kind of obsessive, desperate, almost dreamlike hope that the very old and the very weak cling to in their fading moments. Woken out of the midst of sleep, Joshua looked gaunter and grayer and older than ever. This good, *good* man was failing quickly, Jonathon thought with a flare of helpless resentment. And there wasn't a damn thing he could do to stop it.

"I'm sure you're right, Joshua. Perhaps with the campaign over, your son might even manage to get home for furlough." Jonathon said it only out of the urgings of sympathy. He himself harbored no special wish to see any Yankee officer, let alone this particular one. Chase Courtland's involvement with Leanna had left behind a bitterness that Jonathon found to be unabating. But Joshua reacted only to Jonathon's words, and the pleasure that lit his face repaid the younger man for the effort of having said it.

"God, Jonathon, how good that would be to see Chase home again! Even if it were only for a little while. There's so much I need to speak to him about." Joshua's smile had faded slightly under the force of his own sudden remembrances. There *was* so much he needed to talk to Chase about. The coalition for one thing. Transferring out of field duty to a safer, closer desk position in the capital was another. "Anyway, thank you, Jonathon, for coming over. Thank Whitney for me as well, of course. I'll see you in the morning at the usual time."

"So now the prodigal son will come waltzing home, perhaps. Strutting his prowess and covered with glory." Elinor's murmured undertone stopped Jonathon in his tracks. Startled, he glanced sharply up the stairs to see if there were a reaction from Joshua, but the older man was already three-quarters of the way up the stairs, too far away for Jonathon to see. Perhaps the Courtland father hadn't even heard Elinor's barb. Or, perhaps, after so many months, Joshua had trained himself to pretend he hadn't.

Jonathon glanced briefly at Elinor's face as she turned, then he too turned, moving for the door. He was careful to say nothing, to show nothing on his face, until he was outside the house once again and concealed by the darkness of the bitter-cold night. It had been an interesting expression he'd momentarily seen on the Courtland daughter's face just now. Not merely jealousy over her brother's possible return to the house. Not joy or forced filial love—that Jonathon would have understood as sham. Instead there had been a certain wariness in Elinor's gaze, displeasure and a sudden caution. As if she were planning something that her brother's return might make more difficult.

The Philadelphia picture was growing ever more complicated, Jonathon thought uneasily. Now he must add the fact of bad blood between the Courtland son and the Courtland daughter. And ever more definitive hints of something new brewing in Elinor Courtland's witches' pot. Suddenly, in a sense, he found himself agreeing with Joshua's wishful hopes. Jonathon hoped, too, that Chase Courtland might come home fairly soon. Otherwise, with the father's health failing and the son a thousand miles distant, Elinor might prove an over-whelming challenge in the months that lay ahead.

Chase Courtland walked slowly by the riverfront deciding what kind of prize this last campaign had won his federal army. His arm was still in a sling but he'd recovered enough otherwise to be enjoying the warmth of the sunny morning and the cool air blowing off the riverhead. Behind him on the roof of the U.S. Customs House, the federal flag snapped and cracked in the brisk wind, and federal soldiers crowded the city with dark blue uniforms. Savannah today was very obviously occupied territory. Smoke still drifted in occasional wisps from the burned CSA navy yard. Warships, burned to the waterline, still drifted erratically along the wide, slate-gray river. Abandoned, spiked artillery lay along entrenchments on Hutchison's Island across the way. There was a faint smell still—like the swamp, a marsh smell, but mixed here with fresh river air. It was a beautiful city, of elegant homes and lush gardens, sophisticated and aged like fine wine, far different than the much newer Atlanta had been. But in many ways he'd liked Atlanta better, Chase decided. Atlanta had been more Northern, more familiar, both in weather and in people. Savannah reminded him of Charleston, which he'd visited years before the war, and a little of New Orleans minus the French touch. The landed aristocracy was strong in these older cities, its code of order omnipresent, the "genteel life" structured to stifling rigidity. Here in Savannah, the antiquity of the Deep South and King Cotton were further laced with the international flavor of a deep-water port, and the English flag flew in abundance here over many of the riverfront warehouses.

Surprisingly—despite Savannah's Deep South traditions—of the city's twenty thousand inhabitants, Chase guessed nearly half were not displeased at the city's fall. The blacks and the poor whites had nothing to lose by Yankee occupation and they had suffered greatly these last few war months. In addition, Barnum's brigade, which had led the way in entering the city and been assigned to patrol it, had done a good job here—looting, pillaging, and arson all were rare. By today, even the wealthier, staunchly Confederate classes were looking on matters with a more hopeful eye. Pretty women abounded, nicely dressed, bolder than in the smaller towns. As in most Southern cities, Savannah showed a noticeable lack of men. Some of the women were hostile, stepping into the cobblestoned streets to avoid walking under the national flag, the boldest jeering, or playing "Dixie" overloudly on fine imported pianos inside brick mansions overlooking Columbia or Oglethorpe Squares. But others he had passed today had offered the hint of an encouraging smile. As well they should, Chase reflected, in practical terms. Before this year, their families had probably been worth millions, but Southern wealth was in land, in cotton, in slaves, fine houses and railroad or Confederate bonds. It had taken a hundred years to structure Savannah's grand aristocracy. One month of the federal march through South Carolina had toppled it forever. Under federal aegis, at least markets and stores had been reopened, the city given something to eat. For the first time probably in their sheltered lives, "ladies" mingled with "trash" out of the shared necessity of eating, and it had provided some stark contrasts today in the market lines.

Here on the riverfront itself, though, there was a noticeable quiet. Federal ships were steaming upriver from the sea, but most hadn't arrived yet. In years past, this would have been the very heartbeat of the port—tall-masted clippers and steamboats both, taking on cotton, or unloading imported goods into the now mostly-empty, shuttered brick warehouses that lined the docks. Factor's Walk, a path of wrought iron, oyster shell and brick that connected the various riverfront offices, warehouses and the huge Exchange—once the haunt of the wealthiest men of Georgia, of plantation owners and their cotton brokers—was deserted today except for federal officers such as himself out sight-seeing. A squirrel ran over the gray cobblestones, collecting the nuts of the live oaks towering on the bank above. It ran practically over Chase's boots and he smiled faintly. Squirrels reckoned nothing of North or South, federal or CSA. And for a moment, Chase envied the creature such blissful simpleness. A good year was any when nuts were plentiful. It must be nice, he thought. Not to balance, not to weigh, not to think. To forget the past and be unaware of a future. Confederacy or Union was all the same to the animal he watched—as it would be, maybe, to all of them someday yet. The fall of this gracious, elegant, old bastion of the Deep South was one step closer. Maybe Sherman was right after all to wage the kind of warfare he'd been waging—hard as it was on all of them caught in its horror. Because this was more than a simple war. In a way, this was a collision of two worlds, two ways of life. Only one could survive. So maybe it had to be fought this way.

The sun went under a cloud, and with the wind from the river the December air was suddenly chilly. Only two days from Christmas, rose-colored camellias bloomed on thick green bushes and live oaks draped with moss defied the calendar. As Chase turned from the riverfront to walk back into the city he put his hand in his pocket to warm it. The paper of letters crackled beneath his fingers, reminding him of home. Mail ships had been among the first in, bringing answers to letters written before they'd left Atlanta. Funny how that seemed an eternity ago. Two letters from his father. Two more from Susan. One, unexpected from his mother's sister in Boston, so lighthearted it had made him smile. Those from Susan had reawakened an old guilt, and now reminded him of an overdue promise. Chase checked his step in sudden decision, turning another way. Maybe he would see snow instead of palm trees for Christmas after all.

"You see, Stewart, you were wrong." Leanna smiled, but bleakly, from the hilltop. Down below, the city of Savannah was only a haphazard blur of greenery and brick. "The Yankees *did* take Savannah. And with very little trouble."

"We didn't need Savannah anyway. The port's been closed for years."

Stewart dismounted to step beside her, and involuntarily, almost unconsciously, Leanna flinched and stepped farther away. Nothing had changed between them since that awful, nightmarish night he'd found Lt. Col. Drake's file and beaten her for the half lies and half truths that it contained. By day, Stewart tolerated her with coldly bitter scornfulness. By night, he made love to her—if it could be called that. "Bred" her would be a more appropriate term, she thought. Like horses, or prize cattle. Even that, he did coldly—as he did everything now, it seemed. As cold as his blue eyes were now looking down on the distant, federal-occupied city. Cold—and cruel. And his hatred of the Yankees had only increased, with each of Sherman's army's successes, with each of his futile attempts to kill the Yankee major who had succeeded in doing what Stewart had been unable to do—get his wife with child.

Down below in the distant city, the stars and stripes of the Union flag were flying over the Savannah customs house. Watching it wave in the breeze coming off the river, Leanna felt a sudden anguish and a sudden compassion for the bitter hopelessness Stewart must feel. Stewart—and all the Southern men who had risked everything in the war, struggled so resolutely against such impossible odds. Because the Yankees *were* going to win, she thought, in something like surprise. That Union flag flew daily over more and more of the South. And all the Confederate gallantry, all their heroism and their sacrifices, would have been made in vain. The Southern world was going to be crushed to nothing beneath the onslaught of Yankee bootheels.

The sudden realization of that future brought tears to her eyes and an anguish potent enough to momentarily submerge her hatred for the man who stood beside her. In a last impulse born out of desperation, Leanna reached out to touch Stewart's lean, sun-browned hand. "Stewart, now that the Yankees are in the city, leave it go. For the love of God, leave it go while there's still a chance to salvage something—of the South, and of ourselves. I *will* try to forgive what you've done to me. I'll *try* to forget. And if you would only—"

"Spare your Yankee lover? Is that what you're about to ask me for?"

He spoke with a familiar but nonetheless unpleasant smile, and Leanna felt equally familiar anger and bitterness toward him surge back all the stronger. She shook her head at it, trying to fight her anger away, trying to express a last desperate appeal in the eyes she raised to lock to his. "No, not him. At least, not Chase alone. I mean *all* of it, Stewart—*all* the past that's brought us to this. What I've done to you. What you've done to me. The ugliness, the bitterness, the destruction. All these terrible years of war. Leave it behind and we could go up to your plantation. Today. Tomorrow. Start to take one day at a time. Work together. Have a family together. Try to build some kind of future where even the Yankees *do* win, they won't be able to take everything away from us."

"It's too late for that, Leanna." There was a sudden terrible anger on Stewart's once-handsome face, and he pulled his hand abruptly away at her touch. He looked to the city instead of to her, and he shook his head in familiar resolution. "I'll never give up to them, don't you understand that yet? My lands, my slaves, my houses. They're mine by right of birth and breeding. If I lost them, I'd be no better than common trash."

"But for the love of God, Stewart, if the Yankees win the war! If the war is over and we *have* to—"

"The war will never be over! Not for me. And not for you. Not as long as there's a Yank alive on Southern soil! I'll hunt them down like rabid dogs! Exterminate them as I would any other kind of vermin! That's the only future *I'm* willing to accept!"

She felt tears burning her eyes and closed them, turning her head away from him. It was no use. There was no chance any longer. No way to even touch them. Maybe there never had been. The desperation of that sudden, unexpected empathy faded slowly, replaced by a now-familiar, cold resignation to living as enemies—she hating him and he her with as violent a bitterness as could ever lay between soldiers of different flags. Oddly enough, though, there was strength in that and Leanna's tears dried unshed. "I give up then, Stewart. Let the future hold what it will. At least with General Sherman in Savannah, your hand is held back from committing such senseless murder as you were determined on. I thank God for that. Not for Chase's sake alone. But for mine. And for yours."

There was a short silence. She looked up finally to find Stewart smiling again, searching the marshy, distant South Carolina shores with apparent satisfaction. "They won't stay in Savannah forever. And when they come out, I'll be waiting. *I* know the Carolina country far better than *he* will. Or maybe I'll arrange something sooner." He turned as he finished speaking and remounted his horse, curtly gesturing the girl to do the same. Long since acquainted with the futility of rebelling, Leanna complied, never looking back at the distant city that now held a man who had once been dearer than life to her. But there was no doubt in her mind who the "he" was Stewart had spoken of. Regardless of what she did to try to stop it, this was a nightmare that seemed destined to continue to its deadly end.

Regimental headquarters were occupying a fine old house on Charlton Street, by Lafayette Square. Ogelthorpe had planned carefully when he'd first founded Savannah in 1733, and Chase had no trouble finding the address. Unlike most cities, sprawling and growing in a haphazard pattern, Savannah, thanks to Ogelthorpe's vision, was neat as a chessboard, streets and park squares laid out straight and wide. It gave even the center of the city a country air. Of course, Chase reflected, it was the industries of the Northern cities that fouled the air and gave rise to their tenement slums, but industry had won the war for the North, too. Even to match Savannah's undeniable beauty, he would not sacrifice the burgeoning industrial might of the North.

Regimental headquarters was always chaotic. Today was worse than usual. At least a hundred soldiers crowded around the open doorway, lining the steep, wrought-iron-banistered steps, blocking the street and extending into the shadows of the live oaks of Lafayette Square. Some of the men had picked pink and red camellia blooms, tucking them into black caps and cartridge belts in gaudy, incongruous contrast to battle-stained uniforms. Chase didn't try to press through the crowd. Rank had some privileges other than the dubious one of being the first one shot at in a battle charge. The door to the ground level—kitchens, laundry, and slave quarters—was also open. He ducked his head to pass beneath the landing of the main entrance and took the half-dozen steps down to enter the damp cellar. Walls of limestone and oyster shells greeted him. Even in midmorning, it was dim, close, and damply cool. But the stairs were where he'd expected to find them, and he soon emerged into the bright and airy main floor of the house, raised above the ever-present dust from the streets outside. Thick walls of plaster kept heat out in the baking Savannah summers, the warmth from burning fires kept it in on such December days, and he found the temperature inside to be about perfect. The house had obviously belonged to a wealthy man—but not, Chase decided, to one of *the* wealthiest. Heart-of-pine-planked floors were only stained dark to mimic mahogany; the plaster molding on the high ceilings was second-rate; and the center medallion from which hung a rather gaudy crystal-and-gilt-chain chandelier was too obviously a copy. Probably from one of the Jay-designed houses, such as the Owens mansion on Ogelthorpe Square. Jay seemed to be Savannah's prestige architect. There were other telltale signs as well, like a center staircase, curved as fashion dictated it must be, but steeper than some, a shade too narrow for wide-hooped skirts. And he wasn't surprised as he stepped into the formal front parlor to note that the fireplace front was not genuine marble but cleverly painted cast-iron. He hid a smile, thinking Philadelphia and Savannah people, though presently divided by a bitter war, were not so altogether different after all. Social climbing and its attendant pretenses were sedulously practiced in both places, apparently.

The furniture, at least, was good. A few Chippendale pieces but mostly older Duncan Phyfe, all were richly covered in heavy satin brocades to match the drapes of the paired, ceiling-high windows. He chose a small corner chair and drew it closer to the marble-topped table where a staff officer worked.

"Be with you in a minute." The staff officer hadn't even looked up as Chase seated himself. He was almost inundated by papers, and as several slipped off the table's scalloped edge

Chase obligingly reached to lift them off the fine oriental carpet and put them back.

"Thank you. Oh—Chase." The harried officer looked up at last and grinned, pushing the papers disgustedly aside. "Damn this stuff. Furloughs, sick leave, new uniforms to get issued. How many men are still waiting outside?"

"About a hundred."

"Oh great." His expression said otherwise and he shook his head. "And what do *you* want from me?"

"Only a furlough and a way to get home to enjoy it." Chase smiled wryly, knowing it was not an easy favor to grant. But McLeod had been Colonel Adamson's aide. And he would at least try.

"*Only?*"

"I've furlough backed up. And don't tell me there aren't ships scheduled north. I know better."

McLeod sighed, reaching across the table for a particular paper, searching to find it. "All of about two. Any chance I can talk you into a second choice?"

For an instant, Chase hesitated. The war was almost over, it had to be. His father had managed without him for this long; Susan had already waited for years. Then came a startlingly vivid memory of the ambush in the swamp, the earlier one on a night-shadowed road. Even a day of this war was dangerous, maybe more so rather than less as it drew down to these last few bitter weeks. Especially with the questions of who and why yet unanswered regarding that last, obviously deliberate ambush in the swamp. "No, not this time, Dan. I wouldn't ask if it weren't important. There are some things up North I've already put off too long. Personal things. I need to get home."

The young captain glanced up, silent a moment, then shrugged. "Furlough's out of the question. General Sherman's said so. We might manage it with sick leave."

"Make it sick leave, then." Chase raised his left arm and gestured to the sling. "That's not altogether a lie."

"Umm. Your whole battalion seems to have come down with something lately, as a matter of fact." McLeod fixed Chase with a suddenly sharp eye, no longer smiling. He glanced to a sheet of paper and slid it across the marble top toward Chase. "Any notion of why? Your troops are usually about the healthiest in the regiment."

94

"Swamp fever." Chase was not smiling either, but he kept McLeod's eye with a steady gaze. "I imagine they'll be recovered soon." He slid the paper back without looking at it. The other man kept his gaze for a moment, then shrugged, sighing.

" 'Bout when you get back from up North, I'd guess. Don't press it any further than that, Chase. Speaking as a friend, someone's going to ask how come, and Davenport isn't the same man Colonel Adamson was. Understand?"

Chase nodded. Colonel Davenport had assumed the command when Adamson was killed. And Davenport cared more for his own reputation than for his men—an unfortunately common occurrence in the federal army. "A ship?"

McLeod sighed again and picked up a mechanical pencil to check. "There's only one possibility. A hospital ship's leaving Christmas morning for City Point. You'll have to get from Virginia to Philadelphia on your own. Shouldn't be any trouble for a man who's already traversed the whole of an enemy state, though, should it?"

"No trouble at all. By horse to Washington. I'll get a train from there."

"All right. Coming back . . ." He frowned, checking the list twice before he spoke. "A shipment of supplies is due out of Washington, D.C., on the second of January. You'll have to board the night before because they're leaving on the morning tide. Doesn't give you much time, I'm afraid, but it's the best I can do."

Chase calculated quickly, frowning. He'd arrive at City Point probably the twenty-eighth. Get to Philadelphia, with luck, late on the twenty-ninth. Have two days, the thirtieth and the thirty-first, and have to leave for Washington again early on the first. Two days? Well, it would *have* to be enough. It was all he had. "All right, Dan. That's fine. And thanks." He stood up and turned to replace the chair. "Personally, I fail to see why scheduling is so tight. As long as Sherman plans to winter here in Savannah—"

"Who said he was?"

The question, delivered in a careful undertone, caught Chase off guard. He turned again, sharply, forgetting the chair. "I see." No comfortable winter quarters after all, then. Not for Sherman's troops. No hot oyster stews, oven-baked biscuits, roasted goose shot along the marshes—cold swamps instead, and bullets, and coffee bitter from boiling too long.

Another march. God in heaven, he was tired of war. "I believe I'll buy a new pair of boots while I'm home."

"Buy several."

"Thanks." Chase shrugged, frowning, as he turned to leave. And no one, seeing the expression on his hard, handsome face as he walked from the headquarters building would have guessed he'd gotten the favor he'd wanted granted. A winter march—through South Carolina, probably, the cradle of the whole rebellion. Through sleet and icy rivers and swamps that would make the one which had almost killed his battalion ten days ago look like a mere mud puddle in comparison. Back out to face Rebel armies and Rebel partisans—and whoever had been waiting in that swamp for them, waiting, probably, still. Two days. And he *must* get everything done, he was thinking. In only forty-eight hours. Because only God knew whether he or anyone else in Sherman's thousands would ever see their homes again after that.

Chapter Seven

It was later than Chase had hoped it would be when he finally arrived in Philadelphia. Dusk had already fallen on the snow-grayed city. Inside the old stone Courtland mansion, lights shed a golden glow that looked warm and inviting. Chase had forgotten the cold and ice of December up North, how the wind went through everything, and he shivered as he stood at the well-remembered front door, watching the moisture of his breath cloud the gleaming brass of the door knocker. He'd sent a telegram from City Point but apparently no one had received it; he had taken a hired coach from the train station home. The door opened suddenly, and anxious to escape the cold, Chase stepped inside. There—just for a moment—the scene that greeted his gaze took him totally aback. He didn't recognize the manservant who stood staring at him, and the foyer furniture seemed all wrong too. New satins covered the hall benches; the old rugs, blood-red orientals, had given way to lighter, rose-patterned Aubussons; the new chandelier over-head was gas. He could hear its faint hissing. For a split second, there was the unsettling feeling he'd entered the wrong house altogether.

"The family is presently engaged in supper, Major Courtland. Perhaps you would care to join them there in the dining room?"

Chase nodded in distracted acquiescence, but he was frowning as he began to walk. It didn't occur to him to wonder how the servant had known who he was—the portrait on the parlor wall, perhaps. But such mundane triviality was lost in the lingering strangeness of things wrong and misplaced, not at all the warm familiarity he'd expected. Had it been so long since he'd been home? He hadn't realized. All the while, he'd thought of home as static, not changing as *he* had. Stupid, he accused himself. But the sensation of it remained—that vague sense of unexpected loss—and it lingered until he entered the dining room. Even there it was only somewhat dispelled. The room was ablaze with light, familiar silver was on the long table, familiar china and Irish linens, and his father was sitting where he always did in the only chair that didn't match the Chippendale set but had remained out of sentiment for his grandfather. Chase managed a smile then, finally, taking his snow-dusted hat off with one hand and watching the surprise slowly register on his father's face. "Father. How good it is to see you."

Joshua only stared for a moment, speechless. Then he found his wits and jerked to his feet to clasp the lean, chilled hand his son reached out toward him. "Chase! For God's sake . . .!"

"Sorry to interrupt your supper. I telegrammed from City Point but—"

"We never got it. But never mind that. You know how it is these war years. Everything's priorities, and red tape." Joshua stared still at his son, as if disbelieving. Then he blinked finally, never releasing Chase's hand. "Good God, what a wonderful surprise! I'm sorry I didn't meet your train. I would have had I known, of course. You know that. Well, how are you? He let go of Chase's hand at last, as if reluctantly, and stepped back. "Your arm?"

"Flesh wound, nothing serious. An advantage, actually, it got me home."

Joshua began to nod, then turned sharply as if remembering, frowning down the table to where Elinor sat. "Can't you say hello to your brother, Elinor? Offer a word or two of welcome?"

She merely smiled, nodding once toward Chase. "You were exuberant enough for both of us, I thought, Father. My beef was getting cold."

"Elinor." Joshua frowned.

Chase reached to touch his father's arm. "Never mind," he muttered. "It doesn't matter." Chase drew out a middle chair, seating himself before turning to glance down to where Elinor sat watching. "Hello, sister." He smiled as he spoke, but dryly. "I must confess my homecoming startled me a little—I didn't know the man who answered my knock, and you've changed the foyer since I left." He glanced briefly back to where his father was reseating himself.

Joshua frowned, then nodded. "Oh, yes. But that's been two years or more."

"Well, no matter. It just . . . surprised me for some reason." Chase shrugged and returned his gaze to his sister. "At least I find *you* haven't changed, Elinor. That's reassuring, actually, in a way."

The smile remained on her face but a sudden coldness hardened her eyes. "I shall choose to take that as a compliment, brother, so thank you. But in all honesty, I must confess I can't return it. You look . . . a good deal older. Sorry."

"I am a good deal older." Chase merely agreed, reaching to take the platter of sliced beef his father offered. Like magic, a maid had stepped forward to set his place—as silently, as unobtrusively, as if he'd been an expected guest. Away from the battlefield, the old world still existed. "By eons rather than years it sometimes feels like."

"And your plans now? Or should I say General Sherman's plans now?"

At his father's question, Chase hesitated so briefly that the pause was imperceptible. There was no reason to worry his father yet with rumors of a new campaign. "On to join Grant at Richmond I would guess. How or when, I don't yet know."

"By boat or by train, obviously. Either way, it doesn't matter—the war must end very soon. The South must surrender, then." Joshua's relief was genuine. Chase felt it from where he sat several feet away and deliberately said nothing to dispel it. "And Susan? She's here, you know, in Philadelphia. Rather unexpectedly came up from Washington several days ago. Did you wire her also?"

"No. But as long as she's home, perhaps I should ride over to Stratfords' tonight."

"Tonight? Well . . . it's late for that, though. What do you want to see Susan about?"

Chase could feel the sudden apprehension in Joshua's words and he looked up, forcing a reassuring smile. "I haven't much time—I have to be back in Washington on the first. I did commit myself to marry Susan on my very next leave, Father. I'm sure you remember that at least as well as I do, and I haven't forgotten that promise, nor do I have any intentions of breaking my word." Even as he spoke, Chase was conscious of an irrepressible flare of reluctance, but he refused to allow the sensation more than a moment's pause of recognition. Then he continued on all the more resolutely. "Anyway, there's no reason to put the marriage off any longer. Nothing happened in Atlanta to make me change my commitment to Susan, Father. If anything, Atlanta worked the *other* way." He paused for only a moment, glancing up to find visible relief spreading on his father's face. In answer only to that, Chase managed a smile. "After this furlough, I may not get home again, I'm afraid, until the war is finally ended. If I go over tonight, Susan would at least have more than a single day's notice of her impending marriage."

Joshua seemed not to notice the strain that underlay his son's words. He'd smiled wider at Chase's answer and now nodded. "Well, yes, of course. It's late for a social call, but under such circumstances, I'm sure that etiquette can be breached. I'll order the carriage drawn up for you at once."

"By the way, whatever happened to Jonathon Penley's fair sister? Leanna, wasn't it?"

The careful nonchalance of Elinor's question fooled no one. That it had been asked simply out of a sympathetic concern was equally unbelievable, no matter how carefully she might feign such. Chase glanced sharply at her in startled reaction, wondering whether anything more than mere spite had lain behind her question. "I don't know what happened to her actually, Elinor." He shrugged finally in the awkward silence, making an effort to keep the expression on his face unchanged. Leanna is only a memory, he reminded himself. And after Atlanta, not a particularly pleasant one. It had partly been in an effort to bury that memory once and for all that he'd come a thousand miles to marry another woman. "Leanna Leighton chose to leave Atlanta before the federal army did, Elinor. And I . . . lost track of her after that."

"Regarding that subject, Chase, you might speak to Jonathon while you're home here. I'm sure he'd appreciate hearing what you *do* know of his sister, at least. He's been quite concerned, of course."

"I'd planned on it, Father." Chase gave his sister only a last, silent glance of inquiry then chose to drop the painful subject. He gestured to the roll basket lying to Joshua's right, pretending more appetite than he actually felt just now. "Pass the bread, would you? If I'm to get to Stratfords' yet tonight at a decent hour, I'd better eat."

*   *   *

The morning of the thirtieth dawned gray and cold, with a fine drizzle some would call sleet—a fairly typical late December day for William Penn's city. Deep snows were rare before January and February, and March began the thaw again. Joshua left orders for the household staff to move on tiptoe, and as dark as the morning was, Chase slept until nearly noon, waking to find the sleet changing to fine-flaked snow, his father briefly gone to the bank and his sister out shopping for the wedding Susan had set for four o'clock Saturday. Tomorrow, he thought, surprised to find the event still totally lacked reality for him. Tomorrow. He unpacked the dress uniform he'd brought home for the ceremony, and quiet, unfamiliar servants came to collect it for pressing, his low, black boots for polishing. The house was quiet. Almost uncomfortably quiet for someone used to the chaotic clamor of an army encampment spread around him. Chase frowned at the thought and tried to repress it as he dressed and descended the stairs for breakfast. It was strange. All of it strange. From the homecoming itself to Susan last night. It had been too late to say more than a dozen words to her, and her parents, flustered and pleased, had not thought to withdraw to offer even a moment's privacy. What he remembered most about the evening, though, was the shock of first seeing Susan's face. Despite the tintype of her that he'd carried now for months, there had been the undeniable sensation of looking at a stranger's face, then the simultaneous realization that she was no stranger at all. In fact, in less than two days' time, Susan Stratford would be his wife. It was something he must accustom himself to. And quickly.

"Major Courtland?"

The servant startled him on the last step of the long stairs and Chase turned, apparently too quickly. Cooke paled and took a backward step. "Excuse me, sir. I only—"

"My fault." Chase acknowledged, interrupting. "I'm used to having to react. To the war, I guess, and to being—" He checked his own words, realizing that Cooke had no idea what he was rambling about. It's habit, Chase wanted to say. You learn to move fast or else you die. Can't you understand that? Hasn't the war touched you people here at all? No, he answered himself. Nor was there any reason that it should have. *He* was the one who'd just walked out of the midst of war, they hadn't. *He* was the one who was out of step with the world. "What is it, Cooke? Did you need me for something?"

"I . . . no, sir. Mr. Penley's waiting in the parlor, though. He says if you could spare a moment, it's imperative that he speak with you."

Preoccupied as he'd been this morning with his other thoughts, Chase had not yet taken time to prepare himself for a meeting with the Penley brother. Apparently, now, there would *be* no time. "Well . . . tell him I will be right in, of course. Bring coffee in and I'll breakfast later, then." Cooke nodded in that formal way that was nearly a bow, and Chase frowned faintly as he watched the servant disappearing down the hall. Jonathon Penley. The name alone conjured up memories Chase would have preferred to leave forgotten. The first time he had ever held Leanna Leighton in his arms had been at the news of her brother's supposed death. And it had been a year ago almost to the day, last Christmas at Blytheswood, when Chase had received the wire from Doc Lacey who had first found, then saved, the young Rebel officer's life in the Washington hospital. At Leanna's plea, Chase himself had traveled up to Washington shortly thereafter to try to talk Penley into accepting federal parole—an offer which, at the time, had been frostily rejected. That was the last time Chase had even seen the man, in that Washington hospital where Penley had almost died. He remembered him now as a stubborn Rebel. Hard-eyed, and seemingly equally hard inside. And the fact that he was also Leanna's brother did not at this point work in the Virginian's favor, Chase admitted grimly to himself. It was *not* how Chase would have chosen to begin his day.

"Major Courtland." Jonathon Penley rose to his feet as Chase entered the parlor, and stepped forward rather stiffly, extending his hand to the federal officer.

"Hello, Major." Chase managed a smile of cordial greeting, but not one produced with either ease or sincerity. Seeing Jonathon Penley, no one could miss the blood ties between him and his sister, Leanna. And at the same time, Jonathon was equally aware of Chase Courtland's blood tie to Elinor. Consequently, before so much as a word had been spoken, the subtle tension had already begun to heighten. Both men felt it. Chase unconsciously straightened his shoulders and took a single step farther away.

"I won't take any more of your time than I need, Major Courtland. But I do need to speak with you about something."

About Leanna, Chase assumed instantly, bracing himself. He kept a frown off his face with an effort. But his brown eyes darkened and grew cold as he remembered a golden locket swinging in a Georgia woman's hand and twenty-eight federal soldiers lying dead nearby. What could he tell the brother about a woman who had betrayed both Chase's country and his love?

"It's about the bank—your father's . . . your family's, rather. There have been some problems there."

The choice of Penley's subject took Chase momentarily aback. "Yes. My father mentioned something in a letter, I believe. Something about the board members and the Southern accounts?"

"No, something that predated that. Something your father doesn't know and which I hesitated to put into any letter I could send you. Your sister, Elinor, was stealing bank funds, to be frank. I believe the correct term is embezzlement. Your father knows the funds are missing. He doesn't know who took them. Nor do I ever intend to be the one to tell him about his daughter's treachery. I was never able to find out exactly what Lady Bennington was doing with the money she took, but I know it had some connection with a war contractor named Roland Hodges. Hodges supplies guns and ammunition for the federal War Department, I believe. Anyway, when I told your sister I was aware of the money's connection with Hodges, she immediately stopped taking bank funds and hasn't taken any since early this fall. It isn't pleasant to hear, I'm sure, but as long as you are home, Major, I felt an obligation to relay the truth to you."

Chase stared—startled, and trying not to show it. Not the shock. And not the anger that instantly followed. "You're *sure?*"

"Obviously, yes—one hundred percent sure, or I wouldn't say it."

Penley's response was flung back like a challenge and Chase flushed, sensing anger that his question had even been asked. Damn these Southerners. Damn their touchiness and their exalted pride.

Cooke chose that moment to enter with the coffee tray—solid silver, crowded with an ornate sterling, steaming pot, fine china cups and saucers, silver bowls of sugar and cream, teaspoons cushioned softly against rich folded linens. The man seemed to take an interminable amount of time at the project. God! Chase thought, all he'd wanted was a simple cup of coffee, not a damn ritual! But there was no way to pursue the conversation with Cooke in the room, and in the tense, lingering silence Chase fought a losing battle to keep his temper held in check.

To Jonathon Penley, also waiting in silence, the break in their conversation enabled him to study the Yankee officer with an eye of cold assessment. He liked this damn Yankee no better than he guessed the Yankee liked him. He could already see anger paling the Courtland son's face. Left to himself, Jonathon wouldn't care if the audience ended in a fistfight, but Whitney's pleas for peace still resounded all too clearly in his mind. "Be cordial, Jon, I beg you. Think of Joshua and of what we owe the family. Remember that when the flames were sweeping the cottage at Blytheswood, it was Major Courtland who risked his own life to rescue Miranda. And Major Courtland who had arranged parole in the North and proximity to the fine Northern hospitals which had resulted, at least, in Bonnie being born alive." Remember then, Jonathon admitted to himself, that in a way Jonathon owed Chase Courtland the lives of both his children. So regardless of Leanna—and what may or may not have transpired between her and the Yankee major either last winter at Blytheswood or again this fall down in Atlanta—regardless of that, Jonathon Penley was prepared to make some sacrifice of pride. He would *try* to be cordial toward the Courtland son. But he already had the feeling that was going to be impossible to do.

"Thank you, Cooke. That's good enough." Chase gestured the servant from the room finally with an impatient nod. He could feel Penley's eyes on him, watching him and judging him, aware of a kind of silent accusation in the ex-Confederate officer's eyes. Damn the man, Chase thought abruptly. He wasn't about to play cat-and-mouse games with Jonathon Penley or anyone else. "Would you insist on viewing it as an insult to your Southern honor, Major Penley, if I were to ask you how the hell you even became *aware* of all these things?" Despite Chase's efforts, anger was all too evident in his voice, and hearing it, Jonathon Penley's own face darkened. "I know my sister fairly well, Major Penley. Suffice it to say that Elinor and I have *never* been close. Even so, I think I have the right to wonder a bit about the kind of accusations I hear *you* leveling at her. Especially since the last time I saw you, you were only a captured prisoner of war who'd been very damn fortunate to even survive. Now I return from campaigning to find you privy to information which even my own father doesn't share. You've obviously spent a busy year here in Philadelphia."

"Your father needed someone very badly." Jonathon no longer troubled to keep forced cordiality in his voice, either. Chase Courtland had started it. Regardless of all of Whitney's pleas, he would not grovel to the Courtland son. "His health was failing, his bank had problems, and his own daughter was robbing him blind. Your older brother was dead already, and you were off with your army busily burning as many square acres of Southern land as you Yankees could find torches for, Major. Regardless of what you may or may not choose to believe, I do have a strong sense of what I consider fair dealing. I did what I could to repay your father and yourself for the generosity you'd offered to my family and myself. You have every right to question the decisions I've made since I arrived here, but you have *no* right now or ever to question whether I've acted honorably. I can show you the bank ledgers if you wish. Or the audits run on funds in the vault. Or widening disparities between listed amounts in frozen Southern accounts and actual deposits. Or you can ask your own sister for the truth, Major. Elinor didn't even take the trouble to try to lie to me about what she'd been doing. She offered me a share of the profits, in fact. You'll have to take my word for the fact that I turned her offer down."

For a split second, anger swept everything else from Chase Courtland's mind. You arrogant, Confederate son of a bitch, he wanted to say. Why the hell should I take a Penley's word for *anything* anymore? But in the next instant, he made a last attempt to regain some sense of sanity once again. It was not Jonathon Penley who should be the primary focus of such blinding fury. It was his sister, Elinor, instead. Chase's personal antipathy toward the ex-Confederate must not be allowed to overwhelm the more important question of what Elinor was doing to the Courtland bank. If it did, then *he* was the fool not Penley. Penley had been a hundred per cent correct in saying that Joshua Courtland needed him; Joshua Courtland would *continue* to need the ex-Rebel until the damn war was finally over, until the South had surrendered and Chase himself could come home. And God only knew how long, yet, that might be.

"All right, Major Penley." Chase spoke slowly, at last, struggling hard to force cordiality back in his voice. The quiet words were a surrender of a sort, and one that went sorely against the grain just now. Even so, he had no choice. Penley had offered plenty of proof. "I *will* take your word for it. I know my sister is capable of having done exactly what you accuse her of." And I thank you for not telling my father. He's obviously not very well." There was a lingering pause and Chase turned slowly, forcing himself to meet the Virginian's unforgiving gaze. "I'll speak to Elinor myself, of course, but frankly I don't imagine it will do much good. She knows I'm required back in Savannah by the fifth. As long as I'm off with the army, she'll probably feel free to make further trouble. And as for my coming home again to stop her . . . well, I don't imagine that will prove feasible until the war is finished. How long that will be is up to your government, really. I'll return as soon as they end the war."

"Fine." Jonathon only shrugged a cold dismissal. "At least now you're aware of the truth. That was my only reason for coming to speak to you." Jonathon was already turning to go as he spoke. The South's surrender was too sore a subject with him to bear discussing, especially with the Yankee officer who stood here with him. And so there seemed nothing else for him to say.

Chase watched the Virginian all the way to the parlor door before moving forward. There was one subject left very obviously undiscussed between them. Reluctant as he was to raise the specter of Leanna, to raise it by his own hand, yet, perhaps it was better to get it over with now and hope it would never have to be raised again. "I'm surprised that you don't choose to inquire after your sister Leanna. My father told me last night that you've been so *very* concerned."

Jonathon Penley immediately checked his step, but for a long moment he didn't reply. Slowly, then, he turned on one heel, finding Chase Courtland's eyes darkly challenging and fixed on his face with extreme intensity. Before Jonathon could think to mask it, anger flashed on his face and Chase Courtland's eyes narrowed expectantly in the waiting silence. "I had already decided against mentioning my sister to you, Major. That particular subject can only lead to even greater unpleasantness between us, I think."

"Unpleasantness?" Chase repeated the word slowly, making a sarcastic question of it. "I've spent the last four years of my life dealing with 'unpleasantness,' Major. I've learned that meeting it head-on is usually safer than letting it lurk behind you with a knife at your back."

Jonathon flushed at the implications of such treachery and gave up all pretenses at further cordiality. "There's no 'knife at your back' coming from this direction, Major. I don't *stoop* to that sort of thing. On the other hand, I'm not about to offer you my approval regarding your involvement with my sister. I owe your family a great deal—but not that."

"Hardly that. And frankly, I don't give a damn for either your approval or the lack of it. I merely wanted to clear the air between us, if I could. There is no 'involvement' any more between Leanna and me, anyway, and since I'm marrying another woman tomorrow, that should end it."

"End what?" Jonathon's temper flared dangerously higher. "End your *commitment* to the affair? How convenient for you. It hardly restores Leanna's honor, though, does it?" He picked up his coat with rude brusqueness. "Not that honor was ever of concern, apparently—especially not to *you!*" He shouldered past Chase, heading for the door. "Good day, Major. I said what I came to say. Now if you'll excuse me—"

But Chase had deliberately blocked his way to the door, every bit as angry by now as Jonathon Penley was. "Whatever you know or *think* you know of the situation, you needn't brood over some fantasy of your sister as the innocent, injured party! Let me assure you, Leanna gave far better than she got—in that regard, at least. I paid a very dear price indeed for the dubious honor of knowing your sister!"

Jonathon took one step backward, ashen with both shock and fury. "If you were anyone other than Joshua's son, I'd demand satisfaction for such from you, Major!"

"If my father didn't need you so damned badly to run his bank and watch his damned daughter, I'd oblige! Most willingly!" Chase hurled back with equal defiance, and the sudden silence between them burned and seethed, ugly and unforgiving. It felt like long minutes, but it was probably only seconds before Elinor stepped into it. She paused at the door, then smiled as she glanced from one man to the other and back again.

"Oh, sorry. Am I interrupting?"

Chase heard her as if from a distance, so intensely had he been focused on Jonathon's anger and on his own. He pulled his eyes from the Rebel's with an almost physical effort, turning toward her. "You wouldn't care if you were, Elinor. But as a matter of fact, I believe our discussion has just ended."

"Oh? I hope you two had a nice chat." She could guess what the obvious tension between them had flared from. She could have told Chase about Jonathon's own indiscretions—about one of the nights when he'd first arrived at the Courtland house, when the handsome young Rebel had spent part of the night in Elinor's arms. She could have turned the tables on such righteousness as the angry Virginian was displaying now. But secrets were weapons, and using one too early, or needlessly, was a waste. She owed her brother no such favors.

"Nice?" Chase only shrugged, making an effort to regain his lost composure. "Part of our discussion concerned you, Elinor, as a matter of fact."

"I hope it was entertaining, then."

" 'Enlightening' might be more accurate, I believe."

Without another word, Jonathon Penley turned and left, walking stiff-legged with fury, his face a rigid mask of barely refrained violence. Elinor merely stood there, smiling and watching him go. "I'm sorry, Chase, I'd love to stay and continue our little talk but I've an appointment at the seamstress's. I only stopped home to drop off a few boxes."

Chase reached for her arm as she, too, turned to go. "I mean to talk to you, Elinor. If not now, then another time."

"I really can't imagine when. I'm very busy."

"*Make* time, Elinor, or I will. I'll drag you out of your seamstress's and into the damn street if I have to!"

Elinor turned at that, no longer smiling. Her eyes flashed daggers of emerald ice. "You wouldn't dare."

"Try me."

For a moment she considered, staring at Chase with narrowing eyes. Four years ago she *would* have tried him. But not, she decided, any longer. Sometime during the war, her little brother had grown up. "Tomorrow morning then, if you insist. It's *your* wedding day. Spend it as you like."

"The wedding's at four o'clock. We'll say ten o'clock then, Elinor. In the upstairs library." Chase only now released her arm, letting his hand drop slowly. She stared at him silently, rubbing the place where he had held her. "I'll try not to keep you overlong. I'm sure you're planning a virtually interminable toilette so you can dazzle all the wedding guests."

"Would I do that? Outshine your mousy little bride?" She laughed shortly, over one shoulder, as she turned for the door. "Until tomorrow then. I can hardly wait to see what subject you've chosen for this week's lecture." As she left she laughed again. Not a forced laugh, either. Chase decided frowning. A genuine one. One that said she had weapons of her own yet unused and wasn't really very worried about what he might try to say or do to censure her. Damn, he thought, watching the arrogant flounce of her topaz hooped silk gown as she disappeared out the door. Damn! Two days weren't going to begin to be enough time. Between Jonathon Penley and Elinor, Philadelphia had its own private war waging. And he'd landed square in the middle of it.

Chase had eaten supper with Susan's family—partly he admitted, out of a severe disinclination to eat where either Elinor or Jonathon Penley might also be. The snow had continued most of the day and only stopped at sunset. The evening now was clear and quiet and stars were beginning to brighten in the sky. It was lovely, and it had not surprised him when Susan had suggested they walk together in the garden outside.

There was no wind at all tonight. Snow lay on bare branches and dusted the evergreens like powder. Cold yes, but not uncomfortably so. He smiled once, slowly, thinking it was the first time he'd really enjoyed his furlough since arriving home to such startling complications.

"Chase . . . I must ask you . . ."

Susan's voice, always soft, was unusually tentative. He held her arm tighter in his as they walked, and he smiled reassurance. "You must ask what?"

There was a moment's pause and she glanced up at his

109

star-shadowed face thoughtfully. Then she made a nervous little gesture of dismissal. "Oh . . . nothing. Never mind."

He smiled still but checked their slow steps. "Now I know it must be important. You aren't so shy otherwise. Whatever it is, go ahead and ask."

She glanced at him again, then began to draw her arm away from under his. For a moment, she almost dismissed her thought. Then she changed her mind. A lifetime lay in the balance for both of them. No, for three of them—herself, Chase and Roger Lacey, too. She had to ask. "Last Spring, in Washington, I asked you then and doubted your answer. . . . Chase, I *must* know. Are you still in love with Jonathon Penley's sister?"

The question seemed to echo in the stillness of the snow-covered, stone-walled garden. Chase stood silent for a moment, startled. "That's not the sort of question I expected."

"I know. Perhaps it was wrong of me to ask. I'm sorry, Chase. You needn't answer." Susan had pulled her arm away to turn to face him. He made no effort to reclaim it, but half-turned away to look back at the snow-silvered garden they'd been walking in. Bare-boughed flowering ornamentals; stiff, perfect rows of hedge. Maybe because of the snow, the night, the time of year, there was a deadly quiet. The only light was from stars and a partial moon, cold silver with no warmth. Chase took a single step farther away from where Susan stood, conscious of his boot crunching in the snow of the path, the slow clouds made of his breath as he sighed. "I'm the one who should apologize, perhaps. Not you." He turned slowly back to face her, watching her face. "Had you asked me so directly back in the spring, Susan, my answer would have been different. Or I would have lied to you. But now"—he thought a moment, trying to be sure and thinking he was when he finally answered—"no. I'm not in love with Leanna Leighton. Not anymore."

She watched him wordlessly a long time, then nodded once. "You mean you were, but you aren't now."

"Something like that, yes."

She thought of Roger in Washington, of what she felt for him, and found some faint reassurance in Chase's answer. It was possible then. Maybe she would stop loving Roger one day, as Chase had Jonathon's sister. "Thank you, Chase. For your answer. I'm sorry if I've upset you."

"You haven't." He managed a smile, only partially telling the truth. Thinking of Leanna was never easy. Not even now, with months gone by. The memory of betrayal still rankled inside him almost as cruelly as ever.

Susan moved toward him, smiling faintly in strained apology. "Yes, I think I have, whatever you say. But I had to know before we married tomorrow."

"I understand. You had every right to ask about her."

Susan looked up, searching Chase's face in the shadowed darkness. She could read pain there and apology . . . but no trace of a lie. How very handsome he is, she found herself thinking in a strange sort of total objectivity. Even loving Roger, then, did not blind her to Chase Courtland's charms. All her life before she'd met Doc Lacey, she'd thought of Chase as a secret god, infinitely kind, also, in a sense, infinitely unknowable. Yet tomorrow she would be his wife. It should have felt like a miracle to her. It *would* have, she told herself, except for the guilt that lingered on, haunting her unbearably from that single stolen hour she'd spent in Roger Lacey's arms. Seven days ago, now. One dreadful week. She had given Roger something that had truly belonged to Chase. For three days afterward she'd lived in a kind of horrified hell, fleeing from Washington and from Roger himself but never able to entirely escape him. There had been the daily terror of too many guilty fears. How long could she stay away from her duties in Washington before someone guessed the truth of her sudden flight? What if Roger himself came after her? God in heaven, what if she'd conceived a child from that single loving? What in the world would she ever tell anyone then? In another day, she would have returned to Roger. Before Chase had come home, she'd already booked passage on two trains she hadn't taken. She would have returned to Washington and to Roger, then, because it was the only possible choice left her.

But then Chase had come home so unexpectedly, speaking of marriage, *assuming* their marriage. There had been only haste and the absolute finality of a hurried wedding. And then, there'd been no time for her to think anymore. No time to weigh her choices. No time, indeed, to really decide if she had any choices left. Susan only knew that she'd found herself floundering in a kind of panicky terror, totally unable to tell Chase the truth. Totally unable to greet his sudden home-coming with the truth of either her love for Roger Lacey or the truth of the betrayal that had already occurred. She'd found herself trapped as surely as she'd ever been, unable to break the bonds that held her. Roger had been wrong in thinking that she *ever* could have broken free.

Chase was still standing beside her in silence. A dull sort of pain still darkened his eyes. In apology for having caused him pain, Susan deliberately lifted her face up toward Chase's, raising her hand in the silence to touch his arm. If he had loved Leanna Leighton still, then perhaps, she might have found the courage to tell him of Roger. Now, even that forlorn hope was gone. As she felt his mouth drop to hers, cold at first, then quickly warm, she closed her eyes in final surrender.

It was cold out now that they'd stopped walking and Chase was warm. Deliberately, Susan pressed closer to him, tighten-ing her arms. She felt his hand beneath her heavy cloak, sliding up her dress from her waist to seek her breast, his fingers cupping it gently against his palm. It was a gentle movement and slow, meant not to startle or frighten an inno-cent girl, and she accepted his tentative touch. It was but a prelude to tomorrow night and she did not object, nor did she wish to. She knew now of the pleasures of love from Roger—that single, guilty encounter. This, sanctified by marriage and unsullied by betrayal, must be even sweeter, she told herself. Whether it was or not, this was now what her future contained. Chase's hand tightened on her breast, his fingers caressing her, and she tasted a rising hunger in his mouth pressed to hers. She kissed him back, feigning more response than she actually felt, and tried to ignore the sick thudding of her treacherous heart. Of all the women who had ever stood here in Chase Courtland's arms, enjoying his warmth, his strength, his undeniable masculine charms, Susan thought it bitter irony that his own promised wife should be the only woman who'd wished instead for another man.

Chase raised his head at last, breaking the embrace with a smile of gentle ruefulness. "In spite of the cold, I'm afraid I may be overheating out here. Perhaps we should go back to the house before your parents glance out and find our affec-tion premature."

For one last moment, Susan wavered on the brink of blurting out that all-important, desperate disclosure. But Chase had turned already, looking on toward the house, his attention already displaced from her. Whatever he was thinking of just now, she realized helplessly, it wasn't about her. And she simply could not find the courage to intrude on private thoughts, especially not with the shocking revelations the truth would hold. Numbed by a feeling of helpless surrender, she forced a smile to answer his smile and nodded to his nod. As she turned she took his arm to walk the short way back, but she was careful to keep her eyes from meeting his.

Chase kept his smile, too, as he walked. But as Susan suspected, his thoughts were far away from either his marriage or the woman who walked at his side. He could do it, he was thinking. He could feign enough emotion to live this lie through to its consummation tomorrow night. These past few minutes had been a kind of test of that, and one which he congratulated himself on having passed. There had not been the burning, blind hunger he had known once in Leanna's arms, but there had been enough at least, a healthy normal desire to continue making love to Susan. It boded well for Joshua's longing for grandchildren, Chase decided wryly. So in another twenty-four hours, he would be utterly and completely bound to Susan Stratford, the woman everyone so confidently believed would be his perfect wife. Maybe then, at last, the ghost of Leanna Leighton would be laid to rest once and for all. The "devil woman" he once had loved would be exorcised even from the haunting recesses of bitter memory. But somehow, even now, he doubted that she would.

"Jonathon Penley informed me yesterday about what's been going on at the bank in my absence." Chase turned to close the heavy library door, locking it against possible intrusion. Ordinarily, they used no locks, but today the house was in an uproar, servants were everywhere. The Courtland home was larger than the Stratford family's, and so it had been decided the wedding party would be given here tonight instead of there. Preparations were in full swing down below: Feather dusters whisking, washed crystal chandeliers dripping, oil lamps filled, and old, half-burnt candles replaced by tall new ones. His thoughts miles away from the wedding preparations,

113

Chase turned back to face Elinor, his expression grim. "I don't know what game you're playing but I want it stopped. I can't speak any more frankly than that."

"What game do you mean?" She spoke sweetly, seating herself comfortably on the burgundy velvet-covered settee, her back to the window. It kept her face in shadow and Chase frowned against the morning glare of sun gleaming off fresh snow outside.

"Let's not waste each other's time. You know what game I mean. Stealing money from the bank vaults."

"*Stealing?*" She raised one brow leisurely. "That's a harsh word to use."

"And what would you call it?"

"*Borrowing*, dear brother. That's all. You know as well as I do that our father is not particularly well. The bank is ours when he dies. I was only making a loan, so to speak, against future expectations."

"An *unauthorized* loan, I might point out." Chase smiled coldly, unimpressed. "Well, I don't care what you call it, Elinor, I want it stopped."

"It is. Is that all you wanted to say?"

"No. I want it to *stay* stopped, Elinor. Penley will keep me informed of any more treachery on your part. Don't make me come home a second time before the war is ended. Understand?"

"That almost sounds like a threat."

"It is. You've taken advantage once already of my absence. Don't do it again. You may think your path is clear once I'm gone, because you've always been able to wrap Father around your little finger." Chase kept her eyes, coldly. It was hard to tell the expression on her face with the window's glare behind her, but he thought she was smiling still. "Father's always been blind to you, we both know that. Mother knew you for what you are—suspected, anyway. It's partially what drove her to an early grave."

Elinor's smile widened, and her green eyes gleamed once like distant lightning. "Yes, Mother. She had her secrets, too, you know. She was hardly the saint you think of her as, Chase."

Anger flashed in his eyes and he held his temper in check with an effort. It was only a ploy of Elinor's. A favorite one.

She'd slander anyone and everyone to turn the finger of accusation from herself. A muscle flexed once in his jaw, white against his bronzed skin, and he drew a slow breath. "We are not here to discuss our parents, Elinor. Neither their virtues nor their lack of them. You acknowledged yourself that Father is in failing health. For the love of God, show some pity. When the war's done and I return, do what you will, or try to anyway. You and I understand each other. It will be a fair battle, then, and one I'm resigned to having. But for God's sake hold your hand now. Let Father at least die in peace!"

"Is that all for this morning's sermon? Or is there more yet?"

Chase closed his eyes briefly, turning away. There was not a trace of repentance in her voice. Only the usual flippancy, light and cool and smooth as silk. Good God, what else could he say to her? What would touch her? Nothing, he answered himself. Nothing ever had. Nothing ever would. He sighed slowly and went to unlock the door. "All right, Elinor. I don't know what else to say to you. Sometimes I think if I had the courage, I should strangle you with my own hands. It could only be to the rest of the world's advantage." He opened the door and gestured her out, curtly. "Just remember what I've said. It isn't a warning you can afford to take lightly. Father may tolerate anything you do—I won't. And the war won't last much longer now."

"Pity." She smiled politely as she brushed past, leaving the familiar scent of gardenias lingering on the air in passing. "Good things never seem to last, do they?"

Chase only stood watching her, grim and silent, until she disappeared from sight down the hall. After he left, Jonathon Penley was going to have his hands full, he had the feeling. Not in any pleasant sense of the term. And there didn't seem to be one damn thing he could do to prevent it.

"Did your friend ever find you?"

Doc Lacey glanced up from the instruments he was collecting for surgery. New Year's Eve might be a holiday some places but not in hospitals. Especially not with the unexpected arrival of hospital ships full of wounded from Sherman's troops in the Deep South. He shook his head. "Friend? No, what friend?"

Peterson shrugged, unconcerned. "Tell you the truth, I don't recall the name. Calvary major. I could tell by the uniform."

Lacey frowned, turning. Not Chase Courtland. The chance was too great.

"Had a nice chat with the fellow, fresh up from Sherman's army in Savannah. He only had a few minutes, though. Had to catch a train. He said it wasn't—"

"A train to Philadelphia?"

"Yes, I think so. I don't recall exactly."

"Oh God . . ." Lacey laid down the instrument in his hand, trying to clear his mind. Not Chase. Not now. And Susan in Philadelphia, too. "When was he here?" He was turning and reaching for his hat and coat as he spoke, and Petersen stared in surprise.

"Uh . . . Thursday, I think. The twenty-ninth."

"Thursday?" That startled Doc Lacey further, worsened the cold fear rapidly spreading in his belly. He wasted a precious moment turning to frown at Petersen. Thursday? And today Saturday. But even if it *had* been Chase Courtland, surely in only two days' time . . . "Cover for me. I'll be back as soon as I can!"

Lacey tried to reason with himself as he hurried down the long corridor toward the outside door. He'd made a mistake letting Susan go north. But he'd thought maybe she needed some time after what had happened between them, time to think it out, to realize her choice had really already been made. He'd had four days of furlough due next weekend and thought he would travel after her to Philadelphia then if she still hadn't returned. Jesus God! Hadn't the wounded soldiers he'd asked told him absolutely *no* personal furloughs were being granted in Savannah? Only sick leaves. And very few even of them.

Doc Lacey hit the outside steps of the building, not feeling the cold damp wind blowing today off the winter-gray Potomac. Purely out of instinct, he began to run. There was a telegraph office two blocks away at Massachusetts and Tenth. It was after four o'clock already but if he could get there before they closed for the day, in time to telegram a message to Susan, everything, yet, might be all right. But somehow, already, he'd begun to doubt that desperate hope.

*   *   *

The church was only a block and a half from the Courtland house—St. Mark's Episcopal, parish of Philadelphia's fashionable society. Built only a few years earlier in 1850, it mimicked the miniature Gothic of an antique English church, stained glass and spires, a massive tower, parish buildings set around a flagstoned, ivy-canopied garden. Silver and brass and ivory spotted the chapel inside, and it gleamed now, beautifully, in the muted church light of the sunny late Saturday afternoon.

Chase knelt on one knee to receive the final blessing. His dress sword hung at his side and he held it back out of the way with one hand, holding Susan's slender, trembling hand with the other. Fear or chill, he wondered? He could understand either. The high ceilinged church was drafty; the marble they knelt on felt like ice. He, at least, had the protection of his tight-fitting, wool dress uniform, high-necked and normally uncomfortably hot, but Susan's shoulders were bare under white lace, and the fine white satin of her gown offered little warmth. And if it were fear, he, too, had known his own strong sensation of uncertainty—standing at the head of the aisle and watching Susan's slow progress up the flower-strewn satin path toward him. For him, it had come as a sudden gut-level warning, an instinct he knew well after four years of war. The ceremony had been unreal, still, until that moment—something that existed only in some vague future. And soldiers learned to dismiss such things as futures, as futures themselves were so often dismissed by cannon shell or minié balls. It was too late anyway by then, watching Susan already approach. And now, for better or for worse, the thing was done. A gold ring gleamed—dull and cold—unfamiliar and awkward feeling on his left hand. Another gleamed on Susan's. The marriage now was utterly final. Right or wrong it really didn't matter anymore. It was too late for that; it was simply done.

". . . till death do you part. What God hath joined together, let no man rend asunder. You may kiss the bride."

Chase rose to his feet, forcing his smile as he turned to Susan and bent his dark head. Dimly he heard the murmurs of rejoicing approval from the wedding guests seated behind them. A sound, somewhere, of a woman weeping. Susan's mother, probably, he thought. Now his as well.

117

The pastor was beaming as he stepped backward and shut the book, and as he moved sudden sunlight streamed from the high, barred window of the nave to fall directly on Chase. He winced in its sudden glare, turning his head away with a frown of pain.

". . . I now pronounce you man and wife."

Chapter Eight

Two of Philadelphia's best families had been joined together in marriage today, and the air of approving gaiety radiating from the church's crowded pews and aisles had a distinctly prewar feel to it. The war had changed things in years past, too often church services were celebrating death not life. And even beyond that, the war had worked to blur the old traditions, to undermine the old order. This wedding was proof positive that things hadn't changed nearly as much as people feared they had—if a Courtland and a Stratford were duly exchanging marriage vows, the world was still turning in its prescribed rotation. As the bells of St. Mark's began to chime, the very music carried an air of near-giddy relief, a frantic kind of jubilation in the day's events, and inside the church as well, people were laughing and talking in exuberant joy, crowding the aisles as they waited their turn to pass through the wedding line on their way out of church.

Amid the clamor and the laughter of the crowded church, Elinor Courtland Bennington felt perfectly safe in seeking out Roland Hodges for a moment's private conversation. Should anyone see them together here, why it was only the happenstance of finding herself next to the wealthy war contractor while they waited for their respective turns to offer congratulations to the bride and groom. It was only courtesy for her to speak to him, or him to her, wasn't it?

"Lady Bennington, you look lovely as ever." Hodges began the conversation with a statement as accurate as it was courteous. People nearby glanced briefly at the speaking pair, then looked away. Hodges noted the movement and smiled, keeping his smile as he continued in a lower voice. "More lovely, I must say, than the bride herself—though I suppose that's not a gallant thing to say."

Elinor dipped her head in gracious acceptance of the compli-

119

ment and allowed a flash of acquiescent amusement to light her emerald eyes. "Actually, *I* wondered if the bride was going to faint, Roland. Odd for a girl to look so stricken on what should be the happiest of days for her."

"Probably a simple case. The pre-wedding-night terrors of the virginal."

"Terrors?" Elinor laughed out loud at the mere notion of such terrors, then threw Hodges a sidelong glance of more thoughtful conspiracy. "I'm not sure I believe that's all there is to the bride's blushing reticence. Not in this case, at least. I happened to mention my surprise that that young doctor— Lacey, I think—hadn't been included in the wedding party. He is Chase's good friend, after all. And Susan's hospital compatriot. You should have seen the look on her face, Roland, when I so much as said the man's name. Sheerly by feminine instinct, I find myself wondering now whether there hasn't been some sort of secret, forbidden *affaire de coeur* between Susan and the young doctor. Interesting possibility, isn't it?"

"Would it prove of any benefit to us if there were?"

Elinor debated the question only momentarily, then shook her head. "No. Not at present, at least. I think things are better left as they are for now."

"Whatever you say. I myself was somewhat surprised that the wedding ever materialized at all. I thought your brother had fallen helplessly in love with that Confederate woman, Penley's sister."

"He did. But then Chase is *far* too honorable to jilt his fiancée, Roland. Surely you know enough of my saintly brother to realize that. Besides, I have the impression something happened down South that temporarily cooled my brother's ardor for Leanna Leighton. I'm not sure what. He was careful to volunteer nothing. Either way, it doesn't matter to me. Chase would never compromise anything as sanctified as his marriage vows, so from now on he'll stay far away from his lovely Rebel, and I'll have one less complication to overcome when I do finally get a hold of Leanna Leighton. And *that* should be accomplished anytime now."

Surprise showed momentarily on Roland Hodges' face though he was careful to keep his voice held low. "I thought that the last wire from the War Department said that the elusive Mrs. Leighton had managed to escape federal capture when their trap outside Atlanta backfired?"

"Yes. Idiots that they are. I wouldn't trust those fools to hold on to their own purses in a crowd." Elinor's mouth briefly twisted in a mocking expression of contempt. "I've taken a different tack since then, Roland. As you know, my husband Hadley is in Richmond, working with the Confederate government on that side of our . . . mutual business there." Even here in the midst of a clamorous crowd, Elinor was taking no chances on betraying herself with an incautious word. She lowered her voice nearly to a whisper before continuing on. "I sent a message on to Hadley in Richmond. He'll arrange to have Leanna Leighton's name placed on the Confederate War Department's list of suspected traitors. Maybe the Confederate War Department will prove themselves more adept at getting that woman than the federal one did. In either case, with *both* sides out to arrest her, our dear Leanna will find nowhere to run to, will she? It can only be a matter of time before one of the two sides has her under arrest. And then, with brother Chase no longer involved, and Jonathon Penley trapped here in the North by his parole, *I* will be Leanna Leighton's sole source of aid. She'll live or die by my orders."

"And Jonathon Penley will dance to whatever tune you pipe, my dear."

"Exactly. I've already begun to lay my plans for that eventuality. Chase will be back in his war by then. Penley will be under my thumb. And my father will fail any day now. When that happens, I shall be waiting to take over control of the bank itself. It occurred to me just recently that I needn't limit myself to a few paltry thousand when it's just as practical to take it *all*."

"Brilliant as usual, Lady Bennington." Even Roland Hodges could not repress a startled sidelong glance at the beautiful, but infinitely treacherous, woman who stood beside him. "I'm glad I find myself your friend, Lady Bennington. I'm quite sure I wouldn't want you for an enemy." He paused a moment, noting that the crowd they moved in was nearing the vestibule finally. They must put an end to the conversation soon. "By the way, I relayed to the other coalition members your warning regarding your father's involvement with the group. I confess at first that I myself was somewhat surprised at your father's willingness to partake in such schemes, but he's balked at nothing the group has yet suggested. Joshua is *your* father, though, and I imagine you know him better than we ever could. If you distrust his true allegiance to the coalition, we'll be very careful what we tell him in the future."

"For God's sake, I hope you never told my father of *our* business?" Genuine alarm flashed in Elinor's eyes as she turned on one heel to stare at Hodges. "That could ruin everything I've done!"

"Of course not, Elinor. I've told him nothing. As far as Joshua knows, I don't even know his daughter as anything more than a casual acquaintance."

"Good. See it stays that way." Elinor was craning her neck as she spoke, looking ahead to where the small wedding party in the vestibule was only now finally becoming visible. Her father was not looking their way, he was talking to someone she didn't even know. Still, if she could see Joshua, Joshua could see her as well. It was time to end her conversation with Roland Hodges. "I'd better go up and offer my best wishes to the lucky couple, now, but I'll be in touch, Roland. In the meantime, take good care of those surplus guns you have stored for me. I think I'll be needing them for another shipment south almost any day now."

In the vestibule ahead of Elinor, Chase Courtland was far too preoccupied with his own feelings and his own private thoughts to spare much attention to what his sister was doing. If Elinor looked a little too questioningly at the continuing pallor of Susan's face as she passed through the line offering her well-wishes, Chase didn't even notice it at the time. The feeling he'd had all throughout the wedding—that sensation of dull warning, of having made a mistake that would cost him dearly—persisted even now with the ceremony behind him. Most of his energy was directed toward concealing that uneasiness. No one else, at least, had seemed to perceive it. Guests passing through the receiving line accepted his frozen smile as a genuine one and offered in return their own unclouded satisfaction and untroubled joy. Two of Philadelphia's best families had been joined together today and few social events this year would equal this occasion. Several women dabbed at tears with fine lace handkerchiefs. Men grinned and caught Chase's eye with the usual gleaming, good-natured envy. Jonathon Penley went through the line, stiff but courteous enough, extending his hand. Following her husband, Whitney was far warmer, but tears glimmered in her eyes, and she avoided meeting Chase's gaze as she kissed Susan's cheek and only briefly touched Chase's hand. Then she turned to hurry the child who trailed several feet behind her. The child's thick, dark curls and wide blue eyes triggered sudden memories, and in startled recognition, Chase stepped forward, kneeling to speak on the little girl's level.

"Hello."

The child stopped short, staring at him, too shy for the moment to offer a reply. "I'm Miranda," she announced finally, almost defiantly.

"Yes, I know." Chase smiled faintly as he studied the little girl's well-remembered features. "We met once before, but that was a long time ago." A *year* ago actually. At Blytheswood. He had climbed a burning roof to get to where this little girl lay sleeping in a cottage being consumed by fire. God, what a year had passed for them both since. "You've grown a great deal since I last saw you—into quite a pretty young lady, now. Good thing I'm married already or I should fall head over heels in love with you, perhaps."

That coaxed a smile, a brief one, but she eyed his dark uniform with unabashed wariness. "You're a Yankee."

"Miranda!" Whitney hushed her, reaching to pull harder on her daughter's hand. "Forgive her, Major. She doesn't—"

"It's all right." Chase immediately shook his head, gesturing to Whitney to please remain. "Tell me, Miranda, do you dislike all us Yankees so terribly still? Or just me?"

She considered that a moment and shook her head, finally smiling and losing her shyness to reach and touch his knee with one finger. "Not you. You're Uncle Chase. Grandpapa shows me your picture all the time, whenever he gets sad for you. It's on the wall in the room where I'm not allowed to play."

"Whenever he gets sad for me?" Chase considered that silently. Country and family. Always a bitter choice to have to make. "Well, pretty soon I may be coming home to stay and your Grandpapa won't need my picture so much anymore. Perhaps, then, if your mother would let us, you might take Grandpapa and me to the circus. It's been a long time since I've seen one. What do you think?"

"You would have to promise to be very good." She nodded solemnly. "And then I might."

"I will promise." Chase nodded as he stood up, glancing to her mother. "She promises to be a beauty, Mrs. Penley. I'm sure you're proud."

Whitney nodded, uncomfortably aware of the long line of people waiting yet to pass through the line, some of whom were staring, not kindly, because of the delay. She was seven months along now, and her pregnancy most definitely showed. Women of good breeding were not expected to parade themselves in public in such a condition. She and Jonathon had never intended to attend the wedding supper, but she had felt Joshua would like them present at the ceremony itself. She'd thought they could slip in and out of the church with little notice.

"And how are you feeling, Mrs. Penley?"

"Fine." She sensed Jonathon eyeing her impatiently.

"And the youngest? I don't see her here."

"Bonnie can be cranky this time of day. We thought it best to leave her home."

"But she's well?"

"Yes, perfectly, thank you."

"Good. I'm glad to hear that." Chase smiled again faintly. He felt Susan's hand on his arm, suddenly, asking for his attention, and he glanced to his bride and nodded once. "I would have liked to have seen the baby, but perhaps another time." Whitney nodded and moved on, but the ghost of Leanna Leighton lingered after her. Watching Whitney and the little girl for another long moment, Chase's eyes grew dark with remembered pain, and he realized the source now, finally, of that strange foreboding. He'd been wrong then to believe his marriage to Susan Stratford was going to be able to change anything. At least so far, it had changed nothing. Leanna haunted him just as surely now as she ever had. . . . God in heaven, would he *never* be free of her?

"Chase, please!"

Susan's soft voice held a note of embarrassment in it. Chase turned to her in startled apology, making an immediate effort to mask the guilty direction of his thoughts.

"This is Dr. Barstow, Chase. And his wife. They're old friends of my parents."

"How do you do?" The ritual began again. Chase extended his hand to the older man with a smile that masked any lingering anguish. "How very kind of you to come."

"We wouldn't have missed it for the world." The doctor's wife was still dabbing sentimental tears from the corners of her eyes. "I don't believe I've ever seen two young people who make a more *perfect* couple together than you two do."

"Was that necessary, Whit?" Jonathon spoke in an undertone as the coach door closed and iron-rimmed wheels began to clatter home over slushy cobblestones. "You know how I feel about Major Courtland."

She glanced to Miranda first to be sure the child was concentrating on the wonders outside the coach window, then turned to reply to her husband. "Yes, I do know, Jon. I happen to feel differently, that's all."

He shifted restlessly on the seat, frowning. "Because you're too trusting, my love. And too forgiving."

"Traits you admire only when they are to your advantage?"

He eyed her sharply, but in the dimness of the coach interior, he couldn't read her expression. "You remember only what he did for Mandy—saving her life in that fire at Blytheswood. You forget he also dishonored my sister."

"Leanna dishonored herself—if dishonor was involved at all, which I still withhold judgment on."

"For God's sakes, Whitney! I nearly came to blows with the man yesterday in a conversation that couldn't have lasted five minutes." Jonathon's anger flashed openly. "Yet you seem determined to treat him as a long-lost friend! He may be Joshua's son, but he is also arrogant, and outspoken, and dangerously quick-tempered. I don't know what else to say to caution you!"

"And he's also a Yankee officer, which doesn't help, Jon, does it?" She replied sharply, then instantly repented, reaching to touch Jonathon's arm. The muscles there were tight as steel bands and she squeezed once, very gently. "Oh, let's not argue, Jon. Please. I think you misjudge Major Courtland, that's all. He's human like any of us. Cruel and kind. Strong and weak. It's not that I think he's a saint, I don't. You are too much alike in some ways, I think, to ever get along. But he's leaving tomorrow for Savannah. We may never see him again. Can't we be as pleasant as we can?"

Jonathon shrugged, still angry as he stared out the carriage window. Maybe Whitney was right in one sense. Maybe Elinor's brother would die in some battle and never be seen

125

again. The thought arose of its own volition, and startled him with its cruelty. And yet, in all honesty, he could not seem to make himself wish it back.

With Chase due back in Washington by early tomorrow, the time was too short for a proper honeymoon. Before the war, he would have been expected to take his new bride on an extended trip, to the South at least, more likely to Europe. But because of the war, they would have only one night instead, and Susan's parents had lent the couple their guest cottage. It was dark and quiet here in the firelit cottage, even darker outside in the December night. Outside, Chase could see only the pale golden circles of the street lamps illuminating the darkness of the icy snow, and the occasional brightness of passing carriages moving slowly on the distant, cobblestoned street. The houses nearby were mostly quiet. Most of their owners were at the wedding supper he and Susan had just left themselves a few minutes ago. There, people would still be chattering away, clinking champagne glasses and dancing in genuine gaiety, waiting for midnight to celebrate all the hopes and promises of the brand-new year. For himself, Chase had found little cause for celebration. The wedding supper had been a long and wearying ordeal he was glad to have left behind him. Ahead of him now lay only the very last duty of what had been a most difficult day.

It should not feel like a duty, Chase chided himself immediately, frowning faintly in the cottage darkness. He owed Susan better than that. He owed himself far more than that. Yet in spite of his effort, the feeling remained. In all honesty, Chase admitted silently to himself, he was *not* unhappy with the shortage of time he would have with Susan. He knew he could make any lie convincing for the short space of a single night, but had there been weeks of the very same fiction to maintain, he doubted he could have done it so well. He had left Savannah partly in an effort to leave the memory of Leanna Leighton behind him. Instead, her ghost had resurfaced all the more stubbornly wherever he'd turned here in Philadelphia, from Elinor to Jonathon Penley. Even Susan herself had called forth the demon of Leanna. It wasn't that he loved her still, Chase told himself again in the quiet darkness of the tiny cottage. Only the greatest of fools would love a woman who had betrayed him time after time, as

Leanna Leighton had done. Following the ambush in Virginia, he had blindly, obstinately, clung to his belief in her innocence. Even in Atlanta, he had persisted in the illusion that she loved him still. But outside Atlanta, where she'd left her locket behind as a deliberate signature to bloody slaughter and gruesome atrocities, he had finally been forced to confront the truth. If she would give her approval to what had happened at the MacRae farmhouse, leave her locket behind to mock him with the irrefutable fact of her presence there among her husband's band of bloodthirsty animals, then the woman he had loved did not even exist anymore. Perhaps she had *never* existed. It had all been deception, time after time. And only the greatest of fools would continue to cling to proven deception.

Well, he was a fool, Chase admitted wearily to himself. Where Leanna Leighton was concerned, he had been a very great fool. But not the *greatest* fool. He believed in neither her nor her love any longer, so it was not that which stood between him and his new bride tonight. Not, at least, the guilt of being in love with another woman. It was only that the wounds Leanna had left were too recent, the scars still too raw. In time they would heal. He had only forced it too fast, asked too much of himself too soon. It was good he was going back to Washington tomorrow, and going back to more months of war. It would give him the time he needed to heal those wounds completely. If he survived Sherman's coming campaign and lived to come home in the distant future, he would be able by then to offer Susan both the love and commitment she deserved from him. God knew there were a thousand reasons he and Susan belonged together—already behind them lay a lifetime, practically, of familiarity and affection. When the war was over and he returned again, they could make a good life together. No, he amended his thoughts instantly with a faint frown of impatience with himself. No, not *could*. Susan and he *would* make a good life together. All he needed yet was just a little more time to forget the past and Leanna Leighton.

The sudden faint patter of soft-soled slippers and the whispering sound of fabric trailing on the floor interrupted his thoughts abruptly. He had lost track of time as he'd stood by the cottage window, and Susan stood behind him already, waiting, while Chase had not even begun to undress as yet.

127

He turned swiftly to face her, forcing a smile back on his face. It was time to perform his husbandly duties. "You look lovely, Susan. Truly you do." Truly she did, too, he told himself. She was a woman any man would be proud to call wife. Susan only murmured something in reply, some wooden courtesy he guessed, but spoken far too softly for him to hear. She had stopped several yards distant from him, just beyond the fire's main light, and she stood there motionless as a statue half hidden by uneven shadows. Her floor-length gown was purest white, as tradition decreed was proper for newlywed virginal brides. Irish lace, expensive and intricate, softened the modestly high neckline and fell over her hands nearly down to her fingertips. In the darkness, it was hard to tell, but the faint fireglow muted the white of her gown to a mellow ivory and it looked to Chase as if Susan's face was even paler than her gown. It looked, too, as if she were shivering badly. Odd, he thought. If anything, the cottage was a shade too *warm* for comfort.

It was not any chill in the tiny cottage that had Susan Stratford Courtland shivering. In fact, she was not shivering at all. She was trembling instead, trembling with uncontrollable intensity, torn between tears and flight and screaming despair. It was not because of Chase himself. It would have been the same for her with any man other than Roger Lacey. If she could have spoken just then, she might have made one last desperate effort to tell Chase the truth, to escape the final consequences of her inability to speak up sooner. But now she was totally unable to utter a word. She was absolutely consumed by the blind, unreasoning terror of a cornered animal. Either way she turned, she found only her own destruction waiting. If she told Chase of Roger, she destroyed herself by her own hand. The scandal that would follow would forever close her world to her. She would be like a leper, unwelcome even in her very own home. Yet if she said nothing, she risked equal disaster, for the moment of the marriage consummation was only minutes away. Chase would, of course, be expecting a virgin bride . . . and Susan, of course, was no virgin. She'd given her virginity to Roger Lacey back in Washington, in that awful instant of unrecallable weakness. She remembered feeling that sharp flash of pain, finding blood on her underclothes in those ensuing minutes of guilty panic. Ignorant as she was of almost every aspect of sexuality—

and obviously unable to ask even her own mother for advice in this case—she knew nothing of the ways a woman might attempt to feign such lost innocence on her wedding night.

Oh dear God, she was thinking now in her desperate terror, would Chase be able to *tell* that when he lay with her? Would he know in that same instant that she had betrayed him? And if so, what then would he do with her? Hurl accusations of bitter outrage at her? Haul her forcibly into her parents' home and demand an annulment to their marriage? Cry her disgrace and her unpardonable shame to the very same people who'd just offered their congratulations to her today? No, Chase would not, she tried to reassure herself fearfully. Even if he could know absolutely that his bride had come to him deflowered, Chase was not the kind of man to react so cruelly. He would try to believe whatever lie she could think up to offer. Pretend to believe her whether he did so or not. But God in heaven, what in the world was she going to offer him for an explanation? The one thing she must *never* tell him was the truth.

Susan could feel Chase's eyes on her still, faintly appraising, and by now, faintly questioning as well. Even the night's darkness did not conceal her face well enough to hide the unnatural pallor it wore. Though she kept her own eyes deliberately averted, she sensed Chase's sudden movement toward her and struggled against an urge for tears as his hand gently fastened on her trembling arm.

"Susan, love, what is it? Are you all right?" Only gentle concern was evident in Chase Courtland's voice as he questioned her. It was not merely just a chill, he had decided finally. In fact, Susan looked as if she might well faint. "What's the matter, Susan? Are you ill?"

For an instant only, Susan almost said yes. It would be so easy, she told herself. It would solve so many problems. No, not solve them, she realized in the same despairing instant. Only postpone them. It would leave her to face God knew how many more months of this same guilty terror. Sooner or later, this moment must come. "No, I . . . No, I'm not ill. But I . . . I . . ."

"Too much champagne, perhaps? I had more than my quota myself, I'm afraid." Chase spoke quizzically but gently, keeping a careful hold on Susan's arm. She shuddered again, more violently than ever, and he reached his other arm around

129

her shoulders. For one brief moment, Susan lifted her ashen face to look at him. Fear that was close to outright terror showed starkly in her eyes and startled Chase with its strange intensity. But without speaking, she looked away again, making no protest at all against his embrace. In fact she leaned even more heavily against him, as if without his support she might actually fall. "Good God, Susan! What's the matter?"

"I . . . I don't know what . . ." Susan made a last desperate effort to force some coherent explanation from her lips. But Lord, what *could* she offer to explain such behavior? "My brother, Chase. I was thinking of my brother Benjamin just now. Of how . . . of how he wanted so badly to see us together. But instead now, he's dead."

For a long, startled minute Chase didn't reply. Ben Stratford was not *newly* dead, he'd died at Chancellorsville some years ago. Baffled, he glanced down to study what little he could see of Susan's face in the firelit shadows and found himself wondering whether she was telling him the truth or not. She must be, Chase decided slowly. Susan Stratford was not the kind of woman to lie. "Thinking of Ben?" She only nodded for confirmation and Chase fell silent for another long minute. "But it shouldn't upset you so to think about Ben, Susan. Certainly not tonight, at least. If Ben were alive, he would be pleased to see us finally married."

"Yes, of course. Yes, I know that he would be. It's what Ben wanted most, all his life. To see his best friend and his little sister together. It's the last thing he spoke to me about just before he went back to the army that time. Back to die at Chancellorsville." That at least was true enough. At least she had fulfilled her vow to her long-dead brother. Susan made an effort to cling to that thought, for it offered her far more strength and confidence than anything else she'd thought of this evening. Briefly, she even managed a smile of sorts and dared raise her head to touch Chase's eyes with her own. "I remember that summer day you came home from England, then, Chase. You and Ben went down together to volunteer for the war. And when you came home, you asked me to marry you."

"Yes. I remember that." The whole conversation was still baffling. He had the sense of groping for something he couldn't quite grasp, some hidden inconsistency he couldn't identify. Nor was he altogether comfortable with the memories of Ben

Stratford the conversation had given rise to. He had his own memories of his childhood friend, memories more vivid and far more painful to recall. He could remember the cold, misty rains of Chancellorsville. Ben's stomach ripped open from heart to groin by a misshot Union cannon shell. The worst thing about gut-shot men was the incredible length of time it took for them to die. Blood pumping out everywhere, clotted blood and lumps of gore as large as a man's fist. Screaming, unholy agony. He'd held Ben Stratford in his arms for how long that day? Hours maybe? It had felt like days, instead. Holding him as he screamed and cursed and cried in unbearable agony, men shouting all around them, cannon smoke choking his breath. Chase's dark blue uniform coat had been entirely scarlet from collar to hem by the end. He had burned it afterward, and gagged in the stench of the smoking fire.

God, I don't want to think about that now, he ordered himself suddenly. I don't want to think about the war just now; I don't want to think about past people or past events. Not Leanna Leighton, not Ben Stratford, not anyone or anything that lay beyond the confines of this cottage. There was something still that waited to be done, right here—the last part of the ritual they had undergone today. And memories of past people and past anguish were not going to help him to get that done. Susan was obviously terrified. Far more so than he'd expected she'd be. Far more so then he guessed most brides would ordinarily be. But standing here in aimless, awkward conversation was not going to do anything to allay her fears. Perhaps the years of separation caused by the war were taking their toll tonight on her. Since their engagement years ago, he had only seen Susan a very few times. He hadn't been home to hold her hand. He hadn't been home to take her out walking alone in moonlit gardens, where carefully bred young ladies like Susan were usually introduced very gradually into the mysteries of lovemaking. He had, in a sense, whole years to make up for tonight. So he would be gentle with her, and he would proceed slowly. But the war waited for him again on the morrow, and this single night was all he had to offer her. Best for both of them to get it over with, then. There was no better way than that, he thought, to convince her that there was nothing to fear.

Without another word or any warning, Chase simply dropped his head closer over Susan's, brushing the top of her hair with

131

his mouth. She stiffened immediately, growing cold and wooden where she stood in his arms. Then he felt the tremor of another deep shudder wrack her. Compassion rose, urging him to abandon his efforts, and for a moment, he wavered on the brink of doing just that. If they'd had more time, he might simply have stopped there to let her accustom herself to his touch more gradually. But as things were, he dismissed that option, impatient at his own self-serving thoughts. To stop now was only the easy way out for him. It was certainly neither the right nor the best solution to disarm the fears of a frightened bride. Chase was not inexperienced at lovemaking. That left him with another option. He would put forth as much effort as he needed to and try to win from her a glad surrender. It was just as well he hadn't undressed yet, perhaps. Now, he would do so only gradually and minimize his chances of offending her virginal modesty. Despite Susan's nursing experience, he doubted she had ever seen much more than a man's bare shoulders. So Chase moved as slowly as he could, only shedding his coat at first and waiting for the fire to die down before disrobing any further.

The fire died down slowly in the darkness of the tiny cottage, long minutes passing while the flames shrank and the wood logs turned a cooler scarlet, and Susan's inexperience yielded only with infinite reluctance to Chase's efforts. She had married a man well versed in the ways of a woman though, and gradually, almost without her realizing it, her body had begun to respond to the caresses of a skillful lover. That did not change the thoughts that still troubled her mind, nor, in her preoccupation, did Chase's lovemaking engender the same high passion it might have in another woman. But Chase was not expecting high passion from his trembling bride. He was expecting only a minimal response, and though Susan trembled slightly still and her face remained as pale and closed as ever, he was well enough content at last with the instinctive responses her unknowing body was returning to lift her up and carry her on toward the nearby bridal bed. He pulled his boots free and unbuttoned his shirt only then, smiling faintly with the silent observation that Susan's eyes had remained so tightly closed that he doubted modesty or lack of it would have posed any obstacle anyway. In deference to that modesty, though, he deliberately left her nightgown on her. He merely untied the ribbons that closed her neck and bodice, and slipped one hand slowly within to cup one small, peaked breast in gentle fingers. Susan caught her breath instantly in a kind of half gasp, half moan, her body tensing again in involuntary protest. Then against her will, her eyes flew open in momentary surprise, finding Chase's handsome face only inches from hers, molded by fire glow and darkened by shadows. There was an expression in his eyes that she had never seen there before, a strange kind of dark intensity that touched the very core of her being with a sudden shudder of responding passion. God, she thought in incredulous shock, what kind of woman was she? Despite all the logic against such desire, Chase's mouth and hands were rousing her body to eager acceptance of everything he did. And yet, not even the realization of that unexpected shame sufficed to stem the tide of her rising hunger. She was only hastening the moment of her own inescapable doom, she told herself, but still, in a kind of dazed disbelief, she felt her arms reaching out to pull him closer to her, felt her mouth yielding helplessly beneath the sudden hot pressure of his mouth. Chase's hand slid slowly down from her breast to her belly, leaving her trembling and breathless with its leisurely passage, and she closed her eyes again, trying desperately to conceal both her passion and her guilt. His hand came to rest finally between her thighs and she moaned aloud in a last, helpless sound of denial, moving her body away from his touch.

"No, don't, sweetheart. I won't hurt you. I swear I won't."

Chase's murmured reassurances accompanied the motion of his hand, a caress that had changed from tentative question to more deliberate demand, a caress that followed her this time as she moaned and tried to move away from him again. She forced her eyes back open, staring desperately out into the cottage room's darkness to make a final, failing attempt to resist her own body's cry for surrender. God, she must say something now, she ordered herself. *Now*. She must at least prepare Chase ahead of time in case he realized the lack of his wife's virginity. Perhaps if she spoke now, at this very moment, he would accept whatever lie she could think to offer, a lie plausible or not. Surely Chase was not thinking a great deal more clearly than *she* was at this particular moment. But before she could gather her thoughts to speak at all, his hand had moved again against her and all she could think to cry then was a startled protest at the slow intrusion he made into her.

The last thing he had meant to accomplish was any deliberate exploration for Susan's virginity, because he had harbored not the slightest doubt he'd find it. He had only thought to offer her a kindness, to prepare her gradually for the greater intrusion which would shortly follow. Now, he knew only a moment's sense of puzzled surprise and an instinctive sense of something not quite as it should be. But that was all. And before he could even crystalize those feelings, Susan had reacted with violent alarm. She cried out a denial and twisted away from his hand, and before he could think to reach after her there came a sudden terrific pounding on the door of the cottage.

Startled, he lifted his head. There was an unexpected brightness at the cottage window, too . . . carriage lanterns outside in the Stratford drive. He had time only to glance once to where Susan lay less than an arm's length away from him, helplessly sobbing, and then the pounding on the cottage door resumed with thundering, insistent demand.

Instinct alone made Chase move as he did. He rolled free of the bed in a single motion, rebuttoning his shirt as he started for the door and struggling to regather his thoughts into some rational order.

"Susan? Chase? Oh, for the love of heaven, one of you wake up! Answer the door! Susan!"

"Mrs. Stratford?" Chase jerked open the shadowed door to find Susan's mother standing on the other side, her face as ashen and as stricken as her own daughter's was on the bed behind him.

"Chase, something terrible has happened! It's your father. He's had an attack!" At the sight of the young man, Mrs. Stratford's tears had begun to flow more urgently once again. Now she reached one hand out to Chase in a kind of panicky demand. "No one seemed to know what to do! All those people are just standing around, now, still at the house. We looked for your sister but we couldn't find her. And *someone* has to take *charge* of the thing—get the guests on their way, find the doctor, direct the servants . . . You've simply got to go back over, dear! Mr. Stratford will ride with you in our carriage, of course."

"What?" In that first single instant, Mrs. Stratford's news had made not the slightest bit of sense to Chase. There had been too much, too fast. Too many things to try to think of at once.

"Oh, Chase dear, I'm so sorry." Mrs. Stratford seemed not to notice his confusion in the preoccupation of her own distress. She merely shook her head and raised her arm to pull more urgently at his hand. "Chase, hurry now. Go get dressed."

He *was* dressed. Mostly at least. But he would have to get his boots back on, of course. Suddenly then, he stood frozen— only for an instant, but entirely motionless as the full import of her words struck home. Oh God, his father . . .? Not now, he thought. *God*, not *now!* There was something too important left unfinished here. He turned back to glance toward Susan. She was still in the bed where he'd left her, but she was sitting up now, staring in silence toward the door. He tried to meet her eyes, tried a last time to read the expression on her face, but in the darkness it was impossible. Whatever questions and comforts should have passed between them at this moment were simply lost.

"Here, son. I'm waiting the carriage for you. Get your coat." Mr. Stratford had appeared at the doorway, reaching past his weeping wife to take Chase's arm. The man's appearance seemed to break the spell of his lingering shock, and Chase nodded sharply in instant comprehension.

"I'll get my boots and be right with you."

"I'll get my cloak, Chase." Even as Chase had turned back for the bed Susan had materialized with his boots in her hand. She did not meet his eyes as she offered them to him, but she touched his hand as if in vague apology to him. "I'll be coming with you, of—"

"In your nightclothes?" Susan's mother moved instantly to block the girl's exit. "No, of course not, dear. You'll get dressed and go over later. You'll do Joshua Courtland no kindness in scandalizing the family name by dashing about in only nightclothes." The mere suggestion of such shocking immodesty seemed sufficient to distract Mrs. Stratford from her earlier grief. She ceased weeping abruptly, pushing hastily by Chase to take her daughter's arm in a denying grip. "I'll order the other carriage drawn up, Susan. Once you're properly dressed, I shall ride over to the Courtland's with you."

"Hurry up, son. We're only wasting time here. Come on."

For only a last, awkward instant, Chase hesitated at the cottage doorway, looking over to where Susan stood, her face still pale, still cloaked too completely by the cottage darkness for him to read her thoughts. Wasting time? He wondered abruptly. Or using it to ferret out some desperately needed answers instead? Whichever it was, he realized abruptly, he had no real choice. There was no time now for Susan. No time now to think things out. No time now for anything except his father. And everything else would just have to wait. This had turned out to be one hell of a trip back home.

It was nearly an hour before Susan arrived at the Courtland house. Cooke knocked on the door of Joshua's room so softly that had it not been for the absolute silence inside the room, Chase probably would not have even heard the sound. Odd, he thought, how abysmally silent the house had become. Eerie, somehow. From the oversoft creaks of the roofbeams outside, to the fire flames hissing in the fireplaces inside, everything seemed equally subdued—as if the house itself were participating in this lingering vigil. It was like the woods were, he remembered, in war. Just before a battle charge. It was the same kind of a waiting quiet.

"Miss Stratf—Mrs. Courtland, sir? She's waiting for you downstairs."

"Thank you, Cooke, of course, I'll be right down." Chase only nodded once wearily, glancing toward where his father still lay comatose and barely breathing an arm's length away. In the long hour he'd sat by his bed, there'd been no change. No change. Neither good news or bad. Neither living nor quite dead. Joshua lay somewhere in between the two . . . where would he eventually end? Chase drew his thoughts away from his stricken father at last with an effort, trying not to frown as he looked down to find Susan waiting silently in the darkened foyer below him. He hesitated only a moment, and then descended the stairs to go to her.

"Chase . . . your father?" Susan had seemed to sense the house's edict of silence, and it suited her own mood almost perfectly. Even from some distance away from Chase, she'd spoken in a tone barely above a whisper, and Chase had strained merely to try to hear her words.

"He's alive still, but I understand he had one attack already earlier this past summer. He chose not to tell me of that, I guess. And regardless, this is a much more serious one." There was far more than just the strain of Joshua's illness between them. Chase could feel the awkwardness that hung like an invisible curtain between him and Susan, noting words did nothing at all to pierce it. Eye contact might have done so, but Susan kept her eyes from meeting his as if she feared the contact might betray some secret.

"The house is . . . so deserted." At Chase's approach, Susan had turned nervously, partially away, glancing as she moved toward the rooms off the hall. Half-filled champagne glasses still littered the tables, half-carved roasts and other debris littered the buffets. Candles in silver candelabra stood only half burned, hurriedly snuffed. It looked like what it was—a house of sudden catastrophe . . . but then, she reminded herself, of course it would. Perhaps of more than one catastrophe this night.

"Yes, I know." Chase noted both the direction of Susan's glance and her ensuing expression and shrugged weary dismissal to both of them. "I told the servants to just leave it be. I did get the musicians packed up and out. And I saw all the guests to their carriages. No one seems to know where Elinor is. Someone said they saw her dancing with a widower friend of your parents' . . . but God only knows where she is now. I've got half the servants out looking for her, and the other half out looking for Dr. Stevens—Cooke tells me that's my father's usual doctor now. At least Dr. Barstow has been kind enough to offer his services until we can find Dr. Stevens . . . very thoughtful of your parents to have invited along a medical guest for us." He heard the bitterness in his own voice, and in an effort to dispel it, he dropped his head to his hand to rub his eyes in weary silence. God, he thought suddenly, I should never have come home. It's been one disaster after another, with hardly enough break to pause for breath. Penley, Elinor, the bank problems, my father . . . and you, Susan. Just what in the hell is wrong between *us*? Couldn't this much, at least, have gone smoothly? Why in the hell won't you even look me in the eye anymore when I talk to you?

"I . . . Chase, I'm sorry." Susan made a nervous little gesture of apology, tried to force herself to meet her husband's eyes and found she was simply unable to do so. A faint blush of shame and of guilt rose to stain her face and she blinked at the tears that threatened to fall. "About your father, I mean. And about . . . this evening, earlier, too. My behavior tonight was unforgivable."

Unforgivable? Chase wondered in swift disagreement. No. Mystifying, he would have said. He could neither forgive nor condemn something he didn't understand and he didn't understand Susan's strangeness today. But this was hardly the time for questions and answers. Hardly the time for bridging the distance that had inexplicably arisen between them in the last few days. Even if his father hadn't been lying upstairs close to death, Chase was still expected to leave for the war again only a few hours from now and even if he hadn't been leaving he simply didn't have either the time or the energy left tonight to try to break down whatever defenses Susan was hiding behind. Whatever it was would have to wait now until he came back from the war again . . . *if* he came back from what Sherman had planned for them next. And that was a big if. "Susan, I won't pretend to understand exactly what went wrong tonight, but I certainly don't hold you entirely to blame. I'm the one who should apologize, perhaps. I took it too fast. Or I took it too slow. I don't know which, maybe you don't know either. We've a lifetime behind us, and a lifetime of being married ahead of us. We'll work it out somehow when I come back again."

Two conflicting emotions rose simultaneously in Susan's mind at Chase's weary words. Relief was the first one—and she wasn't sure it wasn't the major one. Oh God—her thought rose irrepressibly in bitter self-reproach—what a *coward* you are, Susan. You'll stand here silent and let Chase assume blame that's rightfully yours. But also, inexplicably, she was seized by a nearly overwhelming urge to cry out in despair, because Roger Lacey was now utterly, hopelessly, lost from her . . . for the rest of her life.

"Are your parents waiting? Shall I have Cooke signal to have the carriage brought up?"

"No." At last, Susan seemed able to force her voice above a barely audible whisper. She drew a deep breath, conscious of the shudder within it as she used the brief instant to regather her thoughts. "No, I told them to leave me here. I *am* your wife, Chase. I ought to be here with you . . . and I wanted to

138

be here with you." Strange perhaps, she thought, but that much at least was entirely true. "I won't intrude on your being with your father, Chase. I'll wait down here in the parlor, instead. But I'll be here in case you should have need of me."

For a moment that was almost bittersweet, Chase felt an absence of the tension between them, a resurgence of the deep bond of affection that had bound them all their lives. It would be all right yet, maybe. They had a very sound base to build upon. "Thank you for that, Susan. If you don't mind, I'll go back up to my father then again. I'll let you know if there's any change."

"Chase, I do love you! It's important to me that you understand that!"

Chase turned sharply on the stairs, glancing back in startlement to where Susan stood staring up at him still from the parlor doorway. There had been such a vehemence in her tone, but a vehemence coupled with some strange sort of sorrow. . . . "I know that, love. I've never doubted that." For a moment, Susan seemed on the verge of saying something more, then seemingly thought better of it and let the conversation lie instead where it had ended. For himself, Chase stood a much longer moment on the shadowed stairs, watching even after she'd disappeared into the parlor darkness. Without understanding it all any better than before, he finally turned at last to resume the vigil in his father's silent room.

It had to be nearly dawn by now. The last dimly audible chimes of the downstairs clock had indicated six o'clock, or maybe six-fifteen, Chase wasn't sure which. Despite that fact, the darkness of night outside Joshua's bedroom window seemed disinclined to give way to increasing daylight. Another storm, perhaps? An iron-gray dawn that presaged more snow. Even the weather seemed determined to be contrary today. How many hours had it been then that he'd sat here by his father's bed? Four? Maybe five, maybe six. He'd thought time only moved this slowly before a major battle; Antietam, Fredericksburg, Chancellorsville, Gettysburg . . . Kennesaw Mountain and Peach Tree Creek. There would be more yet ahead with Sherman marching the army north. More nights like this one, passing cold and slow and silent. In all that time, Chase's father had never moved, never stirred, never spoken. Joshua just continued to lay there, unchanging. God, Chase demanded in sudden impatience born of exhaustion, *do* something, father. Get better, get worse. *Anything*, just *change!*

The stunning selfishness of such a thought shocked Chase instantly, and he glanced swiftly to Joshua's bed for reassurance that it had not translated into reality. God, I didn't mean that, he thought wearily. I don't even know what I'm thinking anymore. Few fathers and sons were as close as Chase and Joshua Courtland were. Few families shared the depth of genuine affection that Chase and his father had shared with one another through the years. There had not been the same deep bond between his father and his older brother Josh, even though Josh had been the oldest son and trained, of course, as the son and heir. And Elinor . . . well, there had always been a unique relationship there. But not friendship. Certainly not of the gentle, enduring kind that had always existed between Joshua Courtland and his youngest son Chase. Joshua had been more than a father. He had always been a friend, as well. The very oldest and probably the dearest of Chase's friends, surpassing even Susan's brother Ben, surpassing even the affection Chase held for Doc Lacey, who had taken Ben Stratford's place in the course of the past few years. The last thing in the world Chase truly wanted to do was to wish further harm to the unconscious man. He offered another shame-filled apology and leaned forward to brush his father's limp hand with his own. Then he settled back farther into the dark leather wing chair, laid his head down wearily against one hand and closed his eyes.

Perhaps he'd slept for just a moment, he wasn't sure. He only knew that he was conscious suddenly of a gentle hand touching the top of his dark hair in wordless sympathy. A feminine touch, and the soft, swishing sound of crinoline came from nearby. Instinctively, he turned his head sideways, letting his face rest for a moment against the cool silent comfort of the woman's skirt. "God in heaven . . . why this? Why now? Just sitting here hour after hour. Nothing even changes . . . and the worst of it is I feel so damn helpless. There isn't one damn thing I can even do for him."

The hand held his head closer for a moment, brushed his hair again with gentle understanding and then let him go. "I think you're being too hard on yourself, Major. You may be doing far more for Joshua than you even realize. Your love and your prayers aren't such negligible things to offer, and you did come home to him. I've never seen Joshua happier than he's been in these past few days, just having you home with him again."

Chase lifted his head with a sudden start, opening his eyes to find not Susan but Whitney Penley standing in the shadowed darkness close to him. He flushed immediately in embarrassed reaction. "Oh. I'm sorry, Mrs. Penley. I just assumed that it was Susan, there. Forgive my—"

"No, don't, Major. Don't beg my forgiveness. There's no need to, and even if there were, I owe you far more than I could ever begin to repay." Whitney glanced down in the shadows, offering him a smile of gentle dismissal. "I believe Susan is sleeping downstairs. As I came in Cooke was just pulling closed the parlor door, and he gestured to me to please be quiet. Perhaps it's I who should apologize for intruding on your grief."

"No, that's all right. You really aren't intruding at all." Chase only managed to mumble the words, finding both thought and words heavy with the numbness of utter exhaustion. "I told Cooke not to wake you, Mrs. Penley. I saw no sense in disturbing your sleep for such unhappy news."

"Cooke didn't wake us. My baby, Bonnie, is less considerate of my sleep than you are, though, I'm afraid. She was up fussing, and when I got up to go to her, I saw the lights still burning over here, and the servants coming in and out of the driveway. I knew at once there must be something wrong." She stepped away from Chase as she spoke, moving near enough to Joshua's bed to lean over and touch his ashen face with a lingering hand. The expression of her face made the tears glistening in her eyes seem mere redundancy. "Will you be staying, then, Major? Have you wired your army yet to extend your leave time?"

"No, not yet. Cooke's going to do it as soon as the telegraph opens, but I doubt there's much use. Sherman is—" He caught himself just barely in time, reminding himself she *was* a Confederate. He might trust Whitney Penley with such news but he didn't think he would trust her husband with it. "There are . . . reasons I'll be expected to return, regardless of

141

this or anything else. I don't doubt I'll be leaving this morning as scheduled. But it's one hell of a mess to be leaving behind."

Whitney nodded, turning to Chase again as she spoke. "Don't worry yourself too greatly about all of us here at least, Major Courtland. You've got to keep your mind on your own well-being, not on ours. Your father Joshua will be very well looked after, I assure you. I'll take care of him as if he were my own father, and of course, your wife will surely do so too. And Jonathon can take care of any of his business affairs that should require tending."

At the mere mention of Jonathon Penley's name, there was an instant tension that had not marred the conversation earlier. Chase glanced sharply at Whitney's face to see a faint blush rising and then glanced away, conscious of his own sense of awkwardness. It was obvious that Whitney Penley knew of the antagonism that had flared the other day between him and her husband. So she was here now offering Chase her sympathy not because of her husband's wishes, but rather, he guessed, in spite of them. Chase offered her a faint smile in wry gratitude, nodding once to the unspoken exchange. "You're a fine lady, Mrs. Penley. A very fine lady. I thought so from the first time I saw you in Virginia, at Blytheswood." Then a smile more bitter than wry touched his mouth, and he continued as if only thinking aloud. "At least I was right about something there. That should give me *some* consolation I suppose, anyway."

Whitney did not look at him when she spoke, and her voice held a soft note of wistfulness, as if she offered him now some private sorrow only this once to be spoken aloud. "I think you were right about more than you yet realize at Blytheswood, Major. But that's hardly a proper subject for us to discuss any longer. And in light of your recent marriage, perhaps it's best you think what you do." She made a small awkward gesture, a gesture that somehow terminated the conversation. She turned back to face Chase again, and only sympathy showed once again in her blue-gray eyes. "You must be exhausted, Major Courtland. As long as I'm here, why don't you take a few minutes to try to sleep? I'll wake you at once if there's any change."

"There isn't time, I'm afraid. I've got to be prepared to catch the nine o'clock train back to Washington."

142

"At least go rest a bit, then. Take time to change your uniform and get washed up. You don't want to have to travel like that."

Only for a moment longer did he even hesitate. Then he nodded grateful acceptance of her offer and rose to his feet. He was in his dress uniform still. Not something he could very well wear back on the train. And even a moment's rest—would be dearly appreciated. There were a thousand things, too, that he should be thinking about. All the things which his father's attack had simply eliminated from his mind so far. Responsibilities outside of Joshua which he had allowed himself to temporarily forget. His will was one thing. He must have it changed to benefit his wife now—Susan. And then there was Elinor and the treachery Jonathon Penley had accused her of committing at the bank. And in regard to that, Chase recollected with a startled frown, who would vote the family bank stock now that his father was obviously unable to do so? Susan knew nothing about running a bank. And Elinor, he thought, knew far too much. She would be voting her own ten percent interest of course, and nearly fifteen percent lay in the hands of the other stockholders. Chase's proxy for his own twenty-five percent had been given to his father to vote, but that was no longer a practical solution. And after Penley's accusations against his sister, he did not trust Elinor sufficiently to leave that kind of power in her hands. He must think of someone else then to assign his proxy to. But who in the hell was that going to be? Too bad Whitney Penley was not more closely involved in the business of the bank, Chase thought wearily. She was one of the few he could have absolutely trusted with such power, but he found it hard to offer that same kind of power to her husband regardless of how well qualified Jonathon Penley might otherwise be.

In the end, he found that he had no choice. The War Department cabled back their regrets, of course, but it was absolutely impossible to grant any of Sherman's officers an extended leave. Susan he had left sleeping, leaving only a hastily scrawled note on the table beside the sofa in the parlor where she lay. He'd kissed her good-bye, but he doubted she would remember that. At least Dr. Stevens had been found, at last. He had been with Joshua Courtland when Chase had made his own farewells to his unconscious father, and surely

Elinor would be returning home soon—though none of the servants had been able to find her earlier. Chase had stopped off briefly at Epsley's house, rousing the family lawyer from bed to redraw Chase's will for him. And he had also had Epsley draw up the required documents to pass the right of Chase's stock proxy from his stricken father on to someone else. Only now, at the very last moment, standing in the cold gray chill of the Philadelphia train station and waiting to see the steam of the locomotive that would carry him back to his ship in Washington, only now did he fill in the name on the top edge of the proxy. Jonathon Penley. It was a gamble, Chase knew. A simple case of being forced to choose between the devil and the deep blue sea. And if Chase found himself surprised and uneasy at giving the ex-Confederate that kind of power, he took some small comfort in knowing that Jonathon Penley would probably be equally surprised at receiving it. It was not any gesture of friendship still, he thought grimly as he dropped the sealed envelope into the box. It was simply a kind of a truce. For now, that was as much as he felt able to offer the man. That alone had been difficult enough.

So he had gotten everything done at least—the thought occurred to him as he turned away from the mailbox, and it brought with it a grim satisfaction. These precious few days had been sufficient after all—just as he'd told himself in Savannah they would have to be. He was ready now to resume Sherman's planned march into hell . . . and not to worry too greatly about it if he didn't manage to march back out again.

Susan slept on the Courtland couch until nearly midmorning, missing the distant train whistle that marked her husband's return to the war. She had also missed the messenger who had delivered a telegram from Washington, D.C. By the time she'd arrived at her home, her mother had already accepted it for her, and as Susan wearily took a seat by the sitting room fire her mother brought it in along with Susan's breakfast tray.

"I almost forgot, dear. This came for you earlier, by special messenger."

The telegram carried the stamp of its origination—Washington, D.C. As soon as Susan saw it, her hand began to tremble. Not daring to open it while her mother remained in the room, she feigned indifference and simply laid it aside on the settee cushion.

"How is Joshua Courtland doing, dear?"

"No change." Susan managed to make her voice sound relatively normal though her heart was racing in reawakened dread and her mouth had gone as dry as dust. "Dr. Stevens said it might well be weeks before we know either way."

"What a terrible pity for everyone involved." Mrs. Stratford shook her head. "For Joshua himself, of course. For his son Chase, too. Terrible for him to have to leave his father in such a condition. Terrible for you, too, I believe. A woman's wedding night is difficult enough for her, even under the best of circumstances."

Susan sensed more than saw her mother's sharp glance as she spoke the last, but she didn't choose to respond to it. She merely shrugged a silent dismissal to the subtle opening and felt it as her mother looked away. It was too late now to begin telling the truth. All of it or even any single part of it. Better by far to just let it go.

"I've got to send over a condolence letter to the Courtlands, of course. I believe I'll do that now while you're eating your breakfast, dear. I shall only be a few minutes away from you."

"All right, mother. I shall be fine." Scarcely had the sitting-room door swung shut than Susan forced her trembling fingers to reach for the Washington telegram. It was from Roger of course. It had to be. Could he possibly know about her marriage already?

DEAREST SUSAN STOP POSSIBILITY CHASE IS HOME STOP FOR THE LOVE OF GOD, DO NOTHING FOOLISH BEFORE I CAN SPEAK FURTHER TO YOU OR TO HIM STOP WILL ARRIVE PHILADELPHIA ON THURSDAY THIS WEEK OR EXPECT YOUR RETURN BEFORE . . .

She only read it to that point, then heard her mother again outside the door. She crumpled the telegram to throw it hastily into the fire, feeling as if it were her heart instead that lay there burning.

"Congratulations from that young doctor you work with?" Susan's mother glanced curiously to where the telegram lay already in flames, frowning as she stood watching it burn. "Why in the world would you destroy such a . . . oh, never mind, dear. I forget the stress you're undoubtedly under. Still, you mustn't simply dismiss people's kindnesses like that. You must thank the young man properly when you return to Washington."

"But I'm not going back to Washington, Mother. At least not yet." Despite her best efforts, Susan's voice carried a note of oversharp denial. She stole a moment to try to further mellow her tone before she dared continue. "Now that I'm married, I think it best I . . . give up the nursing work. Plus, with Chase's father so very ill, I can't leave Philadelphia for some time, of course."

"Oh? But I thought you *loved* your work?" Susan's mother shrugged her startlement. "Did you speak to Chase about giving it up?"

"No, I . . . there wasn't time," Susan faltered uneasily. "I think he'd want me here with his father, anyway."

"Yes, of course, you may be right. You must telegram back to your doctor friend then, though. You owe him the courtesy of that much response."

"Yes. Yes, I'll send something on. I'll do that today yet. Later."

"Why not simply dictate to me what it is you want to tell him? I shall be happy to do the errand myself and save you the effort, dear. I'm not unaware of how difficult a day this has already been for you, you know."

For only a moment, Susan hesitated. But there was really nothing left for her to say to Roger, nothing at least that could make any difference to either one of them now. All she needed to do was to convey to him the fact of her marriage. He would know everything else just by knowing that much. "Yes, Mother, I would appreciate that if you're sure you don't mind. Send him my . . . thanks for his wishes, and my hope for his continuing . . . friendship. To Chase and me both. Sign it Mrs. Susan Courtland. I think that will do fine."

As Susan watched her mother out the door she gave way only for a moment to the tears that rose involuntarily in her eyes. It was New Year's Day today, she recollected with a start of surprise. It had been 1865 for some hours already, and been one anguish after another for all that time. If this was any sort of a presage for what the rest of the year would offer, she didn't think she regretted having neglected to celebrate the year's beginning.

During the war years, the federal mails—even the local ones— had grown more erratic than they had ever been. The letter Chase Courtland had mailed on New Year's Day in the Philadelphia station was not even sorted until several days later. Cooke picked it up then along with the other miscellaneous Courtland mail on his daily trip to the federal post office.

In the days since Chase's departure, little had changed yet at the Courtland house. Joshua still lay in a coma. Cooke's errands that day had taken longer than he'd hoped and he was both late and increasingly anxious by the time he returned to the house on Locust Street. Remembering the letter he'd picked up for Jonathon Penley, Cooke glanced impatiently toward the carriage house and spied Miranda Penley out playing in the snow. There was no need, Cooke thought, to deliver the letter himself. He would simply have the child carry the thing back over and save himself the additional time. "Miss Miranda?"

The child looked up and came running, offering the servant a delighted smile. Cooke was a familiar figure from her many outings with Grandpapa Courtland; he smiled back a genuine smile. It was impossible not to respond to the child's carefree innocence. "Hello, Cooke! I have made a snow dolly. Want to see her?"

Cooke smiled but declined, shaking his head regretfully. "Later, perhaps. You might do me a favor, though, if you would." He reached in his livery coat for the envelope and held it forth. "Is your father home?"

"No. He had work."

"Your mother, then. Give this to her. It's from the post office and it looks to be important. Be sure you give it to her right away."

Miranda nodded and offered a snow-chilled kiss. Cooke accepted it and watched her start for the house before he turned away. Mandy was three now, three and a half, and she took such responsibility seriously. She held the envelope tightly as she ran inside.

Whitney was just coming down the stairs, Bonnie in her arms, and fear shadowed in her soft, gray eyes. "Oh, Mandy. I was hoping it was Father."

"Cooke gave me this for you. From the post office he said and it's . . ."

"Later, darling, please. Bonnie's fever is back, quite badly. Put that down somewhere and run to Grandpapa's house. See if Dr. Stevens can spare a moment to come over and see her."

"Bonnie Baby?" The two names were one to Mandy and she looked up with solemn eyes. Bonnie Baby was sick a lot. All winter almost so far, but her mother wasn't usually scared like this. As Miranda felt her mother's fear she began to tremble.

"Please, Mandy! Hurry!" Whitney was tired from pregnancy, tired out from Bonnie's various illnesses, and she was distraught at Joshua's recent attack. She didn't mean to be impatient with her oldest child, but even so, her voice was sharp. "Go on, Mandy—now! I can't take Bonnie out in this cold air."

Miranda nodded once, turning with the envelope still in her hand. She remembered it at the door and shoved it on top of some books her father used for his work, not thinking much about it anymore—Bonnie Baby had taken precedence.

Dr. Stevens diagnosed scarlet fever. The rash had already begun to appear and Bonnie to scream with discomfort and fever. Mandy, for her protection, was sent away to the main house and her parents' fears for Joshua Courtland were now mixed with fear for their own child's life—scarlet fever was a notorious killer of young ones. No one gave another thought to the envelope Miranda had brought inside, and in the confusion, Cooke didn't think to mention it either. In consequence, the all-important transfer of proxy which Chase Courtland had so agonized over lay simply forgotten on the Penley shelf, gathering dust. It would be missed most desperately long before it was ever found.

In the meantime, unaware that her brother had even made such an transfer, Elinor saw the opportunity she'd long been waiting for. She ordered the carriage hitched and began to pay visits to the minority stockholders of the Courtland bank.

By Wednesday evening, she was finished. And smiling. And anticipating the board meeting that was scheduled only two days from now on the fifth. The bank would be hers in a matter of mere days. It looked like the New Year of 1865 would be her year.

Chapter Nine

A warm, velvety dusk had settled over Savannah. The fragrance of orange blossoms drifted from shadowed trees to lace the balmy evening air with sweetness. Chase was smiling faintly, unaware of it, as he climbed down from the supply wagon that had detoured to drop him off here at regimental headquarters. After the bitter cold of Philadelphia and the even icier, bone-deep dampness of the ocean-going cargo ship, the semitropical warmth of Savannah was blessed relief—the gleam of brass on uniforms, the raucous confusion of soldiers, the muffled oaths, the distant clatter of a cavalry patrol all infinitely familiar. In a strange sense, this felt more like home than Philadelphia's crystal parlors and Chippendale sofas had felt after so many years. As he stepped through the door of the elegant old headquarters building, Chase heard familiar voices speaking inside, and his smile widened slightly as he steered a path toward them. A step or two later, he found Grier standing by the parlor fireplace, talking to Captain McLeod. Almost instantly, Chase's smile began to fade. The look on their faces was not one that presaged a joyous homecoming.

"Grier. McLeod." Chase scanned their faces more sharply, pausing a moment by the arched doorway before walking through. "Happy New Year, gentlemen. A little late."

Grier only grunted for answer and Chase's gaze sharpened.

"Happy New Year." McLeod shrugged wry disagreement. He was already turning to leave. "Maybe. But I'll withhold judgment on that for a while yet, if you don't mind. Anyway, it's good to have you back, Chase. Grier will be happy to tell you exactly why—I'm already overdue at a staff meeting."

Chase followed McLeod's half-dozen steps out with a thoughtful concern darkening his eyes. Then he turned back to face Grier. Welcome home, he thought, bracing himself for bad news. Welcome home to a war still very much in progress.

Grier's eyes flickered swiftly across his major's hand as Chase pulled his gloves free. A gold ring gleamed in the firelight and he nodded once. "Mission accomplished, I see."

"Yes, most of it." Chase's simple answer dismissed all the complexities he'd left unsettled: his father—living or dead by now?—Jonathon Penley and his sister, Elinor and the bank's future, the doubts he harbored about Susan. He kept those thoughts silent with a shrug. Grier had his own problems probably—every man here did. No one's life was without complications; the interruption of the war had only added another. "What's the matter down here?"

"Davenport. Our new commander." Grier's expression said more. "He's assigned us a little task."

"Such as?"

"Such as we're supposed to leave the city sometime tomorrow and set up camp ten or twelve miles to the west somewhere. Our old friend, Lieutenant Colonel Leighton, sent word around the first of the year—offering to surrender, apparently, but only to *us*."

The last trace of Chase's smile vanished. "He isn't serious."

"Who? Leighton? Or Davenport?"

"Both."

"On the contrary, our fine colonel is perfectly serious. 'Quite a coup', as he said to McLeod. Every regiment down here would like to get their hands on Leighton. As for how serious *Leighton* is, well that's a different story."

"Any fool can see it's a trap."

"Any fool but Davenport, apparently. He's got visions of pretty little general stars appearing on his shoulder straps. He thinks getting Leighton will put them there."

Chase turned to face the fire with a smothered curse. Leanna again—the old ghost rising once more to haunt him. Here or home, she seemed equally inescapable. He watched the flames and remembered Atlanta and his voice was cold when he finally spoke. "Why us, supposedly?"

"Because of our 'fair treatment' in Virginia. Leighton trusts us not to murder him under the white flag—or so he says."

"Uh-huh." The fire hissed and popped, and Chase stared at it without really seeing the flames. His thoughts were turned inward and there was a long moment's brooding silence. "The

151

swamp, then, of course. That's who it was there. I should have known."

Grier shrugged for answer, silent.

"And Davenport expects us to waltz right into another ambush, does he? I think I'd better talk to him."

"Go ahead and try, Major. McLeod and I already have, but we didn't gain an inch for it. Maybe he'll change his mind, but I wouldn't expect so."

Chase finally forced his eyes away from the fire, turning on one bootheel to start for the door. "Maybe he shouldn't change it. Maybe we're better off taking a shot at Leighton any way we can get it—put an end to the thing once and for all, before he devils us all the way to Richmond. But I'll see what I can do with Davenport."

Leanna had overhead only the last few of Treejack's murmured words to Stewart, but she eyed her husband sharply as he nodded once and dropped the canvas edge of their crude shelter. "A surrender, Stewart?"

He didn't look at her but she saw a brief smile touch his mouth—a smile she'd seen before and come to fear. Despite the warmth of the Savannah night air, she shivered as she spoke again. "What are you planning, Stewart? I should at least have the right to know."

He turned slowly on one heel. And she thought, looking now at his face in the dim light of the bonfire burning outside, that all the handsomeness he'd once possessed had gone somehow, been transmuted into sheer, cold, cruelty. And she wondered if her face, too, reflected the ravages of war. It had been so long since she'd bothered to look in a mirror—if she could have found one to look in—she no longer knew. But as he faced her, his eyes, cold and pitiless, flickered over her and subtly changed. She was still beautiful then, she answered herself. More curse than gift, though, like fabled Helen. It seemed to cause only anguish for herself and everyone her beauty touched.

"You have a nasty habit of eavesdropping, dear."

"Then let me go." It was such an old conversation. Old and overused. And the answers never changed.

"My pleasure, Leanna. Just as soon as you're safely bred."

They did not even bother to put the correct intonations into the exchange anymore, she thought. The original hatred,

152

bitterness and fury had worn dull with time. Still, Stewart would not relent. "What are you planning, Stewart?" She repeated her original question flatly. "You aren't seriously contemplating a surrender."

"Maybe I am."

"You'd die first." She watched him take a sip of bourbon from his battered tin cup. Bourbon he drank more and more heavily, it seemed, and kept concealed from the rest of his men. Stewart was possessive with what he considered his: his elite position, his authority, his lands, his slaves . . . his bourbon and his wife. She slowly cocked her head to one side, studying him. "This is another trick of some kind, isn't it? Trying to kill Chase Courtland still. You've grown impatient waiting for the Yankees to leave Savannah."

"Rumor holds they may take a ship up to Richmond to join the Army of the Potomac. And then where would I be, my dear?" He lifted his hand to slap a moth, which had flown inside the canvas walls of the crude tent and was now flying feebly at the brightness of the fire glowing through the closed end. He took it in his hand and squashed it before he let it drop. "Besides, Leanna, you were angry enough at Yankees when you first rejoined me, when you'd first learned that they'd burned your precious Blytheswood. I wish you'd try to remember that fact. It might increase your enthusiasm for what I'm trying to do—to repay a portion of what they're doing to us."

It was never without pain, thinking of Blytheswood gone, but the first terrible anger of it had faded as greater horrors had loomed. "Blytheswood was only a house, really. And some barns." She turned away from Stewart to deny him the pleasure of reading pain on her face. All the decisions she'd made, the sacrifices, the denials—all made to save Blytheswood . . . and she had lost it anyway. "I wonder now if Blytheswood was worth it. Worth"—losing Chase, Leanna could have said. Or worth losing the child she'd conceived by him. But she knew better than to say either of those things aloud. "—Maybe Blytheswood wasn't worth the Confederate lives spent in trying to save it, or the Yankees lost in trying to take it, Stewart. I don't know anymore. I'm not sure of the answers." Blytheswood's magic had been its ability to embody everything she loved best of the Old South: age, elegance, graciousness, serenity, romantic fantasy come alive, chivalry real as well as ideal. And long before the buildings themselves had been burned, those fragile illusions had been shattered. Even with the war not over, they had been lost among the very first casualties. "Killing every Yankee in creation won't give Blytheswood back to me now. I accept that, Stewart." She turned to face him, raising her eyes to meet his and daring the words. "Just as you ought to accept that killing Chase Courtland won't bring anything back to you."

"That's where you're wrong."

"No, I'm not. If you would only listen to me, just *once*. It's over. We've lost the war. Why sacrifice anything else? Only to add to what it's already done to us, taken from us? It won't change anything; it can't any longer. Let it go! Let me go!"

"I am, dear. Doing just that. By offering to surrender." He smiled, though, as he said it, and Leanna closed her eyes helplessly as she turned away. She heard the soft metallic clink as he set his cup down, the muffled step of his boots toward her, then the smell of bourbon on his breath and the touch of his lean, cruel hand caressing her shoulder. For a moment, it lingered there, then slowly dropped to her waist to unbutton the closure of her long, overworn riding skirt. Like a nightmare, she could not wake from, repeating itself a hundred times, and nothing could ever change it. Yes, one thing could—the thought surprised and chilled her. One thing could—and eventually would. He would kill Chase Courtland, or finally, Stewart himself would be killed. And how much longer could it be before one of those two things happened?

Grier had been right: Davenport had remained absolutely adamant. The night of the seventh of January found Chase's battalion about ten miles northwest of Savannah, riding in a cold drizzle, which was the closest the Georgia coast came to actual winter. Despite the rain, the air had stayed warm enough to make the night bearable if not pleasant, and the frown that creased Chase Courtland's face was not put there by his physical discomforts. He had wrangled one concession from the brigade commander—one and only one. They were not under orders to make camp anywhere to await Leighton's arrival. His troopers could and would stay mounted, could and would stay armed and at the ready for trouble. A small concession but an important one. It took them out of the

154

sitting-duck category, Chase thought grimly. But that was about all.

"Grier?" Chase drew rein on his horse and beckoned his captain closer. Dawn was nearing, the Georgia sky finally beginning to brighten to a dark, dull gray. Patches of fog barred the small clearings that spotted the woods, and Chase glanced up once at the leaden sky, saw no break yet in the weather and shrugged. "Better warn the men to keep the rain out of their cartridge boxes. Sticks and stones won't do us much good against Leighton if he shows up."

"I'll bet he won't." Grier grunted. "This isn't his style, is it? He likes dirty tricks better."

"He may have some planned yet. Don't get too relaxed."

Just as Chase spoke, the trooper riding left point gave a sudden shout. "Over here, sir! I see a horseman."

Chase turned instantly to Grier, reining in his horse and raising his hand to signal caution to the soldiers behind them. "You just lost your bet, Captain. I think we've found Leighton. Or maybe I should say, he just found us."

The battalion advanced far more cautiously after that. In the full light of a gray dawn, Chase led the soldiers through a stand of scrub pines and out to the edge of a marshy meadow—wet already, soon to become a quagmire in the slow, steady drizzle that continued to soak the Savannah countryside. At the woods' edge, Chase halted, uneasily, eyeing the clear ground ahead with a jaundiced eye. No trees meant no cover. And no cover, to a soldier, could mean dying. It was a half mile or more to the next grove of scrub, just distant brown and black shadows in the fog—shrouded, faint gray light. And every instinct Chase possessed warned him not to go out in that meadow. "We'll wait here." He decided aloud, searching the scrub beyond the meadow with grim eyes. "We'll make Leighton come to us."

Leanna had been sleeping when Treejack galloped in, exulting, to cry the Yankees' approach. Hearing the shouted news, for a moment, she'd found herself helplessly unable to react; staring speechless as men hurriedly filled revolver chambers and loosened their rifles' saddle straps. She hadn't believed, somehow, that Chase would come, hadn't believed this dreaded moment would ever materialize—and yet now it had.

There was suddenly a kind of excitement in the camp, the

kind she'd felt there before a cock fight—a bloody, but thrilling game about to be played. With a sudden cry, she ran to search for Stewart, found him mounted already, turning his horse to go. "No!" She raised a desperate hand to the horse's bridle. "No! For God's sake, Stewart, give it up! Give it up now before he kills you or you kill him! I beg you! Please! Give it up!"

Stewart's only answer was to reach down and wrench Leanna's hand free of the bridle, half throwing her to the ground with the force of his hand. Leanna stumbled and staggered back helplessly, unable to do any more than to stand watching him go. The spurred horse lunged forward and away, practically trampling her in its rearing passage. Stewart had said nothing; he hadn't needed to. The cruelty and the bitter anger she'd seen flash from his eyes, the cold smile that had curved his mouth to match it—they had said more than words could, been a denial more vehement than any speech. Neither he nor Chase would spare each other, or themselves, or her. Events long ago set in motion were coming down to their inevitable end—ugly, destructive, deadly as it always was when two men staked claim to the same territory. And she was totally helpless, as helpless now as she had ever been, to stop either one of them from this final confrontation.

"Hold your fire."

Grier scowled openly at the order and silently Chase admitted to himself an equal uneasiness with it. He didn't trust Leighton either, but three horsemen had ridden out from the distant pines waving a white flag of truce, and something inside him was unable to order cold-blooded murder—whether warranted by the raiders' past treachery or not. He watched them ride slowly forward into the swampy gray meadow and felt a chill settle between his shoulder blades, a chill he unsuccessfully tried to shrug off.

The Rebels halted. The words came across the meadow in a shouted Southern drawl. "Is that the Eighth Pennsylvania?"

"Yes, it is," Grier shouted back before Chase could, and as Grier spoke, he primed the hammer of the carbine he was drawing to lay ominously ready across his lap.

"Is a Major Courtland there to receive Colonel Leighton's surrender?"

"Yes, he—"

"Yes, I'm here," Chase interrupted, kicking his horse forward.

He had to press him hard against where Grier had deliberately drawn his own horse across to block the way, and for a moment, the two horses leaned into one another, ears back and belligerent. Then Grier abruptly yielded, jerking on his reins to back his horse. "It's all right, Grier. But keep your rifle out." Chase spoke in an undertone to his scowling captain, then urged his horse another step into the open field, shouting across it. "Bring your men out into the open, all of them. Show your weapons and then drop them."

Vague shadows appeared in the distant woods, sharpening to become mounted men as they came forward onto the field. Chase scanned the ragged line and found Leighton near the center, and he nodded to himself as the Rebels raised rifles high and then dropped them with a momentary clatter onto the rain-soaked grass.

Across the field, Stewart concealed a faint smile and cocked the hammer of the loaded LeMat revolver he held beneath his gutta-percha poncho. He glanced sidelong to see Treejack's almost imperceptible nod, then walked his horse slowly forward. All of the men were still armed—with revolvers mostly. Not the equal of Yankee carbines over this distance, but fine for the close work they had planned. The weapons that littered the field were useless ones—captured Yank pieces they had no ammunition for, or CSA equipment that no longer fired. The good rifles had been left back at camp or were strapped close to the horses' saddles where the Yankees wouldn't see them in time.

Across the meadow, Chase watched the Rebels' slow progress in silence. Now what, he asked himself? Was it possible the surrender was a genuine one? Every fiber of his being still said no. "Grier, you and your troop come with me. Tell Cowles and Watson to follow if trouble starts. Leiffer stays here to guard our backs." He started his horse forward as he spoke, not looking to see the disapproval he knew would darken his captain's face. Grier was far less troubled by conscience in such circumstances; he'd have opened fire on instinct alone. "Grier, keep your carbine ready. We may need it."

Chase brought the federal line out of the woods, slowly, closing on the rebel one which had halted at midfield. The white flag of truce still hung there in plain sight, pale, wet gray—drooping and dripping rainwater, but carried too prominently be to ignored. Chase couldn't disregard it as much as he wished, just now, he could. He halted his horse directly opposite Leighton's and said nothing, merely met the man's ice-blue eyes in a silent stare.

Stewart stared back at him for a long moment, unblinking. Finally, a small, faint smile curled one side of his mouth and he spoke. "Major Courtland." Stewart broke the long silence unhurriedly, inclining his head as if greeting an old friend. "Shall we proceed with this unpleasant necessity?"

"You want to formally offer me your sword, Colonel?" A brief, humorless smile flickered across Chase's mouth. Along both lines of soldiers, Yankee and Rebel were eyeing one another sullenly and sharply. The horses moved restlessly, laying their ears back as if sensing the enmity that seethed in the air. Chase held Leighton's eyes another moment, wondering. If the man weren't Leanna's husband, would he still feel the same, gut-level enmity? Impossible, perhaps, to know. But he thought so. There was something missing in the man, some essential humanity. Under *any* conditions, he and Stewart Leighton would be enemies. "Colonel Davenport has authorized me to offer terms for your surrender. You and your men will stand trial for your 'alleged' partisan activities against the federal government's legally sanctioned military activities. If you're acquitted, you're free to seek parole. If found guilty on any count, you will serve an appropriate prison sentence."

Stewart raised one brow as if surprised. Briefly, something like amusement showed in his eyes. "Most generous, Major. You must accept my gratitude."

"Don't thank me, Colonel. The usual sentence for partisans like you is death, and in your case, I think, well deserved. I'm only relaying Davenport's instructions—and personally, I'll do anything I can to see you hang."

"Hard feelings left from Virginia, Major?"

"And from Millen and that swamp outside Savannah. Call it hard feelings, yes."

"That's too bad. We have so many other interests in common."

Grier's sudden shout of warning drowned out Stewart's last words. Out of the corner of his eye, Chase too had caught a hint of motion—the man to Leighton's right drawing something from beneath the cover of his rain cloak. Even as Grier had cried out, a revolver had glinted in the Rebel's hand, and

Chase drew his saber in the same instant. "Open fire!" he shouted. "Defend yourselves!" He saw Leighton's motion in the same moment, his revolver out, being swiftly leveled. From down the line of federal troopers, there was a sudden scrambling jerk from immobility to action, the roar of carbines and the cold scrape of swords being drawn, horses being spurred forward, and behind them the frantic call of the buglers as Cowles and Watson's men burst galloping out onto the field. All of it could not have taken more than a few seconds yet Chase pulled his sword dripping blood from the first man and instinctively began to turn toward Leighton. Then he felt the shock as Leighton's revolver was fired. It felt like taking a brass-knuckle punch from a dockside brawler; Chase choked as the bullet drove deep in his belly, forcing the air out of his lungs. Then he coughed, startled, struggling to regain his breath. He had a momentary glimpse of Leighton watching him, of his faint smile widening. Then there was Grier's horse rearing in the confusion, coming down just long enough for Grier to fire his own carbine, and Stewart Leighton too had begun to fall. Somewhere, someone raised a revolver and fired twice. The first bullet whined by Chase's ear. The second caught his left shoulder, slamming him sideways on the saddle. Simultaneously, finally, pain exploded in his belly, pulsing fire, his vision began to blur and a loud humming in his ears deafened the clamor of the clashing lines. Dimly, he heard Grier shouting once, as if calling to him, but pain overwhelmed it. He felt himself slipping on his saddle, glanced down to see the brown leather bright, wet red with blood, and couldn't seem to save his balance.

Grier saw his major begin to fall and made a desperate lunge to grab him, firing one-handed, wildly and furiously, at the remaining Rebels. Most who remained alive had wheeled their horses already, dashing for the cover of the woods beyond. Cowles and Watson followed them, drawing level with the bloody original line and surging past, shouting and shooting, pursuing Leighton's men at a reckless gallop. After the kind of treachery Leighton had displayed today, the federal troops would give no quarter, and most of the thirty-some men who had seen the morning's dawn would not see the evening's sunset.

Back at the camp, Leanna heard the sudden distant roar of the firing, then the drum of galloping horses drawing nearer,

159

a wild shouting and screams of agony. It froze the blood in her veins and she stood ashen-faced, motionless, staring in that direction. Oh God, he did it, she thought. Nothing she had said or done had served to stop him. It was done. Chase and Stewart—one or both of them was surely dead today.

Horsemen burst suddenly from the scrub pine into the camp clearing—Stewart's men. Leanna saw them and gave a desperate cry of sudden panic. She turned to try to run, grabbing for the feathery tip of a nearby pine bough, trying to pull herself through the impossible tangle of thickets that edged the clearing. A horse sounded loud behind her, almost on her heels, and instinctively she turned with a cry of fear, throwing her arms up to shield her face. John MacRae grabbed her wrist as she raised it, not slowing his horse's gallop as he hauled her up over his lap onto the saddle. Then he reached down for the loaded rifle he'd left propped against the pine's trunk, spurring the lathered horse through the thickets into the shadows beyond.

Behind him, the first of the federal troops reached the Rebel camp and opened fire with withering, scathing fury—a hail of bullets that, in moments, left not even the tent poles standing. It was the last camp Leighton's bloodthirsty guerrillas would ever make—Cowles would make sure of that. Cowles' men wasted little time among the scattered debris that littered the clearing afterward. A few troopers dismounted to loot weapons from the dead men, to pull watches out of pockets and rings from stiffening fingers. But they didn't bury the Rebel dead before they left; they didn't think they owed them that courtesy after today's treachery.

The long, slow rain finally showed signs of stopping by the time Cowles returned to the bloody meadow. In the distance there was still the occasional sound of firing as his men pursued the few Rebel survivors. But it was muffled, inconsequential, and Cowles dismissed it to ride to where Grier knelt on the marshy field. There, the last few raindrops were diluting the scarlet of blood to a watery pink before it drained into the meadow grass. Some yards away, a revolver cracked, killing a horse that had broken a leg in the scramble, but Cowles didn't even glance over at that familiar sight. He merely dismounted to stand in silence beside the lead troop captain, not needing to voice his question.

"Go get one of the wagons, Cowles. We're going to need one to get the major back to Savannah alive."

Grier straightened up wearily as he spoke, half turning, and Cowles glanced down. Between the shoulder and the stomach wound, the whole front of the major's coat was soaked dark scarlet; the ashen grayness of his face testified to the fact that all the blood there was his. "You're gonna need a miracle, Grier, not a wagon."

"Both, maybe. But miracles aren't in your province. Wagons are. Will you go get one for God's sake? *Now?*"

Cowles nodded and remounted, even set spurs to his horse to evidence a show of haste. But the haste was for Grier's sake, not the major's. Personally, Cowles didn't think a few minutes more or less was going to matter much to Chase Courtland. He thought the war was over for him.

Chapter Ten

News traveled quickly these days since the invention of the telegraph—"magic" messages riding thousands of miles over mere wires. From New York to Washington took nine hours by train while a telegram took little more than two. But dispatches from the federal armies fighting in the South took longer. Delays were unavoidable, as both cavalries cut telegraph wires constantly, and from Savannah north, part of any message had to be hand-signaled from federal ship to federal ship up the Rebel-held coastline.

It was Saturday afternoon before Grier led the battered Eighth Pennsylvania back into the city. Contrary to Cowles' prediction, Chase Courtland was still alive. But as the first report of the incident was being telegraphed north, to the War Department, Union doctors were unable to give an optimistic prognosis on the desperately wounded young major. Consequently, the telegram that left Savannah Saturday, relayed then from Washington to Philadelphia, caught Susan Stratford Courtland at the Courtland house on Monday morning. She had come to inquire after Joshua's progress, had sat for a little while with her still-unconscious father-in-law, and now descended the stairs to find Cooke just closing the front door of the house. The servant turned slowly to face her, and instinctively Susan froze on the bottom step of the long stairs. Whatever it was that Cooke was holding in his hand, she realized slowly, it was obviously unwelcome news . . . and it was bordered in the black ink of calamity.

"A telegram, Mrs. Susan. Something relayed on from a friend, he said, in Washington. It's addressed to Mr. Joshua."

Oh God, no, Susan thought swiftly. It can't be Chase. He could have scarcely returned to Savannah by now. A momentary trembling shook her and she fought against the onslaught of a premature dread. Joshua Courtland had many friends in

162

Washington, many contacts there both personal and business-related. Such a missive could well be from any one of them. "Let me see it, Cooke. Elinor isn't home and Mr. Courtland is obviously unable to open it. Perhaps it's only a message from Chase." Still, her hand was shaking as she reached out for the thing, and her fingers were clumsy in opening the envelope. The news it contained was both bitter and brief:

FOLLOWING GUERRILLA ACTION OUTSIDE SAVANNAH ON THE EIGHTH OF JANUARY, INVOLVING THE EIGHTH PENNA. CAVALRY, THE FOLLOWING REPORT OF DEAD AND WOUNDED: FEDERAL MAJOR C. E. COURTLAND LISTED THERIN AS VERY SERIOUSLY WOUNDED. NO FURTHER INFORMATION AVAILABLE AT THIS TIME.

"Oh, my God . . ." Susan had barely enough breath to whisper a stunned denial. "But he was just *here*. He was just fine only a few days ago. He was right here with us."

"It is the young major then, isn't it? Here, Mrs. Susan, let me help you to a chair."

Only at Cooke's interruption of her thoughts did Susan begin to actually react to the telegram's message. She began to tremble, shaking so hard that the fine tissue of the telegram made faint fluttering noises in the silence of the foyer. "Oh, God, Cooke . . . it says Chase is dying!" In irrational but irresistible revulsion, Susan thrust the message back to the servant's hands, as if she might by that simple act cancel the thing's existence. She turned abruptly away from Cooke's proffered hand, turning to lean back on the banister of the stairs she'd just descended. She closed her eyes there in inescapable horror, struggling for breath in the aftermath of the shock, and unable as yet to force her mind to produce any semblance of a more rational reaction. It meant things she must do, of course. Details she would have to assume responsibility for. Arranging for her husband's body to be shipped home. Funeral services at St. Mark's. Other people she must surely notify. But who?

"Here, Mrs. Susan. We must try to take heart." Cooke had read the brief message himself by now. His face, too, was pale, but not nearly as pale now as it had been only a moment before. The telegram specified wounded, not dead. And Cooke was, by his nature, an optimist. "The young Mr. Courtland is healthy and strong. He may even now be recovering from his wounds."

"No." Susan only shook her head. "No, I've been a nurse too long to believe that, Cooke. I've seen too many casualty lists by now. I've learned to read what a doctor means when he says '*very seriously.*' " She closed her eyes more tightly, struggling against tears. " 'Very seriously wounded' is only a euphemism that doctors learn to use, Cooke, when there's nothing they can do to save their patient. 'Seriously wounded' means 'don't blame me when the soldier dies, but there's some small chance yet that he may not.' Doctors only insert the word 'very' when they're awaiting what they regard as the inevitable. It means the doctors in Savannah can't do anything at all to try to save Chase; it means whatever wounds he has are beyond their ability to treat. We can't afford to delude ourselves it's any different than that."

"But then a better doctor might be able to save him still. They must surely have their surgeons with the army in Savannah. Surely one of them might be gifted enough to offer some hope yet to the situation?" It was simply not in Cooke's nature to give up even the faintest glimmer of hope.

"Gifted army surgeons?" Susan's mouth twisted briefly in a grimace of bitter denial. Under other conditions, she might have laughed out loud at the thought. She had seen too much at the Washington hospital. Heard entirely too many stories from Roger about army surgeons' ineptitude, of incompetent butchery passing for medicine. "Oh God, Cooke, you can't imagine . . . the conditions they're forced to practice under. The lack of training. The lack of proper facilities, even. Barnyards for operating rooms. Meat butchers pressed into surgery. God in heaven, I hope they don't even *try* to help Chase. Better they should leave him die in peace than that."

"But with the Courtland family's contacts in the War Department, with their friends there and their influence . . ." Cooke's face creased in a frown of sudden thought. "Who would you say was the best doctor you worked with in Washington, Mrs. Susan? Who would you say was the most gifted surgeon in the hospital there?"

"Roger, of course. I mean Major Lacey." Susan's mind was not even entirely on their conversation by now. Anguish was beginning to pierce the shell of the shock that had gripped her, insulating her until this point. Only one distant portion of her brain still continued to operate, enabling her to understand the servant's questions, even to reply to them with some sort of rationality. The rest of her was beginning to scream inside in silent protest. Not Chase, too, she was thinking. I already gave my brother to the war. Joshua already gave the butchers one son. It isn't fair for the war to take Chase from us as well. It simply isn't *fair* of them!

"And this Major Lacey is more qualified than the surgeons you guess are still in the field hospitals?" Cooke was frowning still in continuing thought. He was silent another moment, then nodded his head in sudden decision. "Then we must simply forward on a request to the War Department, Mrs. Susan. We can have the Washington surgeon sent down to Savannah, or have the young major brought up North instead. Surely that's a small enough favor for Mr. Courtland's Washington people to arrange."

For a moment longer, Susan made no reaction at all to Cooke's suggestion. It took a few minutes even for his words to penetrate her grief. Send Roger down to Chase in Savannah? Oh God . . . she thought slowly. Oh God no, Cooke. No. No!

"We could telegraph down to Washington today. It seems by far the best hope we shall have."

"No." Susan turned to face the servant in instant denial, shock showing in her eyes behind the veil of tears. "We can't do that, Cooke. Not send Roger Lacey down there. We just can't!"

"But we *have* to, as I see it, Mrs. Susan." Cooke rarely argued with his superiors. It wasn't a servant's place he thought to protest even the most outlandish order. But just now he was as shocked by the young woman's refusal as she had apparently been by his suggestion. Sometimes the shock of grief made people thing poorly, he told himself. So, he argued the matter in deferential tones, but still he argued. Even while he apologized for stepping momentarily so far above his station, he spoke again with the same sense of veracity. "Please, Mrs. Susan. I understand how difficult a moment this is for you, but I also feel obliged by my sense of duty toward the family to beg you to reconsider your initial decision. You say that the message in the telegram means that there are no surgeons in Savannah capable of restoring the young major's life, but there is a very fine, very gifted young doctor already under War Department orders in Washington. So what could be more sensible than to have that same fine surgeon sent to Savannah, then? What possible reason is there for us to relinquish what little bit of hope we have? Surely it can do no harm to let this Dr. Lacey at least try?"

For a moment longer, Susan only stood and stared at the servant, unable to coerce any rational thought. A thousand reactions flashed through her mind, jumbled and conflicting, before she isolated any single one. Yes, she thought suddenly, if it weren't for me, Cooke, it would do no one any harm to send Roger to Savannah. And if it weren't for the fact that Chase had just married the woman Roger loved, if the last telegram from her to Roger hadn't been an announcement of that marriage . . . if it weren't for the guilt and the anger and all the secrets she and Roger Lacey shared . . . Chase Courtland had been Roger's closest friend once . . . before Susan had intruded between them. If it weren't for me, Roger probably would have gone to Savannah for Chase, Susan realized in rising dread. But how in the world could anyone ask that of him now?

"Perhaps since you worked with the doctor, you might consent to send the telegram to him yourself? I should send a telegram on to the War Department and assume the liberty, of course, of employing Mr. Courtland's name for the request."

"A telegram? No, I . . ." Susan paused only a last and frantic moment, desperately trying to put order in her turbulent and conflicting emotions. Cooke could not possibly expect *her* to beg Roger for Chase Courtland's life! But God, how, too, could she *not* beg Roger's aid just now? How could she otherwise bear the guilt, wondering for the rest of her life whether she had condemned her husband because of her own sins . . . condemned Chase because she was too fearful of what awful truths might pass between her husband and Roger Lacey if Chase survived. And if they looked too directly into each other's eyes and saw there the secrets Susan had given up everything in order to hide. How had fate conspired so cruelly to put her in this untenable situation? For a moment, there was no answer to that question she had posed herself, and only a sweeping bitterness remained when the answer did come. She had placed herself here by her very own hand, of course. The only real question remaining was whether she would allow it to be Chase or Roger Lacey who paid the price for *her* betrayals of both of them. . . . "No, Cooke. No . . . no telegram, I think." She could barely force her lips to form the words to answer, but she knew her responsibility suddenly, knew it with an agonizing clarity she could not ignore. She could not allow herself to take the easy way out in this case. Not this time. Not any longer. She simply could not live with her guilt if she did. "No. I must travel to Washington, myself, Cooke. As soon as possible. I will have to talk to Dr. Lacey myself, to ask him to go to Savannah . . . to go to Chase. You're quite right in one regard, Cooke. Doc Lacey is an exceptionally . . . talented surgeon. He may be the only doctor in the army with that much ability, I think. If Chase is still alive when Roger reaches Savannah, there may be some small hope for his life after all. We must at least give Chase that, then. Regardless of the . . . the difficulties it might cause for any of us. Of course you're right; we can do nothing else." Susan turned away from the servant, partly in a need to reach for her winter cloak and partly in a need to hide the fears and the anguish she knew must show on her ashen face. "Drop me at the train station then, Cooke, and go on from there to send your telegram to the War Department people. By the time I arrive in Washington, we must have Major Lacey's orders pending. And have immediate space for him on a ship to Savannah. Even if I *can* convince Doc Lacey to go to Chase, the one thing which will still be working against us all is time. Even the most gifted surgeon in the world can't do anything to help a dead man, can he?" Susan had meant the last words only in dread, then found that they tempted her instead with a terrible kind of sudden hope. God forgive me, she prayed despairingly as she followed Cooke outside to the waiting carriage. What kind of woman would wish for her own husband's death? Whatever kind it was, she realized abruptly, she wasn't far from becoming one of them. And she had no one even to blame but herself.

167

*   *   *

There was a new air of expectancy in the federal capital this year, a new sense of the long war finally, hopefully, nearing its bitter finish. Most things hadn't changed yet: there were still a dozen military hospitals within sight of the Capitol; the patent office, which had hosted Lincoln's second inaugural ball, was still being used as a barracks for troops; new graves were filling Oak Hill, Georgetown and Arlington's lawns with white crosses; cattle pens and slaughterhouses ringed the Washington Monument; Foggy Bottom corralled thirty thousand horses and mules; the basement of the Capitol itself was a federal bakery; and supply trains still chugged across the Mall only a hundred yards from the red castle of the Smithsonian Institute. But the South was failing, finally. The federal capital sensed that and responded with a restored dedication to the war effort. Throughout the city there was the quiet expectancy now of a lull before the storm—before the *last* storm, hopefully. Frostbite, starvation, disease and a critical lack of soldiers was crippling Robert E. Lee's once invincible army as no Yankee army had ever quite succeeded in doing. Sherman, in the Deep South, had shattered the CSA army there. This spring should be the end, then. *Should* be, Washington cautioned itself. There had been other hopeful years that hadn't fulfilled that promise before.

In the Confederate prisoner ward of the Washington hospital, Doc Lacey had already sensed a change. There was no longer the same feeling of overcrowded agony and desperate enmity. For one thing, the South was running out of men so quickly that the ward was half empty, and many of the soldiers who were here were convalescent, on their way to prison or awaiting a parole. In one sense, that change was a change for the better; in another, it was for the worse. It served to make the anguish that did remain seem more useless than ever, the agonies futile, the deaths infinitely meaningless. Plus, he admitted frankly to himself, what had happened here with Susan had not left him with easy memories of this hospital, either. He had replaced her as a nurse—with another young volunteer who stood with him now, as a matter of fact, helping him to bandage a wound. But he had not replaced Susan as a companion. He had certainly not replaced her as a lover. In that regard, he wondered if he ever actually would. Perhaps in Denver, he told himself, if that long overdue transfer ever came through. Perhaps if the war casualties countinued to drop so abruptly in numbers, the federal War Department would consider closing a few of the capital-based facilities. Then they might spare a few of their surgeons for reassignment to the western territories. God, I hope so, Lacey thought wearily. It had been six months or more already since he'd initially requested the transfer out of Washington. Then, the reason for that request had been because of Susan Stratford, because of a blind, anguished need to put miles of distance between himself and the fiancée of the man who was probably his closest friend. And now once again it was Susan— now Susan Stratford *Courtland* he reminded himself—that made that expected transfer both so appealing and so urgently desired. Perhaps in Denver it would be easier to finally forget her. At least in Denver, there might be a greater *hope* of doing that.

"Dr. Lacey?" The earnest young nurse who had replaced Susan interrupted Roger's thoughts now in an apologetic manner. "Excuse me, but there's someone waiting to see you, I think."

"Oh, not just now." Lacey frowned without glancing up from the wound that he was bandaging. "I'm right in the middle of this thing here. Whoever it is will have to wait just a minute." Most doctors probably wouldn't have reacted that way; most doctors in 1865 still picked bandages up off the floor if they fell and dressed open wounds with unwashed hands. But Doc Lacey didn't. And he didn't yet trust his brand-new nurse to the degree he once had trusted Susan Stratford. There was an ugly, open wound in front of him, and that in his mind took precedence just now over anything else.

Only when the task was entirely finished and his nurse had already started on toward the next wounded Confederate did Lacey pause to glance over toward the open doorway. And he froze in that instant, silently staring. The woman who stood there was infinitely familiar. The woman in the doorway was Susan Stratford Courtland.

"Roger, I beg you . . ." Even from across the hospital ward, Susan's voice managed to convey the soft hushed quality of a whisper. And her eyes meeting his conveyed a plea of utter desperation. "Roger, please. I *must* speak to you. Please."

For a moment, Doc Lacey was about to simply turn away

. . . and he found himself unable to do so. With a terrible effort, he did finally manage to look away from her. He stared at the empty wall of the hospital ward while both anger and pain flashed over his face. What could possibly be left for her to say to him, or for him in turn to say to her? Congratulations, Susan, on your recent marriage. Have you told my best friend yet that I slept with his bride before he did? What the *hell* had she come back to Washington for?

"Roger, it's Chase. He's been wounded down in Savannah. From the telegram I saw, I'm not sure he isn't dead already."

Susan had taken not a single step closer toward him. He glanced back sharply to her now, startled and for the moment not even believing her altogether. It's an odd thing in war. Even doctors who spent day after day treating nothing but wounded soldiers were still shocked when close friends fell victim to the minié balls and cannon shot. For a moment, that took precedence even over Susan and her unexpected reappearance. "Chase?" For another long moment, he stood shocked and astounded. Then in the same instant, he both believed and dismissed Susan's agonized message. "Then you have my condolences, of course, Mrs. Courtland. Now, if that's all, I've an awful lot of work to do here, I'm afraid."

"Roger, please, for the love of god! Is that all Chase ever meant to you? Is that all *I* ever meant to you? Can't you even manage the decency to come over to me? At least *say* that like you *mean* it!" Susan had been trembling to begin with, her face had been ashen and her eyes had been blurred with tears. Now, suddenly, she was shaking uncontrollably and her voice had risen to a choking accusation. "I came down here today from Philadelphia to beg you as a favor to go down to Savannah to try to save Chase's life! I didn't expect you to make it easy for me. I don't deserve to have it made easy for me— God in Heaven, I'm well enough aware of that! But I did expect you to *care*, Roger. Even if you said no to what I asked you to do, at least I did still expect you to care! What in the hell are you made out of inside?"

"Raw, bleeding, agony," Lacey suddenly wanted to shout back at her. I hurt so damn badly that I'm never free of it either day or night! So what gives you the right to come back down here now and make even further demands on me? What the hell do you *think* I'm made of inside? Granite? Roger Lacey managed to keep his mouth closed at least—managed

170

to keep all of that internal agony from spilling out to fill the sudden silence of the hospital ward—but that was all he could do. And even to do that much, he'd had to turn his back on her in a silent fury. There was a sudden sound from the doorway behind him, a kind of choking sound and then the sudden rustle of moving fabric. "Susan!" Lacey whirled back to face her but it was already too late. There was only the blurred impression of rushing movement from the corner of his eye. By the time he'd turned fully around, the doorway stood empty again. "Susan, wait!" Oblivious to the stares of his new nurse and the dozen Confederate prisoners of the room, he bolted after her, flinging a handful of bandages carelessly to the floor as he ran. "Susan, wait!"

"No, let me go!" Lacey had followed her and caught up to her in a half-dozen running strides, and Susan shook her arm violently against the pressure of his sudden hold on her. "No, Roger, I should never have come back here! I should never have thought this could do any good for any of us! Forget you ever even saw me again!"

"Susan, no. Susan, you can't go out on the streets like this, it's freezing cold out there!" Lacey managed to drag her to a halt halfway down the hospital corridor and only stood there for a moment staring down at her face with stricken eyes. "Susan, tell me again what—"

"It's no use, Roger. I knew it as soon as Cooke mentioned the idea. It was wrong of me to even see you again. Wrong of me to expect you to care anymore. I had no right to ask anything more from you at all." There was the shrillness of rising hysteria evident in her voice now as she spoke to him, and the efforts she made to free her arm from his grip were made with the strength of sheer desperation. "Let me go, Roger. I'll go to Savannah instead of you. I was a nurse, after all. I should be the one that goes down to Savannah. Just forget you ever saw me here today."

"Savannah? What the hell are you talking about? You can't go to Savannah. *I* couldn't go to Savannah, even if I wanted to. Only troop ships and War Department personnel—"

"Cooke is already arranging for War Department clearance. I'll go as a nurse. I'll go as a soldier if that's the only way I can get down to him. He's my husband, Roger. . . . Chase is my husband. I have to do *something*, don't I?" She dropped her head suddenly in her hands with a last anguished moan,

171

leaning heavily against Lacey's hand in sudden surrender. "Oh, God help me, Roger, I know you don't understand. You can't know what I thought of this morning when I heard the news. I think in a way that I wanted Chase to die. That's terrible, isn't it? How terrible for me to wish such a thing on my own husband . . . But it would all be so much easier if Chase did die, Roger. So much easier for me, I mean. I didn't want to come ask you for help at first, mostly because I thought you might go. And I realized then that I'd rather see Chase dead than risk his ever knowing the *truth* about me." Susan shuddered then with a sudden violence, never raising her head from the sanctuary of her hands. "Now if he dies, I can never forgive myself. It will be almost as if I had killed him myself."

"Susan, that's a ridiculous thing to even think about. You didn't shoot Chase—your wishes and your thoughts had nothing whatsoever to do with this! It's a war, for God's sake. You've seen enough of it here in the past months to know that. Men die every day. Nothing either one of us has done has caused this damn thing to happen."

"Hasn't it?" Susan raised her head abruptly to meet Roger's eyes in a terrible gaze of disbelief. "*Hasn't* it? The telegram said Chase was 'very seriously wounded,' Roger. Not dead. Wounded. If it weren't for me you would at least go down to try to help him, wouldn't you? But you won't now. I know you won't." She drew a deep breath finally, a long, shuddering sob, and turned her face away from his again. "God help you, you're as guilty as I am, Roger. You want Chase to die so you can have his wife."

"Susan, that's a goddamn lie!" But even as he spoke, a chill trembled instantly down Doc Lacey's spine and he shivered. God no, he thought. I don't want Chase Courtland dead, I don't. I don't want my friend's woman *that* desperately. It *is* a lie, he told himself again. It has to be. "That has nothing to do with why I'm not going. Savannah is days away from Washington. Even if the magic Courtland name could requisition a berth for me on a ship leaving today, by the time I could get to Savannah it would be of no use."

"When Jonathon Penley was wounded last year, it was weeks before you found him and worked your miracles to save his life. *Weeks*, Roger. And now you're talking about only days to get to Chase."

"No, dammit, I just won't *do* it!" I don't owe Chase Courtland that, Lacey thought in violent protest. I don't owe either one of you any more than I've already given! The abysmal cruelty of his own involuntary thoughts stunned him into utter silence and he pulled away from Susan's grip with a sudden anger of near desperation. Dammit, it *isn't* my fault! I warned Chase last winter! I warned him then that he was heading for this unless he pulled out of the field and took a position in Washington! So it isn't my fault he finally took the bullet he was so damn determined to take. Let him die, then. It was his own damn choice. Let him die.

"Roger, don't let me do this to you, I beg of you! Don't let me poison you with the same guilt I'm going to carry for the rest of my life! Be better than I am; go try to help Chase. Roger!"

The desperation in Susan's voice caught him at the very edge of the open doorway and made him check his step in spite of himself. For a moment, there was only that silence— absolute, brooding, chilling. Then he closed his eyes with a last anguished sigh. And what if I *do* go down to Savannah . . . and Chase dies anyway? Will she ever believe I tried my best? More importantly, maybe, will *I* ever know if I did? There was a long silence, broken at last by another sigh. Doc Lacey nodded finally then, just once, without turning around. "All right, Susan. You win. I'll leave at once then. Go find out for me when the ship's going south." He walked through the door without looking back. He couldn't look back; he was afraid of what he'd see on Susan's face, and more afraid of what she might see on his. "I'll wire you at your home in Philadelphia then—one way or the other—as soon as I get down to Savannah."

Monday morning had dawned clear and blue in Philadelphia; the air all day had been doubly cold because of it. As dusk approached now tiny crystals of ice glazed the glass panes of the Courtland carriage house's single sitting-room window, a delicate filigree of silver lace that glittered in the failing sunlight. Jonathon put another log on the already hot, high fire and turned to hang his coat on the brass hook by the door. In the passing of the week since Chase Courtland had returned to war and to a rain-soaked bloody meadow outside Savannah, little had changed here in Philadelphia. Joshua Courtland

173

remained unconscious; the baby, Bonnie, remained ill with a high fever; Elinor, Lady Bennington, continued to smile mockingly, mystifyingly, whenever Jonathon caught her eye; and the board members of the Courtland bank continued to act increasingly odd.

For the moment, though, Jonathon was preoccupied with a brand-new worry, one outside of both Philadelphia and the Courtland family. He had met an old friend today, a VMI classmate of his, and a fellow ex-Confederate officer. Douglas had, like Jonathon, taken refuge in the North for the remainder of the war and he'd met him quite by accident, in the lobby of downtown Green's Hotel where he'd stopped to lunch with a visiting client. Unsettling news had thrown an immediate pall on the gaiety of the ex-Rebels' reunion. According to Douglas, Jonathon Penley's sister Leanna was in trouble in Georgia. Deep trouble. Rumor held that she was riding with her husband's partisan raiders—dangerous enough just that. But more—just before Savannah had fallen to the Yankees, a strange wire had come over the Confederate telegraph there: Leanna Penley Leighton was wanted in custody by the Confederate government for suspicion of treasonable activities against the CSA. Unknown, of course, to either Douglas or Jonathon himself—or to hardly anyone else outside of Richmond—Elinor Courtland Bennington had achieved her intention to implicate Leanna Leighton in some vague conspiracy against the Confederate government. It hadn't even proven very difficult for her to do. Black-market guns were a vital necessity to the failing Confederacy, and the people who supplied them were accorded every courtesy the Confederacy could offer. From his vantage point within the Southern capital and with his contacts in the Southern government, Elinor's husband Hadley had found it pathetically easy to convince CSA officials of a certain Leanna Penley Leighton's perfidy. So Leanna Leighton would now face the same kind of dangers from her own Confederate War Department that she had earlier faced from the federal one. Both sides would be grimly awaiting her capture now. And Elinor's trap was closing right on its predetermined schedule.

As far as the charges themselves went, Jonathon didn't lend the remotest credence to the notion that his sister had actually betrayed the South. He had been far too close to her for far too long; he knew Leanna as well as he knew himself. She was headstrong occasionally. Too fiery and too passionate to have ever been a model of the ideal Southern lady, perhaps. But there was a soul-deep honesty in his sister, and her loyalties ran deep and strong. It was not just the closeness that had always existed between Jonathon and Leanna that colored his belief in her innocence now. Even outside of the unusually deep affection between Penley brother and Penley sister, he would have trusted her to the ends of the earth. Leanna was far too dedicated to the Southern cause to have done anything even remotely treasonous. And whatever the reasons Richmond had for suspecting her, Jonathon was sure they must be a mistake.

But mistake or not, he realized suddenly, if Douglas were right, such a mistake put Leanna in a very dangerous position. Governments in wartime tended to act first and wonder later. And from Jonathon's position here in a Yankee city, miles from Richmond itself, he was damn near helpless to try to disarm the dangers that might face his sister if the CSA War Department got hold of her now.

As he stood dripping snow onto the tiny cottage's sitting-room floor, Jonathon stared at the crackling fire, preoccupied and silent. How could such a thing have happened? Who in Richmond would even know his sister well enough to suspect her? And more importantly, perhaps, how much actual danger did this put Leanna in? Whitney touched his arm just then, startling him with her closeness. As intent as he'd been on thoughts of his sister, he had been unaware of his wife's approach.

"I heard you come in, Jon, but I was just putting Bonnie down." Whitney's soft gray eyes looking up at him showed instinctive shared concern. "What is it? More bad news of some kind?"

He replied by a shrug and a forced smile, meaning to minimize the thing. If he could do nothing, Whitney could do less; she had enough on her mind with Bonnie and the unborn child she carried, and the day had been shocking enough already with the report of the Courtland son's near death in Savannah. "It's nothing really. Some remote possibility that Leanna's run afoul of the CSA government. Richmond may want her in custody for something. I'm sure it's an error, it has to be. We both know how staunch a Confederate Leanna is."

"Yes, *we* do. But if Richmond—"

"It's a mistake, Whit. That's all. Don't worry about it. Please." He shook his head sharply and turned away. Whitney remained motionless only a few feet from him, and he could feel her shock—and her mounting anxiety in the suddenly awkward silence. "Have you heard from the federal War Department yet, Jon? About those proceedings Joshua initiated back in October to secure amnesty for her? When Major Courtland found her wanted by the Yankees in Atlanta?" Whitney spoke at last in a quiet voice, barely audible above the fire's loud crackling.

"No." He admitted that with an abrupt shake of his head, and moved restlessly toward the fire. It didn't need tending, but he reached for the poker anyway, rearranging the burning logs with sharp jabs. Behind him, the failing sunlight cast the rest of the room into deepening shadow. "There seemed no reason to pursue it really. She had escaped Atlanta and the federal adjutant colonel who had wanted to arrest her, so the danger seemed past. Plus with Joshua's condition—"

"Then the federal army will arrest her still, too?" Whitney interrupted in alarm.

"Perhaps—if they find her again. But I doubt Leanna will allow that to occur now that she knows of her danger."

"But she wouldn't dream of the same kind of danger among her own Confederate troops. Jonathon, I'm worried. It's bad enough she's down there at all, in the midst of both armies. Now, no matter which side she's with, she faces arrest. Imprisonment maybe, or—" Whitney interrupted herself, turning ashen pale, her eyes slowly widening. "They wouldn't hang a woman, would they? Or shoot—?" She interrupted herself again, reaching to take Jonathon's arm in sudden appeal. Her gray eyes were distressed and searching his with a silent question before she finally dared to continue. "Jonathon, we could wire Major Courtland down in Savannah. Cooke said he was only wounded, not killed. Perhaps he could do something we can't do from up here. Perhaps he could at least find out if it's true that Leanna is wanted. If he's alive still, I'm sure that he would—"

"No!" Jonathon pulled his arms abruptly from Whitney's hand as he turned away. "You know that Major Courtland and I hold no particular friendship for one another. Even if he hadn't been wounded, I wouldn't ask him to do one damn thing regarding Leanna."

"For the love of God, it could be her *life* you're talking about!"

"I'll ask Douglas to inquire further. Or if Joshua recovers—"

"Joshua could die! Today, even—tomorrow. And so could his son. What if Douglas *does* inquire further and finds it's true? What then? Do you expect Lady Bennington to offer us any help? She'd laugh herself sick! She'd love to see you squirm!"

"I want Chase Courtland *away* from Leanna and out of her life! He is now, finally. And I won't do one damn thing to change that!"

"You *ought* to want Leanna safe any way you can ensure that!" Whitney did not often go against her beloved Jon, but on this she would. Her usually soft eyes turned suddenly steel hard. And though she trembled at the necessity of defying him, she faced him squarely, resolutely. "If you won't ask Major Courtland's help, *I* will. I swear I will! I'll wire him myself. Whether you give me your approval or not!"

"Mr. Penley?" Cooke's voice calling from outside the cottage's door interrupted the voices of rising anger, leaving only a tense, strained silence remaining inside. Whitney turned quickly back to the fire, wiping tears dry as Jonathon fought shocked anger from his face and moved toward the door.

"Yes, Cooke? What is it?"

"A telegram, sir. From the young Mrs. Courtland in Washington." Cooke's cold-reddened face showed anxiety. "Some particulars she was given this afternoon by the War Department people. I thought perhaps you might wish to see it, sir."

"What is it, Jon?" Whitney had come to stand beside him, her voice soft again but full of dread. The confrontation of the moment before was instantly forgotten as Jonathon read the telegram from Susan Courtland. And he reached an arm around Whitney's shoulders then in silent empathy. It was not a long wire. Neither did it offer any good news.

FOLLOWING GUERRILLA ACTION OUTSIDE SA-VANNAH ON THE EIGHTH OF JANUARY IN-VOLVING THE EIGHTH PENNSYLVANIA CAV-

ALRY, THE FOLLOWING LIST OF DEAD AND
SERIOUSLY WOUNDED:

DEAD: ADEARY, G. PRIVATE
DEAD: CHAPMAN, M. PRIVATE
        COURTLAND, C. MAJOR . . . WOUNDS
        IN SHOULDER AND STOMACH. WOUNDS
        ESTIMATED BY STAFF AS DEFINITELY
        MORTAL.

"No. Oh, my God." Whitney's denial was barely breathed.
Jonathon had the sensation from her of genuine, almost debili-
tating grief, and then she had turned away abruptly from
beneath his arm. He watched her hurried exit from the room,
saw the moisture of tears glistening silver on her ashen face,
and he turned back to Cooke in shaken silence.

"Might it be a mistake, sir?"

Jonathon shook his head once, sharply. "I doubt it. War
Departments usually err on the side of optimism when they
err at all."

Another silence followed, and finally the servant began to
turn slowly for the door. "If Mr. Courtland should regain
consciousness just now, do you think I must relay this discour-
aging news to him just yet?"

"No. No, wait awhile. Such news always keeps." Jonathon
spoke slowly, distracted by his other thoughts. The telegram
solved one dilemma, anyway. He and Whitney no longer
needed to argue over cabling the young Yankee major for
Leanna's sake. Small comfort, though, compared to the other
havoc that this could wreak. Her brother's death would leave
Elinor *alone* to manage the family bank, for one thing.

"And what of the Lady Bennington, sir? I'm afraid if she
were to know, that . . ." Cooke paused briefly, looking away
and then looking back to meet the young Rebel's eye—a
communication of knowledge shared, but never to be voiced.
"In her own grief, mightn't she tell her father, perhaps,
prematurely?"

There was nothing untoward in the servant's words, but
Jonathon felt a shock hit him as physically as a blow. Cooke
knew. All about the Lady Elinor; all about all of them, he
guessed. There were no secrets kept from the servants who
changed the bedsheets and dumped the ashtrays while men

178

were speaking together and placed opened-and-read letters into the trash. And this might well be a dangerous thing for Elinor Courtland to know about. "Yes, Cooke, I quite agree. Let the extent of Major Courtland's injuries remain our secret for a day or two. Surely, it can do no harm to anyone that way."

Cooke nodded once, his face carefully expressionless as he turned to return to the main house again. Jonathon watched him across the dark, snow-dusted drive, and then slowly closed the door against the night's cold wind. Then he turned to toss Susan Courtland's wire into the fire flames and watched it burn. I never pretended to like the Courtland son, he told himself with something close to guilt gnawing at his mind. But I didn't wish this on him, either, at least I don't think I did. Regardless of that denial, the suspicion left a lingering heaviness on his soul. And one more worry Jonathon almost feared to admit the possibility of—it left Douglas's news about Leanna more disturbing than ever. Now, no matter how desperate Leanna's danger from either War Department, there would be *no* one left to ask for aid. If Leanna were arrested by the CSA for treason, he would have to go south after her himself. And for a paroled Rebel, such a journey into active war would be nothing less than suicidal.

Jonathon's troubles were far from over; he discovered that two days later. With no further news from either Douglas or Savannah, and with Joshua Courtland still hovering on the edge of death, all the pieces of at least one particular puzzle came together with stunning suddenness. The annual stockholders meeting of the Courtland bank was over, and over early. Elinor had wasted no time making her move to seize all power from Jonathon Penley's hands. She had initiated a proxy vote, and within two minutes, had taken complete control of the bank. Even now, Jonathon stood half stunned, watching the other stockholders leave. Few of them dared to meet his eyes. None of them paused to inquire after Joshua Courtland's condition. Well, why should they offer that hypocrisy, he thought? They'd already proven they cared only for themselves. Damn you, Elinor Courtland Bennington. It's bad enough you don't give a damn for anyone in the world besides yourself, but must you infect everyone else with the same rotten disease as well? He turned to where she remained standing, alone now in the long, empty board room of the bank. The gleaming length of the polished mahogany table separated them—three yards that might as well have been three miles. A good thing, Jonathon thought. A sudden surge of furious, violent anger finally broke the shock of what had just happened and left him trembling in fury. He wasn't sure, if he could have reached his hands easily around her lovely white throat, that he wouldn't have throttled her for what she'd just done. "You keep proving it to me, Elinor, over and over again. You're as wantonly vicious as any poisonous snake or wild animal. You ought to be destroyed before you do further harm to anyone."

"Destroyed?" She only greeted his anger with a faint smile, her green eyes mocking as they touched his. "Funny, my brother mentioned that same thing when we last spoke. But I won't be destroyed, not by you at least, my dear Rebel. If you recall the votes just cast, you no longer even *work* here."

Jonathon's face flashed deeper anger. "You'd better hope your father dies. If he doesn't, you'll pay dearly for this."

"I can afford to now, can't I?" She showed her amusement openly, almost laughing. "Now that we've elected a new president and a whole new board of directors—and, of course, voted to disperse assets confiscated from our Confederate clients—I find myself quite wealthy again. I wish you luck, Jonathon, finding another position for yourself. I'd hate to see you indigent and returned to that prison camp." She started toward the door, the wide turquoise satin of her hooped skirt rustling faintly—like a rattlesnake before it strikes, Jonathon thought. A most appropriate analogy.

"Oh, by the way, Jonathon." Elinor turned at the doorway as if in afterthought. "Should you harbor any idealistic notions of trying to stop my duly elected bank officers from fulfilling their duties of dispersing the bank profits and confiscated assets tomorrow, let me mention something else. *Two* things actually. First: don't bother trying to wire my brother for aid in Savannah. A friend of mine from the War Department has already relayed the news that Chase is dying, if he isn't by now already dead. That took care of the complication I was most concerned about. And secondly: should you *personally* get in my way, consider this: with my father incapacitated and my brother dead, you and your family have a roof over your heads and food on your table only by *my* generosity. Further, I have good friends in both the federal and the Confederate War Departments, and I've arranged some insurance for myself—in the form of your precious sister. Between the two armies, they should have Leanna Leighton in custody anytime now. And then, if you so much as squeak a little mouselike protest, or if my father *should* recover and you think it your duty to try to convince him of my complicity in this sad state of affairs, I shall see that your sister faces a conviction for treason. A firing squad, or worse. You know a little something about prison camps, Jonathon. Try to imagine your sister's fate if she lands in one."

She began to smile, more widely, a familiar expression glittering in her eyes, and Jonathon had no trouble following the allusions she made in the next breath. "Pretty as she is, and quite without anyone's protection, how many of her jailors, would you guess, will hesitate to accommodate themselves at her expense? Depending on how lusty her guards are, she may not live to see a bullet kill her."

"You conscienceless bitch." It was only a whisper, sick and shaken. And for a moment, shock overwhelmed even the anger he should have felt. Good God, Douglas had been right. Leanna *was* on the Confederate War Department's list of suspected enemies . . . because Elinor Courtland Bennington had arranged to *put* her name there. And Elinor had also arranged Leanna's equal danger from the federal War Department earlier, then. It all made sense suddenly—infinitely appalling sense. No wonder Joshua Courtland's efforts to secure Leanna's amnesty had moved with such heretofore mystifying slowness. Elinor, too, had friends in high Washington places. And if the chance of Chase Courtland's protection had already gone to a lonely grave in Georgia, nothing stood in Elinor's way any longer. Nothing.

"And now I believe you finally understand the point I've been trying to make to you for quite some time." Elinor continued to smile faintly. "I don't intend to be troubled by *your* conscience any longer. And one more thing as well. Now that you're unemployed, how do you expect to earn your keep, Jonathon? My generosity, you know, only stretches so far." She moved her head, leisurely studying him head to toe with an appraising eye. "I might be willing to offer some work for you in the stables. And if I should summon you some evening with a different sort of riding in mind, I shall expect you to oblige such a request both promptly and courteously."

Jonathon could not have replied to save his life. His jaw was locked rigid in sudden violent fury; his whole body trembled with it, helplessly. A stable boy and a male whore. Elinor Courtland's private whore. Service at command. She left him with a last, malicious smile, disappearing into the hallway of the bank—*her* bank, now. Not that it showed on the minutes of the meeting that way, of course. Her father, Joshua, might yet recover, and Elinor was too clever to be so obvious. With her meaningless ten percent, she'd voted against all the motions, but the minority's combined fifteen percent had, unfortunately, overruled her. Bitch, Jonathon thought again, sick and staring at the door where she had stood. Good God in heaven. What am I expected to do now? An ex-Confederate, paroled, powerless—there was nothing he could do. The game was played to a finish and she had won.

Chapter Eleven

It was late in Savannah and the moon was faintly shining when Doc Lacey's footsteps echoed over the gangplank that bridged the dark river water to the mildewed wood and gray, shadowed stone of the dock beyond. Dusk had been falling when the ship reached the river's mouth some thirty miles downstream, and only by sheer good luck had he found a tugboat captain willing to maneuver through Savannah's treacherous shoals and mud shallows in the near darkness, thereby avoiding another full night's delay. Lacey did not waste that precious time by searching out each of the scattered buildings designated as temporary federal hospitals. There were over a dozen of them—warehouses, or hotels, and for wounded officers, the once-elegant but now abandoned town houses of the cotton magnates. Chase Courtland might be anywhere—if he weren't already buried deep in sandy Savannah soil, Lacey reminded himself grimly. He went to regimental headquarters and found Grier already there, as if awaiting him. Chase's captain was standing at the foot of a wide, curving staircase, and was obviously angry, speaking with bare civility to an officer, a colonel, in a spotless, dress-sashed uniform who stood several steps above him on the polished stairs. The troops would call him a dandy, Lacey concluded, and dislike him. Obviously Grier did.

"Sir, I will repeat myself then, once more. I put two Spencer carbine slugs in the man's chest from a distance of less than a half-dozen yards. I saw him fall. Wherever he is, you may assure Washington he is *quite* dead." The dandyish colonel nodded silently, disappearing back up the elegant staircase without another word. Grier remained at the bottom for a moment, only staring after him as if surprised at something. And finally slow anger gathered on the captain's bearded, sun-weathered face. "Yes, thank you, Colonel. Of course I'll be happy be relay your personal concern to your wounded soldiers."

"Grier?" Lacey had overheard Captain Grier's bitter murmur but he tried to ignore it. A lot of commanders were that way—*too* many. That wasn't something any doctor could change. He reached out his hand to meet Grier's grip of startled greeting, and he forced a faint smile. "Glad to see you're still well at least, Grier. Now try to stay that way, will you? That means no fistfights with your commanding officers."

Grier only shrugged, the same anger still showing on his face. "Sometimes that seems a hard rule to remember. You may not know this yet but the major's hurt. Shot a couple days ago outside of the city."

"Yes, I do know. As a matter of fact, that's why I'm here." Lacey nodded once, turning to conceal his expression before he continued. "But Chase isn't dead, then, at least."

"No, not dead. Not yet, anyway. But I'd be a damn liar if I said it looked good for him, Doc."

There was a short, odd silence, and Lacey deliberately kept his eyes from meeting Grier's. He had been conscious of a surge of relief at Grier's words, relief he couldn't quite identify the source of. Relief that his friend was still alive? Or the tone of Grier's voice that said it was only a temporary state of affairs? "Any chance you could take me to see Chase tonight? Right away?"

Grier's frown reappeared. "You aren't going to like what you see."

"I didn't expect to. Field hospitals are never what they should be."

"Not that so much. He took two bullets, one in the shoulder, one in the gut about waist high. They couldn't even find that one, let alone get it out." Grier shook his head angrily. "I'm sorry, Doc, you know I am. But I'm afraid you made a long trip for nothing. And Davenport"—his angry, jabbing motion indicated the officer Lacey had seen on the stairs—"doesn't give a damn. He got Leighton—and a gold star on his record sheet. That's all he cares about. Not his soldiers."

"Leighton?" Lacey involuntarily threw Grier a swift, sharp glance as the captain began to turn for the door. "As in *Virginia* Leighton—Blytheswood?"

"The same."

Lacey was startled to see a sudden brief but bitter enmity

flare on Grier's face as he answered. But Grier volunteered nothing more. And as Lacey followed the captain's hurried strides toward the door, he found himself wondering at such a coincidental happening . . . and wondering if it were coincidence at all. Chase and Leanna's guilty love he remembered from Blytheswood all too well. Only ironic justice, maybe. Or maybe Leanna had been involved somehow—either as participant or as motivation for her husband's private war. Had it been because of loving her in Virginia that Chase Courtland now lay dying here in Savannah? Chase and Leighton. Leanna. Susan and himself. "Oh, what a tangled web we weave when first we practice to deceive." Sir Walter Scott had said it well—Lacey's own anguish was proof of that. On his way to his wounded friend, he stopped at the military telegraph office to send Susan word of his arrival in Savannah:

> CHASE ALIVE, BUT SITUATION NOT HOPEFUL.
> WILL DO MY BEST.

He left it at that—and prayed to God that whatever happened, Susan would believe those last four words.

"Mister Penley?"

Jonathon didn't know the name of the servant who had knocked just now on the carriage-house door, but he knew him for one from the Courtland house, and moreover, one whom Elinor, and not Joshua, had hired. Instinctively, even as he was opening the door, the tension grew in the pit of his gut.

"Lady Bennington wants you over at the house. *Promptly*, she said."

"She didn't waste any time, did she?" It was only a bitter comment spoken softly, and Jonathon expected no answer from the man. God, it wasn't even a full day yet, Saturday morning. And Elinor was already calling due the debt.

"Jonathon?"

Whitney appeared at the edge of the doorway from the kitchen, ashen-faced. "Jonathon, what is it? Not Joshua, I hope? Or news of Major Courtland?"

"No. Lady Bennington. She wants to see me at the house."

"Jon, don't go."

He made no reply, only shook his head in silence. As he reached for his coat Whitney hurried across the room to grab his arm in a fearful grip. "Jon, please, I beg you. Whatever she wants—don't go!"

"I have to. I have no choice."

"Yes, you do, you must! Jonathon, please—"

"*Promptly*, she said." The manservant lounged insolently by the door post, and Jonathon's eyes flashed in anger as he turned to nod once.

"I'm coming." Jonathon pulled away from Whitney's hand. A cold kind of nauseousness was spreading rapidly in his belly, a feeling like fear but with revulsion and helpless anger added in. He didn't bother to button his coat, merely brushed by the servant in the open doorway. And though he heard the whisper of Whitney's last pleas still continuing as he started outside, he only walked the more quickly to get out of earshot, careful not to even look back at her now. If Whitney should read the truth in his eyes, it would be utterly unbearable. God, he thought. This was worse than any part of war had been. He was going to meet the enemy again—but a different kind of enemy this time. An enemy he had no weapons against in this kind of war.

"Excuse me, sir. Would you be Mr. Penley perhaps?"

Jonathon glanced over, but only slowly. Someone in dark servants' livery was hurrying up the drive toward him, but as intent as he'd been on his personal hell, Jonathon hadn't even heard the sound of a carriage arriving.

"Mr. Penley? I'm from the Stratfords, sir. The young Miss—Mrs. Courtland asked me to relay news from a wire she just received from a Dr. Lacey, down in Savannah. The wire concerns the Courtland son."

Jonathon felt something like a shudder ripple through him and he only stood silent, waiting, like a man condemned to be given a death blow. Chase Courtland was dead, then. He had to be.

"It appears that the younger Mr. Courtland is alive, still, at least. Better news for his family than one might have expected to—" The man interrupted himself, beginning to frown as he noted the bleakness of Penley's face. "Oh, I'm sorry. You didn't know he'd been wounded?"

"Yes, I knew." Jonathon's tone was flat, entirely wooden, and the servant's expression subtly changed. He stood another moment as if waiting, then wordlessly began to turn. But behind him, Jonathon came alive again with a sudden intensity. "Wait, I'm sorry—what was it you said? Chase Courtland *is* alive? And the doctor's name? I must have misheard what you said, I'm afraid."

"Dr. Lacey. A friend of Miss Susan's from Washington. He took a ship down to Georgia Monday evening, I believe."

The news had taken a moment to register in Jonathon's distracted mind. It took him another moment to fully assess what the message could mean. The weapon he'd needed. Or the hope of a weapon, at least. Not much maybe, but far better than nothing at all. If anyone could save Chase Courtland's life, Doc Lacey could. Just as he'd saved Jonathon Penley's the year before. Jonathon, too, had suffered a wound categorized as mortal, but Doc Lacey had made a lie out of that grim prognosis and restored the captured Confederate to health. Maybe Lacey could do it again. Maybe he could work a second miracle in much the same manner he had worked the first. At least, as long as there was even a glimmer of that hope, Jonathon would rather continue the war than offer up such a craven surrender. He found himself smiling faintly and he turned once again to Lady Bennington's man. "Go tell Lady Bennington to go to hell. Quote me if you like. Tell her she was a bit overhasty in burying her brother. Tell her that her brother's still alive and just might stay that way. And then tell her I'm going to find a judge somewhere who'll grant an injunction against her bank takeover plans, as well. Can you remember that clearly enough? Or shall I repeat myself?"

Shock wiped the smirk off the manservant's face. Jonathon waited a moment more, then nodded almost pleasantly as he turned back toward the carriage house. He wasn't surprised to find Whitney standing there, framed in the open doorway, her chestnut hair blowing in the chill wind of the cold gray January day. She was shivering with cold but watching him still, and he smiled a kind of grim reassurance as he hurried back toward her. Once a Rebel, always a Rebel, Jonathon thought with cold resolution. And one thing Elinor Courtland Bennington should have learned by now: no matter how lousy the odds they faced, Rebels were damnably slow to surrender. As far as he was concerned, the war wasn't over yet after all.

* * *

The brightness of morning sunlight was unkind to both older women and wounded soldiers. Savannah had both in abundance, and Doc Lacey was frowning as he mounted the stairs of the town-house-turned-officers' hospital, not pleased by that particular insight. Chase Courtland had looked poor enough by the more flattering glow of a single candle last night. This morning, then, he must look even worse. An orderly crossed in the hallway above him and Doc Lacey called out his question in a voice that was already tired and grim. "Captain Reardon?"

The orderly pointed farther down the upstairs hall for his answer. "Busy just now." His continued gaze was a question that Doc Lacey answered over one shoulder as he turned toward the room he'd found Chase lying in last night.

"I'm Doc Lacey, down from Washington to see to Major Courtland. Captain Reardon was off duty when I arrived last night, but when he's got a moment free, would you ask him to stop by, please?" He acknowledged the orderly's grunt of consent with a gesture, not looking back. Two officers—Chase and another desperately wounded young man—shared the first bedroom upstairs on the right. He drew an involuntary sigh as he stepped inside, then froze before he'd even fully closed the door. There was a particular odor in the room, one he'd grown all too familiar with in these past few years. The smell of death. He was suddenly conscious of formulating an anguished prayer, not sure of exactly what he was praying for as he looked toward the bed where Chase Courtland lay.

But it was the other man, not Chase, an artillery lieutenant colonel by the uniform he wore. The death smell thickened as Lacey stepped closer to the lieutenant colonel's bedside. By long habit, he bent to press his hand against the pulse of the neck. There was none, which didn't surprise him. There was only a waxy rigidity to the skin and an unnatural coolness beneath his hand. Lacey turned to draw the bedsheet over the officer's fast-graying face, then glanced up at the sound of a sigh coming from the doorway.

"Captain Reardon?" Doc Lacey straightened up, eyeing the young man who was standing there. Lacey found himself faintly surprised. He'd expected a more typical army field doctor—older, heavier, far dirtier, often half drunk. This young man was in no way typical. "I'm sorry. You just lost a patient, here, I'm afraid."

A vague kind of pain flashed on the young man's face, only momentarily displacing the weariness that seemed a permanent fixture there. And seeing that pain, Doc Lacey eyed him even more sharply. He knew that look; he knew that feeling of defeat. It was rare among doctors who'd seen what they all had these past years—rare to still care—and Doc Lacey was conscious of some vague sense of instant kinship with the young captain. Hardly old enough to be out of school he looked like—but he cared at least, that counted for something. In Lacey's book, in fact, it counted for a great deal. "I'm sorry," Lacey repeated himself, meaning it more this time, as much for the doctor as for the patient. He stepped away from the one bed, starting toward the other where Chase Courtland lay. "I missed you last night, Doctor. I won't take much of your time, but if you could just fill me in on what's been done already for this man—"

"Major Courtland," Reardon interrupted, moving to step toward Doc Lacey. Then he fell silent, frowning either in thought or against the glaring Savannah sunlight streaming in from the nearby window.

Lacey glanced sideways as he slowly nodded. Reardon hadn't needed any medical card to remember Chase's name, and there came a sudden feeling, wishful maybe, that he need not have come down here perhaps—that whatever *could* be done for Chase was *being* done already by this weary but dedicated young man. For an instant, there arose the desperate hope he might yet escape the ultimate responsibility of this particular irony. God knew he wanted to, to let it be someone else, *anyone* else, but him. But the young doctor's next words dispelled that hope.

"I've done all I can, I'm afraid. And it isn't going to be enough." There was frustration evident in the young man's voice and he rather abruptly turned away. "Shoulder wound, there"—he gestured to where white bandages showed on Chase's left shoulder above the blanket edge—"not too bad. I got the bullet out, no broken bones, no excessive bleeding. Sutured it closed. But the other—" He brushed by Doc Lacey almost impatiently, pulling the blankets down. "This is the one. I probed for the bullet but couldn't find it. Only restarted heavy bleeding in the process. I had no choice but to leave it be in the hopes that it would heal itself. Otherwise he'd have died there under the knife. But by yesterday, it was already festering. It's probably worse yet today. That bullet's poisoning him and there isn't a damn thing I can do about it. The man is dying." Reardon straightened up with a crooked smile, his eyes grim and dark as he faced Doc Lacey. "I understand you're down all the way from Washington, Doctor. I hope you hospital surgeons are all you think you are; you won't find this one an easy case."

The responsibility, so desperately unwanted, resettled itself squarely on Lacey's shoulders. He shrugged at it, at the same time trying not to frown at the sting of Reardon's words. Reardon could not know the strain his compatriot was working under. The young man was only tired, and God knew Lacey understood that feeling. Tired and angry and sick to death of being defeated like this time after time, when you cared and you tried, yet you faced the limits of mortality and you just couldn't win. He heard the sounds of orderlies coming in behind him to remove the artillery officer's body and he didn't look around. He'd seen the same sight too many times before. "I was a field medic, too, Doctor—for several years. Major Courtland was my commanding officer. He became my friend. A very good friend. And Washington or Savannah, medicine remains much the same." He paused only a moment, then reached out with one hand, slowly. "Have you scissors? I'd like to look over the wounds with you if you wouldn't mind. Sometimes two heads, medically, are better than one."

Reardon flushed faintly, then yielded. "Yes, of course. Sorry."

"So am I." Lacey spoke softly, not clarifying the strange comment as he took the scissors and turned, forcing himself through every motion. He cleared his throat softly as he examined Chase's shoulder wound, careful not to touch it. Reardon had done a fine job. A clean job, too, he realized. There was only the slightest trace of infection there where the jagged gap showed skin torn from the bullet. He replaced the dressing pad and nodded his approval.

"Some infection, there, though. No matter how careful I am, I can't seem to avoid it," Reardon added.

Lacey nodded distractedly and cut carefully along Chase's stomach bandage. "It comes as a blessed shock to even hear another doctor lament infection, actually. My commanding officer in Washington still commends pus as 'laudable.' I can't seem to eradicate infection either, not entirely. But at least, keeping it to a minimum is a step in—" As Roger lifted the stomach bandages free both his hand and his voice had immediately faltered. There, if ever he'd seen one, was a death wound. "Oh, Christ." Despite himself, his hand shook slightly as he let the bandages fall back over the ugly wound.

"It *is* worse today. Damn. I was afraid it would be."

Lacey had closed his eyes for a moment, and he forced them open again now only with an effort.

"Actually, I guess I *am* glad you're here, Dr. Lacey. I was thinking yesterday that I've only two choices, and I didn't like either one of them. I can do nothing and let Major Courtland die slowly. Or I can try surgery again and kill him quicker." Reardon offered a twisted smile, more grimace than humor, and his eyes were bitter. "Now, you can make that choice. One less on my conscience, thank you."

Oh, God, Roger thought numbly. If you only knew, Captain, you wouldn't thrust that devil's alternative on me, either. Which way would you like to die, Chase? Fast? Or slow? Shall I make Susan a widow today? Or wait out the week?

"Well, Doctor, what shall it be? I'll second your decision either way."

There was sympathy in the young man's tone, but the words still resounded cruelly in the silence that followed. For an absurd instant, Lacey thought of wiring Susan, of letting it be her choice instead. And then he realized instantly how cowardly that was. In his agitation, he turned away too abruptly and knocked Reardon's hand as he moved. The scissors gleamed sharp silver as they fell out of the younger man's hand. Lacey lunged for them, managing only to deflect their fall, and they slashed Chase's bare thigh.

Reardon was ashen, badly shaken by the mishap. "I'm sorry, Major. I'm tired, I guess. Clumsy today." He reached hastily for a cloth, dunking it into a nearby water bowl.

As Roger took the cloth from the young man's hand, he noted its shaking and only shook his own head in dismissal. "Don't worry over it. No harm's done." He washed the shallow wound almost carelessly, frowning with the sensation of something gone somehow awry. Then he raised his head to throw a long, thoughtful glance at Reardon. "Did his leg move? Did you notice? When the scissors hit. Or with the cold water?"

The young captain only shrugged, as if confused. "His leg? No, I don't think so. Why?"

"But Chase moved when I pulled those stomach bandages free."

"Well, yes. He did yesterday, too, when I took a look. I was in hopes, then, he might regain consciousness, but—" Reardon broke off in surprise as Doc Lacey reached to reclaim the scissors with a sudden gesture.

"You watch." Lacey held the scissors point down and made a single, sharp stabbing motion against Chase's leg. Nothing. Not a single damn thing. He turned in the same motion to press the sharp point against Chase's wrist. There, the fingers clenched briefly—almost imperceptibly—but they did move. He was conscious of a faint, but instant surge of exhilaration— gone before he could capture it. But its mere presence reassured him as nothing else in his life had ever done. If he was capable still, of that, then perhaps he wasn't so guilt-lost after all. "He's got no reflex reaction in his leg. It's a guess, of course, but it may mean the bullet is—"

A soft moan interrupted and Roger turned, following the young doctor's startled glance in time to see Chase Courtland's eyes drift open, slowly shut and then reopen once again.

"Chase?" Roger leaned closer, knowing the wounded man's vision would be poor. "Chase, it's me, Lacey. Can you hear me?"

A slight movement of Chase's dark head on the bright, sunlit white of the pillow was his answer. Roger reached to grip Chase's shoulder, desperate for even a moment's consciousness. No matter what he decided it was probably going to mean Chase's death. So let it be Chase's choice, he thought suddenly. God could be that merciful to them all at least. In the years to come it might make all the difference in Lacey's living with himself. "Chase, we've got a decision to make. Today, before you get any weaker. You've a bullet still, somewhere in your—"

"Leighton?"

It was a slurred sound, little more than a groan and Roger didn't understand. He shook his head, impatient, starting to speak again.

"Leighton, did we get him?"

Roger understood Chase's words this time. He hesitated for a fraction of an instant, trying to recall Grier's words and wondering what the best answer, regardless of truth, would be. "Yes. Grier says he did."

"Fair trade, then." Chase had already closed his eyes. Doc Lacey reached to shake his shoulder, forcing him to reopen them.

"Chase, listen to me, it's important. We have to decide whether to risk surgery again. It is dangerous, of course, your losing more blood. But without surgery, I'm afraid that bullet will kill you anyway. It's a gamble I know, but I think it's our only real—"

"No." It was barely a whisper, and Chase's eyes closed again as he spoke. "No."

For an instant, Doc Lacey merely stared at Chase's face, astonished. No? Why not, for God's sake? Why not at least try? "Chase!" There was no further response and he shook his friend's shoulder almost angrily. "Chase!" He stood motionless a moment more, then let his hand slowly drop. Well, he'd wanted Chase to be the one to choose . . . and now in a sense, he guessed he had. But it wasn't the choice he'd expected Chase to make, and all Lacey's instincts told him that it was the wrong one. The surgery—risky or not—was the only chance Chase had for life. By denying that chance, in Lacey's opinion, Chase was only choosing slow death. Damn you, Chase, Lacey swore in silent anger! Couldn't you make it just a little bit easy for me? If it were anyone else but Chase Courtland on that bed, Lacey would overrule that decision without so much as a second thought, proceed instead on his own best instincts . . . but if his instincts were wrong *this* time, if Chase died during the surgery or even because of it, Lacey would always wonder at the motives behind the choice he had made. Medicine, after all, was not a realm of absolutes. At best, it was a realm of probabilities. There *was* some small chance that Chase's choice was the right one. And if Lacey overruled Chase, he would have no one but himself to blame if Chase should subsequently die. Lacey shook his head in abrupt decision, already beginning to turn away from the bed. There were too many years ahead to risk being wrong on this one. Too many years to wonder what he'd done, and why he'd really done it. "I'll be going back to Washington, then, Captain. You don't need me here just to change bloody bandages. Good luck."

Reardon reached for Lacey's arm as he began to brush by,

stopping him. "I don't understand you. You started earlier to say something about—"

"It doesn't matter, now. There's nothing more I can do here; he doesn't want to risk the surgery. You heard him, Doctor, and so did I."

A strange, almost stubborn expression momentarily flickered in the young captain's tired eyes. "No, I didn't hear him. I didn't hear anything. And besides, I usually act on *my* decisions, not on my patients'. Apparently you Washington surgeons reverse that procedure, then, do you?"

That question stopped Roger in his tracks and he slowly turned as Reardon continued. "If you have—even if you only *think* you have a notion where that bullet might be, for God's sake tell me, Doctor. *Then* leave if you want. Go back to Washington. I'll take the responsibility. I'll proceed on my own from there."

There was a long silence, left deliberately hanging like a waiting challenge. In its wake, there was only the sound of water dripping somewhere, and from down the hall, a distant groan. "You mean you'd choose surgery whether or not I were here to perform it?" Lacey's had locked on Reardon's for a long minute before he'd finally spoken.

"I mean if you know where that bullet is, for the love of Christ, *tell* me, Major! The last thing I want to do is to spend an extra quarter of an hour digging around to try to find it. He hasn't got that much blood left to lose."

There was another long silence. While it lasted, a dozen emotions crested and passed in Lacey's mind, but there was no denying the challenge in Reardon's eyes. That challenge mandated an answer. This much of the responsibility, at least, Lacey wasn't going to be able to duck. "The bullet's in his back, maybe, I've seen it before. Men shot in the center of the back sometimes lose even reflex reaction below such a wound. But I'd better remind you, that's only my guess."

"Thank you, then, Doctor. It's been a real pleasure meeting you. Good-bye."

There was another silence, short and cuttingly dismissing. Reardon meant to try surgery anyway, that much was clear. And what if Reardon was right? God, why had Chase said no? Maybe because Chase knew, too, where that bullet had lodged. Maybe because he knew he was risking a long life as an invalid, paralyzed, and he preferred death. And maybe, weakened and drugged as he was, he hadn't even understood the question. Had it only been what Roger had wanted to hear? If it hadn't been Chase, would he even have asked? "No, I'll stay." Lacey cringed inwardly to even say the words, but he forced them out before his courage could break. "I'll stay and do the surgery myself. Because if anyone can pull this kind of a gamble off, I can. I've had a whole year of nothing but practice in Washington." Plus, I'm the one who offered Chase his choice, Lacey continued silently. Rightfully or wrongfully, I did ask. So if I can save him—whole—then the hell with his lack of permission. But if I can't do that, and he still chooses death, then I'll stay to be sure he dies as painlessly as possible. It has nothing to do with Susan either, he tried to tell himself, no sort of bargain with fate for a last chance to claim the women he loved. It was only a compromise he felt obligated to make before overruling a friend's decision . . . but if a portion of Lacey's mind hadn't clung so stubbornly to doubts regarding the real reason for that last agonized and private concession, he would have been far less anguished as he brushed by Reardon toward the door. "No sense wasting time then, I guess. I'll wash up, Captain. If you'd be kind enough to prepare a table and assist, I would appreciate it."

Barely moments later, the thing was upon him. Captain Reardon was not about to give him time to change his mind, Doc Lacey thought numbly. All was in readiness before Lacey's hands were even dry from their bath in lime chloride. But at his first sight of what lay now ahead of him, he hesitated in the doorway of what had once been the house's formal dining room and found himself momentarily unable to move. For the first time since that awful July of 1861, the first of treating battle-wounded, his stomach felt half sick again. And he swallowed against a telltale dryness in his throat. God, don't shake, he ordered his hands in anguished prayer. Don't shake now, please. Not after all these years. But still, they did shake as he forced himself into the room.

Reardon had laid Chase facedown on a pine board, stoked the fire higher and covered the unconscious major with only a single snow-white sheet. A young woman nurse stood looking frightened and pale, waiting in silence by Chase Courtland's head. Brass and silver surgical knives were neatly laid out on a small pile of folded white cloths; bandages lay in careful rolls beside them. Lacey managed to nod to the younger doctor and forced himself forward toward the table. As he stopped there he allowed himself only one swift glance down at the man who lay there beneath his hand. A friend, he thought. A good one. More *that*, he told himself, than Susan's husband. Finally, he felt his hands begin to steady enough to reach for a knife.

"What's your choice for anesthetic if we need it? Ether or chloroform?"

The question startled him out of his private hell, and Lacey shrugged.

"Ether, if it's good."

"It is."

He nodded, glancing down to the knives. Faint shadows of wetness lay beneath them. They had been cleaned then, already. There was no reason for delay. "I've got the Confederate prisoners in Washington. I hear from them that their army's pretty much out of both. And we've got our choice of either. Seems almost unfair, doesn't it?"

It was Reardon's turn to shrug—not a callous gesture, simply one of a horror known and accepted. "They should give up."

"Yes, I agree. Unfortunately, *they* don't." Lacey turned to face the young nurse and slowly nodded. "You've done this before?"

"Only once or twice. I'm afraid."

"All right. Just do what I say, then, but listen carefully. What's your name?" Lacey had glanced back at Chase, reaching to pull the sheet down as he spoke.

"Susan," the nurse answered in a faltering voice.

Her answer startled him. Involuntarily, he glanced up. "Susan?" He caught himself and nodded almost at once, returning his gaze to Chase's bare back. "My nurse in Washington was a Susan also. Susan Courtland. She was a godsend, an invaluable help."

He didn't realize the young doctor was watching him as he spoke, but he was—and Captain Reardon noted the emotion that momentarily softened Lacey's grimly set face. It answered the question he'd asked himself earlier. More than any mere friendship, then, had brought the Washington doctor down to Savannah. "Susan Courtland? The major's sister, I assume?" Reardon smiled.

"No." There was only the most momentary pause. "No, his wife." Lacey's eyes were still fixed on Chase's bare back as he selected a small, razor-edged knife. He missed the sudden, quick reaction in Reardon's eyes, the instantaneous glance of doubt given to the scalpel already gleaming in Lacey's hand. Doc Lacey kept his own eyes fixed on Chase, trying to shut out all the turbulent emotion those last few words had reagitated. Forget her, he ordered himself. Forget everything else. Pretend it's a stranger lying there instead. God, he would have to. Or he would be totally unable to proceed any further. "Are you ready, Doctor?"

Lacey's voice was entirely emotionless and Reardon managed a nod, stepping forward. There was no time to second-guess any decisions now anyway. Doc Lacey was already searching the bare skin of the major's back, with narrowed eyes and a careful hand. Where is the bullet? he was asking himself. And where is that gut instinct that usually tells me? Reardon is right about Chase not losing much more blood. What if I've guessed wrong? What if I cut and I kill him, and then can't even find the damn bullet at all? What will I tell her then? What will I tell myself?

"Look. That faint bruise, there." Reardon gestured down with a jab, repressing a silent sigh of relief. He signaled over Lacey's shoulder to the orderly, calling wordlessly for more light.

Roger saw the bruise and slowly checked for the lump that might be beneath it. It could be; it should be. A long minute passed, slowly, and in silence. The knife in his hand gleamed overbright; he could feel the distant ticking of the foyer clock. God, I can't do this, he thought in final anguished decision. I can't trust myself. Sweat had started on his forehead and palms already. Sweat from the fire, he told myself and knew it for a lie. God forgive me, I just can't do this. What if the damn knife slips?

"Go ahead, Doctor. You're the best shot he has." Reardon had stepped closer to speak in a grim undertone. "Go on, for God's sake! I didn't even get to this part of medical school before I enlisted."

That startled him. Lacey glanced up and read a strange kind of anguished frustration in the younger man's eyes. That silent anger steadied him as nothing else probably could have— reminded him of a time before Susan or Chase or anything else, when he'd been just like Reardon; the only enemy, then, had been death. He drew a deeper breath and then nodded one time in resolution. "All right, watch how it's done, Captain. I'll give you a lesson you won't soon forget."

The bullet was exactly where he'd guessed it to be. It was an ugly black color, surrounded by swollen red tissue and the yellow pus of poison wedged against a mass of what looked like gray hairs that twisted out from the bones of the back—gray hairs that meant the difference of a man walking or lying in bed the rest of his life Lacey reminded himself. So don't force it, he warned himself. Take your time. Don't rip it out like panic would have you do; don't think about how fast the blood is pooling; don't think about how desperately Chase can't afford to lose anymore. He used the probe with infinite care, nudging the bullet slowly loose. Then the forceps could grip its blood-slippery cylinder. With each slow breath Chase made, Lacey moved it out a little further, not noticing that his hand was finally rock steady, not noticing either the intensity or the growing respect in young Reardon's watching eyes.

Chase moaned suddenly, a soft whisper that, in the silence of the room, was like a cannon shot. Doc Lacey didn't move his hand, but the command in his voice snapped like a whip. "Anesthetic—three drops. Hurry!"

Reardon glanced up to make sure the nurse reached for the can of ether, but he didn't notice how badly the young woman's hands were shaking as she poured the anesthetic out. He had already turned back, leaning down to hold the wounded major's shoulders still—because if Courtland moved now, he killed himself. He kept his grip hard, felt a soft, half sigh beneath his hands and only dared to watch sidelong as Doc Lacey used that momentary muscular easing to slide the bullet fully out.

For a moment, Lacey merely stared down at the thing with a vague sort of surprise. Thank you, God. The thought came with a shocking, almost sickening intensity. Thank you for making it be so easy. So quick. It's out of my hands now. Oh thank God, it was over. "Close up." Even his own words seemed strange and distant, the familiar action of turning to drop the bloody bullet into waiting water absurdly anticlimatic. Reardon had turned, offering him a threaded needle, and Lacey blotted at the draining blood and pale yellow poison almost casually. Six stitches. Eight. Nine. His hand froze suddenly in midair. His whole body grew rigid. Instinct. Something was wrong. Something was missing. What?

Doc Lacey lunged for the scissors with a sudden move, severing the thread. Then he grabbed past Reardon for the waiting bandages, merely throwing them over the undressed incision. "Get him over!" He had a momentary glimpse of the young medic staring openmouthed, and he shoved him backward, throwing the long ends of the rolled-up bandages into his hands. "Get him over, damn it! He's not breathing!"

To his credit, Reardon moved instantly, remembering only by instinct to pull hard on the bandage ends as he struggled with Courtland's dead weight. From the corner of his eye, he noticed the Washington doctor's desperate lunge to knock the ether-soaked cloth away from Chase's face, ignoring the startled, frightened cry of the girl as he turned back again toward the table. "Breathe, Chase! *Breathe*, damn you, Chase!"

Reardon had the sensation—almost frightening—of some tremendous, nearly physical energy bursting from the man as he moved. A furious command, an awesome will hurled like a weapon against a merciless enemy. He could only stand frozen, watching him in shock.

"Chase, breathe, damn you!" Lacey leaned across the table, shouting in anger. He raised one hand to deliver a sharp, stinging blow to Chase's paling face. One and then another, with no reaction. He turned then on one heel, making a fist and raising it high, letting it drop like a hammer into Chase's bandaged midriff. A faint whisper of the last air being driven out of his lungs touched the sudden silence like a soft farewell, and Reardon stared, beginning to shake. Then there was another sound. Faint, like the other. A breath being slowly drawn, almost a sigh. Chase moaned softly on the exhale and Reardon glanced involuntarily at the man's slowly moving belly muscles, almost expecting to see something physical, some evidence of the miracle he'd just witnessed. There was nothing except a slow-spreading stain of fresh blood on the bandages. Doc Lacey turned and followed Reardon's gaze, shaking his head slowly, suddenly weary unto death.

"Sorry." His voice was a croak, an immense effort. He cleared his throat, raising his hand to gesture at the blood still very slowly spreading. "I'm afraid I undid some of your earlier work, there, Doctor. I'll repair it later."

Reardon managed to shake his head, shrugging. "That's . . . think nothing of it. What happened?"

"Too much ether. She soaked the damn cloth." Roger drew a deep sigh as he spoke, raising his hand to gesture the orderly to return Chase to his room. It wasn't over, he warned himself wearily. The last test remained to be made. Now he would see whose choice had been wisest—Chase's or theirs. If that leg only moved. If it did, he'd won. Lost Susan, perhaps, but not his soul, not his sanity. Good God, he was tired. Tired of anguish and choices all mired in contradictions. Tired of examining his own soul under a microscope and doubting its honesty. At least he knew that now. At least he knew how he really felt, who he really was, a doctor still first. When Chase had quit breathing, he had not thought of Susan. Had not thought of anything but the urgency, the necessity of forcing that next, priceless breath in and out. "I'll go with him, if you don't mind, Captain. If he wakes, I'd like to speak to him. If not, I'll leave instructions before I go to send a telegram north."

Roger didn't wait long. He stood by his friend's bedside for a few moments silently, gathering the courage to make that final test. With the pressure of the bullet removed, Chase should be fine. And he was. He moaned a soft protest and moved his leg away from the irritation of the ice-cold water. Doc Lacey sighed slowly, and a private pain lingered darkly in his eyes. Almost like a mother with a sick but favored child, he leaned down before he turned to go, touching Chase's bare shoulder briefly. The gesture was affection and apology both, and his voice was a whisper when he finally spoke. "I'm sorry, Chase. I could have accepted your decision and let that solve it, maybe. Save us all a lot of future pain, perhaps. But I couldn't. I just couldn't. I had the best chance in the world and I threw it away, and now we're all left in the same damn mess we started in, aren't we? But the damnedest part of all is that I don't regret it a bit." He waited a last moment, wordless, and frowning now. Then he turned on one heel to send a bittersweet telegram to Susan.

Chapter Twelve

The days since that bloody, rain-soaked Saturday of the ambush had passed as if in a living nightmare for Leanna. Days and nights were distinguishable only by light or the lack of it, for fear of the Yankees who might be pursuing kept the guerrillas moving twenty-four hours a day—waking and sleeping in their saddles, stumbling a few miles on foot beside their equally exhausted horses. Food was infrequent, cold, and eaten out of hand; rest was unthinkable; sleep only dead exhaustion stolen out of hysterical fear. Swampy fields, small nameless creeks, stands of pine scrub, knee-deep marshes— they struggled through them a first time only to see them endlessly repeated. And always, passing like a whisper from one man to the nest, the fear that haunted them, drove them unmercifully, clung to them like a living thing, cold and oppressive as a death shroud: the Yankees; the Yankees. They'd long ago ceased to question whether the fear was valid or not. They did not pause to send back scouts; they did not stop at the ridge of high ground to search the countryside behind them. Leaderless now, the small group—Leanna, still on young MacRae's saddle, and two others from Stewart's shattered band—simply followed their fear instead, obeying its command without question, each man's terror feeding off the next's. Like stampeding animals, Leanna had begun to think, they would run like this out of blind panic until they dropped dead in their tracks. Carrion birds would pick at their flesh, dust would slowly bury their bones, and in a way, because it seemed inescapable, Leanna had almost resigned herself to just such a fate.

But at sunset today, they had crossed the Savannah River out of Georgia and entered into the deeper swamps of South Carolina. And immediately, she had felt a change. The fear had begun to subside, the heat of the panic began to cool.

They were in the very cradle of the Confederacy. Lathered horses were finally slowed to a walk. Men paused to refill empty canteens. And then, with the coming of dusk, they had unbelievably stopped to make camp. Leanna had left a fire burning and supper cooking to seek the nearby creek. Caked by the mud and filth of such reckless flight—and more, dirtied by some less physical feeling of horror and death and shame—she felt she simply must cleanse herself or die. She had washed her hair even, despite the ice coldness of the creek water, and she was shivering now as she reached for her underclothes. North by less than a hundred miles from Savannah where orange trees would be blossoming and camellias blooming, here in the woods of the ever-present South Carolina pine, it was already colder. The few hardwoods she could see had lost their leaves and not yet budded again to herald spring. But more than the chill breeze of the coming darkness made her hurry her dressing to return to camp. Too many ghosts now haunted the brooding silence of the dark woods around her: Stewart, Chase, her unborn child fathered by one man and murdered by the other. She knew by now from John MacRae that both men had been wounded to their deaths in that bloody meadow, and *she* carried the secret guilt of knowing why. Partly for the larger war, yes. North versus South, Union versus Confederacy. But partly, too, for *her*. Stewart, obsessed by revenge, no longer even totally rational. And Chase not the man to back away from any confrontation, angry, perhaps, too, at Stewart—and at her, believing as truth those terrible lies she'd last told him in Atlanta. If she had not killed either man by her very own hand, still the responsibility of setting such a fate in motion could only be hers. And now she could not close her eyes without seeing one of their faces—cold and pale, drawn in lines of a bloody death. Stewart, her husband, whom she had betrayed. Chase, her beloved Yankee, whose hated uniform had not kept her from loving the man who'd worn it. Guilt and sin and terrible shame. Her world betrayed by loving Chase; her love betrayed by leaving him, because she could not bring herself to that final denial of her beloved South, could not love him enough to sacrifice everything else so precious to her. And then, in final bitter irony, she had seen her world shattered, and everything else lost anyway—leaving her now with nothing at all.

A twig crackled somewhere nearby in the shadows, catching her ear, and briefly she glanced up. She saw nothing, and shuddered superstitiously—hurrying more with the buttons of her long skirt. The woods were full of wild creatures, she told herself. Ghosts walked only in children's nightmares. Still, she reached hurriedly for her blouse, trying to ignore the trembling of her hands. Another twig snapped, closer this time, and she turned with an involuntary cry. Only a man stood there, barely visible among the tree shadows, and she dared breathe again, relieved. "I'm not finished yet. I'll be back to camp in a moment."

"There ain't no reason to hurry none." The man stepped forward as he spoke, emerging into moonlight. At his approach, Leanna felt the first whisper of fear brush her soul. For a moment, her fingers paused on her half-buttoned blouse and she glanced in the direction of the distant camp. He was alone.

"I'd have saved me some work, it appears, to have come a mite sooner."

In the moonlight, Leanna had no trouble seeing the way the man's eyes flickered over her half-buttoned blouse, then dipped lower to the dark cloth of her skirt. She felt a moment's utter shock, and took a single, faltering step away from him. "No." At the first realization of the expression glittering in his eyes, her voice was startled, more pleading than angry.

"C'mon, now. Sooner we begin, sooner it's over."

She felt the cold, rough-scaled bark of a pine-tree trunk beneath her hand as she instinctively backed away. Her bare foot caught in a root and she stumbled as she turned to face him. Her plea, and the look of revulsion that paled her face had not deterred him in the slightest apparently. Her heart began to pound in sick horror, and a treacherous weakness trembled in her knees. She spared a last glance behind her, and then another one past him, searching the silent shadows in growing desperation. Only the creek and darker woods lay behind her; and he blocked any escape toward where the others were camped. "You lay so much as one hand on me and I'll scream. I swear I will, and the others will come."

He was only a dozen feet from her by now, close enough for her to see lust in his eyes and a smile on his bearded face. "You do that, Mrs. Leighton." His smile widened momentarily to a grin. "By the time they get here, I'll be done with you anyway and they can have their turn."

Even as he spoke, he made a sudden lunge toward her— feinting first to one side, then catching Leanna's arm with a laugh as she instinctively bolted toward the other.

"No, please!" The words burst helplessly from her as he dragged her down toward the rough floor of the woods. "Oh, God, don't!" She felt his hands fasten on her like iron clamps, hurting as she struggled against his far greater strength. In only moments, he had overwhelmed her, lay panting hoarsely above her, and Leanna's body was pinned beneath his. He buried his face against the soft breasts that curved beneath the half-buttoned front of her blouse, and with a cry, she twisted her face away from his, clawing and writhing but still in his hold. The untrimmed whiskers of his beard scraped her face and her throat raw as he rubbed it carelessly against her, dipping one filthy, calloused hand into her camisole to free one breast to his mouth. As his lips covered it, hot and dripping wet, she could feel his hand sliding downward over her, reaching for the closure of her skirt to unfasten the buttons with clumsy haste. It did not free enough of her body even unbuttoned, so he pulled at it angrily, rubbing himself on her leg in panting anticipation. Leanna felt the shock as he pulled at her skirt, felt a momentary, breathless hope as he struggled with its stubbornness, and she redoubled her own efforts to try to free herself. But in the next instant, the fabric had ripped, and there was the sudden feel of his hands on her over her underclothes. "No, No. Oh, God, no, please." Tears felt like fire on her cheeks, stinging the skin scraped raw by his beard, and she only moaned the words in helpless desperation. His fingers had found the edge of her worn, cotton petticoat. He ripped that and the drawers beneath, with a single easy pull. She felt him move his hand then, touching her hungrily, then retreating to his own trousers to free himself for that final movement.

Suddenly, his head was jerked back from her breast, and he gave a single grunt of snarling surprise. Leanna had a split-second impression of a knife flashing silver in the moonlight and a dark scarlet spurt of blood issuing from a severed jugular. Before she could even open her mouth to scream, he was gone. John MacRae was there instead, looking grim and angry in the silvered blackness of the night. He knelt over her, opening his arms, and Leanna moved into them with a wracking sob.

She had no idea how long she stayed there like that, sobbing and shaking, mindlessly seeking shelter in the young man's arms. But finally, her terror began to lessen, her tears to slow, and she was aware of his hand stroking her tangled, wet hair, aware of her face pressed to the warmth of his shoulder and the soft murmurs he made against her ear. There was some good left after all, she thought in a kind of dazed relief. Someone left in the world who would make the effort to protect her yet. She opened her eyes, looking up to thank him, and she found his pale eyes strangely unreadable. Then she felt him take one arm away from where he'd cradled her, dropping his hand to the tangled, ruined fabric of her skirt as if to straighten it. She realized abruptly that she must be exposed still, and she sat up straighter to try to cover herself. But her hand froze halfway to her skirt. MacRae's fingers were busy at his own clothing, not at hers. He was unbuttoning the closure of his trouser front. For an instant, she could only stare, uncomprehending and bewildered. And even as she stared he unbuttoned the last button and reached in his pants to withdraw his fully engorged member.

With a stunning jolt—like lightning striking her—comprehension dawned. Leanna's eyes flew wide open, and she gave a soft, shocked gasp, instinctively trying to pull away. But MacRae held her in a no less unbreakable grip than had the first man. And the moonlight did not allow her even the kindness of invisibility—it etched all of him and all of her in clear visibility to her horror-stricken eyes. Still holding his rigid member to guide himself within her, MacRae raised his hips to roll over atop her, dropping his head toward her breast. Leanna made a late and futile attempt to escape then, but her hips arching in a struggle to avoid him only accomodated MacRae the more easily. She felt him plunge within her like a spear, her cries and her continued struggles passing all unheeded.

At last it was over. He had the decency to lay still, at least, on her—in her still. She felt MacRae raise his head and she turned her own away—silent, closing her eyes in horror and pain.

"I been wantin' you from the first I laid eyes on you." His voice was hoarse now against her ear, and she shuddered at both its touch and its words. "Now yer husband's dead and yer on your own, so you'll be my woman now. Better get used to that. You belong to me. I won't let anybody else have you anymore. I'll kill anybody that tries."

She made no reply. Not even a denial. There was none she could make that was anything more than a wishful lie. MacRae's weight was heavy on her still, his member still within her, the warm liquid of his leavings trickling slowly out to wet the pine-wood floor beneath her. For a girl who had once stood at the top of a beautiful, unshattered Southern world, it had been a long fall down to this—to being used as a whore on a dirty forest floor. At the thought, something died within her, something was left cold and weary and strangely numb. And though she'd struggled the first time, she didn't the second, nor the third. By the time the dawn came, the once proud, pampered and lovely Leanna Penley Leighton had become as much a ghost as any of the others she'd thought of just earlier tonight. The reality left was only a Georgia guerrilla's unwilling but helpless whore.

By Saturday, the fourteenth of January, Sherman's army was hoping to leave Savannah in a new campaign. Grant, in Virginia, had given permission to his subordinate to chase the Rebels into South Carolina and to deal that first seceded state an avenging blow of what Sherman regarded as divine justice. No less a personage than Secretary of War Stanton had traveled down from Washington for a last visit with the general—some said to ascertain whether Sherman's reported callousness toward black-slave refugees was actual or only imagined by rumor mongers in the North. Some said the visit was prompted by the hope it was *true*. In light of the eccentric general's lightning-swift conquest of Georgia, his political power, should he choose to weild it, could be awesome indeed. A taint of bigotry could help to curb it. But Sherman was not interested in politics. Given a choice, he said, of the White House or a penitentiary, he said he would "take the penitentiary, thank you." The Secretary of the ever-more-powerful Department of War returned to Washington rested and reassured in every way, and passed the comforting news along an ever-growing network of personal and political allies. Things looked better than ever for the Philadelphia coalition and others like it.

But in Savannah itself, the rains that had started the first week of January were still continuing. The river was high, muddy brown and swollen, and a light drizzle fell today again from pale gray skies. Doc Lacey hurried his step from the street to the house and tossed his rain-soaked cloak to one side with a grimace as he entered. "Damn weather," he muttered. "Worse than Washington's."

But Reardon's only reply was an amused, wry smile, and Lacey began to frown a slow question to it. Before the young doctor could speak, though, Roger noticed Grier standing in one corner of the room and he turned in surprise toward the cavalry captain. "What are you still doing here? I thought you were marching out today."

"The pontoon bridge collapsed—damn near drowned Smith's command. So we're not leaving after all, not until the river goes down," Grier explained.

"Oh." Lacey nodded, standing a moment. The rain had some good points after all, then, it seemed. It had delayed the damn war awhile. Good.

Reardon stepped forward to gesture up the stairs, and what he had to say erased Lacey's momentary pleasure. "Your Major Courtland is being uncooperative, refusing to take the morphine this morning. I'm looking forward to seeing how a hotshot Washington surgeon handles mutiny, doctor."

Lacey swore softly, surprised, then quickly frowned. "We hotshot surgeons are inclined to hold the man down and give him a double dose for sheer spite, actually. Give me the morphine. I'll go up and handle my obstreperous major." He stopped on the stairs, glancing over his shoulder at Grier's sudden movement after him.

"Doc, wait! It's my fault, I think. When the march was delayed, I found myself with some time on my hands. I figured I'd come over and help the major pass the morning."

Lacey paused in surprise, holding Grier's eyes. He read wry apology and more—and he slowly descended the stairs again toward him. "So what is it, then? What's the problem?"

Grier shrugged, and replied in an undertone. "I told him . . . well, we were talking about the ambush. Leighton's. And I mentioned that Cowles thought he saw a woman in Leighton's camp just before they opened fire."

Lacey's frown deepened. For a moment, he only waited,

puzzled, and then he nodded slowly. "Oh, I see. *Mrs.* Leighton?"

"Cowles didn't know. Sounded like her though." Grier's expression lay somewhere between anger and apology. "I didn't think twice about it, Doc. I guess I should have after Virginia and Atlanta, but Christ! Since then, the major bedded every warm-eyed widow from Atlanta to Savannah! And he went home and married that girl of his."

"He married Susan. Yes, I know." Lacey had turned instantly away to conceal his eyes. Confusion lingered on Grier's face, but Roger merely shrugged a disinclination to try to explain. He could understand Grier's confusion, but he thought he could almost have anticipated Chase's reaction, too. So Leanna Leighton had resurfaced again. And that old attraction was still powerful apparently. He'd seen Chase and Leanna together last year in Virginia, seen the formation there of an awesome bond between them, a guilty bond perhaps, but nonetheless a compelling one. And like Lacey's own guilty bond to Susan Stratford Courtland, Chase's to Leanna was slow to die. It's not that easy, Grier, Lacey wanted to say, when the woman you love wears another man's wedding ring; maybe you try a little harder to *pretend*—sometimes to yourself, and always to others. But there were times when the pretense slipped—God knew Lacey himself was proof of that. And so, perhaps, was Chase Courtland—in spite of his marriage to Susan. There might well be a bond yet, voluntary or not, that linked Chase to his former lover.

"It wasn't just that, though." Grier was continuing on as if unmindful of any undercurrents of tension in Lacey's long silence. "McLeod on staff asked me to deliver a letter that came for Chase, a letter from the family's lawyer, I gather. It seems like the fellow must have written it not knowing the major'd been wounded. And I guess all hell's broke loose up North since the major left to come back to Savannah and this lawyer was sending down an SOS to try to warn him. The major's sister is giving somebody fits and there's something about bank stock to be voted. This lawyer wanted to know if Chase had ever assigned some proxy he'd had made, or if Chase wanted the lawyer to begin court action to appoint his father's power of attorney."

"What?"

Grier shrugged to Doc Lacey's frown of startled question.

"I don't know. The major asked me to read it to him—and then he got hot enough to shoot somebody."

"That's just about where I came in," Reardon interjected with a wry smile. "And he made a quite nasty suggestion about what I should do with my morphine. Needed his head clear, he said. Not that I understand where he thinks he's going—clear head, or no."

"He's going *nowhere*. For some time yet, actually." Lacey's expression was grim, nearly angry as he started up the stairs again, taking them two at a time in his hurry. "He only even regained consciousness two days ago. Chase is damn lucky that he's even alive."

He had reached the doorway of Chase's room still angry, but there he had paused suddenly, shocked by the agony he could see written inside on Chase Courtland's face. Agony as patent as that could not help but give rise to sympathy that mellowed even a doctor's anger, but still Lacey frowned as he strode toward the bed. He knew Chase well enough to know that he dared not offer even a hint of possible compromise, sympathetic or not. "Chase, you damn fool! What's this about refusing your morphine?"

Until Lacey had actually spoken, Chase had been unaware of the surgeon's entrance. He forced his eyes open immediately now, despite a rising sea of agony that washed his body from head to foot, pain that left him shaking as it surged and passed, then surged again relentlessly. It was an incredible effort to try to think. But think he must, pain or no. "I've got to get up, Roger. Too many questions need to get answered. Everything's come apart up home, I think. I ought to get back . . . straighten it out . . ."

"You're going *nowhere*, Chase, not for some time yet. For one thing, you've got a touch of pneumonia I think. And going anywhere, especially back to the cold dampness of a Northern winter is absolutely out of the question!"

"But pneumonia's common with this bad a wound. And pneumonia or not—"

"Common maybe, but nonetheless dangerous," Lacey interrupted. Even as he spoke he was watching Chase's face—the frown that had gathered more surely there simply with the effort of speech. And shortly there came the soft sound of an expected half cough and the choked moan of pain that immediately followed it. In anticipation of a worse spasm,

Lacey turned to reach behind himself for a bed pillow, holding it in one hand as he hurriedly continued. "I knew last winter you were determined to try to get yourself killed, Chase. And you damn near succeeded *once* already. Now I came all the way down here from Washington to keep you alive, and by God—with or without your help, I'm going to *do* that."

"Roger, help me get up. Please. I've got to get up."

"*No!* Now you listen to me, Chase! I don't care what Grier told you or what that damn letter said either. You're to forget it for now. You'll only kill yourself trying to do anything about it just yet."

A groan was his only answer as Chase made an effort to move on his own.

"Damn you, Chase! Stay put!" Lacey snapped the order like a whip, startled. Chase ignored him, and Lacey moved toward the bed to enforce the command. "Chase, you damn fool, be still! Your main concern just now has to be staying alive. Forget your sister, forget your lawyer, forget Jonathon Penley and that damn bank too! Forget everything else Grier told you this morning. Including Leanna Leighton, if that's partly what's behind this nonsense. If you reopen those wounds and lose more blood, your prognosis could still change in a hurry."

Chase started to speak an angry denial, but the cough came instead—a loose, choking sound. Swearing, Lacey threw the pillow down hard over Chase's still-bandaged stomach and reached one arm tightly beneath his shoulders. Before the first cough had died, he heard the next gathering already, and he gripped Chase harder as others followed in succession, holding him motionless against the wracking agony as the spasm ripped brutally at torn stomach muscles. A moan that was nearly a sob signaled the final end of it, and Lacey shook his head in angry but anguished sympathy. He knew Chase too damn well. What Grier had told him earlier was akin to waving a red flag at a bull. Injured or not, the animal would obey its instincts and charge . . . or try to. Chase was as much a victim of the way he was made as anyone else and was simply not able to dismiss a responsibility he considered rightfully his.

Roger waited a moment longer to be sure the coughing spasm was over, then he slowly reached one hand out toward the small brown glass bottle of morphine. Chase's face was ash-white with pain, his eyes closed against it. Lacey said nothing more, merely measured a strong dose into the nearby water glass and put it to Chase's mouth in silent command. "Here, swallow this. Now." He raised Chase's head in his arm, expecting no further protest and getting none. But he waited in silence until the liquid was fully drained, and only then allowed himself a single, soft sigh of relief. "All right, Chase. I'll make a deal with you. I understand a little bit how you feel, so you obey Reardon's and my orders for now, and later this week, I'll back off on the morphine. I'll wire Susan and ask her what's going on up there, all right? I'll have her relay down whatever information you could possibly need to give you your answers to those questions at least. But you stay here in Savannah for that pneumonia you've got. And you stay in bed until I say otherwise. Understand?"

Even as he spoke he had begun to feel the slight easing of Chase's pain-rigid muscles, the easier rhythm of his friend's ragged breathing, and Chase only nodded once in wordless answer. The morphine was taking hold, quickly, he thought. Thank God. He held Chase a moment more, then eased him back down slowly. Christ, he thought! Usually, the trouble came in taking a patient *off* the potent drug, not in keeping him *on* it. Damn, what a mess! He might be wrong, Lacey warned himself grimly, but he didn't think it was only the letter from the lawyer or the trouble up home that had caused the violence of Chase Courtland's reaction. He thought it had more to do with the news of Leanna Leighton than either Chase or Lacey himself might like to admit. Stewart Leighton might have failed in his efforts to kill the federal cavalry major in ambush . . . but after today, Lacey wondered whether Leanna herself might not still succeed someday where her Confederate partisan husband had failed.

The Swamps of South Carolina were far different from those Leanna had known while riding with Stewart in the Georgia wetlands. For one thing, these were far worse. They seemed unending, stretching literally hundreds of square miles north of the Savannah River rice fields, only rising to swampy meadows, then deepening again to great pools that dropped nearly a man's shoulder height and more. Long gray shrouds of Spanish moss drifting down from snakelike cypress limbs—

omnipresent in Georgia—here in the Carolina Low Country were only occasional. Their place was taken by massive black tupelos, ancient cottonwoods, sweet gums and tulip trees, all thickly overgrown with vines of honeysuckle and sweet bay, tall stands of some waxy, sharp-edged grasses, and huge, feathery ferns. Deep green moss marked every tree trunk. Oppossums, raccoons, deer, deadly cottonmouths and huge alligators—these last two mostly torpid, fortunately, this time of year—all manner of creatures both malevolent and benign rustled the distant boughs and brush, splashed in the swamps' black waters, and added their individual sounds to the insects' constant background whine. More than any normal landscape, the Carolina swamp resembled a devil's maze, trackless and nearly impenetrable, sunless and forbidding. And this was the world John MacRae had brought Leanna to some weeks before.

Even the mighty Yankee army—*if* it came—would be helpless to advance through this, Leanna decided. The South might yet halt Sherman's columns—not with her soldiers but with her swamps. But that was small consolation to Leanna just now, and growing ever smaller as the days dragged on and MacRae continued to claim her. This was hell, Leanna thought, and somehow she had fallen into it, friendless and unprotected. Rescue, even escape, had seemed an ever more distant possibility. Until today.

Today, for the first time, MacRae had left her alone, riding off to raid some unfortunate, impoverished cabin for ammunition and supplies. He had left Leanna unguarded, doubtless thinking the swamps surrounding them would be guard enough. And he had left her no supplies, no weapons, no horse, not even any decent understanding of where she was or what direction she might go to escape. But still it was a chance. And if it wasn't a very good one, it was all she was liable to get—one she must take, or else resign herself to continuing horror when MacRae returned. So take it she must.

The hillock where MacRae had left her had been quite dry, but only a hundred yards away, green-scummed pools encircled the higher land like a medieval moat. At the edge of the first water, Leanna hesitated, shuddered and turned away from it, trying a different direction. She turned a dozen times, probably, in all, often enough that she was no longer sure she had not recrossed her own path, but there seemed no

212

land bridge to carry her over. Everywhere she looked were tangled trees and overgrown brush and water blocking her every route. In desperation, she raised higher the hem of her already swamp-stained skirt and simply plunged ahead into the nearest pool. She could only guess how deep the water was, or what foul creatures might inhabit such a home. But if she died, how much could it even matter anymore, she asked herself. Her world had been shattered by marching Yankee armies and the attendant horrors of war: Blytheswood was burned, her husband dead, her child miscarried, her Yankee lover doubtless buried by now in Southern ground. She had not, at least not yet, conceived a child of her captor's begetting. Her flow the week before had been blessed proof of that small mercy. But she had all too readily conceived Chase's in Atlanta, and she must face the probability that if she remained here any longer, used at least daily to satisfy MacRae's lust, she could all too easily conceive a child to him as well. What MacRae forced her to endure was horror enough. To have to bear his child would be infinitely worse. Better death, she thought, than that. So she had plunged ahead, desperate and determined, forcing her way forward among vines and brush and endless stands of half-dead trees, until death, it seemed finally, was indeed the most likely outcome of all her efforts to try to save herself. She was still in the swamp, she was lost, and it seemed as if the daylight were failing.

Time had long since become completely meaningless; direction had too. If the sun were still shining, it was impossible to prove that in the unrelieved darkness of the swamps below. Fifty feet above Leanna's head, tree boughs laced their branches in an unbroken canopy, vines and dark-leaved creepers trailed around her, and even if she had chosen to give up and return to the hillock and MacRae, she no longer knew the way that marked return. Oozing slime reached above the edge of her calf-high boots, sucking greedily at her feet with every forward step. Snakes hung laconically, occasionally hissing. from nearby branches. Mosquitoes drew blood with sudden bites, and encouraged their success, swarmed around her unrelentingly. And in the ever-deepening shade, Leanna began to shiver from cold and rising fear.

Another of the seemingly endless pools now lay at her feet, and though she'd forced herself to its very edge, her body had stopped of its own accord—shuddering and shivering, refus-

213

ing to take another step. She was not sure she had not gone through this pool already. Once, even twice. Hours ago they all had begun to look alike. She had long since been soaked with stinking, ice-cold swamp water, bleeding and itching from a thousand insect stings, shivering hard and constantly from the numbing cold. And now as she stood at the edge of more slimy, dark water and licked her lips against their sudden trembling, she tasted the bitter salt on them that signified tears. So she was crying by now, as well. For some reason that realization somewhat surprised her, and that only somehow redoubled her tears. Her knees gave way, and she sank slowly down in a shivering heap, sobbing in huge, wracking gasps of despair.

What might have been an hour passed by her unheeded. She was not conscious any longer of time, or thought, or anything else. Only a faint, nearby thud startled her at last, touching some instinct still alive within her consciousness. It slowly brought her head back up, her eyes back open in a last weary effort. The light, faint at best within the swamplands, had faded even further, Day had become dusk in that invisible sky above the dense trees. It was harder than ever for her to see, but about a dozen feet away, it seemed a branch was swinging slowly, and from the long tangled grasses beneath it there came the sudden sibilant sound of something's slow, rustling passage. A snake? Oh no, she thought. No. That was too awful a way to have to die.

With a final effort, Leanna forced her frozen limbs to make one last move, to throw herself toward the blackish water that still blocked her way. This pool was deeper than the others, the bottom of it the usual, stinking slime, but these foul waters reached well above her head as well. For a moment, astonished, she simply floundered in the foul water, choking on what she'd expected to be a breath of air. And even once free of the water itself, she found the far bank of the pool to be green-mold-covered ooze—impossible, it seemed, to either climb or crawl up it, though terrified instinct told her she must. From behind her, already, came a faint, ominous splash— the snake slipping into the pool's farther edge—and in sheer, mindless panic, her desperation forced her somehow up the slimy slope to relative safety. She would not die, at least, by the agonizing venom of the watersnake's bite.

Terror had lent her a last surge of strength. Leanna half-

214

ran, half-crawled her way forward still, pushing herself through tangled vines in a near-frenzied final effort. And then suddenly she halted, openmouthed and staring. The swamp had given way to open ground, ground miraculously both firm and dry, a small clearing lit by a sunset sky. And at the very center of the clearing stood a cabin, not a hundred feet away. The door to the ramshackle structure was just now swinging open; a small, black child came running out. Leanna gave a faint cry, and instantly the child stopped, staring at Leanna as Leanna stared at her, and for a single moment, both were frozen silent where they stood.

Barely an instant later, the cabin door swung open again. A woman appeared in the doorway there, calling something to the child, but still staring at Leanna; the child did not reply. Then her mother repeated herself, in tones that changed from request to command, and hearing it twice, Leanna gasped in sudden recollection of her fear-numbed senses. It was not a language she'd ever heard, but it was words, and if she could beg a night of shelter from these people, her chances for survival, even for escape, were infinitely brighter. She might yet win free of MacRae and the swamp dangers both. "Wait, please!" Leanna moved from the edge of the trees out into the openness of the dusky clearing, raising one hand high in universal appeal for aid. "Please, can you speak English? Can you help me find a way out of these—"

"Don't waste your breath further. Gullah don't speak white people's tongue."

Startled, Leanna whirled to search the swamp shadows for the speaker who had interrupted her. For a moment, there was nothing there—nothing, at least, that she could see. Only a moving branch that drew her eye an instant before a woman emerged to face her. "But you speak English?"

"Well as I choose." A black woman stood facing Leanna, a figure not clearly etched against the deeper shadows of the swamp behind her, just barely visible in the failing daylight.

Almost at once, Leanna felt the warning prick of an instant wariness, a sensation almost akin to fear. But she could not afford to give way to that wariness; she could not afford to jeopardize this chance for aid. She knew all too well she was not likely to find another if she lost this one. "I didn't understand the language they were speaking, so I'm not surprised they wouldn't understand mine then, as well." Leanna shivered as she spoke. But she was freezing in the poor warmth of the January sunset, and uneasily conscious of the picture she must present to the woman—emerging from the swamps, filthy and slime-stained, soaking wet from head to foot. "I certainly don't mean to trouble anyone here. If you'd only be kind enough to translate what I say to them, I need to beg a night's shelter from whoever owns that cabin there."

"Gullah don't want no part of you."

The black woman only smiled faintly as she spoke, and Leanna's uneasiness instantly deepened. "Gullah? Is that the family's name?"

"No, Gullah. The people who live here, all through these swamps, the language they speaks, too. They calls 'em both Gullah. The Gullah don't have no *need* for white folks."

There was something utterly cold in the woman's tone, something even colder that glittered briefly in her eyes, and Leanna felt the same instinctive surge of fear she'd felt on seeing the snake start to slither toward her back in the swamp. The woman took a single step closer as she finished speaking, and Leanna instinctively took a step further away. Still, she continued, because she had no choice. "Please, will *you* help me, then? If they won't, can you? Please. All I need is shelter for the night."

"Fine lady like you here begging my help? Well, fancy that. Must be that glory day come a mite early. What you lookin' for you figure a poor old 'nigger' can help you get?"

Leanna flushed with humiliation, keeping her fear checked and her chin high only with the greatest effort. Tears threatened in her eyes, but she blinked them away, or tried to, and she offered the most candid reply she could possibly make. "I'm running away from a man. Not from my husband. My husband's dead. This man has been . . . forcing me. Forcing me to . . ." She could not say the words, themselves, not even now. Her throat was too tightly constricted by humiliation and tears to even allow her further speech, and helplessly she looked away from the woman's all-too-piercing gaze.

"He been taking his 'pleasures' on you, lady? Well, how the mighty be brought so low." There was little sympathy in the voice, but there was some, and more than Leanna had heard in it up to now. The woman went on as if recollecting old memories, thinking out loud. "Oh, I know how it is 'bout men taking what they want of a woman. That's one thing I

216

know real good. These swamp folk, these Gullah, they're free. Born free. They speak the old tongue, live in the old ways. You hear the drums sometimes at night. You hear them singing. They escaped off slaving ships a hundred years ago. Maybe more. Nobody knows just when. Ships run aground on that Carolina reef out there, and here they be. And a few, like me, runaways come here to join 'em. Even the dogs can't follow the scent in swamp. So the Gullah, they don't know about white men taking what they want from a woman, but I do. How do *you* like being a white man's taken slave?"

It was bitterness, both violent and cruel, the slave's natural response to centuries of bondage. Leanna recognized that bitterness finally in the woman's face and in her voice, and she shuddered in helpless inability to answer. Was this God's justice? she wondered numbly. Was this her repayment for all those years of accepting, even of defending, this callous horror? That her last chance for aid would be denied her because of the lingering poison of Southern slavery? Virginia had not had the huge plantations of the Deep South. Virginia didn't have land suited for cotton or rice where hundreds of slaves were kept like cattle for labor in thousand-acre fields. Slaves in Virginia were house slaves, mostly. Treated kindly and even generously. But even they had been property still, as she herself had become John MacRae's. And now she knew slavery of any kind as a horror beyond all other horrors. There was no answer but honesty, for any apology was too long overdue to be of any possible use—either to her or to the ex-slave who stood staring at her, awaiting Leanna's words in bitter silence.

"I *don't* like it. No better than you did, once. You ran away. And so did I. At least that must make us *something* alike." Leanna drew a moment's breath, driven only by desperation to make a last and probably futile plea. "You needn't put yourself out for me in any way. I have no right to even ask you to. But if I can't take a night's shelter here, then I beg you to give me help of another sort at least. My husband was an officer, killed in the war, but his family lives somewhere north of here, southwest of Charleston. I'm not sure where I am, but the Leighton's home can't be all that far away. Show me a path if there is one in these swamps, or just point out the right direction and perhaps—"

"Leighton's?"

There was a sudden awful silence, explosive as the instant before thunder cracks open a hot summer storm. Then the woman laughed abruptly, a sound more terrible than even that momentary silence had been, and Leanna froze before the abysmal cruelty that it conveyed.

"Oh, yes, indeedy, I know the Leighton place real good! See these marks?" The black woman turned in a fearful jerk, showing bare black shoulders crisscrossed by livid scars. "These was made by a Leighton whip!"

For a moment longer, Leanna simply stood stricken. Then she made a sudden lunge away from the slave—afraid as she had never been before in her entire life. Something worse than death, worse even than John MacRae's possession of her had flashed in the ex-slave's eyes as she'd turned back around to face Leanna. But that instant she'd lost had been an instant too long. A moment later, strong fingers had caught deep in the tangles of her long hair, cruel fingers were pulling her helplessly back. She struggled against the woman's grip, against the hands that were forcing her slowly to the damp ground, crying out a desperate, choking protest even as she struggled and fell.

"Oh yes, don't I know the Leightons! I know all about *all* the Leightons! Young master Stewart, was it?" She twisted the long, black strands of Leanna's hair around one fist, jerking her head back and pinning the girl to the ground. "Yes, I knew your husband, too, 'Miz' Leighton. I was too old for Master Stewart's tastes, he liked 'em young. Young like you, or even younger. Like my sister. She was twelve when he helped himself to her maidenhead one night. I heard her screaming as he took her, screamin' and screamin'. And when I couldn't stand it no more, then I got these whip marks, for interruptin' the young master's pleasure!" She gave Leanna's head a cruel jerk, and Leanna could only cry out, unable to move. "Then the war come and I ran away to here. Even Leighton dogs lose a scent in *these* swamps. And don't God see justice done us 'poor niggers' after all, *Miz Leighton*! He's done delivered 'mine enemy' into 'mine hands'!"

"Dee-ah!"

The sharp command of that alien voice fell like a sudden blow. Leanna opened her eyes with a desperate prayer, hearing an instant's frozen stillness behind her from the slave, then a soft throaty snarl like that of an enraged animal.

"Dee-ah!"

Whether it was a name or a command, Leanna was never to know. But the anger in the Gullah woman's voice cut the air like a razor's edge, and almost imperceptibly, the grip on Leanna's hair began to loosen. A flood of words followed, none of which Leanna could understand. But she understood the hand reaching down to her aid, and she thanked the Gullah woman with a choking sob, slowly shaking her hair free of that lingering and murderous grip. Then she crawled, half stunned, toward the nearby cabin, not daring to look back, hardly daring to breathe. Stewart haunted her still, was all she could think of. The thought held a note of utter insanity, but even recognizing that, she couldn't deny it belief. Even dead, Stewart stood between her and any hope of escape from this horror. Even Stewart's ghost held unceasing power over her. And thinking that, Leanna closed her eyes in another insanity—as desperate, as senseless as her whole Southern world had finally become. If Stewart's ghost would rise to haunt her, then Chase Courtland's ghost must rise to help her. Despite all the cruelty and the anguish that had marred their love by Atlanta, still she found herself appealing now to her once—beloved Yankee. Even if Chase's aid must now come to her, she believed, from beyond the grave, still it would come. He had never before failed her when she needed him most.

Half dazed by shock and fear, utterly exhausted by the day's ordeal, Leanna did not hear either the sudden hoofbeats or the unfamiliar voice that called to her as she crawled on toward the sanctuary of the Gullah cabin door. The first she knew, high black boots barred her passage toward the distant hut. Black boots such as the regulation cavalry of both Union and Rebel armies wore, with gilt-colored spurs strapped around the heel. Boots such as Chase Courtland had worn, she recollected in a kind of numb surprise, and she lifted her head half expecting to see Chase actually there with her. But no Yankee uniform greeted her glance. It was the dusty gray of a Confederate one instead, and as Leanna lifted her head the unfamiliar Confederate captain who stood before her swore out loud. "God in heaven! What the devil is a lady like you doing here?"

He spoke the words softly, as if to himself, and stared for an instant before he moved. "Here, lady, are you all right?"

He moved then with a sudden motion, as if belatedly recollecting an earlier notion to do so. One strong hand fastened around Leanna's arm, lifting her with an easy grace. "We heard some commotion going on over here, and swung on by to see the problem. Lucky for you, I think, that we did. It's damn near dark. And this isn't the place for a lady to be wandering around alone." Puzzled blue eyes scanned Leanna's ashen face, looking for an answer the girl was as yet unable to offer in speech. The conversation of the black women behind him suddenly terminated in an oversharp way, and frowning, the Confederate officer threw one swift glance over his shoulder toward them. As he turned his head back he reached surreptiously to loosen the revolver that hung from his belt, then slowly started Leanna toward the horse he'd left standing in the meadow a bare half-dozen yards away. "Whoever you are, and however you got here is a story that's going to have to wait a bit, I think. Right now, we're going to mount up and rejoin the rest of my men. Come on."

Leanna could not find her voice yet to speak, anyway. And though she tried to force her leaden limbs to move in response to the officer's urging, she found her knees were shaking, her whole body both shivering and weak, hardly able to support her weight even with the aiding hand that was gripping her arm. Once on her feet fully, a dangerous wave of dizziness washed over her. She closed her eyes and bit her lip, making a desperate effort not to faint.

"Here, lady fair, put your foot in the stirrup here. That's a girl. I'll get you up." Leanna could offer him little help, but it didn't seem to matter much. Barely a moment later, he mounted behind her, slid an arm around her waist to hold her, and urged the doubly burdened horse into a hurried gallop. Leanna had a brief, blurred impression of a black face flashing by, awful still with unrelenting hatred. And then it was gone. Trees closed around them again, and there came the sound of horses splashing through the swamp's endless pools, and simultaneously, the deep-throated rising murmurs of other men riding nearer to them. Quite suddenly, then, the effort that Leanna had made up to now to maintain consciousness was too much to ask any longer of her exhausted body and she felt herself drifting into blackness without either energy or sufficient will left to stop her. Her last impression of that terrible journey was strong Southern arms holding her close

220

and safe on a galloping horse, but it was a Northerner who haunted her dreams as she slept that sleep of utter exhaustion.

Far to the North, in distant Philadelphia, Jonathon Penley was not unaware of his sister's desperate plight. He and Leanna were close to each other, closer by far than most brothers and sisters, and through those long years of childhood a very special bond had developed that linked the two ever-closer together. Instinctively now, despite the miles between them, Jonathon Penley somehow sensed Leanna's danger. He replied to it, also instinctively, with a feeling of rising urgency. The decision to go after Leanna had already been made some days ago; he had only been waiting to make a last and failing effort to contain Elinor Courtland's designs on the bank. It looked now, though, as if it had been a week lost in vain, for the temporary injunction which the courts had granted last week ran out tomorrow. Joshua Courtland had regained consciousness finally, just Sunday evening of the previous weekend, but Joshua's recovery was still far too precarious to risk with announcements of his own daughter's treachery. Wires from Savannah had been encouraging about the Courtland son's recovery, but he still was too ill, and certainly he was far too distant, to be able to offer any help against his sister's plots.

Susan Stratford Courtland remained a distant possibility for aid, but in deference to her greater concerns over her husband's life, Jonathon had waited to tell her of the private war that was being waged here. Today he must tell her, and hope against hope that she might hold her husband's proxy and be willing to vote it at the bank meeting tomorrow. But he doubted that miracle was likely to happen. Susan had been totally uninvolved in the Courtland business, and it was not probable that her husband would have assigned any power to her. At least, though, Susan Courtland would have to know the truth. *Someone* here in Philadelphia must know the truth, if only to relay it to the Courtland son when he finally returned home to convalesce. Because after the bank meeting tomorrow, if—or *when*, Jonathon amended grimly—Elinor herself took over the bank, then Jonathon's obligations to the Courtland family would of necessity be over. There would be no more he could do in Philadelphia. And no further reason to have to stay here. He would simply tie up the strings, finish his final entries in the Courtland bank ledgers and go in search of his endangered sister. For an ex-Confederate on Yankee parole to reenter the South was suicide, probably, but it couldn't be helped. There was no other way to get help to Leanna. And even if Jonathon's strong sense of family duty hadn't necessitated his decision to go, he still would have gone out of sheer love alone. Hold on, Lea, he thought grimly as he reached out to knock on the Courtland front door. Hold on for just a few days longer. Or a few more weeks. However long it takes for me to find you. In just one more day, I shall be on my way south. And somehow, God don't ask me how, I will search every damn mile of swamp and woodlands and city until I can find you and bring you, somehow, to safety. I promise you, Lea. Just one more day.

Winter had kept its still-icy grip on William Penn's city, and as Jonathon now stepped into the Courtland foyer he noticed Susan Courtland shivering as she handed her own snow-dusted muff and cloak to the waiting Cooke. Jonathon simply hung his coat on a peg, for he no longer felt like a stranger here in Joshua's house. Susan offered a brief smile of greeting, a strained smile actually, but in Jonathon's preoccupation with his sister's danger, he didn't even notice that brief hint of tension. He merely glanced once up the wide stairs and then spoke to Susan in a very soft voice. "You *are* going to tell Joshua today about what happened down South? It's only been a few days, I know, that he's even been conscious. But Lady Bennington knows now, too, of her brother's misfortune. And I don't think we should risk *her* telling her father the news. She might not phrase it quite as reassuringly as you will." Involuntarily, Jonathon's mouth had twisted in a grimace at the mere mention of Elinor's name. Elinor might well announce her brother's near death in the most dramatic way possible, he thought, if she decided it could be in any way to her advantage to do so. Of course, Elinor would not tell her father about the proxy battle going on down at the Courtland bank—she would do nothing to undermine her own plans for ultimate victory tomorrow there. And without severly risking Joshua's still-precarious recovery, Jonathon could not tell him either. It was a stalemate.

"I brought Dr. Lacey's latest wire along," Susan said. A faint, unconscious frown had creased her face as she handed

Cooke her cloak and turned now to face Jonathon Penley. "Chase gave him some trouble already about following doctor's orders, I gather. He says that's quite normal for Chase, and I should be reassured by it. I brought the wire to show to Joshua—first, I believe. Roger himself suggested the idea." Distracted by both the telegram and the unsettling news she must soon relay to Chase's ailing father, Susan didn't even notice the familiar way she'd just referred to Dr. Lacey.

Jonathon did, and he glanced at her, puzzled. And he noted the strange, soft expression that played briefly on her face as she looked down at the telegram she was holding. "Roger"? Did she mean Doc Lacey? He looked away to conceal the impropriety of the question that instantly came to his mind, and he tried to forget he'd ever thought it. "As long as it's good news, by all means, let Joshua see it."

Susan nodded, refolding the telegram as if strangely reluctant to put it away. Jonathon Penley turned for the stairs, waiting to allow her to precede him as courtesy demanded, but she hesitated, glancing instead toward the nearby parlor. Elinor had greeted Susan's arrival at the house with aloof tolerance. But she had retired quite pointedly as soon as Jonathon Penley had come inside. Elinor was in the parlor now, examining the latest fashion doll she'd ordered sent on from Paris. Skirt hoops were wider than ever; waists narrower; shoulders puffed or bare; and décolletage, for evenings, was bold. Susan made no effort to interrupt her sister-in-law's retreat. Some basic feminine instinct warned she would not be welcome, and there was a very good reason, anyway, to leave Elinor excluded for the moment. The telegram she held asked some very pointed and disturbing questions, questions that Susan would just as soon *not* have Chase's sister overhear.

As she turned back to face Jonathon Penley Susan's frown had intensified, and she spoke in a voice now barely above a whisper. "I must also mention the other reason that I asked you to meet me today. I find myself in a very awkward position just now. Dr. Lacey has asked me to relay down to Chase a detailed explanation of exactly what is transpiring up here, and I find I have no idea what he's even referring to. Evidently, before Mr. Epsley, the family attorney, had heard the news of Chase being wounded, he had written a most unsettling letter to him. Something about a proxy apparently, and a developing power struggle between you and Lady

Bennington? Forgive me for speaking so frankly, Major Penley, but it does seem obvious that there is some ill will between you and my sister-in-law. So if you'll see fit to enlighten me, I think Chase himself should know all the specifics of any problems that have developed here since he himself left home for the South."

For only a moment, Jonathon Penley found himself totally taken aback. There was only surprise at her questions for the space of a minute, and then slow rising anger after that. Apparently, the Yankee major was *not* too ill to be issuing his usual orders again. Chase Courtland had gone back to Savannah, dropping the whole damn thing back in Jonathon's lap, without leaving him either any allies or any weapons to use to fight back against Elinor's machinations at the bank. And now the damn Yankee demanded explanations for how his sister had garnered the upper hand! "I shall be happy to give you all the 'specifics' you could wish, Mrs. Courtland." Jonathon spoke stiffly when he finally, spoke, barely managing to check his temper. "I would have thought your husband far too ill to be dragged into the midst of this mess just yet, but since he's the one so anxious for explanations, I'll be more than happy to relay them to him. Perhaps he can amuse himself with such concerns in between his doses of morphine."

Jonathon paused at that point, obstensibly for breath; in reality he paused to struggle harder with his rising anger. "However, I don't believe that this is exactly the place for any such specifics. Go up and visit with Joshua Courtland as you came over to do. And then when you're finished with that, come over instead to the cottage house where my family and I live. It's not a tale that's short in the telling, nor is it going to make for a pleasant meeting, so we may as well make the thing as comfortable as we possibly can. I'll have some port on hand. I'm afraid you may need some afterwards, Mrs. Courtland."

Susan only gave him a swift glance of shock, then instantly glanced on behind him to the open doorway of the Courtland parlor. For a moment she seemed about to speak again, then apparently thought better of it with her sister-in-law only scant yards away. "All right, Mr. Penley. I shall probably be about an hour here. And thank you."

Jonathon himself watched Susan go up the stairs, preoccupied with anger and deep in thought. As he turned from the wide stairs back toward the Courtland front door Elinor's sudden call from the foyer below startled him. He checked his step abruptly, glancing warily to where the beautiful Courtland daughter stood watching in the open doorway of the parlor.

Elinor only smiled at his glance, motionless for the moment. Then the satin of her gown rustled as she reached out to offer him a half-filled glass of brandy. "You look entirely too grim these days, Major. Perhaps some of that is my fault; I've been thinking so anyway, this morning. Regretting it. I have allowed our quarrel to spill over into the personal realm when I might easily have confined it to the bank alone." She pressed the brandy glass more insistently against Jonathon's hand, and more by reflex than out of any conscious decision, he accepted. As he did, it seemed to him that Elinor smiled more surely. "Let us agree to limit our enmity to the bank board room, Major. And be friends, instead, elsewhere."

Jonathon listened to her long speech, expressionless, remaining silent for a thoughtful moment. "You're feeling generous, perhaps? Because you think this time tomorrow you will have outlasted the injunction and the bank will be yours, Lady Bennington? If that's your motivation for this sudden surge of friendship, I should remind you that your brother appears to be recovering well in Savannah, your father, too. Even if I can't find a way to stop you, Elinor, your victory tomorrow will only be temporary."

"Temporary?" Elinor shrugged, but still spoke pleasantly, and she kept her smile as if unperturbed. "That's all I need it to be. I don't want to oversee the bank as a *career*, Major. I only need a few hours to . . . 'readjust' some of the funds in the vault." She raised one perfect brow in wordless invitation, and lifted her own glass a few inches higher. "Let us drink to a fine distinction, then: enemies elsewhere, but friends here."

She raised her glass to take a dainty sip, and Jonathon remained motionless for a moment, watching her. She *was* beautiful. Framed against the gold and white brocade of the foyer wall, her hair was almost a perfect match for the gold of the fabric, and the soft peach hue of her day gown flattered the subtle peach blush of her cheeks. Beautiful enough to grace a king's court and still outshine the others. But her beauty no longer held any appeal for Jonathon Penley; he knew too well what lay beneath the splendor of that magnificent facade. "Sorry, Lady Bennington." He turned and poured the contents of his glass out into the African violets that bloomed in pots by each foyer window. Poured it quite slowly and quite deliberately, without a moment's indecision. "I have very few privileges remaining to me at this point in the war, but one of the few I yet retain is the freedom to choose my friends. In the South, we aren't quite as facile at separating board-room enmities from personal friendships, perhaps. In any case, I'd just as soon not complicate our relationship, Lady Bennington. I'm perfectly content to remain enemies with you, regardless of locale. Good day."

Cooke stepped through the foyer only in time to see Jonathon Penley pour his brandy over the violets blooming in their polished brass pots. They were his special pride, several rather rare varieties carefully tended. He cringed inwardly but held his tongue and kept his face impassive. He had overheard enough of Jonathon Penley's last words, and now he saw enough of the expression that hardened the Courtland daughter's face as the Virginian turned on one heel and left. It was not a conversation he wished to intrude upon, so he carefully withdrew.

He would probably have thought little else of the occasion, except that that night, as he made his usual last, late-hour check of the house, he noticed all the violets in the one pot were quite definitely dead. Startled, he bent over the pot to check and found a familiar, bitter scent had soured the potting dirt. White arsenic powder. It was commonly used as an insecticide in gardening; there was no mistaking the odor. It was also used as a poison, he realized with a shock of chilling intensity. There had been arsenic in the brandy Jonathon Penley had poured out on these plants. Apparently, the Lady Bennington had decided to escalate their war to a deadly level.

For a long moment, Cooke stood silent and shaken in the darkness of the night-shadowed house, totally unable to think what to do. The Courtland son was too distant and too ill. The master's health far too precarious to risk shocking him with such tidings. Jonathon Penley, obviously, was already at his limit in dealing with the Courtland daughter. So that left only him—a figure of very little visible power as head of the household servants, but wielding a great deal of a more subtle kind of control. Cleaning the Lady Elinor's boudoir, for example, one might easily find and remove any arsenic powder that had so carelessly been mislaid from the downstairs gardening supplies. It would be done of course. And he must watch her most carefully from now on—until her father was well enough to warn, or until her brother could return from Savannah. Apparently, the war had come to Philadelphia, too.

Chapter Thirteen

Cooke didn't actually tell Jonathon Penley about either the violets or their sudden, mysterious demise. Such an outright revelation would have too-greatly compromised Cooke's deeply held commitment to keep inviolate the secrets of the Courtland family who employed him. Moreover, as he'd admitted quite candidly to himself at the time, Cooke knew he really hadn't needed to warn Penley about the dangers of crossing swords with the Courtland daughter—Jonathon already knew that well enough. Jonathon Penley had been a soldier; he'd been living in Virginia when the war had been declared, and he remembered well the subtle difference in the air that came when uneasy peace turned into outright war. He had sensed it instantly as soon as the change had come to the Courtland compound, and he understood too why the battle had so abruptly grown hot. It was now or never for Elinor to achieve her ultimate coup at the family bank. Her father was recovering now—slowly, perhaps, but still recovering. Her brother had survived what all had believed must be a death wound and could return home anytime to block Elinor's moves. So Elinor *must* win the proxy fight at the rescheduled bank meeting. She *must* take control of the bank's fortune *now*. Because even next week might be too late.

Well, Jonathon thought grimly, it appeared she had won after all. Susan Stratford Courtland had been both shocked and horrified—perhaps as well, Jon thought, a shade disbelieving—but she had had no remedy to offer in their conversation yesterday afternoon. All she could promise to do was to send a hasty wire down to her husband in Savannah.

Miranda, with the innocence of children, had sensed nothing of the subtle war that had erupted into full battle in the last few days here at the Courtland estate. She sat in unceasing motion nearby at the cottage's kitchen table, chattering

228

and gaily playing while her father worked in his grim silence. Carriage wheels rolling by the front windows seemed exceptionally loud to Jonathon—it would be Elinor leaving for the bank and the meeting he'd unsuccessfully tried to delay. The temporary injunction he'd cajoled from a judge last week now had less than an hour's time remaining, and Elinor would be watching the clock by now with a silent, smug smile. Perhaps he'd been wrong to resist the inevitable. It obviously had done no good, brought nothing but Elinor's greater hostility. The bank would still fall into her hands, and his resistance had only made the Courtland daughter more revengeful than ever, meaning Leanna would be in more danger than ever. And he had lost a full week's time already in leaving to find her.

Frowning at such unsettling thoughts, Jonathon grabbed angrily for last year's ledger, frowning harder as an envelope, unmarked and unopened, fell from its pages with the sudden motion.

"Daddy, Grandpapa Courtland said I might keep a pony here in the stable if you say I may. He saw a red saddle, he said, and a—"

"Miranda, what's this? Do you know?" Jonathon interrupted.

As her father raised the envelope Miranda's blue eyes suddenly widened, her face becoming pale in guilty remembrance.

"Oh. It was for you. Cooke gave it to me, and then I forgot."

"Well, what is it though? Who's it from?"

"Cooke said it was from the federal post office. But Bonnie baby was sick and Mommy told me to put it down and get Dr. Stephens. Bonnie baby was sick and I went to stay at Granpapa's, then, and I forgot."

A harsher frown began to gather and Jonathon shrugged it off with an effort. Mandy was only three, and three-year-olds are unreliable messengers at best. Anyway, it probably couldn't be anything of any real importance. The envelope didn't even carry a return address. But he knew he was wrong as soon as he unfolded the single sheet of legal vellum. There, in simple black ink lay the solution to the very problem he'd struggled to solve by himself all these past bitter weeks. Here was exactly what he'd told Susan Courtland yesterday that he hadn't had: the voting power he needed to check any move Elinor Courtland Bennington could make, the assigning of proxy for Chase Courtland's own twenty-five percent of Courtland bank stock. Jonathon sat for a moment more, his first reaction sheer astonishment, his second reaction a rising anger. Damn that Yankee, he thought in sudden inexplicable resentment. It was an instantaneous reaction, one he couldn't explain, not even to himself. But the anger he felt was inarguably real. It pricked instantly at his pride; it made instant changes somehow in present and future obligations both. This was not a "gift" given out of sheer generosity. This was only a concession from an enemy—like a postbattle truce for both sides to gather and bury their dead. Power on loan that worked to Chase Courtland's advantage at the same time as it worked to Jonathon Penley's. It made unwilling allies of two erstwhile enemies. But even that realization didn't negate what the proxy meant in terms of Jonathon's responsibility toward the Yankee major's father, Joshua Courtland. Whatever else it meant for the future, for the present that proxy was the answer to a prayer—the one and only hope of controlling the outcome of the meeting that even now must be convening in the offices of the Courtland bank.

"Good God!" At the thought, Jonathon had instantly jerked to his feet, flinging a single glance toward the clock, which ticked lazily, audibly, nearby on the fireplace mantel. Even now, only minutes remained and the bank was still many blocks away. He shoved the proxy paper in his pocket with a muttered oath and snatched his coat down from the foyer peg. "Miranda, run to Grandpapa's house! Tell Mommy I've gone to the bank. I'll be home to explain it all later!" He barely paused to watch her start on her way, then turned for the stables to hurry for the bank.

Jonathon galloped recklessly in the winter-slicked streets. Even so, he was late—but not, as he'd feared, *too* late. The minority shareholders had voted already, but Jonathon opened the gleaming double walnut doors of the office in time to hear Elinor's vote, so the meeting was not yet adjourned. Elinor voted no, as she had before—knowing it would look better so in the records, knowing her ten percent or one hundred shares could not overcome the collective fifteen percent of the others anyway. Then, in the silence caused by his arrival, Jonathon smiled faintly at Elinor's look of sudden wariness and hurried forward to lay Chase Courtland's lost proxy faceup on the table for all to see it. "Proxy voting for your brother, Lady Bennington. His two hundred fifty shares join your negative vote . . . and do I believe, carry the decision, today."

He'd seen it only once before in her eyes, a flash of something quite as deadly as this that came now. Her beautiful face paled to ash, and even as he stood trembling, catching his breath from his reckless ride, Elinor rose with a jerk. "Where did you get that? Even if you could have cabled him in time, my brother is far too ill to—"

"Yes, *now* he is, I quite agree," Jonathon interrupted her, not feeling obliged at the moment to offer any of the usual courtesies due her fair sex. "But he wasn't when he drew this up on the first of January. Due to a misunderstanding with my daughter"—he shrugged for just an instant—"I didn't know of its existence until a few minutes ago. But it's quite legal, I assure you of that."

"Let me see that."

By reflex, he began to oblige. Then he caught a subtle hint of warning flickering in her eyes, and he changed his mind. "On second thought, no. I'll keep it, I believe. If you wish to challenge its authenticity, take me to court."

Elinor's eyes narrowed momentarily, and then, as if abruptly aware of the fearful silence that surrounded them both, she turned for the door. "May I see you privately, please, Mr. Penley?"

Jonathon debated a moment, reluctant rather than fearful, but finally he shrugged and followed her out. He heard the sudden murmured rush of conversation begin among the other men as soon as he'd stepped out of sight, and his expression grew cynical. Most evident among the whispers behind him was the one that cried fear. They had tried—and failed. Despite Elinor's iron-clad assurance of success, they had been disastrously outmaneuvered . . . and God, what Joshua Courtland was likely to do to them if he eventually recovered and ever found out. Typical, Jonathon thought, of such people. Unrepentant of the crime itself, but *very* regretful that the crime would be punished.

"You wished to speak to me, Lady Bennington?"

"Only to give you *one* last chance to change your mind, Major." Elinor's voice, soft as a cat's purr, still carried a threat to make him shudder. "*One* last chance before we declare all out war on one another. Believe me, Major, you don't want to do that. I can make your life most unpleasant."

"I'm sure you can try. You already have. But one blessing in disguise of this current war is that I've very little left to lose, by now. Only my good opinion of myself, which I owe almost entirely to your father's generosity, and which, in thanks to him, I am determined to maintain."

"But you forget your sister. You are rather callously assigning her a thoroughly wretched fate, I promise you."

"No. Actually your brother's proxy solves that problem, too, in a way. Because by voting his shares today, I can virtually close down the bank until either he or his father are once again capable of taking over its control. That temporarily suspends my obligation to oversee the bank, Elinor, and that leaves me finally with my time free. You may have both armies out looking for Leanna, but I'll still make you a wager I can find her first. Obviously I'm going to have to, now. That much, at least, I do understand." Jonathon smiled grimly, nodding cold dismissal as he began to turn.

"You'd better hope you do find her first, Major—or I'll send her to you personally. That I promise. I will send her to you, Major Penley. In little bitty pieces . . ."

"Whitney?" Jonathon's face reflected nothing of triumph as he returned to his carriage house after the bank. It was over and, miraculously, in one sense he had won, but he did not underestimate Lady Bennington's capacity for revenge. He could afford to wait no longer to go in search of the endangered Leanna. In "little bitty pieces"—the threat echoed hauntingly in his mind, had since Elinor had first said it. He had no doubt, if she *could*, she *would*, so it was not the sort of threat that let an affectionate brother rest easy.

He had not noticed it at first, but there was an unnatural stillness about the cottage, a silence that gradually cut through his grim preoccupation with Elinor and her venomous promise. Noticing it now finally, Jonathon began to frown. Something was wrong. Not Elinor, surely, not yet. She could not have struck back so soon. But there was fear in his voice still as he called out again. "Whitney? Mandy? Is anyone—" He interrupted himself at the sound of a soft footfall descending the stairs. No words came back to answer him. No sound. But a moment later, Whitney stepped out of the kitchen and into

232

his view, holding Bonnie in her arms. Her eyes caught his and clung to them as if in wordless supplication. Their expression and the tears brimming like quicksilver there took Jonathon's heart in a sudden fearful grip. "Oh God, Whit . . . what?"

"It's Bonnie. She's dead."

Such soft words, he thought, it should have been impossible for them to do such damage. But he felt a shock run through him, *slam* through him rather—like a physical blow. He dropped his eyes from Whitney's—startled, and for a moment, simply disbelieving. Dumbly, he stared at the small, still body Whitney so carefully held. "Oh God, no." For some reason, both of them stood motionless, a dozen yards apart, as if powerless to move. Jonathon continued to stare at his small daughter, watching her curiously, almost carelessly, still quite sure he would see Bonnie move, see her sigh in her sleep, or fret as she had so much lately. Anything . . . Please God, make her move, he thought suddenly, as the disbelief began to melt away, leaving the first faint rush of what would swiftly mount to a raging torrent of anguish. God, please, make her move!

"Jonathon, my baby's dead." Whitney's whisper ended in a soft wail, a sob, and the choking sound of desolate grief. She began to shake then, violently, holding Bonnie still as she staggered to her knees and Jonathon moved forward in a sudden, desperate rush. He was shaking, himself, as he took the dead child, shaking harder as he reached out to hold Whitney as well. And even in that instant, he realized that he could not go to find Leanna. Not anymore. Not with this. Wherever Leanna was, he could not help her now; he could do nothing to protect his sister from Elinor Courtland's revenge. If Leanna were to survive Elinor's vengence, it must be someone else now who reached out to aid her. For Jonathon's hands were entirely tied. I'm sorry, Lea. God in heaven, I'm sorry. Forgive me for breaking my promise to you.

Jonathon sent an apology in anguish and silence, for he had nothing else left now to send to her.

It was a few days later in Savannah, and a fair morning finally—warm and blue, the breeze from the south a gentle one, which carried the fragrance of orange trees and blooming camellias. It accentuated Savannah's semitropical charm and

Doc Lacey almost regretted the necessity of returning to the cold, gray winter of Washington. Three days from now actually, today, being Friday, for the War Department orders of assignment had specified Monday for the surgeon's return. Federals and Confederates seemed to have forgotten most of their differences in the city and mingled together in astonishingly good humor. Well-bred young ladies watched parade drills or went to hear regimental bands play, and while there, they flirted with handsome young officers regardless of the color of their uniforms. Markets, stores and restaurants were reopened, and the smell of shrimp, oysters and crab issued once again from open windows as he passed. Spanish moss hung motionless from live-oak branches, and a few magnolias were just beginning to bud. One would never guess from the air of normalcy that pervaded the city that there was a desperate war still raging and that Savannah, only weeks before, had been its focus. Savannah had been reassured by General Sherman, enchanted by her charm, that unlike Atlanta, Savannah would not be destroyed. Federal troops would garrison it instead, and the people of the city, fearing utter devastation, were generous with relief at the prospect of a mere Union occupation. Rather than enmity, there was a sense of near celebration in the city; the war was over for Savannah and she had survived.

Not so joyful a humor would be evident in Washington, Lacey mused as he walked. Not yet at least. There the war was far from over, its waging was grim and visible still, its people's faces were hard and drawn as they passed one another in the street. There, still, would be the cattle pens fouling the ground by the unfinished Washington Monument; white crosses spreading across the lawn of Robert E. Lee's prewar home of Arlington; convalescent soldiers in the basement of the Capitol, baking bread for their fellows still in the field; hospitals and omnipresent, black-suited embalmers haunting every block; war contractors, too—ever fatter, breakfasting late on steak and oysters at the fashionable Willard. Washington for some time yet would remain what it was—the hub of the war.

Lacey turned onto Perry Street at Colonial Park Cemetery, noting that Federal Cavalry horses had been stabled in the old graveyard there, trampling tombstones and cropping grass grown on the likes of Button Gwinnett and other Revolutionary War heroes—an ironic reminder, to anyone who cared to note it, how fast the glories of war-won fame disappeared. War was unpleasant, and people, by their very nature, were quick to forget such unpleasant memories. Maybe by this time next year, Washington, too, would match the careless memory Savannah already enjoyed, and the war would be over there as well. At least it was a hopeful thought.

"Reardon!" He checked his step in some surprise as he entered the sudden dimness of the hospital-house's parlor and saw the young man there working. "I thought you were scheduled out today on a boat for Beaufort."

"I was." The young doctor shrugged without looking around from his patient. "But I get seasick. I'm waiting until the pontoon bridge refloats itself instead."

"God, don't let yourself get assigned to the infantry, Captain Reardon. You'll treat bunions and lice all day long." Lacey offered this remark wryly, enjoying the equally wry smile that immediately lightened the medic's overgrim face.

"Better than what you treated for the cavalry, isn't it?"

Lacey only chuckled for answer as he continued up to take the stairs. "Did you remember to skip Major Courtland's morphine today?"

"Yes. He may be regretting his decision by now, but his head should be clear."

"Good. I'll check in with you then before I leave."

Doc Lacey found himself smiling faintly as he took the stairs. Damn if there wasn't hope for the future of medicine, after all, with youngsters like Reardon taking on the challenge—bright, aggressive, open to change. God only knew what strides they could make. How did the blood system replenish itself? Why did tree-moss fungus work such wonders on infection? Why lime chloride? Why did dysentery drop among soldiers who drank only boiled coffee and not fresh water? So many questions, not nearly enough answers. But he was smiling still as he stepped into Chase's room. All Lacey ever asked of life was a chance—with young men like Reardon, medicine would have one. So he was content. "Morning, Chase. How are you today?"

"I've been better—was better yesterday as a matter of fact, I think." Chase turned his head away from the window's view as Lacey entered, and he managed a wry smile to mitigate the complaint. He moved as if to sit up, and Lacey hurriedly crossed the room, shaking his head in caution.

"Here, don't move too fast. Your stitches only came out yesterday." Lacey gestured Chase back down and leaned over, putting his ear to his chest. He listened a moment, then shook his head as he straightened up. "It's better, but not gone. You'll have to stay in Savannah awhile yet, Chase, till the pneumonia entirely goes. Sorry." He expected some sort of a protest, but none was forthcoming, and he frowned slightly, surprised. "As for not feeling as well as yesterday—yesterday you were still on a heavy dose of morphine. It was your idea to get off so early, and if you want to change your mind, say so. I'm agreeable."

"No. The morphine makes me too damn drowsy."

"Then don't complain."

"How about a cup of coffee laced with bourbon, though?"

Even that much of a concession to pain was atypical of Chase, and Doc Lacey eyed him more sharply as he turned to call the order to a distant orderly. "Where's the pain the worst?"

"Stomach, mostly."

Lacey nodded, reaching for scissors to begin snipping at the concealing bandages. Fresh blood stained the dressing pad and he nodded as he carefully worked it free. "What were you doing? Making love to a nurse?"

Chase returned a grimacing smile. "Pleasant thought, but no. All I've seen around here are orderlies, in fact."

"No nurses? How much morphine has Reardon had you on?" Lacey feigned astonishment and glanced up to note the momentary flicker of belief in his friend's eyes, then chuckled wryly as he continued his work. Pain or no pain, Chase's head was plenty clear.

"Fine doctor you are. I'm lying here in agony, and you make jokes."

"Would you feel better if I were grim and glum then?"

"No, but I wouldn't be so damn jealous of you, either."

Chase jealous of him? The notion struck Doc Lacey as bitterly ironic, and his smile faded as thoughts of Susan immediately resurfaced. Stop it, he ordered himself. You're a doctor—*be* a doctor. Forget everything else that's going to stand in the way of just doing your job. "There's a little tearing here." Lacey's face was carefully unreadable as he reached for a cloth to begin washing the wound, apologizing to the immediate catch of pain he heard in Chase's breath. "Sore maybe, but not serious. I can put a stitch back in, but I'd rather not. I'd like to use some tree moss on it, and then let it heal on its own, from the inside out. We'll give it until this evening, see how it is." He nodded to Chase's grunt and finished up, straightening. "Still, I think you'd be better on the morphine yet. Give yourself a few more days, Chase. Be that kind to yourself."

"I would if I could be sure I could afford any more lost days." The resistance Lacey had expected earlier came now. Chase frowned as he spoke and glanced back to the sun-filled window, frowning harder in the glare of the day's full light. There was a moment's silence, and Doc Lacey's smile faded with a growing awareness of trouble soon to come. "Did you get that wire from Susan yet?" So that was it, Lacey thought. For a moment, his only response was a silence and then, almost reluctantly, he nodded. "I'm surprised you even remember that, Chase. I was hoping, actually, I think, that you wouldn't."

Chase shrugged, grimacing at the pain of that thoughtless movement. "You were the one who offered the deal."

"Yes. And I'm beginning to think I may regret it now." Lacey was frowning, too, stalling, he admitted to himself, stalling for time as he eyed Chase intently. What is it, Chase, he wanted suddenly to ask? What is it that's driving you so? Susan? Your father? Your bank problems? Or Leanna Leighton, who had been seen again in the guerrilla's camp? "Forget it, Chase. Whatever it is," he cautioned him finally in a voice soft with concern, not doctor to patient this time. One friend to another. "You're in no condition to do anything yet anyway."

"I may have to be, I think. Let me see the wire, Roger."

"Wait until the bourbon arrives at least. Ten minutes isn't going to hurt."

"Now, Roger. Please."

"But it's a lengthy one from the feel of it." Doc Lacey yielded reluctantly and with a deepening frown. He was slow to reach in his uniform pocket to draw it out, and he stared down at the thing he held in his hand, still frowning. "The glare's bad there for you to try to read so much."

"You read it then. Just tell me what it says."

Lacey glanced up sharply, realizing only now that Chase

had closed his eyes sometime during their argument, and a whitening line around his jaw indicated that pain rather than drowsiness had been the cause of it. A reaction, perhaps, to being off the potent opiate for the first time in nearly two weeks . . . or else Chase wasn't as recovered as he tried to pretend. "All right, give me a minute." Lacey stalled again, moving as slowly as he could, letting whole minutes pass before he even began to read. And then, as he started, he regretted not having stalled longer. It began well enough, with Joshua Courtland improving daily. But Chase's sister had tried to gain control of the bank at the annual meeting; Jonathon Penley had stopped her only at the last minute and Elinor had countered by threatening danger for Jonathon's sister. Elinor had told Jonathon—lied to him, Susan believed—that she had arranged for Jonathon's sister to be arrested for suspicion of treason by not just the federal, but the Confederate Army as well. Surely, Susan added, her sister-in-law, Lady Bennington, neither wielded such power, nor if she *did* would she use it so cruelly. But added as a postscript at the bottom was further disaster. Believing Elinor's threats as truth, Jonathon had meant to go south in search of his sister. But on Wednesday afternoon, the Penley's youngest daughter had died very suddenly of rheumatic fever. His wife, Whitney, was close to term and far too distraught for him to leave her. In short, things were in a wretched state.

"Jesus Christ!" Lacey was hardly aware of speaking the oath aloud as he turned on one heel for the door. Whatever he had promised Chase earlier this week, he had no intention of following through with it after this. "Just a moment, Chase. I forgot something downstairs. I'll be right—"

"Roger?" Chase had caught the anger in Doc Lacey's muttered oath, and he frowned at it, reopening his eyes to find the surgeon halfway across the room already. "Roger!"

"Your coffee, Doc."

The orderly blocked the doorway just as Doc Lacey was preparing to step out. He had a momentary sense of being trapped—of frustration and anger and a helpless, stupid desire to somehow, like a magician, make the damn telegram simply vanish into air. This was not the kind of news people usually sent to reassure a wounded man. What in the hell was Susan doing?

"Roger! What is it?" Chase struggled to one elbow, cursing

238

softly at the pain of such quick movement. Doc Lacey glanced over one shoulder to see him, muttered another curse and stood for a moment, torn between two evils. Then he angrily strode back toward the bed. "Will you stop moving like that! I don't know how many times I have to tell you!"

"I want the telegram, Roger. Whatever it says. It's my family. My responsibility. Let me see the damn thing! Let me at least find out what the hell is going on!"

For a moment more, helpless, Lacey hesitated. Then with an abrupt gesture, he handed it over. Almost by habit, he reached for a pillow to support Chase's back and then turned to the orderly with an frustrated scowl. "Get another cup of coffee—hurry. And bring the damn bourbon with you, this time."

By the time he turned back to the bed, Chase was finishing the wire, his face paler than ever, his eyes darkening as he only skimmed the last few lines. Shock, then anger, slowly brought flushing color back into his face. Unlike Susan, he believed Elinor's every word. "God damn that conniving bitch. She's worse than ever."

"I'll have your wife's head for that wire when I see her next, Chase. Susan's lost her mind, sending on this kind of news to you."

"No. Wire her back, Roger. Today. Tell her I'll take care of it. Somehow. I'm not sure. Then wire Jonathon Penley and tell him I'm sorry. Tell him he should stay in Philadelphia— see to his family, see to the bank. I'll find Leanna for him, here in the South, wherever she is. I'll have to, won't I?"

Lacey shook his head in vehement disagreement. "*You're* going home to convalesce!"

"Give me that bourbon, Roger. Let me take a couple swallows, then help me get up."

"No, Chase. No, damn it. You've lost your mind! You try to get out of that bed and you're liable to kill yourself, and I'll be damned if I'll help you do that!" He turned on one heel, furious, starting for the door.

"Then I'll do it without your help."

"The hell you will!" Lacey whirled back instantly, raising his hand in a wordless threat. "You stay put!"

Chase swore softly, closing his eyes against the ripping agony of trying to force torn muscles to move. The curse ended in a cough, long and wracking, and Lacey watched from the doorway in ever-growing fury. Damn her! He wasn't even sure exactly which woman he meant—Susan, Elinor or Leanna Leighton. Damn all three of them then, he amended. And damn Chase Courtland, too—the stubborn fool was bound and determined to try to get up.

"Chase, for God's sake, please! What the hell do you think you're going to prove?"

Chase only waved a dismissal, angry and curt. The cough ended and he reached for the side of the bed, beginning to try again. Move, he ordered into the protesting agony of his body. Move, dammit! If he could stand, he could walk. If he could walk, he could ride. And as long as he could ride, he could rejoin the army that was preparing to march north. And somewhere there, he would find Leanna Leighton before Elinor's people could. He'd have to . . . if for no other reason than that he owed the Penley brother a fearful debt.

"Here, you damn fool. Stand up first. See if you can even do that." Lacey had recrossed the room, scowling and swearing, but he reached down at last to try to help. "Easy now, for God's sake. Don't pull anything open."

Chase's groan moments later was mute evidence of exhausted effort; his head as it fell against Lacey's shoulder was dripping cold sweat. But he was standing. Doc Lacey held on to him with one hand, grabbing for pillows with the other as he eased him back down. "All right. That's all. That's enough for today, Chase. You understand?"

A nearly imperceptible nod was his only answer, and Roger nodded back, badly shaken.

"But tomorrow—"

"We'll see." He interrupted Chase instantly, easing him fully back into the support of the pillows, then bending to check the dressing over the ugly stomach wound. Incredibly, no damage was done. The raw, tender new flesh had withstood the strain of movement.

"Send the wires." Chase's exhausted whisper was half command, half plea. "Tell Jonathon Penley I'll find her. In a few days. When I can sit on a horse and ride. I'll march with the army."

The command, Lacey could and easily *would* have disregarded. But the fact that a friend was asking his aid he could not ignore. He sighed finally, as if defeated, and nodded once very slowly. He remembered thinking earlier this week that Leanna Leighton might yet kill Chase Courtland. Now Chase's wife, Susan, his sister, Elinor, and Leanna's brother, Jonathon, all seemed determined to move in exactly the same direction. And Lacey alone could not possibly fight them all. "All right, I'll send the wires." He turned for the door, his anger fading into a kind of an eerie superstitious fear. "That tangled web," he remembered thinking. Tangled more than ever now. And none of them, try as they would, seemed able to break its subtle threads. Now Chase's sister had moved them all one step closer to the brink, and there was the sudden, fearful sense that they were helpless to resist, that a play, long ago scripted, was slowly being acted out, each scene closing to further anguish, further pain. But it was not the kind of pain that he, as a doctor, could dispel. He could only move along, as helpless as they all were, caught in a malevolent fate too powerful to resist. One thing he knew; the war, and Leanna Leighton with it, had reached out to reclaim Chase Courtland once again. And now only God could see any final ending to the continuing anguish.

Susan Stratford Courtland felt sick again this morning—not incapacitatingly so, just sick enough that it was annoying. She pushed her plate of breakfast away, reaching for a piece of toast instead.

"This is the third morning in a row you've breakfasted on dry toast, dear." Susan's mother smiled faintly, almost secretively. Her eyes studied her daughter's face momentarily before she turned her attention back to her own meal, and her smile lingered.

"It was the worry, I guess, over Chase." Susan shrugged with a faint frown, replying carelessly. "Or a virus, perhaps." She was distracted, oddly lethargic these days, and she didn't trouble to even glance up.

"A virus?" Her mother questioned softly, her own eyes doubtful as she managed to catch her daughter's eye. "Perhaps a virus rather common among married women, dear?"

Susan only frowned in reply, momentarily puzzled. Then she understood, and found it irritated her—both the allusion and the patent approval that lit her mother's face. A Courtland-Stratford marriage. Now a Courtland-Stratford child expected from her. She resented both suddenly with a surge of rebellion and set her toast aside with overt annoyance. "Sorry to disappoint you, but don't pain yourself with false hopes, Mother. Chase and I only had the one night after the wedding, and with his father's—" Susan interrupted herself at that instant, falling very abruptly silent. She'd been on the verge of admitting that she and Chase had not consummated their marriage, so it was impossible she could be with child. But there had been that other time *not* with Chase. In Washington— with Roger. Her face paled, then flushed with guilty color, her stomach contracted in a sudden spasm of fear. Oh God, it couldn't be. Just *one* time. Surely nothing could come of that.

"One night can be enough, Susan, dear." Her mother was smiling still, noting the sudden blush on her daughter's face and assigning an entirely different cause to it. "And if I'm right and you're wrong, I suggest you and Chase should resign yourselves to owning a rather large brood of children in the years to come. Better plan on a roomy house."

Susan didn't dare look up, but her stomach heaved again, worsening, and she left even the toast on her plate uneaten. God, no, she couldn't be! She recounted mentally, in fearful haste. When had her period been due. Sometime in early January, only a day or two after Chase had left again for Savannah. She remembered that now, remembered now that she'd been concerned about having to schedule the wedding so close, but it had never come. And she'd not thought of it since, not in the confusion of Joshua's attack and the ruined night that had followed, not in the anguish of returning to Washington and to Roger there . . . with the news of Chase being wounded or killed, no one even knowing for certain which one. God, what could she do now? What if she *were* pregnant? However would she explain *that* to Chase? "I think . . . I think I should travel to Washington, after all. In case Chase should be coming back on that ship next week." Susan rose to her feet quite suddenly as she spoke, and across the table her mother laid down her fork in surprise at the unexpected announcement.

"But I thought you'd decided to wait for Chase's return here in Philadelphia, dear? And anyway, you can't possibly go just now. The Penley's daughter's funeral is planned for Sunday and you simply *must* be here for that. You are the only representative of the Courtlands who can attend. And it would be unspeakably rude for you to miss it."

242

"Oh. Yes, of course, I'd forgotten. I meant Monday of course. The ship isn't even due to leave Savannah until Monday anyway." She managed to speak rationally, even to keep some sort of composure on her face, though she did not dare to meet her mother's eyes.

"Well, I confess I'm completely confused now, Susan." Her mother was sighing, that slow sort of sigh that signaled blossoming disapproval. "I can understand your being anxious to meet Chase's ship, but I thought from the last wire that it was fairly certain he would not be well enough yet for weeks to travel. Stay here in Philadelphia until you know for certain that—"

"I'm a grown woman, Mother! I'm perfectly able to make my own decisions about whether I wish to go to Washington or not! And on the chance that Chase will be there, *I* intend to be there, too." Susan heard the sharp edge in her voice, and was quite unable to mellow it. She saw her mother merely raise one brow, a faint, humoring smile playing now on her mouth, and she fought a sudden, violent urge to slap her—for that expression only magnified her own silent fears. Instead she turned abruptly for the stairs and the privacy of her own room. But her hands shook and her knees were treacherously weak as she hurriedly ascended the stairs. She recounted the days mentally a dozen times, praying she would find an error. But she didn't. It was only *once*, she thought again in growing horror. Oh please God, I mustn't be, I can't be! Only once!

The next morning, she felt no better—worse if anything, for she hadn't slept well. But feeling her mother's shrewd eyes on her, and seeing the repetition of that faint, hopeful smile, she was desperate to deny to her mother and to herself what that smile might mean. Consequently, Susan ate everything set before her, even the sliced, sugared bananas doused with heavy cream. She ate until her mother finally shrugged and sighed and looked away in fading hope. Then Susan went upstairs, both frightened and crying, and vomited it all back up into the washbowl once again. And very quietly, she packed her traveling bag and made her plans to take the train down to Washington, hoping—no, praying—that Chase would be there. And that wounded or not, he would be as eager to consummate their marriage as Susan herself had suddenly become. It was the only solution that she could imagine, and even at that, *eight*-month babies and *seven*-month babies were not easily mistaken one for another. And seven-month babies looked *not at all* like a child carried nine. The disaster of her marriage to Chase was rapidly escalating into sheer catastrophe already.

Chapter Fourteen

It was blustery cold, black and late in Washington when Doc Lacey's troopship finally docked on the pier of the Potomac. Thursday night had been their scheduled arrival; today was Saturday, no Sunday, Lacey corrected himself wearily, for it was well past midnight by now. Winter storms plagued the Atlantic coastline this time of year, and they had been caught in one for several days off Hatteras, the ship groaning and moaning like some great, anguished animal, the mainmast snapping finally in a sudden gust of wind. Thank God for steam engines. Even with the sails reefed and the mainmast down, the chugging engine had managed to keep the ship's bow into the waves and saved the ship itself and God knew how many human lives. Days late, yes, but at least they had made it home.

No hired cabs were loitering at the Washington docks, not this late at night, and Lacey had no choice but to walk the long blocks back uptown toward his more familiar haunts. One advantage of the miserable weather was that no dockside roughs were prowling the darkness, but still, the surgeon frowned as he walked, and hurried his steps toward the distant hospital he called home. This was a fitting conclusion, he thought, to a trip that had turned sour before he had even left distant Savannah. Friday had begun it—Friday and that damn, disastrously candid wire from Susan. The succeeding days had been no better. On Monday when he'd arrived at Captain Reardon's hospital– town-house to say farewell, he'd found Chase Courtland dressed to ride, his horse standing saddled and restless, tied to an iron horsehead post by the curb of the wide, cobbled Savannah street. If Chase were to have any chance at all to find Leanna Leighton, he must rejoin Sherman's army when it left any day. And that meant he must be able to ride, able to keep up the pace of a marching army. It was crazy; it was a decision born of desperation and not of logic. But nothing Lacey could say had dissuaded his friend from the reckless resolution of pursuing just that course . . . and starting that day. Frustrated and angry, Lacey had finally given voice to both professional and personal disapproval, and there had followed a hot-tempered quarrel on both men's parts.

"You're a damn fool, Chase! With six weeks of sick leave coming, there's no damn reason you can't let Sherman march without you and plan to rejoin when you're better able!"

"There're a hundred reasons, and you know them all as well as I do. You read the telegram before I even did."

"But there's only one reason that's sufficient to require quite such an idiotic decision as this! And the name of *that* one is Leanna Leighton! Jesus Christ, Chase! You're a blind, damn fool for that woman! Admit it!" He'd not meant to say it, not like *that* exactly anyway, but in his anger the words had come of their own volition. They'd snapped like a whip in the sudden silence of the lazy Savannah sunshine, and Chase had turned from the horse to throw Lacey a look of silent warning. Ordinarily, Roger mused regretfully, that single glance would have more than sufficed to make him back off. He knew Chase Courtland; he knew to the inch how far he could press the man he called his friend. But at that particular moment, a forbidden love took precedence over even that friendship, and Roger had been beyond caution. "And while we're on the subject Chase, tell me this, too: how did you word the wire you sent on to your wife in explanation of this suicidal venture? How exactly did you tell Susan that you preferred riding after your old love instead of coming home to your new wife? Were you honest enough to tell Susan just that? Or did you cover it over with your usual excuses about duty and conscience and honor instead?"

Violence had flashed momentarily in Chase's dark eyes. He'd even taken several threatening steps forward before the bond of an old, strong friendship had checked his step. But startled to his very soul, Lacey had already begun to back away and the incident left more than merely a greater physical distance between them. Something of their friendship was irrevocably lost as well.

"Leanna Leighton as such means nothing to me, Roger. And consequently, when I *do* make a final decision and wire

246

my wife of it, I don't mean even to mention the woman's name. If it weren't for Elinor's involvement in this damn thing, I wouldn't feel obliged to so much as walk across the street to help Leanna Leighton anymore. But it's *my* sister that put Penley's sister in such danger—and my responsibility is therefore to get her out. As for Susan, I'm every bit as cognizant of my responsibilities to my new wife as *you* are certainly, Roger. When—or even *if*—I find Leanna Leighton, you may assure your overactive conscience that there will be nothing but the most distant courtesies exchanged between the two of us. Now whether you choose to believe that or not, I don't care. But understand this for the future at least—neither my commitment to my marriage or my commitment to my wife is any more of your goddamn business!"

Lacey said nothing more. He would have liked to. He would have liked to offer an apology of sorts, for overstepping what should have been the limits of even the strongest friendship. But Chase had turned without another word, mounting his horse with the awkwardness of a man who moves in pain, but with the tension of one who moves in anger also. And that had been all. Before Roger could collect his own thoughts to speak again, Chase had been gone on the dusty, wide street—cantering a horse when the man should barely have been out of a hospital bed. Damn! He'd thought. It was a rotten way to say good-bye to a man he might well never see again, an especially rotten farewell to a once-close friend. Between Susan and Leanna Penley Leighton, he acknowledged wearily, the two absent women had managed to set two friends snarling openly at each other's throats. And as for Chase Courtland's assurances of how little the lovely Rebel now meant to him, Lacey didn't entirely believe them. Yes, obviously something had happened since he'd last seen them together at Blytheswood in Virginia, now nearly a year past. Something had intervened, obviously, to sour the affair, to poison much of its initial sweetness. Chase's marriage to Susan, though, had told him that much before. But whatever that bitterness was, it was still balanced against an attraction as strong, as mysteriously compelling as any attraction he'd ever seen. Stronger, perhaps even, than Susan's and his. Few people lived with the extraordinary intensity as Chase Courtland and Leanna Leighton. And bonded together, as it once had

247

been, that depth of combined intensity had been sheerly awesome.

Winter roses, he'd thought. The phrase had been his grandmother's favorite for anything that ran counter to nature, anything that shouldn't have happened but did. What had bloomed between the Yankee officer and the fiery Virginian Rebel had been a case of winter roses . . . And where they'd bloomed once before against all odds, Lacey frowned, they were all the more likely to bloom again. He had left Savannah shortly afterward, deciding he was glad after all to be going back home.

"Roger?"

He checked his step with a startled motion, surprised to find himself on the very steps of the hospital already. As deep in thought as he was, the blocks had gone quickly by, and only now was he abruptly conscious once again of the darkness and the misting sleet, and the slender silhouette of a woman emerging slowly from the doorway there before him. "Susan?" He could only stare for a moment, oddly disoriented by both his recent musings and by utter emotional and physical weariness. Then, in an instant, he shook his head, raising one hand to keep her distant. "You shouldn't have come down, Susan. Chase isn't with me. I thought my wire had made that clear."

"Yes. But I was hoping, still, he might . . ." Susan shivered suddenly, looking over Roger's head to some invisible point in the black Washington sky, then abruptly back again to him. "Anyway, on that hope alone I had to come. And for . . . for other reasons. I wanted to say thank you, too, for what you did. And a little bit, I think, to say good-bye."

"Probably I should thank you instead. You were the one who pressed me to go. If I hadn't, I would have spent a long time asking myself why not." The wind died as he spoke, whipping the icy mist against his face, stinging where the flesh wasn't already numb from the long walk. "At least I have the satisfaction of knowing that I practice what I preach. That's something, at least. And I suppose now it will have to be enough."

Susan made an odd sound, not quite words, a brief, pained sound as if in denial of what he'd said. There was only a moment's pause and then suddenly she moved forward to him, swiftly, in a rush, as if unable to check herself. One slender hand reached out from beneath her cloak to touch his arm. "No, Roger, don't. You give yourself too little credit—you always do. I could read between the lines of the wires you sent; you saved his life, I know you did. Don't take that away from yourself. Please."

"Saved his life?" Roger had moved instantly away from her hand on his arm, feeling her mere touch in a bursting flare of anguish that was not untainted by some vague and lingering anger at her. "Did I, Susan?" There was sudden bitterness in the words he had returned to her, a question where her words had been a statement. He was recalling the last sight he'd had of the man—riding when he should hardly have been walking yet. Saved Chase's life only to see him risk it again, so carelessly, so needlessly—riding back into war as if none of it had ever happened. Riding back into war because of the telegram that Susan had sent. "Maybe I extended his life, temporarily at least. Maybe that's all God ever allows us doctors to really do. But if it hadn't been for that last damn telegram you sent down, Susan, I'd have been a lot more content with how the whole thing ended. I might even have managed to keep Chase as a friend."

"Telegram? What telegram do you mean?"

"*What* telegram?" Lacey raised his head slowly as he spoke, feeling first disbelief, then the faint flaring of outright anger at her. For a moment longer he was silent, letting it all flash back in stunning clarity—the whole damn week, the surgery itself, the angry parting there on a dusty Savannah street. That first God-awful moment on Friday a week ago, reading the telegram that Susan had sent—the damn, stupid telegram that had started it all unraveling again. All that effort and all that anguish and doubt, all spent for nothing. The agony showing all too clearly on Chase Courtland's face on Monday as he'd dragged himself up on his horse to ride back into war. The near fight he and Chase had had over Susan herself that day. And yet Susan now could so innocently ask "what telegram," as if it were an item of insignificance. "That telegram you sent down to Savannah about a week and a half ago, Susan. The one that damn near *killed* your husband when he got it. *That* telegram. Why in the hell you'd send something like that, though, I swear I'll never understand. After all that I did in saving his life. After you were the one that insisted I go down there! Why throw it all away like you did with that damn wire?" There was another silence, a sense of startlement coming from where Susan stood, still motionless as stone. She was slow to reply, and when she did, she spoke in a tone of incomprehension—as though it was not something she'd ever thought to question, nor something she'd thought she would be asked—especially by him. "Why I . . . but you asked me yourself for a more detailed report, Roger. I was only doing what I thought you wanted."

"I was expecting you to use some common sense in the thing, for God's sake. You're a nurse. Even if Chase had been a total stranger to you, you've had experience before with wounded men."

"But it was all Chase's family, Roger. It was all things he had to know about sooner or later. And knowing Chase, I simply knew he would find a way, even from Savannah, to handle all the problems that had come up since he'd gone south."

"*Handle* them?" Lacey surprised himself by feeling a surge of sudden incredulous anger, a flaring heat that instantly dispelled the freezing cold of the dark Washington night and the physical weariness, which up to now had laid on him like a second cloak. He turned sharply on one heel, flinging a single, long, disbelieving glance in her direction. But the night was too black, the mist too thick. It shrouded her face too well for him to be able to discern the expression that paled her cheeks as he continued. "*Handle* them? Damn it, Susan, Chase almost killed himself trying to get up out of bed not two minutes later! And I last saw him trying to ride before he should hardly have been walking yet! Yes, I guess you could say he was going to 'handle' them, even if he died in doing it!"

Susan said nothing, only her body did. Even in the dark of the lightless Washington night, Doc Lacey could not miss the sudden stiffening of her slender frame, the sudden rigidity of shock and astonishment. It was a statement of innocence more undeniable than any words could be—whatever she'd done, she'd truly meant no harm. In some odd way, that only seemed to make it worse, he thought. All the pain, all the risks, all had been so innocently set in motion. "God, Susan, you're *married* to the man! Don't you really know Chase any better than that?" He stared at her a moment more, with a strange kind of anger in his eyes. "Chase Courtland is not a

250

god, Susan. Regardless of what you seem to think, he's as mortal as any of us. I'm mortal, too. I was lucky in Savannah, that's all. I'm not infallible. Neither is he, For the love of God, if he does come home safely and you get another chance, don't ask us for miracles, Susan. Not again. Not me. And in the future, not Chase, either."

"What do you mean? Roger, wait! What do you mean by that? I don't understand what you're so angry at!" Lacey had already begun to turn for the door in farewell, reaching one hand out to grasp the cold brass of the heavy latch. Susan's hand on his arm checked his movement. There was a kind of sudden near panic evident in her grip, and almost reluctantly because of that he glanced back to face her. "Roger, where *is* Chase? What do you mean by another chance?"

"He's hoping to rejoin the army now, Susan, instead of coming home here to rest. Surely you had to know that already. That was the final consequence of that telegram you sent down to him."

"No . . . God, no. He can't *do* that." Susan's hand dropped abruptly from his arm, and even in the darkness, he could sense the sudden anguished incredulity she answered with. "He *can't*!"

"Can't he? Well, I wish I had your confidence in that. According to your wire, thanks to your sister-in-law Leanna Leighton is wanted now by both armies down there. Chase felt compelled by all his unbendable obligations to family honor to rejoin Sherman in hopes of offering some protection to the woman if the federal army should chance to get its hands on her." Lacey spoke without apology, stung himself by Susan's obvious dismay at the news. "You had to know, Susan. I can't believe Chase wouldn't at least wire you before he made a final decision on whether to go."

"I've been here in Washington since Tuesday. Perhaps, at home . . ." Her whispered words trailed off into sudden silence. Then she turned away from Lacey with a sudden sob, a wordless, incoherent cry of pain and utter desperation, and for a moment, she seemed to forget the surgeon who stood beside her. Instinctively, she'd turned to look south, as if somehow she might span hundreds of miles to reach Savannah. "God, no! Chase, you mustn't! I need you here! You must come home!"

Desperate as her words were, they were barely whispered.

Amid the sound of the fine sleet falling and the wicked northeasterly wind, Lacey could scarcely hear them. But he felt her anguish, and he heard her call Chase Courtland's name, and a shock of pain stabbed through him, exploding into vicious anger. "So wire him again yourself, then, if you've finally decided you do want him home so badly! But personally, I've done all I'm going to do for either damn one of you. Good-bye."

"Roger, no. Roger, wait . . ." As if startled, Susan turned back to the present from some distant place, but even as he spoke, he had already reached for the hospital door, hauling it open to start on inside. "Roger, you don't understand. For the love of God, wait—just listen to me for a—" He only jerked away from the hand she reached out to grasp him with, the gesture as coldly final as his words had been. "Roger!" Susan reached out once more in desperation as he disappeared inside, but he didn't stop, he didn't even turn his head. In the sudden light that streamed from the hallway, she had a single, shocking glimpse of his face. Anger and pain and weariness all lay etched upon it in overt display, and momentarily, the depth of the anguish it conveyed struck her dazed and motionless. An instant later, she recollected herself, but it was too late. He was gone and the door was closing in her face, shutting out whatever pleas she would have thought to make, leaving her still and stricken, barely able to think "Oh, God," she whispered to the lonely silence of the misty night. "Oh God, Roger, I think I'm with child. What in the world am I going to do? How am I going to get Chase home now? And what am I going to do if I can't?"

There seemed to be no answer to her last question. It merely echoed in her mind, lingering like the howl of a distant wolf, fearsome and oddly chilling. She would wire Chase again, of course, first thing in the morning. Pray that Sherman's army hadn't marched yet. Pray that she could convince Chase to come home. And pray that her monthly flow would still come . . . because there was nothing else left for her to do.

Chapter Fifteen

At least one part of the nightmare was over—Leanna knew that MacRae was dead. Three days after the Confederate Cavalry patrol had rescued her during her desperate escape, they had found MacRae's body floating facedown in a blackened pool of shallow water. The other man was lying nearby. Their horses were gone, their weapons stolen, and only a single small leather pouch remained on MacRae's grisly corpse. The world had turned vicious, and nowhere more vicious than here in the wilderness of the swamps. Summer Ashton stood between Leanna and that viciousness now, though. The Confederate captain was a bastion of sanity in a world gone mad, and daily Leanna thanked God for her fortune in finding him, or in his finding her—for whichever way it had actually transpired, she did not doubt that she owed Summer Ashton her life.

Originally from an area around New Orleans, he was the eighth child of wealthy Louisiana planters, and his parents— exhausted by offspring—had run out of names by his August birth and simply named him for the season. He had a younger sister, too, called simply Autumn. He was the rarest of all things left in the war—a decent man. And to Leanna, Summer was blessed proof that while the Old South might be dying, it was not yet entirely dead. His men were disciplined, honest soldiers, reflecting their captain's own restraint, and thanks to Summer and his Confederate Cavalry patrol, Leanna once again began to entertain real hope for survival in these cursed swamps.

Rumors had reached the Confederate high command of Yankees scouting the Savannah River shore, of forays into the swamp itself. Consequently, Summer and his men were here on a sweeping patrol, for no one knew what the Yankee General Sherman was likely to do next. That he or any other

253

general might actually attempt to send a large number of troops through this impassable hell seemed unlikely. But all too often, the Yankees did the damnedest things, and no one in South Carolina wanted to guess wrong on this one. Sherman had done too much damage already. South Carolinians were desperate that he be contained.

But much of Leanna's sympathy for the Deep South had faded. There might be charming cities, of undeniable grace and elegance, with walled-in gardens, whimsical wrought iron, cobbled riverfronts and dark leaved magnolias. There might be genteel sophistication among the upper strata of the cotton aristocracy. But there was also this raw and hostile outcountry, covered with tangled and thorny brush, gravelly earth and stands of scrub pine that barely clung to existence; snakes, mosquitoes, alligators and virulent fevers; the drums of the Gullah, faint and foreboding in the darkness of night; and runaway slaves, so embittered by hatred that they'd murder any soldiers who strayed from their company and were unlucky enough to run into them.

Instinctively, Leanna clung to Summer for survival in this hell. This was a world without civilization, without courtesies, where a woman was only as strong as the man protecting her. She rode at his side during the day; she shared his tent durng the night. And she and the Rebel captain had become close in many ways. Summer spoke good-naturedly of life in New Orleans before the war, of the whiskey and women and gambling, which had won him his parents' horrified disapproval. He was young and he was handsome, and there were times when Leanna nearly fancied herself in love with her gallant rescuer. But there were too many nights when she still dreamed of another soldier, one who wore a different-colored uniform than Summer did, and in the first, anguished honesty of awakening each morning, she knew her heart still lay with another man—even if that man were believed dead and buried.

It was the same dream most times. It was Blytheswood again, before the conquering Yankee armies had torched the grand old house to the ground. The elegant old white-columned house of a thousand memories, of Jewel, and Jonathon, Whitney and Miranda. And a man once beloved, whom Leanna could only believe now was as dead as Blytheswood itself. Dark-haired and so incredibly handsome, the hated blue of his uniform always an unsettling contrast to the graying white

254

of Blytheswood's paint. Amber eyes that could soften to near gold, warm and liquid, or harden to frozen black. He would be standing on the open front porch faintly smiling as he sometimes did, opening his arms to offer Leanna safety and welcome within them. But in the dream, she could never move, never force her frozen limbs to go to him, and as she stood, anguished and desperate, she would watch him fade into insubstantial shadows and be lost. "Chase? Chase?" She called to him, sometimes out loud, she knew, for more than once she had awakened Summer with her cries and he would gently hush her and tell her to go back to sleep. It was all right, Summer would say, and there was something in his tone that usually let Leanna believe his words. But some nights, though she tried, sleep would not come again for some time. And it was then she'd hear the distant throbbing of the Gullah drums, the splash of something nearby in the swamp or the muffled murmur of the soldiers walking sentry duty. And then the fear would come again—a fear not so much for the present as for the future, for she had seen her world shattered into infinitesimal pieces and there was no way she could imagine that it could ever be rebuilt again.

By now, it was nearing the end of January. And though Summer's men had scoured the swamp dutifully, there had been no sign of Yankees, either in force or singly. Another day or two, Summer had promised, and they would begin to head northwest out of the swamps, looking for the main body of Wheeler's cavalry to rejoin their usual command. They would be leaving the hell of these swamps behind them at last, and for herself, Leanna was more than anxious to go. It was another of those all-too-frequent nights tonight, when something had awakened her and she lay in her blankets frightened and uneasy, listening to the silence of the swamps outside the dark tent walls. At least it had not been the usual dream of Chase and Blytheswood that had awakened her this time. She felt none of the anguish that always lingered after that dream's passing. And whatever it was had not disturbed the Confederate captain at all; Summer was asleep still beside her, an arm's length away. In the quiet, Leanna could hear his breathing in the lazy rhythm that signified sleep. He was wrapped in his own blankets, a decent distance from hers, for she shared the Confederate captain's tent only for her own protection at night. Summer was a gentleman, and though she could and, in fact, occasionally did, catch a flash of desire gleaming in his unguarded eyes, he had never made the slightest attempt to force himself upon her.

Other than Summer's quiet breathing, the night was very still—unusually still, Leanna thought. There seemed to be an absence of the usual sounds she would awaken and listen so uneasily to. No Gullah drums disturbed the night. No horses neighed. No creatures rustled in the tangled grass or vines. Whatever had awakened her was no longer present. Still vaguely uneasy, she closed her eyes and tried to ignore thoughts of the swamp outside. This time of year in Virginia, there would be snow at night. There was always a deep, soft stillness then as the snow was falling, muffling out the usual sounds of the surrounding Valley. She did not fear the silence then, not in Virginia, and there was no reason she should fear the silence now, she told herself.

Then suddenly it came again, catching her in that twilight moment between wakefulness and full sleep. A distant laugh, strange and chilling, and the snatch of a song sung in a language she did not speak. Treejack's song. And Treejack's laugh. And Leanna bolted upright on her blankets with a soft cry of fear, reaching instinctively for Summer before she was even entirely awake.

Summer was a soldier and years of war had honed his reflexes to a razor edge. One moment sleeping, the next he was reaching to pull Leanna close with one arm, cocking the heavy hammer of his Colt revolver with the other hand as he watched the flap of the tent hanging motionless in the waiting darkness. "What is it?"

For a long moment, Leanna didn't answer his whispered question. Fully awake now, she began to doubt whether she'd heard anything at all. Only a dream, perhaps, a product of her fears that replayed a bad memory in the night's eerie silence. And now, in fact, even that strange silence was gone. From outside the tent came the usual sound of soldiers and horses and the distant splash of an animal traversing the swamp. She doubted herself, suddenly. Doubted herself almost entirely. But she couldn't deny the fearful racing of her heart, still, pressed so close to Summer's shoulder.

"What is it, lady fair? What's the matter?" Summer's hand was slowly lowering the revolver even as he spoke, cautiously disarming the cocked hammer. Leanna could hear the faint click of it as he finished and laid the gun to one side of his blankets again, then she felt the warm security of his other arm, too, coming to encircle her trembling body. "Lord, you're shaking like a leaf in a storm. What was it? Another dream?"

"No. I don't know. Maybe it was only a dream. I thought I heard someone laughing out there." She shuddered violently, finding it an effort to even speak of it. Treejack had always terrified her, his cruelty and even more, his relish in his cruelty. She had thought of him as dead, somehow. Now she wished she were surer that he were.

"Someone laughing?" There was a moment's pause, as if Summer was considering asking another question, and then he seemed to shrug the notion away. Leanna had made no effort to move away from him. If anything, she had molded herself even closer to him, trembling still in the safe circle of his arm. "Well, hell, if someone out there can find something to laugh about in this place, more power to him, I guess." Leanna's sleep-tangled hair was pressed against his face in the darkness, and Summer moved his head slightly without letting go of the girl. "Want me to go out and check around?"

"No! No, don't go out there!" In an instant, the mere suggestion had given rise to an uncontrollable surge of fear and Leanna's body was momentarily rigid with it. "Don't go out there, Summer, please!" There was an awkward silence and Leanna struggled sharply against the unreasoning fear that continued to grip her. Finally, she closed her eyes hard in a determined effort to regain control. It was only a dream, she tried to tell herself. Only your imagination. Forget it. Let it go. And at last, she felt it fading. "I'm sorry, Summer. It must have been a dream, I guess. You must be beginning to find me a most tiresome companion these days, always interrupting your sleep like some fearful child."

"Tiresome? No . . . Actually, I'm beginning to wonder if I'm not in love with you, lady fair." There was only the briefest pause, and Summer continued, his voice low and slow as if he were finding himself somewhat surprised by the words he was hearing himself speak. "Actually, I think if it weren't for this damn war that's keeping me a shade too busy, I'd ask you to marry me."

Leanna froze within his arms, conscious of a dozen different emotions that came in the wake of Summer's soft words.

Surprise was one of them, but far from the most pronounced, for she'd been aware of the closeness that had developed between her and the Confederate captain. A sudden sweet pleasure was another, and that one gave rise to a sudden sense of blissful security, an inner warmth that seemed to surround her quite as physically as Summer's arms did. Yet simultaneously, there surged a strange reluctance, too, instinctive and indefinable, and there was a moment's helpless memory of the Yankee who, even dead, continued to haunt her dreams almost nightly.

"Maybe when the war's over, lady fair. Maybe then we'll talk about whether you might like to try New Orleans with me. I don't feel I can rightfully offer you more than that till my life and my time are my own again and not the army's."

Leanna nodded wordlessly, unable for the moment to offer any surer answer to Summer than that. But she was conscious suddenly of the deep contentment she felt at being in his arms, and conscious of the surprising warmth that seemed to start within her belly, spreading slowly through her body—the first desire she'd felt for any man's love for too long a time. She turned her head in the hollow of Summer's bare shoulder, offering a tentative touch of her mouth on his throat, and waiting, almost fearfully, for his response. He stiffened for an instant, then abruptly relaxed again, keeping his embrace quite carefully unchanged, and only dropping his head slightly to touch her hair with whisper-soft kisses, lazily and leisurely, as if there were years to spend at this, and not just a single halcyon night snatched from the storm of war.

Summer had talked of New Orleans women, and a little of "fast" New Orleans belles. Beneath his quiet hands, Leanna knew it had not been just talk. Summer knew women, and he was putting that knowledge to good use with her. He touched her only with his mouth for a long time, caressing her face, her throat and her mouth with his own, slow kisses, which gradually negated the lessons of fear and cruelty that Leanna's body had learned at the hands of Stewart and then MacRae. There was no sense of urgency from Summer. His hands, as they finally moved to her breasts, were infinitely kind, infinitely gentle. She had told him little of her relationship with MacRae, nothing about the horrors of the last months with her husband, but she thought now that Summer must have guessed at least a portion of those brutal days. And in his own

258

quiet way, he would first dispel those fearful memories and teach Leanna to once again trust the touch of a man's hands on her body.

It was dark in the small pitched canvas tent. Even with her eyes fully adjusted to the night, Leanna could see Summer's face as only soft shadows, the line of his strong jaw, the momentary gleam of moisture glistening on his mouth. His dark gold hair was sleep tousled and soft where it brushed her face and throat in the wake of his kisses. She had been conscious of his scent before, riding close to him or sharing the tent at night, but now in the darkness as he held her in his arms, it enveloped her like a welcome mist—male and faintly musky, with traces of sweat and horses and leather and the acrid, lingering odor of burnt gunpowder. His bare shoulders were warm and smooth, and as he kissed her hair and nuzzled her throat and breast she pressed her own face gladly into the hollow of his muscled shoulder and returned his gentle kisses.

Above all, Leanna was conscious of feeling warm and safe. Only gradually did the more strident demand of desire make its presence known as well. It might have been close to an hour she'd laid with him, his hands slowly exploring her, his mouth wordlessly reassuring her, when his hand finally touched and lingered on the rising peak of her breast. At first, only the tips of his fingers caressed her, teasing that sensitive mound until slow shivers coursed from it at each further touch, traveling from her breast deep into her belly and adding slowly to the fires that had begun to burn there. Unaware of her action, she began to arch her back, presenting her breasts to Summer as a kind of elemental gift, coaxing his hands to take fuller possession of them and sighing with soft pleasure as he did so. Somehow Summer had managed to banish the outside world. Neither the swamp, nor the soldiers' camp, nor the laugh Leanna had thought she'd heard intruded any longer on her consciousness. One gentle hand cupped her breast, his thumb teasing the uppermost peak, his fingers kneading the soft mound of her flesh. With an unhurried move, he lifted his head at last from her mouth and dropped his lips to her breast, his teeth hard, his tongue caressing her warm and wet. Pleasure coursed through her in such sudden violence that she trembled for a moment with it, raising her hand to hold his head against her and lifting her swollen breast higher into his waiting mouth. Her arms around his shoulders tightened slowly, until she was not merely holding him but was actively pulling him closer to her, seeking the feel of his warm, bare body pressed to hers and molding her own ever closer.

At last the touch of Summer's hands was more demand than question. She had offered, he had taken. His hand on her breast took full possession there, his mouth sucked hard on her throbbing nipple, his teeth nipped delicately at the swollen bud. His other hand roamed the length of her trembling body, imperious now, exploring as he willed—her belly, her thighs, and everything she had kept a mystery from him until now. At the first touch of his fingers on her there, she moaned in helpless submission, and merely shifted her body on the rough wool blankets to offer him greater access. His hand lingered only a moment, then traveled on, denying her urgency as he was denying his own. Leanna lifted her body to him in mute desire, finding the edge of his bare hip and pressing herself against him there, her hand dropping from the smooth muscles of his back to caress the hard-drawn flatness of his belly, the line of fine hair that rose to a silky mat on his upper chest. Her hand played there a moment, touching the hard peaks of Summer's chest, then restlessly dropped again, down his taut stomach to seek his hips again. He had kept himself away from her, fearing perhaps to frighten her with the evidence of his own arousal if he'd displayed it to her too soon. Now Leanna found it with her fingers, though, the rock-hard flesh, warm and softly pulsing, and she enclosed it with her hand. Only for a moment, Summer trembled violently in her arms, his body freezing in swift response. Then he continued on as he had been before, only the quicker pounding of his heart and the sudden shallowness of his breath mute evidence of how her touch was stirring him.

Leanna moaned a coaxing plea, rolling her hips closer to his, her hands on him drawing his rigid member toward her. Summer dropped his hand instead, and the sudden action of his strong fingers left her helpless to move at all. She could only open her legs to him in moaning submission, arching her hips, and raising herself against the teasing movements of his busy fingers. There was momentary shame in this, that she should be so wanton under him, but the thought was gone as quickly as it had come. This was nature and it was elemental, and this was how the joining of a man and woman was meant to be. She was conscious now of nothing but the yearning, the throbbing demand of her body, the need to be one with him. Every touch of his fingers merely stroked the fire hotter, less controllable. Her body pouted beneath his hand, dark and wet, offering whatever it was he sought of her. And still he played a kind of waiting game with her, bringing her to the very brink of culmination and then leaving her there, deliberately, retreating to hot kisses on her throbbing breasts, penetrating kisses that took possession of her mouth. And only then he would return his hand to her, driving her higher into ecstasy once again, until a desperate hunger wracked her soul.

At last as he teased her once again and then began to draw his hand away, Leanna reached to hold his hand, demanding fulfillment, and with a sudden motion, Summer raised his hips above hers and drove within her. The sudden sensation of the fullness deep inside her brought shattering pleasure. There was an instant's utter lack of thought or awareness, only her hungry body receiving him in blind delight. Then as she came to her senses once again Summer was moving within her, thrusting in long, slow power, teasing with short, swift jabs. And as his body drove within her his hands worked as well, bringing her swiftly to another, shuddering ecstasy more total than anything she'd ever known before. This time, though, he took as well as gave, and there was a special kind of joy she found in that, holding him fiercely as Summer shuddered and moaned once in her arms, finding his own culmination now as well.

For a long moment afterward, there was only a kind of gentle quiet. Once again, Leanna could hear the sounds of the camp and the swamps that lay outside the tent walls, but they seemed oddly distant and not as fearsome as they had been before. At last, without a word, Summer raised his head from her breast and kissed her mouth, just once, and very gently, then reached to draw his blankets close to hers.

"Thank you, Summer." Leanna whispered the only words that broke the lingering quiet, and she spoke them from the pillow of Summer's bare shoulder as she curled to lie against him in the blankets. He gave her only another kiss of answer and raised one arm to circle her shoulders in the darkness.

He kept his arm around her, holding her, and a few minutes later, she could feel the rhythmic rise and fall of his chest beneath her head as he slowly drifted into sleep. She, too, was tired suddenly, content and physically spent. But a lingering echo of uneasiness kept her from the easy sleep that Summer had fallen into. What would she have said if he had pressed her farther about marriage? What if the war should end tomorrow and she should wake to find him waiting for her answer? Yes, she thought. She would simply tell him yes. If she did not love him with the same helpless compulsion with which she had once loved Chase Courtland, still Summer was a good man and she thought she loved him in a different way. Anyway, it was not, nor would it ever be, a choice between Confederate captain and Yankee major. Chase Courtland was dead and buried weeks ago. And if he weren't? The insistent echo of uneasiness would not be stilled. And if Chase, by some miracle, should rise and stand before her at this moment? Still she would choose Summer Ashton, she told herself. She would have to. Chase Courtland was a Yankee, and part of the army of hated invaders that had shattered her world. She had Chase Courtland to thank for the anguish she had known in Atlanta, for the child she'd conceived there to him and lost later to Stewart's brutality. She had Chase to thank in a way for Stewart's cruelty, and for Stewart's death. And for her own desperate dangers, for MacRae and the swamps and everything else. It had been Summer Ashton, not Chase, who had rescued her from the hell she'd fallen into. And it was Summer, now, to whom she owed all her future love and all her loyalty. On that thought, Leanna closed her mind to further doubts and nagging questions. She nestled her face deeper into his bare shoulder, feeling safe and protected for the first time in far too long, and there she fell into a deep and dreamless sleep.

"Morning, lady fair. Rise and shine."

Leanna awoke to dawn's faint light brightening the interior of the tiny tent, and Summer kneeling on one knee close beside her. She opened her eyes with a drowsy, gentle smile, not noticing at first how grim and drawn Summer's own face seemed to be. "You're dressed already." She reached to touch his hand for a moment's gentle caress, an innocent gesture of memory left from the night before.

And only for a moment, Summer's own face reflected that same gentle memory, and a smile touched his hard-set mouth.

It was in the smile's passing, the return to his face of some grim preoccupation that Leanna finally realized that something was wrong. "What is it, Summer? What's the matter?"

"Nothing too awful. We've got a long, hard ride ahead of us today, that's all. We're going to rejoin Wheeler before the day is out." But he did not meet her eyes as he spoke the reassurance, and as he turned to leave, Leanna reached a restraining hand out to take his arm.

"Summer, why? What is it that you aren't telling me?" There was a moment's awkward pause, and her hand tightened on his arm. And that quickly, a familiar vague sense of dread rose to steal the smile from Leanna's face as well. "Summer, please. Tell me what's going on."

"One of the pickets came in at dawn this morning. He'd found the body of one of Wheeler's couriers nearby in the swamp. All cut to pieces, he said. We buried the poor devil this morning already." Summer spoke tersely, with a kind of anger sharpening his reluctant words. "He never had a chance, obviously, to deliver any message, but the only reason Wheeler'd send someone out after us is to tell us to hightail it back to the rest of the army. The Yanks must be getting ready to move."

"Treejack." Leanna only breathed the hated name to herself, and occupied with sudden memory and instant horror, she hardly reacted to the rest of Summer's words. God, she *had* heard him last night, after all. And now, it was not only the Yankees, apparently, that need fear his mad brutality. Like a rabid animal, he would attack whatever crossed his path. "God, Summer, we can't stay in the swamps any longer. You're right to get out. I'll get up and dress. It will only take me a minute." Even as she spoke she was moving, reaching for her swamp-stained clothes for the day of desperate riding. Summer waited, silently, as she began to dress, and at last she paused to glance back to him, only now aware of an undercurrent of rising tension. "What is it, Summer? I have the feeling you want to ask me something or tell me something, and I don't know what it is."

"You told me your husband's family lived near Charleston, remember? I told you I'd try to escort you up that way when we were done patrolling here in these swamps." There was a momentary pause and Summer's shrug was tightly given. "I won't be able to make good on that promise now, Leanna. I'm

263

sorry. Whatever it is out in this damn swamp, and whatever it is that the general wants us back for, we won't be able to go the long way around. We'll go north for only a couple hours, then due west. Try to make the high ground, hopefully, before another nightfall stops us."

There was a moment's waiting pause. Leanna knew the question Summer was reluctant to put into so many words. She had thought originally to seek refuge at the Leightons' home, but mostly because she had no other place to go. Last night, she'd debated the choice between Summer Ashton and Chase Courtland, and that had been a question fraught with anguish, the answer colored by lingering self-doubt. This was a far easier choice to make. She owed neither Stewart nor his family the slightest continuing loyalty. "I'd rather go with you if I may, Summer. Wherever it is you may be going."

He nodded, and there was a noticeable easing in the grimly drawn lines of his expression. "That's a good decision, lady fair. We'll probably end up around Orangeburg or Columbia, and you'll be safer there anyway than you would be in Charleston. There's not much question in anyone's mind that when the Yankees do finally move, they'll be heading straight for Charleston town."

Leanna answered him with a smile, at once both gentle and faintly bitter. "I'm not sure there's a really safe place left in all the South anymore, Summer. My main concern now, quite simply, is to stay as close as possible to wherever you are."

He met her glance momentarily with his own, showing a touch of surprise that swiftly faded into a grim kind of understanding. "I'll keep you safe. I swear to God, I will. Or I'll die trying."

"I know." Unbidden tears rose to fill her eyes with bitter salt, and seeing the grim determination that lay so clearly on Summer's handsome face, a sudden ominous flare of anguish tore at her heart. "That's the way this damn war seems to work, doesn't it? Whatever we love most finally seems to lead us to our deaths."

In Savannah, Chase had waited until the last possible moment to make his decision, pressing himself each day just a fraction further, hurting and exhausted by night but able still to climb in a saddle the following day. January ended on a day of dark gray clouds, the kind of sky that presaged rain but never quite delivered it. And in its grayness, he sought out his captains to announce his decision to march north with the army. Of them all, only Grier was close enough to him to argue back, and that Grier did—in no uncertain terms, arguing as though the enlisted men that walked the camp around them, some barely a stone's throw away, must have no ears.

"You're crazy, Major. You shouldn't even consider a damn-fool decision like that! Keep your berth on that hospital ship tomorrow instead. Go the hell home and get some rest. The last thing in the world we need just now is a wounded officer to have to mollycoddle."

"I appreciate your concern, Grier." Chase spoke shortly, the tone of his voice giving Grier little reason to continue any arguments. "But I'm not asking your permission. I'm simply telling you how things are going to be."

"Damn it!" Grier exploded again in grim frustration. "That's damn near suicide and you damn well know it! You can hardly even keep on your feet at night! And the idea of your keeping up with a marching army—Rebels and swamps and God knows what else, damn it, Chase, that's crazy." Grier continued his argument stubbornly as if oblivious to the confusion going on in the camp all around him. But as Grier spoke Chase glanced around. Orders had come to march out tomorrow, the first of February, so picket posts were being called in today. The battalion camp was being hurriedly dismantled—campfires smothered, soldiers hastening to saddle horses, collecting scattered weapons, rolling blankets and loading wagons—and underneath all there seethed that strange kind of excitement that always heralded the start of a new campaign.

Any doubts that yet lingered in the back of Chase's mind were suddenly gone as he stood with his men, feeling their tension and matching it deep in his own gut. Whatever he was, he was a soldier first. He wasn't sending them north without him; he was going. "My first responsibility is here, Grier. For a lot of reasons. The war isn't over yet, and as long as I feel healthy enough to be an asset instead of a liability, I'll be leading the battalion the same as ever. That's an order, so just accept it. Now work on getting the camp cleaned up." He started away to forestall further arguments from his disapproving captain, speaking the last words over his shoulder as he walked. "I'm going into Savannah now. I'll meet the troop there later in the city. I've got some wires to send north. And I'll check with McLeod to get myself reinstated to active duty."

It isn't just Leanna either, Chase tried to tell himself as he rode the broad, shaded streets into the occupied Rebel city. Not just the telegram Susan had sent that had warned of her desperate danger. It was a real commitment, still, to the war.

In Savannah, too, there was the feel of tension and of gathering martial movement. The Rebel civilians knew what was coming: Chase could see it in their eyes as they looked at him riding their cobbled streets. Enmity, which earlier had almost disappeared, was there again. It would disappear in Savannah again, too, in a few days time, once the huge Yankee army had finally made good its ponderous exit, he thought. It always did.

As they'd done in their previous evacuation of Atlanta, the Union high command had cut communication lines out of Savannah, too—to prevent word of their advance from being sent into Rebel hands. With telegrams forbidden, Chase stole a hasty minute to write two scrawled letters, the last that would leave the Union Army now, probably, for many weeks. One was to Susan, explaining his decision to remain as well as he could explain it to a woman who understood nothing of the war that had consumed his life these past few years. The second was a note to Jonathon Penley, not an easy letter to write, but one Chase felt honor bound to put down on paper—his thanks for Penley's efforts to stay Elinor's wicked hand, and his commitment to the brother to offer protection for the sister, if or when he should cross paths with Leanna in the course of the coming campaign.

Any day before a new campaign was busy. This one was especially so, and it was past midnight before staff meetings finished, pickets all reported in and last-minute orders of march were actually issued. Chase still tired easily, and light-headed at last with weariness, he stopped to scrawl a hasty address on each letter before handing them into the waiting mails. In his hurry, he addressed the second letter to Jonathon "Courtland" instead of to Jonathon "Penley," and never even caught his error. The last thing on his mind tonight was Philadelphia and the repercussions such a mislabeling might have when the letters finally arrived up North.

* * *

It looked like a brand-new army that went marching out of Savannah, uniforms clean and crisply blue, brass buttons blazing in the glare of a cloud-free sun. Only that indefinable hardness that sets a man's face after years of war betrayed the lie of newness among Sherman's sixty thousand soldiers, and more than a return to war, the march looked like some kind of grand review, not unlike the one General Sherman had conducted weeks ago upon first taking possession of the Rebel city. Seemingly endless columns of federal soldiers crowded through the willow-leaved live-oak-lined streets, down Broad to the riverfront, there to begin crossing the pontoon bridge that snaked across the broad gray river to the marshy rice islands, and beyond to the South Carolina shore. In addition to presenting a very different picture, Sherman's army left behind a very different city than had the CSA soldiers, whose evacuation of the city six weeks ago had taken much the same route. New Orleans, Charleston and Savannah had once been the three main jewels of a glittering Southern crown. Now two of those three had already fallen to Yankee armies. And Charleston, the last, watched Sherman marching northward out of Savannah toward it, knowing the South had nothing left to keep the Yankees from taking the third and last jewel, too.

In Savannah itself, little had remained the same. It was the twilight of the Confederacy and all but the fanatics knew it. The city felt the rumblings of the ponderous Yankee field guns and the tramping of Yankee boots and saw doom marching upon their once unvanquishable cause. Aristocratic pride, prestige, privilege and the power of once-enormous wealth had all been swept away. Social extremes, light-years apart before the war, were nonexistent now for all practical purposes. The best and oldest names of Savannah, prewar gods and goddesses of the Deep South's world, watched helpless and desolate now as their Yankee conquerors filed past. Most of Savannah's men still wore Confederate gray uniforms, but neither defiance nor any vainglorious gesture had prompted the act. All military insignia had been removed, even buttons, but there were no other clothes to be had in the South any longer, and Sherman, in a position to be generous to the beaten Confederates, had paroled most of the men captured in the Yankee approach to the city and allowed them to keep their uniforms as well.

Sherman himself took no part in the army's ponderous exit. He had left the city days ago by boat, steaming north to the beautiful, quintessentially Southern town of Beaufort. The churchlike Gothic Revival mansion of his occupational headquarters in Savannah was left again to eerie quiet, minus the staccato of Yankee staff bootheels on its hardwood floors and Brussels carpet or Yankee voices in the large formal twin drawing rooms. There, massive matching chandeliers and ornate Austrian gold-leaf mirrors were unlit and empty for the first time in six weeks; the covered outside porch guarded by intricate wrought iron was devoid of the activity that had characterized the commander's headquarters, and dust had chance to settle again on the silver-plated doorknobs within the house. The mansion's design had struck many these past weeks as an ironic reflection of Sherman himself. Churchlike inside, with high-peaked, stained-glass windows and small bays like choir naves, the mansion's exterior resembled a feudal fort, with turreted towers and formidable walls. That same strange dichotomy typified Sherman also—war and church, might and the religious sanction to use it. Gentle and kindly by nature, he nevertheless perceived himself and his army as avenging angels of the Lord, and South Carolina trembled in fear before the wrath of Sherman's coming angels. South Carolina had been the first state to secede from the Union that Sherman loved both passionately and religiously, and his army was marching into that hated hotbed of secession with—as they said euphemistically—"their gloves off." Time would prove that the South Carolinians had good reason to fear the wrath of the coming Yankee storm.

At the South Carolina shore, Chase Courtland raised his hand with a frown, scanning the narrow roadway that stretched northward into sudan grass marsh and finally into distant swamp. At a signal, the front three columns drew weapons and opened fire into the gravelly mud ahead, and buried torpedoes exploded to shower wet dirt and clumps of long-stemmed grass in all directions. Chase nodded grim satisfaction and motioned the troop on. Farther back, Grier overheard murmured approvals from men who'd left Savannah in doubt, wondering whether their major—wounded as he was—was not better left behind. Little doubt, apparently, remained—especially as down the way, other soldiers were intent on joining in with their fellows on a triumphant, vengeful cheer at reaching the shore of the South's most hated state. They disregarded such caution as Chase had taken—and coming off the ferry, several stepped on buried explosives and instantly were blown to mangled bits. It had not taken long for the first casualties of the infant campaign to be registered.

In the Confederate capital of Richmond, word of Sherman's renewed movement depressed an already gloom-ridden government. Jefferson Davis and Vice-President Stephens agreed to offer greater concessions to Lincoln and Seward at the coming treaty talks at Hampton Roads, Virginia. But the meeting two days later would remain a vain effort to negotiate peace. Davis still demanded Southern independence as the price of peace, and Lincoln was less inclined than ever to offer the CSA such a hasty bargain.

In her desperation, the Confederacy agreed to draw on the only source of manpower not already hopelessly depleted—namely, the slaves. Promising freedom for any slaves who fought for the CSA cause, the action sent shock waves throughout the South and was an undeniable admission of the depth of her desperation—arming and mobilizing the very people she most desperately feared. A Richmond war clerk wrote in his diary: "Men are silent, and some dejected. It is unquestionably the darkest period we have yet experienced." But the next few months would be darker still.

On the second of February, General Sherman led the right wing of his army out of Beaufort toward the Pocotaglio lowlands. Rumor reported that he was surprised but exhilarated at meeting so little organized Confederate resistance. On the same day, Chase Courtland was riding with the army's left wing, and by some strange quirk of fate, he was struggling along almost the identical path that Leanna Leighton had once followed in *her* desperate passage through the South Carolina swamps. The same dangers she had earlier faced were now falling without mercy upon the heads of the Yankee soldiers trying to march north. Vines and sunken logs snarled the hooves of the horses; foul water wet cartridge boxes and rifle chambers; paths were nonexistent and direction almost impossible to guess. Horses stumbled with every step, often falling. The weather had warmed to an unseasonal high, awakening the snakes and insects to abnormal activity, and all too often, hard-won progress was only given back to the swamps as the cavalry turned back time and time again to help the infantry columns hopelessly mired behind them.

Field artillery, supply wagons and ambulances all sank in the mud, jammed their wooden wheels on submerged obstacles and fouled their axles on vines and long grasses. Officers shouted helplessly into sheer chaos, usually cursing; enlisted men struggled through the swamp-hell as best they could, most wading in the waist-high waters, trying to hold blankets and rifles aloft, searching for a dry route and failing to find one. Wagons were hauled free by sheer physical effort only to hit another quagmire a few yards further along and sink again. Mules and horses alike floundered in the deeper waters, tangling the slippery leather of their harnesses. Cottonmouth snakes, briefly aroused from their winter semihibernation, were hungry and vicious and struck at anything that moved.

By the end of the first day, hardly a mile had been covered. And all the gleaming newness of the army that had left Savannah had been lost to the muck of the moss-draped swamp. Soldiers were wet from the neck down and stank of stagnant water. Field cannons' open bores were clogged with mud and trailing vines, and as the army behind continued to advance over the pontoon bridge miles distant, adding new crowds of confused troopers to the already hopeless mess ahead, the whole left wing of the army degenerated into a milling crowd of utter chaos. Whole regiments played a kind of tug of war with mired wagons, literally dragging them foot by slow foot through the sucking mud. Officers looked around to realize they'd mislaid their entire command, and soldiers, winning free of the swamp, looked around to realize they'd lost their officers as well.

On the fourth of February, army engineers and the pioneer corps collaborated in an effort that was nothing short of miraculous. Pontoon bridges began to float over the worst spots of seemingly bottomless swamp and anything close to firm ground was made into a makeshift roadway. Felled trees laid side by side made a bumpy, difficult road, but any road was far superior to none. By the fifth of February, impossible as it would have seemed two days before, the infantry began to advance again.

As in the March from Atlanta, Chase's battalion was assigned to ride scouting advance for the Twentieth Infantry Army Corps. They followed a route already marked by

Kilpatrick's cavalry, which had preceded them into South Carolina—namely, the charred remains of dwellings burned, houses looted, farmsteads stripped of all supplies and distant spirals of black smoke to mark what once had been the town of Robertsville. "Kill Cavalry's" boys had shown a liberal attitude toward foraging in Georgia—now, in South Carolina, they'd abandoned most of what little restraint they had heretofore shown. And their general, with his eye on popularity and not on humanity, did not discourage them in any way.

Robertsville was still smoldering when they reached the limit of the totally gutted town. Chase halted only long enough to pass out federal supply rations to the pitiful few folk who'd dared—or been driven by desperation—to await the main Yankee army to beg for food. Pain and weariness showed on Chase's sun-darkened face—but no apology, and little sympathy for the people who edged the road and stared so bitterly at the dark blue columns that spelled their ruin. They were people who'd lost everything to the war, and now, watching the incredible might of the Yankee army passing by, knew that their cause was lost as well. Usually compassionate, he wasn't on this particular journey. Chase was desperately weary—of war and Rebels both. The responsibilities of command were draining, and long days of riding made his wounds slow to heal. He had little pity to spare by nightfall for the South Carolinians who had started the whole anguished conflict, and more nights than not, he merely fell into an exhausted, dreamless sleep little troubled by the agonies of the Rebel refugees. Conscience required energy, and Chase had none just now to spare.

There were roads now at least, narrow and often mud-rutted, but a vast improvement over uncharted swamp. The Union advance proceeded quickly to Barnswell and beyond, joking about changing the town name to "Burnswell" as they left. Occasional inconsequential resistance from Wheeler's cavalry and partisan raiders finally began, pitiful attempts that did little but break the wearying monotony of march for Sherman's columns. Five thousand Confederates trying to overmatch sixty thousand federals was a cause lost before it was fairly begun. Skirmish lines occasionally formed, distant artillery boomed, but the major menace to the Union Army had been the swamps, which the CSA high command had believed to be impassable. Sherman had proved otherwise; by today, the last regiments leaving Savannah found the Carolina swamps well tamed. Corduroyed roads and pontoon bridges allowed the troops to advance with practically normal speed, and Sherman had made clear his point. Quite literally, come hell or high water, *he* was marching north.

Humbled at last by desperate need, Jefferson Davis overcame personal enmity to appeal to Sherman's old adversary, General Joe Johnston to take command of what forces he could gather to meet the unstoppable Yankee army. The brilliant CSA defensive genius would slowly gather nearly thirty-five thousand troops, but not in time, and not enough to balance the terrible odds. As Chase rode with the federal army he no longer saw a South united by a cause, arrogant with riches and power. He found the ruins of once-great plantation mansions, the black smoke of cotton burning in distant barns, and he found the collapse of a world that would never quite manage to rise again from the ashes of its own destruction. He found bitterness and grief, widows and orphans, but he had not yet found Leanna Leighton.

Chapter Sixteen

In the federal capital, the mood was strange. For four years, Washington had been obsessed only with the necessity of winning the long war. Now, victory seemed only a matter of time, so people had the luxury of devoting some attention to plans for bitterness, vengeance and eventual profits. Profiteers had begun to slip southward already, infiltrating all areas of Union occupation, and their numbers were only a presage of the rush to come at the war's end. Western territories, largely ignored for the past few years, began to intrude once again on governmental consciousness. Gold had been discovered in Colorado in 1860. Silver had been found since, in incredible abundance, huge veins a mile high in the Rocky Mountains. Denver had grown in the war years from a mining supply depot to a bustling city; the federal fort there, safeguard against attacks by the Comanche, Cheyenne or Arapaho tribes, would be among the first of the western outposts to be regarrisoned. Casualties from the eastern war were at an all-time low; military hospitals in Washington were half empty, several already closed down. Doc Lacey's long-awaited transfer to Denver had finally come through with unexpected suddenness; now it was tentatively scheduled for the first of April, but tentative, still, because the spring campaign could change the casualty numbers drastically here in the eastern war. Lee's Virginia army, already pitifully depleted, was losing men to desertions, too, now as winter's cold, hunger, scurvy, hopelessness and Sherman's Deep South menace continued to drain CSA Virginia lifeblood. But Robert E. Lee could do more damage with fewer troops than any other general the country had ever known, and every previous spring—somehow, some way—the gallant fighter had managed to deny the odds and continue the uneven struggle. No one in Washington would bet prematurely against Lee's performing the same kind of miracle this spring as well.

But spring was months away yet. Today was only the end of the first week of February, and it was cold and damp and gray as only Washington could be gray this time of year. Doc Lacey walked into his now-empty Confederate ward simply to say good-bye to the place that had been his home for over a year. Now it was closed and silent, the whole ward shut down. The iron-frame cots were left still, looking like long close rows of metal skeletons, the mattresses already gone, probably to the burn heap somewhere. The converted warehouse had always been cold in winter anyway, drafty from the high, open-beamed ceilings, and it was colder than ever today without bodies or fires to warm it. Frost had clouded the northside windows to an opaque gray, stealing what little light the day could have offered. It was an ugly place, Lacey decided, totally unrelieved by light or human warmth, an appropriate setting for the ugliness and anguish it had hosted these past years. He would not miss either the place, the pain, or the war itself when he finally left for Denver and a land unsoured by the violent bitterness of civil war.

"Roger?"

Susan's footsteps had been too soft on the bare wood floors to have interrupted his thoughts before. Lacey turned with a start at the sound of her voice to find her framed in the open doorway a half-dozen yards from him. It had been weeks since he'd seen her—since the quarrel which had marked his return from Savannah—and in a way, he had not thought to see her again. But she was here now, dressed in what looked like traveling attire—somber shades of gray and her long hooded cloak a dark dull blue. Perhaps because of the contrast, her face appeared particularly pale and shadows seemed to ring her eyes. He'd felt a familiar anguish stab his heart as soon as he'd turned to see her, but he'd kept his place, refusing to allow himself to move toward her. Nothing had changed.

"They told me downstairs that they've closed the ward. That you've been given your transfer to Denver. I had to see you before you left."

Doc Lacey nodded once, conscious of the distance between them and glad of it. The bare wood planks of the vinegar-washed floor lay between them like a barrier—the distance between Denver and Philadelphia would be even better. "Chase has changed his mind, then? He's coming back here to Washington instead of marching on with Sherman? You're here to meet his ship?"

There was a subtle change in Susan's face. If possible, she seemed to grow even paler in the dim, grayish light. "No." For a moment more, she was motionless, standing in silence and watching Doc Lacey. Then she shook her head and looked away. "No, I sent Chase several wires. If he ever received them, he never answered them. And then I received a letter from him, yesterday, the first letter I've gotten from him in almost four years. He's gone on with the army. He's reinstated himself to active duty."

There was barely an instant's silence, and Lacey shrugged, speaking softly. "Military dispatches have priority over civilian communications, Susan. Chase probably never even got your messages. And even if he had, I can't say I'd be surprised to hear he went on with Sherman anyway. I was there when he read that telegram you sent. You did it to yourself, in a way. And knowing Chase as well as I do, I hardly doubted he would find a way to rejoin his command before they marched north." He turned away as he spoke, avoiding meeting her eyes. He pitied her suddenly, and he didn't want her to read that on his face. It was not just the war, Lacey was thinking, remembering that disastrous wire and the violence of Chase Courtland's reaction to it. Perhaps it was not even *mostly* the war. It was Leanna Leighton, he wanted to say. You did it to yourself, Susan. You asked too damn much of him. Married to you or not, still there is too strong a bond between Chase and the beautiful Rebel, wherever Leanna Leighton might now be. Just as I can't seem to break the bond that ties me to you, guilty or not, Chase can't break the bond that ties him to Leanna. No, I'm not at all surprised to hear he's gone.

"And what about you, Roger? Do *you* love me, at least? In spite of everything, do you love me still?"

Susan spoke softly, but the anguish behind her words was clearly audible. It brought an answering shock of emotion from Lacey, a stabbing despair that cut as badly as any of his surgeon's knives. "Damn it, Susan, you shouldn't even ask me that. Yes, I love you. God help us both, I do. And I imagine I always will." He turned abruptly away, toward the door-

275

way of the empty room, but he didn't leave. He merely stood and looked at its offered escape without quite being able to take it.

"And would you do me a very great favor if I asked it of you?" There were tears evident in her voice, and he could only close his eyes in helpless pain, bracing himself, but for what he wasn't sure. There was a sudden silence, and when she spoke again, her words tumbled out in a sobbing rush. "I'm pregnant, Roger. And it isn't Chase's child. I want you to kill the baby somehow, Roger. Get it out of me. You're a doctor; you must know a way to do that somehow. Please."

Whatever he'd expected, it wasn't this. It felt like a dozen different emotions tearing at him in unison, flaring agony and furious pain. "God, no, Susan. You can't be serious!" He wasn't even sure what he was denying—her pregnancy, her anguish, or her solution to them both. He'd jerked back to face her instantly, his own face as bloodless as hers, his mind shocked and stunned and slow to work.

"Kill the baby—or kill me, Roger. I've considered that, too, already. Do one or the other; you owe me that much. I beg of you. Please!"

"For the love of God, Susan! Murder the child or murder you? You really think I would ever agree to such a horror?"

"But you've got to! Oh God, Roger, you've got to do something!" Doc Lacey shuddered once violently, turning away from Susan in a blind desperation to deny that recourse. She reached after him as he started for the door, holding his arm in a desperate grip. "Oh God, no, Roger, don't leave me! What else do you think I can do? Chase and I have never even consummated our marriage! So, what am I going to offer for an explanation whenever it is he finally returns home? What?"

"The truth! Dammit, tell Chase the truth; is that so hard to finally figure out?" Lacey had whirled on one bootheel to face her, the words exploding from him in an uncontrollable burst of anguish and anger together. It left him shaking as he spoke, but he couldn't seem to stop the words. "Stop the lies, Susan! Stop them now! Yours to Chase, and his to you! If the marriage isn't consummated, then it isn't too late after all! Tell him what's happened, and tell him the *truth*! Ask him for an annulment. Let me marry you, then—take you on to Denver with me! There's another solution for you, Susan— take it!"

She stared at him as if in shock, her hand dropping from his arm as she took a single, slow backward step. "An annulment?" She searched his face with frightened eyes, then slowly, very slowly, she shook her head and backed another step away. Had she shouted a denial, her answer couldn't have been more clear.

"You just told me that the marriage hasn't been consummated yet. So an annulment now is the only solution," Lacey continued, almost harshly, reaching out to grasp her arm in a painful hold.

"No, I can't, Roger. I have no grounds! Chase was of age when we married, and I had my parents' full consent!"

"But Chase has grounds." His words came clearly, dropping like individual pebbles into a pool of rising tension. He held her eyes with his own, relentlessly, commanding her. After an instant's frozen silence, she shook her head again, but fitfully—as if trying to deny him, but unable to look away and break his gaze. "*Chase* has grounds," Lacey repeated it once more, barely above a whisper. "Let *him* move for the annulment. Susan, please. We *still* have a chance, now."

Her face had drained totally bloodless. Open-eyed and staring, it looked nearly like the face of a corpse. "You mean to actually confess to him of my infidelity? My love for you?"

It was only a whisper, but sounded strangely loud in the room's sudden cavernous silence. Doc Lacey looked across an arm's length of distance into Susan's eyes and what he read there made his stomach heave and rise in desperation. "God, Susan, it's better than your dying. Or our murdering our own child, isn't it? *Isn't* it? It's not like we've got a world left of choices?

"They've cut communications to the army, I'm sure. They did before. I'm sure they have now as well. And even if they hadn't, I couldn't do that, Roger. Not tell Chase what I've done. I couldn't. I *couldn't*."

"But *I* could."

"No . . . No, you mustn't! I'll find another—"

"There *is* no other way, Susan. Face it now before you add worse horrors on top of it! For the love of God, just once in your life, have the courage to tell Chase Courtland the truth! If you don't owe it to yourself, then dammit, you do owe it to him!" He reached out suddenly to grasp her arm, breaking her sudden lunge toward the door. Susan whirled back to face him with the desperation of a cornered animal.

"No! I won't! You have no right to ask that of me! I'll find another way!"

"What other way? Throwing yourself into some damn river? I won't let you do that, dammit! I won't!" He pulled her back, struggling against her rising efforts to break free. Susan sobbed and writhed in his grip, kicking and clawing to get away. The very violence of her struggles convinced him beyond any shadow of a doubt that he must not let her go, and he held on to her with a desperation that matched her own and then exceeded it. "Susan, you've got to accept what's happened. Maybe it's even for the best in a way. I *love* you. I *want* you and I *want* our children. Do what has to be done and then come to Denver with me as my wife. We'll leave it all behind us, all of it. Chase and the war, the hospital here. We'll build a new life, a good life, and no one out there will even know about the past. Susan, I beg you! Susan, please!"

She collapsed suddenly in his grip with a last anguished cry, and he reached out with a sudden motion, pulling her to him and wrapping his arms around her trembling body to keep her close. His own arms were trembling by now, too, his whole body shaking with such violence that he could hardly stand.

"If they've cut communications to Sherman's army, how could we even get word down to Chase?" Susan was sobbing harshly in Roger's arms, her words punctuated by a dozen anguished gasps for breath.

"If they've cut communications already, then we can't. Then we'll have to do it another way." He closed his eyes momentarily, allowing himself one long, deep sigh of pain. "Nor can we afford to wait for Sherman's campaign to end, Susan. My transfer to Denver is slated for the first of April, and there's no guarantee we'll be able to even get a letter through to Chase by then. Down in Savannah, though, Chase told me his father has full power of attorney for him. We'll have to speak to your father-in-law about it, instead. We'll go up to talk to Joshua Courtland."

He felt her freeze abruptly in his arms, and felt her begin to raise her head. "No . . . No, wait and talk to Chase, Roger. Not to Joshua Courtland, please. Chase might understand— because of your friendship, and because . . . because you did, after all, you saved his life. You might make him understand, I think, a little of what has happened. But I can't stand in Chase's father's house and tell Joshua Courtland face-to-face that I cuckolded his son before I ever even married him." As she'd spoken her eyes had widened to great, dark pools in an ashen face. Beneath his hands, Roger felt her begin to shake again, more violently. "Oh God, I *can't*. I can't do that, Roger. I can't!"

For one blind instant, he felt a rage so violent he almost struck her, actually had one hand raised and tensed for the blow. In the next, the anger had passed, leaving him deeply, emotionally, drained—but rational once more. He reached to pull Susan against him again, her face pressed to the hollow of his shoulder as she gave a last, small cry. Maybe it was what made him love her so dearly—that part of her some might label weakness, or cowardice. An inability in her to refuse, to disobey, to admit reality when it contradicted fantasy. She could not take the ultimate responsibility for her own life into her own hands. And maybe there was an overabundance on his part of the usual professional compassion—an inability in him to resist such vulnerability. Whatever it was, he loved her. For exactly what she was. And anger held no future place in what he felt for her.

Susan was crying softly against his shoulder, murmuring what sounded like pathetic, childlike apologies, muffled in the dark cloth of his uniform. Thank God, he thought suddenly, that Chase Courtland had never actually managed to love her. For his sake, for Susan's, for them all. At best, it would have doomed both Chase and Susan to a lifetime of hell. Beneath the quiet, strong stability of Chase's facade lay an awesome inner intensity—powerful, seething, deeply passionate. And the force of that let loose on Susan's emotional fraility would have been like a hurricane unleashed on the fragile camellia blooms he'd seen in Savannah—overwhelming and destructive beyond measure. Chase's choice of Leanna Leighton had been far more sound. There he'd found a strength and a spirit more than able to match his own. Perhaps, once freed of his own marriage as Leanna had been freed of hers by her Rebel husband's death, perhaps with the ending of the long, bloody war that had split asunder the country for nearly four years, perhaps despite the bitterness and the anger that had marked them before, Chase and Leanna

Leighton might yet manage to achieve a private peace with one another—as both North and South would have to do on a larger scale in the months ahead. He would have to hope so, at least.

Notwithstanding the pathetic naiveté of Susan's thoughts, Lacey understood as a man that his talking to Chase could accomplish very little. It would not undo what had occurred; the bleak fact still remained that Susan was Chase's wife . . . before that she had been Chase's fiancée. Yet she was carrying Lacey's child. It was not a fact that one man conveyed to another and had any portion of a friendship remain. That farewell had been final, then, that bitter day long ago in Savannah. Lacey'd had the feeling at the time it would be—he just hadn't known the reason for the feeling back then. And now he did. His friendship with Chase Courtland was only another casualty of the war.

He felt Susan's sobbing quieting finally in his arms, and he brushed her hair with a kiss before he spoke. "You needn't speak to Joshua Courtland yourself, Susan. That's not even what I meant. I can go alone and say whatever needs to be said to him." She made a small moaning sound against his shoulder, turning her face closer against him. There was a long silence; the sun passed under a cloud outside, plunging the dingy gray of the room into depressing shadows, then came free again to offer faint light. Finally, Susan nodded once, but without being able to lift her eyes to meet his.

"You'll tell your parents . . . whatever you wish to, love." Lacey's eyes were dark above her head as he spoke. "Tell them nothing about the child if you'd rather not. We'll be in Denver for its birth, after all, and we can as easily write an announcement in November as in September, if that's what you'd prefer."

"But . . . what will you tell Chase's father then, Roger?" Must you tell him what I've done? Done to him . . . and done to Chase?"

Lacey's face was bleak and drawn. A kind of grim, dark sorrow lay in his eyes, and he was careful to keep Susan's head down close against him so she couldn't see the expression on his face. "Maybe not, Susan. But I'll tell him whatever I have to to convince him that an annulment is the only possible answer for the marriage," he spoke softly, brushing her hair with a last, soft kiss. "I won't lie anymore: to him, to

Chase or to you. I'll tell him whatever I have to, to ensure Joshua Courtland's consent to annulment. I'm afraid it's time at last, for *all* of us to tell ourselves and each other the absolute truth. Our lies haven't helped any of us anyway, have they?"

That same afternoon in Philadelphia, Joshua Courtland awoke and was surprised to find a letter from Chase lying on the nightstand by his bed. The sun was setting outside, the shadows in the room dark gray and lengthening, and he reached to turn the light up higher. He'd dozed off, he guessed, going over the ledgers Jonathon had brought up to him earlier, faithfully, as the young Rebel brought them up twice a week. Joshua had been pleased but vaguely bored with columns of numbers that no longer held much meaning for him. The bank was simply in Jonathon Penley's more than capable hands. Jonathon had weathered Bonnie's death decently well. Neither he nor Whitney blamed Joshua, or the North, or anything but vagrant fate for the baby's fatal fevers. And Joshua had been grateful for that—fearing bitterness, and hiding the secret guilt of wondering himself whether the terrible dampness of a Philadelphia winter had been partly to blame for the infant's death. Whitney had suffered more, he thought. Her soft, gray eyes were shadowed lately as if haunted always by secret troubles. But with another child's arrival imminent, she made a show, at least, of keeping her spirits up. And Miranda, of course, with that magic, irrepressible radiance of only the very young or the very foolish, had somehow expanded her presence as if to fill the void left by her younger sister's death. By now, too, it was the end of the first week of February, Joshua reminded himself. The new baby's arrival would come anytime now, and it would do much to alleviate the lingering anguish of the parents' loss.

As Joshua reached across to take up his son's letter he was preoccupied by other thoughts. Jonathon Penley had continued to shield him from all knowledge of either the near disaster he'd so barely averted at the Courtland bank or from the part played by Elinor's hand in creating the confusion there to begin with. Joshua knew nothing of either Leanna Penley Leighton's danger, Jonathon's foiled hopes to go to her rescue or of his own son's reaction to those recent events. He was smiling faintly as he began to read Chase's note, expect-

281

ing to find there reassurances of his son's health and perhaps finally a definite date of his return to health. What he found there was not at all what he had expected.

. . . well enough, I feel, to rejoin my command. We will march out tomorrow, approximately at dawn. In all candor, I must admit that my main reasons for such an action are not generous, but simply required, as I see it, if I am to do my duty to my country and to the soldiers under my command. Our differences of opinion in that regard are too well known to both of us for me to bother further delineating them here, but regardless of our disagreement, my decision to go on with the federal army may have advantages for you in one way. Due to your participation in the war and your subsequent parole, you are essentially imprisoned in the North for the duration of the conflict. Due to my commission in the Union Army, I am required to remain in the South. You have undertaken an obligation to benefit my father and family, there, and conscience requires me to offer my same services in return to your family. By marching on with General Sherman tomorrow, I shall, at least, remain here in Confederate territory. And so long as you remain in Philadelphia guarding my family's interest against the treachery of my sister's designs, I will stand in your stead here in the South. Should your sister, Leanna, be unfortunate enough to cross the path of our marching army once again, I will do everything in my power to assure her safety, regarding either your army or my own. Whatever other differences may lie between you and me, I would hope at least that you will acknowledge me gentleman enough to find reassurance in that promise of aid. Had it not been for my sister, your own would be in far less danger. And surprising as you might find it, we "Yankees" too have our own sense of honor to uphold. You may communicate this, too, if you will, directly to my sister, Elinor: that I hold her absolutely and in every way accountable for this course of events and that she will have every cause to regret her treachery when I return.

Your servant, etc.
C.E. Courtland, Major
U.S.A.: 8th Penna. Vol.
Army of the Tennessee
Camp of the 20th Corps."

It was a letter uncompromisingly cold in tone, and completely bewildering to a man who knew nothing of the events that had preceded its writing. Joshua knew only a sudden shocking sense of confusion and deep, trembling anger. Something was wrong. Something had most definitely, most desperately gone wrong in this long month in which he'd lain in bed. The possibility that he had been lied to, even if for his own good, was intolerable to him . . . doubly intolerable was the letter's reference to treachery on the part of his own dear daughter, written here in his son's own hand. While he'd lain convalescing, a storm of disaster must have swept his world, menacing everything and everyone he held most dear. Exactly how or what, he could not begin to understand just yet. But he would find out, Joshua promised himself. Before another day had gone to rest, he would know *exactly* what had happened. It was time, no *past* time, he amended grimly, that Joshua Courtland arose from his sickbed.

Heart pains flared with his sudden anger. As he reached across the nightstand for the bell that would summon Cooke he found his hand was trembling in uncontrollable violence, giving the normally mellow tone of the bell a strident edge. He ignored both the pain and the trembling, swearing in impotent rage at his body's weakness. Such weakness had kept him in its isolated, helpless cocoon too long already. It would keep him there not a minute more.

"Yes sir, you rang?" Cooke had arrived with a hurried step, as if sensing the impatience of that strident call. At the edge of the room, he hesitated, seeing Joshua already rising from his bed. Cooke stood there a moment in startled disapproval.

"Fetch me my normal clothes, Cooke. It's time I arise from this damn sickbed."

"But the doctor was most adament, sir, that you remain resting for several more weeks, until—"

"I don't have several more weeks to spare, Cooke." Joshua interrupted the servant sharply, gesturing him toward the nearby wardrobe. "I want my clothes and I want them now. You needn't look so stricken. I'm not going to die just yet. Nor have I lost my mind. Ask Jonathon Penley to come by. Also my daughter Elinor. Tell them I shall await them downstairs in the parlor. I think it's time the three of us had a little chat."

"But Lady Bennington is not presently at home, Mr.

Courtland. She left a few minutes ago. And I would not expect her to return before . . . it will be late, sir. Probably morning."

"Oh. I see." Joshua found the implication of that discreet wording only momentarily surprising. You've known for a long time, he told himself bluntly. Known that much about your daughter's appetites. You simply chose to ignore the obvious, hoping you might manage to die before something sufficiently untoward forced you to confront it. "Well, we must leave my daughter for tomorrow then. Is Jonathon in?"

"Yes sir. I just saw the carriage as a matter of fact. I believe he's at the cottage by now."

"Fine. Tell him I've a letter from my son, Cooke. Tell him it's addressed to him, but by the grace of God, erroneously labeled and delivered to me instead." Cooke nodded, ashen-faced but ever the obedient, unquestioning servant. "And now my clothes. Tell Jonathon I shall await him in the parlor, at once."

"But sir—"

"Don't argue, Cooke, it only wastes time. And I have very little left. Some men are fortunate, you know; they get to die in some peace. But I'm not to be one of them. I don't mean that bitterly, Cooke, but simply as fact. You know a poet said once that a man's life isn't measured by what a man lives for but what he's willing to die for. I've always said that honor and real justice were that important to me, and perhaps it's time to prove that. You've got to fight for something besides yourself, Cooke, something greater than your own survival—or you're doomed before you begin, even the cleverest of us, by our own mortality."

Joshua found himself speaking with sudden vehemence to the pale Cooke. He grimaced then, falling silent, and then gestured abruptly for the servant to be on about his errand. Damned old fool, Joshua accused himself angrily. What does Cooke care about your prattling philosophies? What do any of them care, he asked himself in sudden, shocking bitterness. The world's outgrown such idealistic notions. Honor and justice belonged to a bygone age, as much an anachronism now as Joshua himself. Look at the coalition, men frantic with greed and selfishness. Look at the country torn bloodily asunder by war. Look at his own family—Chase and Elinor—look at Jonathon and his sister Leanna—all, somehow, at war. And

284

he'd only seen the tip of the iceberg yet, he reminded himself. God only knew what lay below, submerged and veiled, waiting only for the final reckoning now to surface. But he was not a man who'd lived a peaceful life; he'd had no reason to expect that he should die a peaceful death. It was a world at war, and while he remained still a part of that world, there would be battles ahead that he must fight and try to win. Anachronism or not, it was the only way Joshua Courtland knew how to live.

Cooke had been right in his guess regarding the Courtland daughter's absence. It was midmorning, actually, before Elinor finally returned home, smiling a secret catlike smile and entirely satisfied with the night she had just spent. She had gone to Roland Hodges to talk business, and met a fine young man there up from Washington on some errand for Lafayette Baker's secret police. Kindred spirits, they'd decided together. And they'd proceeded to enjoy various pleasures far more physical than spiritual in the ensuing hours. Another shipment of guns was already on its way south, their earlier schedule somewhat accelerated by brother Chase's overly quick recovery to health. Once Chase came home, she must take care to do nothing he could actually *catch* her doing. Fear of his father's health might hold Chase's hand to some degree, and for a little while, with any luck, Chase might even be ill enough to be confined to bed. But Elinor would play a careful game these next few months, because the stakes were high enough to warrant such caution. Chase's suspicions, even her brother's outright anger was one thing. In and of itself, totally insignificant to her. But the slightest chance that he might be enraged to the point of confronting their father with his suspicions—*that* must never happen.

As of now, her father's will was very impartial. Chase got half, and she got half. Compared to the fortune Joshua would be leaving for an inheritance, even the profits of wartime gunrunning were peanuts. It would be even nicer, Elinor mused thoughtfully, if she could arrange to inherit *all* of it. But Chase would have to die, first, of course—something she doubted he would be much amenable to arranging for her. Instead, he showed the most damnable determination to survive.

She began to reach for the door—and suddenly froze, struck by the possibilities of such a thought. Stupid, she accused herself. She had never even considered it before, and the war had presented such a splendid opportunity. How had she missed something that should have been so very obvious? She could mention it to Roland perhaps? Or to her new friend, the one she'd met last evening? Of course, it would probably be too late by now unfortunately. Chase was scheduled home any day to convalesce. She should have thought of it sooner, while he was still fighting in the field. Well, if the war lasted long enough this spring, perhaps he would go back into it, and she could arrange something then. And in the meantime, she would be very, very nice to her brother while he was home. She would behave with complete decorum, be the model sister, and for her father, the model daughter. She would even wear black in mourning for Chase, and hold her father's hand as they buried one brother beside the other over in the cemetery behind St. Mark's.

Yes, she decided quickly. In fact, she would mention it to her friend tonight—casually, at first, to assess his reaction. He was staying one more night here in Philadelphia before returning to Washington. Perhaps, if he were willing to assist her, they might even manage to have her convalescent brother take a sudden turn for the worse before he got on a hospital ship out of Savannah. That might be the best of all.

The door opened suddenly, before she'd rung the bell, but busy with her thoughts, Elinor scarcely noted either her omission or the expression Cooke's face wore as he stood to one side and gestured the Courtland daughter on inside. Preoccupied as she was with her own thoughts, her first clue of something gone amiss came with Cooke's rather imperious gesture toward the Courtland dining room. "Excuse me, Lady Bennington. Your father is breakfasting in the dining room this morning, and he has requested you join him there—as *promptly* as *possible*."

It was instinctive with Elinor. She paused with one foot already on the stairs and one hand already on the banister. Taken aback, she made a small gesture of delay while her mind flew in rapid thought. *Promptly?* That meant *now*, with her father. It was a bare courtesy, cloaking a rare demand. Had something somehow gone wrong? What was Joshua even doing downstairs? "I should change, though," she murmured. "Perhaps to a more suitable—"

"I would guess your attire inconsequential, Lady Bennington.

Shall I bring breakfast into you there? Or do you prefer to breakfast later in your room?"

Something *must* be wrong. Cooke's insolence was subtle—both his interruption and his assumption that she *would* proceed directly to the dining room in compliance to his request—it left her with no way out of obeying her father's order now. Elinor managed a cordial smile, inclining her head as if she were graciously acceding to a wish rather than responding to something far more nearly a command. "Of course, Cooke. But tea and a croissant, perhaps. Something light." She turned even as she spoke, but spared a single, sharp glance back at Cooke's face. Surely the servant's exquisitely orchestrated maneuverings just now had not been deliberate. If they *were*, she thought suddenly, she must pay far closer attention to what he saw or heard from now on. Servants with brains could become most tedious. Perhaps it was time to have Cooke "replaced."

"Father! How delightful to find you dressed and downstairs once again!" Elinor had deliberately armed herself with her most dazzling smile, barely pausing in the dining-room door before crossing to where her father sat at a nearby table. But Jonathon Penley sat there, too, and noting his presence, Elinor's step involuntarily faltered. Jonathon rarely bothered to conceal his expression; he didn't now. He looked grim and sleepless, and hostility lay open and cold there in his tired eyes. She glanced warily to her father and found Joshua's expression a near match to Penley's, and braced herself for a difficult time. Never in her life had she seen her father look that way at her.

"I have a letter here from your brother, Elinor. It was meant for Jonathon, but fortunately or unfortunately as the case may be, it was delivered to me, instead. I'd like you to read it. And then I'd like to hear an explanation of just exactly what it is that Chase is referring to here." Joshua did not move to hand her the letter. It lay, dirty beige on the snow white linen cloth, and he merely gestured curtly toward it.

For a moment, Elinor was conscious of a lack of movement, very nearly a lack of thought. Then she recollected herself quickly, pretending not to notice her father's extreme discourtesy in refusing to reach the letter toward her. She picked it up and read the thing swiftly, acutely conscious of both men's eyes on her, eyes burning with dual intensity: Jonathon Penley's with accusation, her father's with suspicion. She read Chase's errant letter a second time, too, to be sure she knew the contents of it well. She did not want to catch herself in the old trap of volunteering more knowledge than the letter actually held.

It was a disaster, of course, she recognized the fact of that quite clearly. But thank God, the letter was fairly vague. And one piece of splendid luck—Chase had apparently gone on with his army, so he wouldn't be bringing any more specific accusations home with him shortly. I'm sorry, brother—she suffered only a moment's odd compunction—but if any doubts had lingered from her earlier consideration of arranging Chase's death, they lingered now no longer. She simply could not afford to chance his return now. The letter she held in her hands was his death warrant.

To Joshua watching her, none of those thoughts had shown on her face. Above all else, Elinor was a consummate actress. Her hand trembled now as she reached to replace the damning letter on the table linen, and her green eyes glittered with genuine tears. She looked up at him finally, meeting Joshua's eyes in a long, lingering silence. She had always had this power over her father. She knew she had that power still. The unshed tears glistening in Elinor's eyes were like a knife turning in Joshua's heart, and in the face of that silent wounded innocence, an awful wrench of doubt blunted his earlier anger. He had to force himself even to hold his ground. "Jonathon and I have spent the night awaiting your return, Elinor. Passing the time by discussing certain events that relate to the contents of the letter you have just read. He's told me you've taken money, unauthorized money, from the bank. He's told me you've arranged to endanger his innocent sister, Leanna, for the sole purpose of blackmailing his cooperation in your taking even more. And I know that because of that vicious arrangement, your brother has been obligated to drag himself out of practically his deathbed to try to protect Major Penley's sister if he can."

But you don't know about Roland and Hodges and the guns then, father, do you? And that's the only thing I think you wouldn't finally forgive me for. Elinor made a show of struggling for composure, allowing a single tear to roll down her cheek, and clearing her throat before making her answer. "I don't doubt you found Jonathon Penley more than delighted, too, to vouch for all these absurd accusations, Father. This little drama was probably all arranged before Chase ever left this house to return to war."

"I don't believe there was any arrangement, Elinor." But challenged, in that instant, Joshua's voice reflected defensiveness along with anger. "Jonathon volunteered nothing. No more than your brother, Chase, meant to. What I know now is simply fact."

"What you 'know now' is Chase's and Penley's word against mine, Father," Elinor countered instantly, sensing a weakness and pressing it further. "Of course, how could I expect my poor truths to carry equal weight to Chase's lies? I was never anything to you, anyway, was I? It was always only your sons you loved. Not me, but Josh Jr. and Chase. Even when the war broke out and they left you, both of them, riding off with their uniforms, and bands playing, off to the glories of war, it was I who came back from England so you wouldn't be left here alone. I who left my home, my husband. Because I thought, if you lost Chase, too, that you would need me finally—not to be alone. I loved you better than anything else in the world and you never loved me at all! This is only the final proof of that. And now there's some Confederate stranger you put before me as well, and you love me less than ever!"

"That isn't true!" Joshua's knuckles whitened abruptly where he clutched the edge of the table. Pain flared in his chest, and his eyes sparkled with sudden tears to match those tears of his seemingly frantic daughter's. "This isn't a question of whether I favor you or Chase! God help me, if I loved any of my three children more or less, it was *you* I most favored! God help me, Elinor, in a way, I loved you better than *both* my sons!"

Something quite cold and calculated flashed for a heartbeat in Elinor's eyes—Jonathon sitting, watching, noticed it and instantly felt his blood run cold. But in his pain, Joshua didn't seem to see it at all. "Prove to me you haven't done these things, then, Elinor!" Joshua was the one pleading suddenly—a strong man breaking, desperate to justify a love he couldn't dismiss. Evil or not, he loved her still—a parent's curse, a heart that refused to recognize flaw in its most dearly prized possession. "Oh God, I would sell my soul to Satan himself to prove such accusations only lies, Elinor! Don't you understand that?"

"And *how* shall I prove them lies?" She turned away, her

voice shrill and sharp with rising bitterness. "Shall I pluck brother Chase up from wherever he is now with his precious army? Shall I have Jefferson Davis drop by to explain what reasons he had for suspecting Jonathon Penley's sister of treason?" She gave a small, stiff shake of her head and another sob. "Read the minutes of the bank meeting for your proof if you need it, Father. Read the part where I voted, *both times*, against the minority interests. Ask your doctors who sat up with you most nights while you lay unconscious. Not Chase. He left. Not Jonathon Penley either—he was far too busy seizing ever more power at your bank that seems, soon now, to be *his*. And Chase was far too busy chasing Leanna Leighton and covering himself with glory fighting Rebels in Savannah." She turned abruptly, looking around at Joshua and seeing him trembling, ashen pale—an old man, she thought, nearly beaten, who would soon die and leave her very, very wealthy if she could only escape this very last trap. God, why hadn't he died from that last attack in January? Soon, she assured herself. *Soon* now, he must.

"God help me, I don't know what to believe anymore. I don't know who. And I don't know what." Joshua's anguished words were barely whispered into the sudden silence that claimed the room. He was neither young, nor at this moment, particularly well. He was old and tired, agonized by his son's letter and the shocking revelations that had followed in its wake. It had been a long and sleepless night, and Joshua had the sudden frightening sensation that he was losing his grasp on the issues supposedly under discussion. Someone was lying. Someone *must* be lying. But who? It would be different if Chase himself were here making the accusations. Different if Chase were sitting where Jonathon Penley sat just now. With Chase away, Jonathon had become like a second son. But Elinor was his daughter by blood.

In the terrible, palpable, lingering silence, Cooke chose that moment to enter the room. The servant's face was impassive, and if he sensed the fury of the gaze Elinor had immediately turned on him at his untimely entrance, he didn't betray it. Fool, she wanted so badly to scream! Just as I was on the very brink of breaking him!

"Your breakfast, Miss Elinor." Cooke gestured politely as he set the tray on the table before her, acting as if he were totally unaware of the tension seething in the room all around him. He began to turn and then stopped as if on impulse, turning back to face the elder Courtland. "Oh, excuse me, sir. If you could spare just a moment, Mrs. Eaton needs to speak to you. Something about one of the sterling pieces being gone? I believe it's quite important. If you've a moment to see her about it, perhaps? Do you Sir?"

From deep in the anguished hell of Elinor and treachery and doubts of everyone most dear to him, Joshua frowned faintly, hearing Cooke's words as if they came from an incredible distance away. Quite important? Sterling could be quite important? God, he thought suddenly in a rush of nearly unbearable anguish. God, I wish it were! I wish that were the most monumental problem I knew! In the continuing silence, no one said anything. Joshua glanced almost dazedly toward Jonathon Penley, who was returning his gaze with one of dark concern and sorrow—shared or personal, Joshua was too stunned just now to try to guess. Elinor was silent, too, breathless almost. But Cooke stood stolid and expectant, one hand already resting on Joshua's chair back. "Oh." It was the only sound to break the silence, but in some indefinable way, it cut the tension in the room into little pieces—not dispelled exactly, but accessible now to reason. Why not, Joshua asked himself in sudden desperation? Why not go see Mrs. Eaton about the urgently important mislaid sterling? Time might be the answer he most needed now. Moreover, as his reason slowly returned he was suddenly conscious of how desperately weary he was, of how threatening the worsening pains were that clutched his weakened heart. "Yes. Yes, of course, Cooke. I shall see to Mrs. Eaton with you. I'll come now." He didn't look back as he left.

Jonathan had stayed seated at the table, watching Joshua Courtland's unsteady exit with anguished eyes. For a moment longer, he stayed that way, looking at the now-empty doorway. And then abruptly he glanced to where Elinor stood. He grimaced then, a strange expression to play over the anguish and the weariness that lingered on his ashen face. With a sudden motion, he rose to go. "Congratulations on a magnificent performance, Lady Bennington. Truly remarkable. I think in another moment, you'd have had your father apologizing to *you* instead of vice versa."

"Don't go just yet, Major. We may have a thing or two left to discuss. Something, perhaps, we may have in common."

"No. We haven't."

"But *yes*, Major. I beg to differ." Elinor moved sharply to block his exit, considered only another moment, then plunged ahead. She rarely was at a loss for ways to escape out of any trap, but this was an especially difficult one. And most importantly, she could not allow her father too much time to think this thing over. He must not make any changes in his will based on such sudden doubts of her. So she needed Jonathon Penley now—he was the only key which could completely unlock the doors of the trap. She must convince him to play the fool just one time for her, to recant whatever damning evidences of her duplicity he'd offered to Joshua in the night's long course. There might yet be a way to convince him to do that . . . but only one. A dangerous one, she warned herself, but the circumstances necessitated her taking this last and desperate gamble. "You've put me in a thoroughly untenable position here, Major Penley, and you don't even realize exactly what you're doing. You're undermining your own country. Betraying your very own cause. You see, I'm working—secretly—for the South, Major. Running black-market guns and medical supplies to Virginia. I have been all this time. Have I your undivided attention now, at least?" She saw shock momentarily widen Jonathon Penley's eyes, then saw disbelief narrow them again only an instant later. But that disbelief faded to sheer astonishment as she continued, and before the interview was at an end, Elinor held rising hopes that her desperate gamble would pay off.

Chapter Seventeen

Whitney sensed trouble as soon as her husband stepped in the door. Jonathon looked different, more than just weary from a long sleepless night. He moved awkwardly, like a man stunned by loss or grief, and she hurried toward him in anxious question. It wasn't Leanna surely—the news about her had been reassuring in a sense. Of all the people involved, Whitney was probably the only one who had felt such unalloyed relief at Chase Courtland's promise of protection, for Whitney trusted the Yankee officer with all her heart. Wherever Leanna was, Chase Courtland would find her somehow. Not Leanna, then, something else. "What Jon? What is it now?"

"Elinor Courtland's running guns to the South. She just told me. Proved it, practically. I didn't believe her at first, but it's true."

Whitney simply caught her breath. And as if her startlement communicated itself to the child she carried, she felt it roll restlessly in her belly, and she pressed her hand by habit against the hand or foot that seemed, by now, to press back. She was only a week from term and the baby seemed lower and heavier tonight than ever.

"*That* was the connection then to Roland Hodges. I should have guessed, I suppose, but it simply never occurred to me. She's sent thousands of guns across the Maryland border. Ammunition, medical supplies. And she wants to send more . . . if I lie to protect her from her father. If I deny what Major Courtland's letter says and deny what I myself told Joshua just last night." Jonathon turned away with a sudden movement, anger and weariness both showing on his face. "Why didn't she tell me that in the beginning, damn it? Why didn't she tell me she was working for the South? I could have helped her all this time instead of working so damn hard against her!"

"Helped her?" Whitney's eyes opened in shocked reaction. For a moment, she doubted whether she'd heard him right. "Helped Lady Bennington by betraying the kind of trust Joshua Courtland and Major Courtland both put in you? Betrayed the vow of parole you took when you—"

"My parole only states I won't take up arms against the federal government, not that I won't give aid to the South. I don't owe Chase Courtland one damn thing. And as for Joshua—it may be more kindness to deny what she's done, deny what she is. Elinor's his daughter, Whitney, but he lost a son to Confederate guns. So Joshua's going to lose something either way. And, anyway—my first obligation is to my country, *was* to my country. I'm not sure it isn't, still."

Whitney felt a coldness stealing upon her, a kind of breathless horror at the implications of her husband's words. For a moment, there was only silence. Then she reached to grasp his arm in a hard grip. "You can't actually be considering giving in to her? Lying for her and calling her brother a liar as well! What of Leanna, Jon? What of the danger Elinor put her in?"

"It was a bluff, she said. No real harm would have come to her."

"I don't believe that. And neither did Major Courtland. He was concerned enough to write his father from Atlanta about it. Concerned enough now to drag himself half dead on with his army to try to *help* her!"

Jonathon moved again, abruptly, his eyes anguished as he turned to face her. "I don't expect you to understand entirely, Whit. But those guns, those medical supplies . . . I was a soldier, too, remember. I *know* what those supplies meant to us. Do you know what it's like trying to fight a seven-shot Sharps with an old squirrel musket? Seeing your friend die because the quinine's run out and there's no way left to reduce a fever? God, Whit, the helplessness, the frustration of it! I'd sell my soul to give the South an equal chance! *I* never really had it. Maybe Elinor Courtland can give it to the soldiers there who are still fighting. And if she could, how can I stop her?"

There was a long pause. Whitney searched his eyes and felt her own fill with tears at what she read there in his. For a moment, she could say nothing. Tears choked her throat and when she finally forced herself to speak, her first words were almost a sob. "Oh Jon . . . it's over. It's too late. You said it yourself that day I first arrived in Philadelphia, remember? The South *never* had a chance. *Never*, Jon. Not from the very first shot at Fort Sumter. Maybe Elinor *has* sent guns to the Confederacy, but it hasn't changed anything really, has it? A *hundred thousand* guns wouldn't have changed anything. And I do know this: whatever she's done for the South, it wasn't out of patriotism. It wasn't even done out of mercy. It's profiteering and she's only doing it for the money. It's only further proof of how irredeemably evil the woman truly is: she's sold out her own side even while she's already buried one brother for it. And she wants to *continue* selling it out even while her remaining brother is ducking bullets from those very guns! Jon, for the love of God, face the truth! Elinor cares for nothing besides herself, *nothing*! This is only another ploy she's trying to make you check your hand!"

"Whit, I'm not unaware of any of those things you've just spelled out! There's no doubt in my mind about Elinor's motives! But that doesn't change the dilemma I'm facing— Lady Bennington may be the devil himself for all I know, but if the devil's prepared to help the Confederacy, Whit, then maybe I've got to help the devil! Can't you see that, yet? It's just that simple!"

"Yes, it *is* that simple, the way I see it." Whitney's eyes had turned suddenly cold. So cold that Jonathon was startled by the fearful hardness he saw now reflected in them. "And in this case I wonder whether that comparison you just drew shouldn't be taken as more than just a figure of speech. If you help Lady Bennington, you *do* help the devil. You'd better realize that's exactly what you're going to do. Elinor Courtland would use anyone and anything to further her own filthy ambitions. You, me, her father, her brother, even this awful war. But the ends *don't* justify the means, Jonathon. You used to believe that yourself. You've lived your whole life until now on those very convictions. So you can't help the South by lying to protect Lady Bennington, now, Jon. You can't lie to Joshua for her sake either. You simply can't."

But an anguished sort of stubbornness had set on his face as Whitney spoke, and Jonathon shrugged now and turned away. "I may *have* to, Whitney. As long as there's a Confederate government still viable and operating in Richmond, Confederate soldiers still in the field, my first allegiance has to be to

295

them. Right or wrong, that may mean I *have* to protect Elinor Courtland for their sake. I'm sorry you don't understand how I feel." Jonathon's eyes showed the anguish of his dilemma all too clearly as he paused at the window to stare across to the silent Courtland mansion. Behind him, Whitney waited only another moment, then quietly, helplessly, she turned and left. There was a gathering silence, only broken at last by the sound of a sigh, and something close to tears stood in Jonathon Penley's eyes as he murmured his doubts aloud. "God, I don't know what to do. I don't know which is right, which is wrong. I don't even know at this point what the hell I should tell Joshua Courtland."

By the afternoon of that same, eventful day, Elinor stood in the downstairs parlor, admiring the dark elegance of the new burgundy-toned oriental carpet, the rich rainbow sparkle of the massive cut-crystal chandelier and the fireplace sconces, the sophistication of Chippendale's new curved-back, deep blue chintz-covered settees and—of course—*herself* in the large, gold-leafed wall mirror. She would redo the room yet again, she decided, when her father finally died. The dining room, too, where she'd given—she congratulated herself at the memory—one of the finest performances of her life. She would get rid of the too-massive mahogany table with its stupid unmatching head chair. Hire an artisan, perhaps, to edge the high-ceilinged room with decorative plaster, perhaps fresco the ceiling as a few of the very finest European mansions had done. It would be truly splendid in time, she thought, outshining Roland Hodges' mansion even—a showplace that would be the whispered envy of all of Philadelphia.

She'd taken a dangerous gamble, earlier, revealing the true nature of her business here to Jonathon Penley. She studied herself in the mirror, reflecting, then watched her own slow smile appear. A dangerous gamble that would pay off, she thought. She'd read his confusion in his eyes as he'd left. And with dear, ever-honorable brother Chase gone a-warring once more, incommunicado with his advancing army, no one would be available to assess her duplicity again for months. She would finally have the free hand she'd sought for so long. Her father—guilt-stricken, repentant, and apologetic after Penley's recantations—would say not a word, regardless of what she did from here on out. And Chase would die, or her father would, before the two of them could combine to rediscover the hidden truth. Ah, she thought, the future shines with infinite sweetness.

She was too intent on those thoughts to notice the sound of the front door opening. When, therefore, the parlor door swung open quite suddenly, it startled her. For a moment, she froze, staring straight ahead into the mirror, which reflected a man standing in the doorway behind her. Then with a startled cry, she whirled on one heel so quickly that the hooped flounces of her azure-blue gown blurred in the mirror's cold reflection.

"Hadley!" She could only gape for a moment, astounded. It was the one possible ruination to her plans she had never even considered could occur. Her husband had disobeyed her every order, left Richmond and come to her here in Philadelphia. This could be unqualified disaster. "Hadley! What the devil are you *doing* here?"

"Ah, the warmth of your welcome enfeebles me, my love." Hadley looked a different man than the one she'd last seen in Savannah nearly a year ago. He was learner, grimmer, somehow more hardened. Life in the capital of the dying Confederacy had left its indelible stamp on him. His hands and face were browned by wind and sun, his blond hair and beard streaked now with gray, and there was a kind of anguish lying heavy in his eyes. "You look well, of course, Elinor. But then, I assumed you would."

"Why in the hell aren't you where you belong—in Richmond?"

Hadley's smile turned fainter, and what little was left of it, more cynical. "Because Richmond is about to collapse, my dear. Because the city's starving and desperate, and stricken with grief you wouldn't begin to understand, and I couldn't remain there any longer."

"But I was planning another shipment yet of guns and you've ruined—"

He interrupted her hissing furtive whisper with a shrug and a voice carelessly loud. "It's over, Elinor. Your little empire is finished. It's time we go home."

Elinor glanced at him, startled, silent for a moment. Be cautious, something warned her. This is not the same old Hadley you used to lead about on a golden leash. "Well . . . whatever you decide is best then, of course, my dear." She walked forward to offer a kiss and a belated welcoming smile, hardly noticing how stiffly Hadley received either one. She was thinking too hard about how to turn this unexpected development to advantage instead of to absolute ruin. "How ever did you get here, by the way? It must have been a difficult trip." She turned as if artlessly, leading him by the hand farther away from the parlor door. She'd remembered Cooke, and remembered that unseen ears could be listening even now, just outside the parlor door. As she moved she spared one sharp glance to check for the crack of uninterrupted light that showed beneath it, and then she relaxed.

"Not very difficult, at all, actually. General Grant apparently has about a hundred thousand soldiers trying to get *into* the city, but very few people are wishing to get out. Being English, of course, and so officially neutral, I had no problem arranging the necessary passes to exit Richmond."

"You brought the money, of course? Three hundred thousand dollars in gold?"

"Two hundred fifty thousand dollars, actually. Plus the cotton, of course, already shipped to Nassau and thence home to the mills."

"Two hundred fifty thousand dollars?" Elinor forgot the need for caution momentarily. Her voice rose as she turned with a startled and disapproving frown. "That's not right, Hadley. There should be at least three hundred thousand dollars."

"I gave them the last shipment free, Elinor. *Free*. The CSA coffers are dry as dust. Many of the men I've lived among, dined among this past year, have pledged their last cent to their failing cause. Millionaires will be left penniless. I have to live with myself. I had to give them back something."

"But fifty thousand dollars? Couldn't you have contented yourself with a more *token* generosity?"

He looked at her silently, for a long, long moment, and distaste flashed in his weary eyes. "No. I couldn't. Do you know how they paid for the shipment before that? Women donated their wedding rings. Men their belt buckles, watch fobs, anything gold."

"Well, it's their choice, Hadley. It's *their* war, not *ours*."

"It became mine, too, for a while, my dear. Living there for so long, I couldn't help it, I'm afraid. I admire those people. I grew to despise myself for profiteering off such gallantry and such suffering."

Elinor saw what she thought was an opening and smiled, reaching for his arm. "Well, since you have grown so fond of the South, why leave now, darling? The war will be done anytime now, and think of the opportunities to follow. We can buy whole plantations—twenty-five hundred to three thousand acres apiece—for practically no more than the back taxes owed. We shall live in the South like kings! I've spoken to some people about it already. People who have agreed to help. You should see what they have planned, and we can be part of it—with the money we have already, come the war's end, we can easily quadruple it!" It was her fatal flaw, the one aspect of Elinor that could make her surprisingly naive. Concerned only for herself, she had a difficult time empathizing with another person—even one she knew as well as she knew her husband—an impossible time understanding the impulse behind any genuine show of compassion. Even as she stood aglow with the inspiration of such a fine idea, from the corner of her eye, she saw Hadley raise his hand as if to strike her. She cried aloud, more in surprise than fear, moving aside to avoid the blow.

"Lord Bennington!" Joshua entered at that precise moment, and his voice cut like a knife into the consciousness of the two people in the parlor, freezing them. Hadley turned on one heel, staring momentarily like a blind man at Joshua. Then he blinked and slowly lowered his hand to step away. "Mr. Courtland." He *had* become Southern by now; he'd lived too intimately among them. The cordial greeting he offered so woodenly to Joshua was heavily marked by a Virginia drawl.

Joshua noted that drawl with a swift, startled frown. There was a moment's awkward silence, and then he stepped forward to take the viscount's hand. There had never been warmth between the two men before, but strangely enough, now—just for a moment, perhaps because of Elinor—there was. "Cooke told me you had arrived, Lord Bennington. May I offer you a meal, or perhaps you'd prefer a glass of brandy?"

"Nothing, thank you. I'm on a fairly tight schedule. I've a carriage waiting to take us to the night train, both Elinor and me. We've passage to England on a ship scheduled to leave Washington on the morning's tide."

"Tomorrow morning?" Joshua turned instinctively to glance

at his daughter's face. He saw shock register there, then an instant of unconcealed, bitter fury. Her green eyes were malevolent as she shot her husband a single glance.

"I cannot possibly leave just now, Hadley. You shall *have* to go without me, then." Elinor's protest held more steel than velvet in its tone, but Hadley merely shrugged indifference.

Joshua felt an instant's shock and then, quite suddenly—like a light going on in a darkened room—there was a surge of desperate hope. "No, go, Elinor. Go with your husband." Joshua spoke it like a prayer, with genuine fervor. "Go back to England. It's for the best."

"And leave you hating me for things I haven't done? Leave Chase and Jonathon Penley free to slander me at will, and me not even here to defend myself?" The tears that rose in Elinor's eyes were genuine. Rage rather than sorrow caused them, though, and despite her best efforts, her voice was shrill as she continued. "I won't do that! I simply won't! I demand that you order Jonathon Penley to recant *all* his accusations! If he admits to lying, then I'll leave. But not unless!"

Joshua blinked, taken aback, feeling like a blind man, groping and fearful, stumbling on the edge of an abyss he could sense but could not see. No, he wanted to say. No, I don't want to ask any more questions; I'm afraid of what the answers may be. Just go, Elinor. For the love of God, just go . . . so I can try to forget this whole awful day, try to pretend you're the daughter I've always wanted you to be—as beautiful inside as you are outside.

"I haven't any idea what you're ranting on so about, Elinor. And to be frank, I'm weary enough that I don't much care." As he interrupted the rising tension Hadley's drawn face wore only a faint expression of distaste. He abruptly reached for Elinor's arm to pull her carelessly toward the door. "You've barely enough time to pack, my dear. Go do it."

Elinor pulled free from her husband's hand at the doorway, turning her head again to fix Joshua with a gaze of genuine desperation. God no, she was thinking. Hadley, you incredible fool! Don't you realize what's hanging in the balance here? Half a million dollars! "Father, please! I beg you! Don't force me to leave now! Please!"

There was a moment's long silence. Joshua could sense impatience emanating from the English lord, and genuine desperation from his daughter. *Genuine?* he asked himself. How could he be sure of that? How could he be sure of anything anymore regarding Elinor? His sigh broke the silence, and he was conscious of a bitter, painful feeling of defeat. He had never been able to deny her anything . . . and he could not deny her now. "All right then, Elinor. I shall ask to speak with Jonathon then—one last time. I'll have Cooke go over and ask to see him."

True to his word, Joshua had reluctantly sent Cooke over to the carriage house, but Jonathon Penley was not at home. Despite the icy chill of the February day, he had saddled a horse and gone riding—down along the Susquehana River, on rime-whitened winter grass amid trees bare-boughed with winter's cold. It was a trick he had used since childhood, when questions loomed he could not answer. He would ride alone and think of the horse, the earth, the trees—anything but the problem at hand. And by the time the ride had ended, he always knew the answer he had sought, as if by magic. But not today. Returning to the house, the last few blocks he rode were in darkness. Dusk was already fading to twilight. The carriage lamps at the drive ahead were lit. For *him*, he thought at first, and then, turning the horse's head into the long, graveled drive, he saw the carriage—trunks being lashed to the top, horses harnessed, steaming and stamping restlessly in the cold night air. Frozen by an inexplicable sense of sudden dread, Jonathon reined his own horse to a sudden stop and merely sat there, shivering cold and silent. Joshua Courtland turned to see him there at last.

"Jonathon?"

Joshua did not move as he spoke. And for an instant, Jonathon did not move either. There was a split second's desire to turn his horse's head and ride on, to ride away as if he hadn't heard Joshua's call. Then the others clustered by the carriage block turned too—slowly, one by one. Whitney was among them, and he could not act out such utter cowardice in front of her. Reluctantly, he moved the horse toward them. "Joshua. Hello." He rode to within a yard of the carriage and slowly dismounted, standing where he was, and simply waiting.

"Elinor is leaving. Going back to England with her husband who arrived just this evening." Joshua too was shivering, but only partly from the cold, and he moved slowly, as if with equal reluctance, toward Jonathon Penley. And as he moved, Whitney and Elinor both followed, not together, not even as if either woman was conscious of the other's movement. Elinor moved to stand close at her father's elbow. Whitney took a place apart. Even without sparing a glance, Jonathon could feel their eyes—Elinor's intense, challenging, threatening and inquiring; Whitney's merely waiting, anxious and sad. A split second before Joshua Courtland spoke, Jonathon already knew the question he was going to ask. His stomach contracted in a sick spasm of dread, and he saw the instant of pitiful, desperate fear that now flashed so clearly in Joshua's eyes.

"Elinor begged me to ask you again, Jonathon. To confirm or deny the allegations raised by my son's errant letter. She wants to know the resolution of those questions before she leaves to return to Europe. Demands it, actually. Or she says she won't go."

It was a peculiar moment, Jonathon would think later. A single second, probably, that passed as slowly as an hour. He could feel Whitney's eyes still. Without looking at her, he sensed tears rising as she stared at him in silent sympathy. Elinor watched, too, but with a far different expression, as if sensing his indecision and relishing it. It was a strange feeling, cold and deadly, and in that instant, Jonathon knew Whitney was right about the Courtland daughter. She and the devil went hand in hand. There came an instant's thought of Chase Courtland; of Leanna; of the Confederate soldiers still gallant and desperate, fighting a war they could not hope to win; of a night-shadowed woods on the Virginia-Maryland border and wagons full of guns and medicines slowly and silently passing over that invisible line. But most of all, it was Joshua himself— the fear he simply could not hide in his eyes, the sudden, tragic look of despair that seemed to age him a century in less than a moment's time as he stood in the cold night, waiting for Jonathon's confirmation of guilt.

Jonathon was conscious suddenly of holding his breath. He released it, forced it out and turned his head away from Joshua's eyes. "Don't ask me that, Joshua. Please. I can't swear to either your daughter's guilt or to her innocence, not without chancing a lie on either side. I may have been right last night about her, and may have been wrong, too. Ask your son when he comes home. He may be surer of things than I am. But I can only offer you guesses at this point. Circumstantial evidence only. I won't condemn her on the basis of that and I would think, perhaps that you shouldn't either."

Elinor's triumphant smile flashed and was hidden again, all in less than a moment's time. He thought he heard the soft sound of Whitney's sigh. Joshua blinked once and paused—as if debating whether to ask again—for Jonathon's guess. For a moment, he almost did, actually heard the question formulating in his mind. Then Elinor touched his arm, and his courage, already wavering, simply broke. He merely nodded acknowledgment and turned back in silence toward the waiting carriage. "All right, then, Jonathon. We'll leave it at that. Chase may know more when he returns. And until then, and unless he does know more, Elinor, I shall follow the country's tradition of believing you innocent until proven guilty. Go back to England with my blessings then. And my love. And Godspeed." At the edge of the carriage, Joshua offered his kiss and accepted hers in return, his face expressionless, an unshakable feeling of dread still heavy on his heart as he watched her queenly march to the mounting block. Coward, he acknowledged to himself. Coward. But there was more than Elinor's mere guilt or innocence now to wonder at, he'd realized fearfully. Something in Jonathon's voice and eyes had hinted at a secret worse than any which Joshua had even yet discovered about his daughter. Something that Jonathon now knew that he hadn't known the night before . . . and something he did not wish to share with Elinor's father. God help me, Joshua thought abruptly, whatever it is, I don't *want* to know it! Let Elinor leave, cloaked by her lies. Let Jonathon Penley in his own honor-rigid, Southern way avoid offering either truth or outright fiction. There were a great many things suddenly, which Joshua found himself anxious to forget: Hadley Bennington speaking with a Virginia drawl, money missing, Elinor's connections not only in Washington but in *Richmond* as well, sufficiently strong to enable her to have endangered Leanna Leighton through them. God, I don't even *want* to put the pieces of that particular puzzle together any longer, Joshua thought suddenly. I'm too damn afraid of what the final picture will be. You damned old fool, he accused himself, spouting such fine, brave sentiments to Cooke yesterday.

Damned old fool—only a liar and a cheat. You should have died when you had the chance back in January. And spared yourself, at least, the humiliation of knowing yourself for what you really are.

"Mr. Courtland. Good night. And good-bye." Hadley startled Joshua with both his words and his sudden presence.

Joshua looked up and blinked, strangely befuddled. The night was dark, the winter air bitterly cold. Whitney and Jonathon Penley had disappeared. The door of their carriage house was just now closing. Elinor was gone, seated in the carriage already. Hadley, weary and oddly grim, was standing alone, offering his hand in courteous farewell. Cooke was waiting a discreet half-dozen yards away on the flagstone path, and other than him, Joshua had the sudden, anguished sensation of being left completely alone. Old. Afraid. And alone. Deservedly so, perhaps. He was only a sham now, wasn't he? "Thank you, Lord Bennington. Have a safe trip home." Joshua stood aside, watching in silence as the carriage door closed with soft finality, the coach jolting forward as it always did, then rocking a soothing rhythm as the wheels rolled, crunching on the silver-glazed gravel of the drive. He watched until the lacquered black of the carriage paint blended invisibly into the night's shadows down the street, and then he turned. Feeling infinitely defeated, Joshua Courtland made a slow retreat back into his empty house.

From inside the cottage, Whitney watched, too, as the Courtland daughter's coach made its slow, unhurried disappearance down shadowed Locust Street. Elinor herself was gone. But the effects of her presence would not be so quick to depart, Whitney thought. In Lady Bennington's wake was left Joshua's anguish; the turmoil and seething bitterness lingering on at the Courtland bank; Jonathon's awkward compromise between truth and lie tonight—and unless she was mistaken, Joshua's full awareness and most sadly, his near gratitude for Jonathon's uneasy equivocation, there. Maybe more yet, she mused. Leanna's danger. Perhaps Major Courtland's now as well. How far would Elinor go to to conceal her crimes? She thought she knew, and she didn't like the answer she had. She spoke without turning to where Jonathon stood silent and shadowed behind her, lost in thoughts little happier than hers. "I think I do understand, Jon, why you said what you did. Perhaps it was the only merciful thing for her father to hear. But you've put Chase Courtland in a very dangerous position, I think—put the whole nasty business squarely on his shoulders. Elinor must see that. She's only safe until he comes home and Joshua asks *him* for the truth."

"It was the only way. It *should* be Joshua's son who tells him. Not me. I've done as much as I should rightfully do." Jonathon was frowning faintly as he spoke. Across the drive, the lights were going out in the Courtland mansion—slowly, room by room. He watched until the last was extinguished and then turned from the window, keeping his frown. "Anyway, Chase Courtland is well out of Elinor's reach, Whit. Especially with her once more in England."

"Perhaps." Whitney's lack of confidence showed itself plainly in the single doubting word. There was a moment's pause, the sound of a slow breath being drawn, and then she turned, bracing herself for a probable fight. "*Perhaps*, Jon. But I'm not sure of that. Elinor had enough power with the War Department to endanger Leanna. She might turn the very same weapon on her brother now as well. And as I think we owe him better than that."

Jonathon's shrug held the tight, cold dismissal Whitney had expected. "He's a grown man. He's been through four years of war. I expect he's quite capable of taking care of himself, Whit. And if he isn't, that's not *my* business, it's his."

"You ought, at least, to try to warn him of what's happened here. Forewarned is forearmed, Jon. You do owe him that."

"I owe him nothing. Plus he's gone on with his army; there is no way to warn him. Sherman's marching incommunicado again, remember?" He turned as if to end the conversation and Whitney reached to take his arm.

"Promise me though that you'll try?" Whitney's words came with a sudden gasp. She closed her eyes against the sudden, surging pain that rippled across her swollen belly and pressed one hand hard against the rock-rigid flesh. Oh God, she thought, not now, not just yet. Just a few more minutes . . . it could be so important. "Jonathon, promise me. Please. Make that much of a peace with the Courtland son."

Preoccupied, he'd missed Whitney's first gasp, but Jonathon had caught the second. He turned in surprise, stood silent and startled for only a moment, then turned on one heel to

305

reach for his cloak. "I'll send Cooke out for the doctor, love. You wait for me here."

"Jonathon, please! Promise you'll—" Another wave of pain interrupted her words, and before she could catch her breath to speak again, Jonathon was already at the door. The baby had waited for Elinor to leave. Now, apparently, it would wait no longer. Whitney turned for the day room she had prepared and moved slowly, awkwardly, biting her lip to keep from crying out and frightening her daughter who was sleeping upstairs. Despite all the fears that had haunted her for so long, by midnight, she had delivered a healthy, beautiful son, and seen him safely laid in his father's arms before she'd closed her eyes to blissful sleep. The future held what it must for Joshua, or Chase Courtland, even for her beloved Leanna. Whitney had fought and feared and won *her* war— the others must do the same or perish. She could not live their lives for them. She could not even warn them for sure. All she *could* do for them now was to wish them well, and to wish them luck. The rest must now be up to them.

Chapter Eighteen

In South Carolina, the weather, which had originally promised to favor the marching Yankees, had now capriciously turned against them instead. It became bitter cold. Winter rains on the fourth, sixth and seventh flooded the Salkehatchie River to a swamp nearly three miles wide. Twenty-four bridges were constructed for the troops' crossing, and roads mired by rain needed to be corduroyed. Still the Yankee army averaged an incredible dozen miles' advance per day. And in their front, CSA General Johnston regarded such unobstructed progress with ever-failing hopes, ending a bitter note to Richmond with the observation that "there had been no such army in existence since the days of Julius Caesar."

By the sixth of February, Chase's battalion had advanced finally into "civilized" South Carolina. Here the roads were good, the country rich, level and wet; pine and oak dominated the forests and plantations were both large and fine. There was occasional skirmishing now with the Confederates—Wheeler's cavalry mostly, which hung on the left flank like an innocuous but annoying pest. But no Confederate force came forward in strength enough to halt the advance of the Yankee army.

Ahead of that army, South Carolina roads were thronged with panicked Rebel refugees: men, women and children; horses, stock and cattle; long lines of dilapidated wagons barely rolling; half-naked people cowering from winter's cold in brush tents or thickets, beneath the eaves of houses, in railroad sheds or abandoned, broken-down railroad cars. Some few stayed behind in response to federal assurances that occupied dwellings would be left unmolested, but regardless of federal assurances, the houses rarely were. Occupied homes were not burned, perhaps, but at least they were looted very thoroughly. Refined young women holding frightened children huddled by the gates of once-grand plantations, implored protection from any passing officer. And failing to gain that, they begged a handful of grain with which to make the child's breakfast porridge. Often enough, such children, before the war, had been heirs to bushels of cereal grain, and to plenty more.

On the twelfth of February, hundreds of miles north, Doc Lacey had traveled up to Philadelphia for his dreaded interview with Susan's father-in-law. Still shattered by the recent confrontations over Elinor, Joshua Courtland had heard the young doctor's explanations of his and Susan's affair with no more than dazed acceptance. There would be scandal, of course. There always was in such a case. But Joshua could not seem to collect his anger to argue or even to protest what had occurred. As Doc Lacey finished his anguished tale Joshua heard himself quite expressionlessly agreeing to the necessity for an annulment. Epsley, the Cortlands' lawyer, would begin appropriate proceedings at once. Joshua even accompanied the young doctor to the door, sincerely thanked him for all his efforts in treating Chase back in Savannah and saw him out with every courtesy. As Joshua watched the young man's hired coach roll away down frozen Locust to turn at the corner and pass from sight, he realized belatedly that no bitterness had even marked the brief interview, yet more of the Courtland future now lay in ruin. More dreams were shattered, more hopes foiled. But none of it, not even this anguish, was able to touch him anymore, it seemed. Joshua turned from the window stiff and slow, like the old man he had become, and simply went back to his usual chair in the empty parlor. From there, he wrote a letter of explanation to Chase with no idea of when, if ever, he would even receive the shocking news.

On the same day in South Carolina, Chase was watching the pincers of Sherman's crab begin to close on Columbia. Sherman's feints, once more, had been successful. Southern newspapers, the few still printing, reported chaotic terror spreading like an epidemic. Charleston, sure it would be the Yankees' target, saw thousands flee in a space of hours. Grand and arrogant only four years ago, Charleston had become a ghost town, reduced by blockade and bombardment to rubble. Augusta, too, in the west, had panicked under threat from

Sherman's advancing left wing. But it was Columbia, suddenly, which found itself actually facing the Yankee horde, and with only cavalry and militia left there to defend it.

Sherman's left wing had turned around in their tracks, abandoning their pretense of a strike at Aiken to make a sudden, lightning-swift stab at Orangeburg only thirty miles to the south of the South Carolina capital. The right wing captured the low banks of the Congaree River—Columbia's southern border—and from there, lobbed artillery shells across the water to bombard the practically defenseless city. Wheeler and Hampton were still visibly in the capital. Scouts on the high ridges could see Confederate gray still riding the streets of Columbia across the flooded river. Hampton—Jeb Stuart's successor and Robert E. Lee's pitiful contribution to the Deep South's effort to stop Sherman—was a native South Carolinian, hot-blooded and bold. He had sworn to defend the city by fighting house to house, hand to hand, if necessary. But gallantry rarely held where guns had failed, and the state government quietly removed all the documents and military supplies it could.

By Friday evening on the seventeenth, Hampton too had abandoned Columbia. Wheeler's cavalry was the last CSA force to flee the doomed city, exchanging a last sharp skirmish fire, as they rode galloping out, with the first of the federals who were then galloping in. There was cotton to be burned, powder magazines to fire, arsenals, still, that needed to be torched. The evacuating Confederates needed just a little more time, and it was Wheeler's cavalry that tried to buy it for them. The price of such gallant, last-ditch resistance was often high. It was this time, as well. One of the Confederate soldiers who paid the price on this occasion was Summer Ashton—shot out of his saddle by a Yankee sharpshooter taking aim from the high ground across the river.

Leanna, too, was in besieged Columbia still. Summer had managed to keep her one step ahead of Sherman up to now, riding from Robertsville to Barnswell, to Orangeburg and finally here. On Tuesday night, when the orange of Yankee campfires had first lit the southern shore of the Congaree River, Summer had pressed her to go. But Leanna had reached the limit of something, she wasn't sure exactly what. She had been in the Valley when the Yankees had come, and run from there on to Richmond, racing Sherman's army then to reach

Atlanta. She had been in Atlanta when that city had fallen and run again into the Georgia countryside: Madison, Milledgeville, Millen, Savannah. Into the swamps and run some more: Robertsville, Barnswell and a dozen other tiny hamlets. She was tired of turning tail and fleeing before advancing Yankees. As long as Summer was staying in Columbia, then so was she. And even if she had thought to leave, there'd been precious little chance to do so. The governor and legislators had commandeered most of the available transportation, and the Columbia train station had been the scene of incredible, screaming, desperate pandemonium these past few days. Hardly any civilians had managed to get out.

As darkness fell now on the embattled Southern city Leanna stood at the window of a once-elegant town house and watched the last of the Confederate Cavalry, torches in hand, galloping pell-mell down the street to flee the city. Unaware yet that Summer had fallen only minutes before, she watched the troopers gallop out of sight, wishing them Godspeed and good fortune, to Summer Ashton in particular. But Summer Ashton was not among the soldiers that were fleeing the city less than a dozen blocks before the line of entering Yankees. He was too badly wounded to take along, and these days the Confederate surgeons—all too aware of their pitiful lack of medical supplies and facilities—left more and more of their badly wounded soldiers behind for their well-equipped Union compatriots to treat. A Columbia surgeon in an abandoned warehouse had set up a poor excuse for a Confederate hospital, and Summer's lieutenants had taken him there. As full darkness came and the Yankees took triumphant possession of the South Carolina capital, someone finally thought to send word to Leanna Leighton of where he was and what had happened to the CSA captain she'd grown so close to.

But by nightfall, too, Columbia was swarming with exultant Yankee soldiers, freed Yankee prisoners and slaves celebrating their sudden emancipation. Looting and rioting filled the night streets. The moon began to rise in a crystal-clear black sky, and the long eerie shadows the moonlight cast only added to the terror and confusion as Columbia began to burn.

At ten o'clock, riding over the pontoon bridge that crossed from the burnt-out Saluda River factory ruins to the peninsula itself, Chase could see only single, isolated, orange bonfires in the city ahead. But by midnight, crossing the federal-built bridge over the Broad River, the whole jagged skyline seemed ablaze—wreaths of flaming ash spiraling into the night clouds, screams and explosions shattering the night quiet. The odd, hollow sound of horses' hooves on the wooden bridge were lost to the soldiers' ears, and by the time they reached the suburbs of the city, even the bugle calls were scarcely audible. In the distance, miles away, Chase could see Confederate Cavalry General Wade Hampton's plantation burning, an orange glow in the outer blackness. Here in the city, though, there was no darkness left—fire, by now, had consumed that, too. The high clock tower before him abruptly brightened from within, chimed one o'clock and then suddenly fell inward with a roar, sending bright gold embers shooting into the gusty wind to carry its destruction elsewhere. The long streets of wealthy homes, once-fine hotels, the courthouse, the old capitol building where the first order of Southern secession had been passed, its library and archives, even churches and convent buildings had disappeared into fiery ruin. Hundreds of Rebel wounded lay in improvised warehouse-hospitals, their cries of helpless terror adding to those of the Columbia civilians who thronged the streets, the back yards, the parks, the lunatic asylum and whatever other few acres the fires had not yet set ablaze.

It was like Atlanta, Chase thought, with one difference: Atlanta had at least been evacuated first. Here, there must be some twenty thousand people still—plus the hordes of liberated federal prisoners, new-freed slaves, drunken most of them, crowding the shadowed streets like demons freed from hell. Uniformed men, almost mad with greed and glee, were rushing from house to house, seizing all valuables and then usually firing the building itself. Other men were bedecked with gaudy flowers from looted millinerys, some dancing in the street to the accompaniment of stolen musical instruments of every kind, old violins to huge pianos. Invalids and the aged lay on shadowed street corners, dragged from flaming houses, suffering both the winter cold and the windborne fiery ash, plus the tormenting jeers and laughter of their exulting conquerors. Columbia had possessed wealth in abundance, sent up for safekeeping from Savannah, Augusta, Macon, Charleston and a hundred other isolated small towns and plantations. There were jewelry, gold and silver plate— soldiers staggering now beneath the stolen weight of it—huge waiters, vases, ornate candelabra. Refugee families wandering the street were quickly surrounded, rings pulled from women's fingers, jewels from around their throats, tiny bundles carried by wide-eyed frightened children instantly seized. Shots and shouts, groans and wild laughter from soldiers enjoying the orgy of drink and thievery rose in the air.

To Chase, entering the city weary but sober, it looked like a scene from hell itself. Terrified young women grabbed with desperate hands for the edge of his officer's coat as he passed, weeping, begging him for protection when he could offer them none. And ahead, the fires still looked to be spreading, driving on ahead of the flames those pitiful people Chase saw littering every vacant yard—some standing, shivering, ashen pale with incredulous agony, some huddled on the cold ground, a fortunate few laying on feather mattresses saved from the flames, but bare and blanketless, and presenting a view of rather absurd desolation. The prideless importunities of the Rebel women somehow shamed him; the ceaseless, seemingly omnipresent crying of frightened children was even worse. A crowd of drunken Union soldiers lurched past, carelessly trampling nearby civilians, calling obscene jests to the crying women and jeering at the few desolated men. Witnessing it, Chase swallowed a sudden blinding surge of nausea. Even last winter, he had still somehow doubted it, still cherished some obscure, reasonless hope it would not come to *this*. But it had. The dogs of war were rabid, now. Barbarism and atrocity had replaced honor and cause. And Columbia was paying a bitter price for the war she had begun so jubilantly not four years since. Smoke was so thick on the air that his own eyes burned from it. Whole pieces of ash drifted in the night wind to blacken his face in steaks, and gusts of a changeable breeze—by turns winter-cold and fire-hot—eddied crazily in the street, drying the cold sweat that had broken out on his forehead.

"Grier. Go that way. Take the men. I'm going to try to find someone who knows where the hell the provost guard is. If there even *is* a provost guard. I'll find you later." Chase had to shout to be heard over the surrounding din, his voice breaking. Smoke stung his throat, his mouth was dry from dust and ash. Grier hesitated and Chase shook his head, gesturing angrily for him to take the troopers on. He reined his stallion aside as they passed, then turned back the way they had come, pressing his horse back slowly through the throngs of people, soldier and civilian alike. He saw no signs of any patrol. No signs, in fact, of any organization among the Union soldiers. He swore softly, choking on ash, and standing in his stirrups to better search the shadows of the streets ahead. No one, anywhere, seemed to be trying to control either his own drunken soldiers or the flames that continued to consume whole blocks of the Southern city. Anarchy and chaos ruled the night—drunkenness, terror, thievery and despair. He had a moment's sudden blind impulse to turn his horse and gallop on, a moment's sharp fear of being the only sane man set alone in the company of lunatics. Sane or not, he could not stop the lunacy being enacted around him. And alone he couldn't do one damn thing to turn, even to restrain, the course this war was taking. He'd better find Grier. Find headquarters. Maybe there, there would be someone with answers to make sense of this nightmare. Pray to God somebody would still have some answers. Pray to God somebody was still at least *trying* to control this monster.

The sound of a woman's cry in the shadowed park behind Chase caught his ear as probably nothing else at that moment could have. Without thinking, by instinct alone, he immediately checked his horse. For a moment, there, he sat silent and startled, thinking he'd found that voice familiar. For a moment, too, that possible familiarity took precedence over all other thoughts. But then the voice ceased, blending indistinguishably within the clamor of others, and he slowly lifted his reins again as if to ride on. Perhaps it was only fitting on such a night that bitter memories should rise to haunt him, he thought. Memories of Leanna Leighton were appropriate to the hellish background of the flames roaring, the distant bricks crashing, people on all sides of him shouting and wailing. But wherever else Leanna might be in the South, certainly she would not be here. She surely wouldn't allow herself to be caught again in a contact point between both warring armies. That much, at least, she would have learned of the war by now.

But even as he thought that denial, the voice came again from behind him, and almost against his will Chase turned his head to search the distant darkness of the Columbia park with an anxious glance. And only a moment after that, he was off his horse and pushing his way back on foot, running and stumbling in the pitted, shadowed street, shouldering through a crowd of staggering, raucous soldiers. Shock was one thing he was conscious of feeling. And shock was probably the strongest thing that he *would* feel. But he was also partly, desperately, fearful for her and also partly, desperately, angry. Chase found himself both thanking and cursing God simultaneously, as he fought a slow path back toward the night-shadowed darkness of a huge live oak at the edge of the park. "Leanna?" Chase had come up from behind her, reaching out to seize a woman's shadowed shoulder, shouting to be barely audible above the deafening clamor of the confusion that surrounded them both. As he reached for her, he was shaking with reaction, momentarily unable even to force further speech. "Leanna!"

Frightened by the fires, frightened by the ugliness of panic and Yankees and darkness, Leanna reacted instinctively to the hand that had so abruptly and so unexpectedly gripped her shoulder. She turned with one hand raised high to strike against the importunity of that unknown Yankee hand. But even as she turned, the distant glow of fire was throwing its harsh, glaring light on Chase's ash-streaked face, and his familiar features were just dimly visible in the darkness. Instantly, her hand simply froze where she held it, and she stood staring at him in disbelieving silence, catching her breath and unable, it seemed, to release it again. He *was* alive . . . or was he? It was an unholy night. A nightmare night. Summer wounded. Columbia burning around her. Chase Courtland should be ghost not flesh, yet he seemed so real standing, staring at her. Perhaps she had utterly lost her mind. "Chase? . . . no. No, it can't be you. It can't . . ."

"Leanna! For the love of God, what are you doing in Columbia, here?" Chase's grip on Leanna's shoulder was quite abruptly knocked loose by a drunken soldier who came lurching between them. Chase swore at the soldier as he stumbled for his lost balance, and in that very instant, Leanna believed. No ghost could have taken her in the same strong grip that Chase Courtland had momentarily had on her arm. He was real, then. He was alive. He had not been killed after all then in that bloody little meadow outside of Savannah. MacRae had been wrong. But with that realization came a sudden, shocking surge of reawakened anguish, a kind of blind panic that swept her from head to foot and left her trembling in the wake of too-turbulent, conflicting emotions. "No! No, I can't stay here with you! I have to go to Summer now!"

If Chase even heard her protests against the din of the surrounding clamor, he gave no sign of it to the startled girl. He only reached out again as if to reclaim his grip on her arm, and in instinctive response to that, Leanna herself moved sharply away. "No! No, I have to go to the hospital first!"

If Chase Courtland had heard her cry of startled denial, or if he had not instinctively still reached out to grasp her, Leanna would probably not have reacted as she did. But in the light of the distant, uneven fire flames, she could read a kind of anger on his face and a kind of grim determination there as well. And the hand that reached out toward her seemed instantly threatening. "No!" Even as she cried out, she was pulling away. There had been too many men who had reached for her in just that way these past months. In the shadowed confusion of the hellish night, somehow Chase blended too closely with all of those others. Leanna was not conscious of making a decision to flee from him, she was not conscious of making a decision of any kind. It was only panic that caused a sudden, fearful jerk away from his hand. Like a wide-eyed doe already frightened by the sound of distant gunfire, Leanna turned from Chase with a last startled cry, pushing her way through the crowded park in blind, panicked flight away from him.

"Leanna, no! Leanna, dammit! Come back here!" Chase lost a long, precious minute simply to shock as Leanna first turned to pull back from him. He wasn't sure what reaction he'd expected of her after Atlanta, after the bitter violence that had erupted there between them, or after the grisly slaughter he'd found at the MacRae farmhouse where he'd also found Leanna's locket. He probably would not have been surprised at anger. He might not have even been surprised at vicious attack. But the sudden blind panic he'd seen flash in her eyes, the sudden anguished fear he'd seen so briefly change her all-too-familiar, still all-too-beautiful, ashen face— that was a reaction he had *not* expected. And for a long minute, it left him standing motionless there in bewilderment. Why the hell would she bolt away from him as if he were suddenly something or someone she feared? Did she think he sought to hold her only to turn her over to Drake and the War Department people who might yet arrest her for treason? Could she believe, even now, that he would ever deliberately seek her harm? "No, Lea, wait! Chase recollected himself in belated effort, trying to move after her through the darkness and the milling, panicking throng that filled the shadowed park. "Leanna, wait!"

But it was too late. A half-dozen drunken soldiers suddenly blocked his path, shouting and shoving, delaying Chase's progress for that all-important moment when he might yet have caught her. As he pushed his way through the men at last, swearing in frustration and rising desperation, he found no sign left of the woman he sought. She had simply disappeared as completely as if she'd never been only inches from his hand. The shadows of the night and the hundreds of Confederate civilians fleeing from the fires had simply swallowed her. "Dammit," he swore out loud in his helpless anger, searching the surrounding crowds still but with an awareness, already, of the sheer futility of any such search. But she was in Columbia, then. At least that much he now knew. Leanna might be able to disappear from him tonight into the confusion of the city, but she would not find it so easy to disappear out of Columbia itself in the next few days. Somehow, somewhere here in the city, he would find her again before Sherman's army marched on. Somehow he must both warn her of her dangers from both federal sources and CSA. Until he could undo the work of Elinor's powerful and treacherous hand, he could not afford to allow Leanna to fall victim to either of Elinor's traps. That much he *had* promised, at least—both to Leanna's brother *and* to himself.

Moved by instinct and spurred by panic, Leanna had run from Chase to the far edge of the park, pushed her way through the crowded street, and taken momentary refuge in the shadows of a town-house doorway to catch her breath at last. There was smoke, ever thicker, drifting on the cold night wind. Around her, the gusty breeze carried ever-larger pieces of glowing ash. The people passing were running now, no longer walking, and behind her she could hear the roaring crash of buildings falling in upon themselves in flames. It was time to move on again already. Time to continue on her way

316

to Summer. And quickly. The blocks were too small, the fire too near. As strong as the wind was, there was no assurance of safety here any longer. Thanks to the Yankees, she thought, there was no assurance of safety anywhere any longer, anywhere in the entire South.

As she began to push across the crowded, noisy street Leanna was suddenly aware that her breath was coming in sobbing gasps, her heart pounding in her breast, and the instinctive bitter anger that had caused her earlier flight away from Chase Courtland had dissipated entirely to a kind of colder despair. For one long moment, she simply stopped and looked around herself with the clear gaze of a desolate sanity.

She had made a choice just now, she realized abruptly. In turning away from Chase Courtland's outstretched hand, she had made a choice without even being aware she was making one. Shock and fear had made a decision, given her an answer to a question she had asked herself once, never thinking then that such a choice could ever actually again confront her. All the same, that choice was the right one, she told herself now. Despite the sudden anguish that flooded her soul at the realization of what she'd just done—turning away from Chase, turning instead toward the South and toward Summer Ashton, as well—still, she knew that choice had been the right one. In a sense, it was the only one she could have made. She could remember too clearly the horror of that day of the ambush. The horror, too, of those following days—of MacRae, the swamps, that desperate day of attempted escape, the Leighton slave who'd wanted to kill her, the ominous throbbing of Gullah drums. Chase had not been killed after all, but even so, he had never come after her, never made the slightest effort to ride to her aid. It had been Summer Ashton, instead. Summer who had rescued her then. Summer who had protected her since. Summer who had sworn his very life to continue to offer that needed protection, and Summer who had paid the price of that promise, who lay wounded even now in some poor excuse for a Confederate hospital. And it was to Summer still and to the South that Leanna owed her allegiances. Whether Chase Courtland were alive or dead, the essential parameters of that choice hadn't changed. While the war continued, they could never change. It had been easier, in a way, when she'd thought he was dead.

317

Leanna choked suddenly on air so filled with smoke that she could not breathe it safely any longer, and she turned swiftly away from the park where Chase Courtland had found her, turning toward the distant buildings ahead where the fires had not yet reached out greedy fingers. All around her now, as she ran on, she was acutely aware of the people and the panic and ash still drifting on the gusty wind. God, how did we ever do this to ourselves, she asked herself in incredulous anguish. How did we ever allow this to happen? Columbia in ashes . . . as so many of their Southern cities were in ashes by now. Mayor Goodwyn had wanted to surrender the city to Sherman when the Yankees had first assaulted, then captured, Orangeburg. But General Hampton had assured one and all that it was only a feint, that the Yankees weren't coming to Columbia at all. And even, he'd said, if the Yankees *did* come, he would defend South Carolina's capital to his very last man.

So he had lied too, Leanna thought in a bitter anguish. It was not only the Yankees who lied, with their infamous offers of "protection" to captured Southern cities and captured Southern civilians. Now the Confederacy's own generals, the Confederacy's own government was lying to its people as well. And there was only one possible reason that CSA officials would lie like that . . . because they knew by now that the war had been lost. Richmond would fall, too, and then it would all be over. All the dying, all the misery, and all for nothing. The South had destroyed itself to gain nothing at all. Only this. Only burnt-out cities. Homeless children. People sobbing on street corners. Summer wounded, maybe dying. A hatred between North and South which had risen finally to a fever pitch. Hatred that would last to their children's children and maybe beyond. A division bitter enough, deep enough, to have separated her forever from a man she would once have willingly died for. Miraculously, she had found her beloved Yankee alive once again, and then, in a way, killed him a second time by her very own hand.

More than the Confederacy's last feeble hopes had fallen, then, with Columbia here, she thought in anguish. More than a world, a cause, and a flag had gone down to sad defeat here tonight. She had severed the bonds that once had irrevocably bound her to a beloved enemy. Leanna realized that she was crying now as she continued to run toward her wounded Confederate captain. And she knew, too, that not all the tears she cried were for Summer Ashton. At least a few of them were for the very same Yankee who might well have shot Summer.

Chapter Nineteen

Chase Courtland had no way of knowing it yet, but the war had no intention of giving him the time he needed to search the city for Leanna Leighton. In the darkness and the confusion of that same crucial night, several decisions had been made by General Sherman's staff. One of them would involve the Yankee major and his battalion.

The first hint Chase got of something strange in the offing was a summons to report personally to divisional headquarters—Colonel Davenport had something important to discuss with his major there. The summons arrived at dawn—would have arrived even sooner but for the chaos, which had prevented Davenport from entering Columbia earlier. The divisional commander was not the man to needlessly risk either life nor limb. But now at last the gusty winds had ceased and the fires were mostly out and sober troops were riding in patrol of the streets. What little was left of Columbia lay quiet at last, and it was safe enough for men like Davenport to rejoin their troops and rejoin the war.

"Colonel Davenport, sir? You wanted to see me?" Chase Courtland looked like an apparition from hell. Weariness lay plainly on his face beneath a disguising layer of black-streaked ash, and his uniform smelled strongly of smoke from the fires of the night before. Chase made an effort to conceal both his dislike and his contempt for the superior officer who sat staring at him now from behind the sanctity of an official field desk, and Davenport made little effort to conceal his own startlement. For a moment longer, Chase stood in silence, watching surprise and distaste register on Davenport's face. Finally, Chase made a small gesture of apology toward his uniform, which was almost covered by ash, and a faint smile of irony briefly showed on his mouth. "Sorry, Colonel. War can be a dirty business."

"Yes. Apparently so." Davenport frowned as he spoke, grimacing briefly. Then he seemed to make an effort to dismiss the condition his major had arrived in and to turn his attention to another matter instead. "Well, you're not here for a dress review, Major, so I suppose it doesn't really matter." He had managed to look away from Chase finally, looking back to a sheaf of papers that lay opened on his desk. "You're here for a more important reason. According to the reports which Colonel Adamson wrote about you, Major, you can do nothing much less than walk on water when it's required, and I personally was equally impressed with your abilities in the Leighton affair. Word went out from staff headquarters last night that General Sherman needs someone for a very special mission. I suggested to him that you might do perfectly but the final decision must be yours, in this case. Some risk is involved and such an assignment must be voluntary; the general himself has specified that. How would you like to do some scouting for your army, Major Courtland? General Sherman needs someone badly. Very badly. It might be to *both* our advantages if you were willing to undertake the mission which the general has in mind for you."

Instinct cried an immediate warning, and Chase frowned slowly in the lingering silence. All traces of a smile had long since faded from his mouth. "And just exactly what sort of a mission is that, Colonel?" he questioned slowly at last. "What exactly is it that I'm being asked to do?"

"A simple enough expedition, actually. In the event that General Lee's army in Virginia should slip south to join with Joe Johnston's in North Carolina, General Sherman and General Grant will both need to have some idea of the terrain they may fight on. Some idea, strategically speaking, of where the federal armies might also join forces in order to keep the Rebel armies contained. You would be riding overland, Major. With your battalion, of course—I would hardly recommend you set out alone." Davenport smiled momentarily, seeming to find humor in the thought, though Chase did not. "Your main objective will be simply to traverse the Rebel territory, keeping accurate logs and good maps as you go. You'll be a hero if you make it, Major Courtland. You'll be a full colonel at the least, I'll wager, from the moment you ride into General Grant's winter encampment. Maybe even a brigadier."

"Ride overland all the way to City Point, Virginia?" For a

moment, shock overwhelmed every other possible thought. Chase stared at his commander as if the man had totally lost his mind. Grant's encampment, City Point, lay damn near four hundred miles north. Four hundred miles of solidly held, yet-to-be-penetrated Confederate territory . . . with one battalion for total troop strength? Such a plan must be the conception of either a madman or a fool!

"General Sherman himself proposed the plan, they say. It could be a great opportunity for you in a way, Major. It isn't every day a mere major gets a chance to advance his career by obliging a two-star general, you know."

"But I'm not a professional soldier, Colonel. I'm perfectly happy with the rank I've already attained, thank you." But even as Chase shrugged off that particular aspect of the mission his mind was quickly reevaluating the mission itself. A madman or a fool, he'd thought initially. But General Sherman was neither of those. If the idea was his, then the plan had both merit and genuine need behind it. Sherman, unlike Davenport, was not the type of officer who asked his men to die for nothing. The plan might be a desperate one—no, *was* a desperate one, Chase amended grimly—but then war sometimes required such desperation, didn't it? And the war would continue to require it until it ended. If such a mission would help to hasten this end, maybe it would be worth the risk. "When would such an expedition be sent out, Colonel? How long do I have to consider the request?"

"Today, Major. Tonight you'd ride out."

"Tonight?" Chase Courtland's eyes reflected immediate shock once again, and his first impulse was to simply shake his head in outright refusal. Even if he were personally inclined to volunteer for Sherman's journey, he would not commit his men to the same course without at least first determining the extent of their willingness. And if they did agree, they would need more than mere hours to collect themselves for such a risky business. There would be preparations to make, plans to draw up. Letters to write to homes they might never see again. Plus, Chase remembered uneasily, there was Leanna Leighton still to find, and that duty alone might well take him a week. "Any chance we might move that timetable back just a bit?"

Something changed then in Davenport's eyes. A kind of sly comprehension showed in his face and he nodded once as if to a new understanding. "Oh, I see, Major. You've made plans for tonight already, then? Plans that supersede the importance of your commanding general's need for you? How odd—I had you figured for one of those fanatics who would sacrifice almost anything for the Union. You've grown less fervent and more cautious since you were wounded in Savannah, apparently."

It took Chase a moment to follow Davenport's insinuations, and it was the look of comradeship in the officer's eyes finally, more than his words, that clarified the colonel's sudden about-face. Davenport was assuming that Chase was no different than his commander. Assuming Chase, too, shared the same kind of self-serving attitude the colonel himself so badly suffered from. Davenport would understand entirely if his major chose to refuse the dangerous assignment . . . but he would understand the refusal in all the wrong ways. A sudden surge of mingled anger and contempt for the man rose nearly to the breaking point as Chase stood staring down at him. Davenport was practically accusing him of outright cowardice! This same goddamn son of a bitch who wouldn't even ride into captured Columbia last night with his own division! Certainly Col. Davenport would understand Chase's reluctance to volunteer, because it had never been devotion to the Union that had moved the man to offer his crack troop to Sherman in the first place! Davenport wouldn't even give a genuine damn if they *took* the mission, and then never made it to Grant's army in Virginia. All the colonel wanted out of this mission was a little gold star on his record sheet and the chance to curry favor with Sherman himself! Chase struggled suddenly to control a reckless impulse to tell his commanding officer just how wrong he was about their supposed similarities, to tell Davenport once and for all how much Chase really despised him, his boot-licking attitude, and most of the whole damn war effort by now. He conquered most of that dangerous impulse, but only after an overlong silence, and the effort it took to restrain actual violence left him trembling as he finally managed to speak again.

"No, I don't think you *do* understand entirely, Colonel. I'm *not afraid* of your damn mission, sir. I'm not afraid of fighting out the rest of this war. I'm not even particularly afraid of dying anymore; I've seen enough of that these past few years that I've long since made my peace with that possibility. If it makes you rest easier, Colonel, I'll probably end up accepting the mission and earning another gold star for you with high command. But I won't be accepting it as any favor to you, Colonel. Not even as a favor to the general. And not in an effort to earn some higher rank for myself, either. If I do go, it will be a decision that I make for myself, because it seems to me to be the right thing to do. This damn war is turning barbaric, Colonel. If you'd been in the city with us last night, you could have seen that fact for yourself. Atrocities are rampant now. Brutality is officially sanctioned. It occurred to me last night, riding through it all, that this war has got to be ended *soon* because it only gets worse now from one day to the next. There's no way to reinstitute honor or restraint, especially not with men like you in command, so our only hope is to get this horror over with, to get it finished now as soon as possible, before it degenerates even further. I'm afraid if we don't get it ended soon, neither the conquered nor the the conquerors are going to have any shred of human decency left to claim. We'll have destroyed ourselves in destroying them. Not a happy thought that, don't you agree, Colonel Davenport? But not something that one man like myself, alone, can do much to prevent. Now if General Sherman says this damn mission of yours will help bring the war to a quicker close, then so be it—I'll go. But I'm going to see how my troops feel about it first. They do have some rights about such a decision. And I've got a few things to do myself before setting out for Virginia. If those two things don't entirely suit you, then you'd better find yourself another 'volunteer' . . . *sir*." It was vaguely surprising to Chase how utterly clear and cold his mind seemed to be as he spoke. Every detail of the moment was minutely focused—from the haphazard stacking of the papers on Davenport's desk to the tic that throbbed now suddenly in the man's right eyelid. The sunlight was bright through the town house's back window, a single, faint streak of dust marked the colonel's uniform, and outside somewhere now, Chase could hear the muffled cadence of a regimental drill.

"You're an arrogant, insubordinate, son of a bitch, Courtland." Davenport rose slowly to his feet behind the desk, as shock, then sudden rage, brought flooding color to his ashen face. "I hope to hell you *do* go north, now, Major. Because if you don't, I'm going to find the dirtiest jobs in the whole army to assign to you, I promise. And I don't envy General Grant's army even what slight chance they may have of having to deal with you eventually either. Though I most sincerely doubt you'll ever get there to begin with."

"Oh, I'll get there, Colonel. If I take my men out of Columbia, I'll get them up to Grant. I would never ask them to go if I weren't damn confident I could manage to do that somehow. Good day, Colonel." Chase stood only a moment longer, coldly, refusing to look away from the threatening rage in Davenport's eyes. Finally, in his own good time, he turned on one bootheel, deliberately offering his commander no salute as he left the town house to find Grier.

In a sense, Chase realized grimly, he had just eliminiated any real choice regarding General Sherman's mission. But then, in another sense, there had never been any real choice to begin with. The dangers of such a journey through Rebel territory notwithstanding, if such a journey had to be made and Chase believed—as he did—that he could *make* it, his commitment required him to volunteer for the duty. Davenport had been right about precious little else, but he had been right about that. And as for the rest of what Chase had just told his commanding officer, he regretted not a word of it. It was a fool's hope to think it would change the man, but even so, it had been an indictment long suppressed and long overdue. Whatever else might lie ahead on the long ride north, Chase would not regret having left the colonel's command.

Only now did he abruptly remember another commitment he'd temporarily forgotten in the flaring heat of earlier anger. He'd forgotten his commitment to Leanna Penley Leighton. Forgotten both his promise to Penley and his promise to himself that he would somehow subdue the dangers to her that Elinor had set in motion during these past months. That promise now might have to be broken, he realized. It might be the work of whole days trying to find the Rebel woman in Columbia, and he did not have whole days to spend in the city. He had merely hours instead. And most of those hours must be spent in other ways: in briefing his captains, preparing the logs, speaking to General Sherman's staff and organizing both plans and supplies for a long and dangerous journey north. Once again it appeared that the exigencies of war had intruded between him and Leanna Leighton.

* * *

It would have eased Chase Courtland's mind considerably just then if he could have known what his sister Elinor had only herself learned some hours before, and what no one else other than Elinor and her husband knew as yet. Hadley, Lord Bennington, had met the lovely Penley sister just once in Richmond, a meeting now almost a year fully past. But Leanna Leighton was a woman whom men remembered meeting. Hadley Bennington had remembered her, too. Before he had left Richmond to come north to collect his treacherous wife, Hadley had followed the instincts of both conscience and memory, and had quietly arranged for Leanna Leighton's name to be removed from Confederate War Department rolls. It would be one less burden, he had decided, to carry along on an already overburdened sense of dishonor. Elinor's subsequent rage at the news bothered Hadley not at all. In fact, he had been conscious instead of feeling a grim kind of satisfaction at having so obviously thwarted her schemes.

Entirely coincidentally, activity regarding Leanna Leighton from the federal side had been shelved temporarily also. She was wanted still, by Washington, for questioning regarding her involvement with her notorious guerrilla husband, Stewart Leighton. But with reports of Leighton's death, that inquiry seemed relatively incidental now. Most important of all, the money that fueled Leanna's notoriety, the money Elinor poured into the "cause" of making Leanna suspected of espionage, was no longer forthcoming since her return to England. Leanna Leighton was now no more important to the federal people than a thousand other names on a lengthening list.

But it would be weeks before the slow-moving wheels of either War Department would actually notify its forces in the field of such changes regarding Leanna Leighton. And it would be *months* before Chase Courtland would have access to sources that could report such changes to him. In fact, it would be months before Chase Courtland had access to *any* of the far-reaching changes that had swept his home in distant Philadelphia, and in consequence, as the war moved on toward a final close, those months would see anguish and pain and an ever-rising sense of desperation for him and Leanna Leighton, both.

* * *

"I'll go with you, Major. And the boys in my troop have voted aye, too." Grier's usually ruddy face was paler than usual as he spoke to his major in the ruined parlor of a Columbia town house, but his eyes held Chase Courtland's eyes with wordless determination. "Watson and Leiffer's troops have both voted no. Cowles himself would come with us, but only half his men are willing to come. He wants to know what you want him to do."

"I want him to stay in Columbia then, with the rest of his troop." Chase shrugged flatly, nodding once in acknowledgment of the numbers Grier had just relayed. "In a way, I don't blame them, Grier. They've all been with Sherman and his Army of the Tennessee since the war started. We're the only ones who started out in Virginia. The only ones, probably, with any desire to try to rejoin that part of the army. The Potomac may be our home base, really, but it isn't theirs. And besides, I'm not sure it won't be easier to get one troop through than it would be to get the entire battalion to Virginia, anyway. We wouldn't have had sufficient strength to fight our way through, even with the entire battalion along, and it's a lot easier to try to hide sixty men in Rebel countryside than it is to hide two hundred and fifty. We can eliminate food wagons, for one thing. Live off the land as we go. That means that we won't be tied to the roads so much, and we won't be held back by a wagon's snail pace. In a way, it may be even for the best."

Rain had begun to fall today on ruined Columbia, a light drizzle that only added to the woebegone look of the devasted city. From outside the town house came a dull roar of distant explosions as Sherman ordered the further destruction of all public buildings which had escaped the holocaust of last night's fire. Only the new, unfinished marble capitol building was to be spared. Oddly enough, General Sherman was somewhat of an aesthete, a devotee of art and beauty. The new Columbian capitol was superbly designed, magnificently sculpted, and so it would be spared destruction. Chase laid his head back wearily against the curved wood frame of a Queen Anne settee as he finished speaking to Grier and he closed his eyes. The settee's pale blue satin cushion was ruined by water stains and streaked with black ash—almost emblematic, Chase thought now, of the whole war-torn world. And it would get worse yet before it got better.

"I met a girl last night, trying to save her house from some drunk flat-footers. I stayed on awhile to help her out. She's a Rebel, I'm afraid, but she's about the pluckiest woman I've ever seen. I may just come back here after the war and marry the girl, I think."

Grier's irrelevant comments brought a reminder of another commitment to Chase's mind and a brief, bitter grimace to his mouth. Grier had reminded him of Leanna Leighton, and he murmured a warning without even opening his eyes. "Grier, take my advice in one thing at least. Rebel women are a thousand times more dangerous than their men. Try to forget you ever knew the girl's name."

"Well, maybe so." There was a long pause. Grier shrugged and his voice was flat when he spoke again. He knew who the major was thinking about, though he did not know that Chase had seen her here in Columbia and did not know that his major would spend most of the day's ensuing hours in a futile effort to find her. Grier cursed himself for having made a thoughtless comment and changed the subject back to the journey that lay before them. "What do you really think our chances are of making Virginia, Major? Give me a conservative guess."

"Conservatively? About a hundred to one." Chase managed to force a smile to disarm the pessimism of such discomforting odds. He reopened his eyes at last, glancing wryly at Grier as he got to his feet.. "Be an optimist on this trip, Grier. Please. We'll both like our odds a lot better that way." Chase raised his hand a last time to his eyes as if he could rub the weariness away with a gesture. "Better start rounding up the men, then, Captain. Pack plenty of ammunition; that's one thing we aren't liable to find anywhere along the way. I'll go over to general headquarters and find out what the staff knows about where in the hell we're supposed to be going. And then I've got something personal to take care of. If I don't see you before then, I'll meet you and the men back here at the house about sunset tonight."

Chase Courtland would have no luck that day in finding Leanna Leighton. He had little better luck in his efforts to secure more detailed information from General Sherman's staff at headquarters. It turned out that no one there knew much more than Chase himself did—in other words, precious little. But they gave him all that they had: namely, a single, rough-scale map of South Carolina and the states above it. Mountains bordered the western side, the ocean the far eastern. In between were a few dots marked by names: Cheraw, Goldsboro, Layetteville, Durham and finally, near the top, Richmond. No roads were marked. River courses were only guessed at. And there was only a vague concentration of pencil marks where they thought Joe Johnston's army might be encamped.

Dusk had fallen finally, and the gathering troopers spoke in low murmurs to one another, apprehensive undertones that were punctuated periodically by the snap of stirrup leathers and the tinny jangling of metal bits and brass saber rings. They would wait only for darkness, then leave the city on their long trip north. Wheeler and Hampton's cavalry were still close by, occupying the ridge of high ground just to the north. And throughout the drizzly day, there had been occasional flashes of dull silver from the lenses of field glasses there. Chase was not fool enough to ride out in daylight for the CSA troops to see. The lone Union troop would need all the advantage the darkness could give them—it would most likely be a difficult enough journey even with that.

"Spare horses, ammunition, field rations, water . . ." Chase ticked off items from a mental checklist with the ease of long years of war, pausing only long enough after each item for Grier's nod of assurance. Both men were careful to avoid meeting the other's eyes too directly in the process. Men feel a certain awkwardness when they are riding into possible death, as if secrets might show in their eyes that they do not really wish to share. As Chase finished the long list he paused, frowning, glancing up into the darkening sky for a moment's silence. "We should probably take some medical supplies along, too, Grier. We're liable to need them." He made the grim observation matter-of-factly, and Grier agreed in the same flat tone.

"Already done, Major. Whiskey, bandages and morphine— it's about all any of us know how to use anyway."

"True." The single word preceded a longer silence. Chase stood waiting, watching the pearl gray of the Columbia dusk darken slowly to the ominous shade of ashes—the color of the sky matching the color of earth finally in the burnt-out city. It was nearly time for them to go. He must leave both

Sherman's army and a broken promise to Leanna Leighton behind him. 'We'll ride out the same way we came in—to the west. Try to make the foothills or at least get close before dawn breaks." Chase turned to reach for his gloves, pulling them on as he spoke the quiet orders. "Tell the men to muffle their canteens, their sabers, their bits—anything that makes a noise. I'll take a last look at the map and then I'll be over to join you."

"Major Courtland?"

Chase turned his head to see the young Savannah surgeon, Captain Reardon, step suddenly from out of the shell of a burnt-out town house across the street. Once outside, Reardon seemed to hesitate a moment, searching the darkness.

Little light was left by now, and the gathering shadows were undisturbed by either street lamp or fire tonight. Two officers had turned at his call to face Reardon from across the way—two black shapes in a dark gray night, and it took him a moment to discern their faces. As Reardon recognized Major Courtland and started toward him he could hear his boots making a faint crunching sound on the cinders left in the street from last night's fire. He saw Major Courtland gesture to his captain and then start forward across the street to meet him.

"Captain Reardon. Good to see you again."

Chase wore a faint smile—very obviously forced, Reardon thought—as he extended his hand in greeting. It was hard to be sure in the darkness, but Reardon thought the cavalry major's face looked especially weary and grimly set. Even as Chase had spoken he'd glanced after his departing captain, and following his glance, Reardon saw what looked like a full troop, busy readying themselves as if to ride. "I've caught you at a bad time, I think. About to take a scouting patrol out?"

There was only a moment's pause, as if Chase were making a decision before making the reply. "Not exactly, Captain. Not a patrol, as such. We've been reassigned to the Army of the Potomac, and ordered to ride north tonight."

Reardon couldn't help the portentous silence that filled the time between Chases' words and his own. "Ride overland? But that's rather hopeless, isn't it?" Even as he spoke he regretted the tactlessness of his question, but Chase Courtland seemed unperturbed. He merely shrugged at Reardon's muttering efforts at apology, half turning away to glance at the soldiers gathering barely a stone's throw from them. Despite the darkness, Reardon caught a hint of the wry smile that briefly played on the officer's mouth.

"No, not so hopeless, I don't think. Though I'll admit that seems to be the general consensus here in Columbia, Doctor."

There was an air of preoccupation about Major Courtland even as he replied, Reardon thought. And an air of restlessness, as if, hopeless or not, Courtland was anxious to begin the long journey.

"I don't mean to be rude, Captain Reardon. I'm not ungrateful for the efforts you made in Savannah on my behalf, but I haven't much time just now, I'm afraid. Is there something specific you came to see me about?"

There was, but Reardon was uneasy now about adding to the man's rather obvious concerns. He hesitated for a long, awkward minute before making the decision to continue. There were too many lives at stake not to risk troubling Chase Courtland with still one more consideration of the city and the army he was about to leave behind him. "Yes, I'm afraid I'd like to add to your concerns tonight, Major Courtland. I wouldn't have bothered you if I didn't feel it was absolutely necessary. And I really don't know anyone else to go to instead. You see, I've been assigned care of a hospital full of Confederate wounded, and some refugees homeless from last night's fire. If you'll step inside with me for just a moment, I'll try not to take too much of your time. There's a problem I've got and you're one of the few men left in this army, I think, that might care enough to help me solve it."

Even in the faint light of the shadowed night, Reardon couldn't miss the frown of impatience that darkened the young cavalry major's face. For a minute, he thought Chase Courtland was going to refuse his request. Then, abruptly, he raised his hand instead in a wordless signal to his waiting troop and started toward the nearby town house. If the surgeon hadn't already been aware of Chase's impatience, the hurried length of the officer's strides would have made it clear. Reardon, too, was hurrying, stumbling in the debris that littered the dark Columbia street, and still he arrived at the steps of the burnt-out town house some distance behind the Union major. As he began to move inside, then, Reardon suddenly froze. One foot was still on the outside step, his hand still lingering on the black charred door frame. He had brought along a nurse from the hospital as a guide, a Mrs. Ashton, for he himself had no familiarity with the streets of the South Carolina capital. And waiting inside, Mrs. Ashton apparently had not heard either his or the Union major's entrance. She sat still and silent, looking like a marble carved by a master's hand, her face weary but lovely still, framed in mellow silhouette by the soft light of the single camp lantern they'd brought to light their way.

Unquestionably beautiful, Reardon thought. But it was not her beauty that had so startled him just then; it was the momentary flash of recognition he'd caught on Chase Courtland's shadowed face. Recognition, then relief of nearly miraculous intensity. But at the same instant, a desperate pain had flashed as well. Pain near to agony, issuing from a place far deeper than any surgeon's knife had ever touched. And then, as quickly as Reardon had seen it come, all the emotion was swiftly gone. As the young Federal major stepped forward into the light where Leanna could see him, there was no expression showing on his face at all.

"Major Courtland. One of my nurses, Mrs. Ashton." The introduction was unnecessary; Reardon understood that even as he spoke. The same recognition had flashed in *her* eyes instantly as well, widening them momentarily in startlement. Reardon felt the tension and tried to ignore it, but in the sudden silence of the ruined town house, the shock seemed to linger like a living thing.

Chase Courtland stood as if unaware of the surgeon behind him. He looked only at the Confederate woman, and when he spoke, it was to her and not to Reardon. "Mrs. *Ashton?* You didn't linger long enough to mention that last night. Apparently, some congratulations are in order. "Leanna."

"No. Not just yet, actually." Leanna had to make an effort to steady her voice before she replied. She succeeded remarkably well, she told herself, considering how badly her heart was pounding at the sudden shock of seeing Chase again. She had never thought to ask the name of the officer Captain Reardon had been so anxious to see, and she cursed herself now, futilely, for that all-too-innocent oversight. She felt like some cornered animal now, brought unexpectedly to bay by the hunters' hounds, but there was no escape from this, no way to bolt away from Chase as she had last night. She had only her pride left to deal with the circumstance, the pride

Summer Ashton had given back to her by loving her. Leanna flushed despite herself, but she raised her head high as she spoke, and the look in her eyes was one of defiance and not of apology. "I was . . . not very anxious to retain my husband's name with Yankee soldiers swarming all over the city. I'm sure Summer won't mind the use of his name, though, since we are only waiting upon the legalities of a ceremony."

"I see." Chase managed entirely to conceal whatever anguish Leanna's announcement might have caused him. He simply shrugged a reply, a shrug overquick and overrigid. To Reardon watching him, it failed to convey the indifference it seemed meant to convey, and baffled, the young medic stared from one to the other in rising uneasiness. "Well, perhaps, that's for the best, Leanna. Since we last saw each other in Atlanta, I've married someone else as well. Chase frowned sharply, though, as he glanced back to where the young medic stood waiting in uncomfortable silence, and then he glanced more slowly at Leanna once again. "So you're one of the Confederate nurses, now, Leanna? I seem to recall your saying once that you could hardly bear the sight of blood. That was just a lie, too, apparently. Just one of many?"

"No, it wasn't a lie." Leanna flushed again with the denial but she kept her voice both soft and steady. "None of it was a lie, Chase. Not in Virginia at least, it wasn't. But time passes and things change. The war makes things change all the faster."

"If it wasn't a lie, why leave Atlanta like you did, Leanna? And why leave your locket for me to find at the MacRae farmhouse? Along with two dozen dead and mutilated corpses?"

Involuntarily, Leanna closed her eyes against that day's memory, and her face paled to ash at both Chase Courtland's words and at the bitterness they were spoken with. She simply shook her head helplessly, not choosing to explain. Chase had married in the meantime, and she was committed to Summer Ashton now. Perhaps it was better to leave things as they were. "It doesn't matter now, Chase. Must we rake the coals of all those old angers? Believe whatever you chose to believe."

A grim sort of anger immediately set Chase Courtland's shadowed face at her answer. With nothing more than a curt nod of farewell, he turned sharply on one heel as if to rejoin his waiting troop outside. Startled, Reardon moved to catch his arm, checking his step before he could reach the town-house door. "Major, wait." Reardon didn't understand most of what was under discussion here but he didn't really need to. He understood that something had gone awry and he made a hurried attempt to bring the conversation back to its original purpose before Courtland left altogether. "Before you go, Major, the reason I came to see you still remains. I need your help for that Confederate hospital I've been assigned to. I need it desperately or I wouldn't have troubled you. I've got no supplies, hardly any personnel. If it weren't for the volunteer nurses such as Mrs. Ashton, I'd practically be on duty by myself."

There was a moment's pause, as if Chase had to make an effort to remember what Reardon was talking about. He frowned then finally, glancing restlessly toward the waiting darkness before replying. "And what exactly do you expect me to do about that, Doctor? You haven't caught me at the best of times. I'm not even going to be *in* Columbia five minutes from now."

Reardon flushed slightly at the curtness of the officer's response, but sensing the strain that had caused it, he ignored it as best he could. "Still, I thought you might be able to arrange some remedy for such sheer brutality. There must be someone, still, that you could speak to on my behalf?"

"We're here to kill Rebels, not to nurse them. Or hasn't anyone in 'high command' told you that by now?" Chase had turned completely away from Leanna Leighton, facing Reardon only as he spoke. Even in the lantern's dim, uneven light, Reardon had seen the grimace on the young officer's mouth as he spoke, seen the hint it conveyed of deep regret, but from the deeper shadows where she sat, still, Leanna Leighton had not.

"You don't even *care* anymore what atrocities your damn Yankee army commits, now, Chase?" She had risen to her feet, her face paling further in the parlor's dim light.

"No, of course not. But surely you thought no differently of me, Leanna. Why should you even be surprised?" Chase threw the words over one shoulder, and in the momentary glance that passed from his eyes to hers, Reardon sensed anger again—striking like a lightning bolt.

"Major, please!" Reardon interrupted once again, sparing only a last, swift glance of uneasiness toward his nurse.

"Surely you can do something. Anything. I've got a hundred wounded prisoners there, and ninety of them are going to die unless you can help me to provide some decent care for them. Please."

There was a sudden commotion in the dark streets outside the town house, the sound of soldiers mounting their horses, and even while Reardon was speaking to him, Chase Courtland was glancing around sharply. The anger that had momentarily suffused his face at Leanna's accusation was instantly gone, and Reardon saw sudden grimness rise to take the anger's place. As Chase turned back to face him his words conveyed a greater impatience than ever.

"I'm afraid our discussion time is almost at an end, Captain Reardon. My troop is ready and waiting to ride." There was a moment's pause, the sensation, to Reardon, of swift calculation on Chase Courtland's part. "Nevertheless I may still be able to offer some aid, Doctor. I have a good friend on Davenport's staff. He may be able to give you what you need, but I'm putting a condition now on offering that help. I want your assurance that Mrs. Leighton, or Mrs. Ashton, will no longer be volunteering at your hospital."

Reardon was taken aback. Before he could move to speak, Leanna herself had interrupted. "You have no right to make that kind of condition, Chase, please! Why should it matter to you what I choose to do?"

"Because you're still wanted by the federal War Department, Leanna. And because you're wanted now by the Confederate War Department as well." As Leanna stared open-mouthed and incredulous from across the shadows of the dimly lit parlor Chase met her eyes in bitter, almost begrudging anger. "It's what I wanted to tell you last night when I saw you in the park, Leanna. What I've spent most of the day scouring Columbia to try to find you for. To relay a warning. And to offer you my protection if you'd needed it." He offered a shrug now, rigid and unrelenting. "It's a long story, Leanna, and the particulars are not consequential anyway. It has to do with my sister and your brother and some problems that surfaced in Philadelphia recently. Whatever the reasons, the results are the same. Whatever name you choose to go by, you're still the same woman. There are probably a hundred men in Columbia who would recognize you on sight, and no place in Columbia is going to have more federal War Department people going in and out in the next couple days than a Confederate hospital full of captured prisoners. You can't afford to be caught working there."

"You can't be serious, Chase. I don't believe you." Leanna finally managed to gather her shaken thoughts to offer a denial. That the federal War Department should be prepared to arrest her did not surprise her any. But her own government? Her own beloved Confederacy? Never.

"I'm afraid it's the truth. Your brother Jonathon was prepared to break his vow of parole and come down South here to relay the same warning. You'd have believed him, Leanna. Believe me, too. It's partly to fulfill a promise I made to your brother that I'm standing here in his stead. You relay that warning to your new financée, Leanna, and then listen to whatever he tells you to do. He should be far more able to ensure your safety among the Confederate people than I presently am."

"But I'm afraid Captain Ashton is in no condition to ensure much of anything, Major Courtland." Reardon's soft interjection caught Chase already turning on one heel for the door. The young surgeon met the federal officer's eyes in a moment of silent communication, and then Reardon shook his head in further warning.

"You mean that Captain Ashton is among those hundred wounded Rebels you're trying to find some help for, Reardon?" Chase's question came slowly and left a lingering silence in its wake. "Oh, Christ . . ." To Reardon at least, it was obvious that Courtland had not made that connection before between the woman's financée and her nursing efforts. There was a too-sudden change now in Chase Courtland's expression, and a too-ominous feel of rising tension. He saw the federal major glance once, almost too sharply, toward where Leanna stood silent, and Reardon could sense a sort of gathering heaviness in the dark room around them.

"And yet this wounded Captain Ashton is the same man you're depending upon to serve as your protection from not merely one but *two* armies, Leanna? He's going to be able to offer you precious little protection as a captured Confederate prisoner of war, I'm afraid. Even less if he's dead."

From across the room, Reardon could see the woman's face pale to ash, and it seemed to him that she'd begun to tremble. But she remained composed, returning the Union officer's

336

hard gaze with cold defiance, and when she spoke, her voice was low and soft but clearly audible in the waiting silence. "Summer won't die, though. I won't let him."

"Sometimes death doesn't bother to take a vote first." There was another moment's gathering tension, and though Reardon thought the comment an unnecessarily cruel one—especially to the man's fiancée—he couldn't refute Chase Courtland's observation. "Tell me something, Doctor. I'd like a medical prognosis from you. How much assurance can you give me that Captain Ashton is going to live?"

There was a heartbeat longer of the same expectant silence. Then Reardon slowly shook his head, his expression wholly grim. "None, Major. Very few of the wounded Confederates are going to live at this rate. And Captain Ashton is more sorely wounded, I'm afraid, than most."

In the dark shadows of the room, Leanna felt the sudden intensity of Chase's gaze more than she saw it. For some reason, she began to tremble harder, trying to deny the fear that as yet, had no real cause to rise.

"And even if his wounds don't kill him, trying to offer you protection in his position probably would." There was a sudden absolute cessation of anger emanating from where Chase Courtland stood, replaced by a sense of some deep reluctance, some anguished decision that now, unexpectedly, must be redecided all over again. Reardon saw the Union major make a slight movement, as if setting his shoulders to assume an unwanted burden, and even masked by shadows, his face looked older than it had looked only moments before. "You'll come with *me* then, Leanna. I can get you out of Columbia. Away from *both* armies, North and South. You'll have to ride out with the troop, tonight. It's the only solution I can think of now. The only protection I can offer you."

All Reardon could see of Chase Courtland just now was his back and the rigid set of his shoulders beneath the dark blue wool of his uniform coat. Across the room, he saw Leanna Leighton freeze in utter shock, and there was a curious frozen quality, suddenly, to the entire tableau that stood before him in the ruined Columbia town house.

"Raise your hood up to cover your face, Leanna. I'll pass you off to the sentries as one of my troopers."

"What? Ride out with you on some damn Yankee patrol? How in the world is that going to help any of us?" As the first wave of sheer and stunning shock slowly receded Leanna was conscious of a rising anger. "I don't intend to leave Columbia. I don't intend to go anywhere other than right where I am—especially not with your Yankee soldiers! I'm staying here with Summer Ashton!"

"You *can't* stay here, dammit! Haven't you listened to a word I just said? Haven't you seen enough of what this war has turned into to understand that you can't afford to be caught here by either army?"

"I understand that Summer's wounded and I'll be dammed if I'll leave him in Columbia alone!" Inexplicably, Leanna found herself on the verge of sudden tears as she struggled to speak a denial. "You've relayed your warning, Chase, and for that I should thank you, perhaps. But that's all you need do. My 'protection' isn't your concern any longer."

"The hell it isn't! Whether you like it or not, whether *I* like it or not, the fact remains that your safety is very much still *my* responsibility. I can't leave you here in Columbia with no one but a wounded prisoner of war to protect you. Even if your Captain Ashton does live, he's going to have his hands damn full just worrying about his own survival. You'd be doing him a favor in a way to come with me."

"And leave Summer wounded, maybe dying—"

"It never bothered you so damn much to leave me behind in the same condition!" For only that instant, past bitterness intruded involuntarily into Chase's anger. Leanna caught her breath at his words with a sudden soft sound of shock, and wide-eyed, she stared at his face in momentary silence. Almost instantly, then, she looked away before Chase could see tears rise in her eyes. "Now I've run out of time to argue the issue, Leanna. I'm taking you out of Columbia tonight."

"Maybe you think that by forcing me to leave Summer you'll pay me back for having left you, Chase. Maybe you think that if I leave him that I'll come back to you again instead of—"

"Neither one, Leanna. I'm married now, remember? I have no interest in anything any longer except your protection. And after Atlanta and the MacRae place, I'm only interested in *that* for reasons that have very little to do with you personally." If there was any doubt of that, somewhere still in Chase's own mind, he allowed none of that doubt to show on his face. "And regardless of the reasons you may or may not

338

think are behind my decisions, the fact remains that you're coming with me. Now come along."

"And what if I refuse to do that, Chase?" Leanna forced her breath out finally in a long, slow, considering sound, forcing her eyes to hold his for a single instant of rising anguish. "Suppose I simply refuse to leave either Summer or Columbia? What could you do to me that you haven't already done at one time or another before?" The reference was a deliberate reminder of Chase's violence in Atlanta, and a moment's flash of darkness in his eyes assured her that he had understood the reference all too well. But the resolution that hardened his eyes remained unchanged. She took a single step closer to him, a wordless challenge, and her long cloak fell around her in shadowed folds. To Reardon, watching her, it gave the sudden impression of a vanquished medieval queen. Even in defeat, she retained an incredible dignity. To Chase Courtland's mask of unbending determination, she now returned outright anger and open defiance, and bitterness showed on her shadowed, ashen face. "What can you do if I simply refuse your 'protection'?"

"If you refuse to come with me, then your wounded Confederates will get no aid from me, Leanna. If you want my help for your captured countrymen, then you're the price I'm putting on that favor. We'll make the decision just as simple as that."

There was a silence again, and Reardon caught her sudden, anguished glance of disbelief as she turned toward him for aid. But he was too deeply confused, too desperately uneasy. He only looked away from her, glancing sharply back to try to read Courtland's face in the shadowed silence. He couldn't read an answer there, but he thought he caught a single instant more of desperate pain. Whatever Chase Courtland's reasons were, he didn't think cruelty was actually among them.

"You'll ride out of Columbia as one of my soldiers. When we get to a place I think is safe for you, I'll leave you there. It's not a plan that affords much discussion, actually. It's that or nothing. I've precious little else to offer you."

"And if I refused your damn bargain, you'd let all those helpless soldiers simply die?"

"Yes." Reardon frowned faintly at Chase Courtland's uncompromising answer. He himself didn't believe the Union major. But apparently Mrs. Ashton did. Her gaze held more contempt than anger suddenly as she stared at him in silence from across the room. Then, she glanced once toward the darkened doorway as if listening to the sounds outside of the Yankee troopers ready to ride, and when she looked back to Chase, there was hatred and defiance both showing in her eyes. "I don't know why I should have expected any different of any Yankee. Even of you, Chase. But I confess I did. Now I've learned better, I suppose. No Yankee is capable of honor. Least of all you."

"I haven't found war to be a very honorable sport on either side of late. It isn't covered in the etiquette books, and as for one side being any worse than the other, it was your own cavalry that started the fires last night, not us. At least not originally. Now it's time for me to lead my troop out, Leanna. Come or stay—that's the only choice you're going to get from me tonight."

Reardon saw the defiance that flashed in her eyes beneath the thin, shimmering layer of her tears. He saw the sudden rising of her chin, the reckless pride that was liable to cost her her life if he understood anything of what was actually transpiring here. It was a guess mostly, but he threw his support behind the weary-looking Union officer, and he shook his head before she could speak. "No. Go on, Mrs. Ashton. Major Courtland's right in one sense: it may be far kinder of you to leave your captain than to have him kill himself in an effort to save you. If you're in the kind of danger I'm beginning to think you are, you'll be far safer somewhere out of Columbia."

Chase Courtland had not waited for an answer. Even as the young surgeon had spoken and come forward to take Leanna's elbow, Chase had turned on one heel, nodding once as if realizing that further speech would only be effort wasted. "I'll get a horse saddled and brought up here to the curb."

Still half in shock, Leanna simply watched Chase as he disappeared into the ominous shadows of the waiting night. She said nothing out loud. She didn't need to. The expression in her eyes was comment enough, and it was Reardon finally, who broke the lingering silence.

"On behalf of our wounded Confederates, I thank you, Mrs. Ashton. You've bought them what they needed most." He paused a moment, deeply uncomfortable, and groping for what else to say. "As for Captain Ashton, I'll do my very best, I swear to you. With the proper supplies and personnel, I'll have a damn good chance of saving his life now. And I'll tell him you stayed by him, nursing him yourself, for as long as circumstances would allow."

"You mean as long as Major Courtland would allow."

Reardon's eyes darkened at the bitterness he heard so evident in her voice. He frowned at it, and shook his head, even while he knew his arguments would probably be futile. "Don't be too hard on him, Mrs. Ashton. He's looking at possible death tonight, riding out of this city. And men facing death can grow strangely ruthless about some things."

"Everyone in this war faces death every day, Dr. Reardon. I fail to find that any excuse for this damn bargain."

"But it's not exactly the same thing as this. It's not just a routine scouting patrol he's got on his mind tonight. It's . . . it's somewhat more than that, I think."

Leanna glanced sidelong at the Yankee doctor, her thoughts mostly consumed by anger and anguish and the helpless frustration of the night's shocking outcome. She had paid scant attention, actually, to Reardon's words. It was more the uneasy, deliberately vague way he offered them that touched her consciousness and claimed her attention now. "What exactly are your trying to tell me, Doctor? Is there something more specific you want me to know?"

"No. No, never mind. You are a Confederate still, after all. I may have already said too much to you. I just think you shouldn't judge Major Courtland too hastily or too harshly, tonight. There might be better reasons for his actions than you are aware of."

Leanna had time only to glance once more at him, puzzled and then suddenly, inexplicably, deeply troubled. Something was strange here tonight. Something Captain Reardon apparently had an answer to, but she didn't. "Doctor, please, if there's something you think I ought to—"

"Good-bye, Mrs. Ashton. Good luck." Reardon simply shook his head, letting the denial of the gesture itself interrupt her. It was Grier, not Chase, who had brought over Leanna's horse to the shadowed curb. Grier held the reins, too, as she mounted but in pointed silence. Cloaked as she was, and amid the darkness of the moonless night, there was not terribly much to betray her identity, and Reardon nodded once in uneasy approval. It might work. Major Courtland might get her out of the city safely. Much of the plan's chance of success would rest on the shoulders of the officer who was leading the troop, and Reardon could not help but wonder how long a man might carry so many responsibilities before he broke down.

Chase Courtland sat now on a restless bay stallion at the head of his shadowed troop, one gloved hand held high in wordless command. As Grier handed the reins of the horse to Leanna Leighton he gestured her curtly to ride up to the waiting major. However reluctant the major had been at the necessity of taking the Rebel woman along tonight, it was obvious to Reardon that his captain was even more displeased. Grier's dark eyes flashed apprehension and now even open anger as he watched her ride away.

Reardon glanced at Grier with a deepening frown, keeping his own doubts deliberately unvoiced. Camp rumors told ugly stories of Confederate prisoners unfortunate enough to land on the War Department's enemy list. Altogether, Reardon thought, it was a very grim business. And if the subterfuge was caught tonight, if Col. Drake learned of Chase's aid to Leanna, the major's head would surely roll . . . right beside the woman's own.

"The major asked me to give you this." Grier's terse statement startled Reardon out of his thoughts, and he turned sharply to face the cavalry captain. Grier handed over what looked to be two letters, scrawled in haste, the addresses unreadable in the darkness.

"If you'll pass this one on to Davenport's staff, to a Captain McLeod, he'll slip it in with some dispatches when he's a chance and send it north for the major. You'll speak to McLeod, too, about your hospital problems. Tell him Chase Courtland sent you to him. You have shortages, I assume, of medicine and men both?"

"Yes. The usual. A little worse than usual, maybe. Every month it seems to get worse." Reardon spoke the truth with a frustrated grimace.

Grier only shrugged as if unsurprised. "Well, McLeod will do what he can, and Sherman's staff owes us a favor after tonight. That should be enough for now. One of the Rebels especially, a Captain Ashton?" He paused for Reardon's nod, not seeming to notice the young doctor's sharp questioning

342

gaze. "The major wrote this note to McLeod about him. He'll get special care. Field-officer care, and a parole whenever he's well enough to take one."

"I see." It was all Reardon could think of to say, and Grier seemed to take his puzzled silence for dismissal, remounting his horse to ride away. Why, Reardon wanted suddenly to ask. Why pretend such callous indifference to her wounded captain in front of the woman, and then turn an abrupt about-face when it was too late for her to know the truth? It was a question Reardon had no ready answer to, and precious little time to spend in trying to puzzle any answer out. Wounded men were waiting, maybe dying. And he held in his hand what he'd come to Chase Courtland to get. Reardon watched in silence only until Grier rejoined and the troop moved suddenly on into the invisibility of the Columbia night, then he turned and started back to his waiting hospital.

It was slow going out of the dark city and was closing on midnight before the lone Union troop gained the Saluda River bridge and rode westward past the last picket post of Sherman's huge army. Columbia lay behind them, the ruined city quiet tonight with numerous—and sober—patrols of cavalry riding the streets. Behind them, too, was the most feared army the country had ever known. An army that had broken all the old rules to wage a new kind of war both brutal and also incredibly efficient. Also behind them was Sherman himself, that eccentric but brilliant man of paradoxes—religious and ruthless, always radiating his characteristically intense nervous energy. The man whom history books would label either the war's greatest hero or its greatest villain, depending on which side of the Mason-Dixon line they were written on. Sherman of the sudden, startling moods—red hair and short-cropped beard bristling like porcupine quills, his head wrenched sideways on a scrawny neck—a watching pose, oddly like a hawk's. If the troop made Virginia, they would be under Grant's command instead—the ne'er-do-well, the alleged drunkard who'd worked such miracles for Mr. Lincoln's battered army. The general who was expected this spring to match wits with the brilliant Robert E. Lee. The general Lincoln prayed could capture Richmond from Lee and so end the long war.

From her position, riding amid the Yankee soldiers of the moving troop, Leanna had the bizarre sensation of time and place losing their boundaries, of a nightmare well remembered, now to be repeated. Only the uniform color had changed. All else remained so much the same. It was just as it had been riding with Stewart's band: moonless shadow, the muffled drum of horses' hooves, the cold chill of sunless air, that ever-present sensation of war—fear and wariness and a queer kind of blood lust. They'd had no trouble slipping her past the sentries. Her dark blue, hooded cloak had disguised her femininity from such casual glances. Not even all the men of the troop she rode with knew yet that a woman rode among them. They must realize, she thought, come dawn's light, but every passing hour of continued ignorance reduced the trouble such knowledge might cause.

Chase rode ahead of her by a dozen yards, neither speaking nor apparently even aware of her presence behind him. Grier had ridden with her for the first mile, growling and curt with ill-concealed disapproval. On his major's orders, he'd deigned to brief her—as coldly and cursorily as he would have any troublesome and unwelcome green recruit. As long as she rode with them, Grier would regard her as he would any one of his soldiers. There would be no deferential treatment. Such treatment was too unaffordable a luxury at present. If the troop could dare to stop for sleep, she would awaken to the bugle call. And as long as she rode it, she was responsible for her own horse, expected to provide its forage, grain, water and grooming. Sore back, hoof rot, grease heel and founder were the usual ailments that plagued hard-ridden horses, and unless Leanna wished to walk, it was up to her to prevent such equine catastrophes, for Grier had no intention of sparing her another horse. She would dismount whenever the men did—to walk her horse up steep hills, to wade where the footing was treacherous, and wherever else and whenever else she was ordered by an officer to do so. The men of the troop carried a Sharps breech-loading carbine repeater, a saber and an extra .44 revolver—Colt or Remington—one hundred plus rounds of ammunition, a few days rations in a haversack, twenty-five pounds of grain for their horses, two extra horseshoes, two blankets, an oilcloth, and a gutta-percha poncho for rain. Leanna, quite pointedly, was given nothing besides her saddled horse. Apparently, she thought, neither Chase Courtland nor Grier welcomed the thought of her carrying any sort of weapon tonight while she rode along at their unprotected backs.

344

Between the darkness of the moonless night, the hard pace the officers set and her own shock and bitterly desolate anguish at leaving Summer Ashton and being forced into the company of hated Yankees, Leanna didn't notice any of the things that could have signaled this to be no ordinary cavalry patrol. The darkness hid the bulky sacks of coffee, flour and sugar carried on the spare horses. Extra rounds of ammunition were carefully muffled to avoid what could be a lethal rattling noise. Medical supplies, replacement leathers for tack, spare weapons and the like had been distributed unnoticeably among the various individual troopers. That they rode hard, and due west, didn't surprise her—she, too, knew where Wheeler and Hampton sat with their main body of Confederate Cavalry. It was only war, and she had known nothing else for so long now that the desperation and the grim fatigue of such a desperate ride seemed only normal.

Dawn broke with more gray drizzle, finding the troop thirty miles west of the occupied South Carolina capital and entering the fringes of the pine-covered sand hills of what natives called the Up Country. Here, Chase dared order the first brief halt, momentarily safe in the concealment of the dense pine forests. Looking back, Columbia was no more than a low, distant blur of ash gray and black on the dawn horizon, and miles to the northwest, he could see the first, telltale silver flashes from Confederate field glasses—but directed to the city still, and not to them. They had, at least, made the first, all-important separation from the main Union Army. And that, far more than Leanna Leighton, was the main thing on his mind just now.

It would stay the main thing, too, until he got them to the mountains, he ordered himself grimly. And then, *maybe* then, he would try to decide what to do with the Confederate woman who rode silent and bitter, unwilling and unwelcome, among them. One thing he knew already; regardless of what he'd said to Leanna earlier, there was no safety for her anywhere below the Mason-Dixon line. Until this war ended, there would be no safety for anyone in all the South. The Confederacy was dying, and even its own people would have to beware being destroyed in the coming death throes. In addition to having to work the miracle of safely getting his men to Grant in distant Virginia, he must also manage to get Leanna there as well, despite her defiance, and once there, arrange to clear her of any federal charges still hanging over her head.

Well, Davenport had told him that the deceased commander, Adamson, had written in his reports that Chase could just about walk on water if the situation required it. Chase himself smiled now in bitter irony, remembering the comment. He wished he were surer than he was of such abilities. Between the mission, Leanna herself and the federal War Department, he was going to need a few miracles.

Chapter Twenty

To Leanna's surprise, Chase had not halted the troop on that first dawn in the pine hills. Instead, the Union troop had ridden hard for day upon day out of Columbia—riding almost due west before turning warily north, not stopping to make their first real camp until the third morning just after dawn. Leanna had kept up with the others, but barely. She was aching and sore from learning to eat and to sleep as the Yankees did—on their horses—during the long dark westward march in the Carolina night. Her monthly flow had come, further ruining clothes already filthy and adding to her resentment of this journey. Yesterday, she'd had to accept one of the young Yankees' offer of an extra uniform while she washed and dried her own clothes, and this morning had found her clothes still too wet to wear.

Consequently, as she stood now on a ledge of rock in the fitful sunshine of the twenty-first day of February she looked to a casual observer like any other soldier of that same Yankee army she so bitterly hated. Her long hair was drawn up and tightly pinned beneath an overlarge black slouch hat. The dark blue of the Yankee uniform she wore was already stained by mud and powdered by dust. Boots came to her knees. And most surprisingly, as she stood on the ledge watching for signs of any Rebel Cavalry out scouting in the forest below, a Yankee carbine rested awkwardly in her two hands. The rifle was a gift from Captain Grier—a "gift" that made her frown all the harder as she stood on the high, domed rock of Carolina sandstone. From here, rifle in hand, she looked down on a world she no longer understood at all.

She had been born Leanna Elizabeth Penley, a woman destined to stand at the top of a beautiful, idyllic Southern world. Then war had come and that idyllic world had abruptly crumbled beneath her feet. She had married a man who

347

should have been a god in her world, and in the course of the war, seen him become a monster. She had loved a soldier who should have been her enemy . . . and then found another man only to have him torn from her arms by a Yankee bullet in the streets of distant Columbia. And now she rode with those very same Yankees, any one of whom might have been the soldier who'd fired the bullet that had struck down Summer. And more than anything else, even more than bitterness, as she stood on the high rock and tried to understand why it had all happened and especially, why it had happened to *her*, Leanna felt like the small child who has wandered too far into the woods by mistake and now, lost, frightened and confused, searches desperately for the way to return home again. It had become a world she could neither predict nor understand. A world that moved at the whim of Yankee soldiers, and her with it.

They had already passed close to several small villages, and each time, thinking this was the place where Chase Courtland would let her go, she'd questioned him. Replies to her questions were always curtly given—and the answers even vaguer than they were curt. And each day found her farther from Summer, farther from Columbia and farther from any explanations of the Yankee major's inexplicable actions. Below her now, the tops of the pines looked like waves of a great, green ocean, moving and restless in a gusting breeze. To her right, she could see a portion of the road the troop had followed today, but the part of it where the main portion of the soldiers waited was hidden from sight by trees that crowded to the road's very edge. Only a faint, uneven line in the treetops showed where that unseen road cut the forest, and she turned from that to scan the rest of the woodlands instead.

Rebel Cavalry was supposed to be nearby somewhere. The dawn's light had shown the smoke of telltale campfires. What she would do if she spotted her own countrymen was a decision she hadn't made yet. Fire the carbine, perhaps, to draw their attention? Pay the Yankees she rode with back in their own bloody coin? But Grier had given her the rifle and so deliberately given her that opportunity. And that very action had changed a simple decision into a far more difficult dilemma. Now it was a question of conscience and honor. What did she owe to the Yankee troop she rode with? And what did she owe to her country and to her failing Confederte cause? It would be far easier if Grier and the other Yankees would simply treat her as the enemy she wanted to be. It would be far easier, then, for her to act as one if she got the chance.

A jagged ridge of sandstone cut the ledge by her left shoulder, and sudden bootsteps crunching on gritty, loose gravel around its corner made Leanna turn to face the rock. The sky today was pale blue, aquamarine, and streaked with grayish clouds—it gave the impression of a painted background, framing Chase Courtland as he stepped around the edge of rock just then to see Leanna. Momentarily, he seemed to freeze, motionless against the colors of the South Carolina blue sky. "What in the devil are you doing up here?" Anger had replaced shock with barely a moment's pause in between, but then Chase's eyes had dropped sharply to note the carbine that lay cradled in the crook of Leanna's arm. And his question was followed now by a sudden long silence.

Leanna smiled in slow irony at that silence, enjoying the wariness he conveyed at seeing her armed. For a moment, she even debated the unexpected opportunity the Yankee rifle gave her. "I'm watching for Confederate Cavalry, of course, Major. Just as I was ordered to do."

"Ordered by whom?"

"By Captain Grier." Leanna had had too much practice at reading Chase Courtland's face. She recognized instantly the expression that flashed so sharply in his darkening eyes, the flicker of white tension that made his grim mouth immediately grimmer. Chase had not known, it appeared, what Grier had done. And Grier, she guessed with a faint, bitter satisfaction, would get a tongue lashing upon their return to camp. Chase knew better than to give her such an opportunity as this. . . . Chase Courtland had seen her choose before.

"Well, apparently Grier didn't consider what a fine target you'd make for Rebel snipers up here, sunbathing in a blue uniform against solid gray rock. Or what a fine target *we'd* make for *you*, either." Recovering from his surprise finally, Chase reached to pull her roughly past him on the narrow edge, pushing her around the jagged sandstone abutment. "Either way, you can get moving, now, thank you. I want you down off this damn rock."

Leanna had little choice but to do as he ordered, for Chase's grip on her arm was painful. But as she made the broader

349

ledge of the rock's western face she pulled angrily against him, trying to shake his hand free. "You needn't haul me around like baggage, at least. I got up here on my own. I'm quite capable of getting down the same way."

"Don't tempt me to let you try, Leanna. After all I've already risked for your sake, I'll be damned if I'll let you break your neck falling off this damn rock! Now give me your rifle. I'll precede you on the climb back down."

"No! You get your damn hands off me, Chase, and get them off *now*, or I *will* give you this rifle—bullet first!"

"You so much as cock that damn lever, and I'll—"

"Major!" Billy Matson's sudden appearance on the ledge's far side interrupted whatever threat Chase had been about to make. His eyes snapped instantly from Leanna's face to the young trooper's, but he kept his grip tight on Leanna's arm. "There're horsemen to the southwest. Looks like about a dozen or so."

"A patrol? Ours or theirs?"

"Too far away to tell, but unless Davenport's found some more soldiers to excuse from his army, I'd figure they're Rebels."

"Damn!" Chase dropped Leanna's arm then, practically threw it down as he stepped to the rock's very edge and scanned the woodlands stretching below. "Of all the luck! How far are they? And how fast are they coming?"

"Fast enough so it'll be touch-and-go trying to make it back to the rest of the troop."

"And where's Green? Isn't he down yet?" The patrol corporal had climbed the steep rock above to gain the highest possible vantage point. The other men gathering just now on the wide ledge looked at each other in silent question, finally shrugging collectively. "Well, somebody go get him, then. Johnson, you go down fast and grab the horses. Bring them up closer, and watch they don't—"

"Rebel Cavalry!" The corporal in question made a startlingly sudden appearance on the rock above, his warning punctuated by the sound of gravel rolling down from beneath his boots. "They're coming right toward us, Major."

Chase had turned instantly on one heel, frowning in the direction of the coming Rebels. Now he turned again to look over one shoulder toward the rest of the troop. They were distant, hidden by trees, miles away by the road. "We'll run

350

for the horses. Try to rejoin the others." He decided, gesturing as he spoke. His voice was sharp and he kept his frown. "It's a lousy option, but we can't stay here. There's no cover on this rock at all."

"We might not be able to make it, Major." Billy Matson nodded toward the edge of the rock he'd been guarding. "And if we don't, we'll be on foot and right in the Rebs' path."

"There's a cave up farther. I passed it coming down. We could probably hide in there." Green, too, spoke hurriedly, and without looking at Chase. His eyes were on the forest below, his voice edged with that peculiar tension men display before an expected fight. "If we could climb up there before they spotted us, Johnson and the horses might manage to go down unseen into the woods."

Leanna saw the momentary glance Chase Courtland threw her, guessed his immediate doubts of her, and felt her face flame with the implications of that silent assessment. She was a dangerous liability at this moment—she and he both knew that. First of all, she was an avowed Confederate. Plus, she couldn't keep up with the other men if they risked a dash for the horses and the comparative safety of the larger troop. She couldn't shoot well enough to defend herself here. And she couldn't climb rock face to reach the cave with a man's strength and quickness. You deserve it, Chase, she wanted to say. *You* insisted I leave Columbia with you, I didn't.

"No. Too easy for the cave to become a trap. The rest of you make a run for it. I'll stay here with her and give the rest of you cover." Chase nodded sharply in hurried decision, reaching for Leanna's carbine to cock the lever. "Go."

"Too late, Major. Here they come."

Leanna never knew whether Billy Matson had lied or not. She didn't have time to question anything before the young trooper shoved forward, grabbing and lifting her toward the next higher ledge.

"Scramble up there. Move," he hissed in her ear. Shocked into startled obedience, she did so, clawing at the rock with urgent hands. Billy Matson climbed below her, pushing on the soles of her boots one-handed, literally shoving her up the sheerest portions. Leanna didn't have time to look down as she climbed—and she didn't dare to. Her face was ashen pale, and she trembled from more than the effort of exertion. It was a long way down. And here, the rock was dangerously sheer. If she lost her grip, there was nothing to break her fall but the forest floor nearly a thousand feet below.

She gained the top ledge and only for a moment lay gasping and light-headed, flat on her belly. Then someone had her arm in an urgent grip, pulling her forward, and the next instant found her crawling on her hands and knees through a low jagged opening that led from sunlight into absolute blackness. Something tittered shrilly above her head as men crowded in behind her, jostling her in the darkness and shouldering her roughly against what felt like a wall, damp and soft with invisible moss. Chase's voice intruded softly, a grim whisper ordering a roll call, and though she blinked and strained her eyes to hasten their adjustment to the shadows, she still could not see anything. Chase was whispering more orders; time was passing—slow or fast, she couldn't tell. There was a sudden sound of voices from down the rock face—distant, echoing incomprehensibly among the vaulted rocks. But the drawl they spoke with was unmistakable. The sound was greeted by sudden, ear-splitting silence from the federal soldiers within the cave, and accompanied by an almost palpable, rising tension. In the midst of that tension, a softly piercing, inhuman shriek sounded above Leanna, interrupting that waiting silence. She jerked at the sound of it, bumping the man next to her as she warily raised her head to search the darkness. But there was nothing there. No, she could *see* nothing, she corrected herself uneasily. But something was most definitely there.

She sensed more than saw the sudden movement of whatever it was in the air above her. There was a faint whirring noise, like the sound of a bird taking flight, and then there was nothing. But as it came again, closer this time, she felt the faintest breath of air in motion as well, and that was only inches away from her ear. She moved her head sharply away at the sensation, biting her lip and closing her eyes. Outside, the soft scrape of boots against rock on the nearby ridge reverberated in the tiny cave like an announcement of doom. Even breaths were drawn now in absolute silence. But the puff of air against her face came once again, so close this time that she could have sworn something actually touched her, actually fanned her hair as she bit her lip to keep her silence. Oh God, just go away now, she prayed suddenly to the Rebels outside. Oh God, please, go away. All I want now is

352

to get out of this cave. It could be anything in here. Snakes, spiders, birds . . . *bats*. The realization came with stunning force. Oh God, there were bats in the cave, of course. Disturbed by the Yankees' entrance, they were flying in the darkness all around her. She felt sick suddenly, cold sweat dampening her filthy uniform. One came closer to her face, brushing her skin with a leathery wing tip, and she struck at it with one hand, blindly, trying to hide her face in her shoulder. A single gasp that ended in a sob broke from her lips at last, loud in the otherwise silent cave. All she could think of was a time when she was a young girl, long before the war had come. Late on a summer's dusky evening at Blytheswood, when she and Jonathon had been playing in the barn loft, the bats had come out. One had become tangled in her hair and scratched her face until she bled before Jonathon had come running to her screams to pull it free. It had left nightmares—gone now, at last, for years. But now, as if memory somehow recreated the reality, there came the sudden, well-remembered jerk of a wing tip catching in her pinned hair, a sudden shrill "yeep," and the buffeting blow of the creature's wing striking her face. She gasped again, merely a prelude this time to screaming out loud, as she raised one hand up in panic to hit at the thing. Only an instant later, came the shock of a man's body slamming hers down onto the cold floor of the cave.

Chase had started forward at the sound of Leanna's gasp, making a desperate lunge to silence the scream he sensed building in the cave's silent darkness. For the first instant as he reached her, he felt only blind, sweeping anger that left him shaking with the effort of restraining actual violence. Rebel soldiers were outside, and it appeared that Leanna had made her choice once again. But in the next instant, shock replaced anger. Something came hissing at his ear, and sharp claws were raking his neck above his uniform's collar. God in heaven, he thought. It was a bat. He could smell the filthy thing instantly, the stench of an unclean creature. And as he turned his head instinctively toward it he saw eyes, tiny and staring, red in the cave's artificial night. Without thinking, he reached to grab for the thing, then jerked his hand hard away as the enraged and terrified bat struck back viciously, seeming all teeth and claws in its panic.

Pain had shot instantly throughout his hand and beneath

him, Leanna began to fight his hold on her. The weight of his body was crushing; his shoulder over her face was nearly smothering the girl. But his only response was to tighten his hold on Leanna and to reach out once again in the darkness for the bat. This time he expected the pain and ignored it as he wrapped his fingers around the bat's furry body, taking the creature in a brutal grip. Drawled voices were echoing from the very ledge just outside the cave's mouth as he threw the bat back into darkness and high in the air. Then that hand, too, dove back down to Leanna, holding her head ever tighter against the dark wool of his uniform, his head bent close over hers though he dared not offer so much as a single syllable of reassurance. Miraculously, he managed to keep most of her cries muffled against his chest. The Rebel voices sounded again at last, but distantly, thank God, this time. There was the soft scraping sound of bootsteps retreating, and then a long, fearful silence. Only the continued soft whirr of bat wings, and an occasional screech from one of the creatures as it flew above broke the waiting quiet.

It was then that Chase felt it—a shock to watch the finding of the bat ensnarled in Leanna's hair. Leanna's body beneath his was warm and achingly provocative. The scent she exuded was soft and feminine, her throat was warm where his face was pressed closely against it. She trembled now in fear, much as she'd trembled once before beneath him in yielding passion, and for an instant, unexpected but undeniable, he felt the shock of wanting her still—the blind, burning hunger to hold her in a far different embrace. Neither the wedding ring on his finger nor the legacy of bitterness toward and betrayal by Leanna were able to protect him the way he'd thought they would. Doc Lacey had been right in Savannah. Winter roses *could* all too easily bloom again, couldn't they? In reaction, as if the touch of her body had suddenly burned him, Chase let Leanna go and rolled away onto the cold rock floor. Damn it, he cursed at himself in the silence. Forget it. Forget *her*. Or you'll get yourself and the rest of the troop killed.

"Grier, go out and see if we're clear yet." The whispered words had a harsh edge in them, harsher than usual, and behind him, Chase sensed Leanna move away with a grim relief. He didn't turn to look at her. He pulled his revolver out instead to crawl toward the cave mouth after his corporal.

Behind him, he heard muffled murmurs—Matson he thought, and the softer whisper of Leanna's faltering answer. Matson spoke again, with some sympathy it seemed, and Chase swore once again at himself in angry silence. Stupid, *stupid* idea to bring her along. He should have left her in Columbia, left her to face her own fate, as she'd wanted him to do. Leanna was still a Confederate; she wouldn't even deny that allegiance. And still a woman, subject to all the strange instincts of her sex. Putting her in man's uniform didn't change her essential nature. Whether by conscious decision or not, she'd just about gotten everyone of them captured or killed in here. Yet Matson would offer kind sympathy. His own body would burn with hunger to possess her. And they were not even a week yet into their long, difficult journey north.

"All clear, Major."

The words came through the shadows with startling volume. "All right. Matson, go." Chase nodded his head toward the outside, backing up to let the young trooper pass. There was a momentary pause and the soft murmur of voices again. And not Matson but Leanna started forward, crawling past him toward the faint light that marked the mouth of the cave. Chase's frown reappeared and he reached out sharply to grab her arm. "No. The least you can do is to wait your turn."

"It's all right by us, Major." One of the other men interrupted quickly, motioning toward the bats still flying invisibly in the air up above, wheeling and shrieking in continuing agitation. "Ladies don't like 'em, and we don't mind 'em so much, sir."

For a moment, Chase's hand tightened on Leanna's arm as if in incipient denial. Then very abruptly, he released her instead, motioning her on with a single curt gesture.

She was still trembling as she reached the blessed sunlight and sweet fresh air of the outside ledge, and she drew a deep, shuddering breath before she even tried to stand. Behind her, the other soldiers were emerging gradually from the cave. One paused on the ledge, looking down, and bending over to pick something up.

"Them Rebs were close enough to smell us. Lookit here. Somebody lost the heel off a boot."

Leanna looked over, but more by instinct than out of genuine curiosity. It was hand-cut leather, obviously Confederate, for the federals machine-produced their uniforms. There seemed to be a mark on one corner, worn and faint, and she frowned faintly at seeing it. Something about the thing triggered a vague, mostly forgotten memory, but she didn't pursue the thought any further than that. She was preoccupied with another thought, the uneasy prick of conscience that told her she'd behaved badly in the cave just now, and that she owed Chase Courtland both apology and thanks. That it had been Chase and no other she'd known instantly. She had remembered all too well the familiarity of that male body lying heavy over hers, a familiarity once treasured, from a time before the anger of Atlanta and Savannah and the devastation of Columbia. It had reawakened a buried sorrow and replaced most of her earlier anger with remembered anguish. As Chase emerged now from the cave behind her Leanna forced herself to turn and offer reluctant repentance. "Chase, I—"

"I'm sorry, Leanna," he interrupted her apology curtly, as if he hadn't heard her speaking to him. Neither did he look at her as he spoke. He glanced down over the edge of the rock instead, frowning as if he still half-expected to find Rebel Cavalry in the woods below. Only a small portion of his attention seemed directed to Leanna herself. "I'm afraid I may have been unnecessarily rough with you in the cave there. So I apologize. But I thought at first that you had decided to call out a warning to the Rebels on the ledge."

Her glance sideways was more startled than anything else, and there was a momentary pause before she collected her thoughts to answer. Actually, it had never occurred to her to cry out a warning . . . but now, thinking of it, she wasn't sure exactly why not. Because she didn't want to see Chase die, Leanna realized slowly, regardless of the anger she bore him for Columbia. She didn't want to see him bloody and agonized, dying in front of her very eyes, dying perhaps in her very arms . . . for if it came to that, she realized with a slow sense of rising surprise, she *would* hold Chase once again. Summer and all else notwithstanding. Chase was a Yankee, yes. For that and for the bitter anguish he had caused her in all this year now finally past, she might continue to hate him. But not that much. Never that much. She'd loved the man himself too dearly once, carried his child in her belly and gladly. There would be something of that once-compelling bond that would never be entirely gone. Something of that must always remain.

"No. No, I never meant to betray all of you like that . . . although I'll admit that I did spend most of the morning with that rifle in my hands wondering what I would do if I *did* spot some Confederate troops. I think then that I had about decided I would alert them if I had the chance. But there in the cave it was only the bat in my hair. It's important to me that you understand that. Maybe I'm not as fanatic a Confederate as I once was. Or maybe I've just seen too much dying in the course of this war to want to be responsible for causing any more deaths, on either side, in either army. I'm not sure I know myself what all the reasons are. But I won't betray either you or your soldiers, Chase, unless I feel that I have no choice, unless it's a clear-cut choice between Yankees dying or Confederates dying. As long as it isn't that, you needn't fear I have any ambitions to seek your death, Chase. I don't."

Chase looked at her now suddenly, a sharp glance of dark intensity that conveyed both doubt and also something else, something Leanna might have indentified if there had been so much as a moment's time to examine it. She had seen it in his eyes once before. But he didn't keep her gaze long enough to allow such remembrance. He barely met her eyes before he looked away again, and now he shrugged as if in disbelief. "*Really*, Leanna?" There was both instant and familiar bitterness in the question he now returned sharply to her. "If I could believe that entirely, it could make things a lot easier the next time. Maybe for both of us." But he only shrugged as he spoke the words, already turning to walk away from her protests.

Startled, Leanna caught at his arm, holding it to force him to turn back to face her. "Chase, what in the hell do you expect from me? It appears I'm damned if I do and damned if I don't! Why won't you even listen to what I'm trying to say to you?"

"Because a few minutes ago you were threatening to blow my head off with that damn rifle Grier gave you, remember? You're just going to have to forgive my seeming inability to follow these changing moods of yours, Leanna. I don't seem able to go from anger to apologies quite as quickly as you do!"

"But of course I was angry! In a way I still *am*! And I think I have a right to be! You forced me to leave Columbia, to leave Summer there wounded. You forced me to come along on some damn Yankee patrol to God only knows where, while you seek out some miracle oasis of safety for me from the war. Dammit, Chase, of course I'm angry—I'm just not quite angry enough to want to see you killed for it. That's all." She paused only a last moment, trying and failing to read his eyes. "I'm *not* altogether your enemy, Chase. I never was. And I'm not now either. For whatever that's worth, it *is* the truth."

"Even if I could believe you entirely, Leanna, I'm afraid it's too late to be worth very much. In fact, it might be better for both of us to simply remain enemies from now on. Let's leave our relationship as uncomplicated as we can, shall we?" He pulled away from her hand without glancing back, and she did not see the flash of anguish that momentarily had darkened his eyes. She let him go this time without trying to hold him any longer and watched in helpless frustration as he strode swiftly to the rock's outer ledge where the other soldiers were waiting for him.

"Here, Major, I'll take that rifle down for you." One of the troopers reached out as he spoke, taking what had been Leanna's "gift" from Grier. "Maybe I'd better unload it first, though."

"No need to, Piers." Chase merely handed the carbine to the soldier with a shrug of dismissal. "I checked. It was never loaded in the first place."

Leanna's eyes widened in surprise, a surprise quickly followed by a realization of new anger. But Chase was gone before she could speak, and she made a hasty effort then to simply forget Grier's not-very-subtle communication of distrust. Most of the other Yankees were already following their major's descent from the rock, but two of the troopers were waiting behind as if assigned to accompany Leanna's return. As she started to follow the others she could not help a single, frowning glance at the rifle, which one of them held, and the soldier seemed to misinterpret her glance.

"It's been a hard ride out of Columbia. And a hard ride still ahead of us to Virginia. Those wounds the major took back in Savannah still kick up on him now and again when he's tired, and I figured it would be easier on him to have his hands free for the climb back down. Billy here can take care of you all right without my help."

Leanna had begun to nod already, preoccupied still with

the frustration of her recent confrontation with Chase, hardly even listening as the soldier spoke. But as she started down over the edge of the ledge, she glanced back in sudden startled puzzlement as the trooper's words did finally register. Wounds in Savannah? Ride to Virginia? What in the devil was he talking about? Whatever it was, it was obvious the two Yankee troopers assumed Leanna, too, knew all about it. And it was equally obvious to her she did not. Back in Columbia, Dr. Reardon had warned her that this was no routine scouting patrol, but in the anger and resentment of the past few days, she had thought nothing more about his vague warning. "Virginia, you said?" Despite herself, Leanna's voice betrayed her startlement, and she offered a hasty shrug to try to conceal that. "I mean, do you really believe you will make it that far north?"

The young trooper named Matson, the one who had helped her earlier in the climb to the cave, simply shrugged at her question, as if such doubts did not surprise him or even concern him overmuch. He grinned as he answered, a good-natured grin. "The major says we will. So I figure he's right. He usually is."

"Don't you worry, Mrs. Leighton." It was the other man now who was speaking again, the one who had taken the rifle from Chase moments earlier. "We'll get to Virginia, all right. And we'll get *you* home, as well. You probably don't remember me, but I was quartered at your place in the Valley last winter. Quite a few of us were. Your lady, Jewel, was mighty good to us there, tending our sick and baking things now and again. We sorta made a deal with her, see. We told her we'd look out for you if the time came you needed lookin' out for. It sorta surprised us you coming out of Columbia like you did with us, but we figure our deal still holds. We'll be keeping an eye out for you on the rest of the trip, don't you worry none."

Leanna could only stare in startled silence, trying to keep shock concealed on her face. Virginia? Good God! Reardon's warnings now were only too clear. Chase couldn't leave her in Columbia because he wasn't going to return to Columbia . . . and between Columbia and Virginia lay miles and miles of Confederate territory! No routine patrol, indeed. Some of the questions were beginning to find answers indeed. "And his

359

wounds in Savannah? They don't seem to slow the major down at all."

"Don't seem to much anymore, ma'am. We thought he was a dead man at first in Savannah. Even the captain gave up on him then. But damn if he didn't crawl back in his saddle to rejoin the army when it left for Carolina. Nobody could figure it then, 'cause the major could hardly keep his saddle those first couple days. But he was bound and determined he was comin' north with us, and nobody could do much to tell him he wasn't. Good thing he did, of course. We'd have missed him sorely as the trip turned out. I wouldn't want to be trying to make Grant's army, now, with anyone but the major himself."

A sudden surge of nearly overwhelming anguish rose without warning in Leanna's soul. There was a sudden memory of that bloody day of ambush, the distant sound of rifle fire and MacRae's assurance that the Yankee commander had died. Chase nearly *had* then, after all. When she had seen him in Columbia, it had somehow never occurred to her that he'd even been wounded. It had never occurred to her he'd made the effort he had to come after her as soon as he could. She had blamed him for that, instead, thinking Chase had not cared, had not heard the desperate cries for help which her soul had sent out to him all during those days of horror before Summer had come. Nobody else might know why the major had "crawled back in his saddle" to rejoin his troop . . . but now, abruptly, Leanna did. Regardless of the anger, regardless of Chase's beliefs of her betrayal in Atlanta and afterward, regardless even of his marriage in the ensuing months, he had somehow by instinct sensed the desperation of her need for him. And as she had thought once before on a long ago day in a tiny clearing marked by a Gullah cabin, when she needed him as desperately as she had then, Chase would find a way to come to her aid. So he had done that—just as she'd prayed he would. And she had repaid him in Columbia by running from him first, and repaid him afterward with anger and scorn.

"Mrs. Leighton? Mrs. Leighton? Are you all right?"

It was like waking too suddenly out of a dream, or out of a nightmare really. Billy Matson was staring at her with puzzled eyes, and Leanna blinked, breathless and conscious of the continued hammering of her heart. The sky was blue still.

The sunshine was glaring off the rock, making the day warm, and down below, the tops of the pines still waved like a restless green sea. But it was like opening her eyes to a picture only, and it took a moment for it all to become real to her once again. "Oh. Yes, I'm sorry. Yes, of course, I'm fine. And I thank you for your offer of kindness on the way to . . . Virginia. I'll try not to get in your way too greatly."

"We better climb down, then. Last thing we want to do is get left up here alone."

She nodded numbly, obediently moving, but her knees remained weak, her hands shaking, and the climb back down was doubly slow. Matson had reached the bottom. Leanna was still on the rock face when another soldier appeared below.

"You wanna stay here mollycoddlin' that Rebel bitch, Matson, you do it. But the major's gone, and he can shove his damn orders. I ain't staying to cover you. I'm getting my ass back to the rest of the troop."

Leanna finished her descent just then, dropping to the forest floor in time to catch a last glimpse of the unknown soldier's back. She was trembling still and trying to conceal it, and as Matson reached to take her arm he misinterpreted the cause of her fears.

"Oh, here now, ma'am. Don't let Hazen scare you. He's a bad apple, worse even than Banks, but we'll keep you safe. Don't you fret."

Banks she remembered from the winter in Virginia. If Hazen was as bad or worse, he was trouble indeed. Trouble from *within* the Yankee troop as well as from without? If so, she thought instantly, then Virginia and Grant's army might as well be a hundred thousand miles away. All of Chase Courtland's abilities and confidence notwithstanding, to Leanna this seemed like a suicide mission. And mutiny from within his own troop would only offer it the final kiss of death. As she'd just been reminded by the news of Chase's near-death in Savannah, even the best officer was only mortal. Officer casualties were running abnormally high in both armies by this point in the war, and it wasn't all due to the danger they faced when they led their troops into battle. Bullets weren't dyed blue or gray, and "friendly" fire at an unprotected back could be just as deadly as any other kind. Chase Courtland might find his death coming at him from either direction on the long trip north.

Far away from the dense pinewood forests of South Carolina, and totally unaware of the dangers that faced his son there, Joshua Courtland sat quietly in his upstairs study. The christening for the Penley's baby son was to be this afternoon. He was dressed for it already, formally, for he had finally acceded to Whitney's gentle insistences that he attend. The boy was to be named Joshua Douglas—a combination of the North and the South—and Joshua was to be the child's godfather. He did not really wish to go, but neither had he any genuine reason for absenting himself. It merely seemed a bother—as everything these days seemed a bother. It would be easier, he thought, when he was dead. Except that then he must explain to God why he'd so badly mismanaged so much of his life—living by codes that had proven meaningless and even hypocritical by the end. One son was dead because of his idealistic sham. Another was still at war yet, risking death on the strength of those convictions his father had taught with such holy fervor . . . until that father himself, too late, had found Don Quixote merely mad after all.

Joshua recognized the fact that it was his own daughter who had beaten him in the end, forced him to retreat and not with honor. And the result of that moment's weakness had been to turn his entire lifetime into sheer, unpardonable hypocrisy. He did not hate Elinor for that. In fact, he found himself so incapable of reaction to anything that he did not even hate himself. He despised himself merely—with the same, strange, mild objectivity he would have once regarded a slug oozing slime beneath a damp garden rock.

Brandy stood now in a cut-crystal decanter on the marble-topped table by his elbow. A small fire was lit in the Carrara marble fireplace, and the hissing of gas jets provided illumination from the chandelier overhead and eliminated both the camphor scent and the inescapable black smoke of oil lamps. Luxury surrounded him, entirely without easing him. A newspaper, stiff and crackling, lay open on his lap, and the black of its ink had smudged his thumb and forefinger to a pale gray. Sherman's army had taken Columbia with little Confederate resistance, the headlines proclaimed, and Joshua admitted to greater hope for the war's end and his son's return. But even that had failed to crack the shell of the strange, apathetic melancholy that had encased him since the night of Elinor's departure. Nothing ever would, he thought. It was like living death—cold and numb. The only difference was that now, of all times, his heart refused to cease its beating.

"Joshua? Thank God I've found you in time!" An ashen, pale, trembling Henry Walters burst without warning into the cold seclusion of Joshua's study. In startled reaction, Joshua rose from his comfortable burgundy wing chair to stare at the man. "They know that I know about them, Joshua! I think they're trying to kill me!"

The elderly Walters was wild-eyed and frantic. His distraught appearance and barely coherent words painted a picture more akin to madness than to reality. Joshua simply stared at him, speechless, conscious of a vague sense of annoyance at being so rudely imposed upon by anyone's problems—real or imaginary. His life was over. All he wanted now was to be allowed to die in peace, and Henry Walters seemed indisposed to let him, suddenly.

"Joshua, for God's sake, you've got to do something. We've got to do something. Roland Hodges, Mortimer, Fields, Dolan—a dozen others, some of our own group, some not. I lied to you that night, Joshua, telling you I hadn't heard them clearly enough to be sure. I was too afraid of them. God help me, I think I still am. But now that the war seems close to ending, they're more serious about it than they ever were before!"

"More serious than ever about what, Henry?" Only for such a very good, very old friend would Joshua have made even this much of an effort. For anyone else, he would simply have rung for Cooke to see them out. "I'm not sure I have the vaguest notion of what it is you're so distraught about, Henry. Is it something to do with the coalition?"

"Don't you remember, Joshua? For the love of God, don't you even remember that night? It was one of the last meetings you attended. Shortly before you had your attack."

It had been too long ago for Joshua—not in terms of the length of time, but in terms of the complexity of events. Worries about the coalition had been long since overwhelmed in importance by crises much closer to home: his own near-death, Chase's return and marriage, then the annulment, Elinor, Jonathon Penley. It seemed like that night had been years instead of months ago. "So there's a problem, now, with the coalition, Henry?"

"Yes. No. Not the larger group, I mean, Joshua. Not the one you and I actually joined. They're hardly even organized anymore. With the fall of Savannah and the profiteering that started there, it was every man for himself, you know. Very few of the members even came to the meeting last month. But there's another group—the one I told you about before." Walters calmed down a little as he spoke, regaining some color in his face and accepting the brandy Joshua offered with a nervous nod.

"Hodges, yes, of course. You said Mortimer and Dolan, as well?"

"Probably more names that I don't know. Some from New York, a few from Boston, from Baltimore, from Washington, too. Some of them are from the War Department itself, I'm sure of it!"

A faint, cold shudder touched Joshua's spine, the first emotion he'd felt in too long a time. A few drops of the brandy he was pouring for himself sloshed over the edge of the snifter to spot the ivory-colored fringe of a Persian rug, and he set the decanter back with an abrupt, shaken gesture. The War Department? Yes. Sudden memory came flooding back. God, Joshua, you saw it yourself! Saw it and forgot it. A sudden thrust of fear pierced the apathy that had frozen around his heart since Elinor had left his life in ruins. Fool, he damned himself! Regardless of what personal hell has dominated your thoughts in the meantime, how *could* you have forgotten that premonition of approaching evil?

"There's about thirty of them, Joshua. That includes the Washington people—the 'first echelon,' Lafayette Baker calls them. Stanton himself may be involved. I don't know."

"But what can they do, Henry? The president keeps a close eye on his War Department. So does Secretary of State Seward."

"*Too* close an eye apparently." Walters paled further and set his brandy aside with a sudden movement. "They have plans to kidnap the president, Joshua. And Seward, too. God, don't tell me I've gone mad—I have considered that possibility already myself. Whether I'm dreaming this horror. Or imagining it. Maybe I am. I wish I knew for certain that I was." Walters reached for a crumpled paper, drawing it out of one pocket to push it at Joshua with a trembling hand. "God, read it, Joshua! Then tell me I'm mad! There's an actor named Booth involved, and one of Baker's operatives—a Lewis Paine. That's Baker's handwriting, though he signs himself 'Watson,' and they've met once or twice already up in New York. Set the damn *date* already! For the love of God, Joshua, you've got to do something! You've more influence in Washington than I do—you've got to stop them—while someone still can!"

Joshua's own face drained slowly bloodless. His own fingers shook holding the crumpled paper. Yes. It was Baker's writing, he knew that well. Kidnapping Abraham Lincoln, the president of the United States? Early March? Suddenly, that earlier paralytic apathy was entirely gone. "Where in God's name did you get this, Henry?"

There was a short silence, ended by the sound of a broken whisper. "I stole it from Hodges at the last meeting. He'd shown it to a few of the men—not to me. Not to most. Then he crumpled it up to throw in the fire. I walked by on the pretext of drawing a fresh brandy, and I kicked it out of the ashes with my boot. I picked it up later when I thought they weren't looking." Walters blinked as if at tears, abruptly turning away. "It's God's vengeance, Joshua. We did a terrible, wicked thing, joining that group. Me worse than you. I dragged you into it as well, because I was afraid to be involved with those men alone. Dear God, I wish I had never done any of it, now. I'd undo it if I could. All of it. Give back all the money I got from their schemes. Every penny." He rambled on like a madman, broken and terrified, sounding oddly like he was praying out loud. "I don't want to take over the South! I don't want to live like a king off the Rebels' defeat! I don't want to rival the Russian czar for wealth or for power, or create some abominable, unchallengeable tyranny in—"

"Henry, stop it!" Joshua's voice was involuntarily harsh—partly from his own sudden fear and partly from the guilt of underestimating this horror, of allowing himself to have forgotten it for so long. *Two* crimes, he accused himself. *Two* abysmal failures: Elinor, and now this as well.

Henry Walters turned with a jerk, freezing there to stare disbelieving at his friend. "Oh God. Joshua . . .? You're in it, too?" Joshua blinked for the moment, utterly uncomprehending. Henry Walters stood staring, motionless, pale as a corpse. He began to shake then, slightly at first—an instant later violently. "I'm a dead man, then, aren't I? That's how they knew. You told them. I told you and—"

"For the love of heaven, *no*, Henry! Get hold of yourself!" Joshua stepped forward to seize the man's arm, shaking it violently. "Don't be a damn fool. I never said anything! I only joined the wretched group to try to keep an eye on what they were doing, to try to stop them if they went too far! You've known me for years! I despise men of their caliber. *Despise* them!"

Henry stared a moment longer and finally blinked. Relief and color flooded back into his aged face together. "Yes. Yes. I believe you. Oh yes, thank God, Joshua, I think I understand. I had wondered, you know. I had always wondered why someone like you would join them." His words faltered and died, and sudden stark horror returned to his eyes. "But what can we do then? Nothing. We can do nothing. They'd kill us, Joshua. Kill us both. And never blink an eye."

Joshua offered a smile of bleak acceptance. "That doesn't matter so much to me, Henry, since I'm dying anyway. I've known for some time already that it's only a question of when for me." He shrugged brusquely to erase any overtones of self-pity in the admission. "So they can't do anything to me that nature isn't already doing. Let me keep that paper. I may need it to convince some people in Washington that there's more to this than ugly rumors and panicky old men."

"Yes. Yes, keep it, by all means." Henry handed it over as if the paper were contaminated and sighed deeply with relief as Joshua took it. "Thank you. Thank you, Joshua. At least now if they get me, you'll be left. And you know, *you* can stop them, somehow, I think. That makes me feel much better. Maybe God will forgive me, now. At least, I hope He will." He paused a moment, looking at Joshua strangely. Something akin to tears glistened in his eyes, and he reached his hand out most abruptly to shake a farewell. "God bless you, Joshua. I'm proud to be able to call you a friend. I hope—despite all this, despite what you must think of me because of what I've done with that group in the past year or so—I hope you can still think of me as a friend and not despise me too greatly. Can you?"

A dozen different emotions surged through Joshua's mind, some of them those that Henry Walters feared. But who was he to despise any other man for weakness, he asked himself bleakly. God gave weakness and strength out to mortals in uneven measures, and Henry had done well enough with what he'd been given. It remained to be seen how well Joshua himself would do. Up to now, his record had been unenviable, hadn't it? "Of course, Henry. We are such old friends. I counted on you to be an ally always if I ever needed one." He managed a smile to cover what he privately thought could have been a lie. "Now, you must calm down. Go take a rest somewhere. Go to the country, even abroad. Stop worrying so. If you drive yourself mad, it will help nothing."

"Yes. Maybe the country. I've a farm near Lancaster. The one I used to take your son, Chase, out hunting on, remember? I'll go out there, I think. Away from the city."

"Good, Henry. Good day, then, old friend." Joshua glanced anxiously at the mantel clock. It was already past time to leave for the church and the Penley baby's christening, so whatever needed to be done must wait these past few hours. But no more than that, he promised himself. This failure, at least, he would see put right. Too many men had died, too many once-fine things had crumbled into ruin in this war to allow such misery to have been all in vain. Somehow—*somehow*—he must find a way to cripple the coalition's plan. Elinor was not the only battle, apparently, that God had given him to fight in this life. And regardless of how badly he might have lost the first, he had every intention of winning the second.

Chapter Twenty-One

Leanna hadn't believed the lone Yankee troop would even make it as far as they did. It was a testimony, quite simply, to the man who was leading them that at least they'd managed to cross the border from South Carolina into North Carolina, she told herself now in silent anguish. The pines of the South Carolina sand hills had given way to mountain hardwoods, bare-boughed and just now beginning to bud in the first hint of coming spring. The twilit sky above the trees was streaked with long gray thickening clouds—bars over a rose and lilac background. The men had ridden hard all day, without the benefit of much sleep the night before; there had been nearly two weeks of this pace now. Since the revelations that had followed the incident of the bat cave, many more days of danger had swiftly passed. It was now the Yankees' twelfth day out of Columbia. Twelve long days of hard, hurried travel, dangerous flirtations with far-flung fragments of Rebel Cavalry, hours of hiding silent and shivering in a cold drizzling rain, always another seemingly endless night march. Exhausted horses stumbled in night-darkened woods, and weary soldiers dragged themselves over endless miles. Yesterday had seen near-disaster again. They had found themselves on the bank of some nameless river, the waters ice cold and swollen by winter rains, Rebel Cavalry coming behind. Two horses had been lost to the fearful current of the rushing water, and several troopers as well. But each time that danger had reared its threatening head, Leanna had found a dozen soldiers ready to aid her. And she had thought to herself that if Jewel could only somehow know how her past kindnesses were continuing to keep Leanna safe, she would lie far more easily in her distant Virginia grave.

It was a good thing, too, that those Yankees did so conscientiously honor the promise they'd made to the woman now dead. For Grier regarded Leanna still with a kind of careless hostility, and all too often, Chase, overburdened and preoccupied, seemed to forget her very existence for whole days at a time. After the bat cave, he had simply avoided her. Often the Yankee major was not even to be seen. He might be scouting at the extreme front, riding as rear guard, detouring to overlook the surrounding countryside from the vantage points of the higher ridges they came upon, taking a foraging detail out to search for food from either the few farms they passed or hunting the forest's white-tailed deer. When Leanna did see him, he looked distracted and grim, silent and weary. She might pass within a dozen yards of him without a word or even a flicker of recognition. Most often these past two days, she'd seen him sitting on his restless bay stallion on one side of the forest-lined road, looking not at his troop as it filed by, but looking instead to the distant east.

Rumor had reached them, even out here, that Johnston had gathered a growing Confederate Army, and it lay somewhere to the northeast of them in North Carolina. No one knew where it was exactly. Even the black slaves that appeared occasionally, materializing out of the shadows as if by magic, did not know exactly where Johnston was planning to entrench. And if *they* didn't know, then no one did, for an unofficial army of blacks had aided the federals from Atlanta to Savannah and beyond, providing the Yankees with both knowledge of the local countryside and remarkably accurate information on the whereabouts of any Confederate troops that happened to be ranging in the area, and the slaves' underground ordinarily surpassed any official scout reports in both immediacy and truth.

All anyone seemed to know of Johnston was that he and his army would concentrate somewhere in the central part of North Carolina. And as long as he did that, it would allow the lone Yankee troop to hug the edges of the Blue Ridge Mountains in some small degree of safety. On the basis of that, Chase kept them near the mountains. But always, in the back of their minds, there was the understanding that this was only a guess, at best. A good one, hopefully. Obviously, the best Chase Courtland could make under the circumstances. But if he'd guessed wrong, then the entire troop would pay for that error with their lives. The equation it made was grimly simple.

Leanna knew to look for it now, and as the days had passed she'd seen the toll Chase's recent wounds was taking on him in both pain and fatigue. How he'd even kept up the pace he mandated for the troop was a question she had no answer for. Nor was he the only soldier now showing that weariness—and maybe, she thought, it was that mounting fatigue that had made the edge of difference today. Reactions grew just a half-second slower. Tired brains refused to think quickly enough. Barely an hour past the fork of the roads, they'd ridden into a Rebel ambush—rifles opening a startling, roaring fire from beneath dark-shaded forest branches, horses rearing, men screaming and falling and blood staining the dusty North Carolina road. Somehow Chase and Grier had managed to keep the men from blind, panicked flight and together had gotten most of them into the protective cover of the nearby woods.

Here in the forest that bordered that bloody road, the shadows were deepening already from gray to charcoal. The small clearing ahead was still and the Yankee soldiers surrounding Leanna on this side of the clearing were muttering and restless, a few groaning already with the pain of their wounds. Mosquitoes came out with the fading light, whining faintly in the air. Somewhere in the distance, a snake or some small animal slithered through underbrush, and even more distantly, an owl had just hooted. The last sound startled Leanna, and she anxiously searched the woods in that direction, for Confederate troops often used the owl's hoot as a signal to one another. The Yankees thought it was only local men who had ambushed the troop on the road—local militia, perhaps. But if regulation CSA troops were involved, Leanna knew that the Yankees' situation here was close to hopeless.

Ahead and on both sides of her, the sixty men of the troop lay motionless—on their bellies most of them, a lucky few sitting up where a tree trunk offered some small protection from the Rebel fire. Chase and Grier both crouched ahead in the front line by the shadowed clearing. She could barely see Chase in the gathering dusk. He was only a gray-black shadow, a silhouette with the long, slim shape of a cavalry carbine protruding out at an ominous angle. In between her and Chase lay the rest of the men, and behind Leanna were the Yankees' horses. She herself held four of them. Two slightly wounded men held a couple more each, but the rest were simply tied. Usually in a battle, one trooper in four stayed back to hold horses, but here Chase could not spare one full quarter of his troop for such duty.

A dog padded over soundlessly, whined softly and licked Leanna's hand. She grimaced at the wet cold of the animal's nose but patted him absently in distracted reassurance, never taking her eyes off the ground just ahead. Hound dogs, once prized, now abandoned, roamed the whole South. Food was scarce—too scarce to share any longer with an animal. Homes were abandoned. Owners had fled. The dogs, like walking skeletons, stalked the towns and the roads, usually getting a brutal kick or a bullet in thanks for their trouble. Life became cheap in war—even human life, let alone a dog's. A lucky few of the starving animals found new protectors among the federal troops as this one had today. Pathetically grateful, the dog had followed the troop's hard ride—after bolting down the scraps thrown to it at the end of the morning's meal.

The only difference between this dog and hundreds of others was that this one had come with a boy attached to it—a youngster of eight or nine, orphaned by war and then ravaged by fever, starving and lost. Leanna could not help but wonder if the boy might not be regretting that morning meal now, finding the Yankees' bacon and pan bread not worth the price of finding himself sharing the Northern troop's desperate danger. That thought gave rise to a discomforting question, and Leanna turned slowly, searching the woods behind her for some sign of the child. If the boy were around, the dog should have stayed close to him. For the hound dog to be wandering about, the youngster must not be where Chase had put him, back beyond where the horses were tied. Misgiving grew to fear as she searched the shadows a second time with no more success. Where was the boy, then? Not creeping up into the soldiers' lines, she prayed suddenly. Not thinking to play soldier among his newfound Yankee friends? Invisible rifles from the other side of the clearing fired instantly at anything that moved over here. If the boy disobeyed Chase and tried to play soldier like the older men of the troop were doing . . .

She didn't take time to complete the thought but reached to tie her horses to a nearby tree. And even while she was pulling the last leather into a hurried knot, she was searching over her shoulder for the child, scanning the federal troopers that studded the forest and the edge of the clearing that lay ahead. There was Grier. There was Chase. Billy Matson, just ahead of her. Lt. Harper. Bates, Simpson, Foss, Ryan, Piers, Taylor, Erling, Grissom, Hazen . . . Her eyes went on from Hazen and then snapped back, her heart sounding an instantaneous warning. "No!" She had no time to more than gasp a denial, grabbing her skirts to allow a lunge forward. Directly ahead of her, Billy Matson glanced back, saw the ashen color of Leanna's face and turned to follow the direction of her stare. Hazen lay there, his carbine muzzle raised and aimed—but at the broad, unsuspecting backs of his own federal officers rather than at the Rebel guns concealed across the way. Just as Leanna had feared days ago, the desperation and dangers of such a mission had brought an answer of mutiny from within the troop itself. Hazen wanted out of the mission. And there was no easier way for him to accomplish that purpose than to kill his own officers there where they stood.

Leanna herself had taken no more than a single step forward, and Billy Matson had just gathered himself for his own sudden lunge to prevent Hazen's treachery if he yet could. But ahead of Hazen's leveled rifle, Chase had already begun to raise his one hand in a signal for the troop at large to open fire. And the rest of it happened so fast that she was never sure afterward what had transpired or in exactly what order. The hound dog suddenly burst into the clearing—chasing a squirrel perhaps, or a rabbit—barking madly, its long ears flying, the white of his spotted coat a dull gray in the dusk. In the next instant, Billy Matson had begun to scramble forward to throw himself full-length on Willy Hazen—fists flying, rifles and bodies slamming together in an ominous and startling thud. Chase turned his head at the sound of the fight, his hand freezing in midair. And the little boy they'd picked up on the road dashed out of the middle line of soldiers suddenly, running after his dog, calling him and chasing him out into the very center of the deadly clearing. Leanna had screamed and Chase had turned. But a bare instant later, a deafening volley of shots had shattered the air and acrid-smelling gunpowder had obliterated any sight of either the clearing or the child within it. Leanna could only hear the child's weak cry as Chase jerked to his feet as if to go after him. Then she saw Grier lunge to pull his major back down as the next volley exploded in less than an instant.

Luckily, veteran troops don't always need to be given the order to fire; they develop their own sense of timing after years of a war. Barely had the echoes of the second Rebel volley died than the federal soldiers were returning it with interest, scrambling to their feet to run as they fired, dropping to reload as their back lines fired cover, scrambling up once more to charge the far side. There was no time just now for anything else. Chase was shouting above the confusion for horses, and Grier was seconding his commander's shouts with his own urgent gestures. Leanna turned back to grab the tied reins free, unaware of the tears that streamed down her face. Hurriedly, she half-stumbled, half-ran the horses out into the smoke-filled clearing, with no time to wonder at anything else.

It was not regulation CSA troops facing them, at least not this time. Under the withering power of the federal repeater-carbines' fire, whoever was over there quickly gave ground, retreating immediately as fast as they could.

In another instant, Leanna felt hands shoving her upward into her saddle, and the troop surged out from the woods to the road. They moved at a dead gallop, formationless and desperate, mud flying in huge clots from iron-shod hooves as they gained the road itself and raced toward the setting sun. Animals running in that kind of crowd sense fear quickly, communicate it and magnify it one to another, and Leanna had no need to touch her horse with spurs or whip to urge it on. As if escaping some primeval predator, the cavalry horses ran at their own prompting—wild-eyed and sweating, flecks of lather flying back in the wind from bits wet to dripping with it. They galloped at that break-neck speed for what seemed like hours, sunset fading to twilight, the uneven ground of the road treacherous in the growing shadows. Then finally they dared draw rein to a less reckless gait. But even so, they did not stop. Black against the ever-darkening sky lay the mountains, and it was becoming apparent to her that Chase meant to reach at least the foothills before he dared to stop and rest the troop. Only militia, perhaps, which lay behind them. But militia would pass the word quickly enough on to Wheeler's regulation cavalry. And then time would be precious, and every mile toward the safety of the densely wooded, uninhabited mountains would be fraught with ever-greater danger.

Ahead of her, Leanna could barely identify Chase. He was riding, she thought, with the child in his arms, and she thought she recalled some confused memory of his stopping his horse, of his picking the boy up from the clearing's long grasses. But she could recall no more than that. Whether the youngster lived yet or had died, she had no way to know.

The night darkened further, the shadows punctuated by no more than faint starlight by now. Still they rode on, until Leanna could barely keep her saddle with exhaustion, and the darkness hid all but the soldiers riding closest to her. Chase, with the child, was lost in the darkness ahead, and so was Grier. Only the large, blackish outlines of the nearby horses could still be discerned, and even their riders' faces were cast in deep shadow. Willy Hazen she had last seen somewhere behind her, with young Billy Matson riding grimly behind him. Piers and Taylor rode nearby—all three watchful of the traitor among them. Others of the troop, too, she knew would have passed the word along, and if Chase or the other officers did not know yet what Hazen had meant to do today, then they were probably the only ones in the troop now who didn't.

Finally she came almost without warning into a camp. The soldiers of the foremost rows were already fanning small fires to fight the night's coming chill and to cook what little food remained from yesterday's foraging. Horses were being unsaddled hastily, water emptied from canteens into coffeepots, blankets unrolled—all with the strange silence of men laboring under extreme weariness. She slid from her horse at the edge of the circle of growing light, stood motionless a moment to gather what reserve of energy yet remained in her, and then began to search among the shadows of the moving soldiers. Her heart sank to see Chase nowhere, and sank further as she realized the orphaned child was also absent. Grier she found, standing by the farthest fire, imposing some kind of organization on the troopers just now riding in. But as she turned to her horse, loosening the tight girth of the animal's saddle and slipping the dripping wet bit from his mouth to allow him to graze on the forest weeds and grasses, she still could find no trace of the federal major.

She did see Willy Hazen's arrival into camp just then. Wordless glances passed from man to man at Hazen's closely guarded entrance, and Leanna thought she could guess what those glances might mean. Hazen had long had a reputation among the troop as a shirker, a bad apple, as Billy Matson had called him once. But what he had done today, or what he had *meant* to do today, was something far more serious than the petty disobediences he had offered before. If either the major or the captain were to learn of Hazen's attempted treachery, there would be a court-martial, perhaps even an execution. But a lone Yankee troop in Confederate territory had no time to waste for prolonged legalities. And with the many dangers already inherent in this journey, the troopers themselves had no inclination to add yet another—by dragging along to Virginia a possible traitor. What Hazen had meant to do today, then, would not be reported to the officers at all. The enlisted men of the troop would dispense their own brand of justice in this case, instead. By the next morning's dawn, Willy Hazen would either be dead or driven out of camp by his fellow soldiers, and there would be one less danger left to face the federal troop in their long desperate ride to rejoin Grant in Virginia. Swift judgment and brutal justice, Leanna thought uneasily, but preferable, perhaps to giving Hazen yet another chance along the way to betray his fellows. She too, then, would keep her silence about the incident. The Bible itself said 'an eye for an eye,' and Chase Courtland carried enough burdens already that she had no wish to see him carry Hazen as well.

Intent on such thoughts, Leanna did not even notice Billy Matson walking toward her until he reached out to take her arm in a gentle grip, his young face mud-streaked and grim. "You all right, Mrs. Leighton? Hazen won't cause anymore trouble, I assure you."

She turned at his touch with a jump of startlement, but recognized Matson quickly in the overbright glare of the rising fire nearby. "Yes, I'm all right. Thanks in great part to you, Billy. For Hazen, I mean. I was looking for the major, though, to see about the little boy. I can't seem to find either one of them in the camp."

Matson nodded, gesturing her to wait as he turned and stepped aside to speak to a soldier who knelt by the nearby fire. He turned back an instant later, slowly shaking his head. "Sorry, ma'am. Jonah says he thinks the boy was dead when he major first picked him up. Burial detail's over that little hill there, if you care to check. You might find the major there, too, because he usually reads any services needed."

There seemed a sudden chill present in the Carolina night wind, a sense of déjà-vu about even pursuing such a mission of confirmation, Leanna thought. But still she managed to nod her thanks and she turned. Why should she doubt any outcome but anguish, she asked herself now as she slowly made her way toward the hill Billy had gestured to. Why, after all this time, should she still expect war to show any mercy? Why be fool enough to cling to false hopes? Still, she seemed unable to prevent herself from doing just that. Even knowing what she must surely find there, she climbed the hill anyway, her steps making little sound in the leaf-covered cushion of the forest floor and less sound in the long, damp grasses of the open hillside beyond. Even while she cursed herself for a fool, she was praying still for a miracle. Perhaps, *this* time, the war might be kind. Just this once, perhaps, it might spare them some sorrow.

But as she passed slowly beneath the boughs of a lone, huge oak, her eyes adjusting slowly to the darkness beyond the campfire's light, she could see the scooped hollow of a hillock ahead. Three small trees stood there in the darkness. And there, too, just barely visible in the shadows, the pale gray shapes of three crude crosses rose out of the darkness of three new-dug graves. Two were full size. But one of those graves was pointedly small. And she knew immediately what she'd come fearing to know. War should not be allowed to touch the children, Leanna thought now in sudden, sad anger. Somehow, right in the beginning, we should both have arranged that. North and South alike, they had failed equally and dismally in this.

She had closed her eyes for a moment's long anguish, and opening them now, she turned to retrace her steps. But her eyes had finally adjusted to the night shadows, and she could see another person now, sharing the same grassy hillock she stood on, staring out in the chill darkness at the same small grave. He sat motionless and silent, his knees drawn up and his forearms folded to rest on top of them, and there was not even the sound of breathing to disturb the quiet of the night. But she knew by instinct who that shadowed figure was. She debated only a moment, then almost reluctantly started to move toward him, stepping to within a half-dozen feet of

376

where Chase Courtland sat, staring still at the child's new grave.

"Chase? They said in camp you might be up here."

"Oh . . . Leanna. Or is it supposed to be Mrs. Ashton now? I'm never quite sure." He had moved slightly, abruptly—as if her silent approach had caught him unawares—but he didn't take his eyes off the nearby graves. Leanna thought she saw him briefly close his eyes as he spoke, and she thought, despite the darkness, that she read a momentary, greater pain flash on his face. "Whichever it is, you'll do both of us a kindness to leave me alone just now for the moment. Whatever you want from me will just have to wait."

She stood motionless for the moment beside him, but strangely enough no anger arose. She just shook her head finally, never moving. "I didn't come up here to ask anything else from you, Chase. In fact, though I didn't know it in Columbia, I think you've already done a great deal for me. Or you've tried to, at least. I came up here mostly to see about the little boy. I feel badly about him . . . and I feel badly about your soldiers as well. That's why I came."

"So you're sorry about Yankees now? Forgive me for doubting that, Leanna. Maybe it's just been too long a war for us."

Leanna reacted neither to his words nor to the bitterness they'd been spoken with. There was a time when she would have. A time when she would have hurled back returning anger, as she had hurled it at him in distant Columbia, and hurled it before that in more-distant Atlanta. But she had learned too much in the course of this last march, she had understood at last too much . . . and too late. She was simply unable to hate Chase any longer. And as for his anger and his bitterness at her, perhaps, she thought, he had a right to them both. Plus, tonight especially, he was hurting, and badly. Hurting for reasons beyond her tonight. And hurting worse than she'd ever seen him hurt before—even in Virginia, when Stewart had come home. She could almost feel it in the cold night air, radiating from where he sat—anguished and angry and motionless as rock. She stepped forward, closing the distance between them to reach one hand down to him, touching the dark gleam of his hair in an awkward, wordless attempt at comfort. His hair was cold against her fingertips. Beneath her touch, he didn't move—even, she thought, to breathe. The night air moved, though, in a sudden, biting gust of wind. In its chill, she shivered, and then blinked against the burning heat of her suddenly rising tears. A year ago on such a night as this, he would have sought comfort in her arms . . . and she would have offered it. Gladly.

"Leave me alone just now, Leanna. Please. Go back to camp."

The words were barely audible, more plea than command, and they fell softly into the anguished silence. For a moment, she wavered, on the edge of obeying and turning to go. Then she knelt beside him instead, torn in a way she'd thought she never would be again. He was still a Yankee, yes. But he was human too. And she knew better than almost anyone else how *very* human Chase Courtland could be. Glancing once more toward that small grave, she could not help but remember Blytheswood and the little girl, Miranda, who'd nearly died there in a burning cottage. Chase had risked his own life to save hers, and done that long before there had been any bond between them. Children had always been the Yankee major's most dangerous vulnerability. Many—*too* many things had changed since that night. But not his love for children. "I think I can guess how you feel, Chase, but you'll do neither yourself nor anyone else any good to sit brooding about it. What's done is done. You can't undo it. No one can. Come back to camp now with me. Come eat something and get some sleep."

He only shook his head for answer, but even without words, the gesture conveyed an unarguable decision. Leanna remembered too well to press him further at such a point, but neither could she bring herself to rise and leave him alone. So she sat awkwardly, not close to him, and the silence lasted for a very long time. It was cool on the unprotected hillside, almost cold, and her thoughts could offer nothing kind. She thought about the child the Yankees had buried here tonight, and she thought about Willy Hazen and how easily it might have been Chase as well who'd found an unmarked grave on the same lonely Carolina hillside. And she thought of her own child lost—that one not even given the chance to live, not even given the recognition of a grave. *Chase's* child, too, she reminded herself, lost to the war, just as everything seemed fated eventually to be. It was like being caught in a whirlpool, she thought suddenly. Being dragged ever deeper into it no matter how hard any of them struggled to swim free. Choking on its foul waters. Drowning in it. Even the children now were being sacrificed to feed its seemingly insatiable appetite.

"That damn hound dog. I should have shot him when he first came into camp this morning. I should shoot him now before he gets someone else killed, too." It was only a bitter thought, spoken softly, and somehow it did little to break the lingering silence that lay between them.

From where she sat, Leanna shook her head without even looking at Chase. She knew too well the useless anguish such unhappy hindsight brought with it. "No. It wasn't the dog's fault. It wasn't your fault for not shooting him, either. Some things just happen, Chase. You've got to forget it, close your mind to it and just go on from here. Go forward." She glanced sideways in time to catch the sudden, momentary warning of some strange emotion in Chase's eyes the instant before he'd turned his head away. Startled, she watched him as he slowly began to shake his head.

"No. We're not going any further anyway. I've decided to surrender the troop—tomorrow. Before the rest of the men get killed, too. I was wrong in Columbia. The mission *is* hopeless. It's too far. And I'm too tired, too damn tired already and we aren't even a quarter of the way to Virginia yet."

He was getting to his feet even as he spoke, and startled, Leanna reached out quickly to grab his arm. "Chase, no!"

"Leanna, I lied to you in Columbia. This was never to be a routine mission. I knew it was dangerous before we even set out, but I thought I could get the troop up to Virginia. And I thought I could get *you* there as well. I was wrong. I apologize. You'd have been better off after all if I'd just left you in Columbia as you wanted me to do. Not dragged you off on some hopeless damn—"

"It *isn't* hopeless! Look how far you've already brought the troop, Chase! If you'd only give yourself a little forgiveness, allow yourself something less than utter perfection all the time—"

"Dammit, Leanna, you've got to realize it's hopeless! It was hopeless before we ever left Columbia wasn't it? There are too damn many things for me to think about, too damn many places I should be all at once. In front of the troop and behind it. Home and here. In the war and out of it. Too many things to too many people and never quite able to do it all. God help me, I go to sleep at night and pray I won't wake up in the morning to have to start it all over again, but I always do. It's always there. Never any break from it. Never any peace."

"Chase stop it!" Leanna's voice broke with a sudden, startling sense of shared pain, and she fought an instinctive desire to reach her arms out to offer him comfort. He only shook his head sharply, not even turning to look back as he began to rise to walk away. "Chase!" She rose and reached after him with a trembling hand, catching his arm and holding it to force him into turning once again to face her.

"Damn it, Leanna, get back to camp!" For the split second he allowed his eyes to meet hers, Leanna read there a strange, blind sort of desperation. "You don't care about me and you don't care about the rest of any Yankee troop either! We're both committed now to two different armies and two different people! Why the hell must you make it only that much harder on me?"

"And what exactly do you expect me to do? You want me to let you sit up here alone so that you can decide exactly how you're going to kill yourself tomorrow? You can go to hell whatever way you like, Chase Courtland, but don't ask me to pave your way! That's one thing I'm *not* about to do!" She had risen to her feet to stand facing him, never letting go her grip on his arm. She felt him start to tremble suddenly beneath her hand, and she instinctively reached to try to grab him in a tighter hold.

"Get away from me, damn you! Go back to camp!"

He pulled with a sudden, violent movement that nearly tore her hands free of his arm and pulled her off her feet. She swore at him in a voice breaking with anguish but still shook her head in defiant denial. "I don't want you dead, Chase. And I'm not going to let you *kill* yourself over this. Damn you, I'm *not*!"

Chase had begun to turn away. Now, almost in the same unbroken movement, he turned back suddenly toward her, one hand reaching up to catch a fistful of her dark hair, forcing her face upward as he bent his head over hers in a brutal, punishing kiss. For an instant, she struggled in startled reaction, trying to turn her mouth away from his. The salt taste of blood was rising already on her tongue, and she gasped in a single, gulping breath of air as he began to lift his mouth from hers. But in the next instant, she'd reached to

380

hold him to her, stunned and startled, but never doubting the choice she had to make. There had been a terrible, desperate hunger in the Yankee major's kiss, and it was that desperation that had made her choice for her. It was the only way right now she could hope to reach him. And it would mean his life if she let him go.

For a moment only, Chase pressed his face against the pale, naked warmth of Leanna's throat, and she held him there with a desperation nearly equal to his own. She turned to kiss the cold, dark gleam of his hair, cradling his head against her as she might have done a child's, achingly conscious of the anguish that still wracked his body in shuddering waves. Then his arms came around her, a merciless grip as hard as steel could be, and she closed her eyes in desperate reassurance. This was not Stewart, she told herself fearfully. This was not John MacRae. This was a man who had loved her once and whom she had loved in return. And if Chase would take her with this little gentleness, it was because he had none left in him now to give.

Still, she tried to gentle him, tried to disarm the blind anger that seemed to possess him entirely. She failed, knew she'd failed and still refused to struggle against Chase Courtland's embrace. She held him instead, or tried to. She found it like trying to hold a whirlwind, feeling him tremble and moan and rage in her arms. One moment she was on her feet, locked full-length against him in a fearful embrace. In the next, he had lifted her to lay her down roughly among the deep, shadowed grasses of the cold Carolina hillside. It was only then, and only for an instant, that he seemed to remember some past thoughts of kindness. He was still for a second, resting his face between the warm soft shadows of her breasts and drawing an anguished shuddering sigh.

Leanna dared to kiss him then finally, lifting her head to brush his forehead with her lips, her hand caressing him in a grieving sort of tenderness. And it did seem to her that he was more gentle after that. He moved more slowly to pull open her blouse, and the hand that reached to cup her breast was careful not to bruise her tender flesh. He moaned softly, and she thought it might have been her name he whispered, but then he did not speak again. That desperate violence, instead, returned to claim him. He lifted his head to cover the soft peak of her breast with his mouth, as greedy as a child,

381

demanding what Leanna would have offered to him freely. This was angry, and physical, more hunger than warmth. Even in Atlanta, there had been more tenderness than this. Chase took her now as if her body offered him a release from some kind of pain he had suffered from, pain he now found unbearable. His hands were urgent on her body, unmindful, she thought, of anything else existing in the world. His hands were momentarily cold on her there, hard against the velvet softness of her inner thighs, and then intruding into her with the same rough urgency that had characterized his entire lovemaking.

Still, Leanna never thought to fear his touch, and the hands that held his shoulders shook only with his trembling and not with her own. There was little prelude to his possession of her. He raised his hips briefly from hers, and then returned them abruptly to penetrate her. He thrust himself into her almost roughly, as if ruled by a blind sort of violence, and rocked there inside her with desperate hunger. Despite that, Leanna was conscious of a sudden sensation of wanting him, and of welcoming him, and Chase took nothing from her she was in any way reluctant to give.

It was over quickly—far more quickly than she could remember it had ever been before with him. But in a way, she thought she understood that. The more violent the storm, the shorter its duration, and as this raging fury in her arms had finally peaked and then subsided he lay quiet at last within her arms. Against her cheek, finally still, she could feel the damp, warm kiss of his mouth and the ragged whispers of his breath, but he said nothing to her. He only moved his head down to rest his face against her breast and she thought she heard the soft sound of a last shuddering sigh. Then he moved no more except to flinch once from something in a dream. And lying still beneath him, Leanna felt the gradual slowing of his heartbeat, the change of his breathing from the rapid urgency of lovemaking to the deep, slow, healing breaths of an exhausted sleep.

Leanna dared to move then finally, freed by Chase's sleep to do as she willed. She lifted one hand to smooth the sweat-dampened, tousled waves of his dark hair and, almost defiantly, held his head closely on her breast. But as she shut her eyes tears slowly trickled back into her hair and dropped onto the cold grasses of the dark hillside. She could not deny to herself what she'd felt just now. That single instant's vivid awareness was burned into her soul as if by a brand. It had come full circle, then, finally, she thought—from Blytheswood to here. War or no war, future or no future ahead of them, she loved the man who slept now, motionlessly, in her arms. Yankee or not, married or not, she loved him still. In a way, she thought, she had always known that she did. And in a way, she had always known that Chase Courtland still loved her in return. And yet if they did achieve the impossible and finally won through to distant Virginia, he must rejoin his own side and return to the woman whose ring even now Leanna could see glistening in the shadowed light. And she must return to Summer and to the South. It was that simple, and that agonizingly inescapable. Whatever else might change in the meantime, whatever kindnesses or temporary peace they could offer one another in the course of the long, grueling miles ahead, Virginia must still be the end for them. Whatever else changed, that never could. It never *had*, she realized suddenly with a renewed awareness of the bitter irony. Despite the passing of a year from Blytheswood to this night, the undisputed resolution of all they'd felt for one another was still the same—eventually, inevitably, the final separation must come. It was now, as it had been from the beginning, only a question of when. And now, at last, they had their answer. It would end where it had begun, in distant Virginia. *If* they even got there at all.

Chapter Twenty-two

"So good of you to fit me into your busy schedule, Roland."
Joshua Courtland spoke with more than a trace of sarcasm.
He'd been left sitting in Roland Hodges' parlor for over an
hour—deliberately, he guessed—and he was not a man accus-
tomed to be kept waiting like that. The smile he offered the
other man was cool, and he extended his hand with a faint
feeling of distaste. What an awful house, he'd spent most of
the hour thinking. An almost embarrassingly honest reflection
of the man who owned it. "Money" screamed from the
overlarge, ornate gold-leaf Austrian mirrors, the too-heavily
beaded, Louis XIV chandeliers, the flocked velvet fabric on
walls, the Chinese Chippendale of tables and furniture. *Plain*
Chippendale, Joshua liked. And he liked some of the genuine
oriental pieces—with the flourishing tea trade with China,
oriental silks and furnishings were fashionable just now. But
the English Chippendale's conception of Chinese, that was
altogether different: grotesquely ornate, an unhappy combination of the West mimicking the East, without a true understanding of what constituted beauty in the alien culture.
Roland Hodges' marble-columned mansion was more the showplace of a Sybarite than the home of a gentleman, and Joshua
had found the hour spent in forced study of it oppressive.

"What can I do for you, Joshua?"

Joshua hesitated only a moment, then decided that tact
would be wasted. He wanted to get out of Hodges' gaudy
house. And he had—in his condition—no time left to waste.
"I want you to forget your plans to kidnap President Lincoln,
Roland," he stated flatly. "I won't allow you or your group to
do anything of the sort without blowing a very loud whistle
on such endeavors." Hodges' florid face never changed, but
something in his eyes did. Joshua noted it and offered a wry
smile, unafraid. "Henry Walters told me. Before that un-

happy 'accident' he had last week up at his country place. I'm afraid you were too late with that, Roland."

"I can't imagine what you're talking about." Roland Hodges responded with an easy smile and gestured to a nearby decanter. "Brandy, Joshua? It's French. Very good, if I say so myself."

"No, thank you. Now, about the president—"

"Really, I should insist you have a glass of brandy, Joshua. You are obviously completely overwrought about some nonsense poor Henry fancied he knew. Even if there were such a dastardly plot afoot—and that's ridiculous to begin with—how would you think to block it? Men who'd consider kidnapping their own president would be utterly ruthless men, Joshua. They'd hardly allow anyone to thwart them easily."

"Did I say *easily?* I didn't mean to, if I did, Roland. As for denials from you or anyone else, spare me. I really don't expect repentance, or even the honesty of admitting what's afoot. I simply want it stopped, Roland. Now. Or else."

"Or else what?"

Joshua only smiled to the unspoken threat of Hodges' question. It was an advantage, he thought, being doomed already and conscious of it. How free one was to shrug off further threats. "Or else?" Joshua raised one gray brow, still faintly smiling. "Perhaps a full-page ad, here. And in the New York *Times*, of course. The Washington paper, too. With the simple statement of your plans and—well, how about a list of names, beneath it? About thirty of them. Official titles included. All eight senators, War Department personnel, etc."

Hodges' smile was humorless. "I doubt you'd find papers willing to print such libelous gibberish."

"I could buy them, I suppose, couldn't I, Roland? If I owned them, I could print whatever I liked." Joshua shrugged and reached inside his coat to produce a bulky envelope. "I'm not Henry Walters, Roland. I've far more ammunition than he had, poor old friend. You could squash Henry's opposition as carelessly as you could a bug—and you did, quite probably. I don't doubt that for a moment, 'accident' or not. Unfortunately for you, he shared his knowledge with me before he left for Lancaster—and beyond. And you'll find me a little tougher to dispatch, or to frighten off. I've friends, too, in Washington. And a great deal more money than Henry had. And a touch more foresight. Copies, for instance, of several very damning pieces of evidence. And a complete list of 'who's who' that isn't much unlike the official book of names of influence. Well, Roland, I need a decision from you. Are we at war, you and I?"

"For the sake of our old friendship, Joshua, I hesitate to make such a declaration. It's common knowledge, your failing health. If you should suffer another attack, for example, who would even question your death? Or continue such a senseless 'war'?" Hodges smiled patronizingly, and with maddening calm. "Not the young Rebel who's running your bank, I hope. We could swallow Penley without pausing to chew."

"No, not Jonathon." Joshua shook his head in honesty. Jonathon might try, but as an ex-Confederate he could not hope to win. It would be suicidal to try. "I've a son, though, someday to be home from this endless war. More than capable of assuming my place if he needs to, Roland—especially with all the documents I could prepare to assist him. Chase could—and would—beat you at any game you wanted to play, I believe."

"*If* he comes home from the war—*alive*, that is." Hodges' reminder was sharp and unsmiling, an open threat—and the first display Joshua had yet seen of anything close to that. Hodges, evidently, was done playing games.

Joshua stood in the gaudy parlor, momentarily silenced by the shock of Hodges' threat. Henry Walters had not known whether the War Department itself had been involved in this or not. But if it was, Joshua realized suddenly, then Chase was left in an extremely vulnerable position—serving with an army that marched under the command of the very people Joshua had just so boldly threatened. "Should Chase fail to remain that way, Roland—alive I mean—then I would be *forced* to move—instantly and openly. And most vindictively, I assure you, too. I won't risk taking this kind of information with me to the silence of my grave, and those are the only two choices you're going to get from me. I either swing the ax right now or you back off on all your plots."

For a moment, the two men stood in the silence of the overdone room. Neither man smiled any longer nor maintained any pretense of cordiality. Joshua felt the tension in the tightness of his chest, and his sudden fear for Chase weighed on him like a thousand tons. But still he stood firm, more committed to this confrontation than he had been to any in his life. He was running a bluff, mostly—an awesome, dangerous one. He had few specifics and less real evidence to back up any of the threats he'd made just now. In effect he was gambling. But the next few years of the country's future were all-important: the end to the long, bloody war of division; the rejoining of the two halves of the Union—bitter North and shattered South; the necessity—vital, deadly difficult, but compellingly crucial—of disarming Secretary Stanton and his war-bloated Department of War, of stripping their awesome, tyrannical powers away, and blocking their attempts to reseize such frightening controls over the nearly shattered young nation. More important than any battle headlined in these last four years: Manassas, Chancellorsville, Gettysburg, Richmond—this was a secret one. It would never see the light of day in the New York *Times*. But this one, above all the others, simply *must* be won. Chase had been willing to risk his life for the visible war. If he could know of this one, Joshua could only pray his son would be willing to face its dangers.

"All right, Joshua." Roland Hodges spoke at last, with deceptive graciousness and an abrupt, impatient gesture of one ring-bedecked hand. "We shall say—for *now*—I find your point well taken. That's not a promise of any kind. Merely a temporary condition. You may die sooner than you hope. Your son may even now be dead somewhere with his army. Your only daughter, Elinor, however, is very much alive, and she and I enjoyed a most harmonious relationship while we were running black-market guns to the Confederacy." Hodges gestured as if reminding himself of a pleasant fact he had briefly forgotten. "There is that side of it to consider, too, Joshua. If you think to expose us, you expose yourself as well: your own involvement in the group, your daughter's activities, which were hardly exemplary, and we shall find other things, too, never fear. Drag us down into the dirt and you drag yourself and your daughter down there as well."

Joshua had felt a sudden, stunning, piercing pain at Hodges' careless admission of Elinor's guilt, but not a trace of shock. It was as if he'd known for some time and simply not admitted it to himself before. Yes, Elinor would do that. Providing weapons for the enemy, who had killed one of her brothers and could at any time kill the second. That explained that sense of a puzzle he'd feared to put together. Jonathon's hedging,

Hadley's Virginia drawl. Of course. Where had she gotten the money? From his bank? The money missing from April on, from the Southern accounts? Chase and Jonathon Penley both, he realized abruptly, had suspected something without knowing exactly what. And then, even so, struggled to conceal it from Joshua. Wanting him to die, perhaps, with that last, lovely illusion left intact.

Now even that illusion was gone. But in a way, it didn't matter much anymore. Elinor had beaten him once, perhaps. But she was not going to beat him again. Not twice. "Don't count too much on my lovely daughter's eventual assistance, Roland. To be quite candid for the moment, I've found that Elinor has a nasty habit of turning on her friends if it happens to suit her. And if you ended up with *her* as an enemy, Roland, you might find I look like a turtledove in comparison." Joshua had turned away even as he spoke, with a bleak but resolute smile still lingering on his lips. "Good day, Roland. Pass the word along if you will. You may consider our war declared."

Jonathon Penley was waiting in the parlor of the Courtland home when Joshua finally returned. Joshua was some several hours later than he'd anticipated being—he'd stopped by Epsley's house to change his will. Not Elinor but her husband Hadley inherited a portion of his fortune now. He'd not thought very highly of the viscount in years past, but the last visit had changed his mind somewhat. Anyway, *someone* must control Elinor when he was dead and gone, and there was no better control over the woman than money. With what Joshua had left to the Englishman, Hadley ought to have a fairly good chance at it. A better chance, probably, than anyone else had ever had.

Joshua stopped abruptly as he turned to enter his parlor. Two ornate, ceiling-to-floor mirrors covered an entire wall. An addition, he realized suddenly, of Elinor's. And almost a perfect match to the pair that Roland Hodges owned. They only reminded him all the more sharply of his daughter's connection to the man, of the guns she'd shipped to the very army that had killed his son Josh Jr. and even now was shooting at Chase. Unbelievable that she could have the sheer effrontery to have hung them in this house. "Cooke, they're grotesque." Joshua gestured curtly to the mirrors, frowning.

"Get them down, Cooke. As soon as possible, please. What did we used to have hanging there?"

"The portraits, sir. Of the children."

That took Joshua aback. He had never realized they'd been missing. "Well, put them back, then, Cooke."

"All three of them, sir?"

Joshua hesitated again, considering. It was a strange question for Cooke to ask. Even stranger that for a long moment Joshua debated its answer. "Yes, Cooke, all three," he decided with a soft sigh. She was what she was, Elinor, but still she was his daughter. He could not deny her that even now. Her picture should hang with the others; life was not all the sweetness of victories.

"You've a letter, Joshua, from your son, Major Courtland. It came to the bank this afternoon." Jonathon Penley interrupted a lingering silence uneasily, stepping forward to offer a battered-looking envelope. He could not help but remember the last such letter, misaddressed and misdelivered, and the anguish it had caused. Jonathon was unconsciously frowning as he continued. "From all the scribbling here on the envelope, Joshua, I would guess the letter's been forwarded along with the army's military dispatches. And that must mean that someone thought the news it's carrying was very important."

Joshua opened it hastily, speaking aloud even as he read it, with no time to react to the news it carried. "Chase has left Sherman's army. He's taking a troop north. Rejoining Grant up in Virginia." He paused only a half second, not looking up as he finished the note. "Your sister, Leanna, is with him."

"Leanna's with a troop of Yankees?" In the instant that followed, a dozen uneasy questions flashed through Jonathon's mind in rapid succession. "When does the ship arrive in Washington?"

"They aren't on a ship." Joshua simply handed the disquieting letter over to Jonathon, only now looking up to see the young Virginian's frown, and aware of a matching one beginning to form on his own face. "They're riding overland, he says. From Columbia to City Point."

"Overland?" Jonathon had taken the letter from the older man, but now he was too astounded to look down at it. He held Joshua's eyes instead, unbelieving. "But that's hundreds of miles of solidly Confederate territory!" Joshua said nothing, and in the sudden silence, Jonathon began to believe what he'd heard. With the belief, too, came a sudden, surging awareness of anger and fear, and he was trembling suddenly as he met the older Courtland's unwavering stare. "That's suicide! He has no damn right to endanger her like that! How would he even explain Leanna to the federals in Virginia if they *did* get there? Present her to their sentries as a Rebel spy?"

Joshua shook his head in a kind of vague denial. "I don't know, Jonathon. But I doubt very much that Chase would ever even consider such a thing." Actually, he thought, that problem would be the least of it. If they got to Virginia, Chase would think of something. Cooke offered a brandy wordlessly, and Joshua accepted it in the same fashion. He was frowning, but more in thought than in despair. He did not agree entirely with Jonathon Penley's bleak assessment. There were factors to consider which the young Virginian knew little about. Chase's own extraordinary abilities, which the father, naturally, weighed more heavily than would Jonathon. And, too, following the confrontation today with Hodges, the sure repercussions of which would rock the pillars of the War Department itself . . . maybe it was for the best in a way. Chase was out of Hodges' reach. Out of even Secretary Stanton's reach. At least now, they could not use the son as leverage against the father. There was a ray of sunshine even in the blackest cloud. "I don't agree that it's a hopeless journey, Jonathon." Joshua broke the silence finally with a softly composed tone of voice. "Knowing my son, I would guess they've at least a slight chance of making it. And your sister's traveling with them probably improves that slight chance to a fairly decent one, I imagine. Men will press themselves to astounding capabilities when they're trying to protect something they love."

Jonathon looked at him as if in sharp surprise, and Joshua returned the glance with a very faint smile. "Or perhaps you didn't know that Chase was in love with your sister, Jonathon? Anyway, he is. I believe I heard a rumor she was in love with him, as well. Now they're out of reach of both armies for a while, hopefully. Out of reach of *our* meddling as well. Maybe they'll find some kind of peace with one another. At least, for the first time, they'll have the *chance* to do so, won't they?" That reminded Joshua suddenly of something Epsley had given to him earlier when he'd stopped on his return from

Hodges' house. He put one hand in his coat pocket to withdraw the bulky annulment papers that made a legal end to Chase and Susan's marriage. "This was more my fault than anyone else's, you know, Jon. I knew Chase was in love with your sister, Leanna. He practically told me so last winter. But I pressed all the harder for his marriage to Susan Stratford, thinking that would end the affair, and quite candidly, I wanted the affair ended then. This was the result instead—more agony for everyone involved."

Joshua frowned down at the papers in his hand, then put them back away with a final sigh. "I was planning a trip to Washington anyway, Jonathon. Now, I think I'll leave tomorrow. I have these annulment documents to give on to that young surgeon and Susan. And I have some of my own business to attend. Also while I'm there, if there are charges still pending against her, I shall procure a presidential pardon for your sister. I've let the wheels of the War Department move far too slowly for far too long. I won't wait any longer."

Joshua turned on one heel, slowly, trying to decide exactly what he must do. Clear Jonathon's sister, first. And also speak to Ward Lamon, obviously. Lamon was one of Lincoln's closest advisers—an old friend and a good man. A *trustworthy* man in a city awash with treachery. He must warn Lamon about both the abduction scheme and about the larger evil of the coalition itself. Warn Secretary Seward, too. The arrogant secretary of state might even listen if he believed his own wife was endangered. "I shall write to Chase again, Jonathon. Only this time I'll write to Virginia. I'm going to believe that they'll make it—Chase and your sister both. And you should, too." Joshua spoke softly, over one shoulder, and without looking around at the young Virginian as he left the parlor.

But Jonathon refused to second such optimism, and he watched the older man walk out of the room in continuing silence. Alone at last in the Courtland parlor, he glanced uneasily toward the portraits, which the unobtrusive Cooke had quickly rehung. There had been a time, Jonathon remembered now, when he had wished the Courtland son's death in Savannah. A time when the color of uniforms and lingering enmities from the war had superseded all else. But now, looking at a grim young face in a painted portrait, Jonathon knew that he had been wrong. For a long time now, Chase Courtland had made an unceasing effort to protect the woman

391

he'd had no right to love, and up to now, Jonathon Penley had offered the Yankee no thanks for those efforts. But Jonathon had reached an impasse at last, a final impasse, which required that he make some changes. Confederate and Yankee were no longer divisible, suddenly. He could not afford to regard the Courtland son as an enemy, unless Jonathon could disregard his sister's now-total dependence on the man. And that, obviously, was simply impossible. More clearly than ever, Leanna's own life lay now on the same perilous line as the Yankee major's did, and neither Jonathon's pride nor his allegiance to a dearly held cause could be allowed to overwhelm that simple fact. It was past time, finally, for one war to be ended.

"All right, Yankee." Jonathon spoke softly, meeting the eyes of the Courtland son's portrait, "My sister is that important to me. I'm willing to declare a truce if you are. I'll even offer you an overdue bargain. If you can get Leanna home safely, out of the Deep South and out of the rest of this damnable war, we'll be allies instead of enemies, I swear it. For Leanna's sake, I'll be ready and willing to call you a friend. Good luck to both of you getting back to Virginia." Jonathon only wished, as he spoke, that he were more confident he would someday be called upon for payment of that private wager.

Standing in the hallway of the sadly dilapidated White House, conveying his news in an anxious murmur, Joshua had found Ward Lamon more than receptive to his warning of plots against the president's life—disturbingly receptive. It was not the first Washington had received, obviously, and yet Lincoln was casual about disregarding such threats. Maddeningly casual for those men who cared so desperately, so genuinely for the gawky, gentle genius. A fatalist at heart, Abraham Lincoln would take not a single step to protect himself. He was too busy, he said, with the country's problems. And he didn't like to worry Mary, either, by appearing to believe in such doomsayers' notions.

And so with the war drawing to its last, dangerous death agonies, Washington, D.C., seethed with rumors, each more ugly than the next. Radical Republicans were reaffirming their allies for a hard-line stance behind both Seward and Stanton, the Cabinet's two major powers. It would be a close

nd bitter struggle, at best, come the war's end—Lincoln
reaching compassion in answer to conservatives' cries of
evenge. And spurred by any move against their beloved
resident, the people would throw their power into the radi-
al camp, and into revenge against the South. Unleashed, that
vould be frightening to imagine. And exactly what Hodges'
oalition hoped for, Joshua knew. One of the reasons they'd
o carefully picked the Confederate Booth for their plans.

He stood now outside on Pennsylvania Avenue, staring
cross the street at an open drainage ditch. He was silent,
ustrated, mostly, because there seemed so damned little else
e could do. A carriage rattled by, splashing mud up out of
ne potholed road. Federal soldiers on leave appeared briefly
own the street, spilling out of one tavern to head for the
ext. A crier sauntered by, carrying a billboard advertisement
or a new show opening next month at downtown Washington's
ord Theatre. Inexplicably, Joshua shivered as the man walked
y, and he frowned. A newsboy scampered up, then, like a
uppy, wide-eyed and hopeful, and Joshua nodded with a
rudging smile. Then he reached down in his waistcoat pocket
or a nickel change. The paper was only three cents, but he
estured the boy to keep the extra pennies and then stole a
noment simply to enjoy the youngster's exuberant delight. It
armed him somehow, gave Joshua a moment's uncomplicated,
eaceful pleasure before he turned his attention to the serious-
ess of newspaper headlines still screaming war.

The date on the paper was the last day of February. Tomor-
ow would be the first of March, 1865. Traditionally, March
as the month of the war's renewal in Virginia, the month
nat began the bloodshed and the agony all over again. Battles
f the spring campaign were usually among the most ambi-
ous and bloodiest of the entire year. Last spring had seen the
Vilderness, Spotsylvania, Yellow Tavern where Jeb Stuart
ad died, Cold Harbor, the start of Sherman's march on
tlanta. This spring found Lee still trapped in his lines
round Richmond and Petersburg, an estimated thirty-five
nousand Confederates facing Grant's Union Army of over
ne hundred thousand. The winter had seen Grant's slow,
realthy extension of the Union flank line, an action that had
orced the Confederate general to do the same. Grant was
eliberately stretching the gray defense lines ever longer, ever
ninner, until somewhere, like an overused rubber band, there

must come a sudden snap and a break, and the federals would pour in toward the Confederate capital.

There was never any question of Joshua's loyalties—this year alone, only two months old, he had contributed over ten thousand dollars to the Philadelphia Union League; that building was finally nearing completion, now, after all these years. He had buried one son already in the Union's name and risked the other even now. Yet suddenly, perversely, he was conscious of a deep, strange, kinship with the besieged Southern general. He knew Lee's feelings well, he thought. Compelled by honor, by that same unsilenceable internal demand of conscience. Both he and Lee were facing patently superior and insurmountable odds, yet unable, because of honor, to lay down their fight, either. Joshua could not defeat the coalition. No one man alone could. There were too many of them—too ruthless, and wielding together far too much power. He could only delay the inevitable just as Robert E. Lee was doing—scrambling desperately to steal one day's delay and yet another, but without hope of final victory. And, too, he had lied to Hodges about having Chase continue the fight. He couldn't. He wouldn't even ask such sacrifice from his son come the war's end. Joshua had spent a lifetime collecting powerful friends, building an unassailable personal reputation, a long list of private "debts" due upon demand, and yet even *he* found the odds in this match too great against him. To ask any young man—even Chase—coming home, already tired from four years of war, to take up this fight was senseless—worse, suicidal. And that, out of pure selfishness, Joshua refused to do.

No, the coalition fight was his alone, one to be fought to the last breath of his failing body. And if it was without final victory, still every day of delay was a kind of triumph. One more day for the people and the government to anticipate and plan for the coming peace. One more day for Lincoln to preach compassion, to show the direction that the country he so loved must follow. One more precious day to clarify his programs, to convince a few more fence sitters of kind and gentle justice for the shattered South. If Lincoln lived only to the end of the war, it might be enough. If *Joshua* lived only that long, he might manage to wrestle just that much precious time from the coalition. But time, which had been his enemy since the beginning, was his enemy still. Chase had guessed he end of the war in early Summer in his last letters. June. Perhaps July. Joshua could not possibly last that long—he knew that quite unarguably, and with little emotional reaction other than a faint sense now of frustration. The heart pains, which used to flare only at times of anger or stress, now—since the December attack—were constant, worsening often to breath-catching intensity. His left arm pricked oddly as if always asleep, the vision in his left eye would blur without warning, and his hand began to tremble. The race would be close, he thought, his own death versus the war's ending and the beginning of reconstruction. Very close. Only time would tell who had finally won.

And Chase, Joshua's hope for a more personal future, rode in peril somewhere in the distant South. Sixty men against Confederate thousands, and there was nothing, now, that his father could do to help him. Joshua turned on the curb, looking down Pennsylvania Avenue to Eighth Street, to the marble-columned War Building gleaming dull white in the fitful Washington sunshine. Three days ago, he could have spent ten minutes there and had a regiment ordered out in search of his son's lone troop. Now he was helpless. He had declared himself an enemy to the only people who could have reached out an arm long enough to aid Chase, wherever he was. Stanton himself might be involved in the conspiracy against Lincoln; maybe Major Eckert, his right-hand man; definitely, Lafayette Baker was—the War Department's chief of internal security, with his legions of unscrupulous operatives and the kind of power distilled from treachery and practiced subterfuge. So Chase was on his own, and maybe that was for the best. God bless you, son, Joshua thought with a kind of sudden, anguished pride. God bless you. And good luck. I have my fight in the days ahead. You have yours. And neither one of us can in any way help the other, nor even know perhaps if the other is succeeding or failing.

He remembered the annulment document then, glancing down to the corner of the envelope that showed above the edge of his waistcoat pocket. With a soft sigh, he slowly turned and went to deliver it to the woman he'd once insisted would be his son's perfect wife. And that task done, Joshua took the next train home to Philadelphia. There was nothing more in Washington that he could do for Lincoln, for Chase, or for anyone else.

*   *   *

The last hours of February in Washington, D.C., were black and cold with a sleeting rain. The only people abroad in such weather were those whose business simply could not wait, and Doc Lacey and Susan had chosen to be among those urgent few.

"Have you written yet to Chase, Roger? To explain what happened?"

Susan was compelled to question that—even now, Roger thought with a silent, sad regret, even standing in the cold sleet here in the federal judge's office minutes before the civil ceremony that would make them man and wife. Susan still did not understand. Deliberately, he thought, chose *not* to understand. But he did. "Yes, love. I addressed it to his home, though, in Philadelphia. It should wait until after the war ends, I think. He'll have too much else on his mind up till then."

"Yes. Yes, you're probably right." A little color seeped back into Susan's pale face, denoting relief, and she managed a small, frail smile. "He'll understand I think, Roger. Truly I do. There was never anything really between us—he and I, I mean. Only my brother, Benjamin, maybe. And as close as he was to you, your saving his life in fact, I'm sure he'll accept what's happened."

Roger offered a smile and a nod, and the kindness of keeping his thoughts to himself. Chase might accept what had happened, yes. But he would never understand, nor would he forgive—not in the sense Susan so wistfully hoped. Men were different that way. Strangely archaic. Even good men like himself or Chase. They could be civilized, yes, about most things, but not about their women, especially a woman who took their name. Whatever friendship had existed between the cavalry major and him, whatever debts on either side, this more than canceled them all. And if they ever met again, it was more likely now to be in enmity than in friendship. Roger regretted that deeply. But regret didn't change things. He was still in love with Susan, still going to marry her. And it was still *his* child she carried in her now slightly rounded belly. *That* above all he wouldn't change even if he could. "I got a wire this morning from my family in Chardon. Still willing to add to our trip by stopping off there?"

"Yes." Susan smiled more freely now, taking his rainhilled hand. "Of course, I am. I'm anxious to meet them. And once we get settled in Denver, it may be some time— years, probably—before we'd make a trip back east. With the baby and all."

"Until the railroad goes through, I imagine. But that won't be long now, once the war finally ends. Four or five years, I'd guess."

"We must have Chase come visit us, then. He may be married, too. Perhaps he could even bring his wife, if he has one." Her soft brown eyes searched Doc Lacey's almost anxiously, as if asking him a final question, seeking his final reassurance.

"Of course. We'll have to do that." Roger said it, though he knew it for an absurdity. He even nodded once for emphasis. Then the dark mahogany door of the judge's chambers swung softly open, and Susan's face was suddenly, blissfully radiant. And all the lies were suddenly worth it to him, seeing that. "Come on, my love. Let's go get married." Even amid the war, he thought, they at least had found their place. He could only wish that the others trapped in the same tangled web would find theirs, too.

Chapter Twenty-three

Rebel Cavalry had dogged every step of their way. Sudden skirmishes left a trail of Yankee blood and new graves to mark the passage. Nights were endless and often bitter cold, rests were infrequent, horses and men were pushed to the breaking point day after day and then week after week. Forced marches became the normal activity of every day's dawn. Poor, cold meals were eaten on horseback; what little sleep there was was on horseback as well, snatched a minute at a time and all too often not at all, for they all knew well that to stop was to die. But there was no further talk of surrendering the troop to surrounding Confederates, either. Instead, after that one night of anguish, it seemed to Leanna, as each bloody mile crawled by, that Chase Courtland displayed a greater determination about the journey he had volunteered to make north—a grim, almost desperate intensity to complete the troop's mission, to win through to Virginia and to the federal Army of the Potomac. Part of that desperation, she realized, was due to herself, and to Chase's unspoken but nearly obsessive resolution to ensure her safety. Though he never again spoke of it, she knew it was there still. And she knew why as well— though that, too, remained unspoken.

But the other reason for Chase's redoubled determination was something Leanna could not possibly be allowed to know— the realization, beyond all doubt, that this untamed, mountainous forestland of the interior of the Carolinas was impossible ground for any Union Army to ever try to fight upon. Sherman himself could not know that as yet. His huge army was too many miles to the south and east of Chase's troop, closing on Cheraw now if local rumor spoke the truth, pursuing a line of march that would eventually take it to Fayetteville and then Goldsboro. Between the lone troop and Sherman lay Joe Johnston's thousands of Confederate soldiers, readying themselves for a last, desperate and doomed stand against the federal army marching north. So it was mandatory for survival alone that Chase keep his troop in the wilderness of the Carolina Blue Ridge, out of the way of those two mammoth armies who were slowly, but inexorably, closing in on one another, for the lone Yankee troop would be crushed, unmourned and unnoticed, if it got in the way. Sixty dead soldiers would be an insignificant addition to the lengthening rolls of the war's casualties, but the warning that would be lost with them might mean the difference of many thousands more. With every day's passing, Chase Courtland grew surer, that they had confirmed the grim suspicions that had probably prompted Sherman to send the troop out in the first place. Union troops would be helpless here in this rebel wilderness.

If the CSA armies concentrated here, Union troops would be unable to follow. Huge numbers of transported soldiers required almost astronomical numbers of support items: wagons, ambulances, field tents, telegraph wire, artillery, food, horses, mules, oxen, gunpowder, cannon shot—the list was virtually endless. And moving those things required good roads, or better, good railroad lines. But here, by the edge of the Blue Ridge, there was only untamed forestland, rocks and trees and countless creeks. If the Confederate Army under Robert E. Lee managed to cut loose from Virginia to join Johnston's army down here, the war would be extended by months, more likely, by years. Someone *must* warn Grant's distant army not to let Lee come south. . . . And there was no one else to convey such a warning but the single troop commanded by Chase Courtland.

As they came farther north they found snow in the mountains. Not much at first, but more as they went. In South Carolina, only eight inches or so fell in a winter, but the Virginia Blue Ridge, which lay between Chase and his destination would be treacherous at this time of year. Chase had had no intention of daring those mountains. At best, even a ground cover of snow slowed down their passage and left too many tracks for Rebel patrols to mark. So, across the area of the Cumberland Gap, Chase had intended to bring his weary troop down, to circle the Confederate garrisons that held the Gap against Yankee intrusion and then to turn east, out of the mountains and into the rich, rolling farmlands of Virginia's interior. But the fortunes of war decided differently.

By bitter coincidence, scarcely three days earlier, Sheridan's Union Cavalry had invaded that same Virginia Valley in a lightning strike, thrusting all the way to Staunton and beyond. During that same first week of March, General Custer's troopers had chased down the pitiful remains of Jubal Early's once-grand Confederate Army in the sleet-slicked streets of Waynesboro. Rumor said they'd saber-beaten Rebels there until Waynesboro's muddy streets ran red with men's blood, captured sixteen hundred Rebel prisoners and twenty battle flags—flags which Sheridan displayed like gaudy prizes as he withdrew his Union Army farther north, burning and destroying every mile he traversed.

So the Shenandoah Valley was finally dead. And what few Confederate soldiers had escaped Sheridan's cavalry were now concentrated near Roanoke, in the very same area near the Gap that Chase Courtland's troop was forced to cross. Sheridan had stirred up a hornet's nest of bitter Southern anger and humiliated Southern pride, and it was Chase's troop that was stung. The heightened Confederate activity there simply closed the door to Virginia's flatlands, and the Yankee troop was forced back into the mountains once again. Like it or not, they must risk the dangers of an early-spring blizzard covering the Blue Ridge with yet more snow, slowing them down and aiding their Rebel pursuers. And once again, sleep, or hot food, or even so much as an hour's rest became only a distant and elusive dream. And then the weather turned against them as well, and the march through the night's blackness was sheer hell as liquid ice poured down from invisible clouds in the night sky, and horses and men began to go down.

At least the Confederate Cavalry riding pursuit had finally given up, for the moment, as well. As a gray dawn began to lighten the sky, troopers riding picket positions reported sighting a cave. Reluctantly, Chase signaled an order to rest. Exhausted men and horses stumbled blindly into the comparative luxury of a large, sheltering, limestone cavern hollowed deep into the side of the Virginia mountain, and in the first stolen hours between dawn and morning, not a single soul in the troop thought of anything but sleep.

Gradually, the men had awakened, but to a morning even darker than the earlier dawn had been. As Leanna rolled over ow on the cold, stone bed of the cavern floor she heard the uneasy murmurs of the soldiers, and she blinked her eyes against unexpected darkness. For another long moment, disoriented and exhausted, she could not figure out what had stolen the daylight. But as she sat up in her blankets to stare out to the cave's mouth she saw other men, too, staring out to the same sight: the sky outside growing ever-more ominous, the peculiar, leaden gray color of approaching storm clouds. Spring would not come to the Blue Ridge just yet.

Instinctively, she turned around slowly in her blankets to look for Chase Courtland, not entirely surprised when she was unable to find him. He would not be sleeping—that was a luxury he could not afford. The other troopers as they woke were clustering within the cave in small groups, some tending a pitiful excuse for a fire, some few tending horses by the rough, limestone walls. Despite the light of those several poor campfires, the cave seemed to look more like night than day, and the cold winds stealing in from the mountain outside overwhelmed what small warmth the fires could offer. Even as Leanna sat shivering and silent, it seemed to her that the light faded further, like a kerosene lantern about to die out. It was in the rising darkness, finally, that she found Chase with her eyes, standing with Grier by the cave mouth and staring out at the weather beyond. In the shadows, identities were scarcely distinguishable, but she knew Chase by instinct more than by sight. And in the grueling weeks past, she had learned to expect to see Grier standing beside him. At the same instant she saw them, another thought struck her, one nearly as grim as the weather they watched. Against the Confederate gray of the Virginia morning, their Union blue made an alien and intrusive contrast. They had reached Virginia after all. And it would now—as she'd long known it must—be a homecoming for her, well-laced with anguish. She was home at last, miraculously. But this homecoming was only bittersweet at the best. She had gained . . . but she had also lost.

Leanna rose slowly and silently to her feet, keeping the Yankee blue blanket wrapped close around her shoulders as she started forward to where Chase stood, staring out so grimly at the darkening sky. Grier passed her, but in silence, his eyes alone acknowledging her with a momentary flicker of relentless dislike. From Columbia on, Grier at least had never

401

changed his opinions. He would be happier tomorrow when she at last left his troop. Small comfort, she thought, but at least someone would know no anguish at the coming parting.

Chase said nothing at all as she came to stand by his side, his eyes never moving from the storm clouds. But though he neither looked at her nor spoke to her, Leanna knew he was well aware of her presence. He had been, she thought, from the instant she'd come to him. Strangely enough, too, she had sensed no surprise from him at her presence—it was more as if he'd been expecting her, expecting her long before she'd actually come. For a moment, she longed to reach out and touch him, but that would only make the words all the harder to say—and those words of farewell would be difficult enough.

For a long minute, she only stared out at the sky, following the direction of Chase's own gaze. And then she looked at him, still in silence, studying the familiar grimness that had hardened his face since Columbia, the lines of weariness that she doubted would ever quite fade entirely. How long had this beloved face haunted her, both waking and sleeping. Even in Summer Ashton's arms, she had still dreamed of him. She would dream of Chase, yet, she thought now. . . Probably for years to come. "You look tired, Chase . . . as usual. And somewhat grimmer even than most times, I think. Despite her best efforts, there was an abnormal stiffness in the words she forced finally, a barely perceptible catch in her breath. And she could not bear to look at him while she spoke. Like Chase, she looked up to the leaden gray skies. "You needn't worry about the storm, I think. I'm somewhat of an expert on these mountains, remember? This late in the winter, it should only be an inch or two."

For a moment, Chase did not answer at all. But had Leanna been watching his face still, she would have seen some brief involuntary pain pass over it. He remained silent so long that she had begun to believe he would not answer her, and just at that moment she thought this, he spoke. "The snow? Yes *partly*, I am concerned over that. It might even be easier on both of us if I pretended it was the snow *entirely*. But I'm afraid we would both know that was a lie."

As he spoke he moved stiffly, leaning his right shoulder against the rough edge of the cave wall, an obvious and poor attempt to try to ease sheer physical exhaustion. The Savannah wounds were still taking a toll on him, and the desperate

402

haste of the journey from Columbia had taken an additional toll on him. Between a reawakened consciousness of his weakened condition and the effect of his words, Leanna felt a momentary surge of anguish simply close her throat to further speech. Perhaps worst of all, she thought suddenly, it was simply unfair. If there was ever any soldier from any army since the dawn of time who had fought harder or better in the course of a war, who deserved every kindness that the gods could give him, it was this Yankee who stood so wearily beside her. Yet the gods had not offered him kindness at all. And neither, in this last, inevitable moment, could she. "No, we won't end it on lies, Chase. Not this time, at least. In a way, I think I'm glad that you understand. That you already know what tomorrow's going to mean for us both. It will make it easier for me, too, if you remember that neither of us has any real choice."

"You're wrong, Leanna. I knew you were thinking that as soon as we crossed the Virginia border, but for the love of God, I wish you'd listen to me once. You think you're safe now because we've made your home state. But you *aren't* safe. No place in the South is going to be safe now until the war is finally over. And Virginia is going to be even less safe than most. Once Grant begins his spring campaign, all hell's going to break loose all over this place. There is another option, yet. Come with me on to City Point, let me take you into the camp itself there. I can clear you, somehow, with the federal people and put you on a train to your brother in Philadelphia. Stay there in the North and stay out of the war, Lea. Give me that much at least. Let me have that assurance that at least you'll be safe."

She closed her eyes momentarily against rising tears, only able at first to shake her head in anguished answer. It was not only Chase—the gods, she thought bitterly, had offered no kindness to *either* of them. "No, Chase, I beg you. Don't even ask me for that. You said it yourself once, back in North Carolina: we're committed to two different people and to two different countries. That hasn't changed, and it can never change. I'm still a Confederate, Chase. I belong in the South, and that's where I'm staying. Where I *have* to stay. Just the same as you *have* to go back now to *your* Northern army. I accept that inevitability and you must, too."

As she spoke a single tear rolled down her cheek, dropping

to fall on Chase's left hand. He flinched abruptly, as if startled by the touch of its unexpected wet heat, and then slowly raised his hand to allow the tear to roll on, very slowly, off the side of his hand. Leanna had turned to look at him once again, but he kept his own eyes on his hand, not on her. Looking at the tear, she thought. Or looking at the wedding ring that glistened dully on the fourth finger of his same left hand. Whichever one it was exactly, Leanna could not be entirely sure. Nor, she told herself in silent anguish, did it even matter, did it? "Tomorrow when we get down from the mountains, Chase, you'll go east toward City Point, toward the coast and your army. And I'll go west, instead, back into the Valley. There might be something left of Blytheswood yet. I'd like to know that; it's important to me. And if there's nothing, not so much as a tree left standing, I'll still be safe here. I've got distant kin all over the Valley. Old family friends. I'm home. And I'm safe. And that's all you can possibly do for me, Chase. Except to remember me kindly, if you will, in the years to come. Just as I expect to remember you." She almost left it at that, leaving so many things entirely unsaid and deliberately so. Nothing could change the inevitability of their separation. And nothing she said could offer either of them anything now but further pain and more biting anguish. But one thing, alone, she would allow him to know. One thing she wanted him to remember in the long years ahead. "Chase, if it weren't for the war, it could have been different. I believe that with all my heart. If it weren't for the war, it could have been very . . . very good. For both of us."

Chase had already begun to turn on one heel, not looking back at Leanna, but he suddenly stopped. To Leanna—her eyes fixed on his face with all the anguished intensity of the moment—his face had showed a desolation she had never seen on it before. "Yes, Lea. In one way, at least, I think that you're right. If it weren't for the war, I would never have *known* you. And I think, actually, that that was the only real chance I ever had. . . ."

He was moving again, even as his murmured words were dropping into the silence he had left behind him. He had not meant them in cruelty, Leanna knew that. They had been spoken only out of honesty and out of the depths of his own terrible anguish, but still they seemed to linger on the cold, damp winds of the graying morning, burning indelibly on her heart like acid etches metal. Until the day she finally died, she thought, she would hear the echo of those final words— and remember the pain they had conveyed. And standing there, suddenly, and watching her beloved enemy fade back into the cave's deeper shadows, it all seemed an eerie replay of the dream that had haunted her now for so many months. Standing alone and in anguish while she watched Chase fade into insubstantial mists to be lost to her. And like the dream, as she stood here she could think of nothing either one of them could do to somehow change the inevitability of that bitter ending.

The snow itself started shortly after that. No light snowfall either, despite Leanna's prediction. No mere inch or two to dust the floor of the mountain woods a silver white. Chase was at first concerned about leaving too clear a track for Confederate pursuers to follow, but he needn't have worried about such trivialities. The storm continued all day and on through the night, leaving nearly two feet of wet, heavy snow by the following morning and thus eliminating all chance of further Rebel pursuit, but it also left fifty-one men and horses in snow-covered mountains with nothing to eat, nothing to burn for warmth and nothing to drink except a melted handful of the omnipresent snow. The cave, which had been a luxury, became a trap, and their choices were simple: stay there and chance starvation in the hope that an equally freakish turn of weather would melt the deep snow; or try to struggle through it, out of the mountains and down to the farmland of the Virginia interior that lay miles yet to the east.

But as it turned out, the weather made the decision for them. Even before the clouds of the first storm had entirely cleared, new clouds came sliding in, ugly and gray and blowing the cold, damp winds that presaged only more snow. They *had* to go. And in desperation they tried to do just that.

The Yankee troop rode for about two hours, until the horses, already exhausted, were floundering in snow that covered their knees in level places and came up to their chests in the drifts. Then the soldiers dismounted, leading the horses for hours, exactly how many Leanna had long since lost count of—floundering themselves, struggling step by step in knee-deep snow, staggering in weariness, dragging themselves upright to struggle on another dozen steps and fall again. The storm was finally ending now, too late. Sunshine glared occasionally on the overbright white. And despite the cold, horses and humans alike were sweating, steaming, the panted breaths of exhaustion rising as puffs of mist to hang in the still mountain air.

It was late afternoon, Leanna thought as she noticed that the shadows on the snow were dull gray but lengthening. How many miles had they managed to come? Four miles an hour, the troop usually averaged on level ground. But in this? A total of six for the day, she thought wearily, eight at the most. And they'd only gotten *that* far because of Chase. Left to themselves, most of the troop—herself included, would have simply laid down to die hours ago, exhausted beyond any hope of struggling even one step further in the heavy snow. But somehow, incredibly, Chase had kept moving. And more by habit than by anything else, the men had followed, clinging to their saddle leathers for support, the horses staggering now quite as often as their riders, then blowing and snorting and lurching desperately forward once again.

The sun was setting now. The rosy gold of the clearing sky silhouetted fists of bare granite that thrust upward above their heads and blackened the more distant, rolling darkness of mountains to the west. They would freeze in their tracks come nightfall. Lie down in the odd, seductive warmth of snow that no longer felt cold, and no one would ever know how far they'd come, how well they'd done. It would simply be over, then. And nothing else would matter after that.

Leanna could not feel her hands or her feet any longer. Her face had passed the point where it had stung from the cold and then ached from it with an odd, burning ache. By now it was simply numb. She felt her horse lurch to a sudden stop, dropping its head to drip hot sweat onto the icy snow, and forced her head up finally, only because she became conscious at last of the overlong halt. Ahead of her about a dozen yards, she finally saw Chase. He had surrendered to the inevitable at last, staggered to his knees in the snow, and no longer had the strength to drag himself back up to his feet. She looked across the thirty feet of shining white snow that might as well have been thirty miles instead and felt the sudden burning of tears gathering in her eyes. Around her there was only eerie silence. No one spoke. No one moved except to collapse, helplessly, sinking to their knees in the snow. The wind picked up, whistling faintly, then died again, leaving deeper quiet. Grier stood several yards behind Chase, hanging on to his saddle, unable to help. Leanna glanced slowly to see the Yankee captain there, and the last, faint flicker of her hopes swiftly died. As protective of his major as Grier was, if he could move still, he would have done so by now. So she simply looked back at Chase once again, conscious of the strange lassitude already spreading through her limbs, the odd sense of peace. The snow was warm—amazingly so, compared to the cold of the air. She kept hold of the stirrup with her hand only because it was an effort to let it go, and any effort was beyond her now. She would have liked, somehow, to get to Chase. To crawl, if she had to. To be with him. To tell him that it was all right, he'd done all he possibly could, gotten them all much further than anyone would have guessed he could on this impossible trek. That he must not blame himself for the cruelty of the snow. That he'd done his best—and that was all she'd asked of him on that long-ago night. That she loved him still, and that even now, she was in some strange way content with this ending.

Standing behind his fallen major, Grier could not seem to make even one exhausted muscle obey his command to move. An eddy of wind sprang up to blow stinging needles of snow into his face and frozen beard. He blinked, but didn't even try to turn his face away. The gamble had failed. They'd known it very well might. Known it this morning, he and Chase both, before they'd put the first foot forward into it. No chance at all, they'd decided in quiet, predawn murmurs, if they remained in the cave—not with more snow coming. Not much chance to go out into it either—one in twenty, perhaps. Or less. Not knowing these mountains, they didn't know how far they'd have to go to reach some sort of shelter. Maybe only one mile, then again, maybe twenty. Fate, Grier thought. It had been too far. They hadn't been able to reach it, wherever it was, and so they'd lost. Against the glare of snow, he could see the weary slump of his major's dark blue shoulders, the droop of his head that admitted the final defeat.

In the silence, he could even hear his ragged, panting gasps, breaths gulped out of incredible exhaustion. A good officer. One of the best. That he'd followed him to both their deaths didn't change Grier's opinion. It happened in war. No man, officer or not, good or bad, could command the gods.

Chase lifted his head finally, turning it as if with immense effort to look over one shoulder at the troop behind him. The men were sinking in their tracks. A few were still clinging to their horses, their faces dull and emotionless with fatigue. Grier saw him look back then at the woman for only a second or so, saw her shake her head almost imperceptibly as if denying an apology Chase would have made. Of all the faces, hers was the only one that still showed expresssion. Love and anguish mingled together there, and the narrow, uneven tracks of tears showed on her snow-reddened cheeks. A moment later, Grier frowned in a dull, dazed sort of surprise, watching Major Courtland dip his head once more, very low, his shoulders wracked by a kind of violent shudder. And then with the incredible slow motion one sometimes moves with in a dream, he saw the major begin to get up, pulling himself hand over hand on the saddle to regain his feet, the dark blue of his uniform white with clinging snow from the waist down. Chase didn't speak. Nor did he spare the energy to look behind him. He merely started forward again, slowly, staggering one step and then a second, a third, and slowly then, the fourth. And unbelievably, the troop began to follow him. Long years of war's conditioning were one part of it. Another was simple human instinct. If Chase could move, then so could they. He offered proof, in some strange way, that they weren't as exhausted as they'd thought, after all. There was some strength left deep in their reserves. There must be—because there was in his.

Grier followed, too, he was never sure how. Maybe, he thought, like the men who'd seen Christ walk upon the water, they had been somehow convinced that the impossible was possible. Whatever it was, it worked. A bare quarter mile farther, as dusk was blending the sunset shadows into one gray, formless mass, Chase came to a last, high-drifted ridge, the snow there nearly chest deep. But below that was a sudden, steep drop, forested by tall, snow-sprinkled pines. It was the lee side of the mountain where the snow level dropped abruptly from midthigh to only ankle deep. He stumbled down into it, conscious of the sudden, astounding ease of moving. It felt as if weights had been unshackled from his legs, an odd lightness given back to every step. He kept moving into the forest, never even looked behind him, but by instinct, sank to his hands and knees just as the last stragglers cleared the high ridge and entered the lee ground behind him. Men were too exhausted to think, too exhausted even to feel elation or relief at their unexpected survival. Men simply ceased moving as soon as their major did, dropping as if by unspoken command. There was no thought given to building a fire, no thought even to eating, nor the energy left to do so. But with the last bit of energy men seem to acquire when they realize that with only one more effort they will live to see another dawn, they managed to pull their blankets off their saddles and to roll themselves in the warmth to keep the coming freeze of night at bay.

Leanna moved by an instinct of her own somehow, keeping her feet while others around here were dropping into a sleep so deep that it more resembled unconsciousness. She stumbled forward to the very front where Chase remained motionless on his hands and knees in the shallow snow. His breath was coming in ragged, wracking sounds, more akin to sobs than normal breathing. His handsome, usually clean-shaven face was shadowed now by a dark growth of beard, and it was oddly pale, rigidly set and shadowed in the gathering dusk. Leanna managed to reach across him, pulling the blankets from his horse and drawing them up to cover his shoulders. Still Chase didn't move except to close his eyes. Finally, she fell more than lay down at his side, and then reached up to him, welcoming his head to the pillow of her breast. Once he rested there, he didn't move again at all.

In fact, neither man nor animal moved again throughout the long, cold blackness of the mid-March night that followed. But they lived—that was miracle enough. The treacherous storms of the mountains lay at last behind them. The rich interior of Virginia's farmland lay before them. And they were nearly two-thirds of the way to rejoining Grant's army at City Point.

Leanna woke well after dawn, lifting her head to view an incredible scene. It looked like a child had grown careless with his toy soldiers, letting them drop haphazardly about and not bothering afterward to collect them. Men were sprawled everywhere in no sort of order. Horses stood scattered, untied but unmoving. Above her head in the branches of the pine, she thought she heard a bird call. Other than that, there was absolute silence around her. Chase was a light sleeper normally. Now he did not even stir as she slipped his head down to lie on the blanket instead of on her, and she sat up out of the blanket's warmth into the cold of the morning air. God had been kind in one sense. No Confederate Cavalry had chanced upon them. The Yankees would have been helpless as babies if they had, unable to offer any resistance to either capture or outright death.

Only Grier, Leanna realized slowly, was missing. And even at her thought, she saw him reappear at the edge of the camp, a load of what looked like firewood in his arms. He came toward her and bent down several feet away to begin a fire. Looking up from his task, he caught her eyes only for a moment. But the moment was enough. She saw the lack of enmity, which had always before hardened Grier's gaze. Somehow, at this late moment, finally she had been forgiven for the past.

"I was wrong, Mrs. Leighton. I thought you'd be a liability. Probably even a traitor to us." He shrugged to punctuate his slow, soft-spoken words. "I've been waiting since Columbia, in fact, for you to betray us. I think that maybe I owe you an apology instead."

For a moment, Leanna didn't speak in reply. She glanced back to Chase to be sure Grier's words hadn't woken him. Finding him still asleep, she nodded her head slowly to the Yankee captain, offering him a smile that showed a sadness she could not quite conceal. "I care for Chase Courtland more than you seem to realize, Captain. I have never willingly betrayed him before. And I wouldn't now, either."

"Yes, I believe I heard a rumor to that effect way back in the Shenandoah Valley, Mrs. Leighton. But I've thought many times since that you had a most peculiar way of showing your affection for a man."

Despite herself, Leanna flushed faintly as she shrugged the accusation off. "When that man happens to be an enemy soldier, Grier, one of the very men who are destroying everything else you hold most dear, it complicates things just a tle, I'm afraid. Still, I've never been an enemy if I could elp it."

"Yes, I think I believe that now. In a way, yesterday, you ved all our lives, you know. In that damn snow. He was ady to quit, then. Really, I guess, he *should* have quit. And it had only been us with him there, I figure he would have. ut because of you, he kept on going somehow . . . and so m in your debt now the way I see it. If you ever need a vor from me, you've only to ask. And for whatever time e'll be traveling together, now, I'll be declaring a truce with ou. Truce accepted?"

Before she could reply, Chase moved beside her, suddenly d restlessly, reaching one hand out on the blankets as if arching for her. "Leanna?"

"Yes, Chase. I'm still here." She spared the Yankee captain ly a last wordless glance, nodding acceptance of his offer. hen she returned her full attention to Chase. "Are you all ght, Chase? You slept like the dead."

"Yes, I'm all right now. Just a little stiff, maybe." Chase sat p then, but slowly, reaching his hand out to rest against her p as if he somehow needed that physical assurance of her ntinued presence. Seeing Grier, he nodded a wordless pproval—as much, Leanna thought, to the firewood Grier eld as to the man himself. But though he spoke to his ptain, he did not move his hand from Leanna's leg. "Good ea, Grier. Maybe we owe ourselves a luxury today. We'll aw out with some hot coffee before we have to get moving gain."

"But get moving to where?" Grier reached in his pocket for flint lighter, warming it momentarily between his hands efore reaching it on toward the wood. "Where to now, lajor?"

"To Grant at City Point, of course. It's only another hunred miles or so, isn't it? All we have to do is guess our way, ow, through most of Virginia. Try to avoid riding straight to Mr. Lee's army. There can only be thirty or forty ousand Confederate soldiers between us and Grant at City oint." Chase had lowered his head into his hand, rubbing his ce in a familiar gesture of lingering weariness. To Leanna, atching him now, both his words and his expression took er momentarily aback. Virginia was home ground to her. All

411

through the long and grueling miles that lay behind them, she had always thought of Virginia as sanctuary. If she could get here, she would be safe. It had never occurred to her that it might mean just the opposite for the Yankees she traveled with. For only a moment longer, she maintained her silence, debating her choice. But how much could it hurt the Confederacy to help one lone troop of Yankees rejoin their army? If Leanna had known the warning they carried, even now her choice might still have been different. "Maybe you should consider using the railroads, Chase. Either take a train if you can, or at least follow the tracks to the east." She could feel Chase's eyes suddenly, intensely locked to her face. And he had moved his hand slightly against her as if in surprise of some sort. For her part, deliberately, she did not look at him. This was a last gift from her to him, a farewell gift, and she struggled suddenly against tears as she spoke. "There's a rail line that runs through Danville, I know, and north to Richmond. In Burkeville, it crosses track with the Southside Line to Petersburg."

There was only a long silence in the wake of her words. Grier slowly turned his head to look at his major, but Chase was looking at Leanna still, his eyes dark and unreadable but strangely soft. "Thank you, Lea. Thanks anyway. But we didn't grow up in this state like you did. Danville, Burkeville, even Petersburg—I'm afraid they're only names to me. I don't know where they are. I don't even know of a town with a train station, let alone one that doesn't have a Confederate garrison there as well. I do thank you, though, for trying to help us."

His voice was so soft it might have been called gentle. Hearing the tone of it, anguish redoubled in Leanna's soul and tears rose immediately in her averted eyes. And she struggled suddenly with a decision she'd thought was already made some weeks ago. She had thought, even yesterday, to leave Chase today. Even their near-death in the snowstorm yesterday wouldn't have changed that decision. But she hadn't realized then that while Virginia offered sanctuary to her, it offered only the greatest dangers of the entire journey to the Yankee troop. The next hundred miles or so would be the most desperate of all for the enemy soldier she could not help but love. Greater danger, harder marches, more blood

412

:irmishes lay ahead of him, still. Exhaustion and the redou-
:ed strain of carrying too many burdens and too many lives
١ his shoulders. Chase was a strong man; Leanna knew that.
١o matter what the load he carried, he rarely even stumbled.
ut Grier had said it outright this morning. And Leanna, too,
١ew why Chase had forced himself to such incredible effort
:sterday—because of her. And she knew of another time,
١o, which Grier didn't know. That night in North Carolina,
hen she'd taken Chase in her arms to offer comfort and
:rength when he'd needed them both so desperately. Remem-
:ring those times now, Leanna felt an ominous foreboding.
' Chase stumbled now somewhere along the long road to
ity Point, there would be no one to offer what she had
ffered before. If she left him now, she gambled with his very
fe. He was a Yankee officer leading Yankee soldiers. He
iould be her enemy . . . but he wasn't. And she could not
ave him when he might need her yet so desperately. She
ould see the journey through to its final destination then;
١e would see him safely to his own Yankee lines at City
oint. She would give herself that final gift.

"I won't tell you where the Confederate garrisons are,
'hase. Or their depots. Or their munition works." Chase and
:rier had been speaking in low-voiced murmurs, and at
eanna's interruption they fell silent in sudden surprise. And
١ce again, Leanna was acutely conscious of Chase's eyes on
:r ashen face as she continued. "I won't tell you anything
ɔout General Lee's lines of defense or of his supply lines. I
ɔuld never betray my own people like that. But I can guide
ɔu to City Point. That much I can do. I can help you to find
train still running if that's what you need. I can tell you
'hat towns you ought to avoid, and I'll know what roads are
١e safest to take. If we can make it all the way across the
ate, I'll see you around the edge of Lee's flank near Dinwiddie,
١d I'll leave you there to rejoin my own side."

There was another long silence, a terrible one for Leanna as
١e wondered how great a betrayal this might constitute for
:r own people. Regardless of the need behind it, the love
١at necessitated it, she could not pretend to herself that it
'as any less a betrayal of her beloved South. And even while
١e was resolved to do it, she doubted she would ever entirely
rgive herself. But she'd chosen differently in times now
ast, and found anguish and pain in *those* choices, too. The

413

fact was that she had doomed herself in the beginning, by loving Chase in the first place. She had doomed herself then to betraying someone or something. No, the gods had not offered any kindness to her, either, had they?

"Go tell the men to fix themselves a hot breakfast, Grier. Tell them to use up whatever they've got left. We're coming into good farmland now. We should be able to find something to eat again before tonight." Chase spoke to his captain in a voice barely above a whisper, gesturing Grier toward the other troopers now gathering in the middle of the camp. With only a nod, Grier took his leave, but Chase made no move yet to follow. He waited, instead, conscious of the silence and conscious of the anguish that lay behind it, but for a long minute he did nothing to break it. He was consumed for the moment by his own memories of past choices, perhaps. By his thoughts of anguish. By decisions made and later deeply rued. Conscious of a commitment he'd made to another woman perhaps. A commitment he would have taken back at that moment if only he could have. Finally, he slowly turned his head to study the pallor of Leanna's face. She was instantly, achingly aware of his gaze, and aware, too, of the tears that were burning hot tracks on her chilled cheeks, tears she seemed unable to stop. And she wasn't even sure what such tears were for exactly: for him, for herself or for the beloved South which she had just betrayed. Maybe, she thought, they were for all of them.

"God, Lea . . . If you'd only made that choice a year ago. When it could have made all the difference in the world."

Leanna felt his hand touch hers then, only that and only for an instant, but it only redoubled her tears and left her throat painfully constricted. "But I couldn't then, Chase. There was still too much that stood between us: Blytheswood itself, Stewart, the confederacy and war. Now it seems all those things are dead or dying. I love the South, Chase, but I know that it's doomed. There seems little reason to have you doomed as well." She managed a small shake of her head, turning to look down at the gold ring, which gleamed in the rising light of the Virginia dawn, circling Chase's finger even as his hand lay still against her leg. "It doesn't change anything anyway, Chase. Nothing either of us could do can really change it. Eventually we've still got to say farewell. Eventually, we still have to be enemies once again. Don't we?"

414

There was anguish conveyed in an instant's silence, but 'hase nodded at last to acknowledge the truth. "But I love ou, Lea. God help us both, you know I do. Enemies or not, always will." He got to his feet as he murmured the words, nd he didn't look back as he walked away.

n the evening of March twentieth, the Yankee troop crested e last small hill and reined their horses in to stare down at e winter huts and cabins that marked safety at last—the rmy of the Potomac's left flank. Even with Leanna's guidance, e hundred miles from the mountains to Danville had been overed entirely at a forced march, without stopping, forty iles a day—sleeping, eating, and aching on their saddles, alloping headlong and hiding by turns, narrowly avoiding isaster at the hands of Fitz Lee's Virginia cavalry, which had een called out in response to rumors of Yankee raiders courging the Virginia countryside. The spring weather had een miserable, cold and wet. Roads were almost impassable. ut the weather at least seemed impartial—the mud had ampered the Rebels' search sufficiently to allow a slim fed-ral margin of success. Taking the train had been fairly simple; ivilians were easy prey compared to the veteran soldiers 'hase's troopers were used to facing. And thanks to Leanna, ey had known which train to take.

Then, the last twenty-four hours had been the worst of the ntire desperate journey, from Columbia to here. Since climb-ig off the car just below Dinwiddie, they'd ridden for their ves through mud nearly as deep as the recent snows, dodg-ig the cavalry patrols of Lee's nearby army. Only Leanna ad slept, and she, only because Chase had sat her on his addle in front of him and held her most of the night in his rms.

His action had been motivated by the very real danger of ither ambush or of snipers' bullets, and he'd taken her to nield her more than embrace her. Yet so great was Leanna's xhaustion by now that she had slept as motionlessly and as eeply as an untroubled child, not even waking when Chase alted his horse on the crest of the small Virginia hill and ooked down at Grant's army and the end of what he'd once onsidered a damn near hopeless journey.

"What now, Major? What do we do with her, I mean?" It

was Grier's voice that broke the hush of the moonlit night
He shifted wearily in his saddle, and the faint, squeaking
protest of overworn leather was the only sound for the mo
ment that broke the silence. Chase glanced sharply down to
check Leanna's shadowed face and found her sleeping still
Thank God, he thought in weary gratitude. It made it so
much easier not to have to argue with her now. And there
was no question in his mind what had to be done. Leanna
would expect him to wake her on the edge of the federal lines
to put her on her own horse and allow her to rejoin her
beloved South. And if he did, there would be no anger this
time, none of the bitterness that had marked all of their other
partings. But given a choice between her anger and her safety
his choice was simple. They had no future anyway. Chase
had nothing, in that sense, to lose by her anger. And in term
of her safety, he had a great deal to gain.

"I'm going to take her on with us into camp, Grier
They'll assign me some decent quarters, I'm sure. I'
pass her off as my orderly for the next few days and keep
her pretty much out of sight. Once she's in the camp it
self, she won't have much choice but to do what I tel
her to do. I'd like to get her out of City Point, aboard
a train that's going north. She won't like the idea, bu
all hell's going to break loose around here any time now
and I don't want her caught in the middle of warring armie
anymore."

Grier gave his major only a single, long glance. If there wa
either disapproval or doubt in that glance, he didn't put it int
words. "All right. I'll deal with the pickets, then, Major
You'd better just keep riding if you can."

Chase nodded grim agreement and, without further speech
raised his hand to signal the waiting troop onward onc
again—the last few hundred yards of shadowed darkness in
journey that had seen hundreds of miles of it. Barely fiv
minutes later, Grier was shouting a reply to the picket
challenge, and five minutes after that, the troop was ridin
into the winter encampment of the Army of the Potomac
most westerly flank. The Yankee troop was finally hom
again.

In all the excitement of the unexpected arrival, no one ever
noticed the rather feminine-looking orderly who was left sleep

g in the major's quarters while Chase went on to the camp's
nking officer to relay the warning he'd brought. At all cost,
ee and his army must be kept here in Virginia or the war
ight drag on for additional years.

Chapter Twenty-four

It was almost dawn when Chase finally returned. The fire
that Grier had built in the small officers' cabin fireplace was
only scarlet embers and black ash, and outside there was only
the usual restless quiet of night to be found in any federal
encampment. Leanna turned her head drowsily, awakened by
the soft creak of the cabin door opening and closing. She sat
up slowly, finding Chase standing there tall and shadowed,
barely identifiable in the orange light of the fading fire.

"Leanna?"

"Yes, I'm awake. I'm over here." She began to frown
finally as full wakefulness came at last and she looked around
herself to find only unfamiliar shadows. "Though I'm not
entirely sure that I know where 'here' is exactly."

Chase only nodded once, pausing by the fireplace to add
more sticks to the dying embers. The wood was dry. It
caught almost immediately. And in its sudden glare, Leanna
could read both weariness and a strange kind of tension
etched on his shadowed face. The weariness was normal at
this point. But that tension was not.

"Chase, where are we? This is the Yankee camp, isn't it?"
Even as she slowly spoke Leanna's frown had grown more
certain, and she hardly needed his confirmation. "It is your
damn camp, isn't it? You brought me in while I was sleeping."

Her words held both rising anger and accusation, a reaction
not at all unexpected by the man who had made the decision
to bring her here in the first place. Chase had known he
would face Leanna's sure anger, but he would not apologize
for ensuring her safety how ever he could.

"Damn you, Chase! You know that wasn't our agreement!"

"Agreement or not, this is where you belong, Lea. Because
this is the safest place for you to be. It was as simple as that
when I made my decision. And before you make up your

418

mind to hate me entirely, ask yourself whether you didn't do much the same thing when you offered to help us across Virginia."

"It isn't the same thing at all! How dare you presume to make my decisions for me! What in the hell gives you the right to order my life to suit your specifications?" Despite her anger, or maybe because of it, Leanna found her lip trembling as she hurled the words of accusation at him across the shadows of the tiny room. "Damn you, Chase, you had no right!"

"I had every damn right, Leanna! Every one which was important at the time, at least! I knew you would be angry, but I *love* you, Lea! God in heaven, doesn't that make sense to you? Whatever it cost in your anger, I had to pay it. I had no choice. Whatever it cost me, I needed you safe. Because in the end that's all that can matter to me."

Chase's words had caught her anger still rising, and for a long minute she simply sat there in silence, staring at him from across the room. But suddenly, once again, anguish was warring with the heat of her anger, and very, very slowly did that anger give way. How could she hate him for loving her *too* well? When she loved him the very same way? "Oh, damn . . . I guess I should have known that, maybe. I should never have let myself be caught sleeping just then." Leanna said the words softly, at last, and more to herself than to Chase. She closed her eyes momentarily, feeling more anger remaining at herself than at him. And more than anger, she was conscious of feeling defeated somehow. There was a sudden, vague sensation of having lost something, somehow . . . but what she had lost she could not identify yet. The South, perhaps? Or her chance to go back to Blytheswood? Whichever it was, it had stolen her anger. "All right, then, Chase. It's obvious you must have something else planned for me, then. What is it?"

"I have to go up to City Point in the morning. General Grant is still in winter quarters there, and I'm to speak to his staff. From what I've heard here tonight, Grant is only waiting for Sheridan's return from the Valley to open his spring campaign. It will probably only be days before the war opens all over again, and I have no intention of allowing you to be caught here in the middle of it. I'll telegraph on from City Point tomorrow to check your status with the federal War

Department. If you've been cleared of charges, I'll send you north on the first train berth I can requisition."

"And if I haven't been cleared?"

There was only a momentary pause, as if the decision had been weighed and made many times, and long before this actual moment. "If you haven't, then I'll think of something else, some subterfuge or other that will end up accomplishing the same goal in a slightly more roundabout fashion."

"But either way, then, you still mean to send me north?" Leanna merely spoke the words aloud. She harbored no doubts about this being the actual conclusion to be reached. Oddly enough, she still felt no anger. Or if not none, then so little that in comparison to the other emotions that were storming her soul, it might as well have been none. Mostly she was conscious of a strange, almost numbing kind of shock, that was rising slowly—a kind of piercing anguish that left her nearly breathless with its pain. Something was terribly wrong. But for another long minute, sitting there silent in the flickering orange light of the nearly extinguished fire, she could not identify what. And then, abruptly, she understood. It was not being here in the Yankee camp. It was not the earlier anger that had flared at Chase. It was not even the suspicion that she had lost her last chance to rejoin the South or the realization that Chase intended to send her north to alien safety. It was the fact, instead, that this was the end—the end of the journey and the end for them, too. Nothing had changed because nothing could change. And this was the moment that had long been inevitable. Whether she went north to safety or rejoined the South, the conclusion was the same. This was the end for her and Chase, both, the final end—and *that* was the major source of her anguish. "No, Chase, please, don't send me away from you. Let me stay here, instead. Let me stay with you here in your camp, at least until the war starts again."

"Leanna, no. That's impossible. For too many reasons." Chase turned sharply away as he spoke, shaking his head but almost too quickly—as if before denying her, he had denied himself. And though he'd moved quickly to turn his back to her, it hadn't been quite quick enough. Despite the dimness, Leanna had clearly read the brief flash of pain on his face.

She clung to that pain as a kind of hope. "Chase, please. A

420

ew more days can't make any difference. I'll go north *then*, if ou still want me to."

"I'm not about to bargain with you, Leanna. You're going orth as soon as I can get you there."

"Chase, I'm not asking for anything that you can't give me. And I've never even asked you for this much before!"

"Leanna, no . . . for the love of God—"

"But I'm only asking for a few more days!"

"Leanna, I can't give you a few more days! I can't give you ven a single hour! God, Lea, do you think it's any easier for ne than it is for you? I'd sell my damn soul, offer you my life f you wanted it! But it isn't mine any longer now to give ou!"

There was a sudden anger evident on his shadowed face as he whirled back around to face her in the firelight. An anger o deep and so incredibly violent that it shattered her own ising desperation in a single instant. Not anger at *her*, she hought in dazed shock. Anger at himself, maybe. Or the var. Or the world. But whatever it was, she found herself unable to meet his gaze while it held that kind of pain. She urned her own head sharply away, now, trembling in shocked humiliation at her own prideless pleas, trembling harder in nguish at Chase's subsequent denial of them. The corners of her mouth were shaking suddenly beyond her ability to control them and tears ran helplessly down her ashen face, catching in her black eyelashes and glistening there in the firelight like watery diamonds. She closed her eyes hard to try to control the silent agony that continued to wash over her and merely sat huddled on the camp cot, in unthinking despair.

"How did you lose your baby, Lea?" When Chase's voice came again at last, it had followed a very long silence, and the anger in it had been entirely replaced by a kind of quieter and reluctant grief. "You called out in your sleep so many times. I wanted to ask, but there never seemed to be time."

Leanna didn't bother to try to open her eyes. The question only redoubled the tears that were already blinding her. "It was Stewart. Although Treejack tried too, I think, in his own way. . . ." She caught her breath with another sob and shook her head sharply as if to shake away the pain of the reawakened memory. "It was back in Georgia. Stewart captured some federal adjutant files; one of them was Colonel Drake's. It said something there about you and me being lovers. Stewart only guessed about the baby . . . but he was right." She forced her head up and her eyes opened finally to look at Chase. She saw his slow stiffening and felt his shock of anguish equally matched in her own heart, God, she thought. It hurts even now. Almost like losing the child twice.

"It *was* my child then . . . from Atlanta?"

"Yes, Chase. The child was yours." She whispered the words softly, almost apologetically, closing her eyes against the tears and then slowly reopened them again to meet his gaze.

For a moment more, Chase was perfectly still, his eyes, too, closing briefly and involuntarily against the worsening pain of her admission. "I see." He didn't look at her now as he spoke, but he managed to conceal very little from her, even so. By the growing fire's uneven light, Leanna could clearly see the muscle tensing along his shadowed jawline, the slow movement of a long, forced breath. Pain was written in his every motion. "If only you hadn't left Atlanta, Lea. Despite all that might have happened there between us, you should have trusted me at least enough to *tell* me. I would have done something if I'd known. I'd have *tried* to do something anyway."

"I didn't know it when I left Atlanta, Chase. And by the time I realized, I was too angry . . . standing on the porch of MacRaes' farmhouse and watching Atlanta burning." There was another silence, long and grieving, and Leanna finally shook her head to break its spell. She sighed very softly then, suddenly not feeling desperate anymore, not feeling that raging, unbearable agony that she had felt only a moment ago. She merely felt sad now, and strangely old, and very tired once again. "It was only one of so many decisions. I seemed to make them *all* wrong. From Blytheswood on."

There was a moment's longer pause and then she shook her head, dismissing that unchangeable past. It would not help to dwell on that, she told herself wearily. Nothing but despair could lie in that direction. She rose to her feet to start toward Chase, who remained rigidly motionless, and she touched his arm momentarily as she reached him. It had been such a long year, she thought silently. Such a long, cruel year. A lifetime lived in twelve short months. This time last year, they'd been together at Blytheswood, gentle with each other and not yet bitter—in comparison to now, she thought, very young then, both of them. Chase still hadn't moved away but wasn't truly

422

eacting to her nearness either. Even in the shadows and changing light of the fire, she could see too many lines of weariness and care that she could not remember having seen mark his face back at Blytheswood. Chase's eyes were haunted now by war and pain—and perhaps by regrets for the news Leanna had just shared with him. They were old eyes, she thought abruptly, old eyes in a young man's face. It had not been an easy year for the Yankees in some ways, either. At least not for this particular one. "Was it worth it to you at least, Chase? At least, it appears you're going to win the war. I hope to God all this was worth it for *one* of us, anyway."

"Worth it for myself, you mean?" He spoke as if rousing himself from thoughts still very far distant. "I don't know. If I'd known how the world would change, Lea . . . how damn naive we all were in the beginning, how impossible it would be to wage the kind of war we had in mind. All glory and justice. No cities burned, children dead, the sheer numbers that would be slaughtered . . . I can't give you an answer, I guess. Not now, anyway. Maybe when it's finally over, it will seem like it was worth it. I hope to God someday it will." He was frowning as he finished, and he turned away abruptly from her hand. "I'm tired. And I'm rambling. I think it's time we got some sleep."

He seemed startled when she reached after him, and he turned back sharply to meet her eyes. "If this is to be the end of it, then, give me tonight, Chase. It's all I'll ever have of you now. Regardless of what you said a little earlier, you must have just a few hours that belong to you and no one else, don't you? Let's give ourselves this single night without a damn war always lying between us, without armies between us, or other people, other causes. Come lie with me, just once, like you and I might once have done if none of this awful war had ever happened. Please."

Leanna had stepped toward him, close enough for him to feel the warmth of her, to smell the scent of her freshly washed hair. She stared up at him, pale and beautiful in the darkness, and he could see faint silver marking her cheeks from tears that were not yet dry. His own body responded instinctively, surging with a violent hunger, a sudden shortness of breath and the overquick beat of a racing pulse. "God, Lea. Why must you always make it so damn hard for me?"

She said nothing else, only continued to hold his eyes with

423

her silent question—demand and plea both. In a way, she thought, maybe it *was* wrong of them. Maybe it was selfish. Maybe it was even cruel. But she didn't care suddenly if it was. They deserved something, too, and if Chase was too damn proud to steal those half-dozen hours from himself, then she wasn't. Not any longer. There would be years and years of living apart in lonely honor.

Leanna raised her hands slowly to Chase's chest, her fingers parting around where the brass of "U.S." buttons gleamed gold against the dark blue cloth. Her eyes were locked to his in continuing question. A muscle flexed once sharply in his fire-shadowed jaw. He caught his breath against a sudden blinding wave of wanting her as he'd wanted nothing else in all his life. "For the love of God, Leanna, don't. It isn't right. There're a thousand reasons why not for both of us, and you know them all as well as I do."

There was a sudden anguished huskiness to his murmured denial, and Leanna only shook her head in uncaring denial. "I'm tired of hearing all the reasons why not, Chase. Tonight I only know that I need you, and I want you. And I think, in a way, you need me, too. Can't we be gentle with ourselves for just this once? Can't you allow yourself to bend the rules of your rigid honor just a little? I'm willing to bend the rules of mine for a few hours. Can't you, too?" Tears had started to fill her eyes again. They began to slide slowly down her face as she spoke to him. "Go ahead and lie to yourself if you want, Chase, but don't lie to me. Not tonight. I know how little the rest of it really means to you now. I saw you back there in that blizzard and I know what finally made you keep going then. It wasn't your damn righteousness, and it wasn't your damn Union. It wasn't Susan for you and it wasn't Summer for me. I'm not asking you for a future, I'm asking you for tonight. Give me a gift of it, Chase. Please. Give us both something better to remember than all the pain and all the bitterness we've given one another up to now." She raised one hand slowly as she finished speaking, touching the waves of his dark hair with wondering, loving fingers. Then she reached higher, sliding her hand behind his neck and raising herself on tiptoe to pull his head down to her mouth. At the touch of his mouth on hers, she could feel him tremble. Then his arms came around her suddenly and she could feel his heart pound, urgent and hurried and longing, against her breast. He was able to deny Leanna most things but he had never been able to deny her this. When she demanded his love, he could not help but give it to her, for in a sense, it had always been—and was still—hers to take.

Chase's love—finally, briefly freed to be all that it was—proved as deep as Leanna could ever have guessed it to be. It built around her like a summer storm, swiftly, suddenly, washing over her like a warm hard rain. It held undeniable power, soul-deep intensity. This was different tonight—different from the last time, different even from Atlanta. This was what she'd asked of him—like Virginia but more, as if the bitterness of the past year had never come between them. His hands on her were at the same time both urgent and slow, demanding yet gentle, and lingering as if every new touch must be memorized before it could be allowed to cease. There was no hint of memory betrayed, no concession to either haste or anger. He was warm and heavy lying over her in the narrow cot, and freed of his clothes, his muscles rippled slowly beneath the hands Leanna moved ever so slowly across the bare skin of his back. There was a scar there now, a dark reminder of that other world that must stand between them again tomorrow, but she closed her mind and did not allow her hands to linger there. The fine, dark mat of hair on his muscled chest pressed softly against her breasts, tickling the rising peaks, and she whispered her pleasure as he lowered his mouth to cover them with the warmth of his slow, soft kisses. This was love as she had never known with Chase before, the shadow of a completeness that should always have existed between them but never before tonight actually had. He smiled faintly as he loved her now—a rare, gently playful smile. There were hours yet until dawn and for this night, at least, there was no need for haste.

He nuzzled her black hair as affectionately as a child might, then turned his head to trace the pale column of her throat with sudden, burning kisses. He murmured love to her and explored her body with leisurely hands, until her body began to ache and throb for his possession. Then with another teasing kiss, he would move away again, playing once more as if the night they shared were truly endless.

In return, Leanna whispered smiling, gentle words to this beloved stranger in her arms, in turn half loving, half playing, finally free to know him as deeply as he could ever be known.

She reveled in the gift he offered of that sudden freedom, and found him more than even *she* had guessed him—infinitely patient, infinitely practiced as a lover. It was the equally infinite gentleness that surprised her more, the part of him she had not been allowed to see before. She half-opened her eyes to study his face now in the flickering firelight. His dark hair gleamed faintly, sweet smelling and thick, and tousled now from her caressing hands. The planes of his face were black shadows and fire golds—strong but kind, incredibly handsome, the thick dark lashes of his closed eyes a soft curved whisper of deeper darkness amid lighter shadows. His mouth was slightly parted and glistening faintly from the moisture of her own returning kisses. No enemy for tonight's few hours, she thought quite suddenly. No Yankee, no Confederate. Only himself, Chase . . . and utterly beloved. As if the war had never been . . . and would not ever be again.

She might once again conceive his child in such a night— the thought occured to her hazily, strangely blurred by the mellowness of the infinite contentment she now enjoyed, but she clung to the thought with a sudden sense of wistfulness. She had conceived his child once before after only a single night's loving—in Atlanta, in that sad, doomed, distant city. And if she conceived again, there would then be something left of this precious night, some part of him that she would never entirely lose. That seemed a terribly precious dream suddenly. A future she should reach out and try to make real, something given back to balance what the war had taken away from her.

And with that thought, there was a sudden utter lack of patience in her kisses, a sudden urgency to the hunger she felt for his love. She turned her hips to his abruptly, pressing herself against the bare warmth of his muscled body. And as Chase began to move to her in slow response she moved more swiftly, impaling herself on him in swift demand. There was a teasing pause, Chase poised but waiting against her throbbing flesh, and then, abruptly, there came the longed-for fullness as he rolled to thrust himself deep within her.

Leanna reached out to hold him, only whispering pleasure and locking her arms around his back to hold him there, so deep inside her. And in her arms, she felt his sudden trembling, as if she had startled him with her unexpected urgency. She heard his soft groan of protest as he struggled to regain

426

control, and then there came the sudden violence as he abandoned the effort and began to take her instead with his own desperate need, matching Leanna's breathless passion with his own.

When it was over and Chase lay sleeping in her arms, his face against her throat, their bodies still intertwined together, Leanna struggled against a rising drowsiness to try to pursue some near-forgotten memory that seemed suddenly to nag for her attention. She'd thought of conceiving Chase's child tonight and thought if she did so, she would welcome it. But she'd had her last monthly flow when they were leaving Columbia, hadn't she? And that had been so long ago . . . the eighteenth of February. And today, already, was the twenty-second of March. She froze momentarily, startled fully awake. February was a short month, she told herself hastily. But still, it counted by now to thirty-two. In the rush and the dangers of the long journey north, she hadn't paid attention to the exact number of days. But now she did. Even before tonight, she had already been the better part of a week overdue.

Chase woke late in the morning of the following day, hearing drizzling rain tapping faintly at the roof of the cabin and Leanna's soft, sleeping breathing close beside him. He rose carefully from the bed to reach for his uniform, not wishing to wake her—and for more than the obvious reason of not wanting to disturb her sleep. The night was over and they'd given each other all that could be given. Today, again, they must reacknowledge the barriers of reality that separated them. The dull gleam of gold from his wedding ring caught his eye in the dim grayness of the daylight, and he frowned at it, feeling a surge of something close to loathing. There was a single instant's irrational wish to simply take the ring off and throw it away. But while he might easily rid himself of the ring itself, he could not so easily rid himself of the marriage it signified. God, he thought. How desperately he wished he could. All too clear in his mind was the night he had just spent with Leanna—a night of barely a few hours, but a night in which all the hateful barriers against their love had fallen, a night of deep and mutual joy, a night that bound them, somehow, even closer together.

An ironic contrast to the night he'd shared with Susan; she

427

had trembled with fear at his touch and had finally surrendered her body to him without ever quite surrendering herself. A night that had left Chase only baffled and uneasy, certain something had gone awry but not knowing what. The possibility of annulling his marriage to Susan had crossed his mind more than once in the long weeks past. There would be anger and scandal, probably, but if that were the only price he would pay, he would have paid it. But the annulment of any marriage rested entirely on one simple question—the question of consummation. In an absolutely literal sense, perhaps, his marriage to Susan Stratford had *not* been consummated . . . but only his father's attack had prevented it. And he had known Susan's body intimately in every other way that night. She had denied him none of a husband's rights to her. Chase could not disregard that, no matter how desperately he wished he could. He could not abandon Susan and live with himself afterward. So he was trapped as hopelessly as ever in a marriage that should never have been.

Frowning and silent, he finished dressing and reached for his officer's coat. There was an unusual weight to the coat's left inside pocket, and the weight reminded him of what lay concealed inside. A locket he had carried, now, all the way up from North Carolina, a locket he had found among Hazen's loot, left behind after Hazen's mysterious disappearance. A locket he had last seen in the hands of a Georgia woman amid a scene of grisly slaughter. He hadn't thought to give it back to Leanna when he'd first found it; there seemed too much bitterness and betrayal attached to the thing. And remembering that seemed strange now, suddenly. Strange to remember how certain he had been of Leanna's betrayal that day near Atlanta. Certain enough that he had gone home to marry another woman. Now, too late, Chase knew he'd been wrong that day at the MacRae farmhouse; whatever had happened there, it had not been instigated by Leanna. Now, too late, he was certain that Leanna had not betrayed him, that she would *never* have betrayed him like that. Both the locket and the love it signified belonged to her as surely as they ever had.

Now, without a single doubt still lingering in his mind, Chase took the necklace out of his uniform pocket and laid it slowly, quietly, on the top of the crude cabin table near the bed. The worn inscription on its golden back was barely visible in the dark gray light of the overcast day, and he stood

428

moment in heavy silence above the thing, looking down at it and then back, just once, toward the girl who lay sleeping still on the narrow cot. They had returned at last . . . but only to where they'd started from, he thought in sudden, deep frustration. Despite a full year's passing, the only thing he could offer Leanna was the same damn useless locket.

When Chase Courtland reached City Point later that morning, he found out he'd been wrong in that belief. He could have offered Leanna anything and everything he'd wished to. One of General Grant's staff officers handed him a letter that his father had written nearly a month before, telling him that his marriage to Susan Stratford had been annulled. By the time he returned to the cabin to share the news with Leanna and to ask her to make a last and final choice between the man she loved and the Yankee uniform she hated, he found her gone. It was like it had been in Columbia—the war seemed determined to give Chase no time at all to find Leanna. In the bitter cold sleet of the night of March twenty-sixth, Grant's Army of the Potomac was already dismantling its winter camp and preparing its return to war. This was the last, desperate spring of a long, desperate war. And somehow, amid the chaos and confusion of this final campaign, Leanna Leighton had simply vanished into the cold, dark mists of night as completely as if she'd never been in the federal camp. Long before he managed to find her, the army had already begun its last march toward the final end of the long, bloody war, and Chase Courtland had no choice but to march along with it. Once again, it seemed the war had intervened to separate the federal major from the Rebel he loved.

Chapter Twenty-five

This had been, quite simply, the only solution to offer Leanna Leighton some small degree of safety from the war without having to leave the South. As a nurse in a field hospital, even in a Yankee one, she betrayed neither the South nor Chase. Though she worked beneath a Union flag, she tended at least as many Southerners as Northerners, perhaps more. Food had run pathetically short this past Winter in Confederate Richmond. Droughts in the past two summers had reduced the usual Virginia harvests; the Valley's crops had been lost to Sheridan's torches; Sherman's army had eliminated food and supplies shipped from farther south; and scurvy and disease had run rampant through Lee's few surviving soldiers. CSA surgeons were now almost totally bereft of medical supplies; even the home-grown remedies they'd relied on so heavily in the past year or two were nearly gone. Southern soldiers who fell wounded or ill were cared for almost entirely now by the already overworked and overburdened Union staff. Here Leanna had chosen to spend what she knew were the most desperate days of the failing South, as a last, anguished compromise between a beloved Yankee and a beloved country.

Days ago, on the morning Chase Courtland had left for City Point to debrief Grant's staff, Leanna had awoken to a dreary, drizzling grayness. Her first consciousness was only of Chase's absence. With that consciousness, both full wakefulness and rising anguish had come to her simultaneously. For long minutes, she had merely laid alone in the narrow camp cot, aching and lonely for the man who'd slept the night in her arms. As she opened her eyes to the morning she'd found the soft gold gleam of the locket that lay close by the bedside, a last, wordless message of love from the man who had been taken away from her again. The single night she'd

sked for, Chase had given her. But the night hadn't done
vhat she had expected it to do. It had not made it easier to
eave him. Not at all. Quite the opposite, in fact; it had made
t only a thousand times harder—for her, and probably for
Chase as well. Only now, when it was too late, did she
nderstand what she'd done to herself—done, probably, to
oth of them. She had made a final separation, bitter at best,
ll the more agonizing for herself and for the Yankee unlucky
nough to love her.

No, she'd amended slowly in a kind of fearful, gradual
ealization of the entire truth of what had transpired. No, not
nerely agonizing. Before last night, before those precious,
ittersweet hours that had bound her and Chase all the more
losely together, a farewell would at least have been bearable.
his morning it was not even that. Sometime during the
ourse of those dark, sweet hours, she had given too much of
erself to her beloved enemy, and now she found herself
nable to take it all back upon her command. She had closed
ne door on what she had been, made a final choice for herself
'ithout realizing she had made it. Now she was simply
nable to leave Chase Courtland, despite all the reasons that
till mandated that decision. To leave him and go north or to
eave him and rejoin the South were equally impossible. To
ne north in Philadelphia—Chase's choice for her, she knew—
y safety, perhaps; Jonathon and Whitney, and a world
rgely untouched by the ravages of war. But it was alien
afety there and an alien world. And in Philadelphia, too,
ould be Chase's legal wife—a reminder to Leanna of forbid-
en passions and secret guilts, and a reminder as well of the
uture that lay ahead of her, a future without Chase. To the
outh lay only a failing cause, a desperate army and, accord-
ng to Chase, a possible warrant for her arrest. Blytheswood
as burned and Jewel was dead, the Valley burned to black
sh by Yankee torches. Neither could she go back to Colum-
ia and to the Confederate captain she'd left wounded there.
ven if she could somehow have gotten there, she would not
ave gone. Leanna suspected she might already be carrying
hase Courtland's child once again in her belly, and even
ithout that suspicion, she could never have returned to
ummer Ashton.

If she had not realized it before, the past night had taught
er that truth only all too well. Though she did love her

431

gallant Confederate rescuer in a way—even, she thought, in many ways—it was not in the way she ought to love him, and not in the way she loved Chase Courtland. And having finally learned from Chase what such a love could offer, she would never condemn herself or Summer to a lifetime of so much less than that. Ironic, once again, Leanna had reflected in sudden realization. She had thought a night with Chase would make the bitter choices easier to take, and instead, the night had taken those choices all away. It was as impossible as ever to stay here with Chase as she'd wanted to do . . . but now, it was equally impossible for her to leave him. Somehow, now she must find another course for herself, one that was not a dead end. And she must find it, as well, before Chase returned and forced *his* choice upon her.

Leanna had taken only the locket and her worn, winter cloak to the hospital. Grier had told her once, on just such another cold, gray, bitter morning, that he considered himself to be in her debt. Perhaps it was time, she had decided then, to call on the Yankee captain for that promised favor. If she could neither quite leave Chase nor stay here with him, she had only one alternative. She had to find some way to remain with the Union Army as it prepared to march into war once again. She must find a final compromise between her beloved Confederacy and her equally beloved federal major . . . because in the end, she had left herself no other choices.

Grier had honored his promise of a favor, but he had been obviously displeased at the manner in which Leanna had asked for it. Nevertheless he had found a place for her on one of the regimental hospital field staffs, the only place in the army where women were allowed to be. But he had objected to both Leanna's decision and even more heatedly to her demand that he not tell Chase either what she'd said or what she'd done, or even betray the fact that he'd seen her. Let Chase believe she had gone back to the Confederate side; let him believe she had gone back to Summer Ashton. What Grier considered cruelty, she herself thought kindness. Chase could do much, but he could not change the course of events. His marriage was history, his marriage was simply fact, and he could not undo the commitment he had made. Faced with that irrefutable fact, even Grier at last had fallen silent.

It did not take too many days for Leanna to begin to doubt the wisdom of the decision she'd made that anguished morning.

n some ways, many of Grier's objections had proven to be all too true. Barely a day after Chase's return to camp, despite the rain that continued to soak Virginia, the war began again, right on its bloody, desperate schedule, and all illusions of safety had evaporated into the very air around her. There was a sudden, startling call to arms as the Union Army moved to block an unexpected Confederate offensive. The attack would fail, and it would be Robert E. Lee's last offensive maneuver of the war, but in its wake, Grant would order his Union army into the field to press the advantage.

Only one railroad line still supplied to Lee's soldiers, who now were trapped in their own defense works outside of Petersburg. Sever that vital jugular vein of food and supply and Lee must move, and once moving, must abandon his long defense of the Confederate capital. And if Richmond fell, everyone knew, the Rebel government must fall as well—and the war could end at last.

On March 29, the Union Army made its first slashing attack on that now all-important railroad line. On White Oak Road the two armies met and briefly battled. On the thirtieth, Sheridan's entire command—twelve thousand cavalry, including Chase Courtland's troop and the rest of General Devin's division—bivouacked near the tracks at Dinividdie Courthouse, skirmishing there with the distant Rebels. It was poor country for cavalry action, swampy, scrubby with second-growth timber, riddled by countless tiny brooks and streams. To make matters worse, the Virginia spring rains still continued without letup through the thirty-first. Rations were soaked, blankets wet, camp beds like damp sponges, canvas-tent shelters dripping rainwater. Horses stumbled in knee-deep mud, ambulances and wagons sank to their axles in roads that had become quagmires. Custer's entire division was detached to corduroy roads for supply wagons and the all-important field guns, but the impatient Sheridan would not wait long enough. On the thirty-first, Devin's division was ordered north through the continuing rains to attack the vital CSA junction of Five Forks. Cavalry attacking entrenched infantry had never been a happy maneuver, and now the mud from the Virginia rains made it a thousand times worse. Devin's attacking troopers should have been able to make their charge at a gallop, covering the last, murderous two hundred yards in about fifteen seconds, but their horses floundered in the mud and were barely able to move at all, let alone charge at a full gallop. That left Devin's troops with no choice but to dismount and dig in as best they could, trying to hold an indefensible position on foot. And across the way, entrenched Rebels with their heavier, longer-range rifles were having field day at the federal cavalry's expense.

In the field hospital behind the Union lines, Leanna heard the distant, anguished cry of the Yankee buglers and her heart immediately froze at the notes of alarm and disaster. In sense, she realized suddenly, the Union hospital was going to be the worst place of all for her to be. Every whispered rumor, every cavalry uniform that was carried into the hospital caught her eye with stunning force. And there was always that terrifying half second before the could even look to reassure herself that Chase Courtland was not here among the dead and the dying. This had not been one of Grier's objections to her plan, but it should have been, Leanna realized abruptly, perhaps it should have been the *foremost* one—this relentless fear for Chase's life.

The field hospital of the Twenty-second Michigan was set up on a ridge barely a mile away from the Union front lines. From Leanna's viewpoint there, the actual battle of Five Forks was only a distant, barely visible scene of incredible confusion; the small clearing where the lines of blue and gray were actually clashing was a distant madhouse of smoke and slaughter. Bullets from this distance sounded harmless—like corn popping for a child's treat—but the scene in the hospital soon proved the fallacy of that gentle illusion. There was the pinprick fire of distant rifles; puffs of powder drifting in cold, misty rain; officers shouting; horses panicking; artillery booming and buglers calling. Battle flags were wet and sodden, making groups of men look like chess pieces. And, even at this moment, Chase was fighting there. Leanna knew that suddenly. And she knew it more surely than any camp rumor could ever be—she knew it by sheer feminine instinct that cried out a helpless and a desperate fear. Barely moments later, the first trickle of wounded men was coming into the Union hospital. Before long, the trickle had become a torrent, a flood of agony that poured in from the fighting Union lines ahead. Devin's dismounted cavalry was being driven back, but orders from Sheridan were to fight for every inch. And seeing the incredible numbers of Yankee wounded that crowded the hospital all around her, it was all too obvious that they were doing just that.

Within an hour, the hospital was out of beds, out of stretchers, out of blankets, out of room. Men, Yankee and Confederate both, lay groaning underfoot. Riderless horses trampled the underbrush on either side. Union field guns were moved back. One was booming only yards away from the crude medic station, lurching in the mud, then booming again. Men shouted everything—over the din, it didn't matter. One could hardly hear a word.

In the midst of the chaos, Leanna worked at a frantic pace—partly because she had to, to keep up with the flood of wounded soldiers that were still coming in, and partly in a desperate and unavailing effort to keep her mind from dwelling too long on her growing fears for a particular Yankee. This was the worst of it, she tried to tell herself to calm her ever-rising horror. This was the first major battle she'd ever seen from so close a vantage point. After today, it would be easier. After today she would know what to expect and could prepare herself for the blood and the death and the dying. But still, the moans of the wounded were eerie amid the hush of the overburdened nurses and grim, hurried surgeons. Pain-maddened horses screamed and trampled the underbrush of the surrounding woods. Men cried out in unbearable fear and pain. And occasionally, there was the sudden explosion of artillery fire falling on trees only yards away from them. The agony all around seemed only to grow, as if feeding on itself in cannibalistic frenzy, rising and building until, quite suddenly, Leanna thought she could not survive in its horror as much as a moment longer.

But survive she did. That day, and the day after, and the day after that as well. But it never got any easier. Contrary to what she always tried to tell herself, it only seemed to grow ever worse. And it occurred to her finally that she was paying a very high price for the compromise she'd finally found between a beloved enemy and a beloved cause. It seemed as if the war would take its toll of anguish from her one way or another, regardless of however she tried to escape it.

On the first of April, Sheridan's battered cavalry succeeded in taking the vital junction of Five Forks, and Lee's last railroad line to supplies for his Confederate soldiers now lay securely in federal hands. It left the Confederate Army of Northern Virginia with no choice but to abandon its trenches around the CSA capitol, abandoning its long defense of Richmond, too. Lee's army was a pitiful remnant of its former glory, and now it marched for survival alone. Through the cold, hard rains of the first week of another bloody April in Virginia, the war became nothing more, finally, than a simple foot race between the two opposing, desperate armies. Lee's only hope was to slip out of Virginia and join forces with Johnston's army in North Carolina. Grant's only hope was to keep Lee from accomplishing that maneuver. Both Yankee and Rebel soldiers slept little and marched hard, and on the second day of April, infantry columns broke through the remaining Confederate defense lines to force the evacuation of both Petersburg and Richmond. Rumors swept the Yankee camp that the once-proud Richmond had been left in flames, that Jefferson Davis and the rest of his government had fled the doomed city at midnight, interrupted at church by Lee's grim warning of hopelessness. Federal troops finally entered Richmond on the third, extinguishing the flames that had reduced the once-beautiful Southern city to blackened ruins. Ward Lamon and several other friends were appalled at the needless risk, but President Lincoln insisted on traveling personally to the abandoned Confederate capital on the very next day. Secretary of War Stanton, however, remained in Washington, D.C. Throughout the federal capital, men watched for the end with anxious eyes.

Grant had ordered Sheridan's cavalry to follow Lee's most desperate flight, blocking any attempt the Confederate Army might make to turn south toward Johnston and North Carolina. Leanna had no time to mourn the death of Richmond or the fall of the Confederate government, for the hospital staff followed the cavalry's rear column at the same incredible, desperate pace. The safety she'd thought to find here with the Yankee army seemed to have been only a bitter joke. The air was never still; the hours were never quiet. No one knew where Devin's command was. No one knew what kind of losses they were sustaining. But shallow graves lined both sides of the muddy roads like macabre street signs, pointing out the line of march.

This was war as Leanna had never thought to see it. No pitched battle, no definite start or stop to it. There were only

436

days and nights of an endless nightmare, fighting that never ceased—dirty, exhausting and bloody. Lee marched his Rebel army at a breakneck pace, thirty-five miles a day, littering the roads behind him with broken wagons, abandoned cannon, muskets and blanket rolls, exhausted men and skeletal horses. He tried to escape the federal noose at Annelia Courthouse and again at Jetersville, but both times the federal cavalry held its ground long enough to allow Union infantry reinforcements to entrench, leaving the Confederate army no choice but to push on again to the west, marching for their very existence. In the confusion of the fall of Richmond, the fleeing CSA government had not thought much about providing rations to its defeated army, and consequently, as the Rebels marched and skirmished and died, they also starved. Lee sent wagons and a desperate appeal to the Virginia countryside, but the wagons returned to him virtually empty. Winter and four years of war had devastated all of northern Virginia. Sheridan had already burned the Valley and the area all around Warrenton where "Mosby's Confederacy" had once held sway; many of the people of Virginia were starving. Hundreds of Confederate prisoners were taken by the federal columns—pitiful men, broken and beaten, who simply could not keep up with their army any longer. But most of Lee's soldiers, unbelievably, did keep up, pressing the mounted cavalry to match the march they made on foot.

Several officers on both sides of the war had inspired their men to deeds of greatness. Sheridan's blind fearlessness and rabid aggression brought him reckless fervor from his Union cavalry; "Little Mac" McClellan had been infinitely trusted; Sherman inspired by challenging the impossible and getting it done; Jeb Stuart had set an example of gallantry and fearless courage that his intrepid CSA cavalry had worked to match. But of all the generals on either side, only Robert E. Lee was deeply loved by the common soldiers, and this hellish march was a tribute to him and a mandate to him to continue leading. To hell, if need be, they would march with their "Marse Robert" and die without complaint if he'd ordered it so. But even so, the strain of such a march must take its toll. Pressed by the Union Cavalry divisions, Lee's starving soldiers marched all day and most of the nights as well, stumbling blindly among their wagons and artillery, mumbling incoherently, wandering off into the dark woods in a stupor, panicking and shooting at shadows—and worse, at each other—leaving their dead and wounded where they fell, struggling on for every mile westward. Martyrs to a cause most knew by now was hopeless.

Dawn on the sixth of April brought a cessation, at least, to the rains. For the first time since leaving the distant winter encampments, the Union soldiers were enjoying the fine sunshine of a Virginia spring. At Annelia Station, days before, Chase Courtland had taken a bad fall from his horse while under fire from the retreating Rebels. General Devin had seen it. He had seen the immediate reaction of the Union troop as well, as they'd drawn rein around their fallen major—maintaining a long and desperate covering fire while he'd managed to remount his horse. And Devin understood that only the finest officers won that kind of loyalty from their enlisted men. Grant himself had taken note of the young officer who had led his men on such a desperate journey from one Union Army to another, miles distant, and consequently Devin assigned Chase to a staff position. Good officers were all too rare to risk so casually, and whether it was simply the exhaustion of too many days of riding, or whether, under that kind of strain, the old Savannah wounds flared up again, Chase Courtland could serve the Union better in General Devin's staff room than he could serve it in an early grave.

As Chase rode up now to the troop under Grier's command, it was as a courier instead of as a commander. He had come from Devin only to relay the new orders for the Union march today. Grier's cavalry troopers were mounted already—in the past few days they had scarcely ever been otherwise—and the buglers to the front were already calling the orders to form rank.

Few troop captains were given the privilege of receiving a field officer's personal instruction, but Grier was an exception—at least, to Chase, Grier was an exception. And there were too many years of habit behind them to break that relationship so late in the war. Chase gave Grier the orders, and more, he offered him an explanation of them. Lee's incredible army was faltering at last. The separate divisions were getting farther and farther strung out, one from another. And if those divisions didn't soon regroup closer, it might be possible sometime today to cut the long gray column into edible bites that the Union forces could try to swallow. That hurried

438

explanation finished, Chase offered a last, faint smile and a wordless salute that carried a message of grim well-wishing. He had already begun to turn his horse when Grier's sudden call came after him, and puzzled, Chase pulled his horse back in a brief, rearing halt.

Captain Grier's eyes were on the hand Chase Courtland was holding his reins with, and a startled frown creased his bearded face as Grier continued now to stare at it. In the fine April sunshine, today, the gloves he had worn for that week were finally off. And noting, now, the absence of a ring on Chase Courtland's hand, Grier was conscious of a sudden start of remembrance, of a promise he was suddenly questioning keeping. But before he could speak, the buglers changed their call to a sudden strident cry for action. Something had happened already in the rolling green hills of the Virginia countryside just ahead of them. There would be no time now for full explanations. "Major, your ring, there! Did you take it off or did you just lose it somewhere?"

It took the passage of one long, precious minute for Chase to even understand. It was not a question he had expected. For a moment he merely frowned, startled. And beside him, the Union column Grier rode among was already starting forward into some kind of action. Riders were swearing, horses were snorting and rearing, and there was already the ominous sound of carbines firing in the distance. Chase merely shook his head first, not trying to shout over the noisy confusion that had exploded around both him and Grier.

"Dammit, Major, it's important! *Are* you married still or *aren't* you?" Grier shouted it again in angry desperation, holding his horse back for one precious second longer though the animal reared and neighed its impatience to race on with its companions.

"No, it was annulled. Why the hell should that matter to you?"

"Because Mrs. Leighton is still with the damn army, Major! A field hospital. The Twenty-second Michigan. But she'd asked me not to tell you that!" Grier had no longer to delay; even as he shouted the words across the rushing horses and shouting soldiers he set spurs to his own horse. He left Chase staring after him, his form soon obscured by the dust and distance of the galloping troop. Chase sat only a moment longer, then turned his own horse with a sudden oath of startled understanding. It never occurred to him to doubt Grier's words, for in a sense he had never entirely believed that Leanna had actually left him. It had been too long and they had both learned too much. But he would not have thought to look for her in the Union Army hospitals. And now, knowing she was there, he quietly cursed. A field hospital was probably one of the last places he would have thought to search for her . . . and it was also one of the last places he would have wanted her to be. Her safety was far from assured there, for it was not unknown for artillery shells of either army to miss their mark and land in the medic tents. He would go after her, of course, and see her to safety in spite of herself, but he couldn't go now. As desperately as he might want to, he would be damn lucky now to even manage such a mission before nightfall. Every Union soldier in Sheridan's entire command—including himself—was going to be fighting harder today than they had, probably, on any other day in the course of the four-year war. Leanna had chosen a hell of a spot from which to watch the finale of a desperate war, and right now there was nothing he could do to mitigate the dangers of that foolhardy choice.

In the hospital of the Twenty-second Michigan, Leanna knew only that something major had happened today, that almost every division of the Union Cavalry had been involved at some point in the day's battle. She wasn't sure who had won the bloody scramble. Even when sunset had come, it brought no more than the usual entirely unreliable camp rumors. No couriers galloped by. No sounds of bands announced the outcome. There was only a sudden eerie cessation of artillery fire, and then nothing else. And no one came to her with reassurances.

She waited until dusk, tending the wounded and trying not to think any more than she had to. This was hell here, she thought as she worked, half numb with fear and fatigue. All the men who had voted for war on both sides, CSA and Union, should be required to back up those bloody votes by working here. Both armies were so utterly alike. Blue or gray, they seemed to bleed the same, to suffer the same, to moan and scream and cry out in equal agony, to tremble in fear of approaching death. Lines of distinction once clearly drawn between friend and enemy seemed indistinguishably blurred, and Leanna was weary of it, suddenly, weary unto death of the war and the agony and of everything else. She made herself finish her rounds with the water bowl, washing pain-cracked lips with a moistened rag and ignoring the pitiful whimpers of gut-shot men who would only scream aloud with unbearable agony if she offered them the water they so desperately craved. She spent a long, bitter moment holding a young boy's hand as he murmured incoherently about his North Carolina home and made a broken farewell to the mother and sisters he had left behind there. And then, quite calmly, she got up to fetch her cloak and a lantern, and then left the field hospital far behind her. She was going to find Chase, she knew. Wherever he was, whatever condition she would find him in, she could no longer find any reason sufficiently compelling to make her change her mind. It was more important than breathing now to her. More important than North or South, safety or danger. More important even than the child she carried. She must find Chase Courtland and know whether he lived or died.

The ground was still wet from the icy March rains, and with the darkness it grew colder once again. Leanna shivered as she passed from one camp to the next, walking in anguished silence past the battle-wounded and the usual clutter of the rear lines, past battered army horses, wagons, mules, past soldiers moving in scattered directions, past soft, groaning sounds and the smell of coffee and burning wood from soldiers' cookfires. The answers to her questions were always the same. Devin's division? That way, further west. Yes, they'd fought today. Everyone had: Devin, Custer, Crook, Merritt, Stagg. There'd been a Union victory of some sort, up the hill from little Sayler's Creek. Everyone thought so, anyway, but no one was sure, and no one knew any of the names she asked.

Leanna found Devin's division, finally, just as the moon came up behind moving clouds, but it was a cold victory. Chase wasn't there. Neither was Grier. And in the confusion, no one could say why not. Try the hospitals, someone suggested, and she only nodded, concealing the rising of that terrible fear as she went to search the shadowed, weary faces of the wounded soldiers. Some were ashen-faced with approaching death, some contorted in pain or in the nightmare sleep of opiates. One after another, portrait after portrait of horror—scars and blood and suffering and bandages—until she began to wonder if she'd lost her mind, died and been comdemned to some eerie kind of hell. Twilight changed to night, and still she walked, shivering harder, and the first hard-fought tears began to slip down her face.

It was not Chase but Grier whom she finally found in a hospital close to the battlefield. This one was well lit, at least, for the surgeon in charge was still working. His butcher's apron was brownish-red with drying blood, his arms were covered with gore and the ugly silver of the surgeon's saw gleamed in his hand as he silently worked. In the lantern light, along the long rows, Leanna recognized Chase's captain's face and froze helplessly, only staring. Dark blue blankets drawn to Grier's shoulders only accentuated the pallor of his bearded face, and he was motionless. Unconscious, she thought, or dead. Almost against her will, she reached a slow hand out to touch his cheek. It was warm, almost surprisingly so, for at least half of her had expected the clammy coldness of a corpse. Partly with a rush of relief and partly with frustration that he was here and Chase wasn't, Leanna closed her eyes and bowed her head in sudden overwhelming fatigue.

"Can I help you, dear?"

She opened her eyes, startled, drawing a quick shuddering breath and turning toward the voice that spoke from the shadows. It was an older woman, a nurse by her apron and her air of gentle weariness, and her eyes were kind as they searched Leanna's ashen face. "Can I help you?" she repeated.

"I don't know," Leanna managed to murmur finally, finding the effort of speech an incredible task. "I was looking for someone, a cavalry major named Courtland. I found his captain here, but I still haven't found him."

"Have you been to the division's camp?"

"Yes, hours ago. Or I think it was hours ago. I'm not really sure now if it was." Leanna rose slowly to her feet, fighting a nearly immobilizing wave of nausea and fatigue. It was the first time in her pregnancy that the child had soured her stomach like this, she thought in a kind of dazed surprise. The first of many times, from what she recalled of Whitney's talk. It seemed somehow oddly appropriate that the child should protest now, too, at this instant—as if sensing the mother's fears for the father's life.

"Try the general's headquarters, dear. It's the only other

place I can think of. Follow the road here. Bear left at the wooded crossroads and continue down the hill. There's a little bridge over the creek at the bottom. The house is up on the next hill, to your right." The woman seemed to hesitate, then continued. "The road will lead you through the battlefield, though. If you should fear that . . ."

Leanna only shook her head in answer and rose slowly to her feet. Ghosts held no terror for her anymore. Nor did the corpses of recently killed men. She'd seen too many. And there was only one now that she really feared to find. She turned, then paused, glancing back to the woman's face. "This man here, Captain Grier. How badly wounded is he?"

"I don't know. He was brought in before my shift began. I think I recall that he should be all right, but I really can't remember more than that. I'm sorry."

Leanna nodded, glanced back to Grier's face and gathered up her skirts for the last, long walk. Now that the wind had died down, the night was no longer terribly cold. Not warm either, not yet, not this early in April. The moonlight threw the tall, just barely budding trees into grotesque shadows, black and gray. The tangled rope of wild grape and wisteria vines looked like child's scribble done against a moonlit sky. Her lantern cast a solitary glow for about a dozen feet around her, and she crested the hill in shivering silence, then froze momentarily, looking down on the scene that stretched below her. From the hill to the tree-lined creek below, the night dark grass was littered with unmoving bodies. Only stretcher parties walked among them, occasionally stopping. And over all of it, as there so often was on a battlefield, there hung an eerie, unending silence. Here and there, a horse stood with a drooping head, guarding a fallen master. From far away, an owl hooted twice. Leanna felt an ominous chill settle on her heart and forced herself forward, step by step, not allowing herself to search the dark, frozen faces of the dead men that she passed.

Down the night-shrouded road she walked, noting the all-too-familiar scent of death carried on a gentle air, the faint acrid smell of burnt powder and, at the bottom of the hill by the creek, the pungent odor of the hawthorne trees. The narrow little creek gurgled beneath the wood of the bridge as she crossed, and finally, up ahead, she could see the pale glow of light from the headquarters house. Her hands were cold as she gripped the lantern ring; her fingers were stiff as she reached the picket-fence gate of the house and switched the low burning lamp to her other hand. At the motion of the light, a soldier stepped forward, his musket raised.

"Who goes there?"

She stopped immediately, startled by the sentry's challenge. "Please—I'm looking for someone. The nurse back at the hospital suggested I might try here." The rifle lowered and the man stepped closer. "A major named Courtland? Assigned to General Devin's division."

"Did you try the division's camp?"

"Yes, I did. He wasn't there. I checked the hospitals, too. Can you just tell me whether he's here or not?" It surprised her that her voice began to break, and she made a startled effort to steady it, trying to keep from dissolving into tears.

"No, you better go on to the house, ma'am." The soldier gestured curtly but not unkindly as he stood aside. "I don't know who all's inside and I'd rather you ask for yourself, truth be told. You ask the orderly that'll open the door. He'll tell you if your cavalry major's inside or not."

Leanna managed to nod, blinked against tears that suddenly blurred her vision and picked up her skirt to see the uneven, mossy stones of the walkway that lay ahead. The door of the white-frame farmhouse had no knocker so she used her hand, once and then once again, harder, heedless of the rough wood scraping her knuckles to bleeding. In truth, she didn't even feel it.

The door to the house swung open so abruptly that it startled her, and for a moment Leanna just stood there in silence. The soldier who had opened the door was an older man, with shortish salt-and-pepper hair and a matching, bristling beard that looked incomplete, somehow, as if it were undecided about whether or not to be a full beard. He wore a private's mud-splattered blouse with what looked like shoulder straps of an officer's rank rather casually sewn over a plain seam. An unlit cigar hung from one hand and in the other was what appeared to be a bowl of sliced cucumbers and cream. She was conscious of a moment's puzzlement at how he had even managed to open the door, and in the same moment was conscious, too, of some vague familiarity in the man who stood before her. But other than the troopers who had served under Chase and wintered at Blytheswood, she could not think of any Yankees she would recognize. And at this moment, she was too weary and too preoccupied to spare the matter further thought. "Excuse me, but I was looking for someone. A nurse at that last hospital said I might try here. Could you tell me whether a cavalry major named Courtland is here by any chance?"

The grizzled soldier looked taken aback momentarily, and the eyes that searched the young woman's ashen face were quickly intense. General Grant knew a Virginia accent when he heard one. He'd heard one years ago in the Mexican war when he'd served with a young engineering officer named Robert E. Lee. "Yes, I believe there is a Major Courtland here, young lady. Shall I fetch him out for you to speak to?"

Leanna would have said no if she could have thought quickly enough to do so. She would have stopped the Union soldier's abrupt turn from the open door into the farmhouse's poor parlor. Chase was alive and well. That was all she had really needed to know. But a sudden surge of relief had struck her so hard in that first instant that she could not seem to say anything at all to answer the old soldier's kindly question. She could merely stand there, helplessly silent and uneasily conscious of the tears that were suddenly streaming down her night-chilled cheeks. Then the soldier inside turned away, and barely a moment later Chase himself stepped into the doorway. And then it was too late for her to try to retreat, even if she'd wanted to.

For an instant, Chase merely stood staring at her, his eyes locked to hers in the frozen silence of startled recognition. Then he moved toward her with a sudden motion, stepping through the doorway toward the trembling girl, and the hand he reached out to take her arm with was as rigid as rock but trembling, too, as if with the force of some sudden emotion. "Leanna, thank God! Where in the hell have you been all this time?"

"With the army, Chase. I couldn't leave you, not again. I didn't want the bitterness of another fight and I could never have gone on to Philadelphia like you wanted me to. I didn't see any sense in only putting us both through another—"

"No, I already know that you've been with the army, Lea. I found out this morning, but only after the fighting had started. But when I got over to the Twenty-second Michigan, no one there had seen you for hours! No one knew when

445

you'd left and no one knew where the hell you'd gone! I looked for you all over this damn army. For hours. Where in the bloody hell have you been all night?"

Standing in the dark, damp chill of the Virginia night, surrounded by armies and the distant sounds of all of war's attendant horrors, Leanna was stricken dumb by a sense of sudden, utter incoherence, a sense of absolute and bewildering shock. This was not the reaction she'd expected of Chase, not even the question she'd first thought he'd ask. She would have understood his anger at her leaving him with no farewell, even understood his anger at her refusal to go to Philadelphia as he'd planned. But this other question simply baffled her, now. "But . . . I went looking for you, Chase. After the fighting today, no one seemed to know . . . I was afraid. And I began to . . . I began to think that—" There was a sudden, surging sense of unbearable anguish abruptly cresting, and without warning, Leanna fell forward, helplessly sobbing. Only by instinct, Chase had raised his arms in time to catch her there before she fell. "Oh God, you mustn't be angry with me, Chase. I couldn't help it! Tonight, I was beginning to think you were dead! I looked and looked for you, everywhere, for hours, and I couldn't find you anywhere! I don't even know what I would have done if I had found you dead—maybe laid down beside you and died, too, I don't know. I looked and looked and I couldn't find you. . . ."

"Hush, Lea, it's all right, now. It's all over now. I'm not angry at you. I'm here and I'm fine . . . we *both* are. That's all that's important. Hush, love, now hush." He, too, had closed his own eyes suddenly, struggling to control his emotions momentarily unable to speak through a throat closed and choked with those emotions. God, it wasn't like he couldn't understand the kind of fear Leanna had been driven by tonight. In the long week past, not knowing where she was, fearing for her everywhere. And then himself, tonight, unable to leave his duties to continue searching the camp for her. Unable to find her, it seemed, in any other way . . . A war still raging all around them. Pickets, and snipers, and shells still exploding yet from the daylight fighting. God what a night . . . for *both* of them. "Hush, Lea. It's almost over now. The war is almost over, finally, and we're both all right. We trapped a third of Lee's army today—cut them off, captured most of them. It has to end soon, now. It has to, and it will."

446

"A third of Lee's army?" Unthinking pain had instantly pierced Leanna's heart despite the turbulence of so many other emotions already there. The war over? The South defeated? As if sensing her instinctive anguish, Chase tightened his arms to keep her close, and now he shook his head once in sharp denial.

"God, *don't* Lea . . . don't wish them hope. Wish them surrender, it would be far kinder. That's why Grant came up tonight. He'll send Lee an invitation to discuss surrender terms tomorrow."

"But Lee won't surrender." Leanna knew Virginians too well—she was one. "Lee will try to cut south to join Johnston, till, in North Carolina. You know he will."

"Yes, I know. But we won't let him do that, Lea. And if he makes the Blue Ridge, I'm afraid he'll fight a kind of guerrilla war there, so we can't afford to let him do that either."

Leanna could hardly react to it yet; it seemed too impossible that it could really be over. She could remember too vividly that first glorious day in Richmond. Remember Verena Davis at the Confederate White House, remember Lee himself there, and Stewart, and Jeb Stuart. All of Virginia's once-unassailable confidence and pride. Now, in her mind's eye, she saw only the burned plantations and the ruined farms of the Valley. It had all been lost to gain them nothing. . . .No, not nothing, perhaps. Just to have it over finally must be worth something to all of them. "No, Chase. General Lee would never countenance any kind of dirty warfare. If you beat him fairly, Lee will surrender. He's too much a gentleman to do anything else. If he can't get to Johnston, he'll surrender the army to you, I know."

In the pain that lingered after that, Leanna closed her eyes against the heat of rising tears. She felt Chase move his head to rest it against hers, and only once there came the soft sensation of a slow kiss dropped across her night-chilled hair. "Lea, this is one hell of a time to have to do this, but I need you to listen to me now for a moment. I have something very important to tell you. I'm not married anymore. My marriage to Susan has been annulled. I want you to marry me, Leanna. Marry me before some other damn thing comes up to separate us once again."

"*Marry* you?" Leanna comprehended his words only very slowly. She was startled and weary and struggling to make

the question he had just asked of her seem real. "But—"
Involuntarily, she turned her head to glance down at the hand
Chase rested on her arm. Racing clouds obscured the moonlight
but a faint golden light from the lamps lit within the house
showed only the shadows of molded flesh there now. There
was no telltale gleam of wedding-ring gold. For a moment
incredulous, she stood and stared. Then she nodded slowly,
almost dazedly. "Yes, I'll marry you, Chase. As soon as the
war is over, of course."

"No, *now*." Instantly his arms had begun to loosen from
around her trembling shoulders. There was a sudden hardness in his voice again, a sudden distance in the eyes looking
down to meet hers. There was only the briefest pause before
he spoke again. "Marry me now or not at all, Leanna. Make
up your mind which one of us comes first. Me? or the
South?"

Leanna needed only a moment's hesitation, though that
single moment was heavy with an unspoken anguish. She'd
made that decision some weeks ago, she realized suddenly.
She just hadn't admitted it either to Chase or to herself. The
miracle had happened and he was free. She would not use-
lessly sacrifice both their futures for a doomed Confederacy
now. There were tears in her eyes but she nodded her head in
unequivocal answer, and pressed her face deeper for a long
moment into the familiar, once-hated Yankee blue of his
uniformed shoulder. "Yes, I'll marry you, Chase. Tonight
even if you want. It's none too soon in a way. I think I may
already be carrying your child again." She caught her breath
with a strange half sigh, half sob, and raised her head to catch
his eyes, offering the barest hint of what she'd meant to be a
smile. "That's one of the reasons I stayed with you damn
Yankees this time. I wanted to stay near you as long as I
could, and I thought this army of yours would be the safest
place for me to be."

There was no answering smile on Chase's weary face, only
a kind of grimness as her words reawakened a forgotten fear.
He kept his arms around her, and finally Leanna felt what
might have been a shudder of some kind run slowly through
him before he spoke. "I love you, Leanna, for just exactly
what you are. In that sense, I suppose I shouldn't want to
change you, but now and then you tempt me. God knows
you tempt me sorely to want to do just that." He kept his

448

ands on her shoulders then, but moved a half step farther
way to look down at her in the golden light. "We'll marry
onight, then. Maybe married to me, you'll be more inclined
o listen to me occasionally, too. Especially now, with the
ossibility of our child involved, I am entitled to have some
nput, I think, into making the decisions for these next few
ays. I am *going* to put you somewhere safe. And there will
e hell to pay if you defy me again." Chase drew a last deep
reath, brushing her hair with another last kiss. "Wait for me,
ea. Wait for me right here. I'll go see if I can't manage to
teal just an hour away from this war so we can be married,
ow."

Though he'd finished speaking, Chase still didn't move
way from her. And now, suddenly, Leanna felt a kind of
esperate tension in his arms around her, a momentary, word-
ss message of all the anguish and the pain he'd known in the
ast year and more, which had led them, at last, to this final
oint. A kind of recurring fear, simply, that to let her go was
o lose her again somehow. As he had so many times in the
ast. Leanna reached out then, too, to hold Chase even closer
gainst her, her face bathed with tears of sudden, anguished
nderstanding and empathy, holding him tight and holding
im hard. And she held him that way for another long minute
n a kind of answering desperation and in a kind of wanton
isregard for armies or causes or for anything else. This time,
hough, they *had* changed the ending, hadn't they? They had
scaped the inevitable, after all. "I love you, Chase. Go get
our hour or your minutes or whatever time you can get just
ow. This time, I swear to you, I will be waiting right here
hen you come back. This time, nothing will come between
s. Not ever again."

Epilogue

It was late in Philadelphia, dark, and nearly midnight before the news came in over the wire from Washington. There was a sudden, scattered sound of shouting in the distant, lamplit streets of the city, the sudden clatter of hoofbeats just outside the Courtland house, and a single cry from the rider, muffled by the doors and drapes of the house to unintelligibility. Joshua sat in the parlor with Jonathon and Whitney. The day was Palm Sunday, and because of that, supper had been late and large, and after-dinner brandy was still being enjoyed. They had been talking of inconsequentials, actually: of the bridge under construction to span the Schulkyll, the May opening of the Union League and Abraham Lincoln's promise to be there, of investments in railroad stock, and perhaps, the war-spawned standardized clothing industry.

Now, at the jubilant sounds in the distant streets, there was a sudden, confused silence inside the house. Whitney rose to move toward the window to try to hear. Halfway there, the first, wild peal of a distant church bell checked her step. An instant later, more bells pealed, closer—St. Marks, probably; the bells there had a distinctive mellow clarity all their own. She turned instinctively to Jonathon, saw him flinch once and then slowly turn pale in the low golden light of the parlor lamps. It was Lee, he had realized. It had to be. News of surrender from down in Virginia. The cause had failed; it was finally over.

Joshua sat motionless and silent, sparing only a single swift glance to the young Virginian opposite him. There was nothing to say, he thought. It would be too hypocritical to offer condolences. Still, just as Grant himself had felt facing Robert E. Lee earlier that afternoon, there was no real feeling of jubilation either. It was a moment that held some embarrassment for him actually—for like Grant, Joshua was as conscious of the humiliation of the Southerner's defeat as he was of the thrill of his own Union victory. All that he could take unclouded joy in was the hope that Chase would be home now, soon. And then suddenly, thinking of Roland Hodges and the coalition, he found an instant of bittersweet humor in it, too. By God, they would be gnashing their teeth at this moment! Furious, but helpless to move against Lincoln; the delay Joshua Courtland had wrestled from them had been enough.

Whatever else happened now, this alone would be sufficient. If Lincoln did not live to see the journey completed, at least he had lived to choose the road it would follow. Even at this very moment, Lincoln would be standing on the night-shadowed balcony of the White House in Washington, addressing the crowd gathered on the dark lawn below, and reiterating his inaugural promise of "charity toward all and malice toward none." Lincoln would approve generous surrender terms, and such terms would be standard afterward. He would remind the victorious Union that the South was not a conquered enemy, not a foreign territory that could suffer revenge. The South, beaten and battered as it undoubtedly was, was still a part of the Union whole, and the South must belong not to its Northern conquerors but to the *people*, the people who had fought for it and over it for the past four years. Whatever ground such radical groups as the War Department and the various coalitions might later regain, they would never now know the kind of victory that they had sought. Scars might linger, but the Union itself would heal, in time. Joshua had won one of his battles, then, after all. He had lived well enough and long enough to delay the designs of the coalitions, and to ensure a decent future for the country he loved. And he could die now, at last, content in that.

"I think I hear the door." Whitney's murmured comment fell into silence like a pebble into a pool, dispelling the frozen stillness. Her movement into the hall was somehow shocking, but then Jonathon, too, rose to his feet, and the awkwardness of the first lingering moment at least, was gone.

"More brandy, Joshua? I think I can use another myself." Jonathon Penley spoke with complete self-control, yet his hand shook slightly as he poured. Defeat. Incredible. Once he would have said impossible. Now simply reality. God, what would the Yankees do now to the poor, beaten South? What price would they pay for their failed rebellion?

"It's a telegram from Virginia." Whitney had reentered the parlor abruptly, crossing the room to reach a hand out to Jonathon, touching him once in aching, wordless empathy before turning back to face Joshua Courtland. As she opened the wire, though, a small smile began to spread on her face. "It's from Leanna. War or not, it seems Leanna stayed in Virginia with Major Courtland, and apparently Leanna's *still* with the Yankee army there—as a nurse of all things. She must love your son a great deal, Joshua. I can remember my dear Leanna fainting at the sight of blood. This says Leanna and Chase Courtland were married just before midnight on the sixth of April, and they're expecting their first child sometime in late November or early December. She also says that Chase has been assigned to General Devin's staff now, so he should be quite out of the worst of the fighting—whatever fighting might yet remain. And they will come up here in person as soon as they can." Whitney stepped forward, bending to kiss Joshua's cheek as gently as any daughter. Joshua was startled, motionless. She pressed the wire down into his hands before she slowly stepped away. "Congratulations, dear. You shall have your own grandchildren after all, it seems. I'm so very, *very* pleased for you."

"Leanna *married* him?" In the double shock of the news of this evening, the words had been simply blurted out. Jonathon Penley flushed and began to make an effort to shrug them away, but as he noticed Joshua's own stunned expression he frowned. "If you're displeased at having a Rebel daughter-in-law, Joshua, I can only assure you that being related to a Yankee officer—"

"Hush, Jon. Don't you understand what those bells mean? There *is* no Rebel or Yankee anymore. Leanna and Major Courtland, at least, had the good sense to realize that. Now we all must, too." Whitney was still smiling faintly, as if to herself, and she reached for her shawl to turn to go. "I, for one, think it's wonderful news. But now we should get home, Jon. These bells are liable to have wakened the children. Mandy will want to know what they mean, and Josh will be hungry. He always is."

There was awkwardness lingering in the silence Whitney's exit had left behind her. Jonathon glanced sharply at Joshua and found an expression to prove he had misread Joshua's earlier surprise. Not anger but a soft, almost incredulous pleasure was showing on the elder Courtland's aged face, and something that might have been tears glittered in his eyes. God *did* listen, Joshua was thinking. Lincoln had lived; the Union was safe. And Chase had survived his desperate journey north and had now assured himself a lifetime with the woman he loved. So God had forgiven him for Elinor—this, to Joshua, was simple proof of that. Both his Union and his family were assured a future again, and more than that, a pretty damn good one.

Jonathon startled him out of his reverie by stepping closer and awkwardly extending a hand that carried apology and affection both. He had made a bargain that day—a secret and a silent one. If the Yankee Major could get Leanna safely to Virginia, he had sworn to accept him as a friend and an ally and not as an enemy. And Virginians' honored their given word, even when the word had been given only to themselves. Jonathon would accept his sister's marriage to the Yankee with the greatest grace that he could muster. In a way, he admitted to himself, Yankee or not, Leanna's choice might not be a bad one. "Whitney's right, of course, Joshua. Forgive me. Anyway, of all the families I know, I can't think of one I'd rather be related to than yours—Yankee or not." He offered a faint, wry smile and Joshua Courtland smiled back, rising to take the young Virginian's offered hand.

"And no daughter-in-law I'd rather have than your sister, Jonathon."

They stood for another moment, silent again but strangely close. As he finally turned to go Jonathon thought in surprise that they had survived the war's waging after all, *both* Joshua and he. And now they had survived its waning, too. Now, as he left, he noticed Whitney had left her locket behind by Joshua's chair—the necklace left open to show Leanna's picture. And Joshua was studying it by the gold light of the nearby lamp, faintly smiling, and searching the girl's face as if to find some hint of the faces the Courtland grandchildren would have.

It was that picture of the man more than any other that Jonathon carried with him after that. In the years to come, when Joshua Courtland was long gone, that memory would remain. And always, when remembering the soft radiance of

Joshua's face just then, Jonathon found reassurance that the Penleys had paid their debts to that Yankee after all—in the best possible way they could have.

On the twelfth of April, the Confederate Army of Northern Virginia made its last march—up the old Richmond-Lynchburg stage road and across the small bridge over the muddy Appomattox River which here was little more than a wide and shallow creek. They marched up the winding hill edged by just-budding trees, tangled brush and the crisscrossed wood of country fences. Farther away, a dozen cows grazed unconcerned on the hill of the sloping meadow.

In the distance was the Army of Northern Virginia's last camp, where Lee had inexplicably chosen to remain behind in his tent. General Grant was not present, either. He had chosen to return to Washington, too shy to seek the glory, too embarrassed to witness the final humiliation of his once-proud and infinitely worthy adversary. But among the federal troops lining the dirt road were most of the other high-ranking officers, staff included, and Leanna sat on the front of Chase's saddle with only a bare-boughed tree and a white picket fence between her and the approaching Rebel army. Paroles had begun two days before. This was only a last formality. Rebel arms and battle colors would be surrendered today in the small crossroads triangle covered with new grass. And afterwards, from the edge of this village of Appomattox, the Rebel soldiers would scatter singly and in small groups to begin their long journeys home.

Grant had ordered the respect of silence. There was to be no exultation over the defeat of men who were once again, by Lincoln's decree, considered brothers instead of foes. And among the dark blue columns that lined the road, there was only a waiting sort of quiet. No bands played, no drums rolled. There was only the chilly spring breeze blowing in bare branches, the muffled tramp of thousands of feet, and the occasional stamping of a restless horse. But as the rebel column crested the hill, there was a collective gasp from among the watching federals. After four years of war, Rebel regiments had been thinned to the size of mere companies, and the profusion of red battle flags carried among so few remaining men made the whole column appear crowned with the color of new blood. As General Gordon's lead corps

454

approached, federal buglers sounded a sudden order to "carry arms"—the marching salute—soldiers on one side impulsively honoring the gallantry and valiant fighting of their long-time foes on the other. The sound of shifting rifles seemed to startle the CSA general for a moment, then Gordon wheeled his horse in a slow, proud turn, dropping his saber to the toe of his boot to return the honor.

This army bore little resemblance to the splendid giant Leanna had watched march out of Richmond barely four years before. It had once contained over one hundred thousand men. Now, less than twenty-seven thousand remained to receive parole. There were no solid ranks of gray anymore—gray cloth had run out years ago under the federal blockade, and most of the soldiers now wore homespun wool and cotton, dyed by butternuts to a rusty brown. There were no spirited, sleek horses, once the pride of Virginia; no rousing speeches; no bands playing "Dixie"; only beaten men and a ravaged land, and an eerie motionless silence as if ghosts not men were marching by. A silence that persisted until the last regiment had stacked their rifles and folded their shot-torn colors and melted away into the April sunshine. It was one nation, undivided, once again.

Leanna looked around her then in a kind of dazed disbelief, seeing the Union soldiers through eyes blurred with tears. Their war-worn faces were hard and closed. And this, she realized suddenly, was the face of the future. For better or for worse, the world of the Old South, the world she had been born in and raised in and learned so dearly once to love, that world of gallantry and gracious beauty and illusion was gone forever. The world of the future was the Yankee world—busy, and colder, but infinitely real. The Confederacy had for some reason, even before the war's end, dropped its charges against her. And Joshua Courtland had procurred a presidential pardon for her with the federal side. And thanks to them and to the man who shared his saddle with her at this moment, Leanna *had* a future once again. Strange, she thought now, watching the soldiers of the defeated South pass in front of her, thanks to the war she had learned finally not to hate better but to love better. To love deeply enough and strongly enough to overcome all the divisions that hatred would have put between her and the man she loved.

Once, on a day now long ago, at Blytheswood, in the

yet-unravaged Shenandoah Valley, a federal surgeon named Doc Lacey had warned her that the war would ask her some painful questions. But now, at last, Leanna had found her answers. She had lost something to the war but gained something too . . . as had they all, she realized, each and every one of them. And she and Chase had each other now, to help put war-shattered lives back together, to heal the wounds the war's horrors had left behind on both of them. In time, the Valley would bloom with springtime again. In time, for love of her, Chase would help her rebuild Blytheswood. Their children and their grandchildren would play there in the silver river and fish the old creek as she and her brother Jonathon had done so many years ago, and the scars of war would be nearly invisible. As if somehow sensing her thoughts, Chase moved closer against her in the saddle they shared, and he tightened his arms around her waist—and the child that lay concealed within it. In response, Leanna turned her head to face him, and she offered a smile even through her tears. An enemy no longer, but only the dearest of friends—her lover and her husband both. Chase Courtland's face was the face of her future now, and it was, in every way, a very, very good one. The gods had offered them a great deal of kindness, after all.

THE WINDHAVEN SAGA
Marie de Jourlet